THIS IS **POYO.**

POYO WAS EXPOSED TO A NEAR-LETHAL AMOUNT OF RADIATION AS AN EGG, DURING THE FIRST STAGES OF A GOVERNMENT EXPERIMENT TO CREATE MUTANT SUPER SOLDIERS--

HI-YA!

HI-YA!

BA-KAW!

--TRAINED IN EXOTIC MARTIAL ARTS TECHNIQUE BY TIBETAN KUNG FU FIGHTIN' MONKS--

--AND GIVEN STRANGE BIO-ENHANCEMENTS DURING A RASH OF FARM ANIMAL ABDUCTIONS BY EXTRA-TERRESTRIALS.

NAH, JUST KIDDING.

WINK!

NONE OF THAT SHIT IS TRUE.

POYO IS JUST REALLY, *REALLY* BAD ASS.

image comics **presents**

The Omnivore Edition
Vol. V

written & lettered by
John Layman

drawn & coloured by
Rob Guillory

created by John Layman & Rob Guillory
design by Guillory & Layman

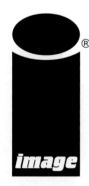

IMAGE COMICS, INC.
Robert Kirkman – Chief Operating Officer
Erik Larsen – Chief Financial Officer
Todd McFarlane – President
Marc Silvestri – Chief Executive Officer
Jim Valentino – Vice-President

Eric Stephenson – Publisher
Corey Murphy – Director of Sales
Jeff Boison – Director of Publishing Planning & Book Trade Sales
Jeremy Sullivan – Director of Digital Sales
Kat Salazar – Director of PR & Marketing
Emily Miller – Director of Operations
Branwyn Bigglestone – Senior Accounts Manager
Sarah Mello – Accounts Manager
Drew Gill – Art Director
Jonathan Chan – Production Manager
Meredith Wallace – Print Manager
Briah Skelly – Publicity Assistant
Randy Okamura – Marketing Production Designer
David Brothers – Branding Manager
Ally Power – Content Manager
Addison Duke – Production Artist
Vincent Kukua – Production Artist
Sasha Head – Production Artist
Tricia Ramos – Production Artist
Jeff Stang – Direct Market Sales Representative
Emilio Bautista – Digital Sales Associate
Chloe Ramos-Peterson – Administrative Assistant
IMAGECOMICS.COM

CHEW: THE OMNIVORE EDITION, VOL. 5. First printing. December
2015. Published by Image Comics, Inc. Office of publication: 2001
Center Street, Sixth Floor, Berkeley, CA 94704. Copyright © 2015
John Layman. Originally published in single magazine form as CHEW
#41-50 and Warrior Chicken Poyo by Image Comics. All rights
reserved. CHEW™ (including all prominent characters featured herein),
its logo and all character likenesses are trademarks of John Layman,
unless otherwise noted. Image Comics® and its logos are registered
trademarks of Image Comics, Inc. No part of this publication may
be reproduced or transmitted, in any form or by any means (except
for short excerpts for review purposes) without the express written
permission of Image Comics, Inc. All names, characters, events and
locales in this publication are entirely fictional. Any resemblance to
actual persons (living or dead), events or places, without satiric intent,
is coincidental. Printed in Canada. ISBN: 978-1-63215-623-5.
For international rights, contact: foreignlicensing@imagecomics.com

Dedications:

ROB: For my buddy Ross.

JOHN: Also for Rob's buddy Ross. Why not?

Thanks:

Taylor Wells, for the coloring assists.
Drew Gill, for the production assists.
Tom B. Long, for the logo.
Comicbookfonts.com, for the fonts.

And More Thanks:

David Baron, Jeremy Bastian, David Brothers, Ryan Browne,
Chris Burnham, C.B. Cebulski, Kody Chamberlain, Kelly Sue
DeConnick, Valentine De Landro, Brian Duffield, Ray Fawkes,
Otis Frampton, Dan Goldman, Paul Hanley, Jonathan Hickman,
Sina Grace, Daniel Warren Johnson, Robert Kirkman,
Jeff Krelitz, Tom Long, Hansel Moreno, Nick Pitarra,
Theresa Peterson, Shaun Steven Struble, Ross Thibodeaux,
Irene Strychalski, Sweet Joshie Williamson, and Kathryn &
Israel Skelton.

Plus the fine foks at Image, especially Eric, Jonathan, Emily,
Corey, Kat, Meredith, Randy and Branwyn.

In Memoriam:

Rufus Jaye Poggles
2000-2015

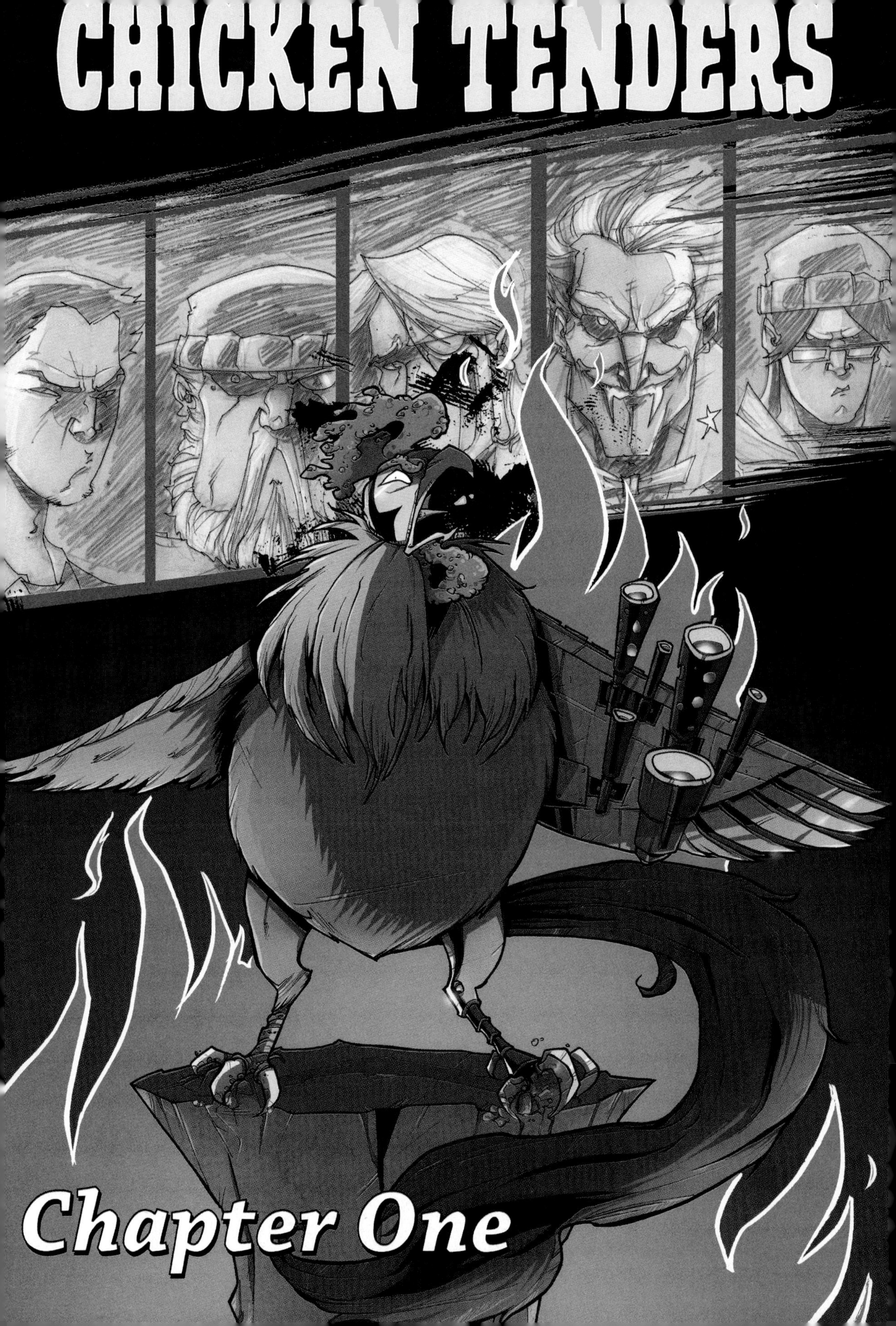
CHICKEN TENDERS
Chapter One

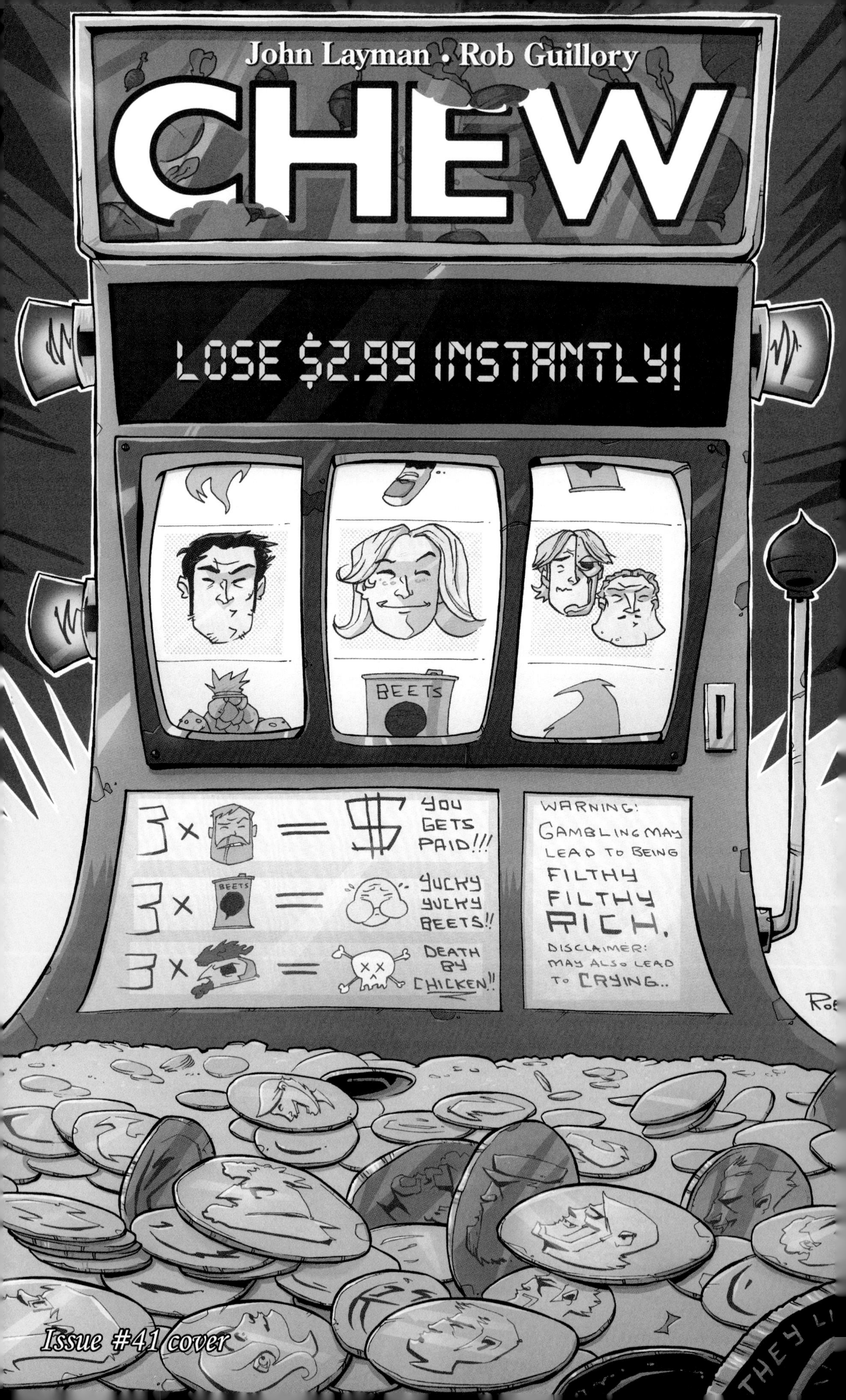
John Layman • Rob Guillory
CHEW
LOSE $2.99 INSTANTLY!
BEETS
3 × = $ YOU GETS PAID!!!
BEETS
3 × = YUCKY YUCKY BEETS!!
3 × = DEATH BY CHICKEN!!
WARNING: GAMBLING MAY LEAD TO BEING FILTHY FILTHY RICH.
DISCLAIMER: MAY ALSO LEAD TO CRYING..
ROB
Issue #41 cover

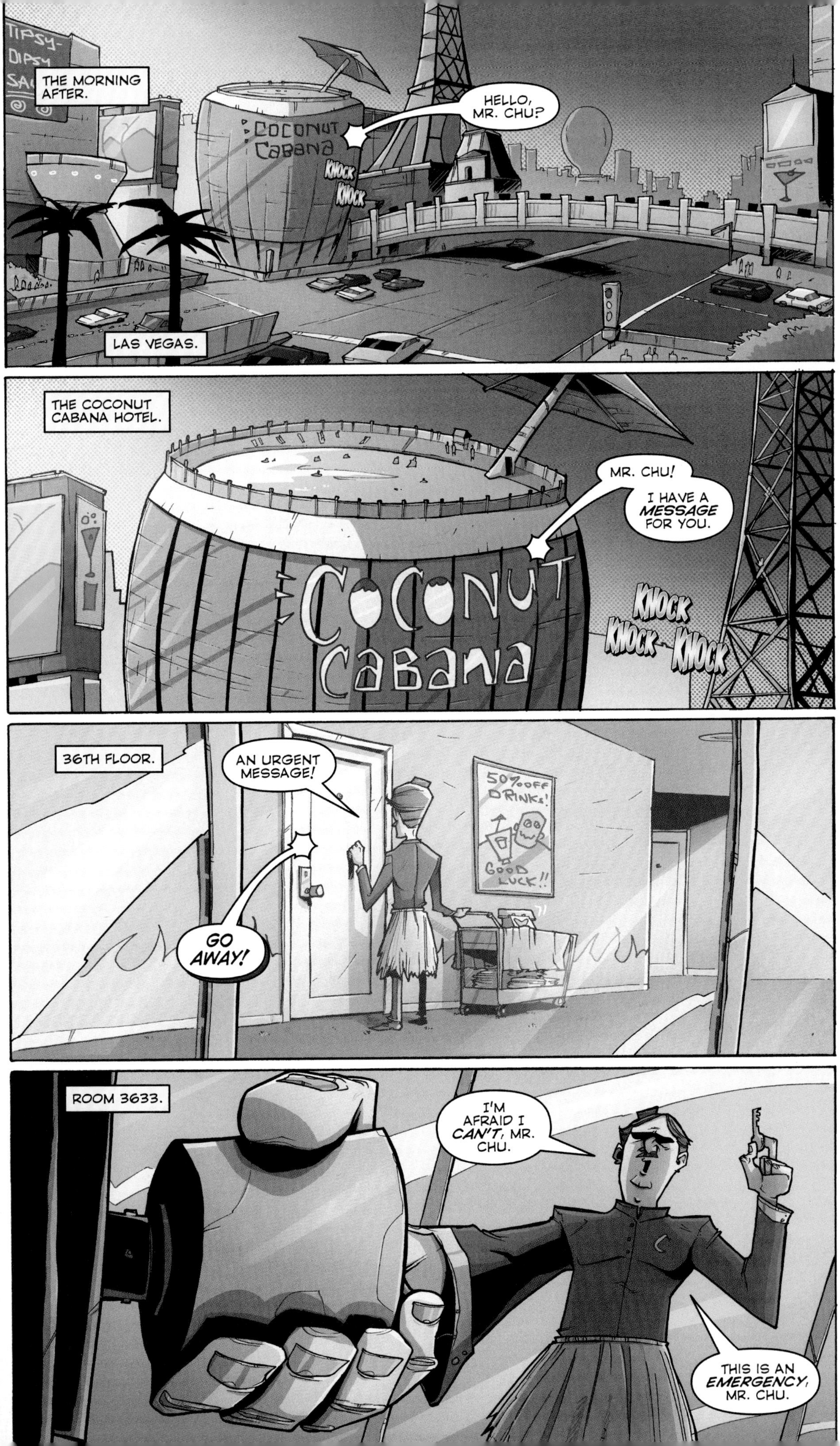
THE MORNING AFTER.
HELLO, MR. CHU?
COCONUT CABANA
KNOCK KNOCK
LAS VEGAS.
THE COCONUT CABANA HOTEL.
MR. CHU!
I HAVE A MESSAGE FOR YOU.
COCONUT CABANA
KNOCK KNOCK KNOCK
36TH FLOOR.
AN URGENT MESSAGE!
50% OFF DRINKS!
GOOD LUCK!!
GO AWAY!
ROOM 3633.
I'M AFRAID I CAN'T, MR. CHU.
THIS IS AN EMERGENCY, MR. CHU.

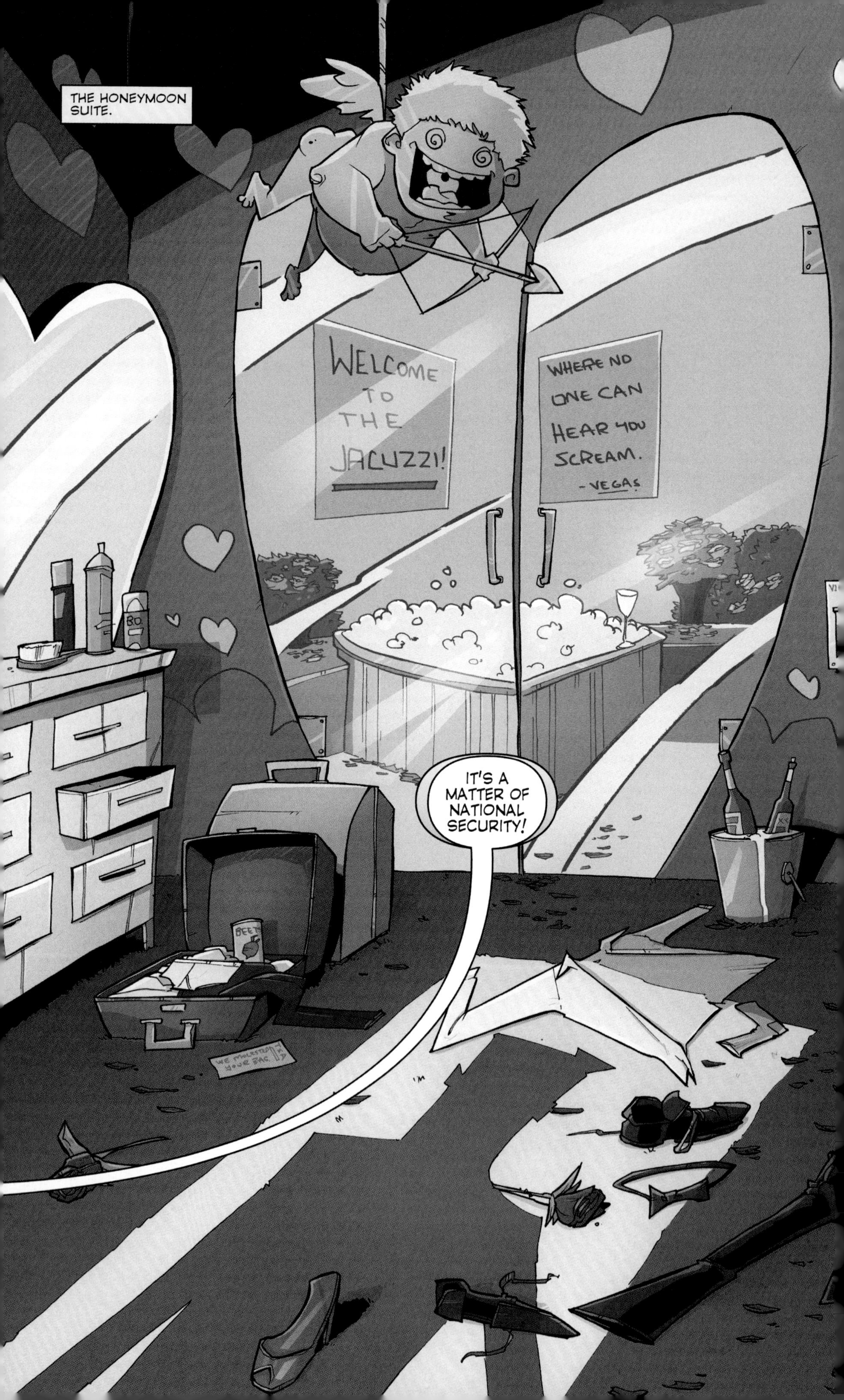
THE HONEYMOON SUITE.
WELCOME TO THE JACUZZI!
WHERE NO ONE CAN HEAR YOU SCREAM. - VEGAS
IT'S A MATTER OF NATIONAL SECURITY!

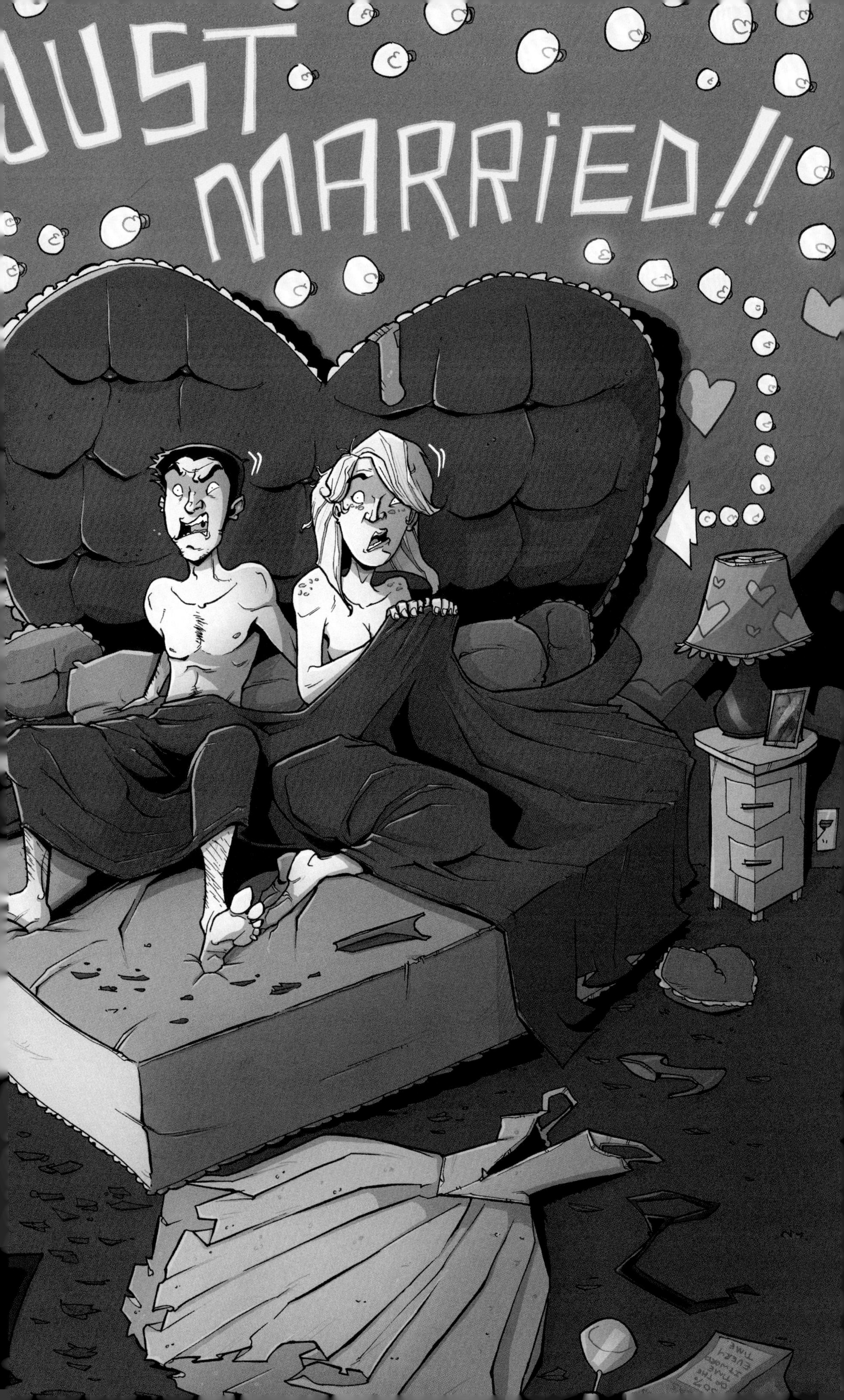
JUST MARRIED!!

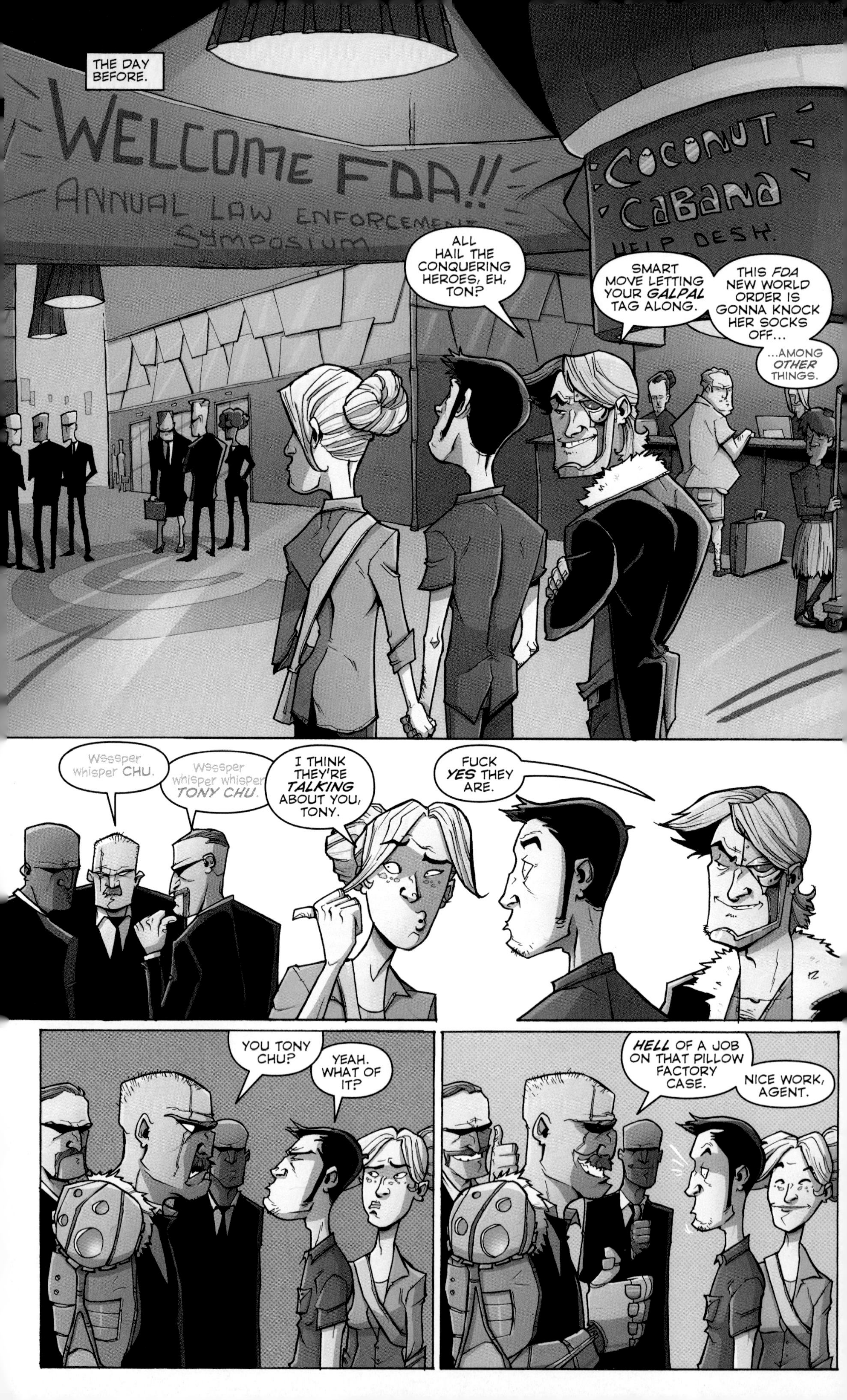
THE DAY BEFORE.
WELCOME FDA!!
ANNUAL LAW ENFORCEMENT SYMPOSIUM
COCONUT CABANA HELP DESK.
ALL HAIL THE CONQUERING HEROES, EH, TON?
SMART MOVE LETTING YOUR GALPAL TAG ALONG.
THIS FDA NEW WORLD ORDER IS GONNA KNOCK HER SOCKS OFF...
...AMONG OTHER THINGS.
Wsssper whisper CHU.
Wsssper whisper whisper TONY CHU.
I THINK THEY'RE TALKING ABOUT YOU, TONY.
FUCK YES THEY ARE.
YOU TONY CHU?
YEAH. WHAT OF IT?
HELL OF A JOB ON THAT PILLOW FACTORY CASE.
NICE WORK, AGENT.

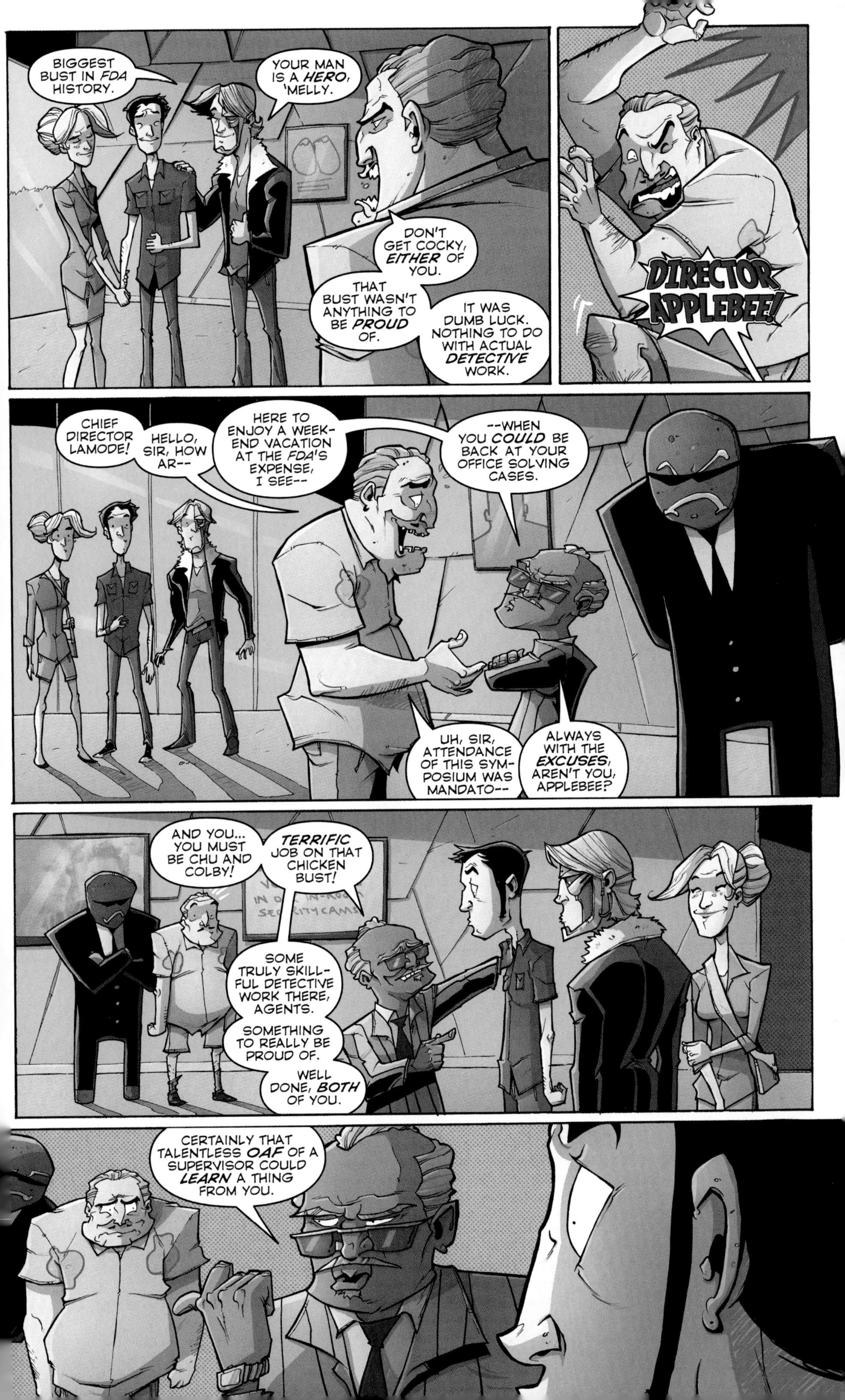
BIGGEST BUST IN FDA HISTORY.
YOUR MAN IS A HERO, 'MELLY.
DON'T GET COCKY, EITHER OF YOU.
THAT BUST WASN'T ANYTHING TO BE PROUD OF.
IT WAS DUMB LUCK. NOTHING TO DO WITH ACTUAL DETECTIVE WORK.
DIRECTOR APPLEBEE!
CHIEF DIRECTOR LAMODE!
HELLO, SIR, HOW AR--
HERE TO ENJOY A WEEK-END VACATION AT THE FDA'S EXPENSE, I SEE--
--WHEN YOU COULD BE BACK AT YOUR OFFICE SOLVING CASES.
UH, SIR, ATTENDANCE OF THIS SYMPOSIUM WAS MANDATO--
ALWAYS WITH THE EXCUSES, AREN'T YOU, APPLEBEE?
AND YOU... YOU MUST BE CHU AND COLBY!
TERRIFIC JOB ON THAT CHICKEN BUST!
SOME TRULY SKILL-FUL DETECTIVE WORK THERE, AGENTS.
SOMETHING TO REALLY BE PROUD OF.
WELL DONE, BOTH OF YOU.
CERTAINLY THAT TALENTLESS OAF OF A SUPERVISOR COULD LEARN A THING FROM YOU.

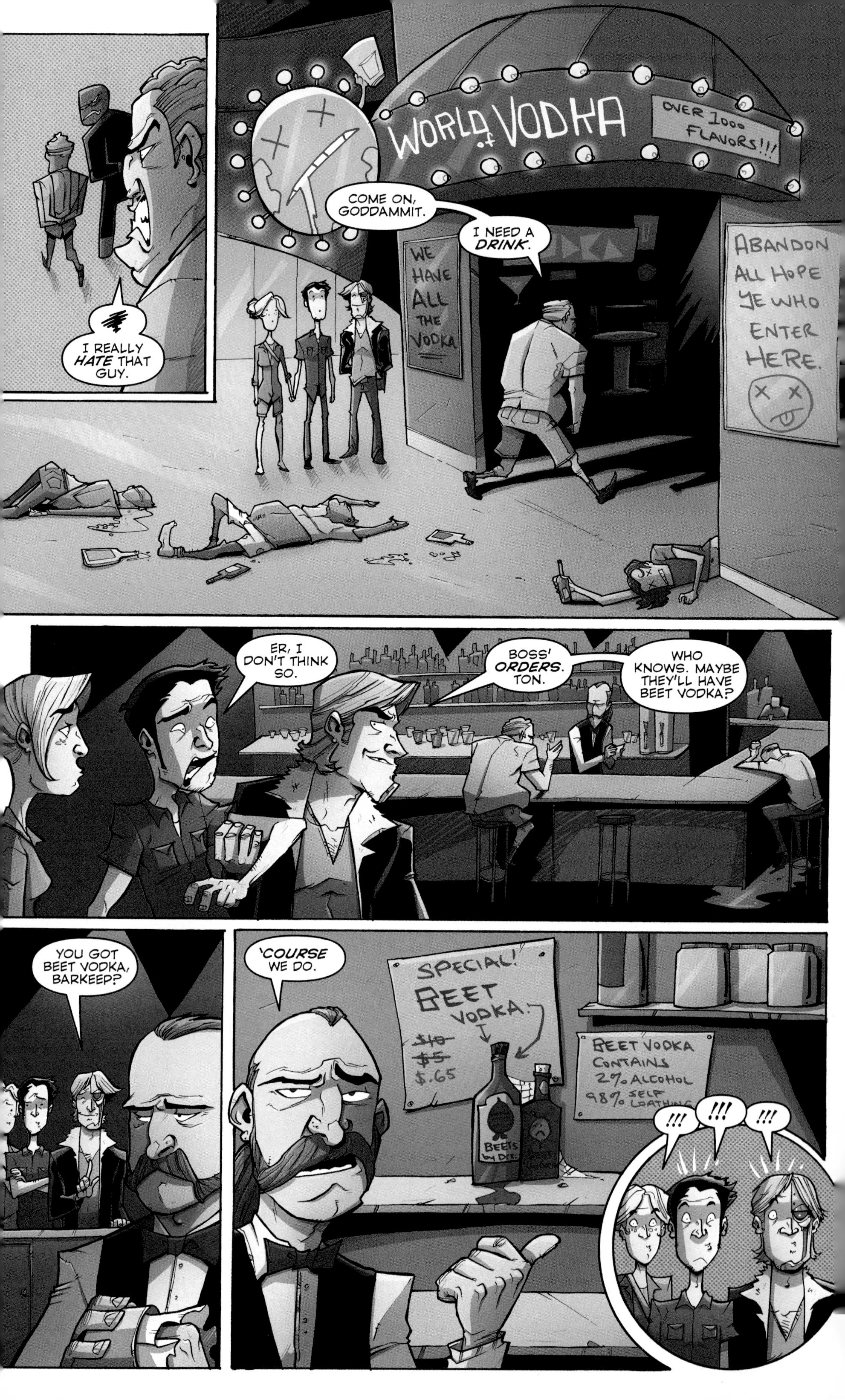
I REALLY HATE THAT GUY.
WORLD of VODKA
OVER 1000 FLAVORS!!!
COME ON, GODDAMMIT.
I NEED A DRINK.
WE HAVE ALL THE VODKA
ABANDON ALL HOPE YE WHO ENTER HERE.
ER, I DON'T THINK SO.
BOSS' ORDERS. TON.
WHO KNOWS. MAYBE THEY'LL HAVE BEET VODKA?
YOU GOT BEET VODKA, BARKEEP?
'COURSE WE DO.
SPECIAL! BEET VODKA. $10 $5 $.65
BEET VODKA CONTAINS 2% ALCOHOL 98% SELF LOATHING
!!!
!!!
!!!

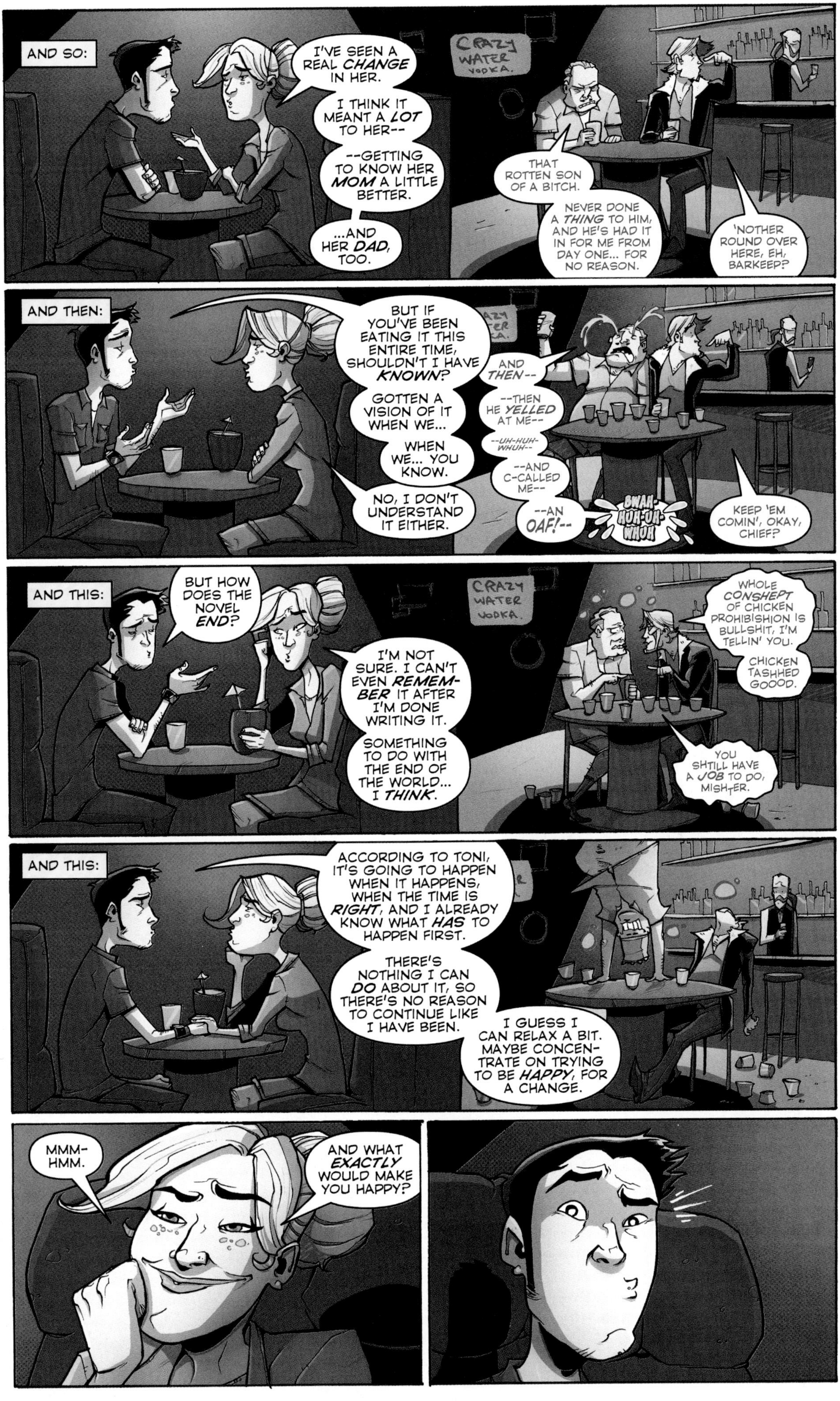
AND SO:
I'VE SEEN A REAL CHANGE IN HER.
I THINK IT MEANT A LOT TO HER--
--GETTING TO KNOW HER MOM A LITTLE BETTER.
...AND HER DAD, TOO.
CRAZY WATER VODKA
THAT ROTTEN SON OF A BITCH.
NEVER DONE A THING TO HIM, AND HE'S HAD IT IN FOR ME FROM DAY ONE... FOR NO REASON.
'NOTHER ROUND OVER HERE, EH, BARKEEP?
AND THEN:
BUT IF YOU'VE BEEN EATING IT THIS ENTIRE TIME, SHOULDN'T I HAVE KNOWN?
GOTTEN A VISION OF IT WHEN WE...
WHEN WE... YOU KNOW.
NO, I DON'T UNDERSTAND IT EITHER.
AND THEN--
--THEN HE YELLED AT ME--
--UH-HUH-WHUH--
--AND C-CALLED ME--
--AN OAF!--
BWAH-HUH-UH-WHUH
KEEP 'EM COMIN', OKAY, CHIEF?
AND THIS:
BUT HOW DOES THE NOVEL END?
I'M NOT SURE. I CAN'T EVEN REMEMBER IT AFTER I'M DONE WRITING IT.
SOMETHING TO DO WITH THE END OF THE WORLD... I THINK.
CRAZY WATER VODKA
WHOLE CONSHEPT OF CHICKEN PROHIBISHION IS BULLSHIT, I'M TELLIN' YOU.
CHICKEN TASHHED GOOOD.
YOU SHTILL HAVE A JOB TO DO, MISHTER.
AND THIS:
ACCORDING TO TONI, IT'S GOING TO HAPPEN WHEN IT HAPPENS, WHEN THE TIME IS RIGHT, AND I ALREADY KNOW WHAT HAS TO HAPPEN FIRST.
THERE'S NOTHING I CAN DO ABOUT IT, SO THERE'S NO REASON TO CONTINUE LIKE I HAVE BEEN.
I GUESS I CAN RELAX A BIT. MAYBE CONCENTRATE ON TRYING TO BE HAPPY, FOR A CHANGE.
MMM-HMM.
AND WHAT EXACTLY WOULD MAKE YOU HAPPY?

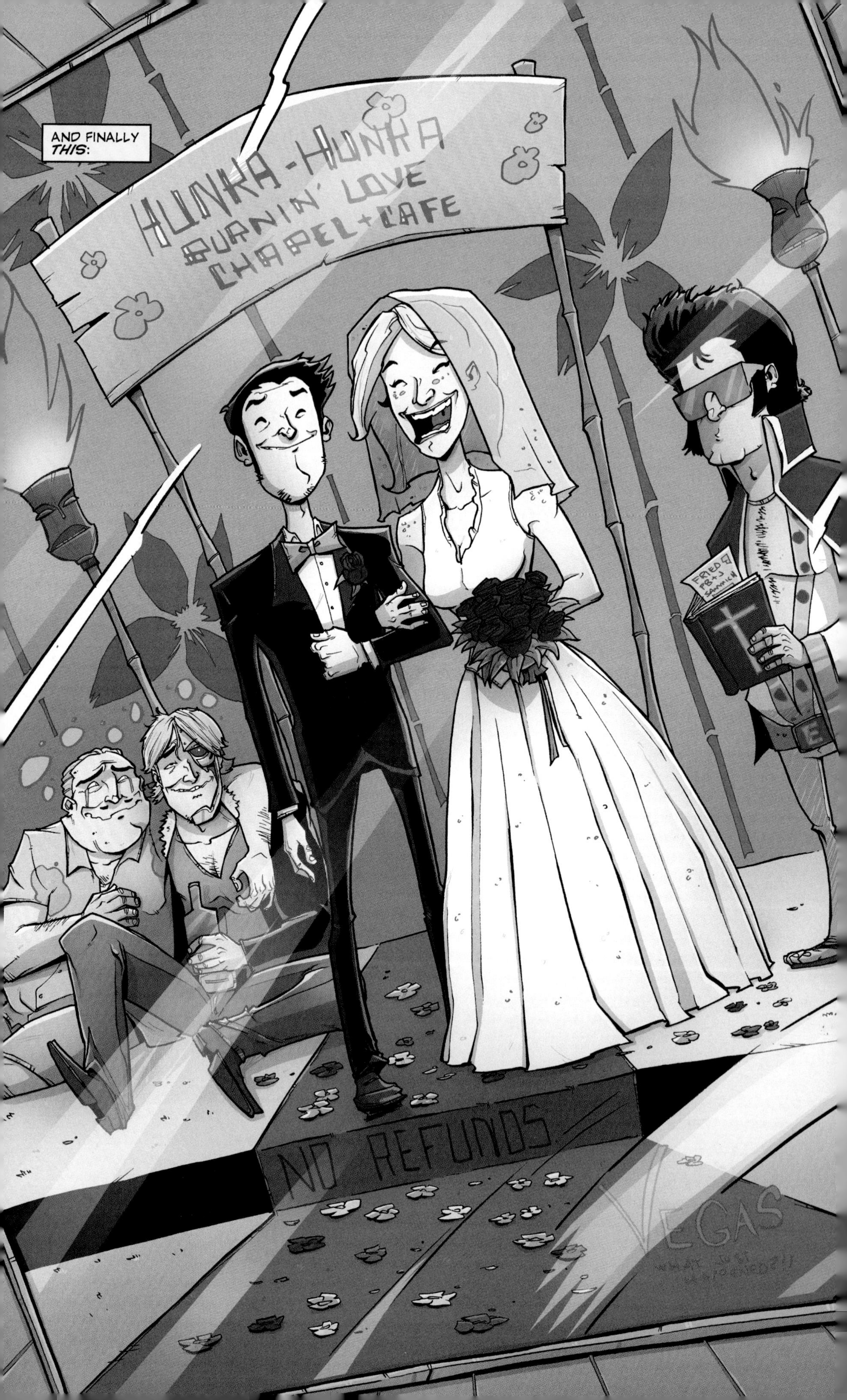
AND FINALLY *THIS*:
HUNKA-HUNKA BURNIN' LOVE CHAPEL+CAFE
FRIED PB+J SAMMICH
NO REFUNDS
VEGAS

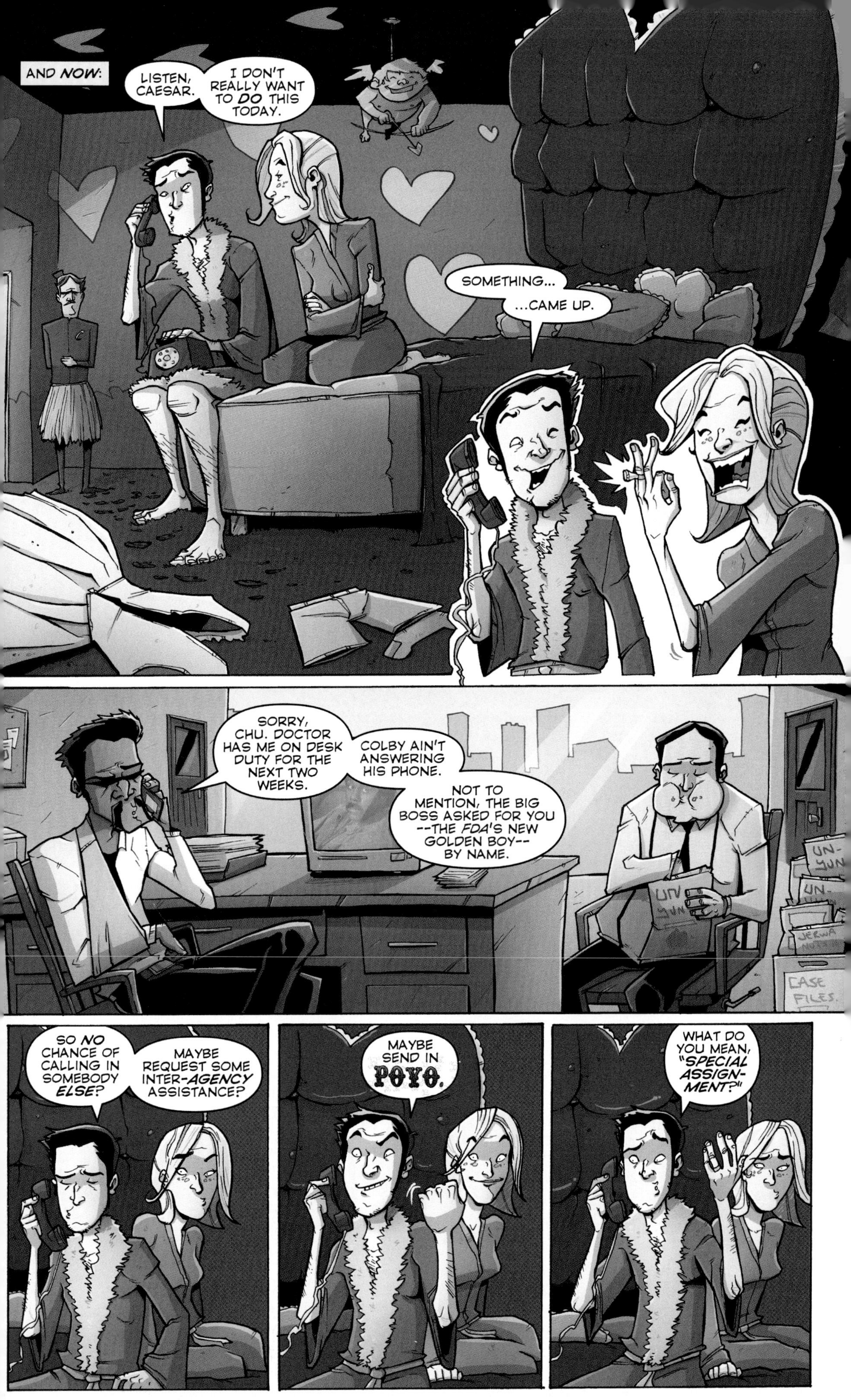
AND NOW:
LISTEN, CAESAR.
I DON'T REALLY WANT TO DO THIS TODAY.
SOMETHING...
...CAME UP.
SORRY, CHU. DOCTOR HAS ME ON DESK DUTY FOR THE NEXT TWO WEEKS.
COLBY AIN'T ANSWERING HIS PHONE.
NOT TO MENTION, THE BIG BOSS ASKED FOR YOU --THE FDA'S NEW GOLDEN BOY-- BY NAME.
CASE FILES.
SO NO CHANCE OF CALLING IN SOMEBODY ELSE?
MAYBE REQUEST SOME INTER-AGENCY ASSISTANCE?
MAYBE SEND IN POYO.
WHAT DO YOU MEAN, "SPECIAL ASSIGNMENT?"

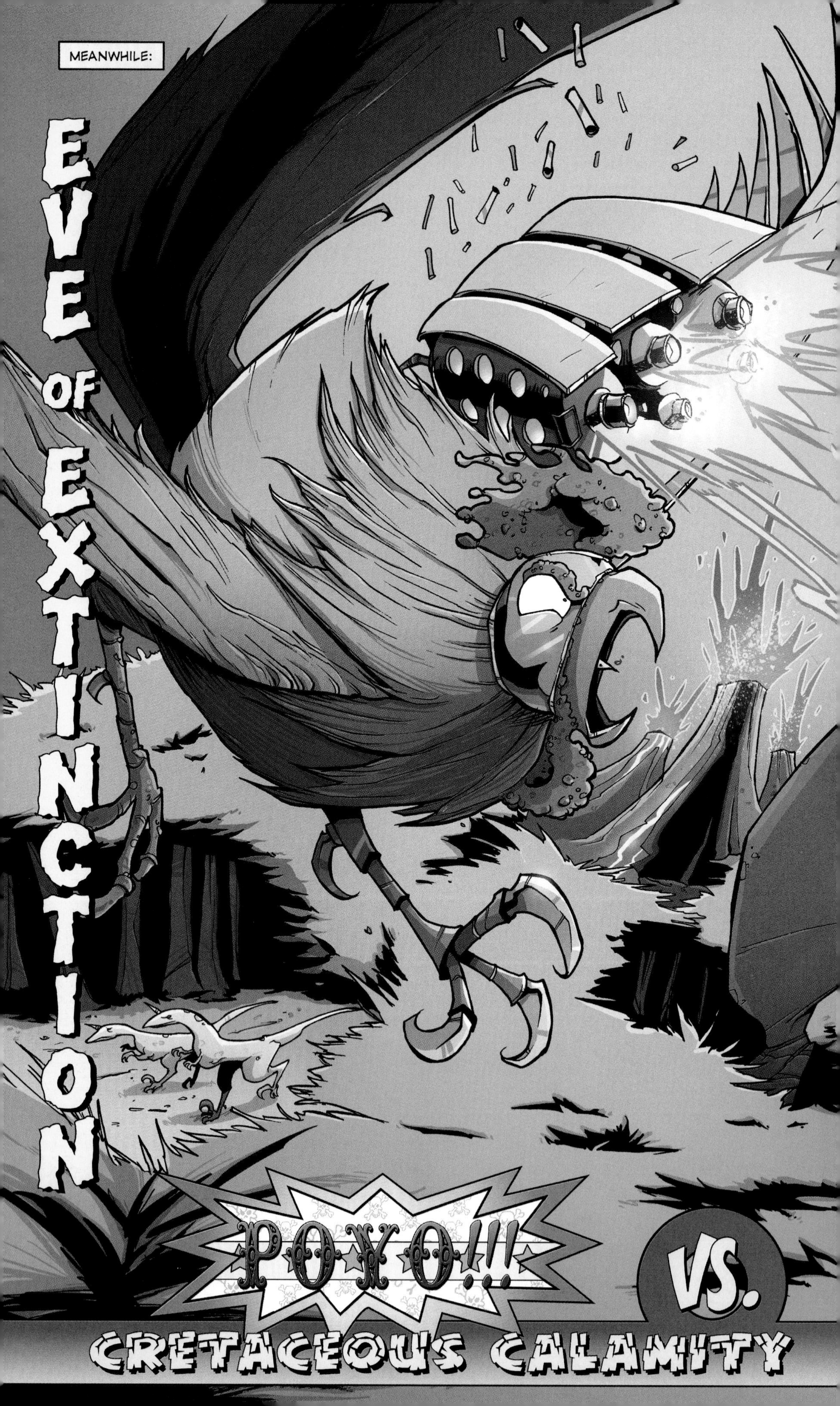

MEANWHILE:
EVE OF EXTINCTION
POYO!!!
VS.
CRETACEOUS CALAMITY

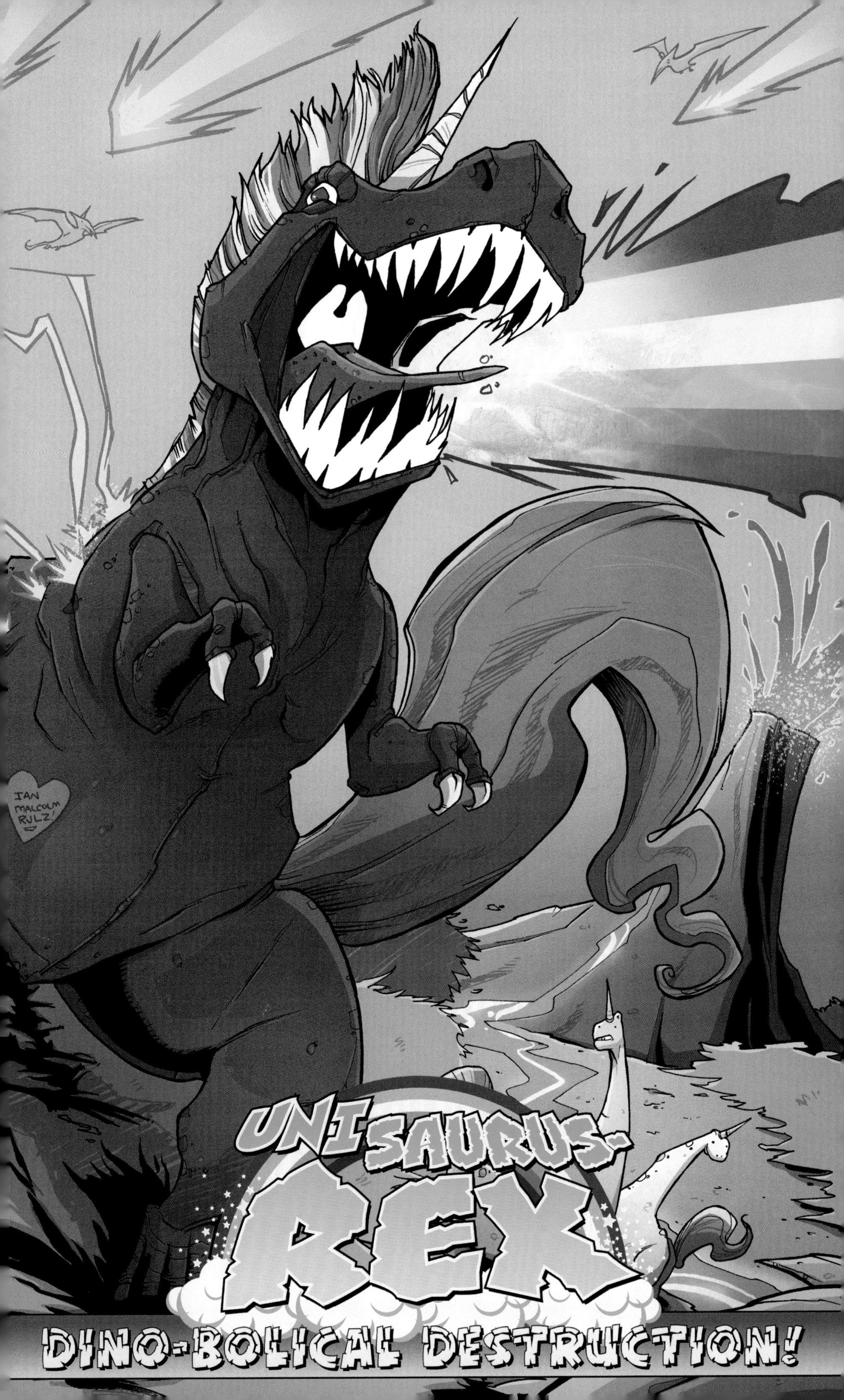
IAN MALCOLM RULZ!
UNISAURUS-REX
DINO-BOLICAL DESTRUCTION!

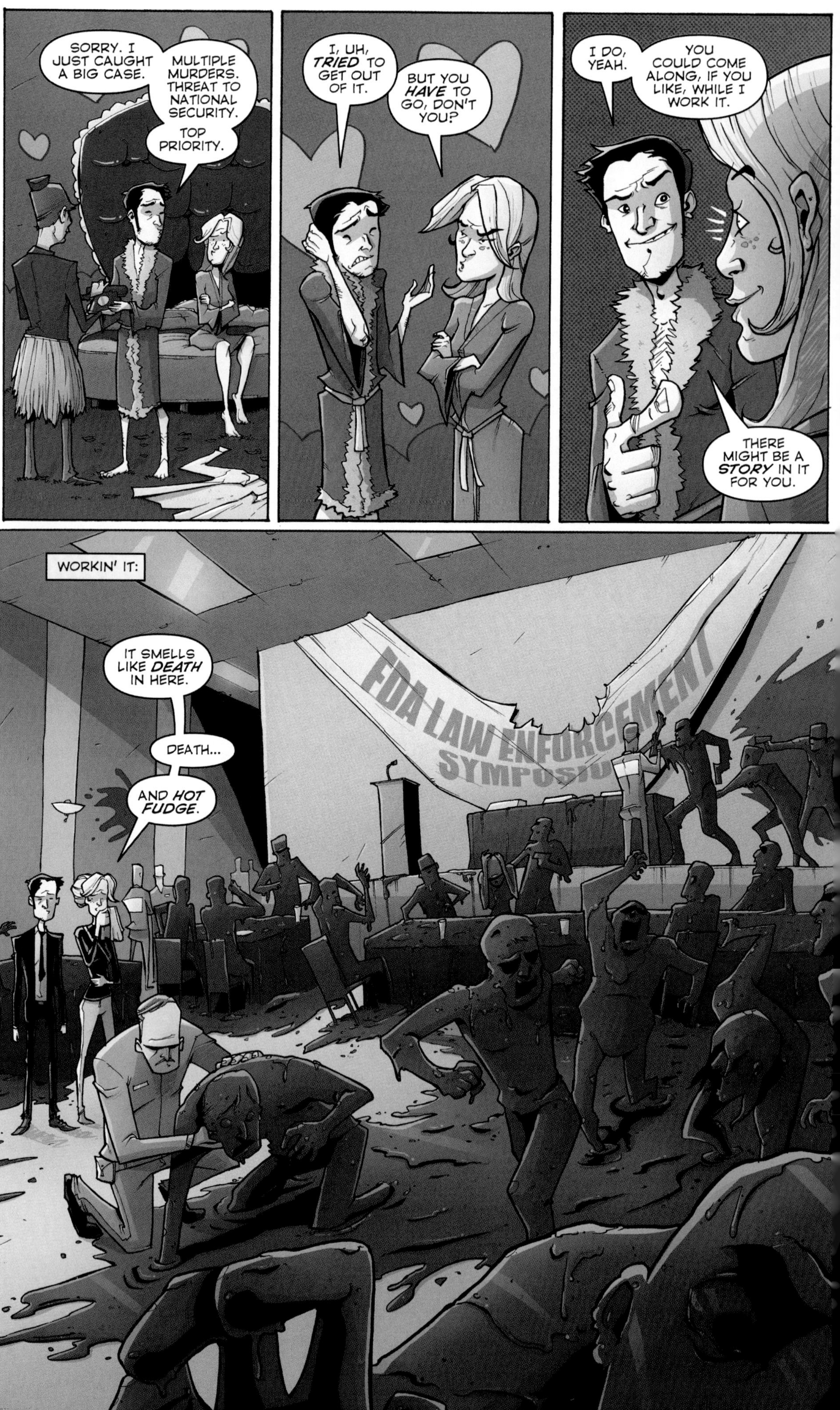
SORRY. I JUST CAUGHT A BIG CASE.
MULTIPLE MURDERS. THREAT TO NATIONAL SECURITY.
TOP PRIORITY.
I, UH, TRIED TO GET OUT OF IT.
BUT YOU HAVE TO GO, DON'T YOU?
I DO, YEAH.
YOU COULD COME ALONG, IF YOU LIKE, WHILE I WORK IT.
THERE MIGHT BE A STORY IN IT FOR YOU.
WORKIN' IT:
IT SMELLS LIKE DEATH IN HERE.
DEATH...
AND HOT FUDGE.
FDA LAW ENFORCEMENT SYMPOSIU

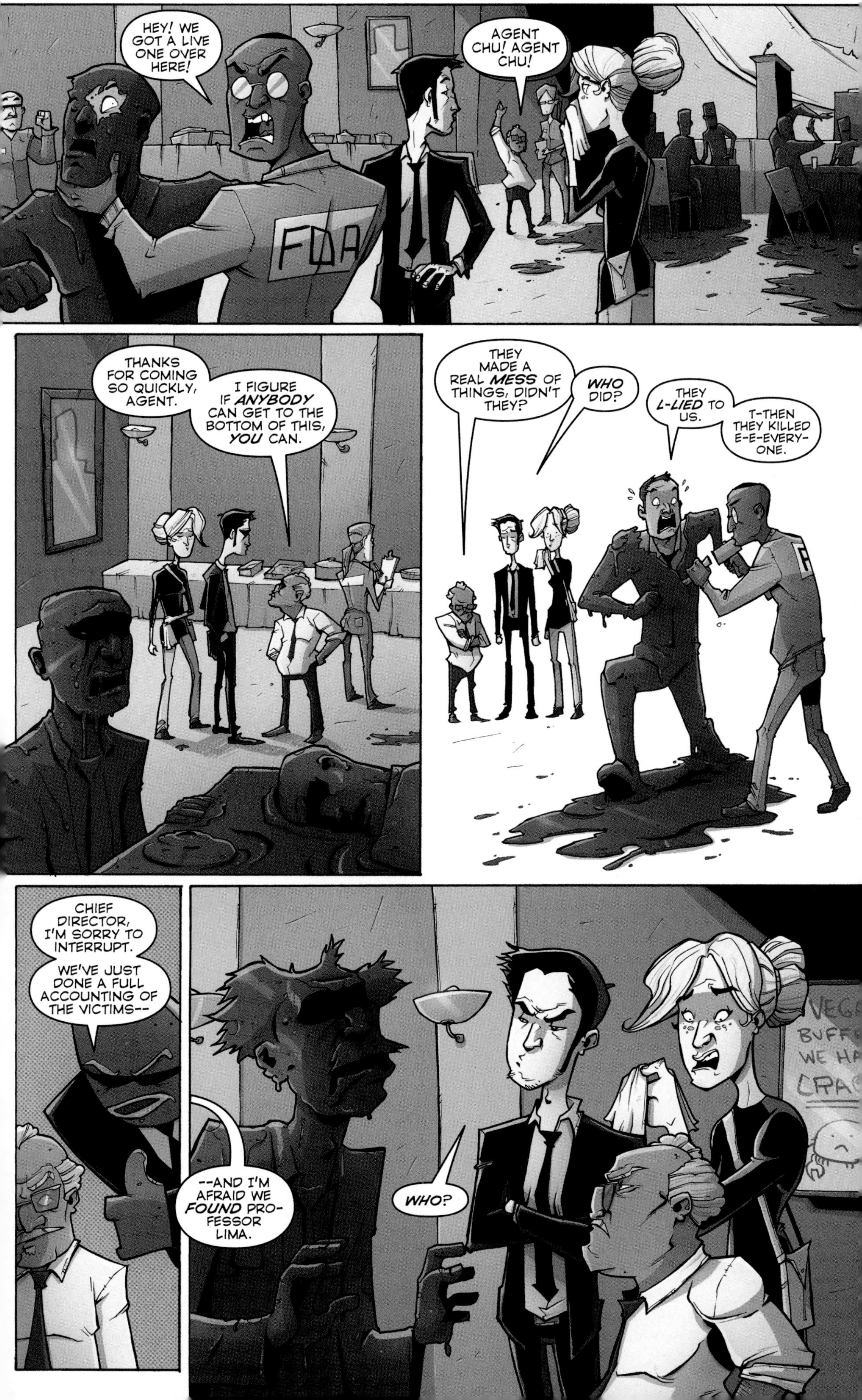
HEY! WE GOT A LIVE ONE OVER HERE!
AGENT CHU! AGENT CHU!
THANKS FOR COMING SO QUICKLY, AGENT.
I FIGURE IF ANYBODY CAN GET TO THE BOTTOM OF THIS, YOU CAN.
THEY MADE A REAL MESS OF THINGS, DIDN'T THEY?
WHO DID?
THEY L-LIED TO US.
T-THEN THEY KILLED E-E-EVERY-ONE.
FDA
CHIEF DIRECTOR, I'M SORRY TO INTERRUPT.
WE'VE JUST DONE A FULL ACCOUNTING OF THE VICTIMS--
--AND I'M AFRAID WE FOUND PROFESSOR LIMA.
WHO?

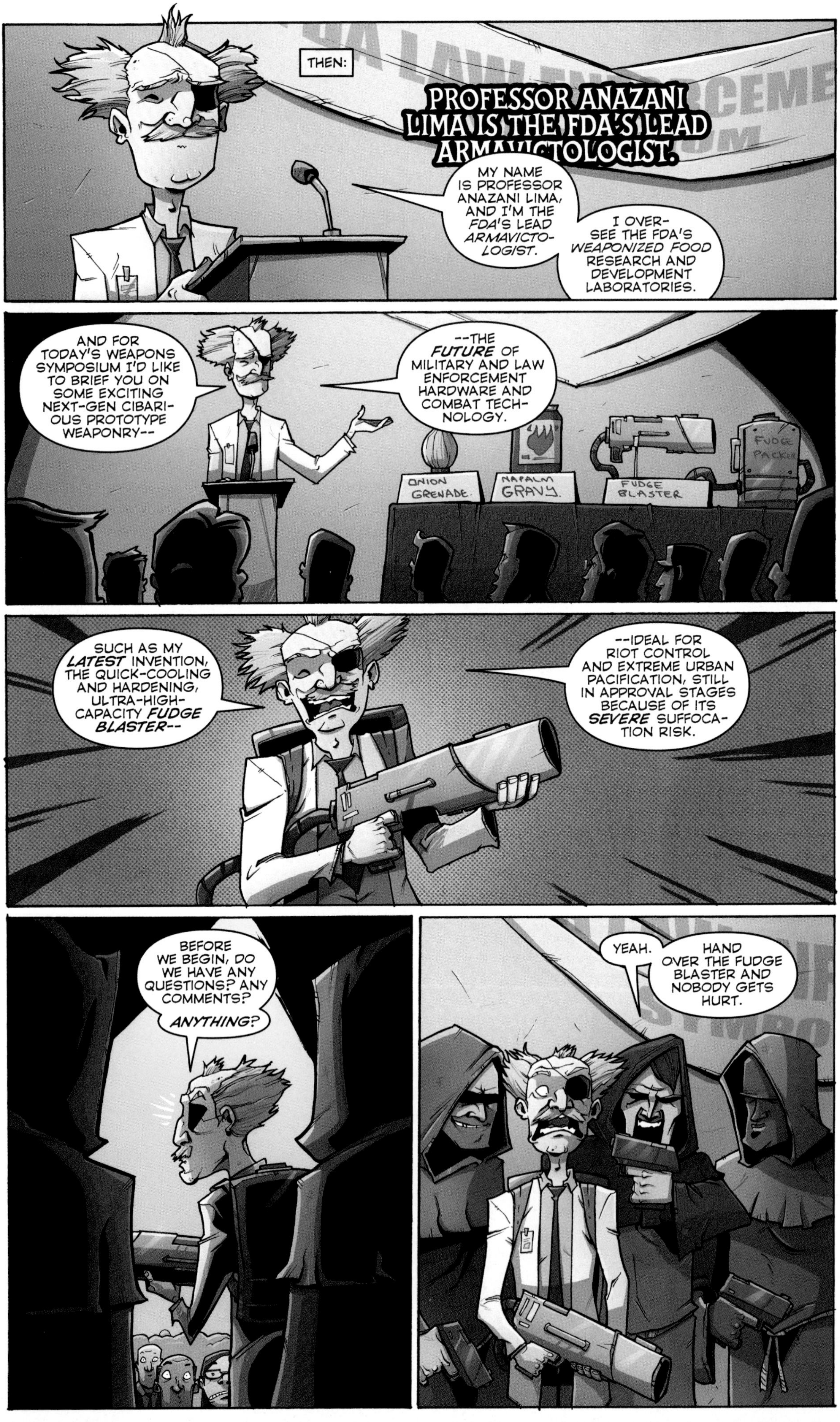
THEN:
PROFESSOR ANAZANI LIMA IS THE FDA'S LEAD ARMAVICTOLOGIST.
MY NAME IS PROFESSOR ANAZANI LIMA, AND I'M THE FDA'S LEAD ARMAVICTO-LOGIST.
I OVER-SEE THE FDA'S WEAPONIZED FOOD RESEARCH AND DEVELOPMENT LABORATORIES.
AND FOR TODAY'S WEAPONS SYMPOSIUM I'D LIKE TO BRIEF YOU ON SOME EXCITING NEXT-GEN CIBARI-OUS PROTOTYPE WEAPONRY--
--THE FUTURE OF MILITARY AND LAW ENFORCEMENT HARDWARE AND COMBAT TECH-NOLOGY.
ONION GRENADE.
NAPALM GRAVY.
FUDGE BLASTER
FUDGE PACKER
SUCH AS MY LATEST INVENTION, THE QUICK-COOLING AND HARDENING, ULTRA-HIGH-CAPACITY FUDGE BLASTER--
--IDEAL FOR RIOT CONTROL AND EXTREME URBAN PACIFICATION, STILL IN APPROVAL STAGES BECAUSE OF ITS SEVERE SUFFOCA-TION RISK.
BEFORE WE BEGIN, DO WE HAVE ANY QUESTIONS? ANY COMMENTS? ANYTHING?
YEAH.
HAND OVER THE FUDGE BLASTER AND NOBODY GETS HURT.

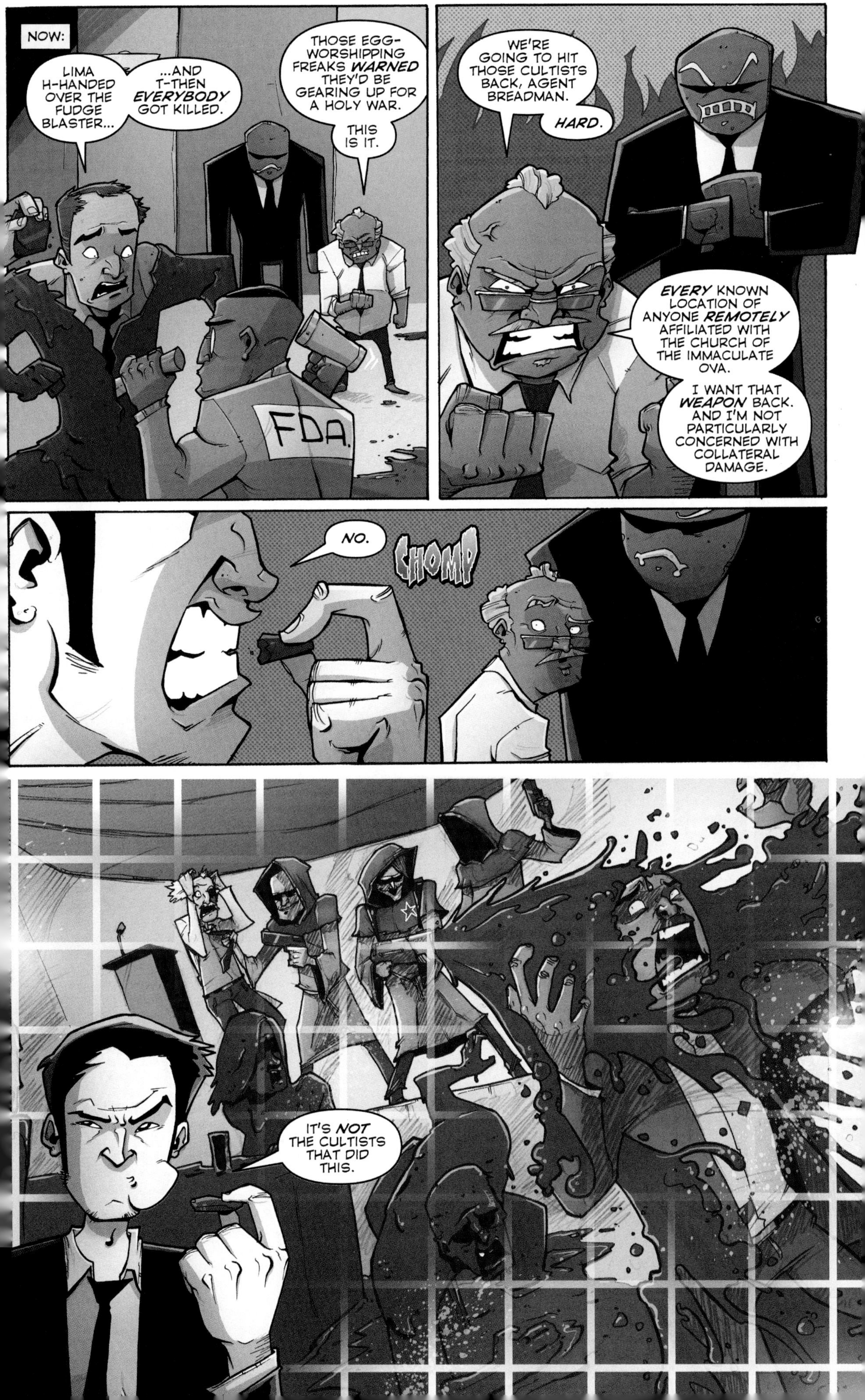
NOW:
LIMA H-HANDED OVER THE FUDGE BLASTER...
...AND T-THEN EVERYBODY GOT KILLED.
THOSE EGG-WORSHIPPING FREAKS WARNED THEY'D BE GEARING UP FOR A HOLY WAR.
THIS IS IT.
FDA.
WE'RE GOING TO HIT THOSE CULTISTS BACK, AGENT BREADMAN.
HARD.
EVERY KNOWN LOCATION OF ANYONE REMOTELY AFFILIATED WITH THE CHURCH OF THE IMMACULATE OVA.
I WANT THAT WEAPON BACK. AND I'M NOT PARTICULARLY CONCERNED WITH COLLATERAL DAMAGE.
NO.
CHOMP
IT'S NOT THE CULTISTS THAT DID THIS.

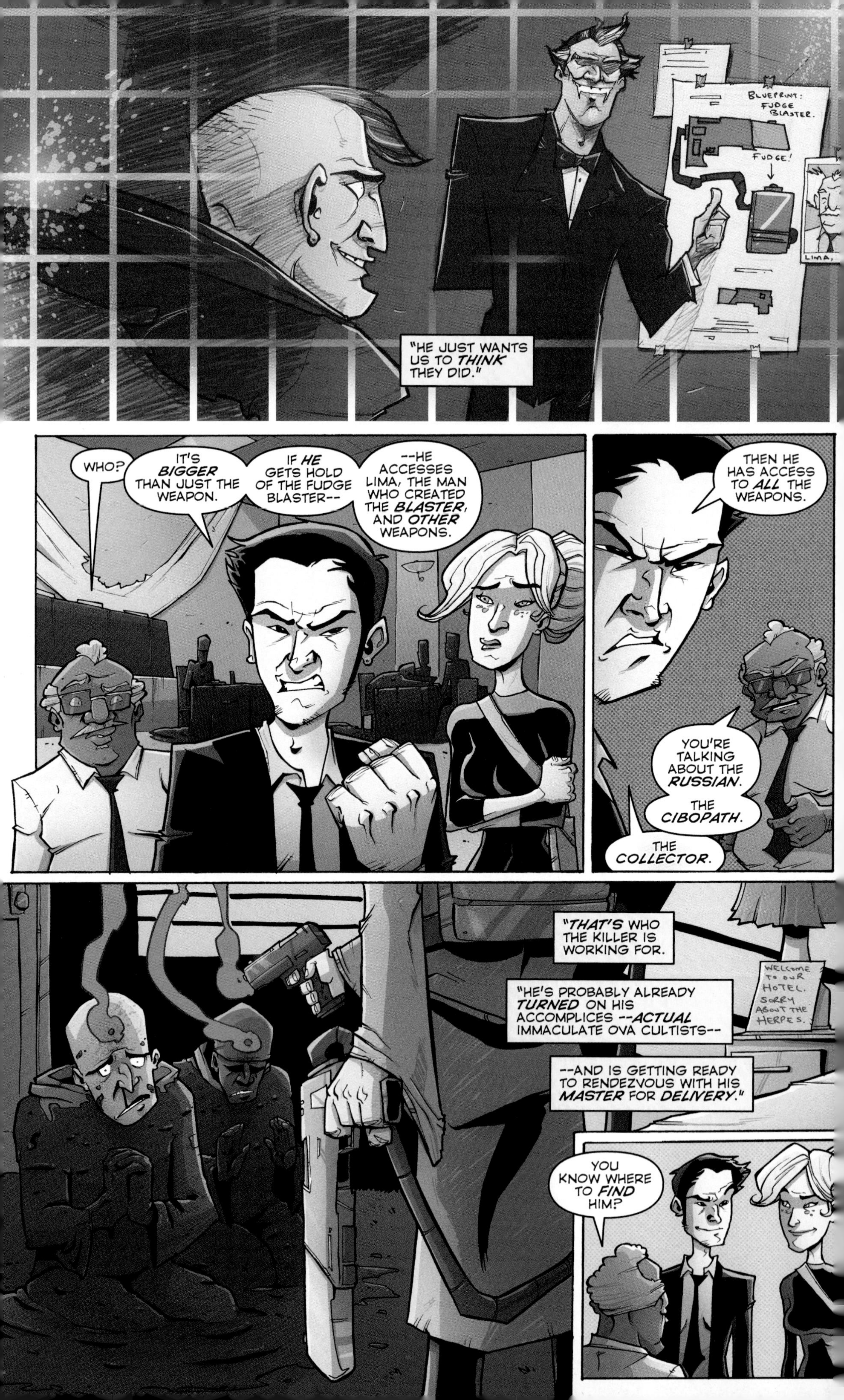

BLUEPRINT: FUDGE BLASTER.
FUDGE!
LIMA,
"HE JUST WANTS US TO THINK THEY DID."
WHO?
IT'S BIGGER THAN JUST THE WEAPON.
IF HE GETS HOLD OF THE FUDGE BLASTER--
--HE ACCESSES LIMA, THE MAN WHO CREATED THE BLASTER, AND OTHER WEAPONS.
THEN HE HAS ACCESS TO ALL THE WEAPONS.
YOU'RE TALKING ABOUT THE RUSSIAN.
THE CIBOPATH.
THE COLLECTOR.
"THAT'S WHO THE KILLER IS WORKING FOR.
WELCOME TO OUR HOTEL. SORRY ABOUT THE HERPES.
"HE'S PROBABLY ALREADY TURNED ON HIS ACCOMPLICES --ACTUAL IMMACULATE OVA CULTISTS--
--AND IS GETTING READY TO RENDEZVOUS WITH HIS MASTER FOR DELIVERY."
YOU KNOW WHERE TO FIND HIM?

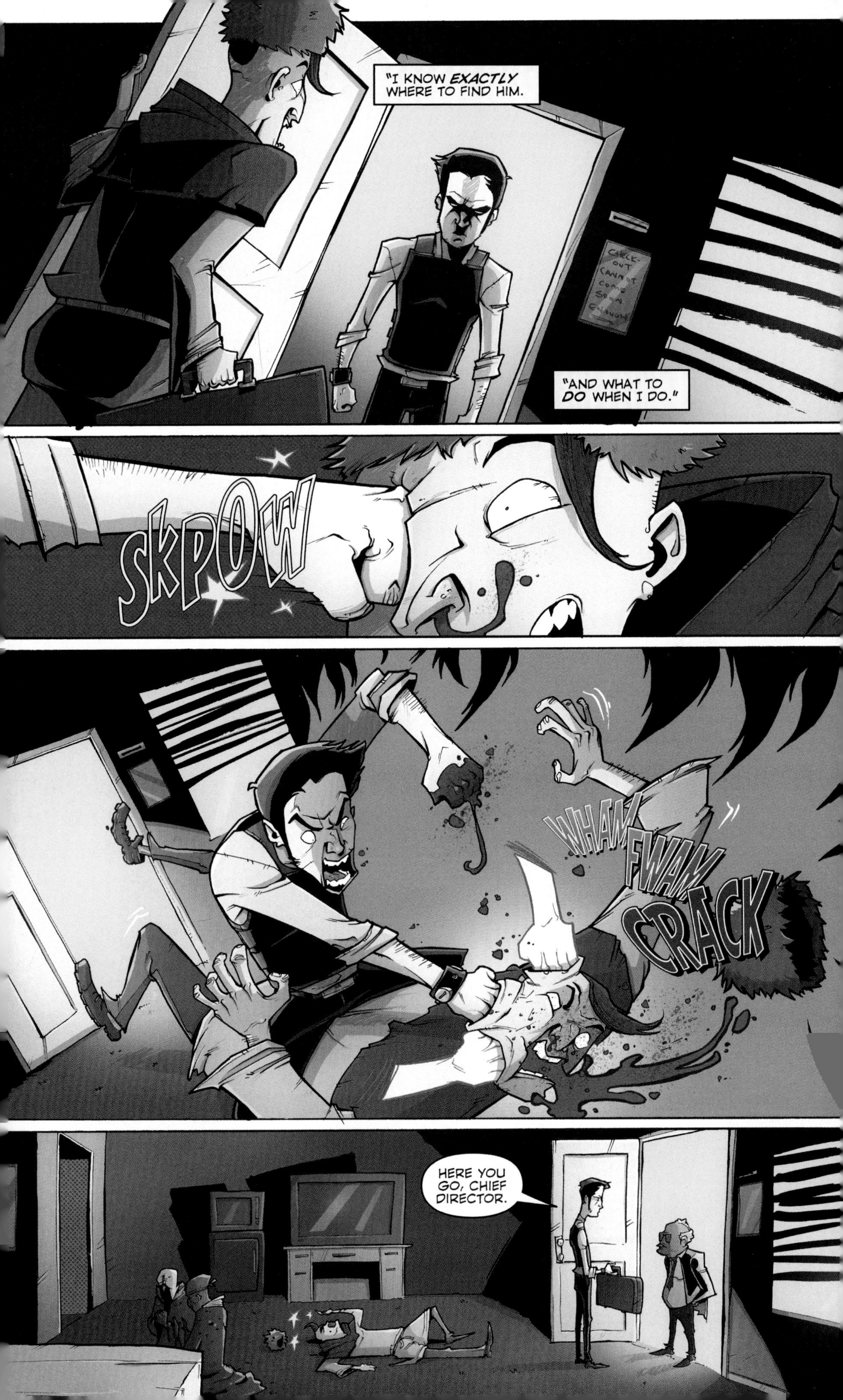
"I KNOW *EXACTLY* WHERE TO FIND HIM.
CHECK-OUT CANNOT COME SOON ENOUGH
"AND WHAT TO *DO* WHEN I DO."
SKPOW
WHAM
FWAM
CRACK
HERE YOU GO, CHIEF DIRECTOR.

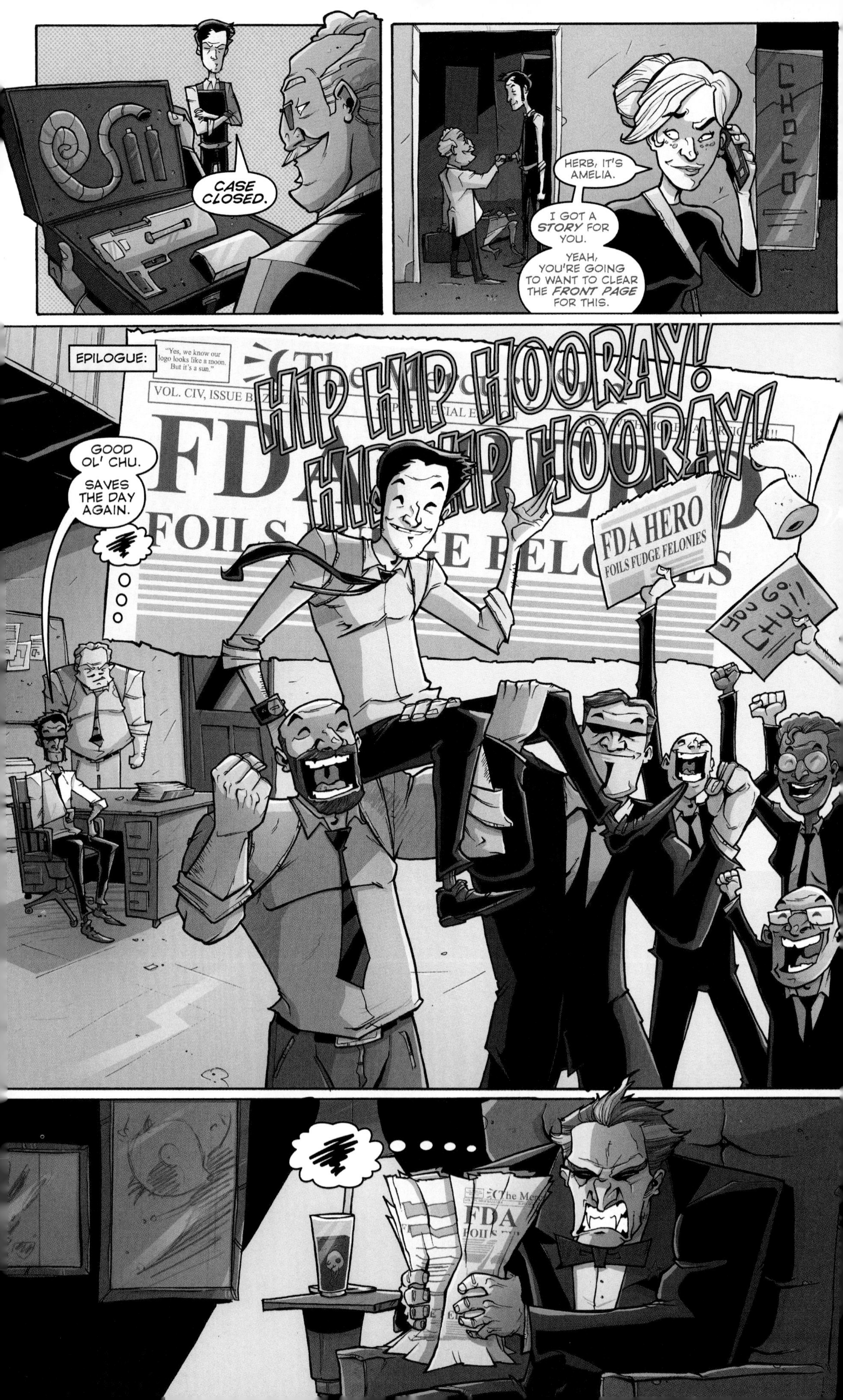
CASE CLOSED.
HERB, IT'S AMELIA.
I GOT A STORY FOR YOU.
YEAH, YOU'RE GOING TO WANT TO CLEAR THE FRONT PAGE FOR THIS.
CHOCO
EPILOGUE:
"Yes, we know our logo looks like a moon. But it's a sun."
HIP HIP HOORAY! HIP HIP HOORAY!
GOOD OL' CHU.
SAVES THE DAY AGAIN.
FDA HERO
FOILS FUDGE FELONIES
YOU GO, CHU!!
FDA

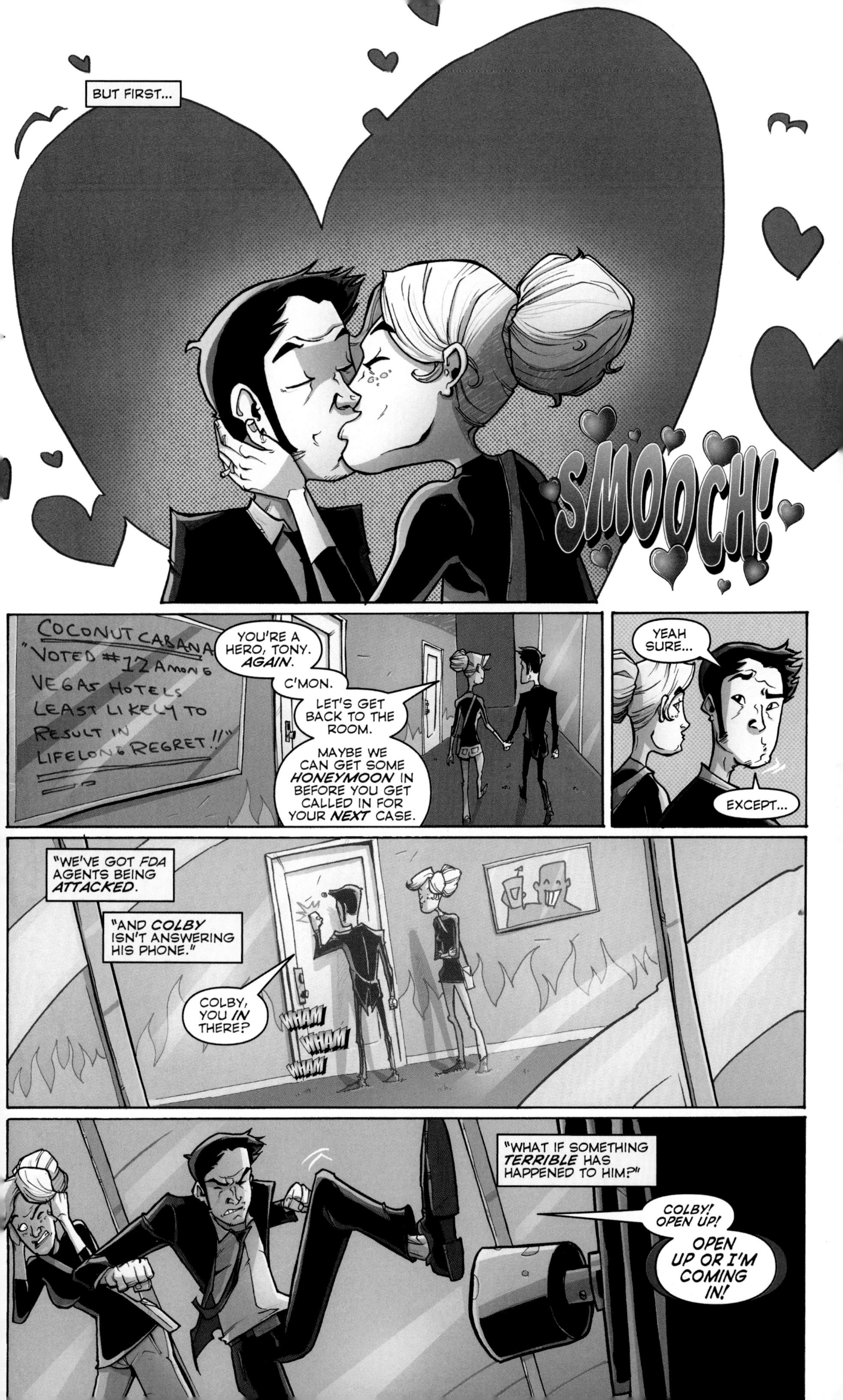

BUT FIRST...
SMOOCH!
COCONUT CABANA "VOTED #12 AMONG VEGAS HOTELS LEAST LIKELY TO RESULT IN LIFELONG REGRET!!"
YOU'RE A HERO, TONY. AGAIN.
C'MON.
LET'S GET BACK TO THE ROOM.
MAYBE WE CAN GET SOME HONEYMOON IN BEFORE YOU GET CALLED IN FOR YOUR NEXT CASE.
YEAH SURE...
EXCEPT...
"WE'VE GOT FDA AGENTS BEING ATTACKED.
"AND COLBY ISN'T ANSWERING HIS PHONE."
COLBY, YOU IN THERE?
WHAM
WHAM
WHAM
"WHAT IF SOMETHING TERRIBLE HAS HAPPENED TO HIM?"
COLBY! OPEN UP!
OPEN UP OR I'M COMING IN!

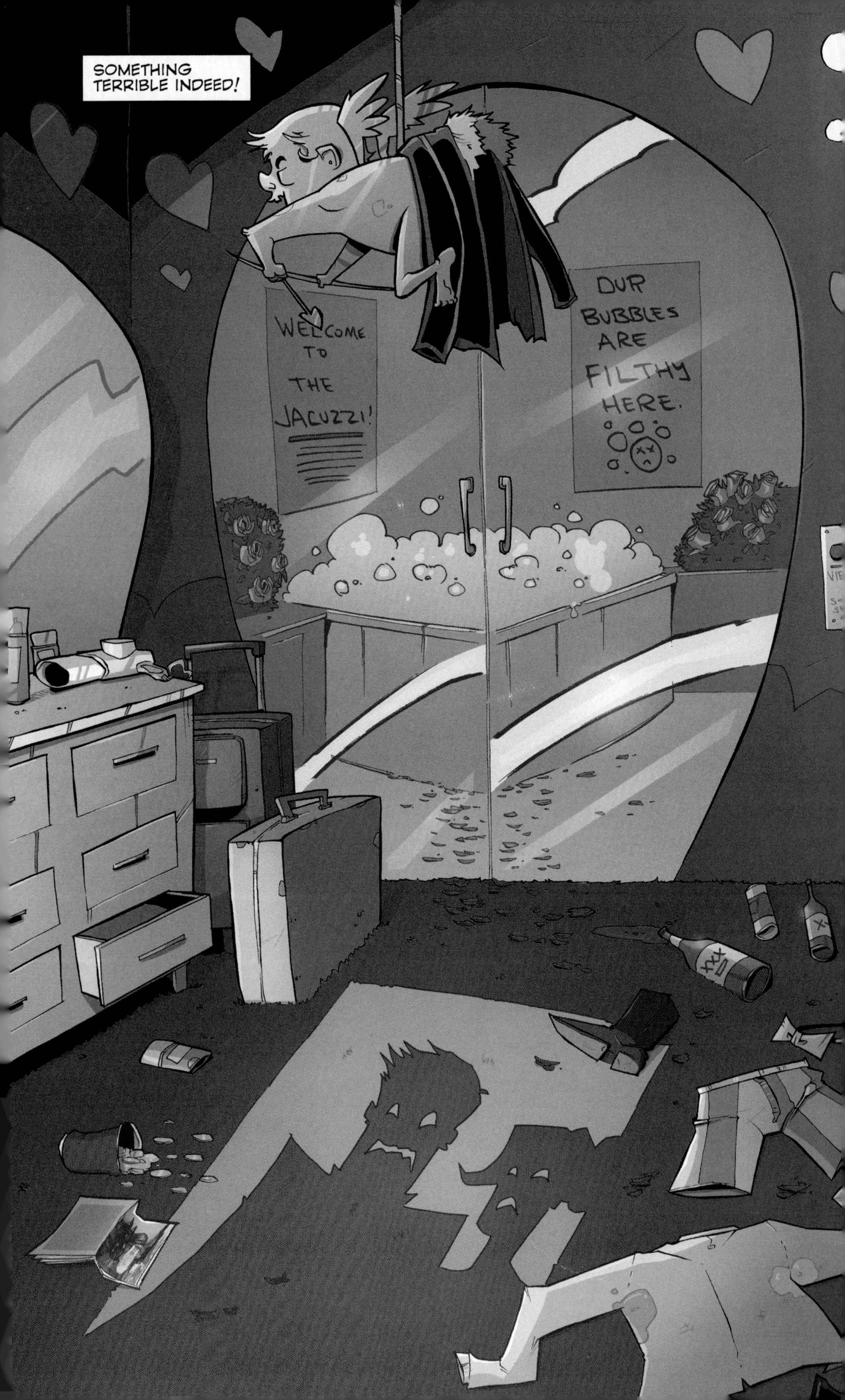
SOMETHING TERRIBLE INDEED!
WELCOME TO THE JACUZZI!
OUR BUBBLES ARE FILTHY HERE.

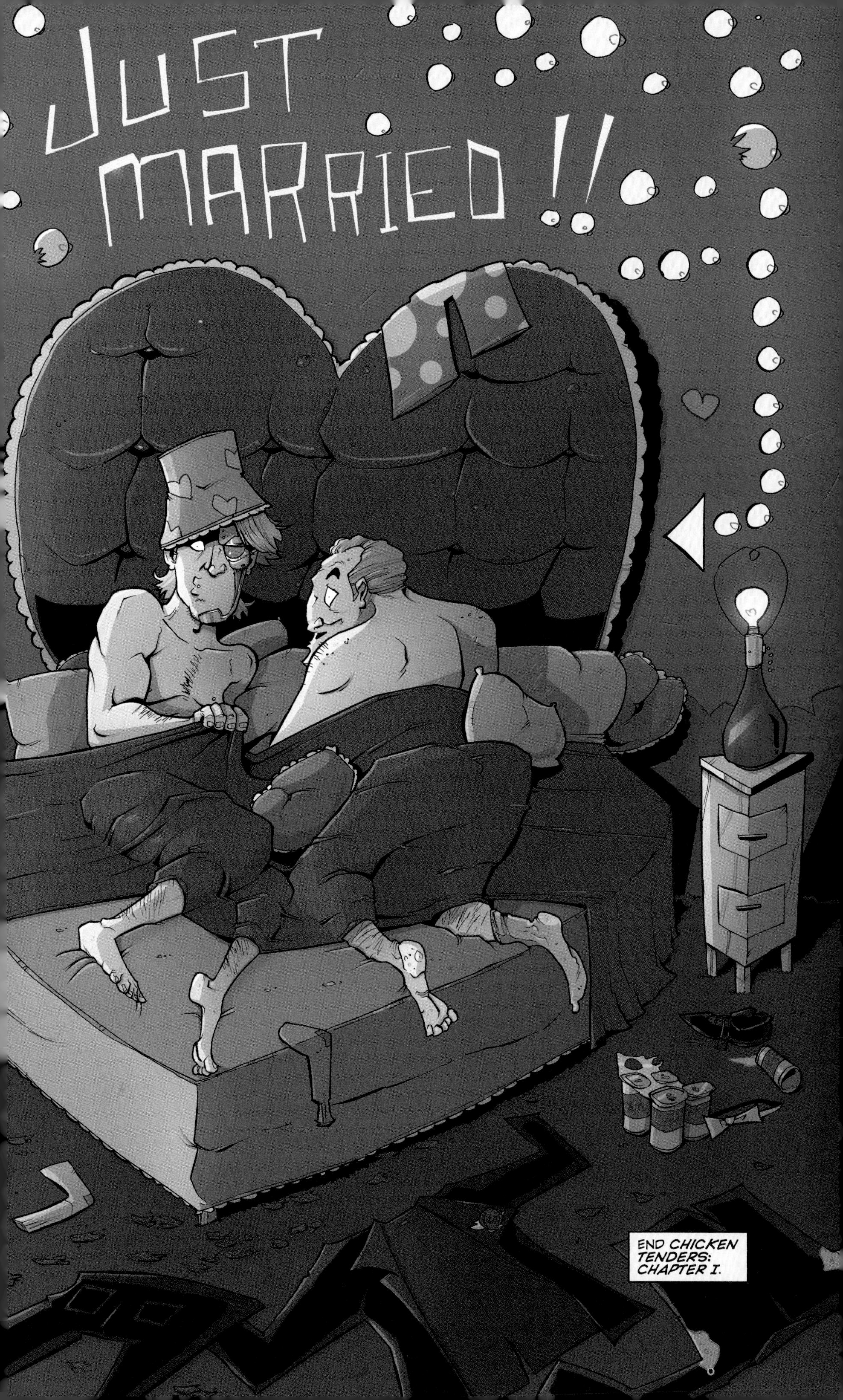
JUST MARRIED!!
END CHICKEN TENDERS: CHAPTER I.

Chapter Two

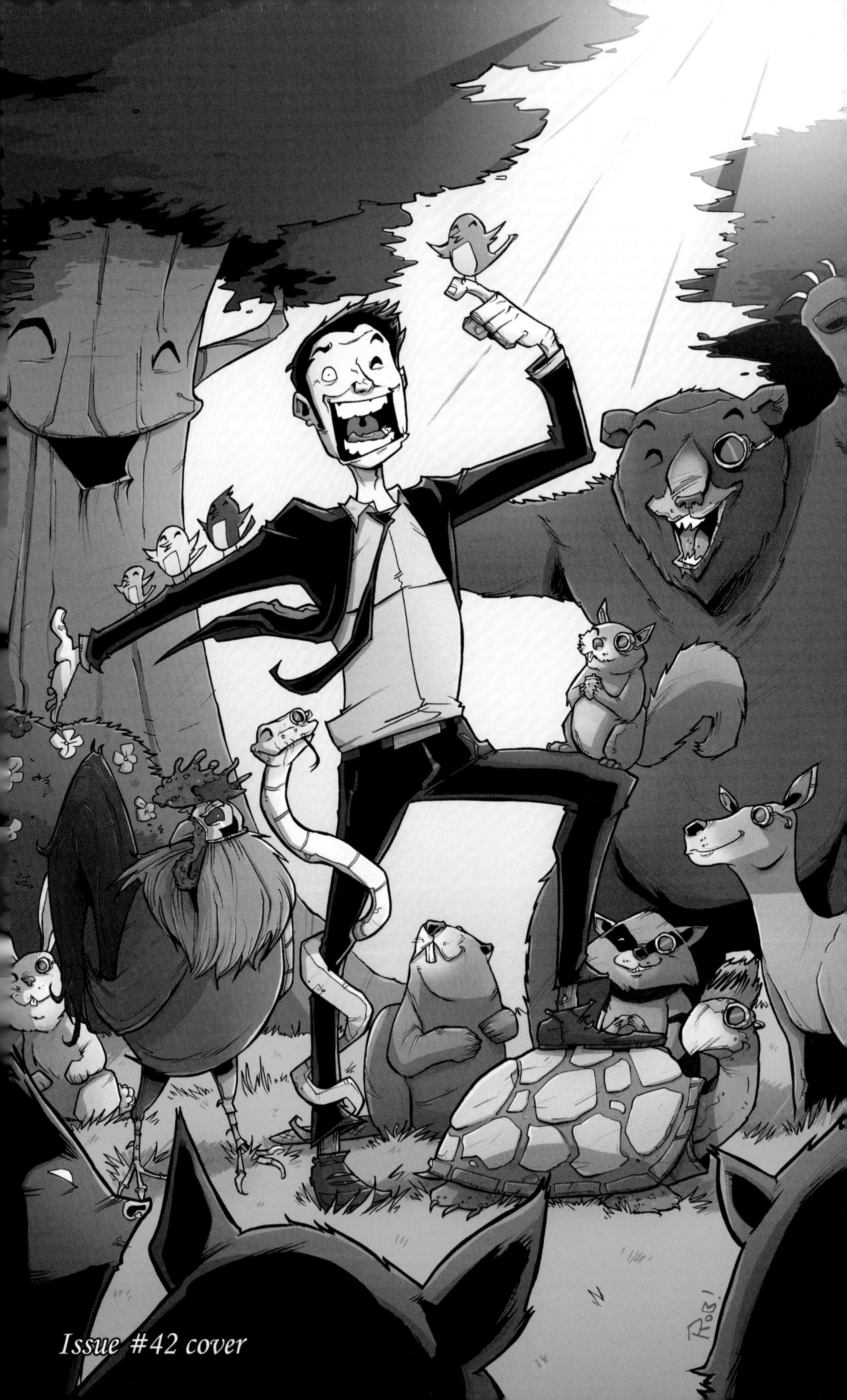
ROB!

Issue #42 cover

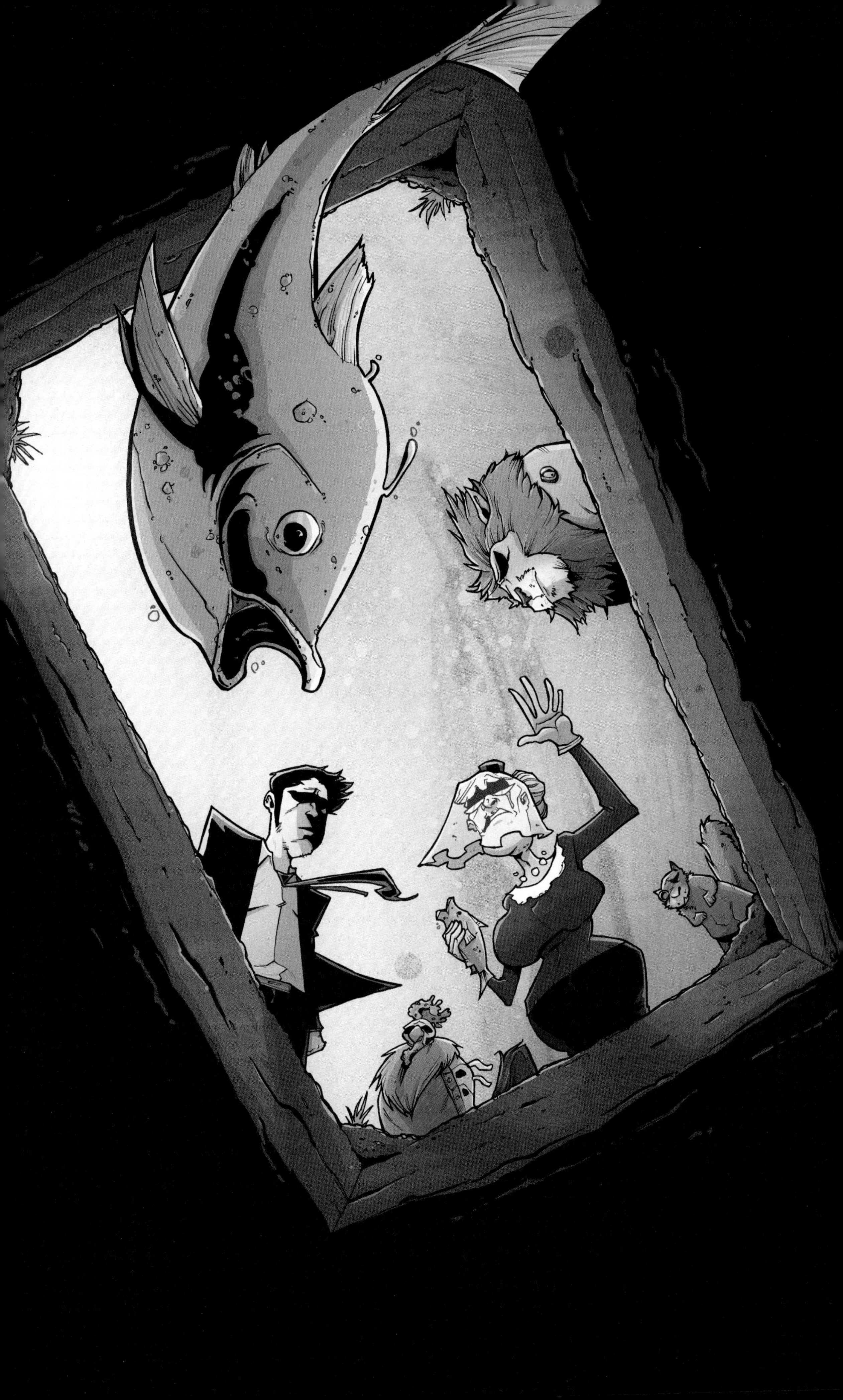

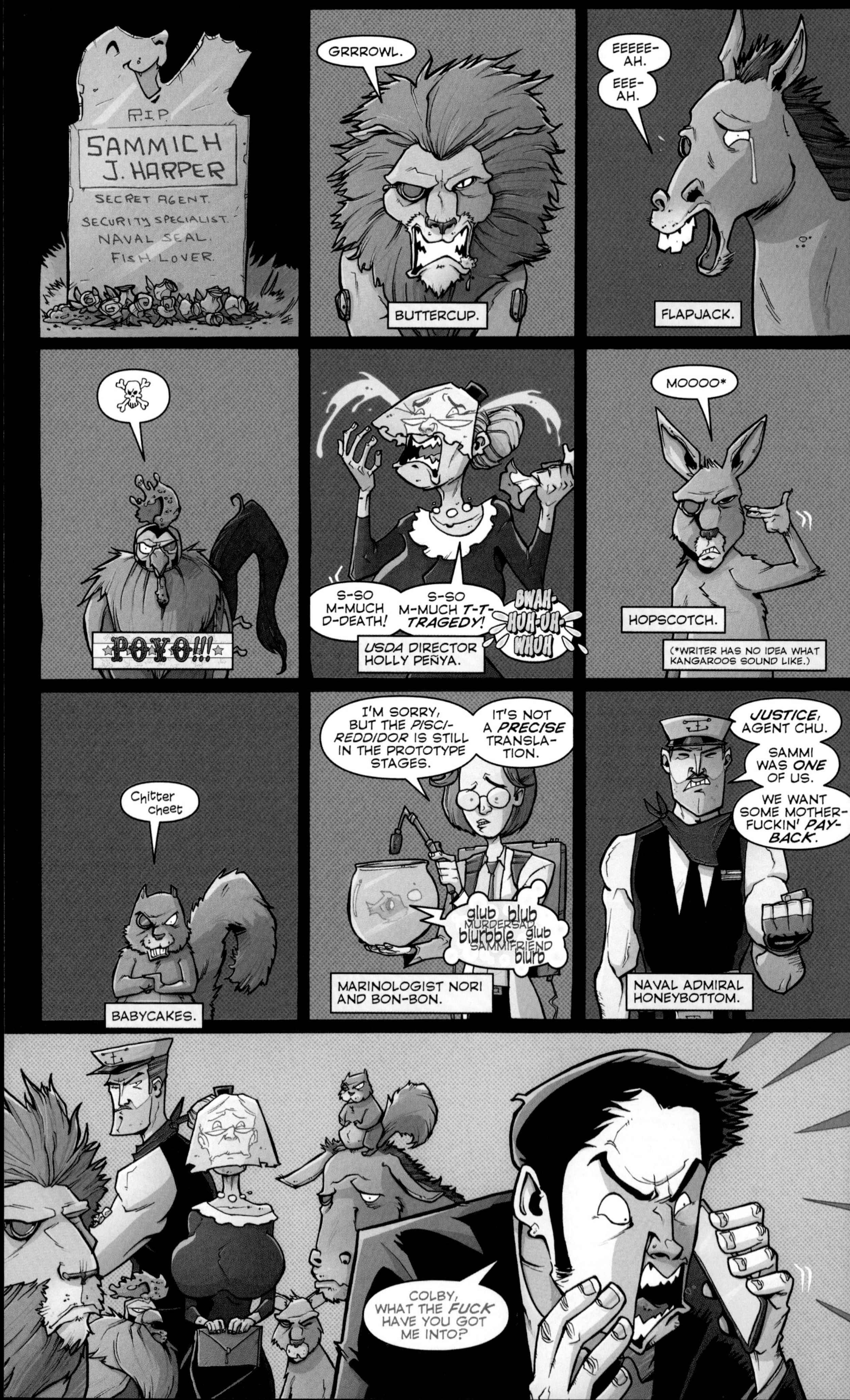
R.I.P.
SAMMICH J. HARPER
SECRET AGENT.
SECURITY SPECIALIST.
NAVAL SEAL.
FISH LOVER.
GRRROWL.
BUTTERCUP.
EEEEE-AH. EEE-AH.
FLAPJACK.
POYO!!!
S-SO M-MUCH D-DEATH!
S-SO M-MUCH T-T-TRAGEDY!
BWAH-HUH-UH WHUH
USDA DIRECTOR HOLLY PEÑYA.
MOOOO*
HOPSCOTCH.
(*WRITER HAS NO IDEA WHAT KANGAROOS SOUND LIKE.)
Chitter cheet
BABYCAKES.
I'M SORRY, BUT THE PISCI-REDDIDOR IS STILL IN THE PROTOTYPE STAGES.
IT'S NOT A PRECISE TRANSLA-TION.
glub blub MURDERSAD blurbble glub SAMMIFRIEND blurb
MARINOLOGIST NORI AND BON-BON.
JUSTICE, AGENT CHU.
SAMMI WAS ONE OF US.
WE WANT SOME MOTHER-FUCKIN' PAY-BACK.
NAVAL ADMIRAL HONEYBOTTOM.
COLBY, WHAT THE FUCK HAVE YOU GOT ME INTO?

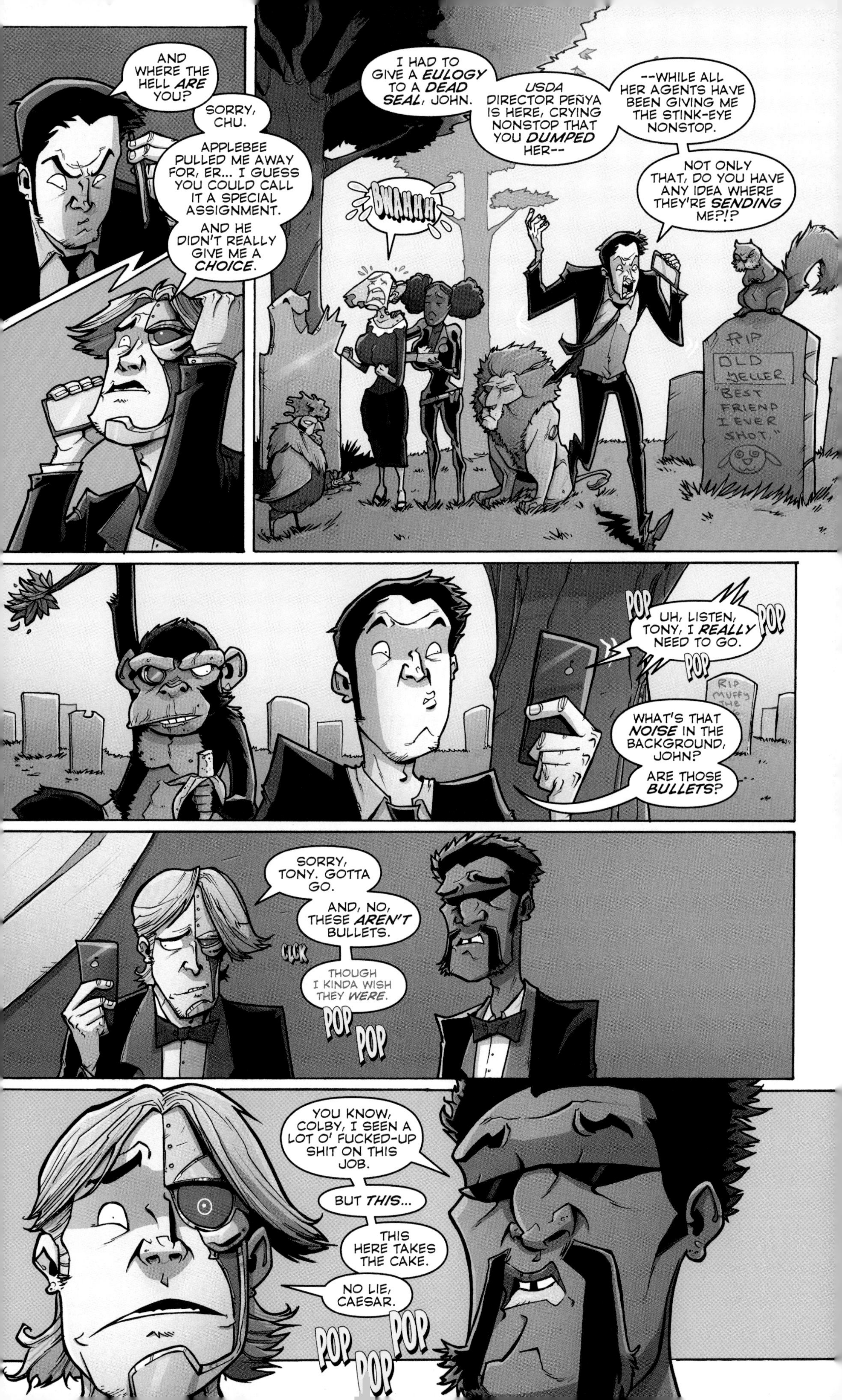

AND WHERE THE HELL *ARE* YOU?
SORRY, CHU.
APPLEBEE PULLED ME AWAY FOR, ER... I GUESS YOU COULD CALL IT A SPECIAL ASSIGNMENT.
AND HE DIDN'T REALLY GIVE ME A *CHOICE*.
I HAD TO GIVE A *EULOGY* TO A *DEAD SEAL*, JOHN.
USDA DIRECTOR PEÑYA IS HERE, CRYING NONSTOP THAT YOU *DUMPED* HER--
--WHILE ALL HER AGENTS HAVE BEEN GIVING ME THE STINK-EYE NONSTOP.
NOT ONLY THAT, DO YOU HAVE ANY IDEA WHERE THEY'RE *SENDING* ME?!?
BWAHHH
RIP
OLD YELLER
"BEST FRIEND I EVER SHOT."
POP
UH, LISTEN, TONY, I *REALLY* NEED TO GO.
POP
POP
RIP MUFFY
WHAT'S THAT *NOISE* IN THE BACKGROUND, JOHN?
ARE THOSE *BULLETS*?
SORRY, TONY. GOTTA GO.
AND, NO, THESE *AREN'T* BULLETS.
CLCK
THOUGH I KINDA WISH THEY *WERE*.
POP
POP
YOU KNOW, COLBY, I SEEN A LOT O' FUCKED-UP SHIT ON THIS JOB.
BUT *THIS*...
THIS HERE TAKES THE CAKE.
NO LIE, CAESAR.
POP
POP
POP

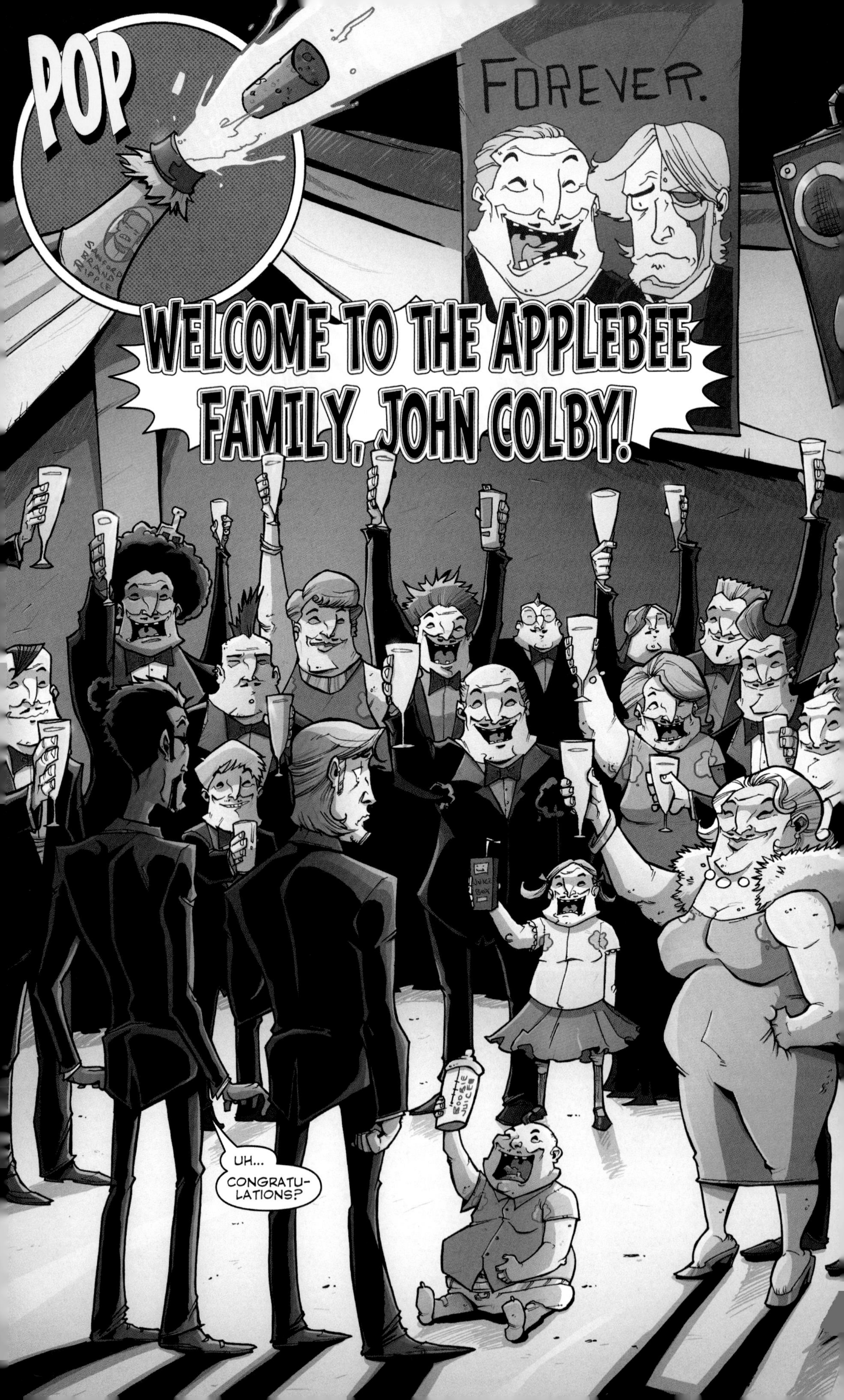
POP
SANFORD BRAND RIPPLE
FOREVER.
WELCOME TO THE APPLEBEE FAMILY, JOHN COLBY!
JUICE BOX
BOOZIE JUICE
UH... CONGRATU-LATIONS?

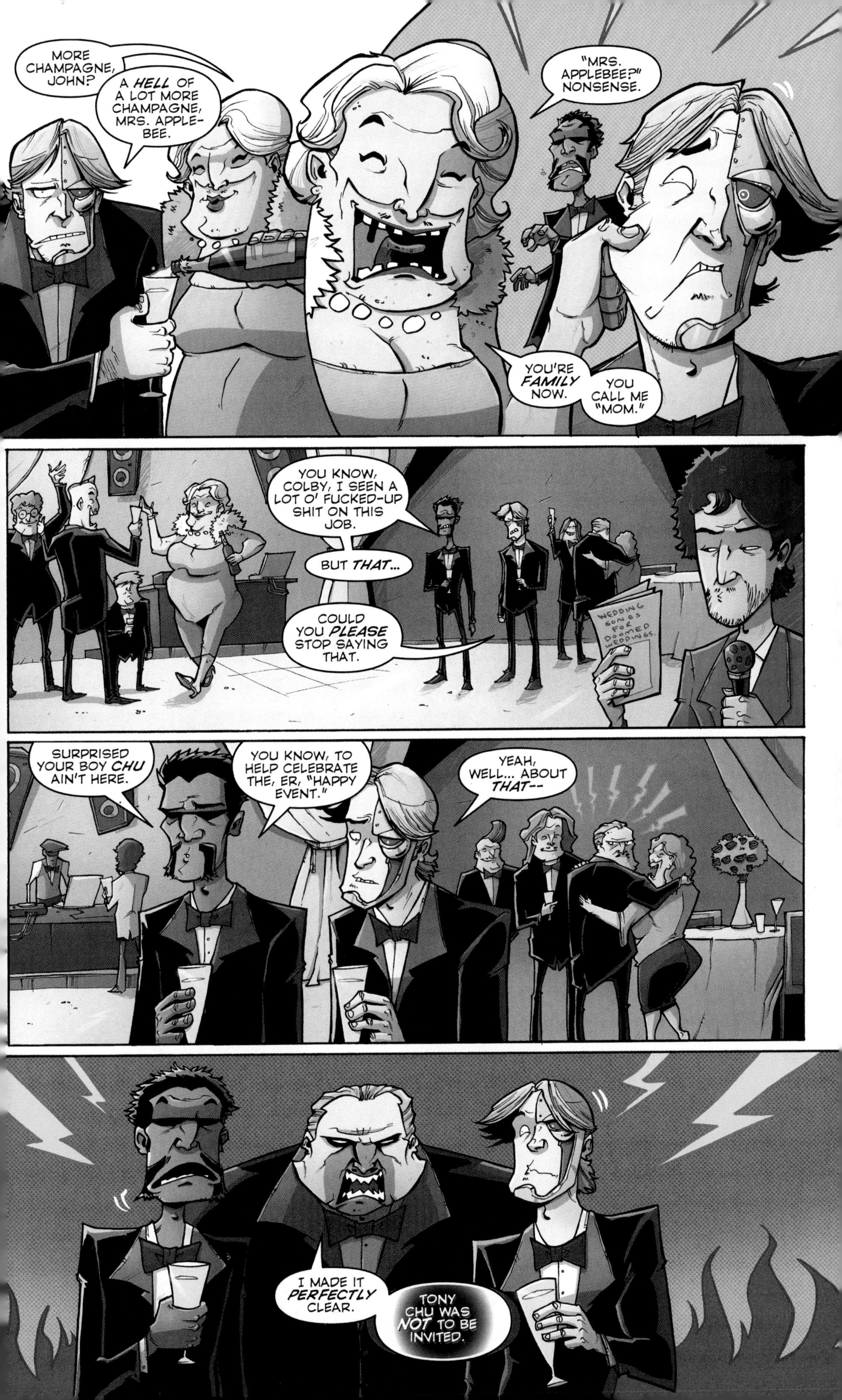
MORE CHAMPAGNE, JOHN?
A HELL OF A LOT MORE CHAMPAGNE, MRS. APPLEBEE.
"MRS. APPLEBEE?" NONSENSE.
YOU'RE FAMILY NOW.
YOU CALL ME "MOM."
YOU KNOW, COLBY, I SEEN A LOT O' FUCKED-UP SHIT ON THIS JOB.
BUT THAT...
COULD YOU PLEASE STOP SAYING THAT.
WEDDING SONGS FOR DOOMED WEDDINGS.
SURPRISED YOUR BOY CHU AIN'T HERE.
YOU KNOW, TO HELP CELEBRATE THE, ER, "HAPPY EVENT."
YEAH, WELL... ABOUT THAT--
I MADE IT PERFECTLY CLEAR.
TONY CHU WAS NOT TO BE INVITED.

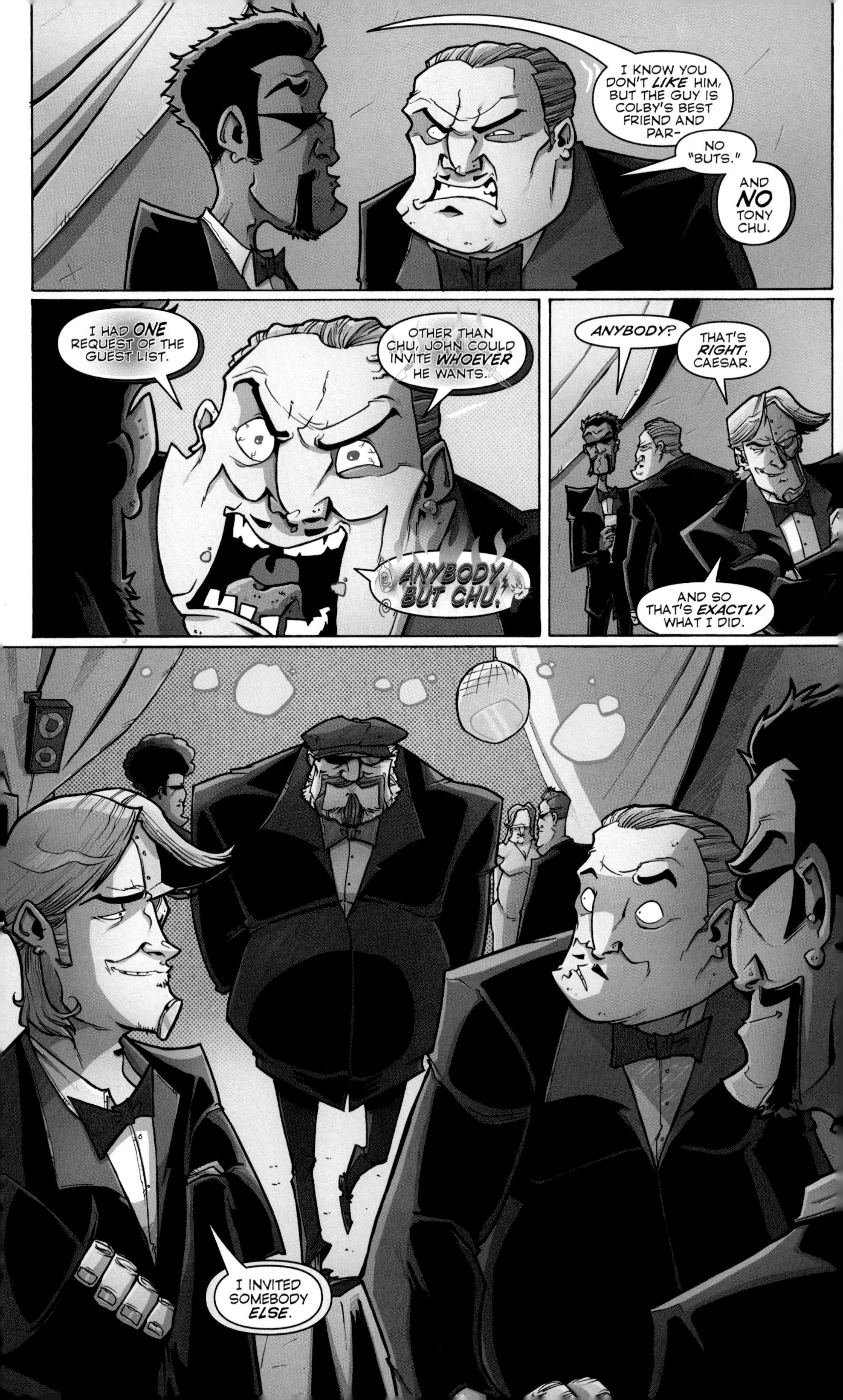
I KNOW YOU DON'T LIKE HIM, BUT THE GUY IS COLBY'S BEST FRIEND AND PAR-
NO "BUTS."
AND NO TONY CHU.
I HAD ONE REQUEST OF THE GUEST LIST.
OTHER THAN CHU, JOHN COULD INVITE WHOEVER HE WANTS.
ANYBODY BUT CHU.
ANYBODY?
THAT'S RIGHT, CAESAR.
AND SO THAT'S EXACTLY WHAT I DID.
I INVITED SOMEBODY ELSE.

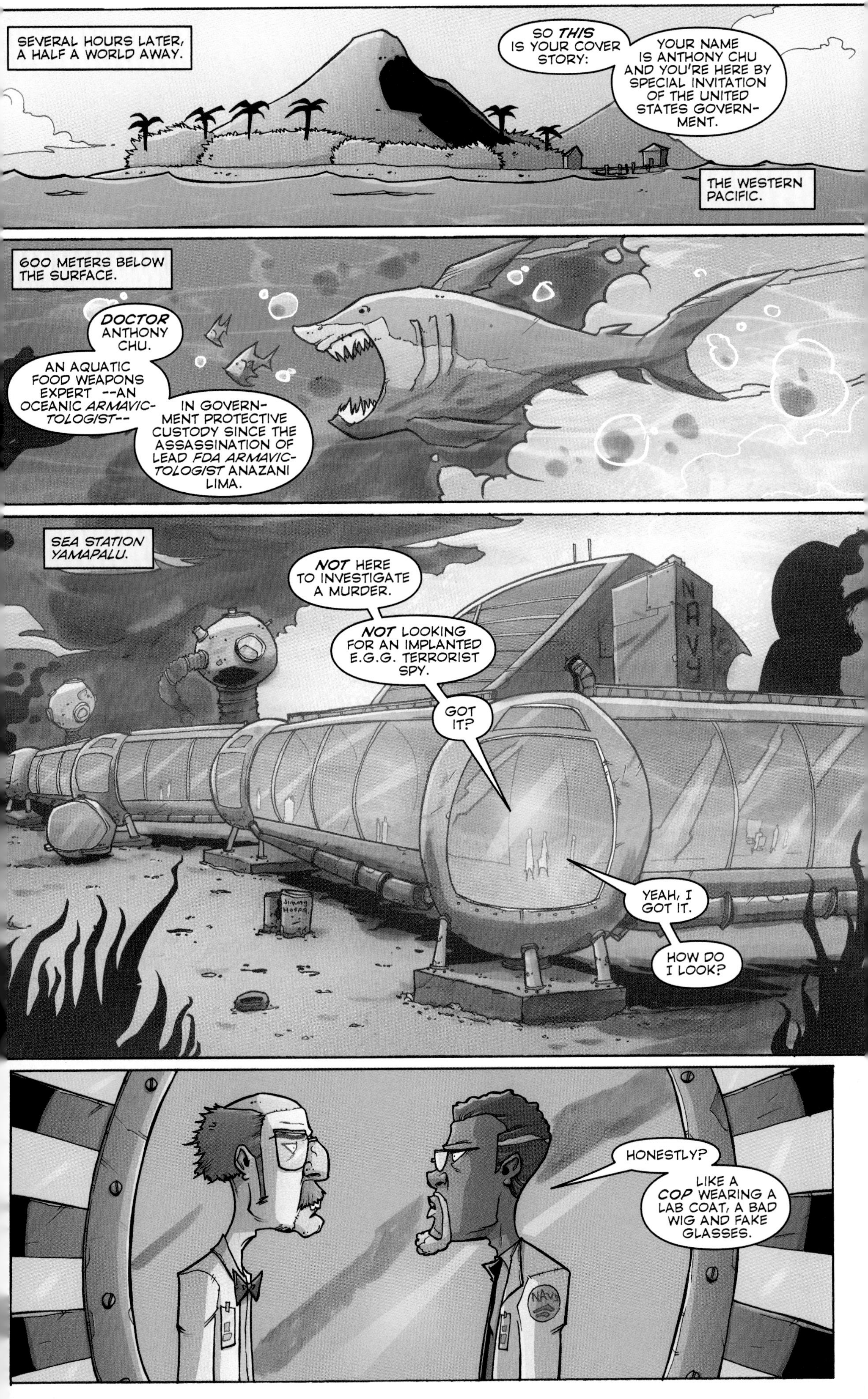
SEVERAL HOURS LATER, A HALF A WORLD AWAY.
SO *THIS* IS YOUR COVER STORY:
YOUR NAME IS ANTHONY CHU AND YOU'RE HERE BY SPECIAL INVITATION OF THE UNITED STATES GOVERNMENT.
THE WESTERN PACIFIC.
600 METERS BELOW THE SURFACE.
DOCTOR ANTHONY CHU.
AN AQUATIC FOOD WEAPONS EXPERT --AN OCEANIC *ARMAVICTOLOGIST*--
IN GOVERNMENT PROTECTIVE CUSTODY SINCE THE ASSASSINATION OF LEAD *FDA ARMAVICTOLOGIST* ANAZANI LIMA.
SEA STATION YAMAPALU.
NAVY
NOT HERE TO INVESTIGATE A MURDER.
NOT LOOKING FOR AN IMPLANTED E.G.G. TERRORIST SPY.
GOT IT?
YEAH, I GOT IT.
HOW DO I LOOK?
HONESTLY?
LIKE A *COP* WEARING A LAB COAT, A BAD WIG AND FAKE GLASSES.

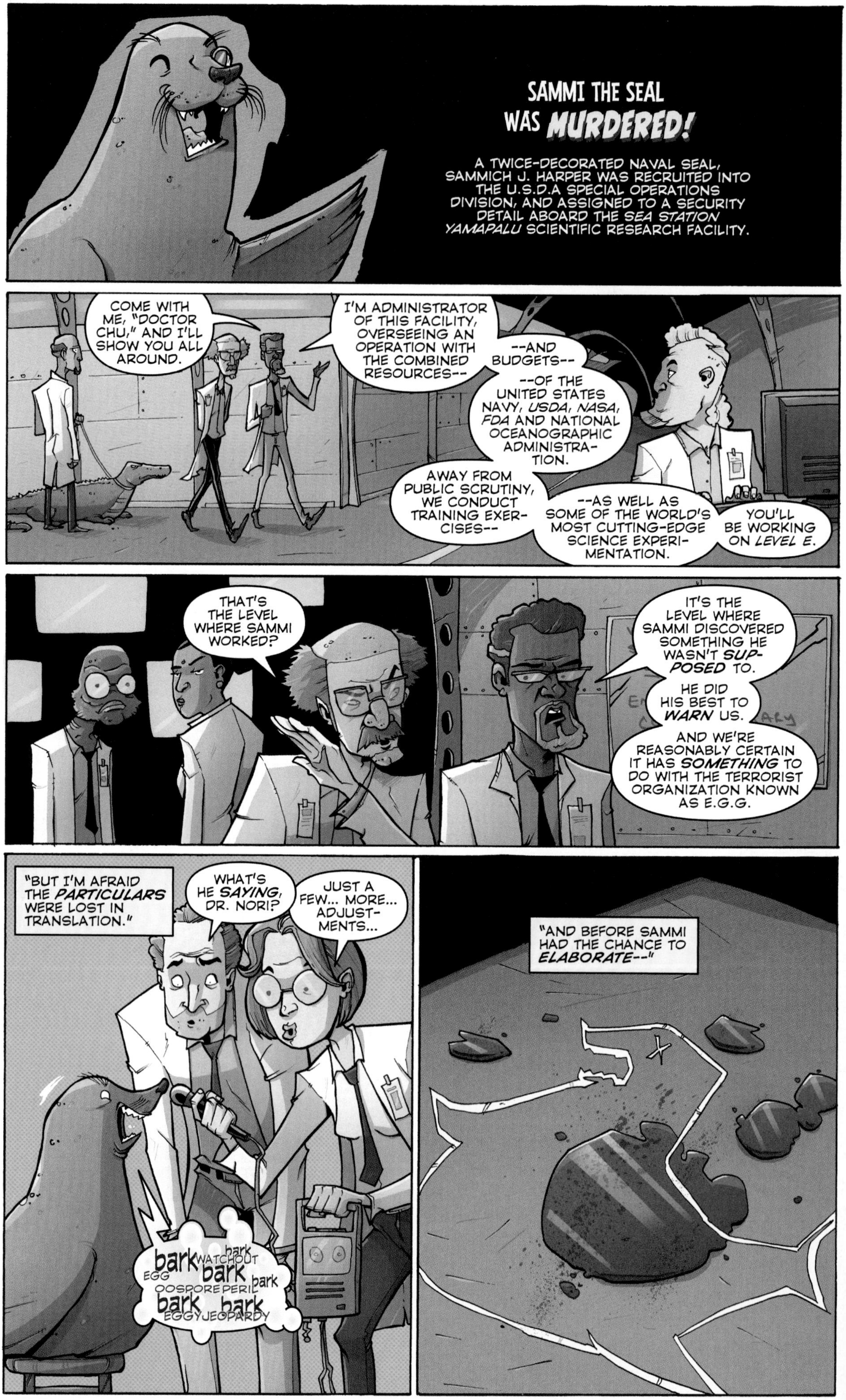
SAMMI THE SEAL WAS *MURDERED!*
A TWICE-DECORATED NAVAL SEAL, SAMMICH J. HARPER WAS RECRUITED INTO THE U.S.D.A SPECIAL OPERATIONS DIVISION, AND ASSIGNED TO A SECURITY DETAIL ABOARD THE *SEA STATION YAMAPALU* SCIENTIFIC RESEARCH FACILITY.
COME WITH ME, "DOCTOR CHU," AND I'LL SHOW YOU ALL AROUND.
I'M ADMINISTRATOR OF THIS FACILITY, OVERSEEING AN OPERATION WITH THE COMBINED RESOURCES--
--AND BUDGETS--
--OF THE UNITED STATES NAVY, *USDA, NASA, FDA* AND NATIONAL OCEANOGRAPHIC ADMINISTRATION.
AWAY FROM PUBLIC SCRUTINY, WE CONDUCT TRAINING EXERCISES--
--AS WELL AS SOME OF THE WORLD'S MOST CUTTING-EDGE SCIENCE EXPERIMENTATION.
YOU'LL BE WORKING ON *LEVEL E.*
THAT'S THE LEVEL WHERE SAMMI WORKED?
IT'S THE LEVEL WHERE SAMMI DISCOVERED SOMETHING HE WASN'T *SUPPOSED* TO.
HE DID HIS BEST TO *WARN* US.
AND WE'RE REASONABLY CERTAIN IT HAS *SOMETHING* TO DO WITH THE TERRORIST ORGANIZATION KNOWN AS E.G.G.
"BUT I'M AFRAID THE *PARTICULARS* WERE LOST IN TRANSLATION."
WHAT'S HE *SAYING*, DR. NORI?
JUST A FEW... MORE... ADJUSTMENTS...
bark hark WATCHOUT EGG bark bark OOSPORE PERIL bark bark EGGY JEOPARDY
"AND BEFORE SAMMI HAD THE CHANCE TO *ELABORATE--*"

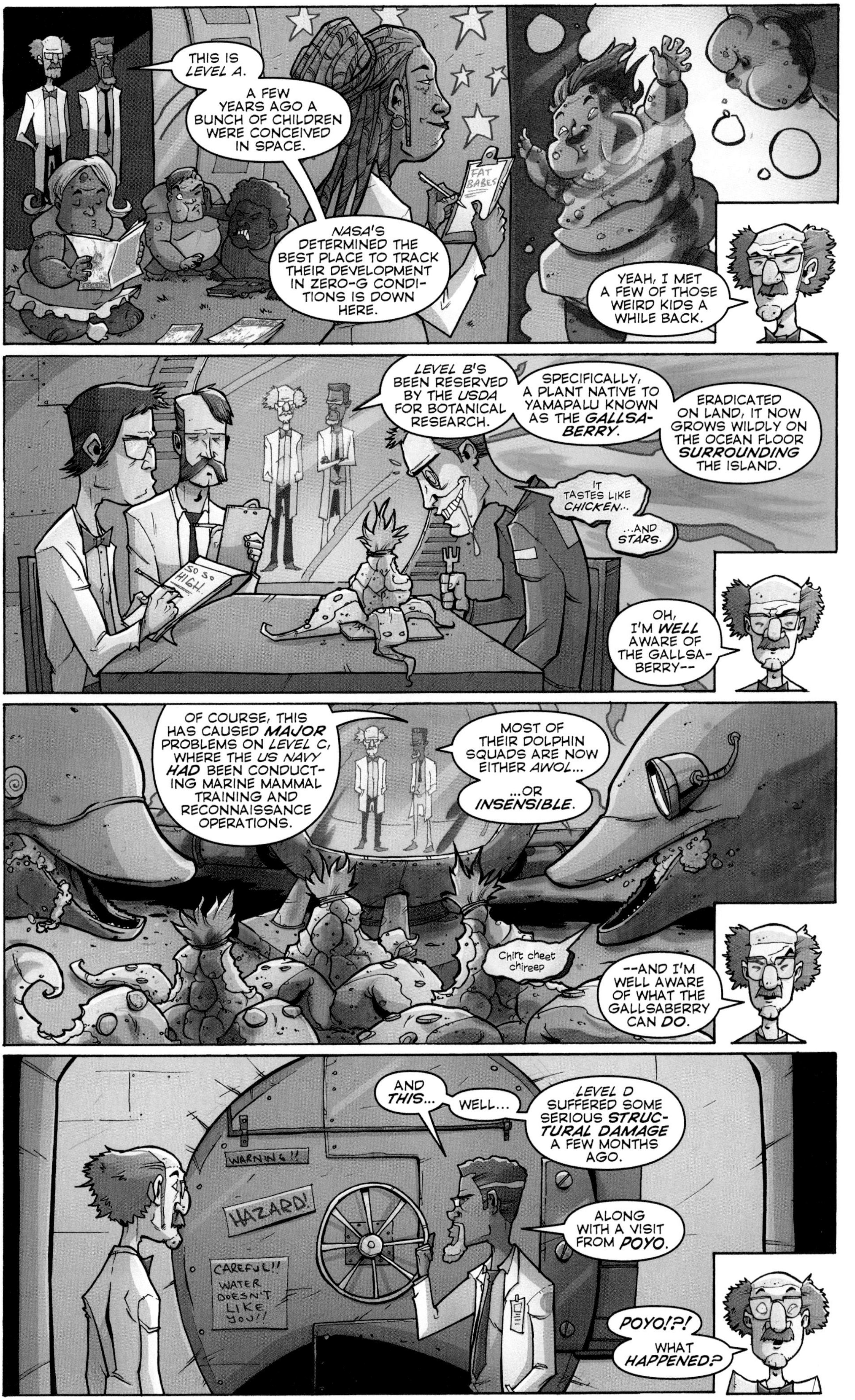
THIS IS LEVEL A.
A FEW YEARS AGO A BUNCH OF CHILDREN WERE CONCEIVED IN SPACE.
FAT BABES
NASA'S DETERMINED THE BEST PLACE TO TRACK THEIR DEVELOPMENT IN ZERO-G CONDITIONS IS DOWN HERE.
YEAH, I MET A FEW OF THOSE WEIRD KIDS A WHILE BACK.
LEVEL B'S BEEN RESERVED BY THE USDA FOR BOTANICAL RESEARCH.
SPECIFICALLY, A PLANT NATIVE TO YAMAPALU KNOWN AS THE GALLSABERRY.
ERADICATED ON LAND, IT NOW GROWS WILDLY ON THE OCEAN FLOOR SURROUNDING THE ISLAND.
SO SO HIGH.
IT TASTES LIKE CHICKEN...
...AND STARS.
OH, I'M WELL AWARE OF THE GALLSABERRY--
OF COURSE, THIS HAS CAUSED MAJOR PROBLEMS ON LEVEL C, WHERE THE US NAVY HAD BEEN CONDUCTING MARINE MAMMAL TRAINING AND RECONNAISSANCE OPERATIONS.
MOST OF THEIR DOLPHIN SQUADS ARE NOW EITHER AWOL...
...OR INSENSIBLE.
Chirt cheet chireep
--AND I'M WELL AWARE OF WHAT THE GALLSABERRY CAN DO.
AND THIS...
WELL...
LEVEL D SUFFERED SOME SERIOUS STRUCTURAL DAMAGE A FEW MONTHS AGO.
WARNING!!
HAZARD!
CAREFUL!! WATER DOESN'T LIKE YOU!!
ALONG WITH A VISIT FROM POYO.
POYO!?!
WHAT HAPPENED?

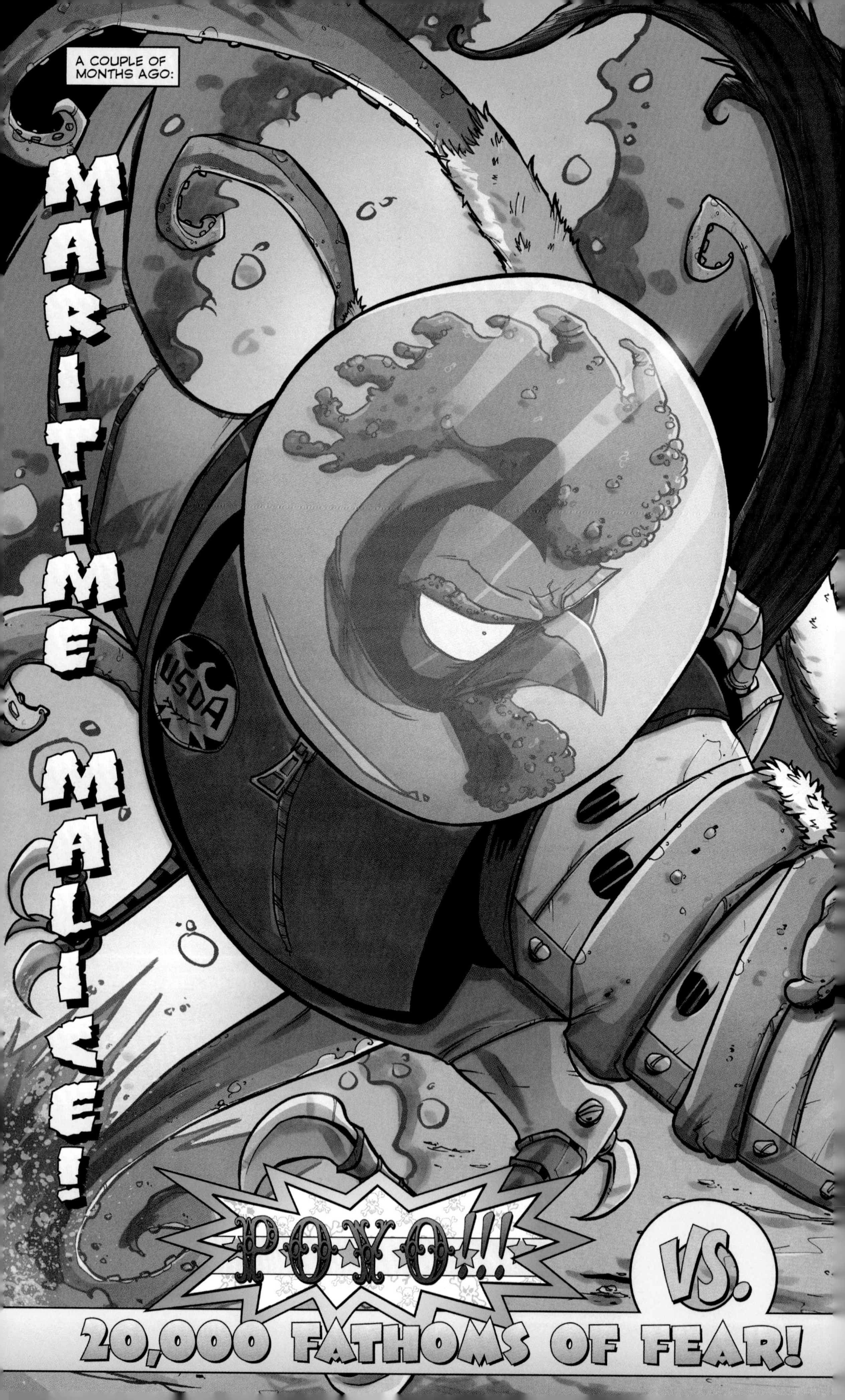
A COUPLE OF MONTHS AGO:
MARITIME MALICE!
USDA
POYO!!!
VS.
20,000 FATHOMS OF FEAR!

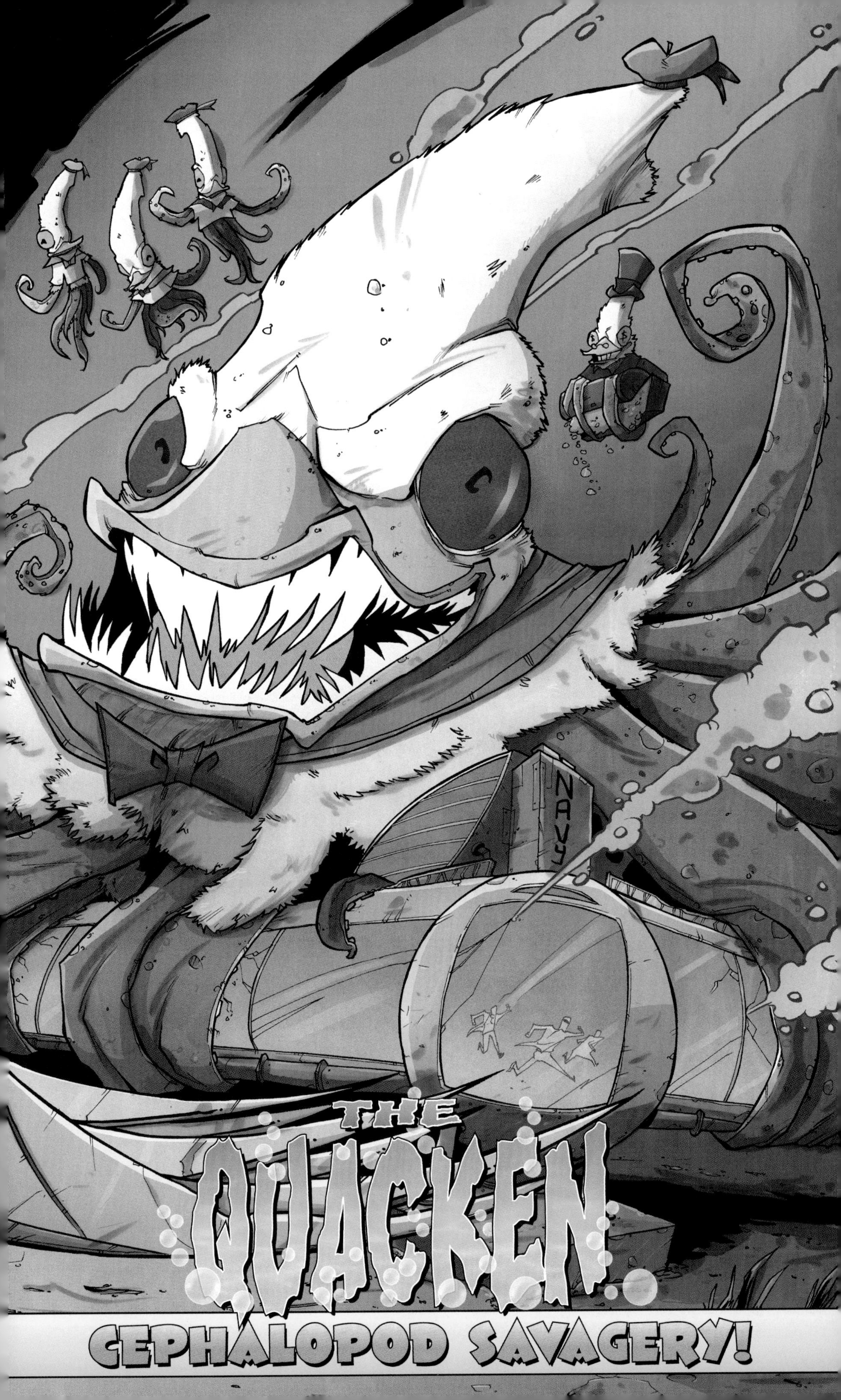
NAVY
THE
QUACKEN
CEPHALOPOD SAVAGERY!

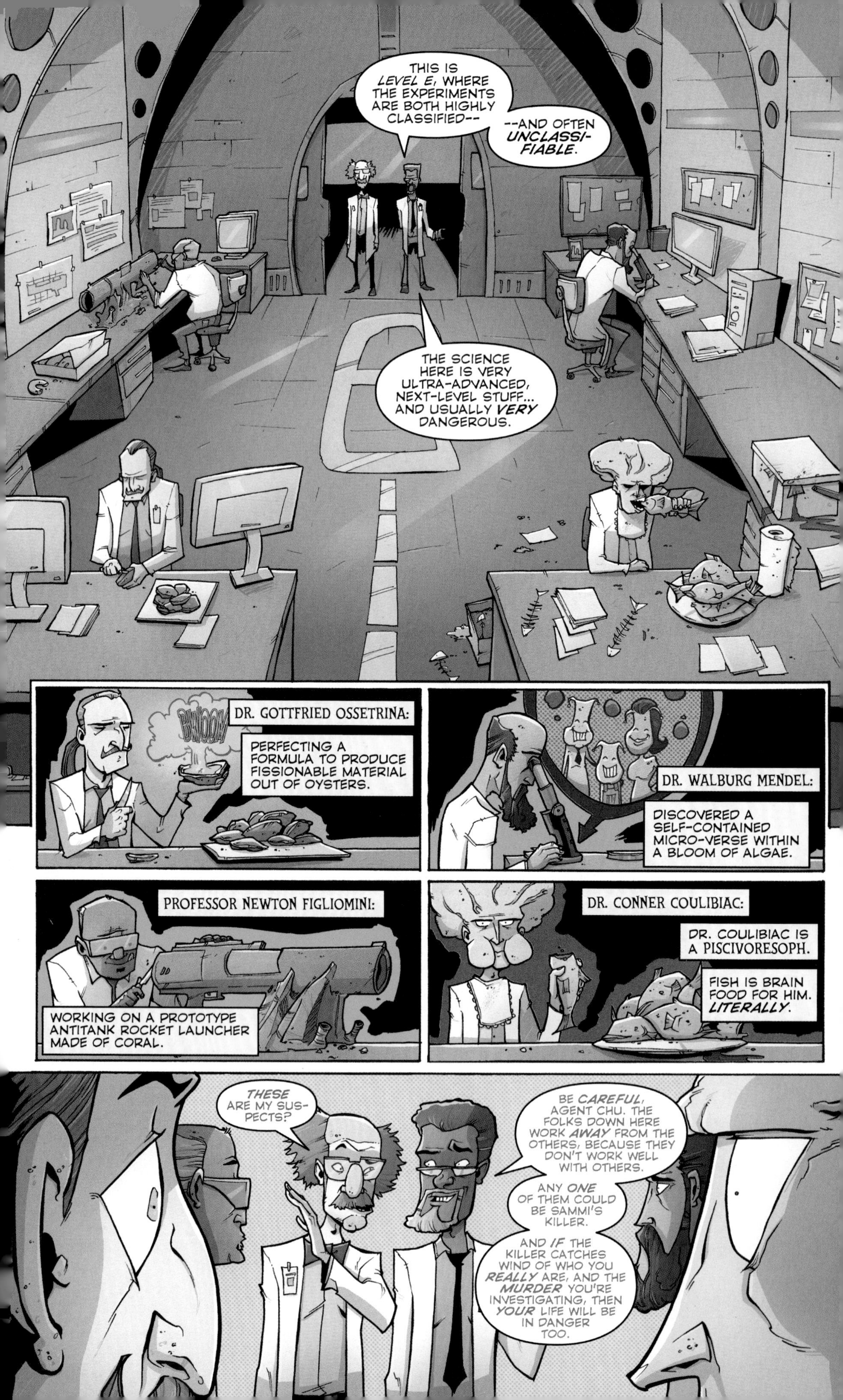
THIS IS LEVEL E, WHERE THE EXPERIMENTS ARE BOTH HIGHLY CLASSIFIED--
--AND OFTEN UNCLASSIFIABLE.
THE SCIENCE HERE IS VERY ULTRA-ADVANCED, NEXT-LEVEL STUFF... AND USUALLY VERY DANGEROUS.
DR. GOTTFRIED OSSETRINA:
BWOOM
PERFECTING A FORMULA TO PRODUCE FISSIONABLE MATERIAL OUT OF OYSTERS.
DR. WALBURG MENDEL:
DISCOVERED A SELF-CONTAINED MICRO-VERSE WITHIN A BLOOM OF ALGAE.
PROFESSOR NEWTON FIGLIOMINI:
WORKING ON A PROTOTYPE ANTITANK ROCKET LAUNCHER MADE OF CORAL.
DR. CONNER COULIBIAC:
DR. COULIBIAC IS A PISCIVORESOPH.
FISH IS BRAIN FOOD FOR HIM. LITERALLY.
THESE ARE MY SUSPECTS?
BE CAREFUL, AGENT CHU. THE FOLKS DOWN HERE WORK AWAY FROM THE OTHERS, BECAUSE THEY DON'T WORK WELL WITH OTHERS.
ANY ONE OF THEM COULD BE SAMMI'S KILLER.
AND IF THE KILLER CATCHES WIND OF WHO YOU REALLY ARE, AND THE MURDER YOU'RE INVESTIGATING, THEN YOUR LIFE WILL BE IN DANGER TOO.

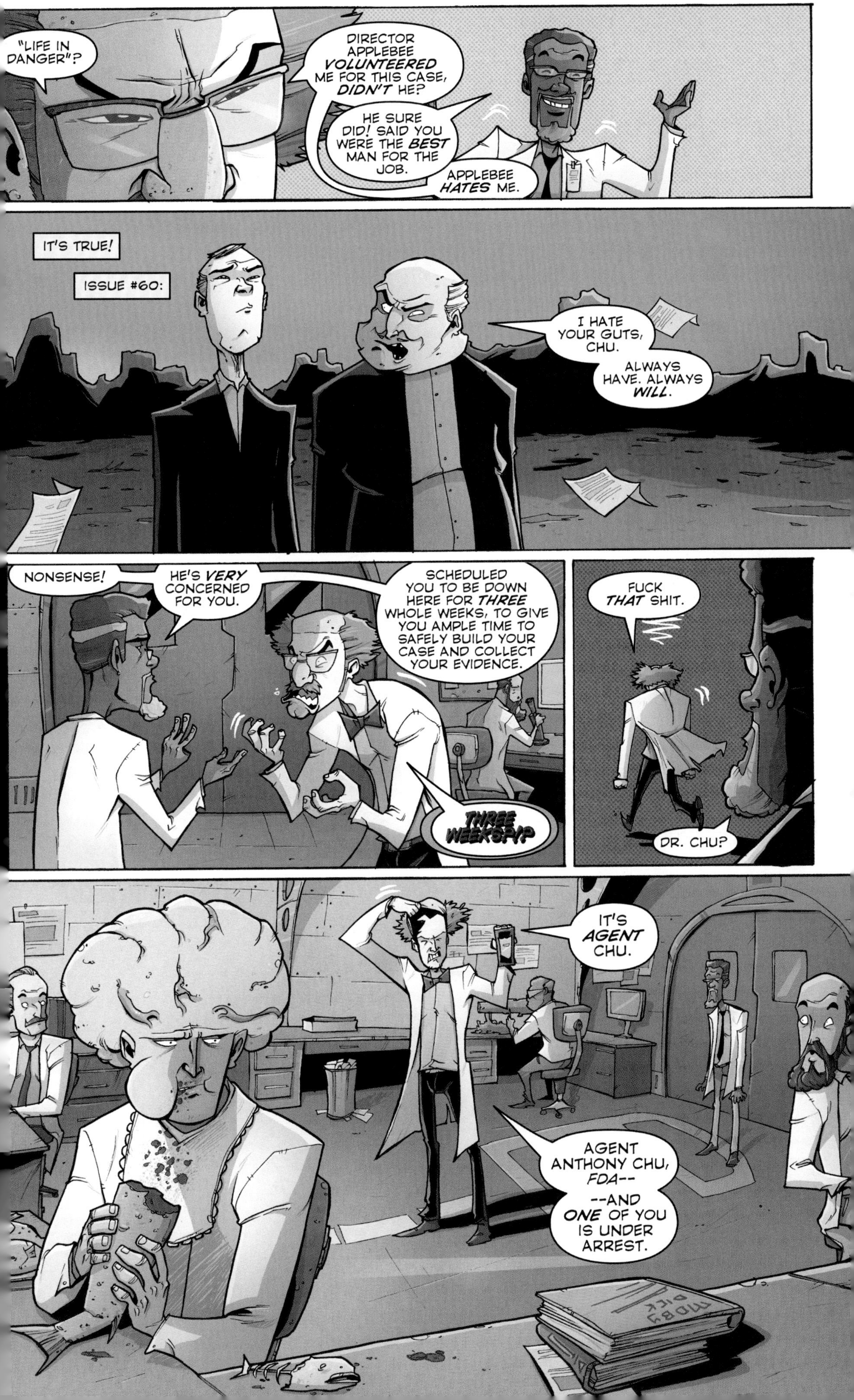

"LIFE IN DANGER"?
DIRECTOR APPLEBEE VOLUNTEERED ME FOR THIS CASE, DIDN'T HE?
HE SURE DID! SAID YOU WERE THE BEST MAN FOR THE JOB.
APPLEBEE HATES ME.
IT'S TRUE!
ISSUE #60:
I HATE YOUR GUTS, CHU.
ALWAYS HAVE. ALWAYS WILL.
NONSENSE!
HE'S VERY CONCERNED FOR YOU.
SCHEDULED YOU TO BE DOWN HERE FOR THREE WHOLE WEEKS, TO GIVE YOU AMPLE TIME TO SAFELY BUILD YOUR CASE AND COLLECT YOUR EVIDENCE.
THREE WEEKS?!?
FUCK THAT SHIT.
DR. CHU?
IT'S AGENT CHU.
AGENT ANTHONY CHU, FDA--
--AND ONE OF YOU IS UNDER ARREST.
MOBY DICK

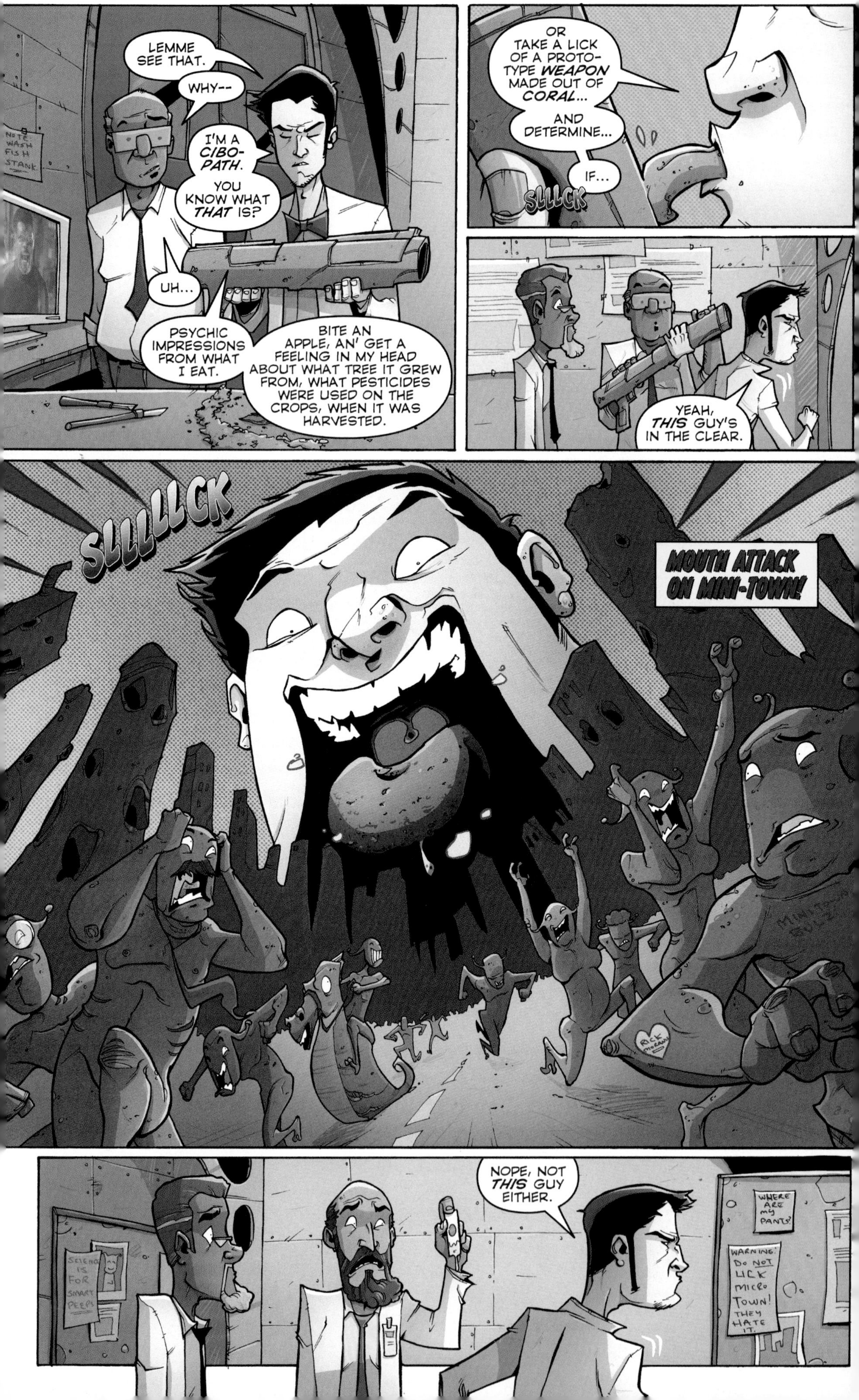
LEMME SEE THAT.
WHY--
I'M A CIBO-PATH.
YOU KNOW WHAT THAT IS?
UH...
PSYCHIC IMPRESSIONS FROM WHAT I EAT.
BITE AN APPLE, AN' GET A FEELING IN MY HEAD ABOUT WHAT TREE IT GREW FROM, WHAT PESTICIDES WERE USED ON THE CROPS, WHEN IT WAS HARVESTED.
NOTE: WASH FISH STANK.
OR TAKE A LICK OF A PROTO-TYPE WEAPON MADE OUT OF CORAL...
AND DETERMINE...
IF...
SLLLCK
YEAH, THIS GUY'S IN THE CLEAR.
SLLLLLCK
MOUTH ATTACK ON MINI-TOWN!
NOPE, NOT THIS GUY EITHER.
SCIENCE IS FOR SMART PEEPS
WHERE ARE MY PANTS?
WARNING! DO NOT LICK MICRO TOWN! THEY HATE IT.

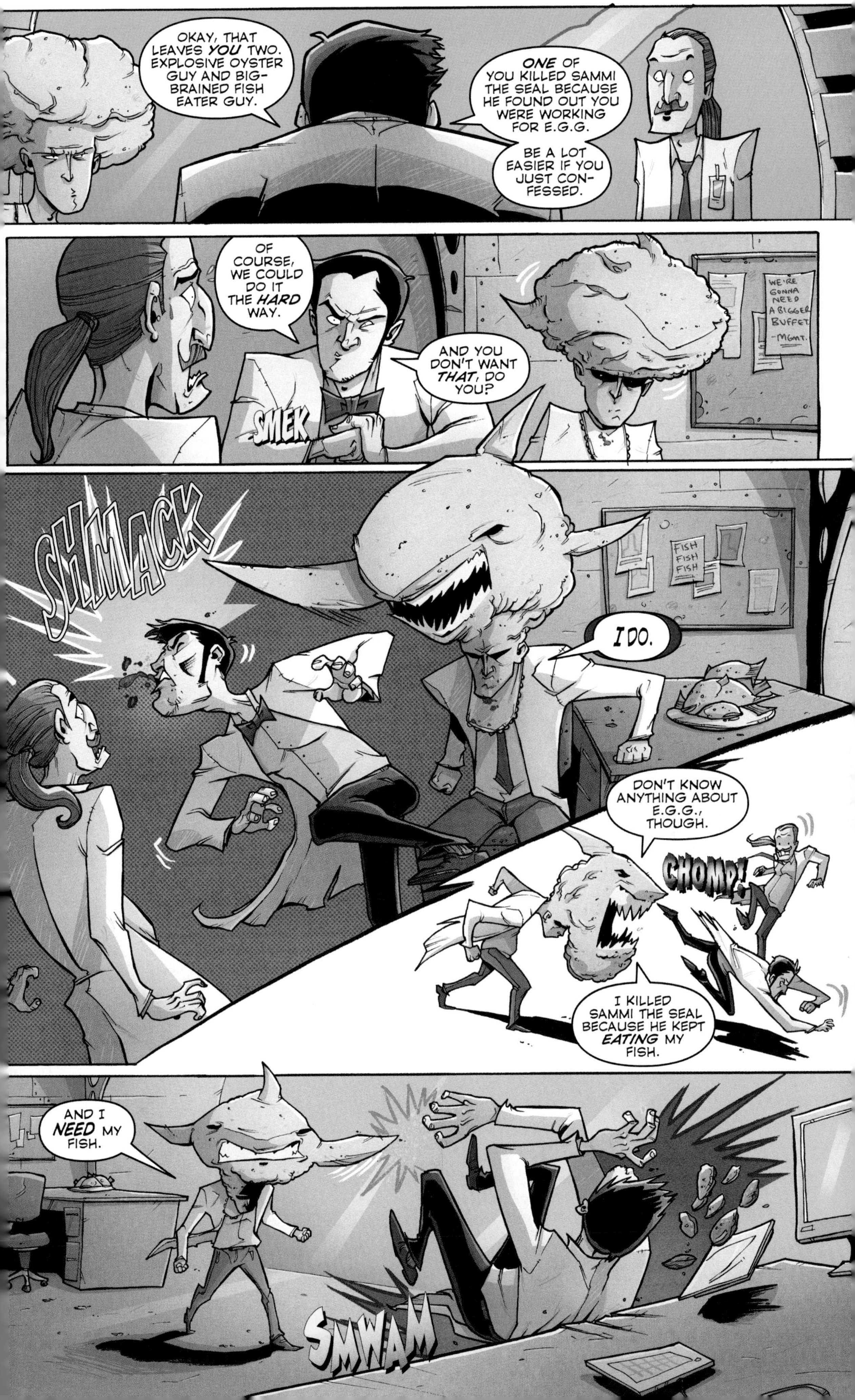
OKAY, THAT LEAVES *YOU* TWO. EXPLOSIVE OYSTER GUY AND BIG-BRAINED FISH EATER GUY.
ONE OF YOU KILLED SAMMI THE SEAL BECAUSE HE FOUND OUT YOU WERE WORKING FOR E.G.G.
BE A LOT EASIER IF YOU JUST CON-FESSED.
OF COURSE, WE COULD DO IT THE *HARD* WAY.
WE'RE GONNA NEED A BIGGER BUFFET. -MGMT.
AND YOU DON'T WANT *THAT*, DO YOU?
SMEK
SHMACK
FISH FISH FISH
I DO.
DON'T KNOW ANYTHING ABOUT E.G.G., THOUGH.
CHOMP!
I KILLED SAMMI THE SEAL BECAUSE HE KEPT *EATING* MY FISH.
AND I *NEED* MY FISH.
SMWAM

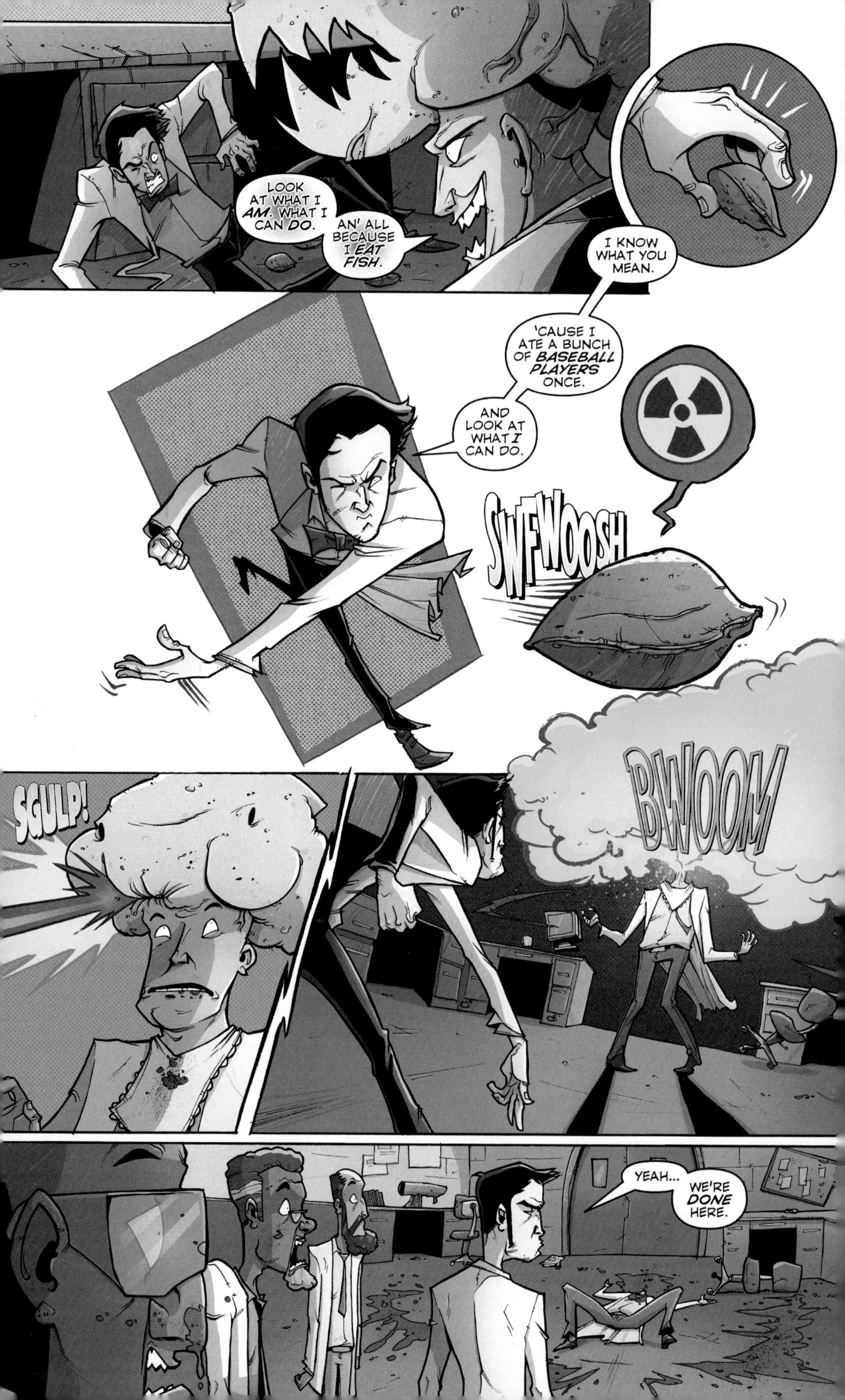

LOOK AT WHAT I *AM*. WHAT I CAN *DO*.
AN' ALL BECAUSE I *EAT FISH*.
I KNOW WHAT YOU MEAN.
'CAUSE I ATE A BUNCH OF ***BASEBALL PLAYERS*** ONCE.
AND LOOK AT WHAT *I* CAN DO.
SWFWOOSH
SGULP!
BWOOM
YEAH...
WE'RE *DONE* HERE.

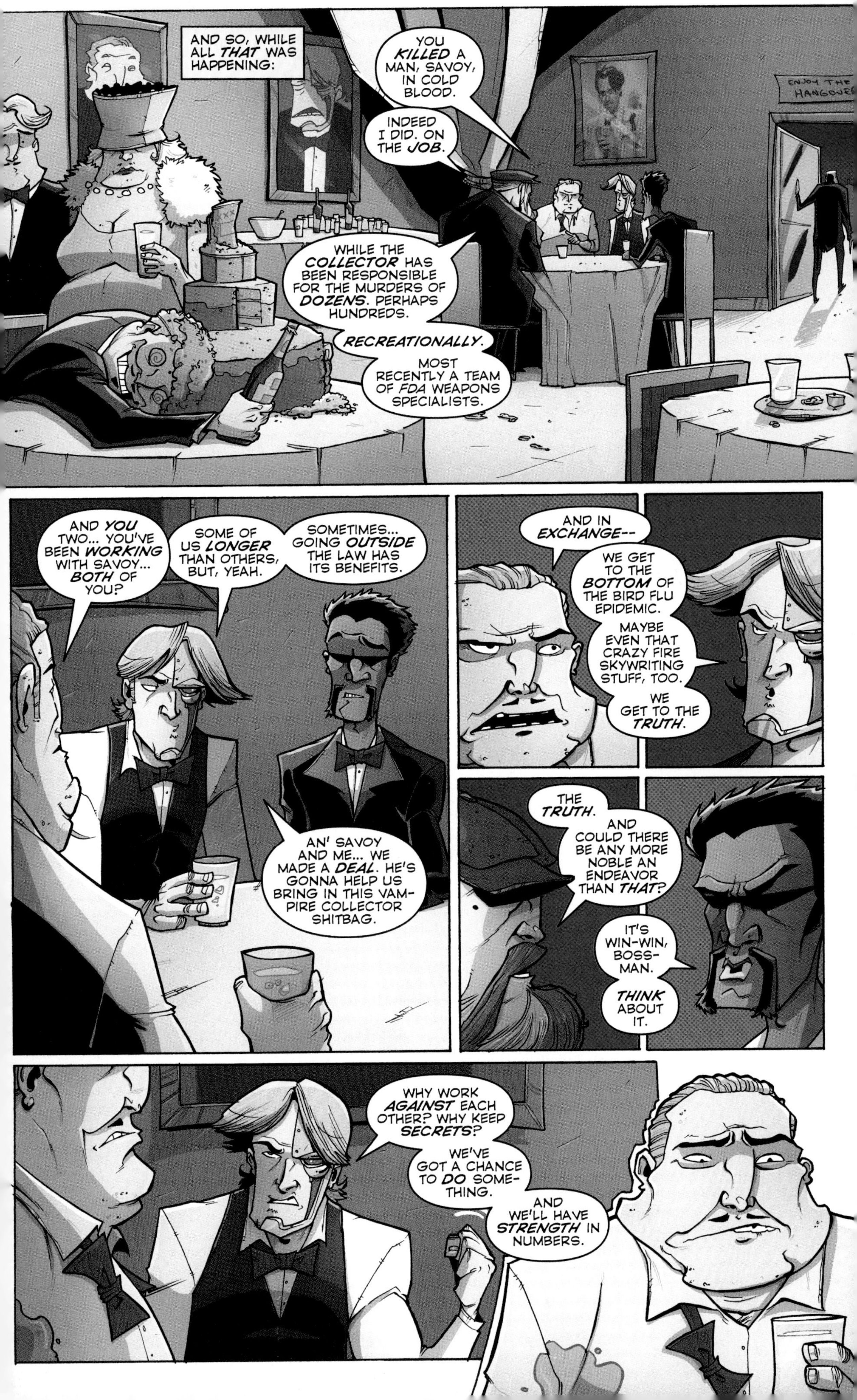
AND SO, WHILE ALL THAT WAS HAPPENING:
ENJOY THE HANGOVER
YOU KILLED A MAN, SAVOY, IN COLD BLOOD.
INDEED I DID. ON THE JOB.
WHILE THE COLLECTOR HAS BEEN RESPONSIBLE FOR THE MURDERS OF DOZENS. PERHAPS HUNDREDS.
RECREATIONALLY.
MOST RECENTLY A TEAM OF FDA WEAPONS SPECIALISTS.
AND YOU TWO... YOU'VE BEEN WORKING WITH SAVOY... BOTH OF YOU?
SOME OF US LONGER THAN OTHERS, BUT, YEAH.
SOMETIMES... GOING OUTSIDE THE LAW HAS ITS BENEFITS.
AN' SAVOY AND ME... WE MADE A DEAL. HE'S GONNA HELP US BRING IN THIS VAMPIRE COLLECTOR SHITBAG.
AND IN EXCHANGE--
WE GET TO THE BOTTOM OF THE BIRD FLU EPIDEMIC.
MAYBE EVEN THAT CRAZY FIRE SKYWRITING STUFF, TOO.
WE GET TO THE TRUTH.
THE TRUTH.
AND COULD THERE BE ANY MORE NOBLE AN ENDEAVOR THAN THAT?
IT'S WIN-WIN, BOSS-MAN.
THINK ABOUT IT.
WHY WORK AGAINST EACH OTHER? WHY KEEP SECRETS?
WE'VE GOT A CHANCE TO DO SOME-THING.
AND WE'LL HAVE STRENGTH IN NUMBERS.

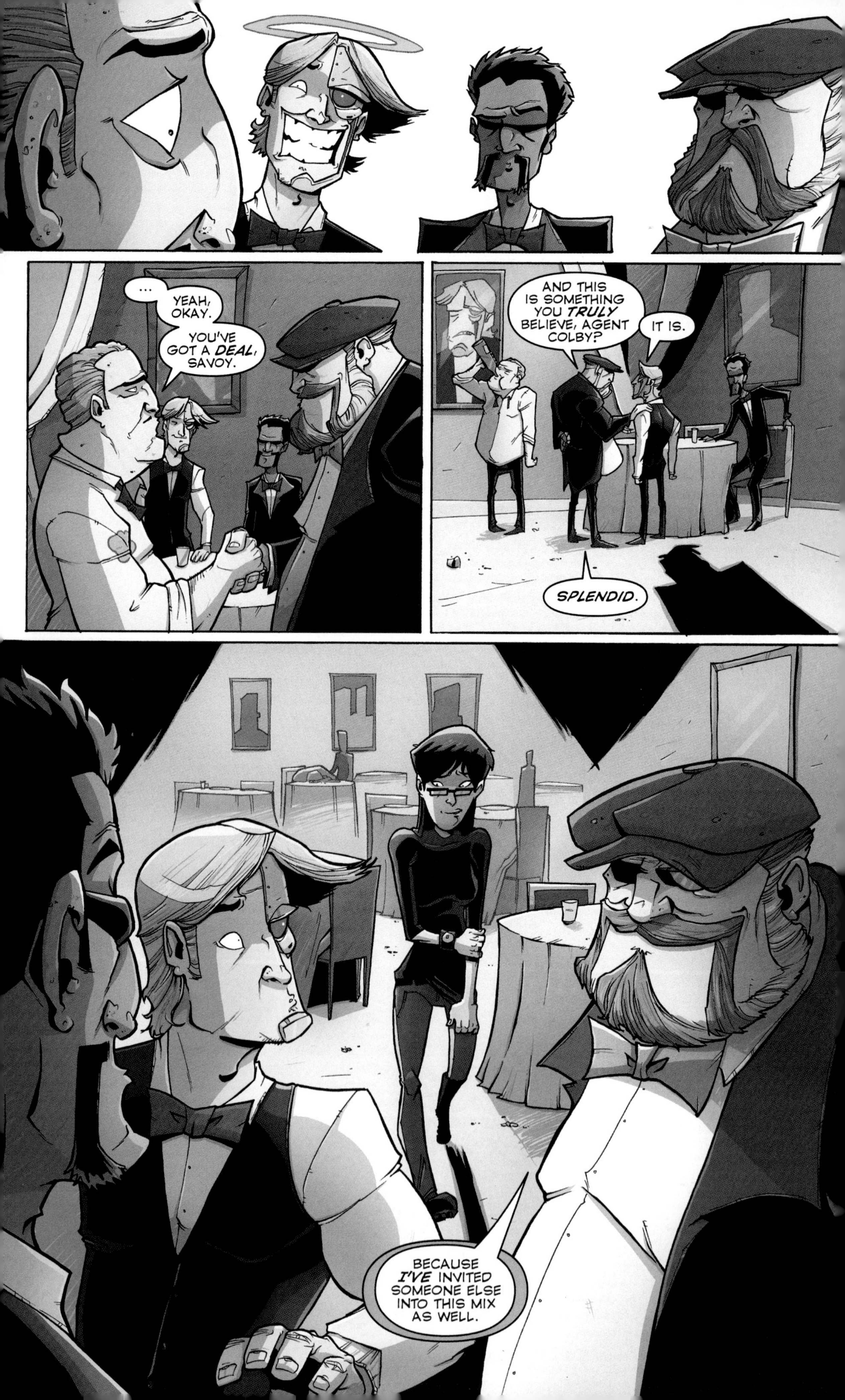
...
YEAH, OKAY.
YOU'VE GOT A DEAL, SAVOY.
AND THIS IS SOMETHING YOU TRULY BELIEVE, AGENT COLBY?
IT IS.
SPLENDID.
BECAUSE I'VE INVITED SOMEONE ELSE INTO THIS MIX AS WELL.

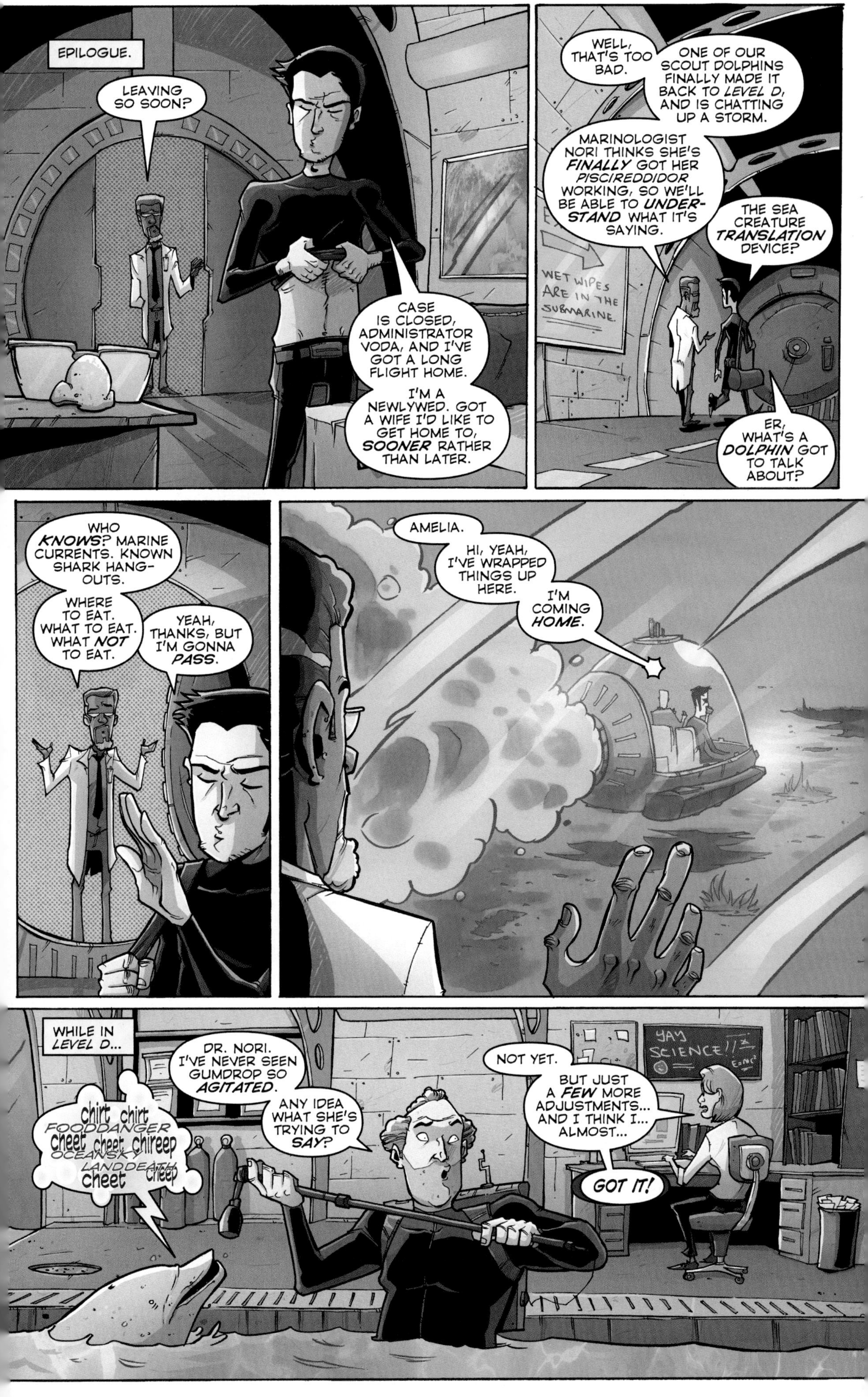
EPILOGUE.
LEAVING SO SOON?
CASE IS CLOSED, ADMINISTRATOR VODA, AND I'VE GOT A LONG FLIGHT HOME.
I'M A NEWLYWED. GOT A WIFE I'D LIKE TO GET HOME TO, SOONER RATHER THAN LATER.
WELL, THAT'S TOO BAD.
ONE OF OUR SCOUT DOLPHINS FINALLY MADE IT BACK TO LEVEL D, AND IS CHATTING UP A STORM.
MARINOLOGIST NORI THINKS SHE'S FINALLY GOT HER PISCIREDDIDOR WORKING, SO WE'LL BE ABLE TO UNDERSTAND WHAT IT'S SAYING.
THE SEA CREATURE TRANSLATION DEVICE?
WET WIPES ARE IN THE SUBMARINE.
ER, WHAT'S A DOLPHIN GOT TO TALK ABOUT?
WHO KNOWS? MARINE CURRENTS. KNOWN SHARK HANG-OUTS.
WHERE TO EAT. WHAT TO EAT. WHAT NOT TO EAT.
YEAH, THANKS, BUT I'M GONNA PASS.
AMELIA.
HI, YEAH, I'VE WRAPPED THINGS UP HERE.
I'M COMING HOME.
WHILE IN LEVEL D...
chirt chirt FOODDANGER cheet cheet chireep OCEANSKY LANDDEATH cheet cheep
DR. NORI. I'VE NEVER SEEN GUMDROP SO AGITATED.
ANY IDEA WHAT SHE'S TRYING TO SAY?
YAY SCIENCE!!
NOT YET.
BUT JUST A FEW MORE ADJUSTMENTS... AND I THINK I... ALMOST...
GOT IT!

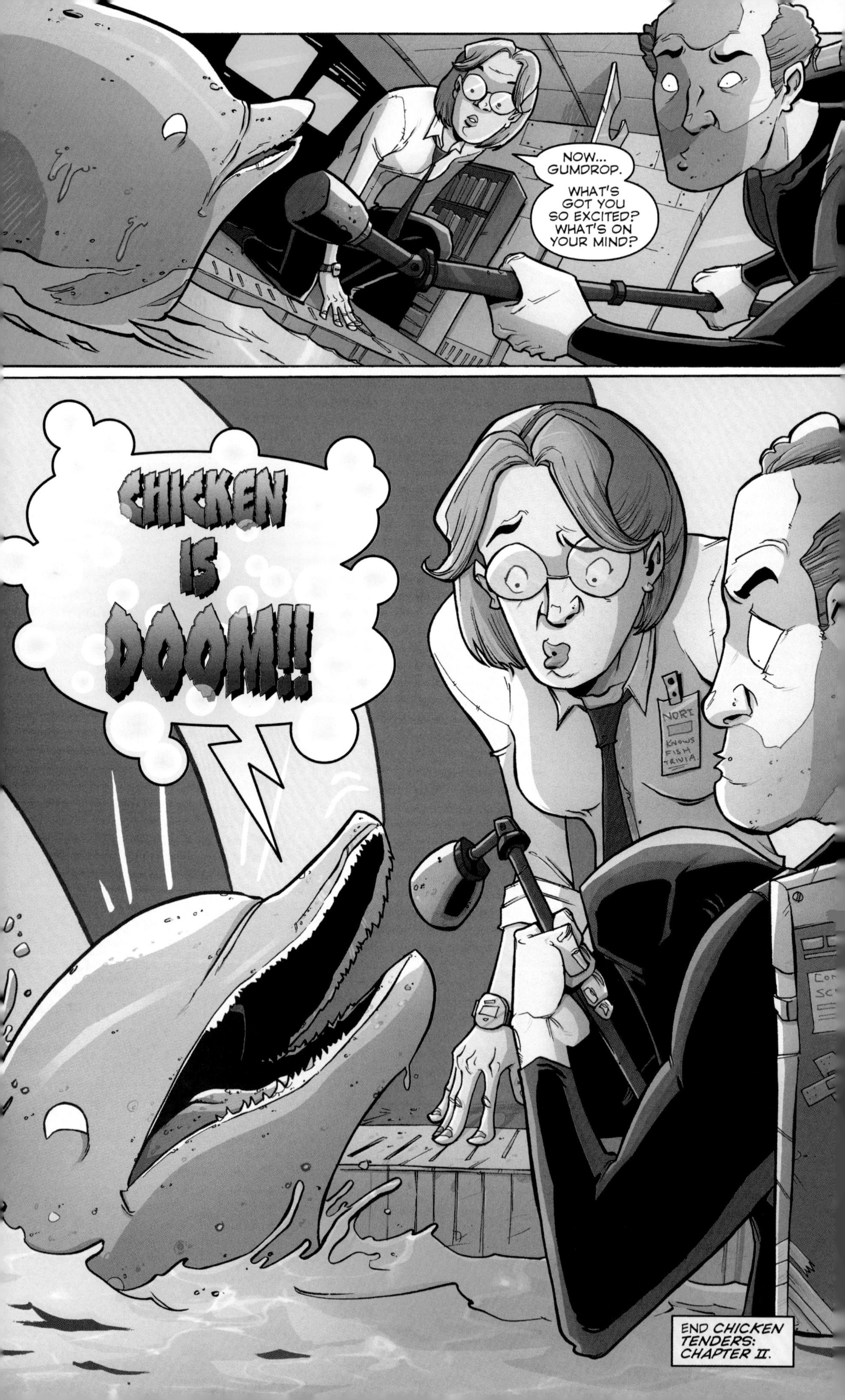
NOW... GUMDROP.
WHAT'S GOT YOU SO EXCITED? WHAT'S ON YOUR MIND?
CHICKEN IS DOOM!!
NORI
KNOWS FISH TRIVIA.
END CHICKEN TENDERS: CHAPTER II.

Interlude

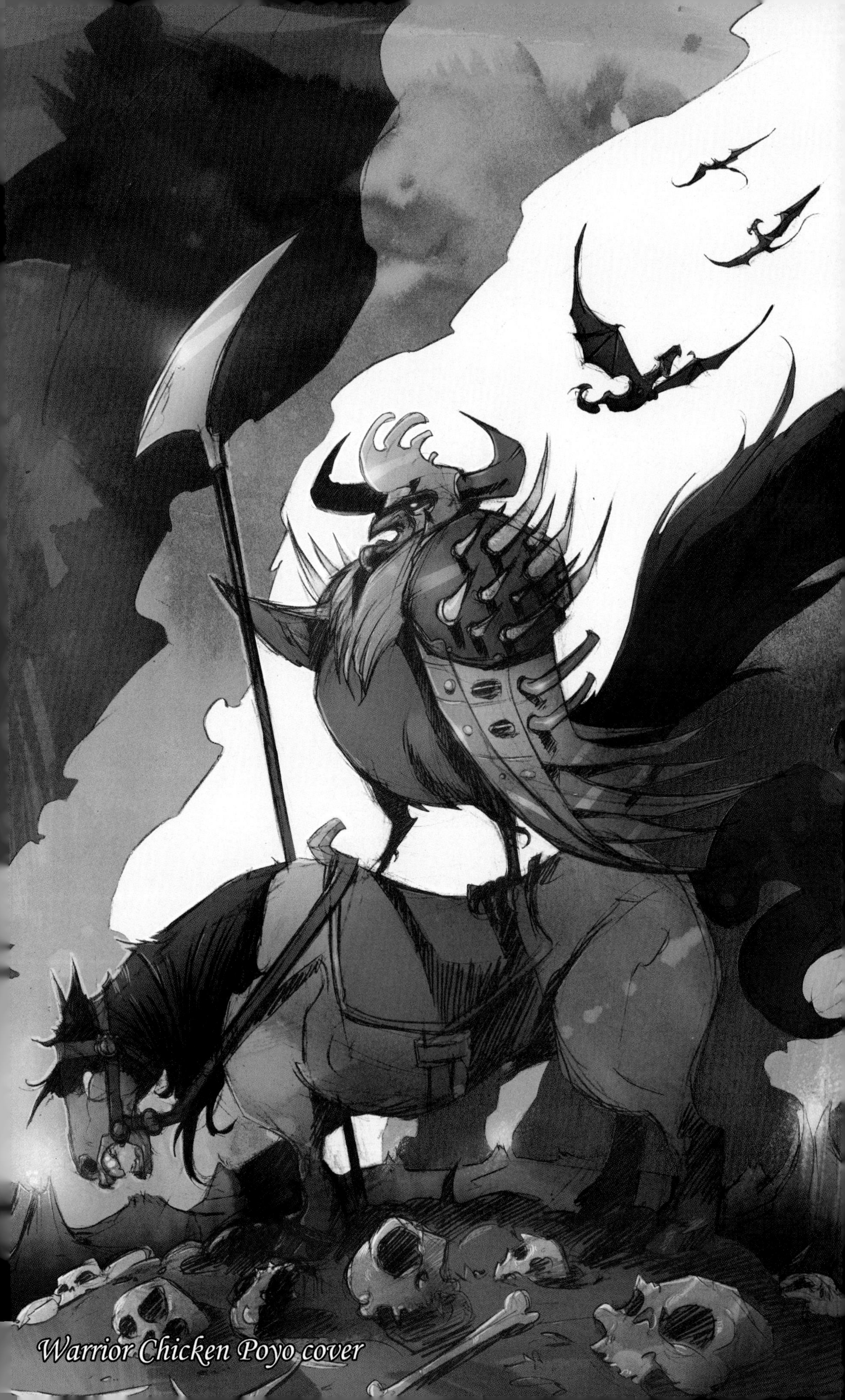

Warrior Chicken Poyo cover

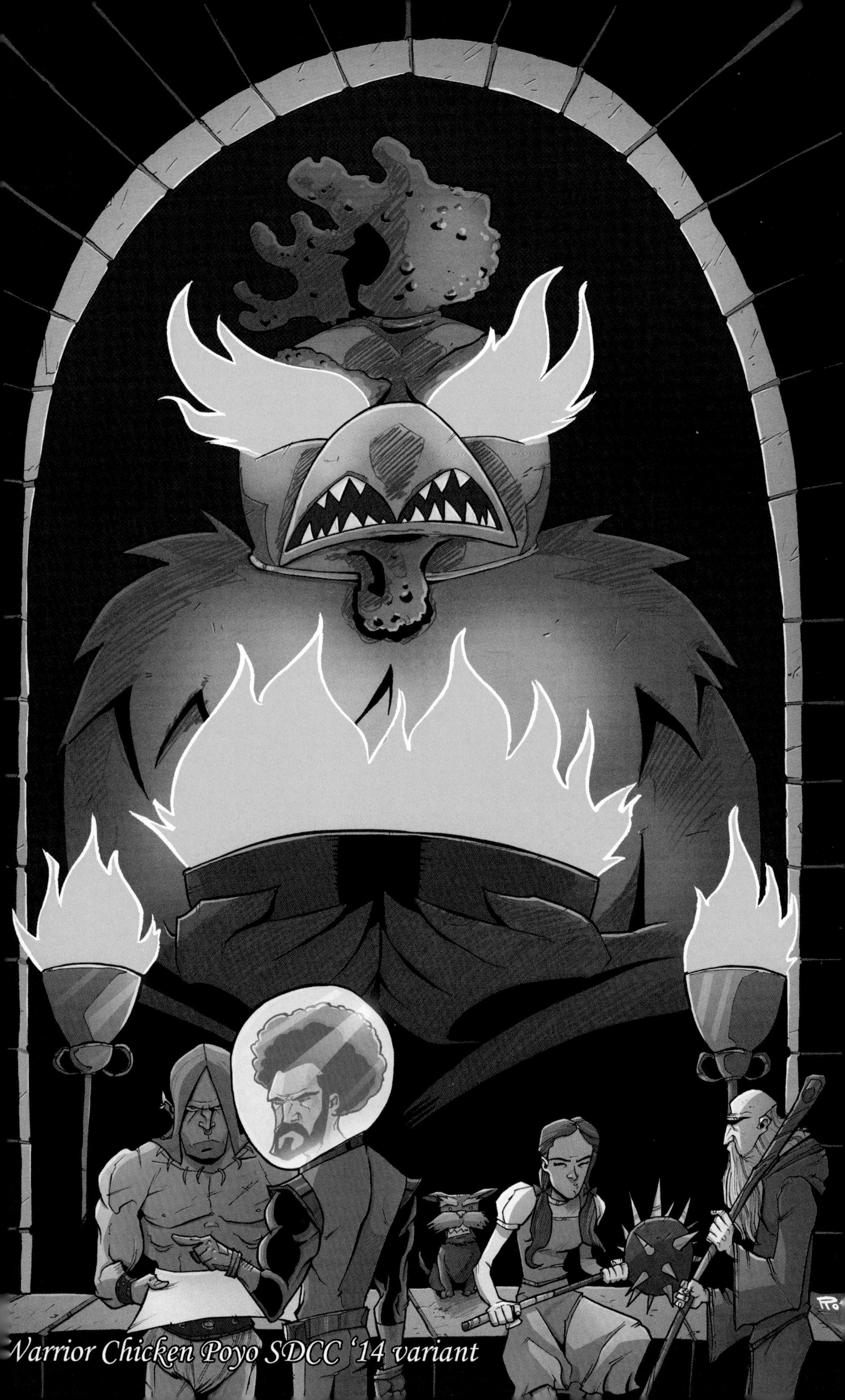

Warrior Chicken Poyo SDCC '14 variant

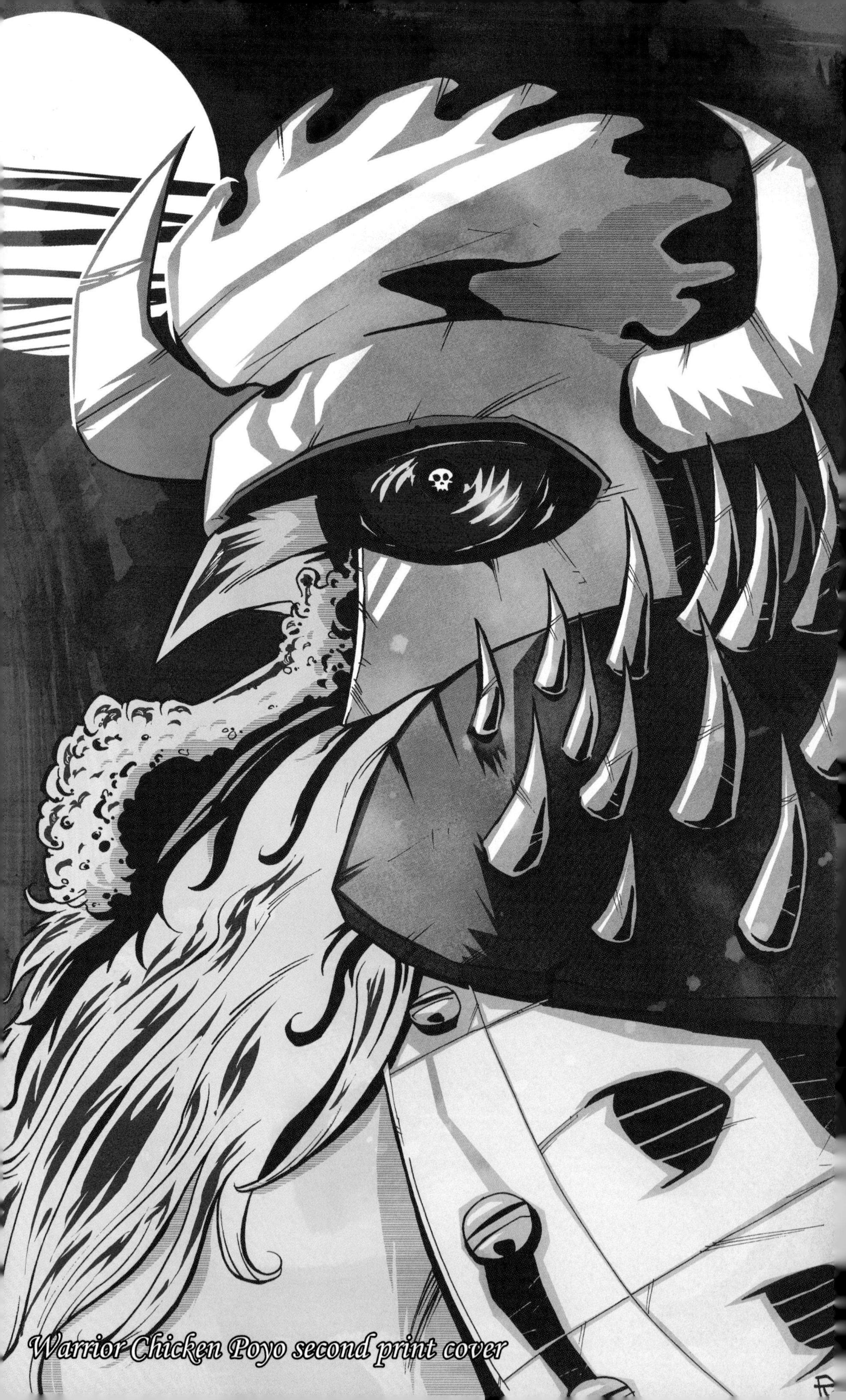

Warrior Chicken Poyo second print cover

WHEN THE TERRORISTS INFILTRATED THE OVAL OFFICE:

WHEN THEY TOOK OVER THE AIRWAVES AND ANNOUNCED THEIR INTENTION TO TAKE OVER NOT JUST THE ENTIRE COUNTRY BUT THE ENTIRE *WORLD*:

WHEN THEY THREATENED TO UNLEASH A DEADLY PLAGUE OF MICRO-NUCLEAR-BATTLE-NANITES:

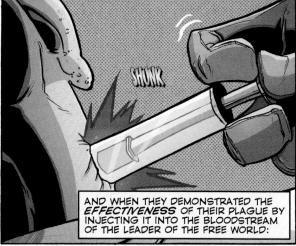

SHUNK

AND WHEN THEY DEMONSTRATED THE *EFFECTIVENESS* OF THEIR PLAGUE BY INJECTING IT INTO THE BLOODSTREAM OF THE LEADER OF THE FREE WORLD:

POYO WAS THERE.

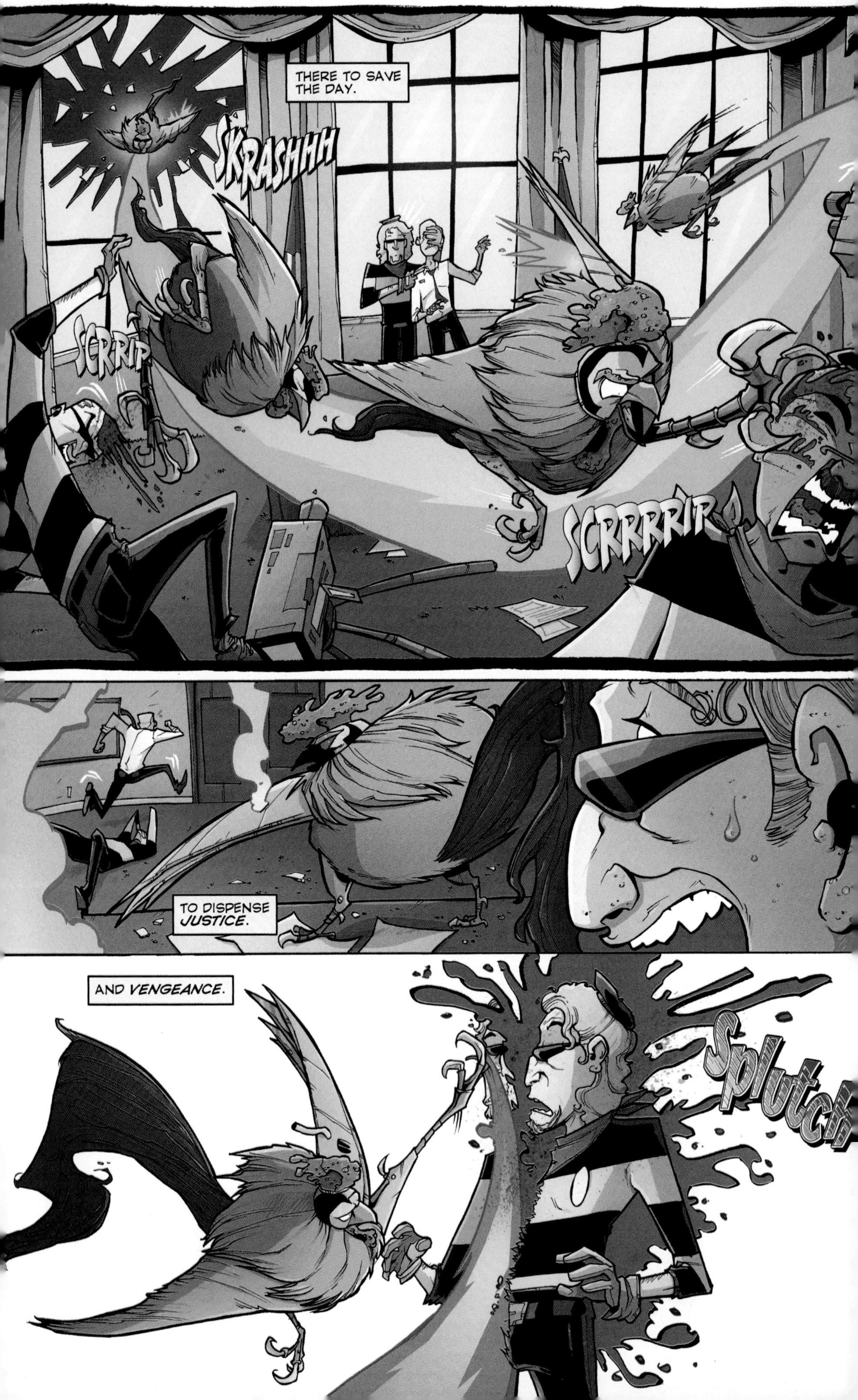

THERE TO SAVE THE DAY.
SKRASHHH
SCRRIP
SCRRRRIP
TO DISPENSE *JUSTICE*.
AND *VENGEANCE*.
Splutch

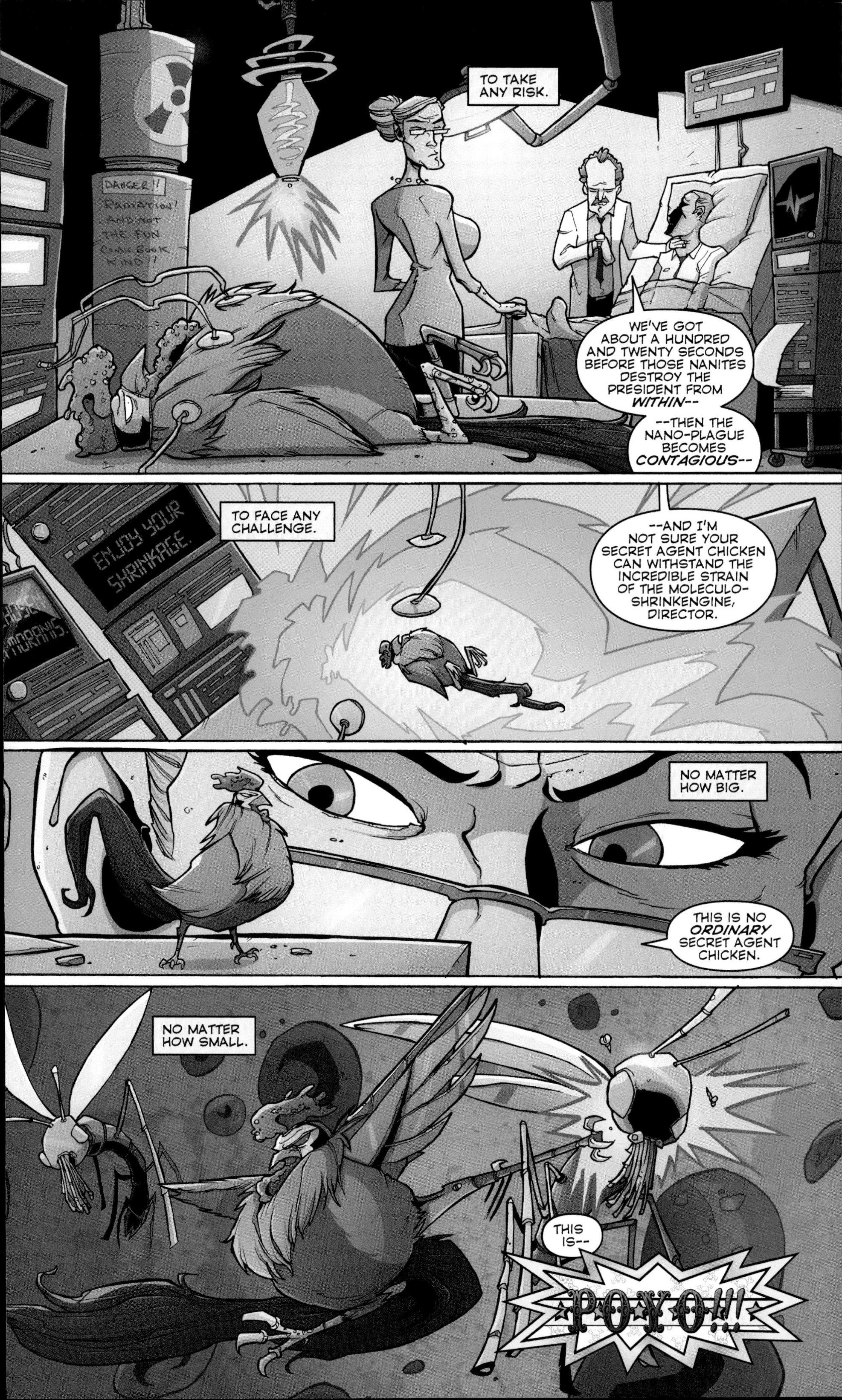

TO TAKE ANY RISK.
DANGER!! RADIATION! AND NOT THE FUN COMIC BOOK KIND!!
WE'VE GOT ABOUT A HUNDRED AND TWENTY SECONDS BEFORE THOSE NANITES DESTROY THE PRESIDENT FROM *WITHIN*--
--THEN THE NANO-PLAGUE BECOMES *CONTAGIOUS*--
TO FACE ANY CHALLENGE.
ENJOY YOUR SHRINKAGE.
--AND I'M NOT SURE YOUR SECRET AGENT CHICKEN CAN WITHSTAND THE INCREDIBLE STRAIN OF THE MOLECULO-SHRINKENGINE, DIRECTOR.
NO MATTER HOW BIG.
THIS IS NO *ORDINARY* SECRET AGENT CHICKEN.
NO MATTER HOW SMALL.
THIS IS--
POYO!!!

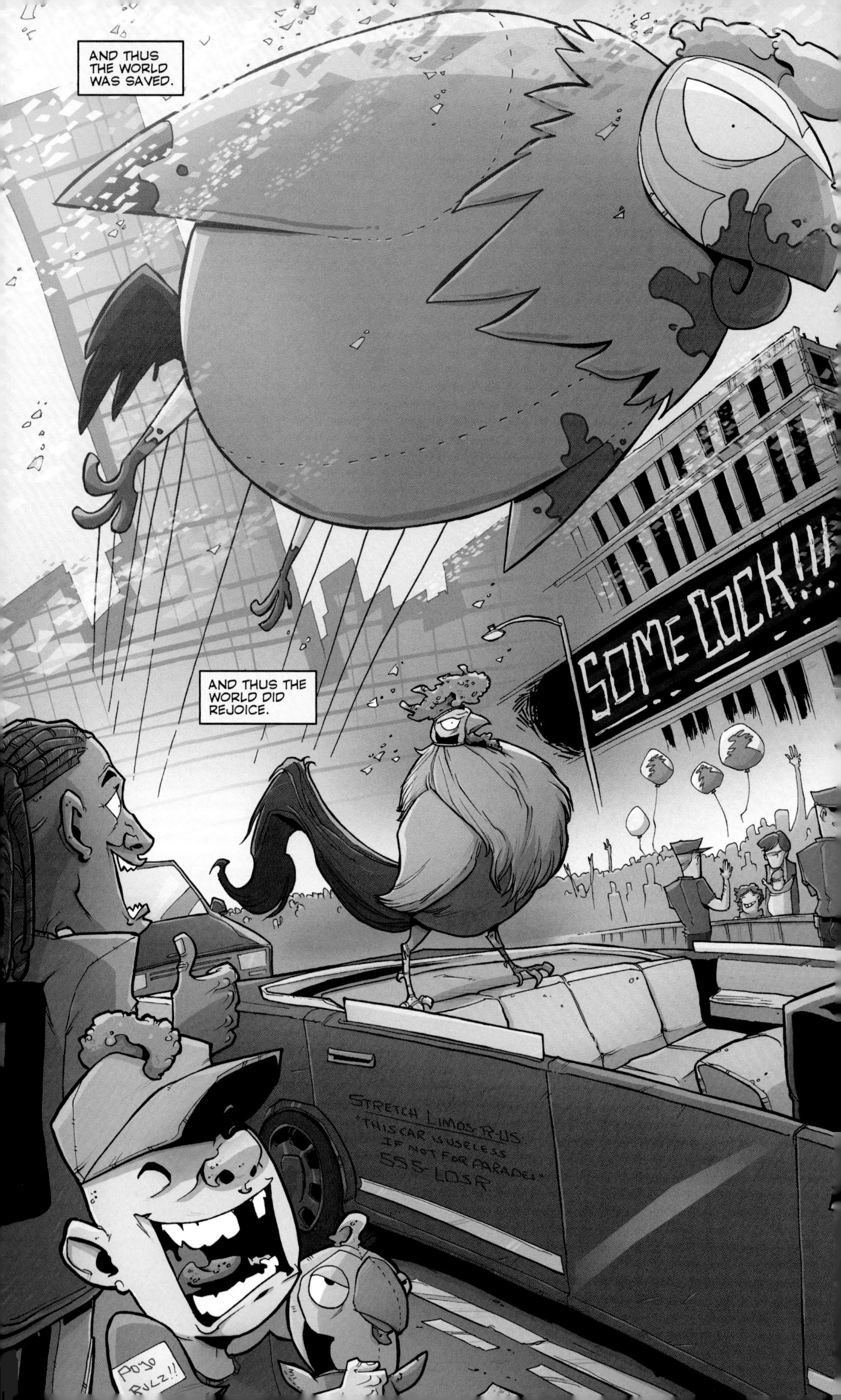
AND THUS THE WORLD WAS SAVED.
AND THUS THE WORLD DID REJOICE.
SOME COCK!!!
STRETCH LIMOS R-US
"THIS CAR IS USELESS IF NOT FOR PARADES"
555-LOSR
POJO RULZ!!

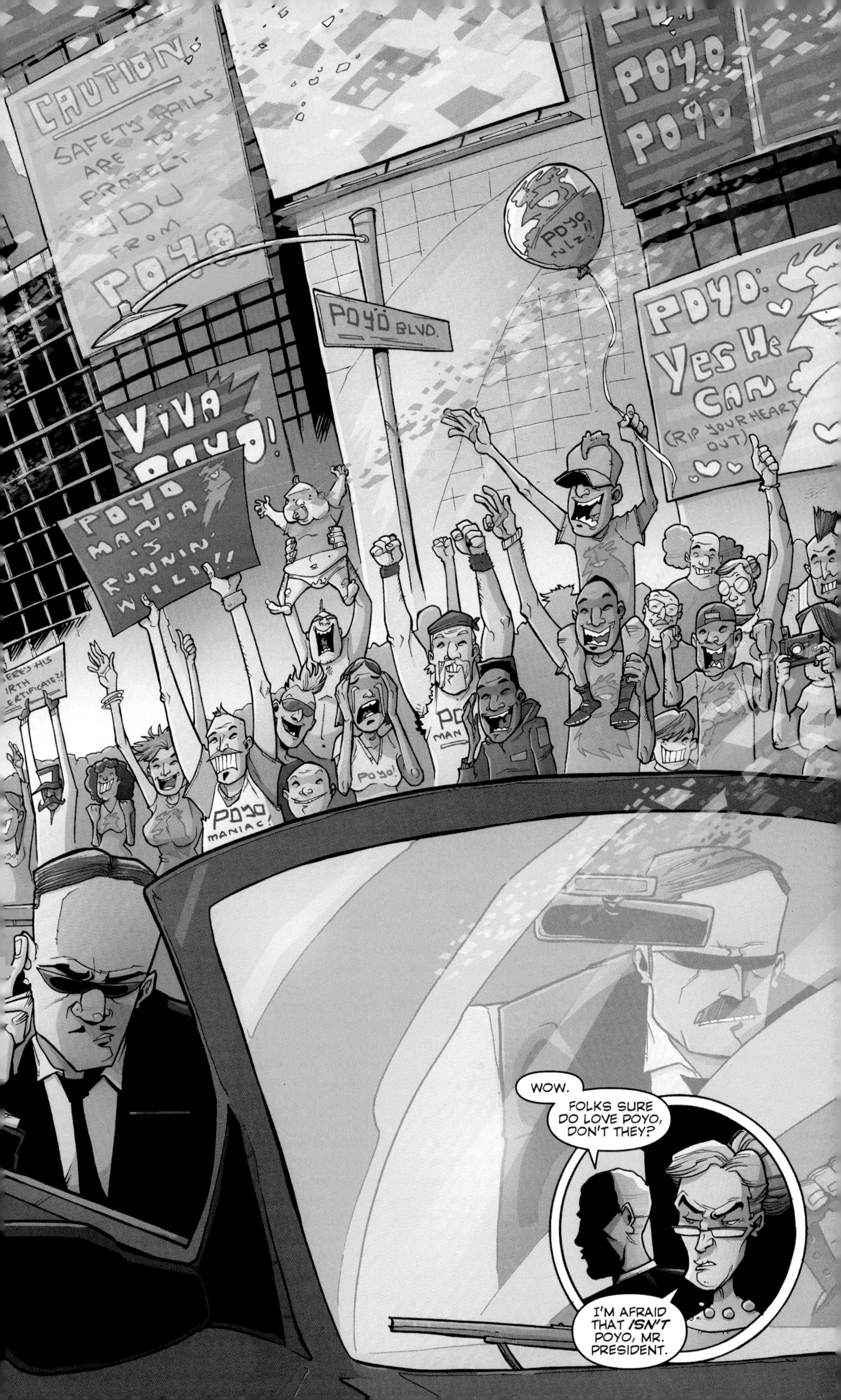
CAUTION
SAFETY RAILS ARE TO PROTECT YOU FROM POYO
POYO
POYO
POYO BLVD.
POYO RULZ!!
POYO: YES HE CAN (RIP YOUR HEART OUT)
VIVA POYO!
POYO MANIA IS RUNNIN' WILD!!
POYO MANIAC!
POYO!
WOW.
FOLKS SURE DO LOVE POYO, DON'T THEY?
I'M AFRAID THAT *ISN'T* POYO, MR. PRESIDENT.

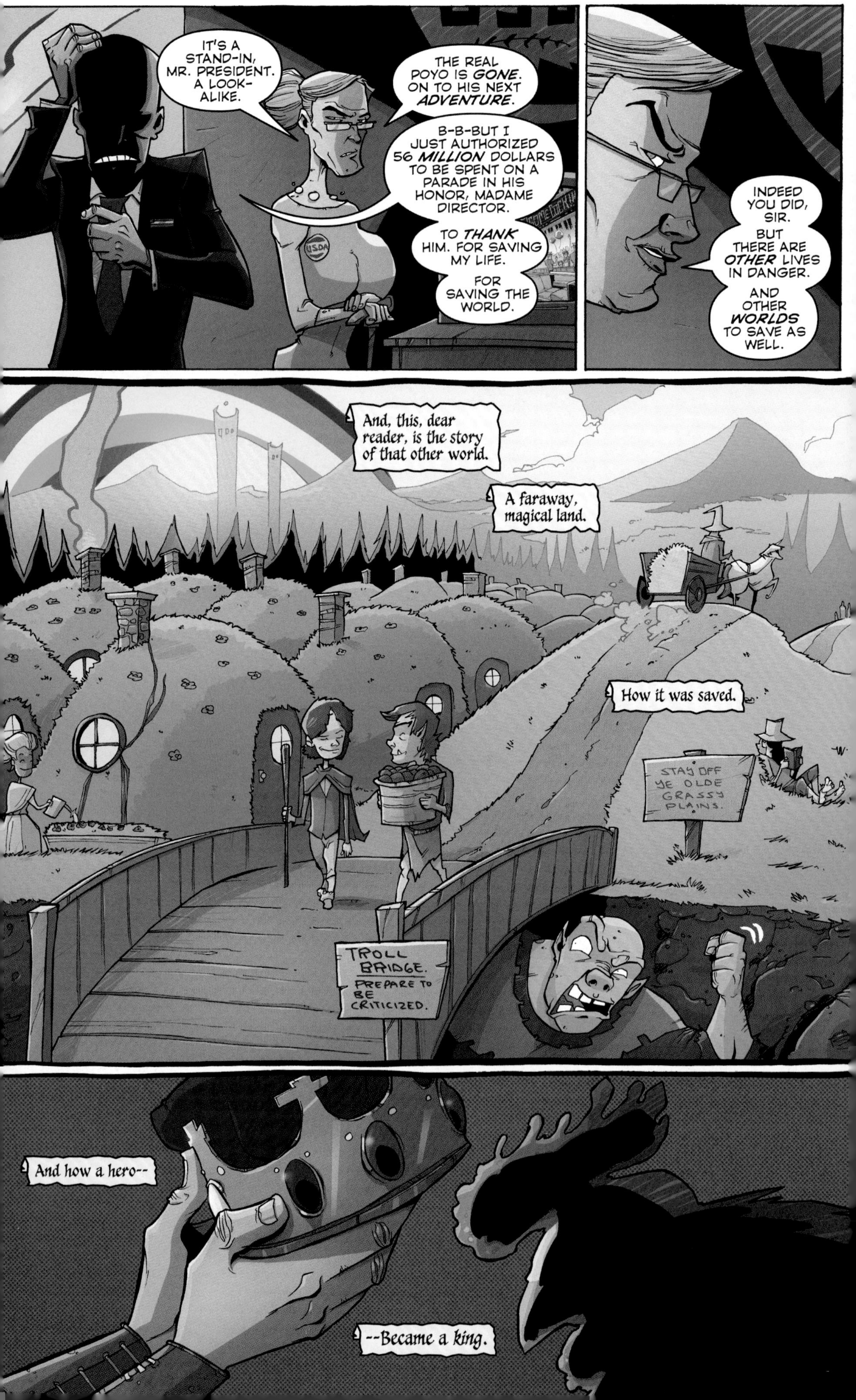

IT'S A STAND-IN, MR. PRESIDENT. A LOOK-ALIKE.
THE REAL POYO IS *GONE*. ON TO HIS NEXT *ADVENTURE*.
B-B-BUT I JUST AUTHORIZED 56 *MILLION* DOLLARS TO BE SPENT ON A PARADE IN HIS HONOR, MADAME DIRECTOR.
TO *THANK* HIM. FOR SAVING MY LIFE.
FOR SAVING THE WORLD.
INDEED YOU DID, SIR.
BUT THERE ARE *OTHER* LIVES IN DANGER.
AND OTHER *WORLDS* TO SAVE AS WELL.
And, this, dear reader, is the story of that other world.
A faraway, magical land.
How it was saved.
STAY OFF YE OLDE GRASSY PLAINS.
TROLL BRIDGE. PREPARE TO BE CRITICIZED.
And how a hero--
--Became a king.

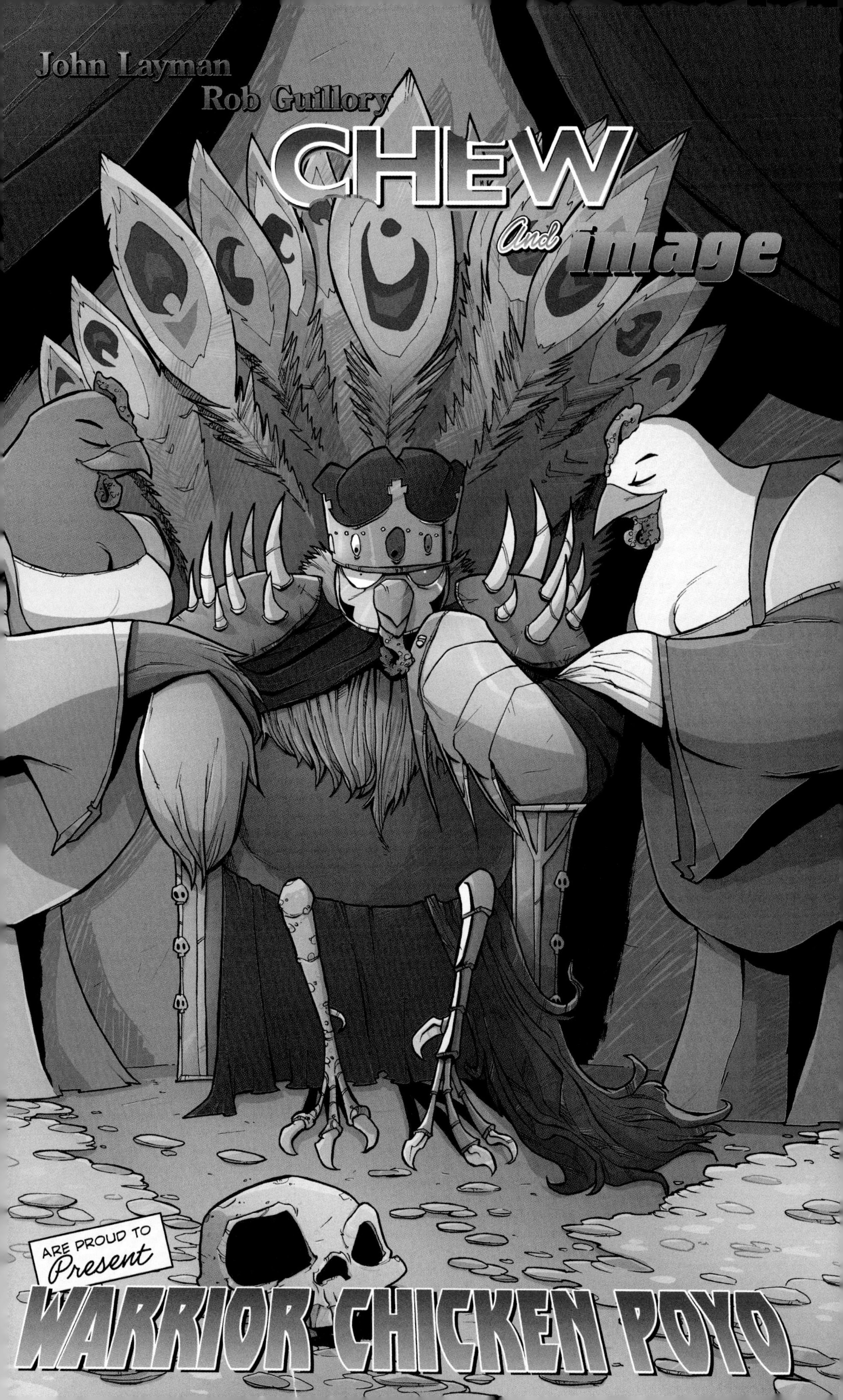
John Layman
Rob Guillory
CHEW
And image
ARE PROUD TO Present
WARRIOR CHICKEN POYO

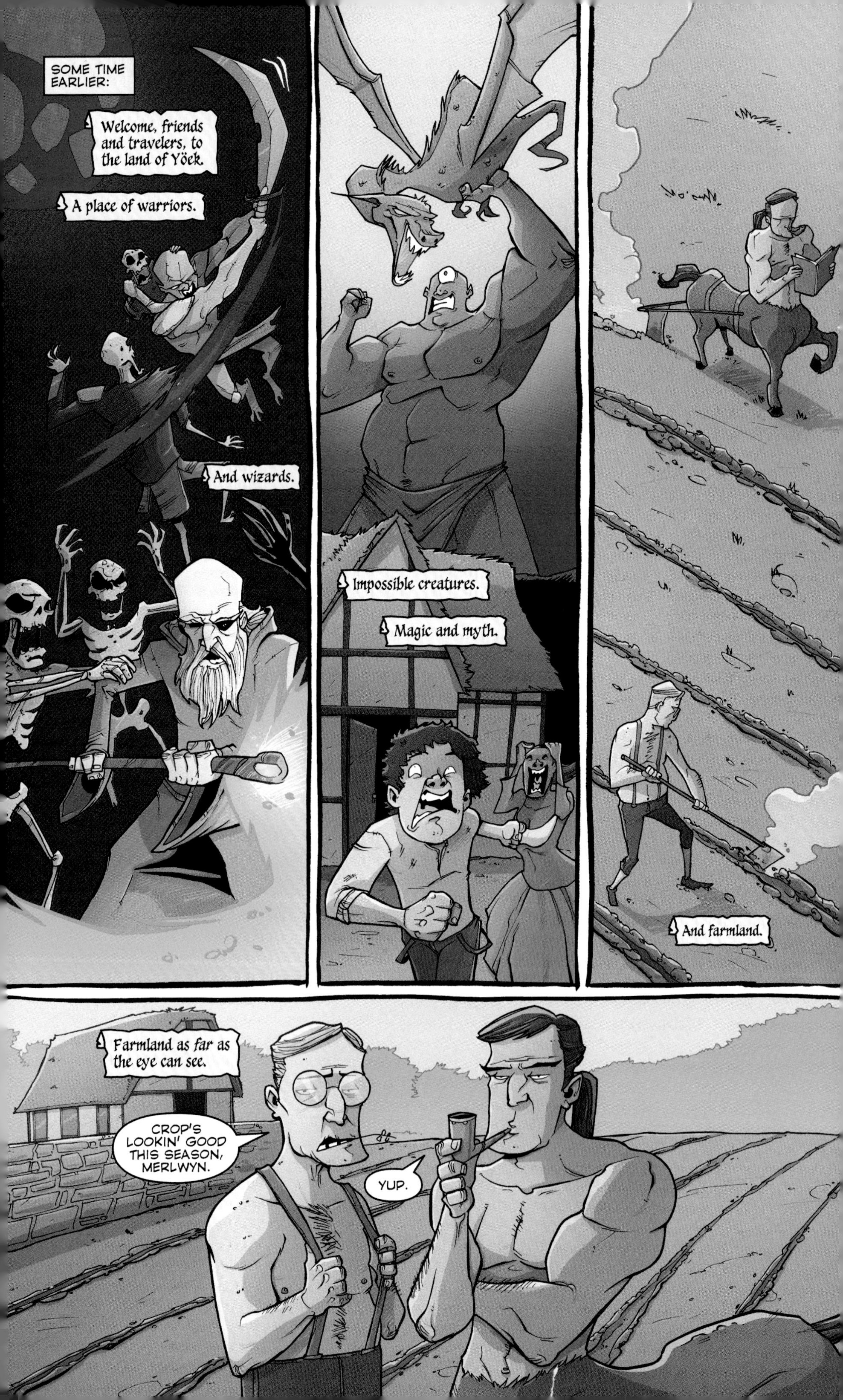
SOME TIME EARLIER:
Welcome, friends and travelers, to the land of Yöek.
A place of warriors.
And wizards.
Impossible creatures.
Magic and myth.
And farmland.
Farmland as far as the eye can see.
CROP'S LOOKIN' GOOD THIS SEASON, MERLWYN.
YUP.

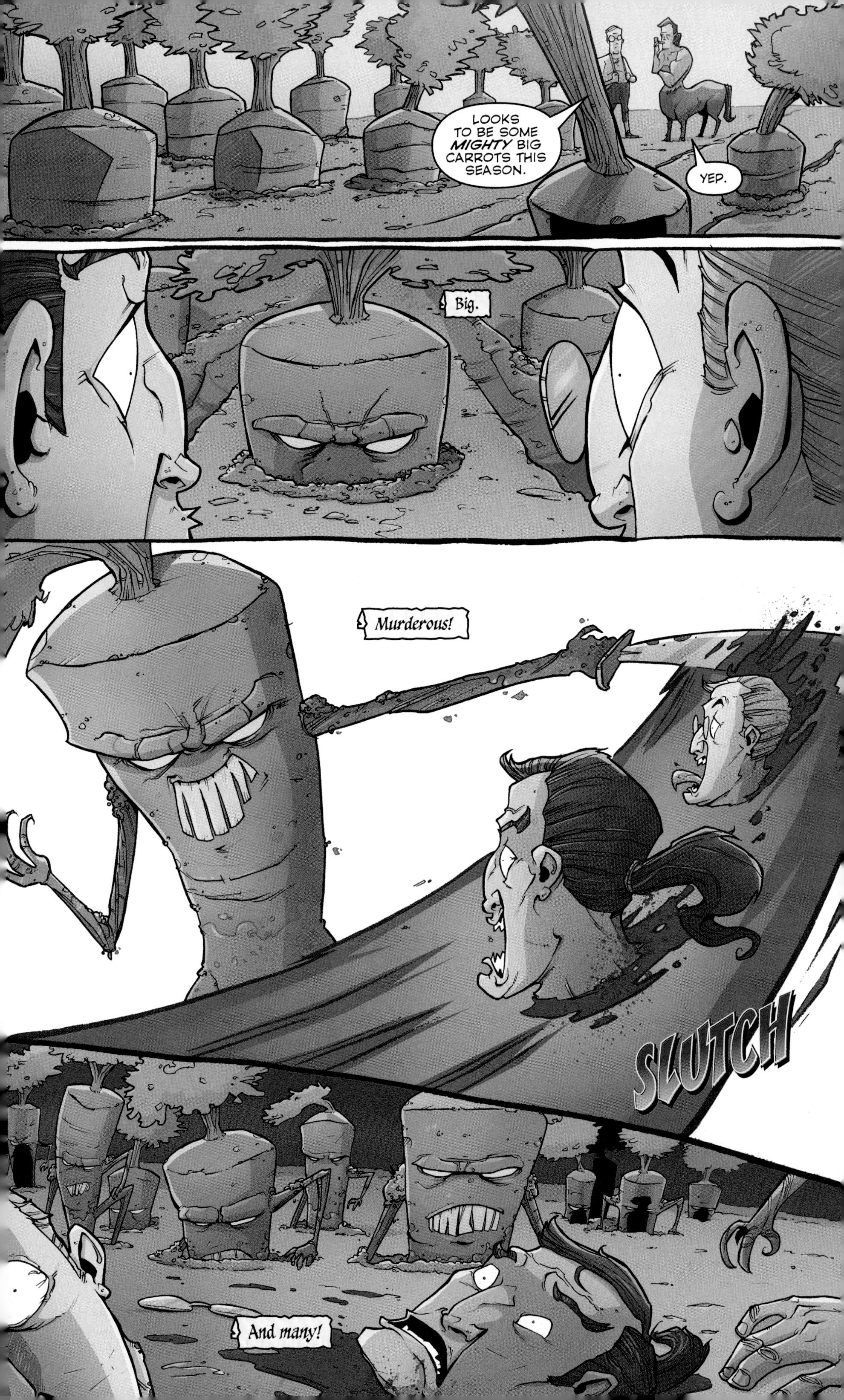
LOOKS TO BE SOME *MIGHTY* BIG CARROTS THIS SEASON.
YEP.
Big.
Murderous!
SLUTCH
And many!

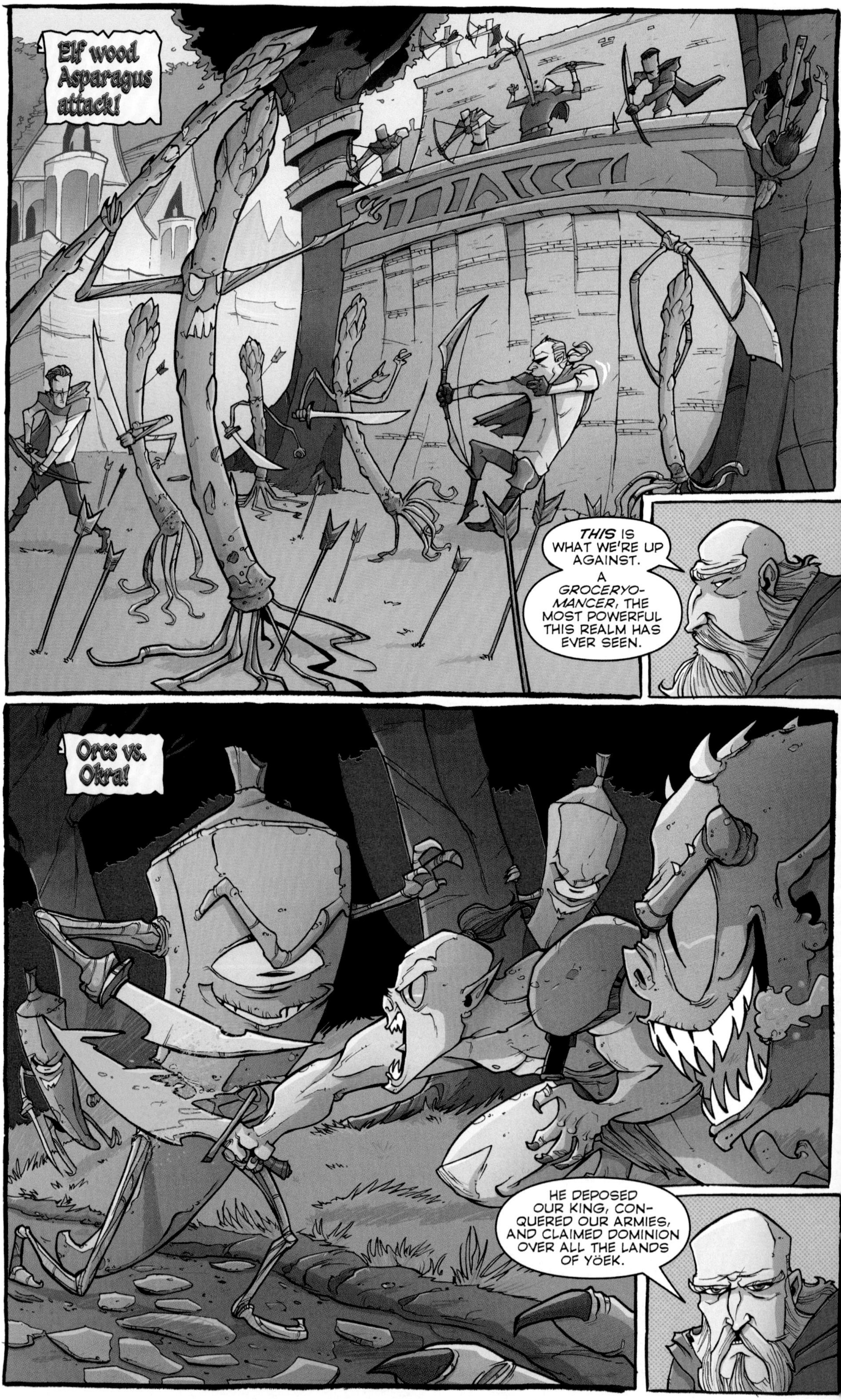
Elf wood Asparagus attack!
THIS IS WHAT WE'RE UP AGAINST.
A GROCERYO-MANCER, THE MOST POWERFUL THIS REALM HAS EVER SEEN.
Orcs vs. Okra!
HE DEPOSED OUR KING, CON-QUERED OUR ARMIES, AND CLAIMED DOMINION OVER ALL THE LANDS OF YÖEK.

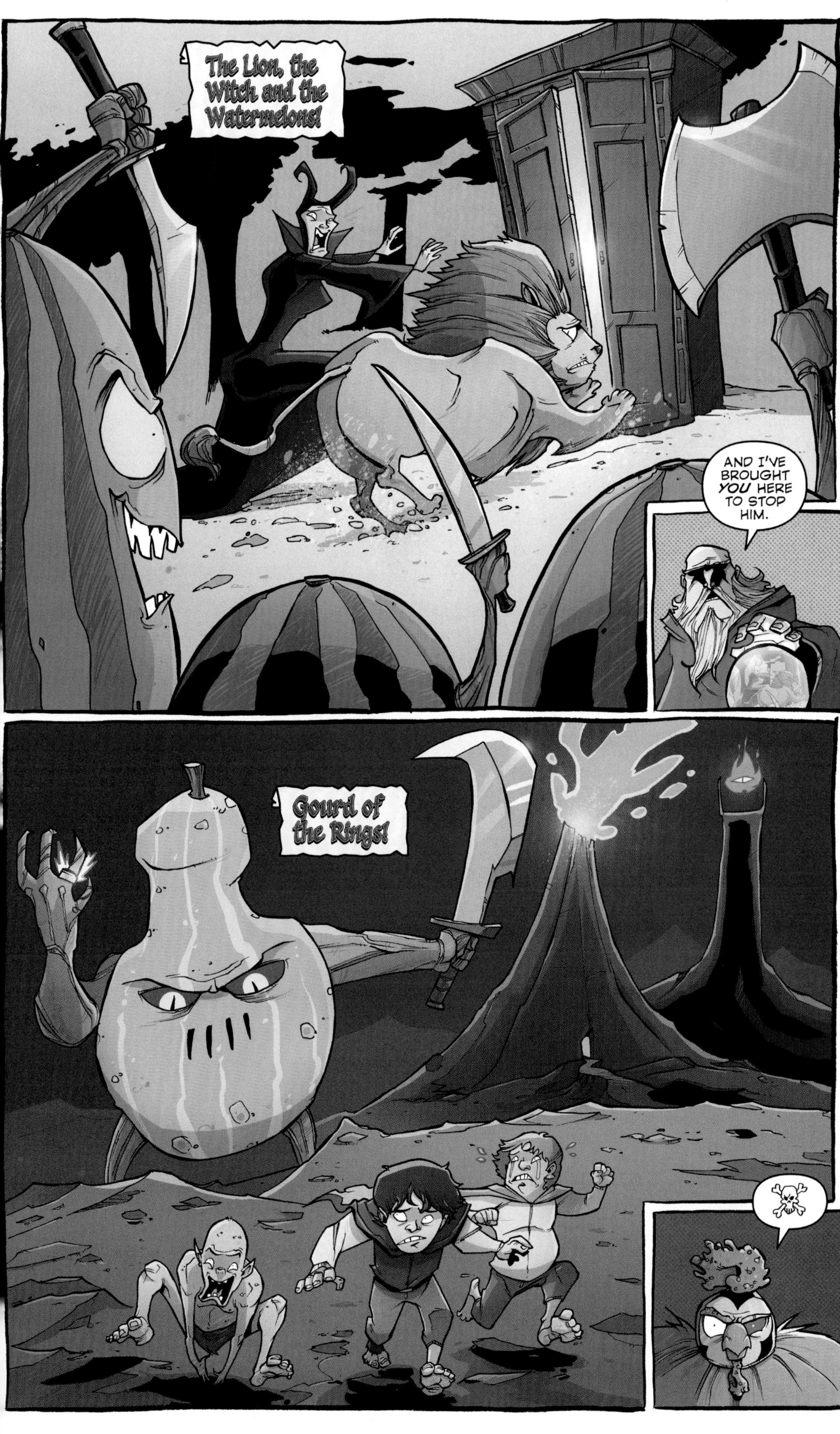

The Lion, the Witch and the Watermelons!
AND I'VE BROUGHT YOU HERE TO STOP HIM.
Gourd of the Rings!

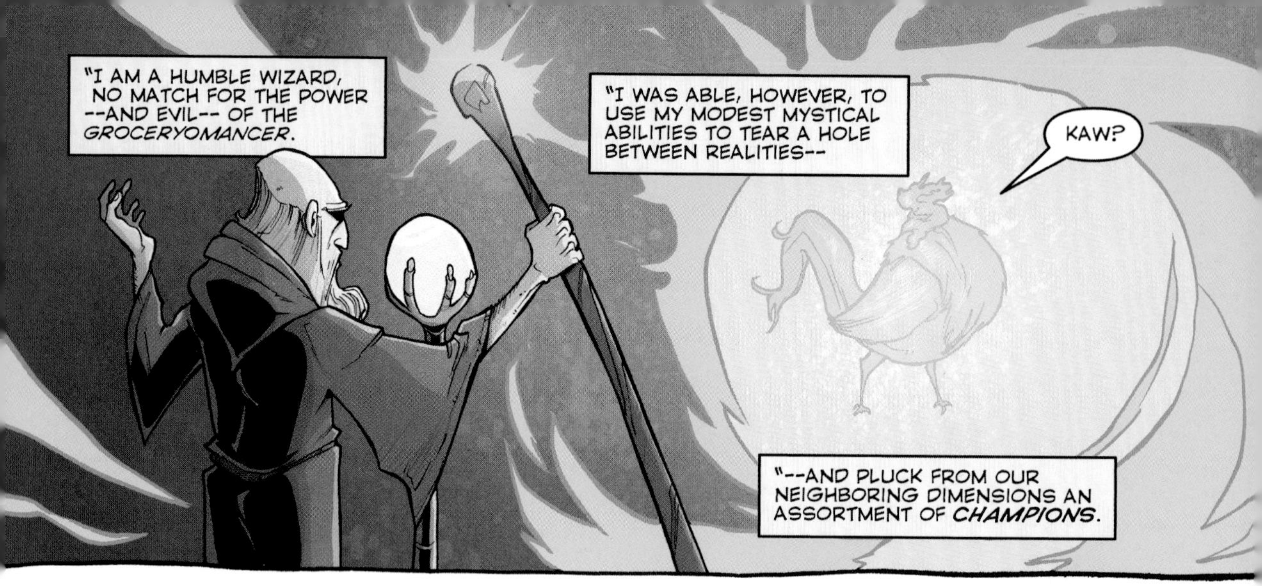
"I AM A HUMBLE WIZARD, NO MATCH FOR THE POWER --AND EVIL-- OF THE *GROCERYOMANCER*.
"I WAS ABLE, HOWEVER, TO USE MY MODEST MYSTICAL ABILITIES TO TEAR A HOLE BETWEEN REALITIES--
KAW?
"--AND PLUCK FROM OUR NEIGHBORING DIMENSIONS AN ASSORTMENT OF *CHAMPIONS*.

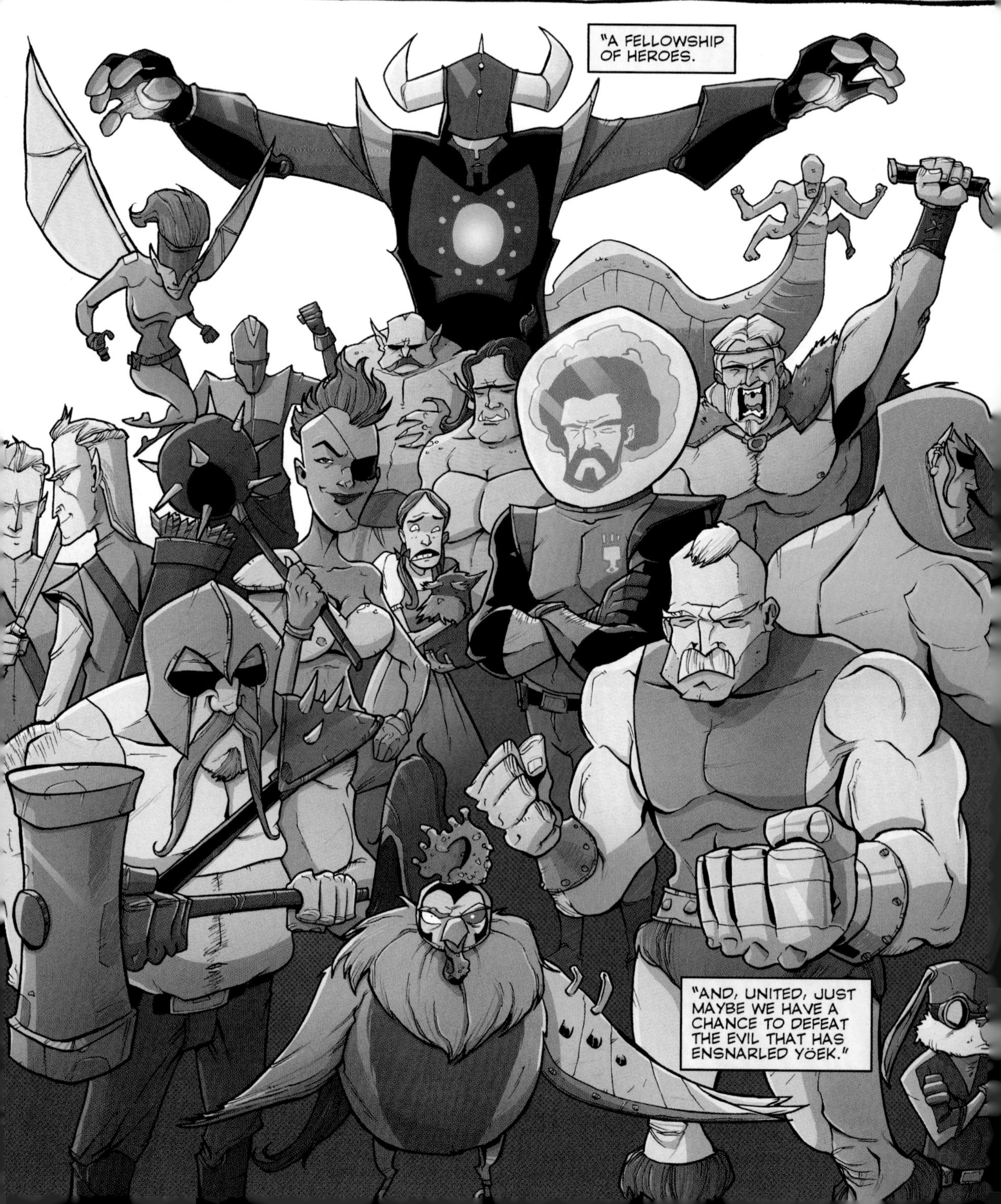
"A FELLOWSHIP OF HEROES.
"AND, UNITED, JUST MAYBE WE HAVE A CHANCE TO DEFEAT THE EVIL THAT HAS ENSNARLED YÖEK."

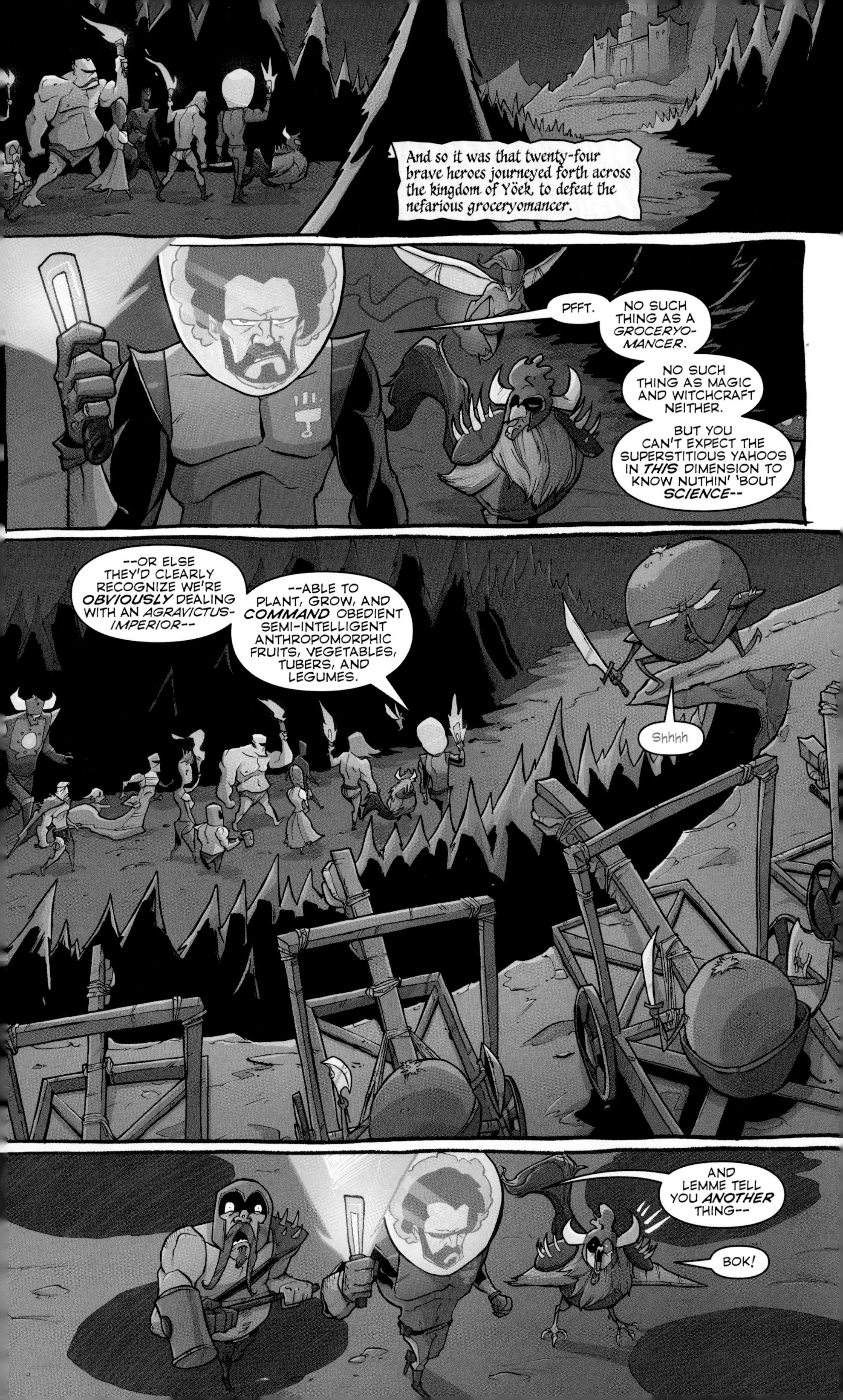

And so it was that twenty-four brave heroes journeyed forth across the kingdom of Yöek, to defeat the nefarious groceryomancer.
PFFT.
NO SUCH THING AS A GROCERYO-MANCER.
NO SUCH THING AS MAGIC AND WITCHCRAFT NEITHER.
BUT YOU CAN'T EXPECT THE SUPERSTITIOUS YAHOOS IN THIS DIMENSION TO KNOW NUTHIN' 'BOUT SCIENCE--
--OR ELSE THEY'D CLEARLY RECOGNIZE WE'RE OBVIOUSLY DEALING WITH AN AGRAVICTUS-IMPERIOR--
--ABLE TO PLANT, GROW, AND COMMAND OBEDIENT SEMI-INTELLIGENT ANTHROPOMORPHIC FRUITS, VEGETABLES, TUBERS, AND LEGUMES.
Shhhh
AND LEMME TELL YOU ANOTHER THING--
BOK!

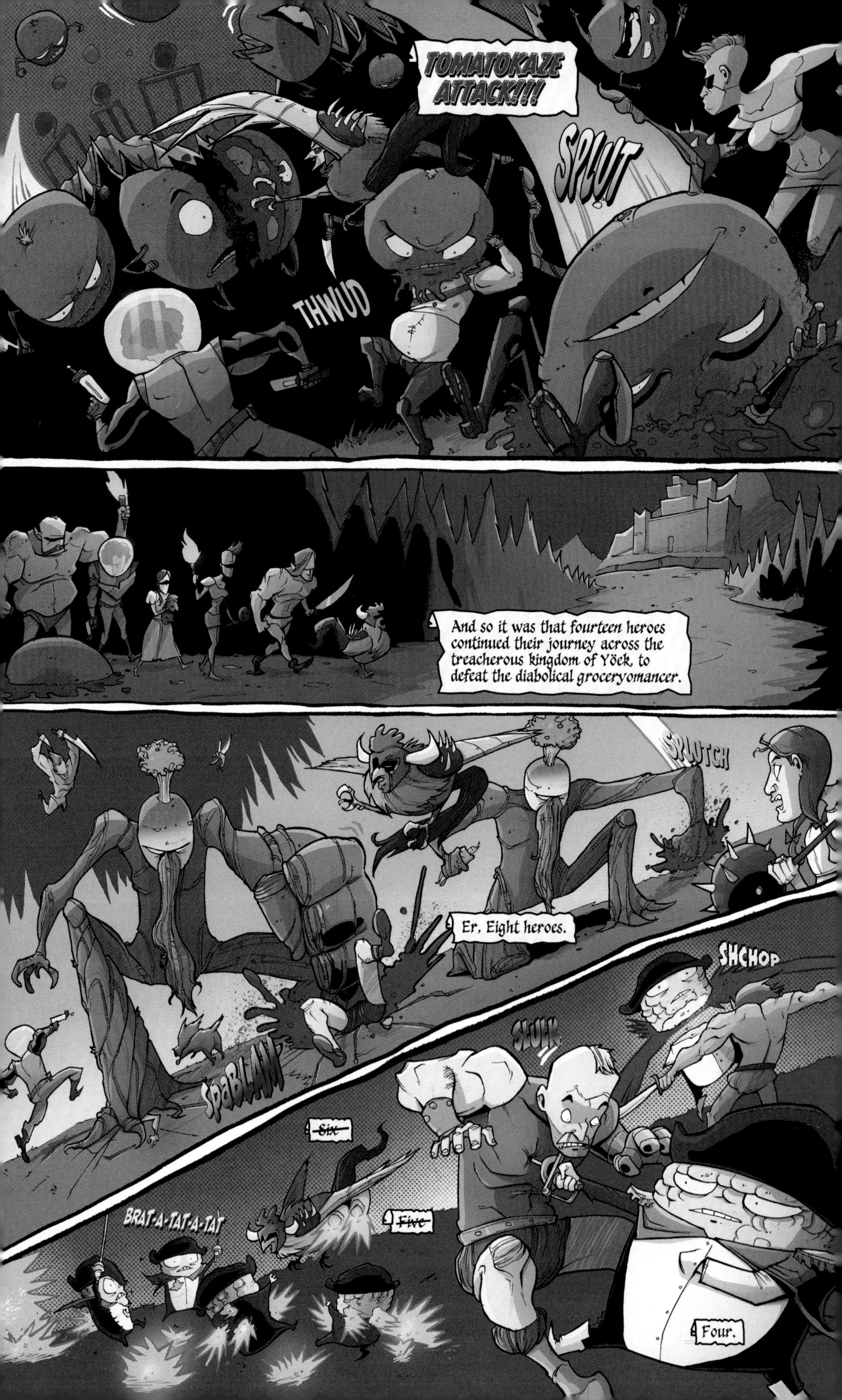
TOMATOKAZE ATTACK!!!
SPLUT
THWUD
And so it was that fourteen heroes continued their journey across the treacherous kingdom of Yöek, to defeat the diabolical groceryomancer.
SPLUTCH
Er, Eight heroes.
SHCHOP
SLUK
SpaBLAM
Six
BRAT-A-TAT-A-TAT
Five
Four.

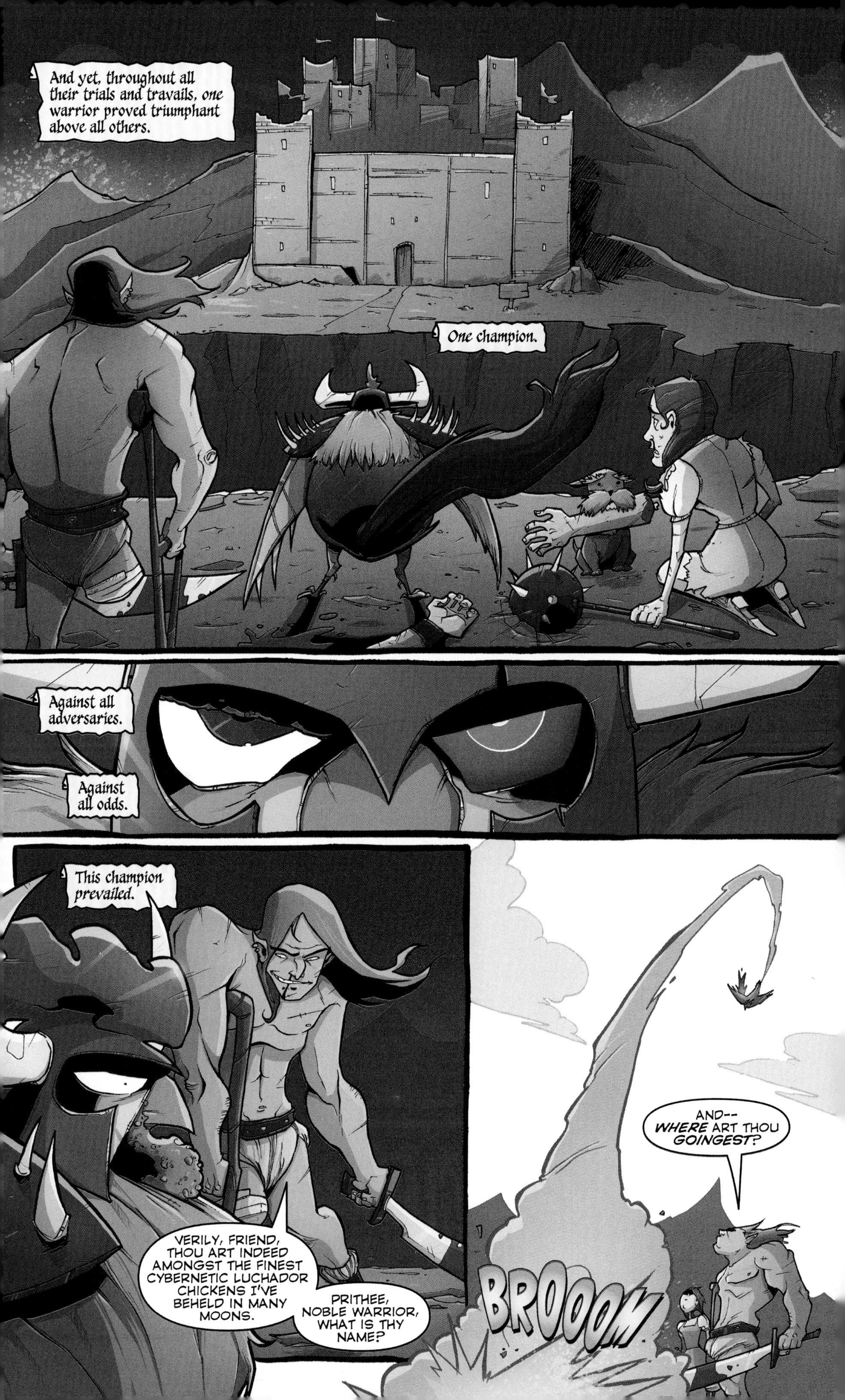
And yet, throughout all their trials and travails, one warrior proved triumphant above all others.
One champion.
Against all adversaries.
Against all odds.
This champion prevailed.
VERILY, FRIEND, THOU ART INDEED AMONGST THE FINEST CYBERNETIC LUCHADOR CHICKENS I'VE BEHELD IN MANY MOONS.
PRITHEE, NOBLE WARRIOR, WHAT IS THY NAME?
BROOOM
AND-- WHERE ART THOU GOINGEST?

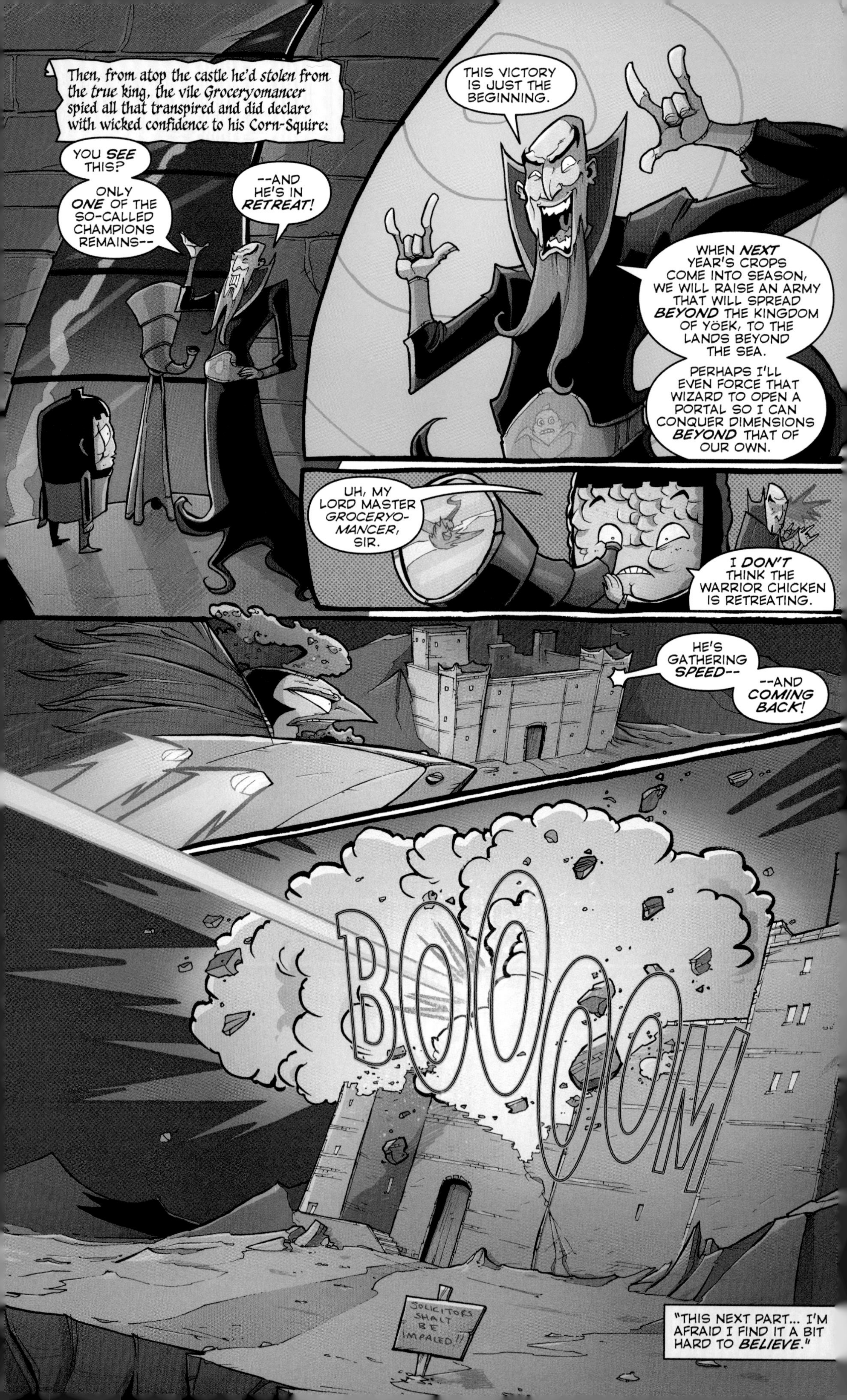
Then, from atop the castle he'd *stolen* from the *true* king, the vile *Groceryomancer* spied all that transpired and did declare with wicked confidence to his Corn-Squire:
YOU **SEE** THIS?
ONLY **ONE** OF THE SO-CALLED CHAMPIONS REMAINS--
--AND HE'S IN **RETREAT**!
THIS VICTORY IS JUST THE BEGINNING.
WHEN **NEXT** YEAR'S CROPS COME INTO SEASON, WE WILL RAISE AN ARMY THAT WILL SPREAD **BEYOND** THE KINGDOM OF YÖEK, TO THE LANDS BEYOND THE SEA.
PERHAPS I'LL EVEN FORCE THAT WIZARD TO OPEN A PORTAL SO I CAN CONQUER DIMENSIONS **BEYOND** THAT OF OUR OWN.
UH, MY LORD MASTER *GROCERYO-MANCER*, SIR.
I **DON'T** THINK THE WARRIOR CHICKEN IS RETREATING.
HE'S GATHERING **SPEED**--
--AND **COMING BACK**!
BOOOOOM
SOLICITORS SHALT BE IMPALED!!
"THIS NEXT PART... I'M AFRAID I FIND IT A BIT HARD TO **BELIEVE**."

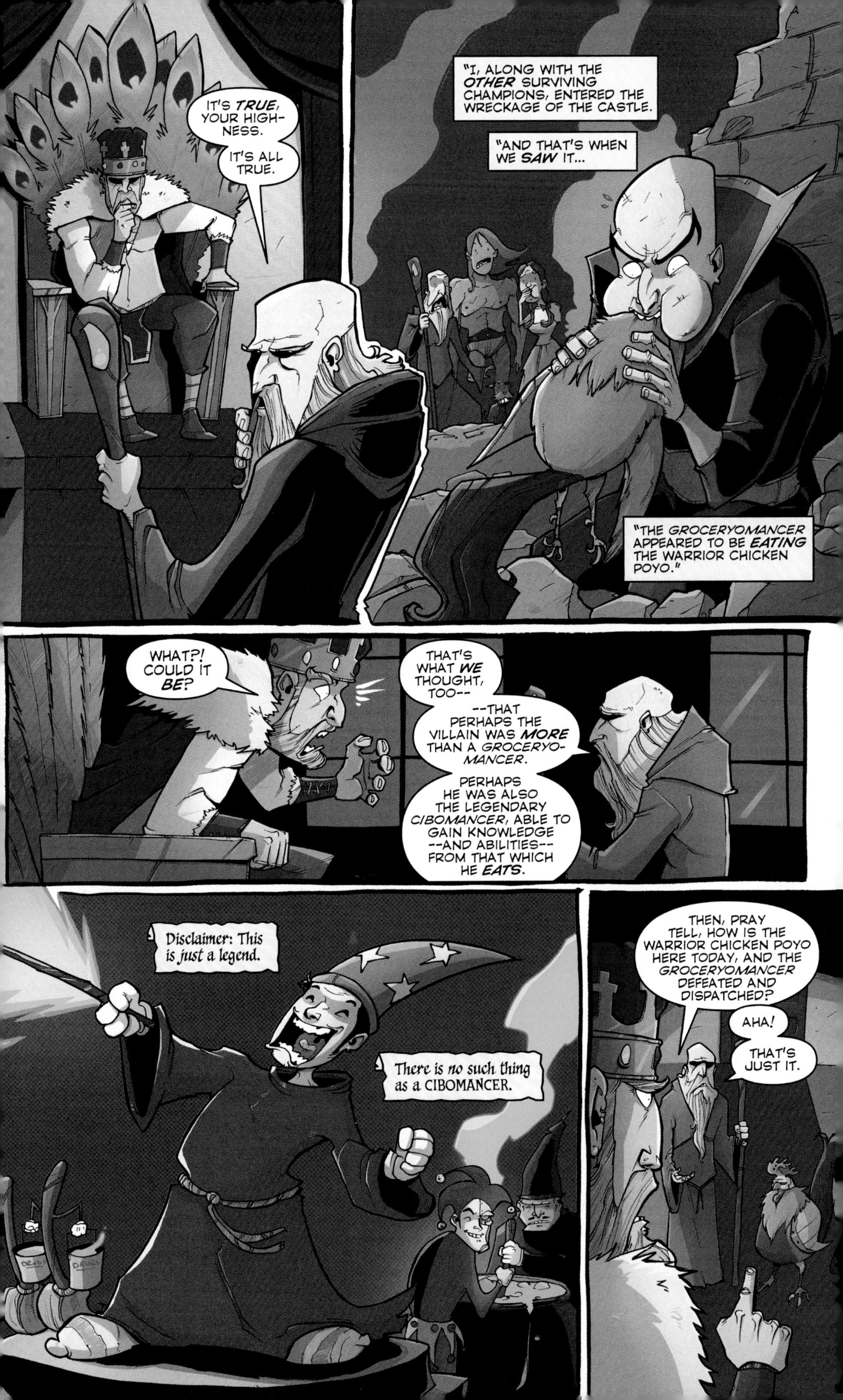

IT'S TRUE, YOUR HIGHNESS.
IT'S ALL TRUE.
"I, ALONG WITH THE OTHER SURVIVING CHAMPIONS, ENTERED THE WRECKAGE OF THE CASTLE.
"AND THAT'S WHEN WE SAW IT...
"THE GROCERYOMANCER APPEARED TO BE EATING THE WARRIOR CHICKEN POYO."
WHAT?! COULD IT BE?
THAT'S WHAT WE THOUGHT, TOO--
--THAT PERHAPS THE VILLAIN WAS MORE THAN A GROCERYOMANCER.
PERHAPS HE WAS ALSO THE LEGENDARY CIBOMANCER, ABLE TO GAIN KNOWLEDGE --AND ABILITIES-- FROM THAT WHICH HE EATS.
Disclaimer: This is just a legend.
There is no such thing as a CIBOMANCER.
THEN, PRAY TELL, HOW IS THE WARRIOR CHICKEN POYO HERE TODAY, AND THE GROCERYOMANCER DEFEATED AND DISPATCHED?
AHA!
THAT'S JUST IT.

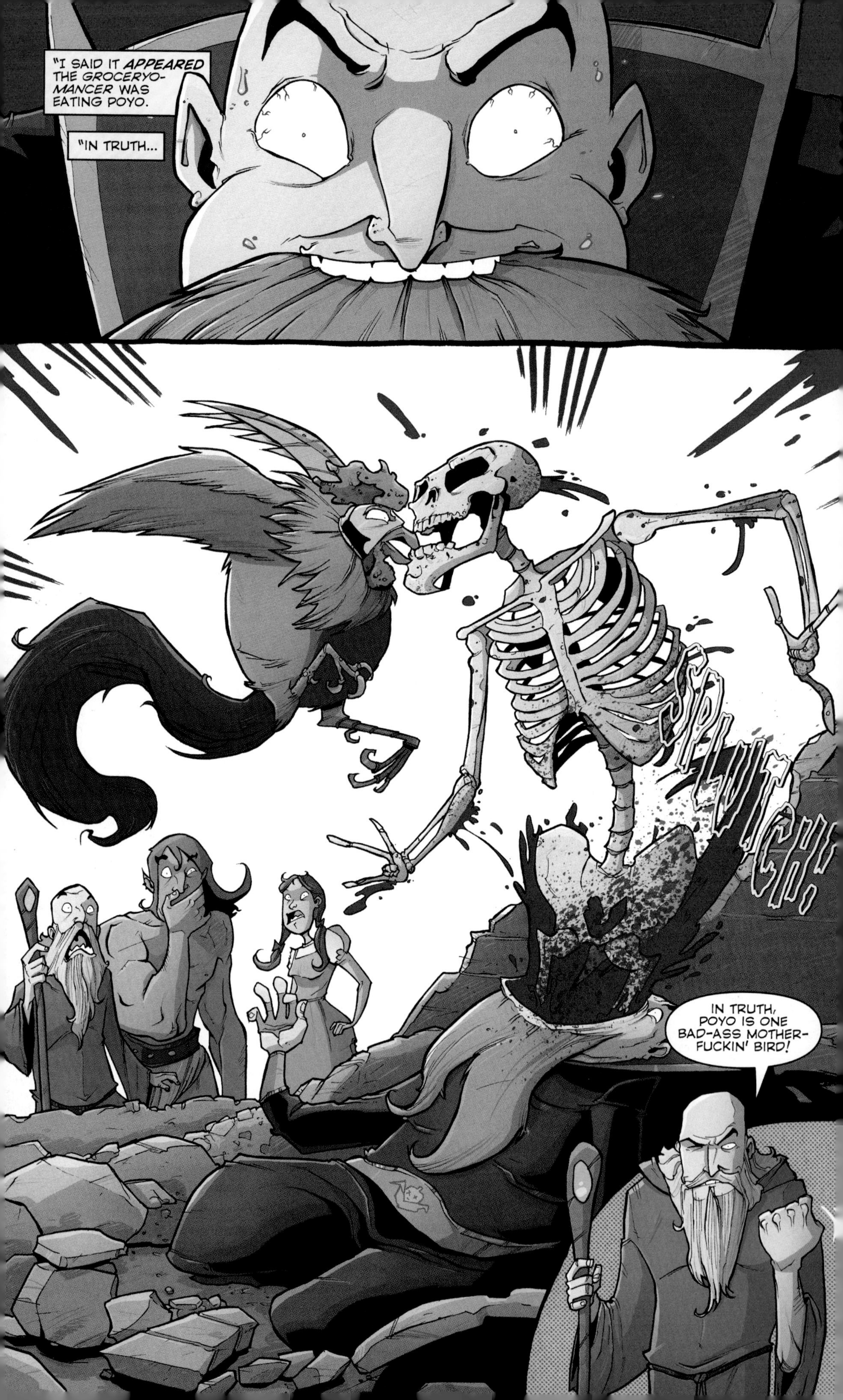
"I SAID IT *APPEARED* THE *GROCERYO-MANCER* WAS EATING POYO.
"IN TRUTH...
SPLUTCH!
IN TRUTH, POYO IS ONE BAD-ASS MOTHER-FUCKIN' BIRD!

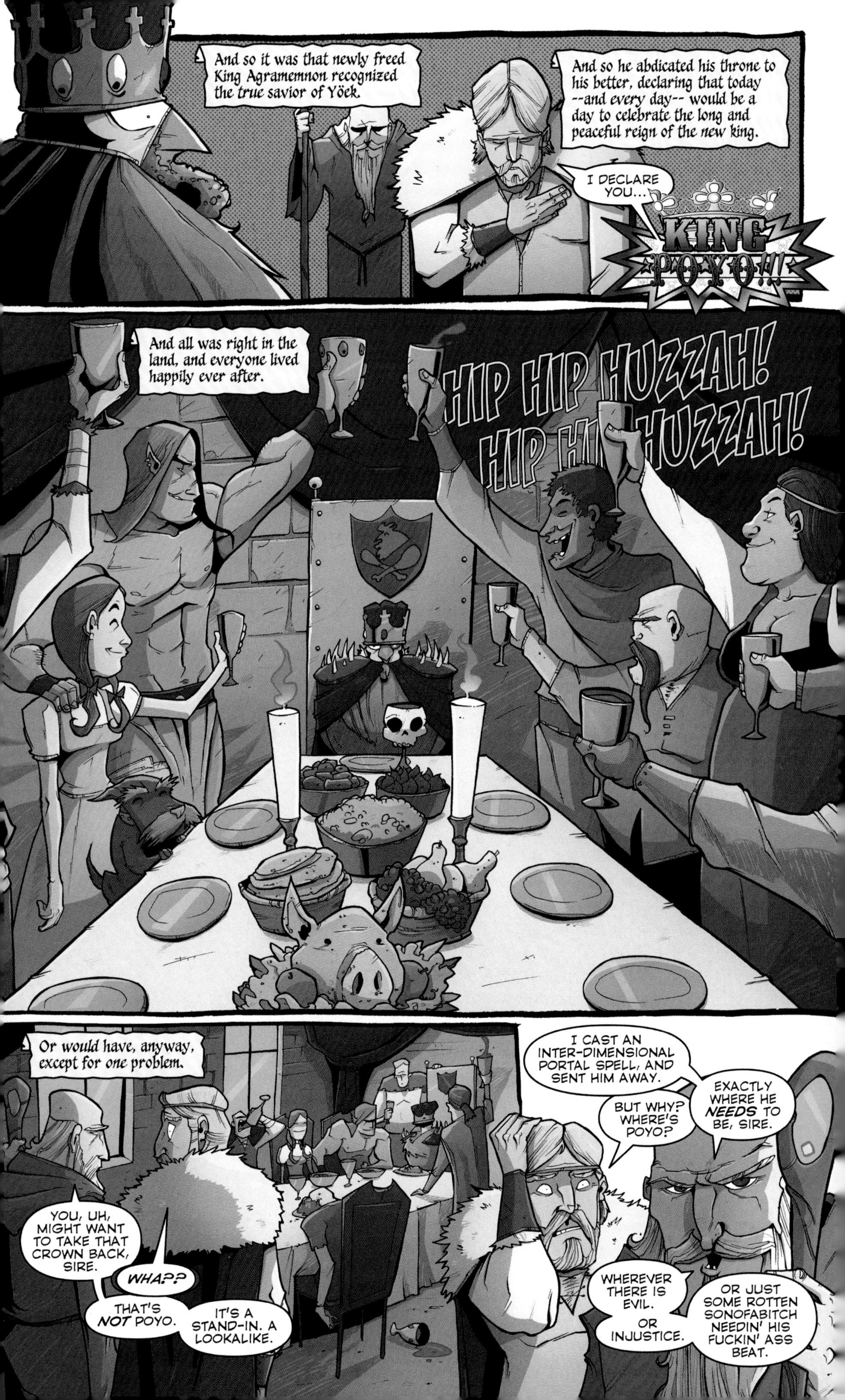
And so it was that newly freed King Agramemnon recognized the *true* savior of Yöek.
And so he abdicated his throne to his better, declaring that today --and every day-- would be a day to celebrate the long and peaceful reign of the *new* king.
I DECLARE YOU...
KING POYO!!!
And all was right in the land, and everyone lived happily ever after.
HIP HIP HUZZAH!
HIP HIP HUZZAH!
Or *would* have, anyway, except for *one* problem.
YOU, UH, MIGHT WANT TO TAKE THAT CROWN BACK, SIRE.
WHA??
THAT'S *NOT* POYO.
IT'S A STAND-IN. A LOOKALIKE.
I CAST AN INTER-DIMENSIONAL PORTAL SPELL, AND SENT HIM AWAY.
BUT WHY? WHERE'S POYO?
EXACTLY WHERE HE *NEEDS* TO BE, SIRE.
WHEREVER THERE IS EVIL.
OR INJUSTICE.
OR JUST SOME ROTTEN SONOFABITCH NEEDIN' HIS FUCKIN' ASS BEAT.

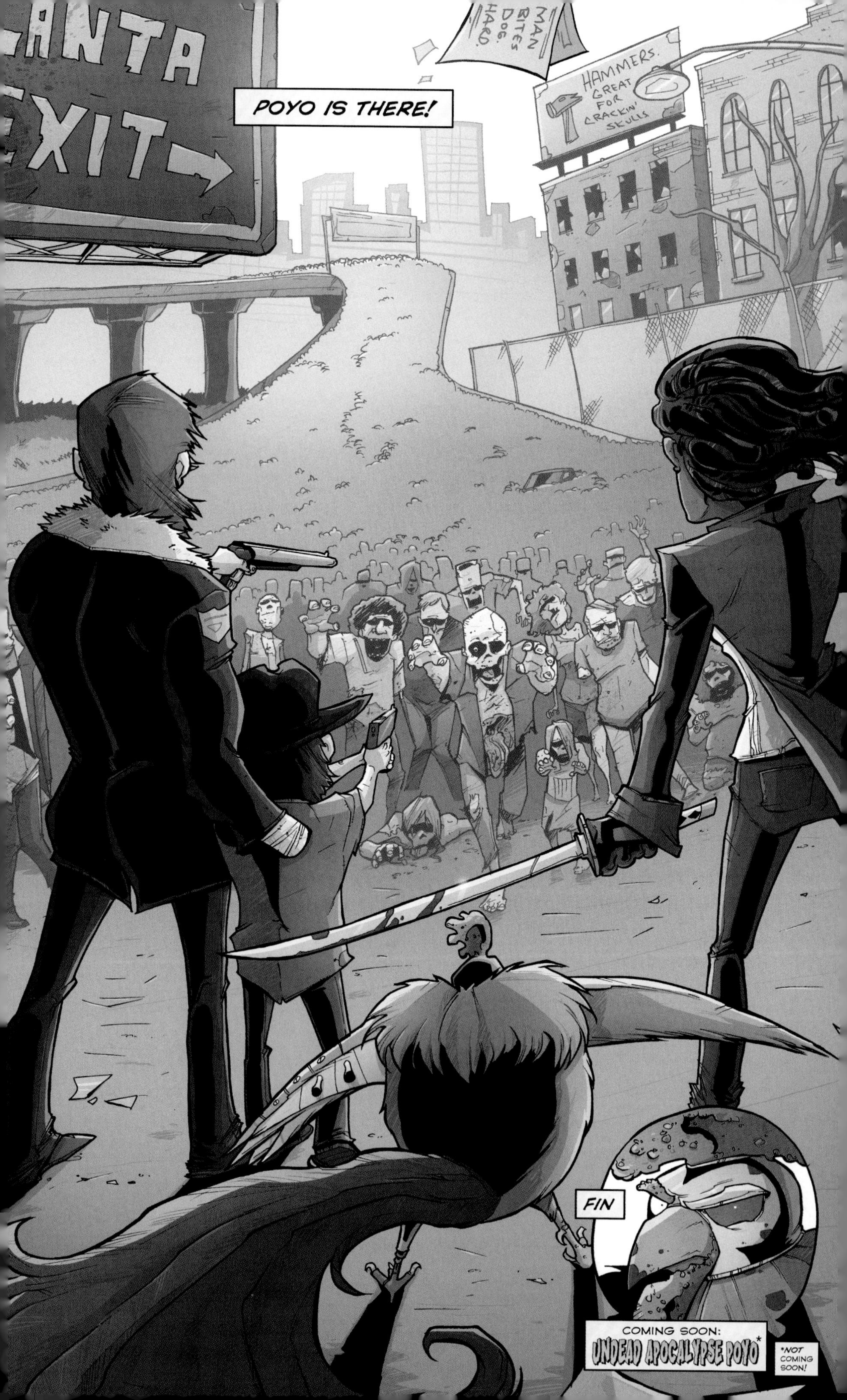

ANTA
EXIT
MAN BITES DOG. HARD.
HAMMERS. GREAT FOR CRACKIN' SKULLS
POYO IS THERE!
FIN
COMING SOON:
UNDEAD APOCALYPSE POYO*
*NOT COMING SOON!

Chapter Three

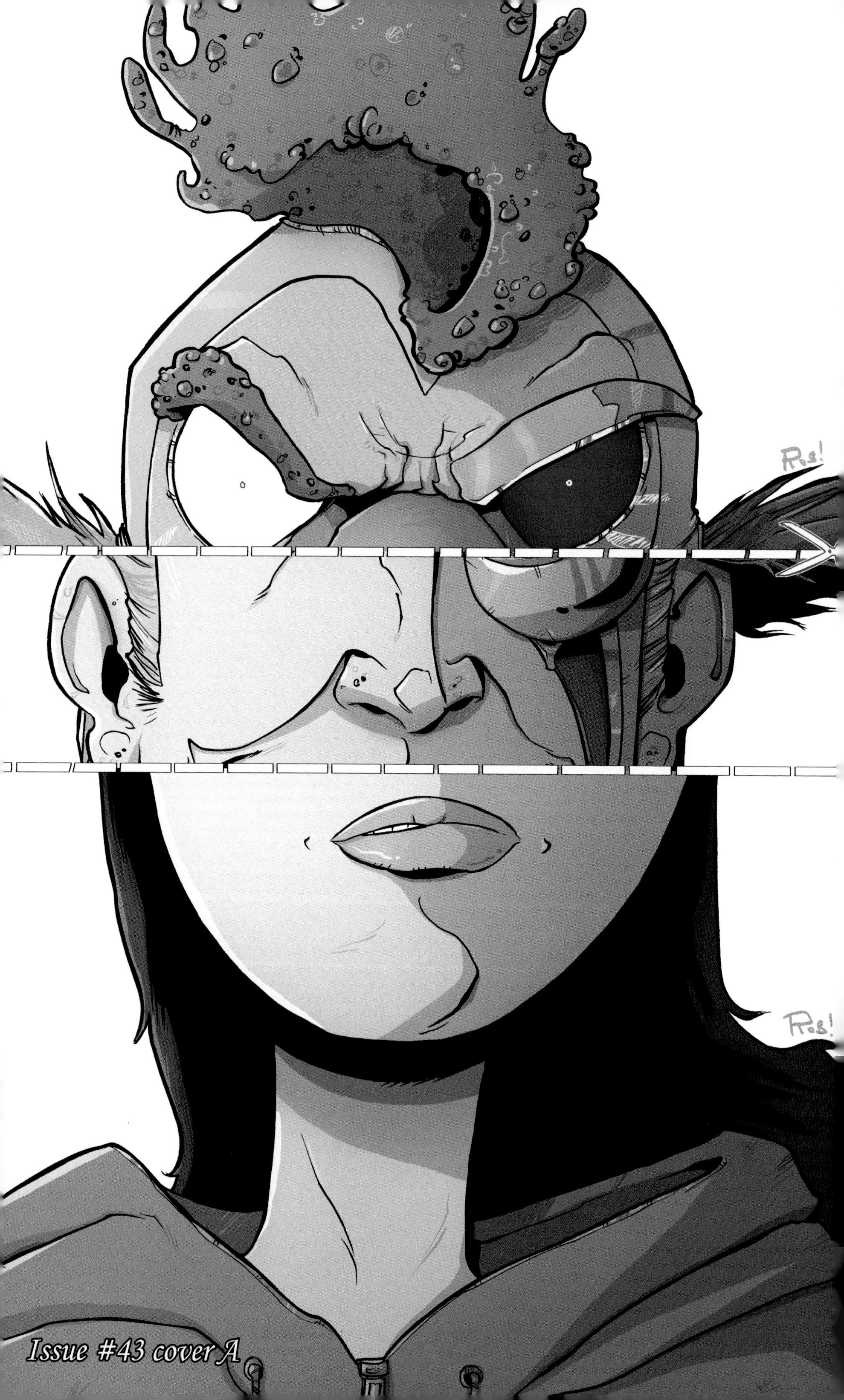
Ros!
Ros!

Issue #43 cover A

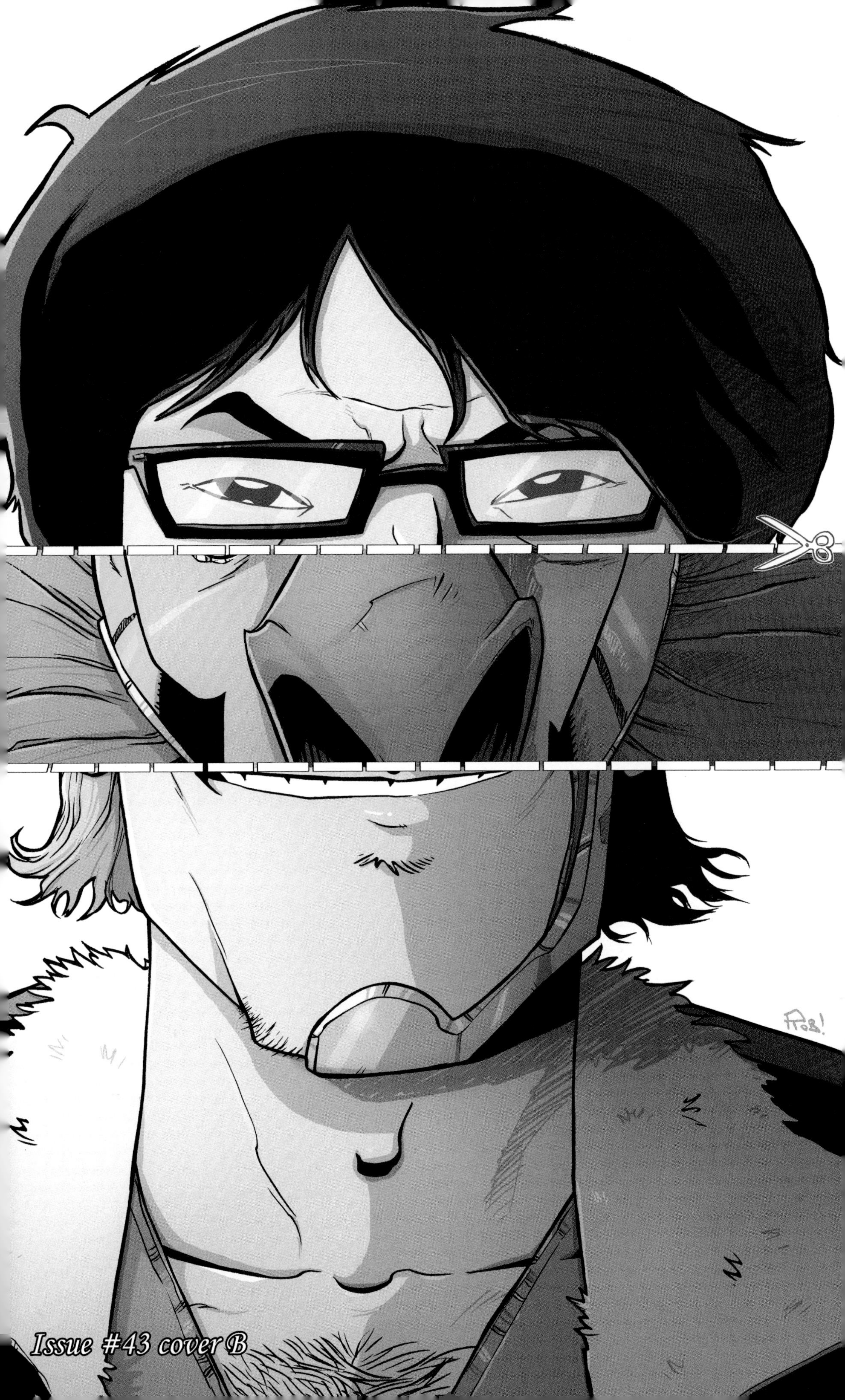

Issue #43 cover B

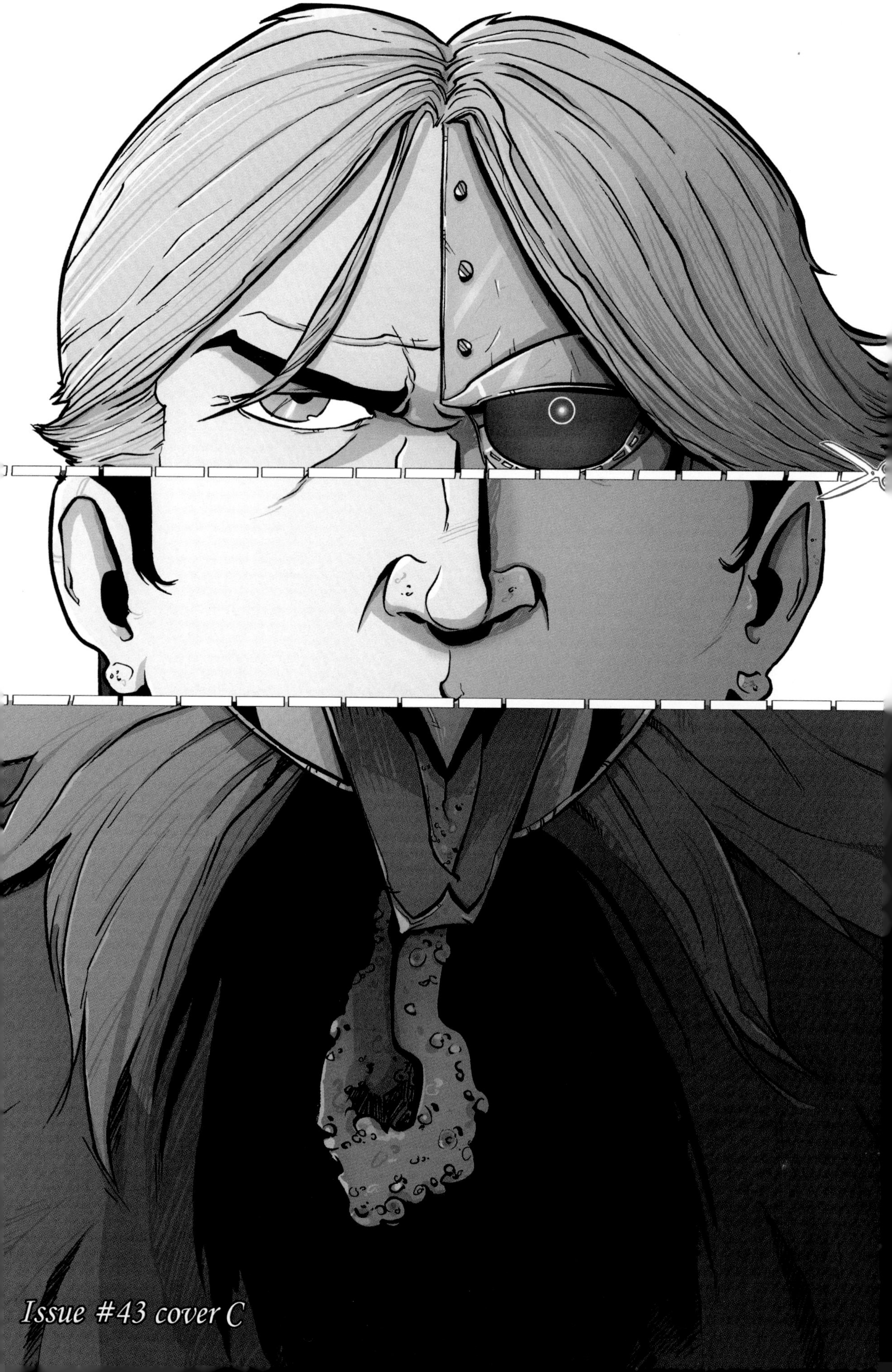

Issue #43 cover C

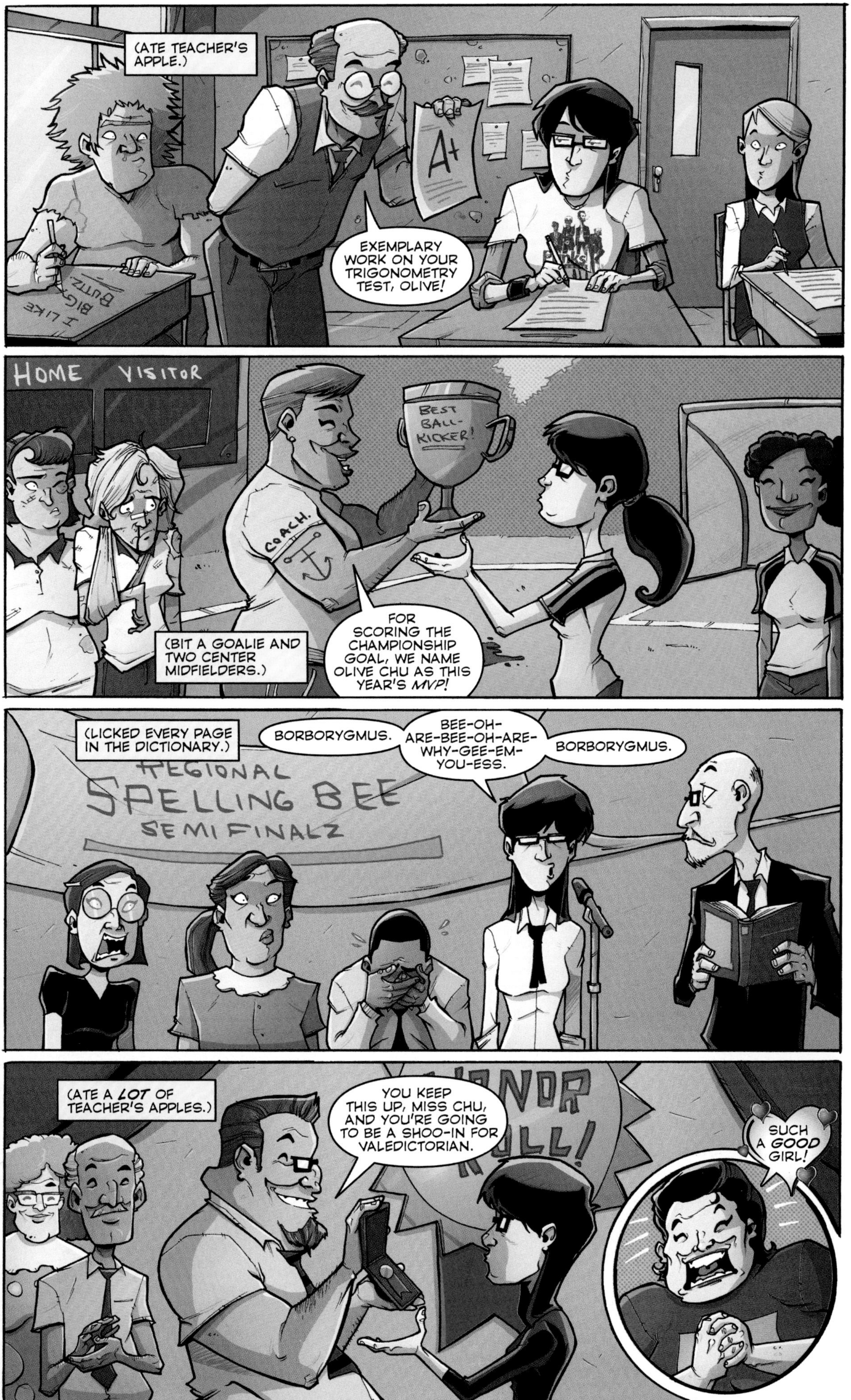
(ATE TEACHER'S APPLE.)
A+
EXEMPLARY WORK ON YOUR TRIGONOMETRY TEST, OLIVE!
I LIKE BIG BUTZ.
HOME
VISITOR
BEST BALL-KICKER!
COACH.
(BIT A GOALIE AND TWO CENTER MIDFIELDERS.)
FOR SCORING THE CHAMPIONSHIP GOAL, WE NAME OLIVE CHU AS THIS YEAR'S *MVP!*
(LICKED EVERY PAGE IN THE DICTIONARY.)
BORBORYGMUS.
BEE-OH-ARE-BEE-OH-ARE-WHY-GEE-EM-YOU-ESS.
BORBORYGMUS.
REGIONAL SPELLING BEE SEMIFINALZ
(ATE A *LOT* OF TEACHER'S APPLES.)
YOU KEEP THIS UP, MISS CHU, AND YOU'RE GOING TO BE A SHOO-IN FOR VALEDICTORIAN.
SUCH A *GOOD* GIRL!

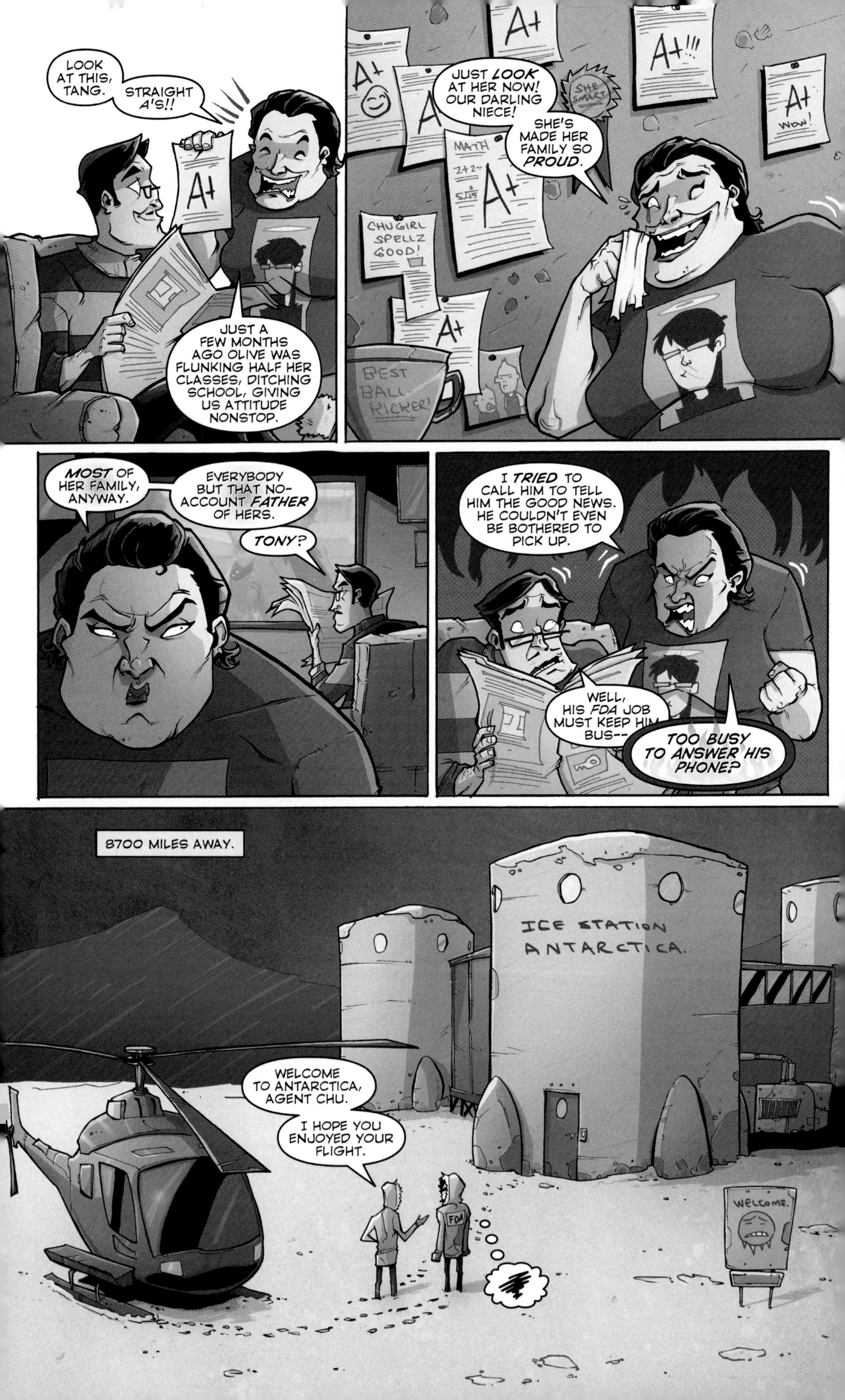
LOOK AT THIS, TANG.
STRAIGHT A'S!!
A+
JUST A FEW MONTHS AGO OLIVE WAS FLUNKING HALF HER CLASSES, DITCHING SCHOOL, GIVING US ATTITUDE NONSTOP.
A+
A+
A+!!!
A+ WOW!
SHE SMART
JUST LOOK AT HER NOW! OUR DARLING NIECE!
SHE'S MADE HER FAMILY SO PROUD.
MATH 2+2= A+
CHUGIRL SPELLZ GOOD!
A+
BEST BALL KICKER!
MOST OF HER FAMILY, ANYWAY.
EVERYBODY BUT THAT NO-ACCOUNT FATHER OF HERS.
TONY?
I TRIED TO CALL HIM TO TELL HIM THE GOOD NEWS. HE COULDN'T EVEN BE BOTHERED TO PICK UP.
WELL, HIS FDA JOB MUST KEEP HIM BUS--
TOO BUSY TO ANSWER HIS PHONE?
8700 MILES AWAY.
ICE STATION ANTARCTICA.
WELCOME TO ANTARCTICA, AGENT CHU.
I HOPE YOU ENJOYED YOUR FLIGHT.
FDA
WELCOME.

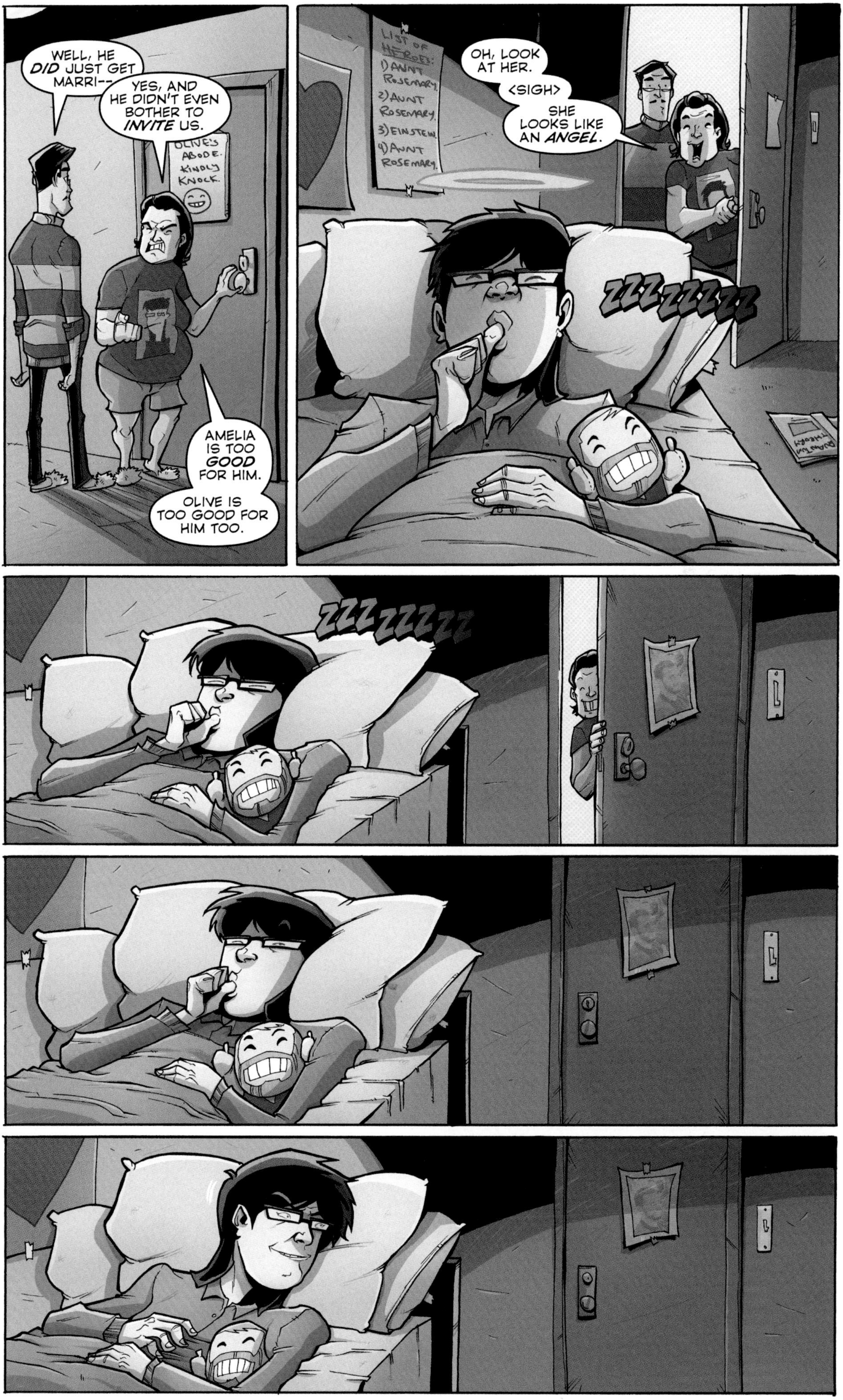

WELL, HE *DID* JUST GET MARRI--
YES, AND HE DIDN'T EVEN BOTHER TO *INVITE* US.
OLIVE'S ABODE. KINDLY KNOCK.
AMELIA IS TOO *GOOD* FOR HIM.
OLIVE IS TOO GOOD FOR HIM TOO.
LIST OF HEROES: 1) AUNT ROSEMARY 2) AUNT ROSEMARY 3) EINSTEIN 4) AUNT ROSEMARY
OH, LOOK AT HER.
<SIGH>
SHE LOOKS LIKE AN *ANGEL*.
ZZZZZZZ
ZZZZZZZZ

SCIENCE BAD. EINSTEIN AWESOME.

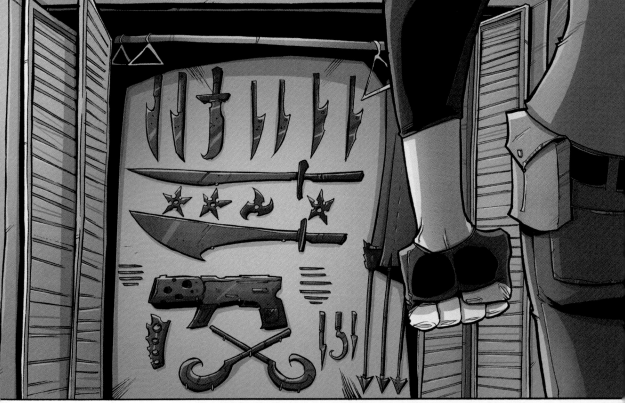

SERIOUSLY? *OLIVE CHU?* SWEET LITTLE FOUR-EYED TOOTHPICK OLIVE CHU?

YOU THINK SHE'S *READY* FOR THIS, FATMAN?

I'LL LET *YOU* BE THE JUDGE, AGENT COLBY.

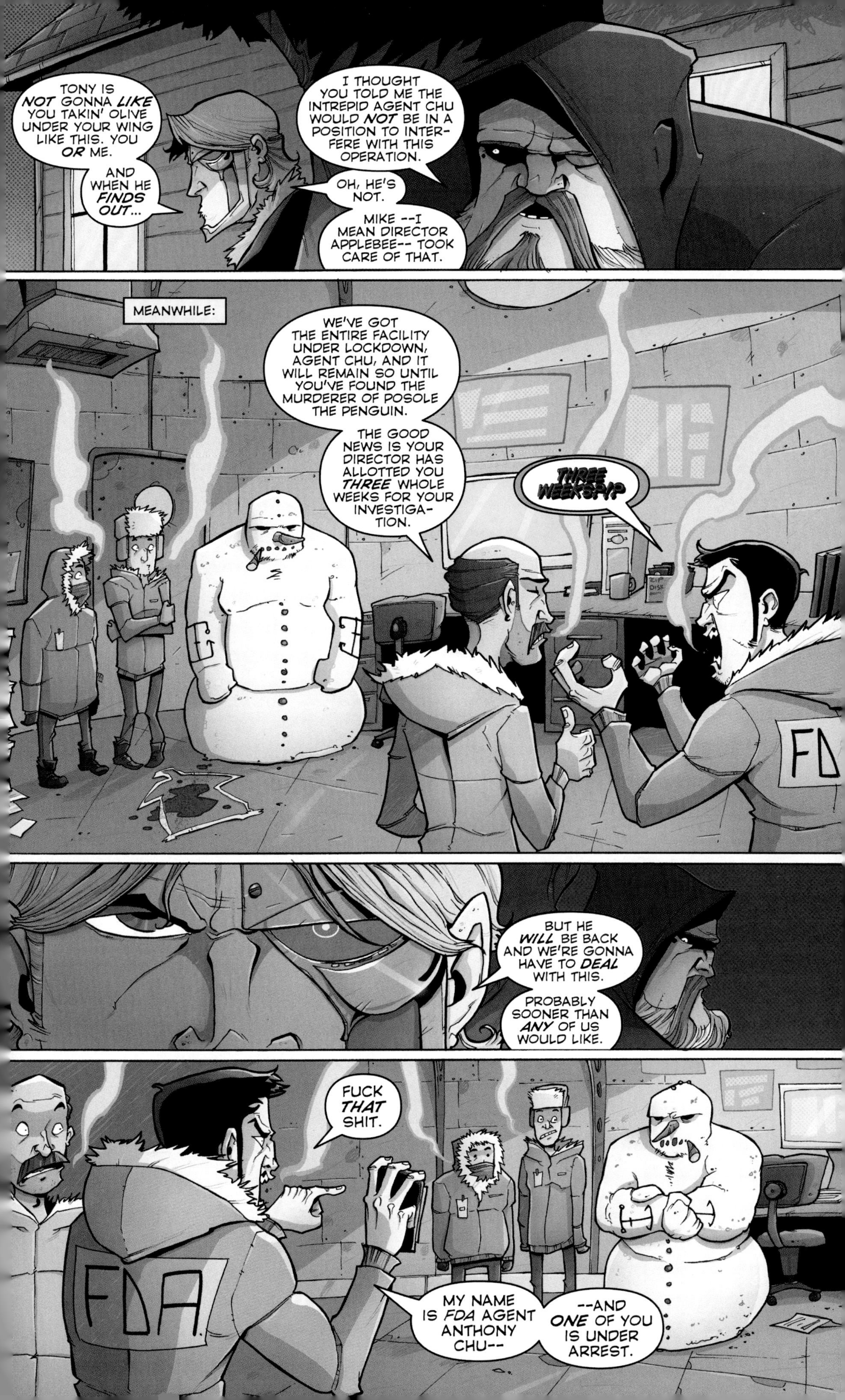
TONY IS NOT GONNA LIKE YOU TAKIN' OLIVE UNDER YOUR WING LIKE THIS. YOU OR ME.
AND WHEN HE FINDS OUT...
I THOUGHT YOU TOLD ME THE INTREPID AGENT CHU WOULD NOT BE IN A POSITION TO INTER-FERE WITH THIS OPERATION.
OH, HE'S NOT.
MIKE --I MEAN DIRECTOR APPLEBEE-- TOOK CARE OF THAT.
MEANWHILE:
WE'VE GOT THE ENTIRE FACILITY UNDER LOCKDOWN, AGENT CHU, AND IT WILL REMAIN SO UNTIL YOU'VE FOUND THE MURDERER OF POSOLE THE PENGUIN.
THE GOOD NEWS IS YOUR DIRECTOR HAS ALLOTTED YOU THREE WHOLE WEEKS FOR YOUR INVESTIGA-TION.
THREE WEEKS?!?
BUT HE WILL BE BACK AND WE'RE GONNA HAVE TO DEAL WITH THIS.
PROBABLY SOONER THAN ANY OF US WOULD LIKE.
FUCK THAT SHIT.
MY NAME IS FDA AGENT ANTHONY CHU--
--AND ONE OF YOU IS UNDER ARREST.
FDA

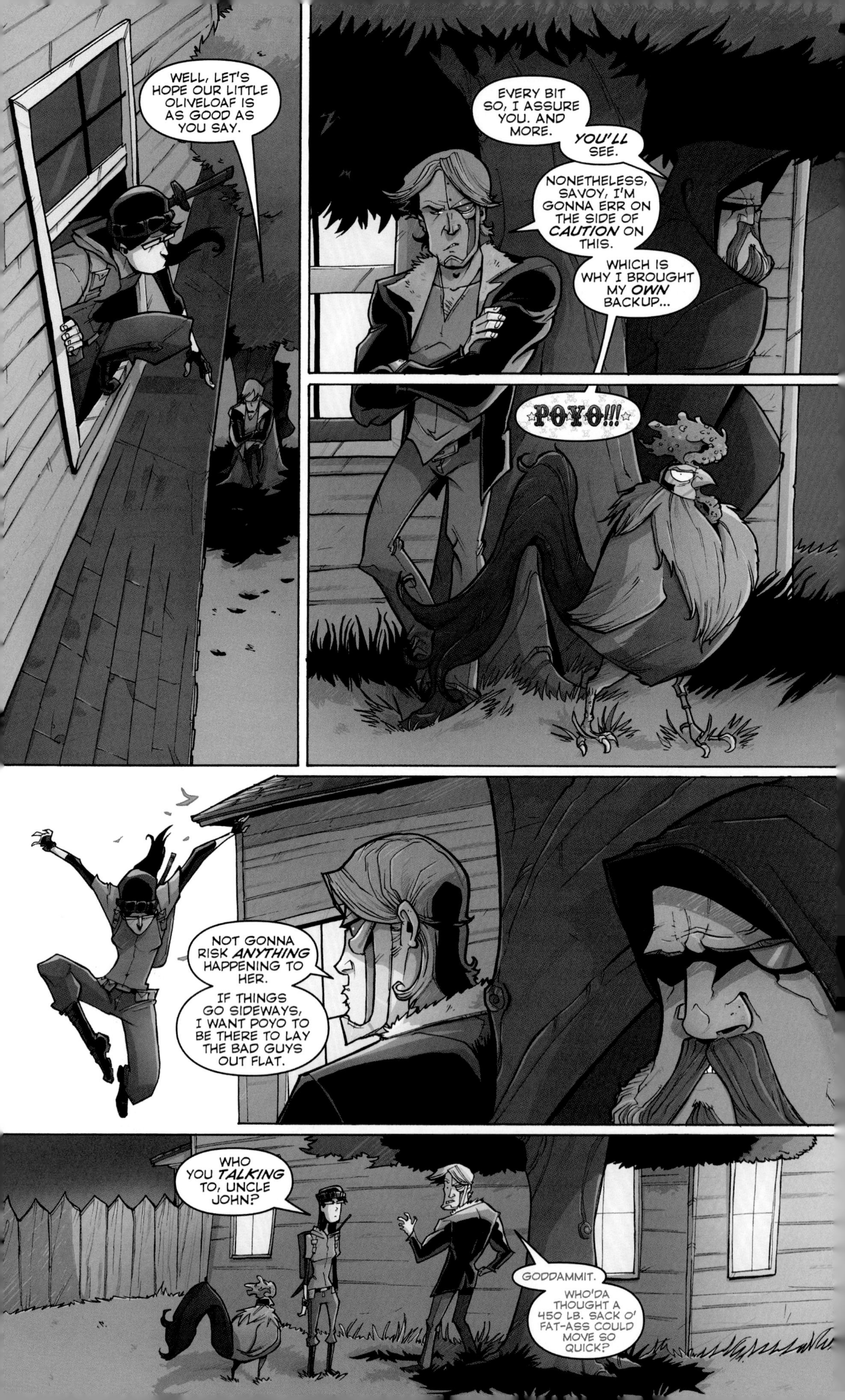
WELL, LET'S HOPE OUR LITTLE OLIVELOAF IS AS GOOD AS YOU SAY.
EVERY BIT SO, I ASSURE YOU. AND MORE.
YOU'LL SEE.
NONETHELESS, SAVOY, I'M GONNA ERR ON THE SIDE OF CAUTION ON THIS.
WHICH IS WHY I BROUGHT MY OWN BACKUP...
POYO!!!
NOT GONNA RISK ANYTHING HAPPENING TO HER.
IF THINGS GO SIDEWAYS, I WANT POYO TO BE THERE TO LAY THE BAD GUYS OUT FLAT.
WHO YOU TALKING TO, UNCLE JOHN?
GODDAMMIT.
WHO'DA THOUGHT A 450 LB. SACK O' FAT-ASS COULD MOVE SO QUICK?

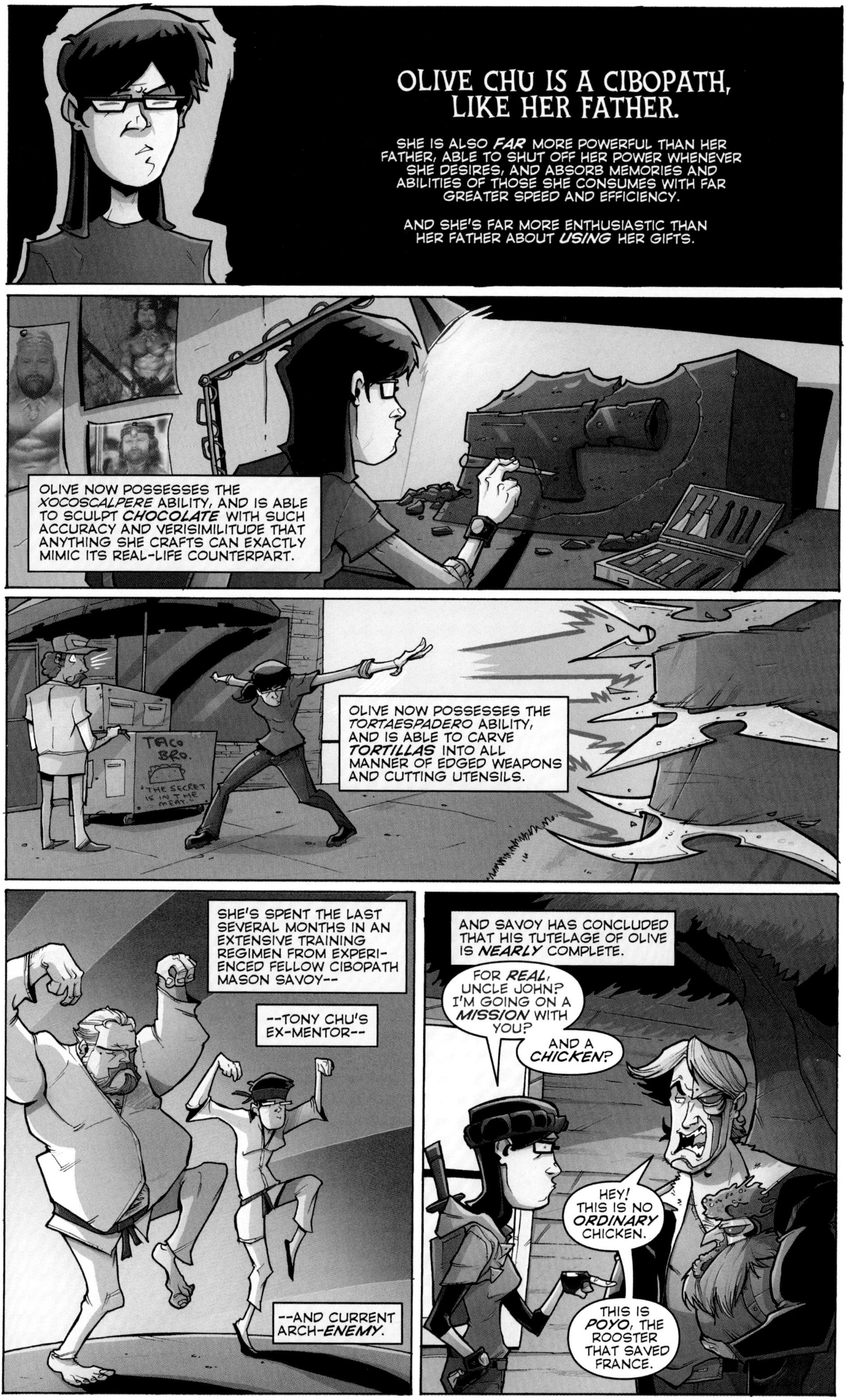
OLIVE CHU IS A CIBOPATH, LIKE HER FATHER.
SHE IS ALSO FAR MORE POWERFUL THAN HER FATHER, ABLE TO SHUT OFF HER POWER WHENEVER SHE DESIRES, AND ABSORB MEMORIES AND ABILITIES OF THOSE SHE CONSUMES WITH FAR GREATER SPEED AND EFFICIENCY.
AND SHE'S FAR MORE ENTHUSIASTIC THAN HER FATHER ABOUT USING HER GIFTS.
OLIVE NOW POSSESSES THE XOCOSCALPERE ABILITY, AND IS ABLE TO SCULPT CHOCOLATE WITH SUCH ACCURACY AND VERISIMILITUDE THAT ANYTHING SHE CRAFTS CAN EXACTLY MIMIC ITS REAL-LIFE COUNTERPART.
TACO BRO.
"THE SECRET IS IN THE MEAT."
OLIVE NOW POSSESSES THE TORTAESPADERO ABILITY, AND IS ABLE TO CARVE TORTILLAS INTO ALL MANNER OF EDGED WEAPONS AND CUTTING UTENSILS.
SHE'S SPENT THE LAST SEVERAL MONTHS IN AN EXTENSIVE TRAINING REGIMEN FROM EXPERIENCED FELLOW CIBOPATH MASON SAVOY--
--TONY CHU'S EX-MENTOR--
--AND CURRENT ARCH-ENEMY.
AND SAVOY HAS CONCLUDED THAT HIS TUTELAGE OF OLIVE IS NEARLY COMPLETE.
FOR REAL, UNCLE JOHN? I'M GOING ON A MISSION WITH YOU?
AND A CHICKEN?
HEY! THIS IS NO ORDINARY CHICKEN.
THIS IS POYO, THE ROOSTER THAT SAVED FRANCE.

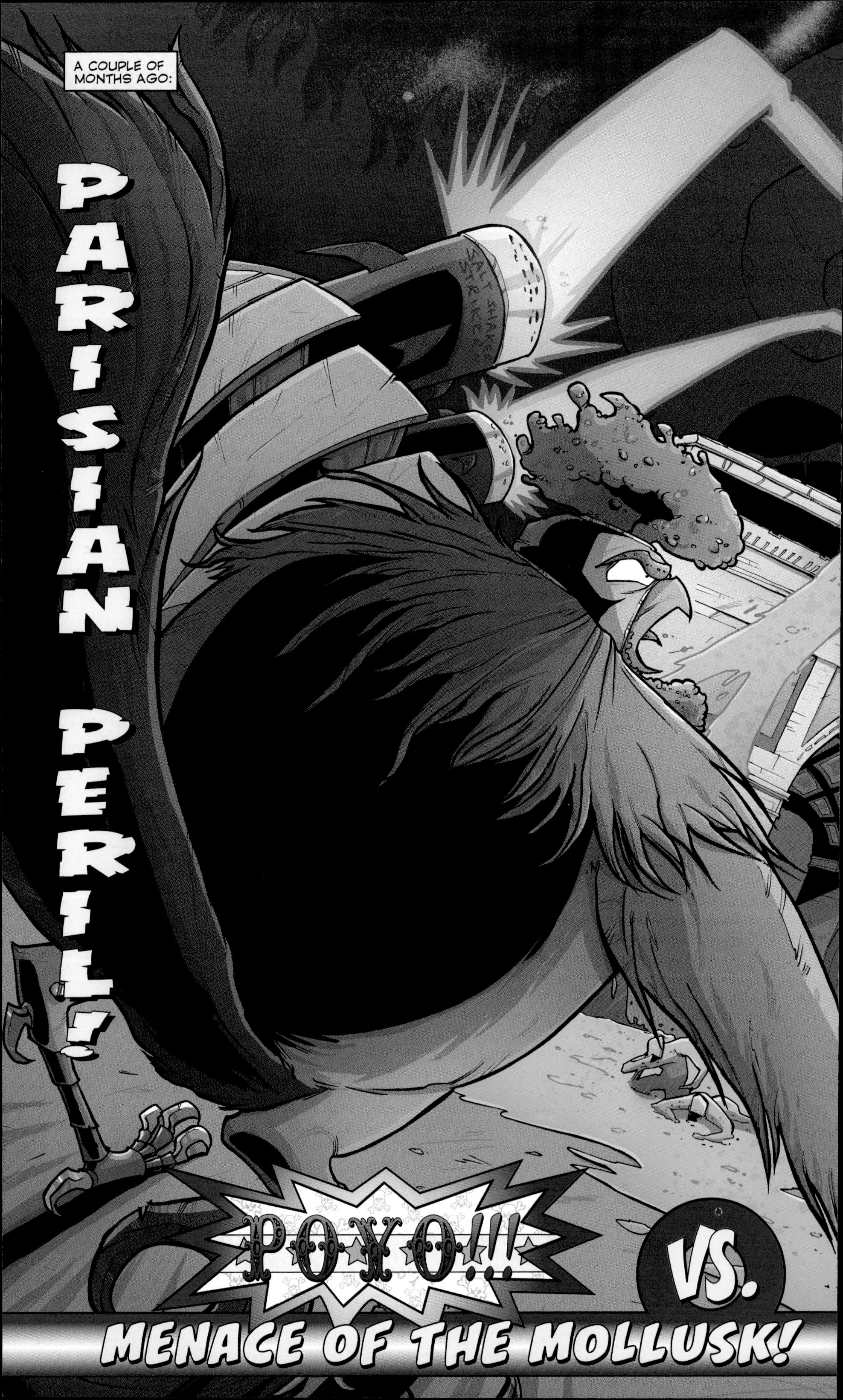
A COUPLE OF MONTHS AGO:
PARISIAN PERIL!
SALT SHAKER STRIKER
POYO!!!
VS.
MENACE OF THE MOLLUSK!

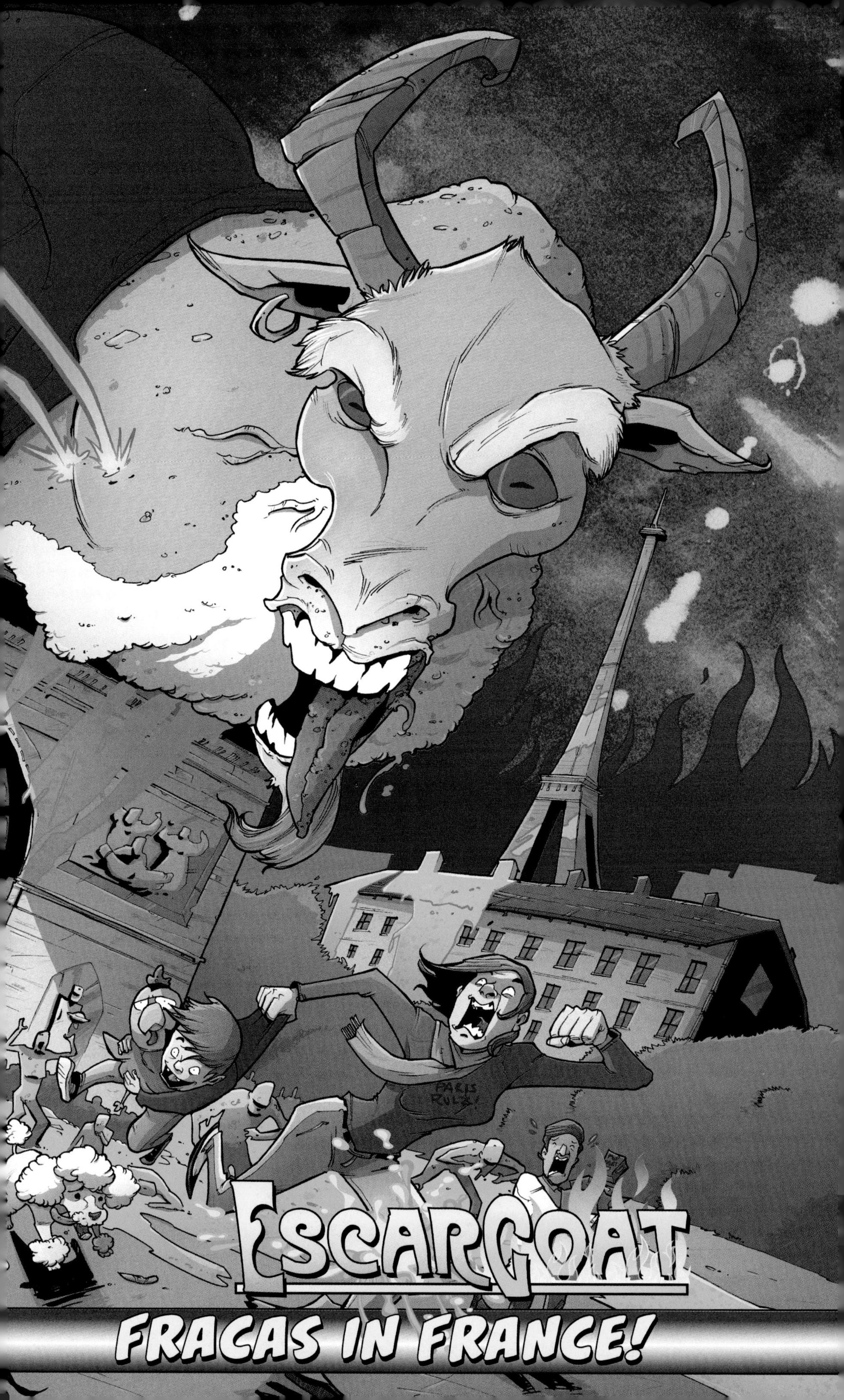
PARIS RULZ!
ESCARGOAT
FRACAS IN FRANCE!

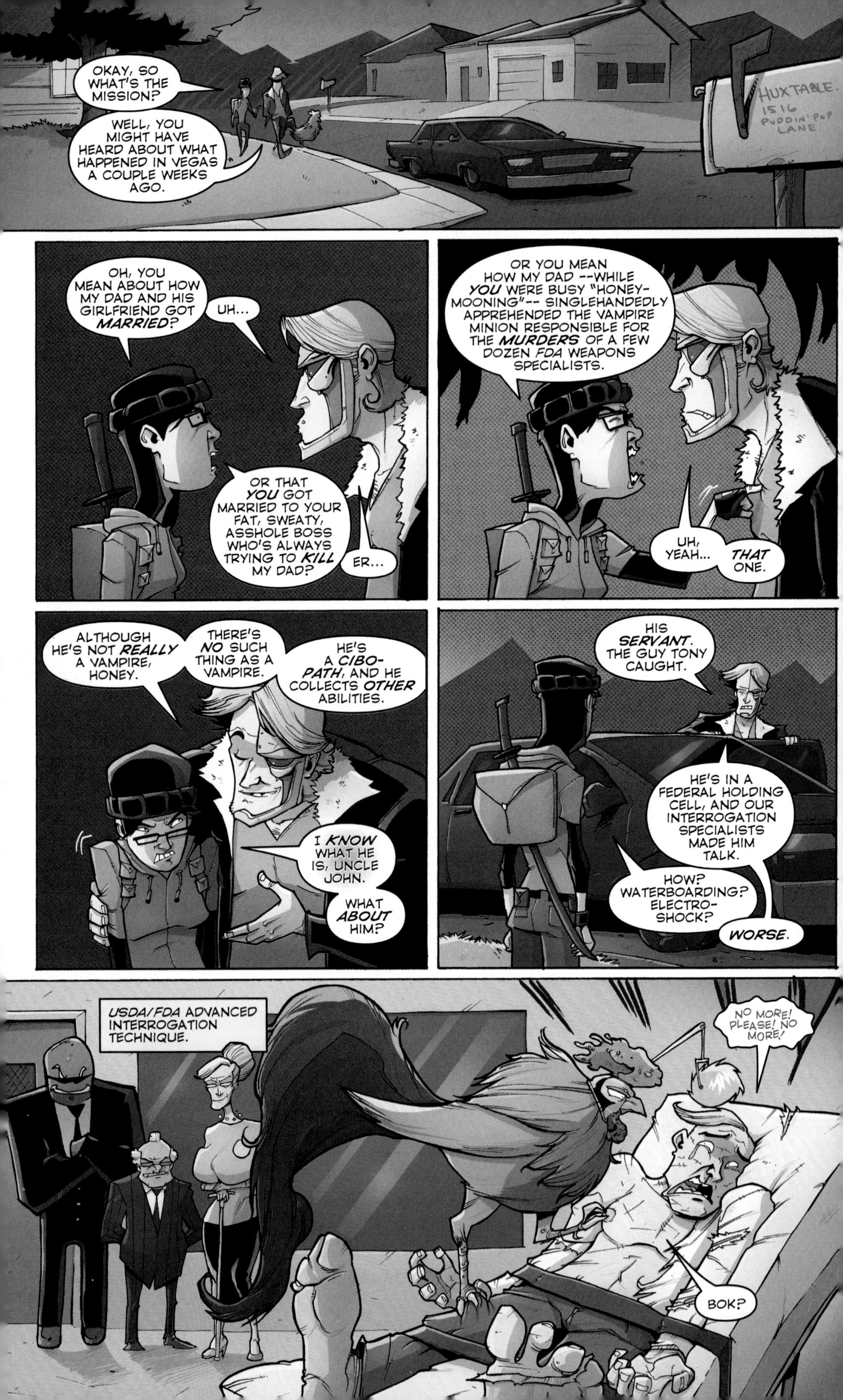
HUXTABLE. 1516 PUDDIN' POP LANE
OKAY, SO WHAT'S THE MISSION?
WELL, YOU MIGHT HAVE HEARD ABOUT WHAT HAPPENED IN VEGAS A COUPLE WEEKS AGO.
OH, YOU MEAN ABOUT HOW MY DAD AND HIS GIRLFRIEND GOT MARRIED?
UH...
OR THAT YOU GOT MARRIED TO YOUR FAT, SWEATY, ASSHOLE BOSS WHO'S ALWAYS TRYING TO KILL MY DAD?
ER...
OR YOU MEAN HOW MY DAD --WHILE YOU WERE BUSY "HONEY-MOONING"-- SINGLEHANDEDLY APPREHENDED THE VAMPIRE MINION RESPONSIBLE FOR THE MURDERS OF A FEW DOZEN FDA WEAPONS SPECIALISTS.
UH, YEAH... THAT ONE.
ALTHOUGH HE'S NOT REALLY A VAMPIRE, HONEY.
THERE'S NO SUCH THING AS A VAMPIRE.
HE'S A CIBO-PATH, AND HE COLLECTS OTHER ABILITIES.
I KNOW WHAT HE IS, UNCLE JOHN.
WHAT ABOUT HIM?
HIS SERVANT. THE GUY TONY CAUGHT.
HE'S IN A FEDERAL HOLDING CELL, AND OUR INTERROGATION SPECIALISTS MADE HIM TALK.
HOW? WATERBOARDING? ELECTRO-SHOCK?
WORSE.
USDA/FDA ADVANCED INTERROGATION TECHNIQUE.
NO MORE! PLEASE! NO MORE!
BOK?

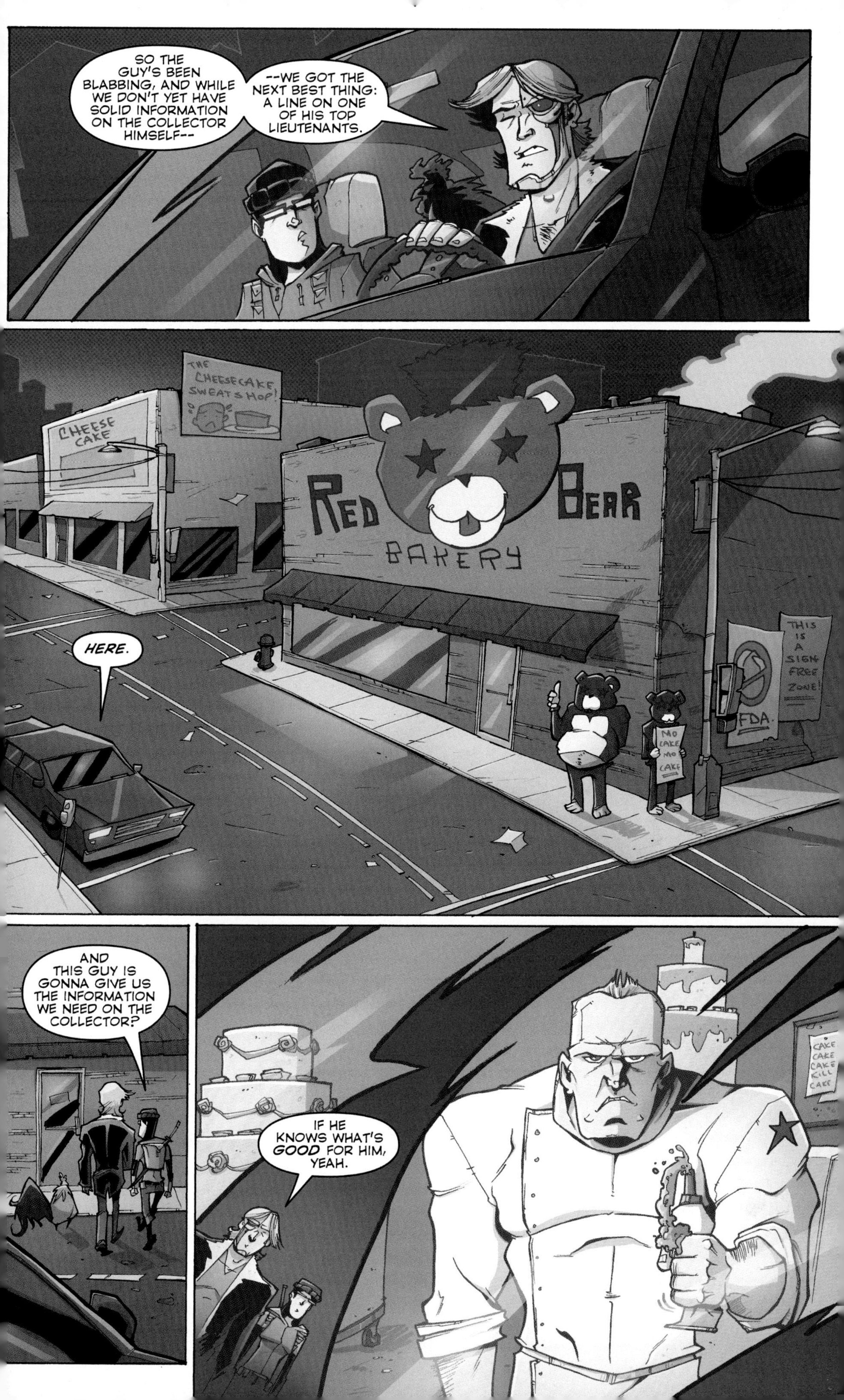
SO THE GUY'S BEEN BLABBING, AND WHILE WE DON'T YET HAVE SOLID INFORMATION ON THE COLLECTOR HIMSELF--
--WE GOT THE NEXT BEST THING: A LINE ON ONE OF HIS TOP LIEUTENANTS.
THE CHEESECAKE SWEATSHOP!
CHEESE CAKE
RED BEAR
BAKERY
HERE.
THIS IS A SIGN-FREE ZONE!
FDA.
NO CAKE NO CAKE
AND THIS GUY IS GONNA GIVE US THE INFORMATION WE NEED ON THE COLLECTOR?
IF HE KNOWS WHAT'S *GOOD* FOR HIM, YEAH.
CAKE CAKE CAKE KILL CAKE

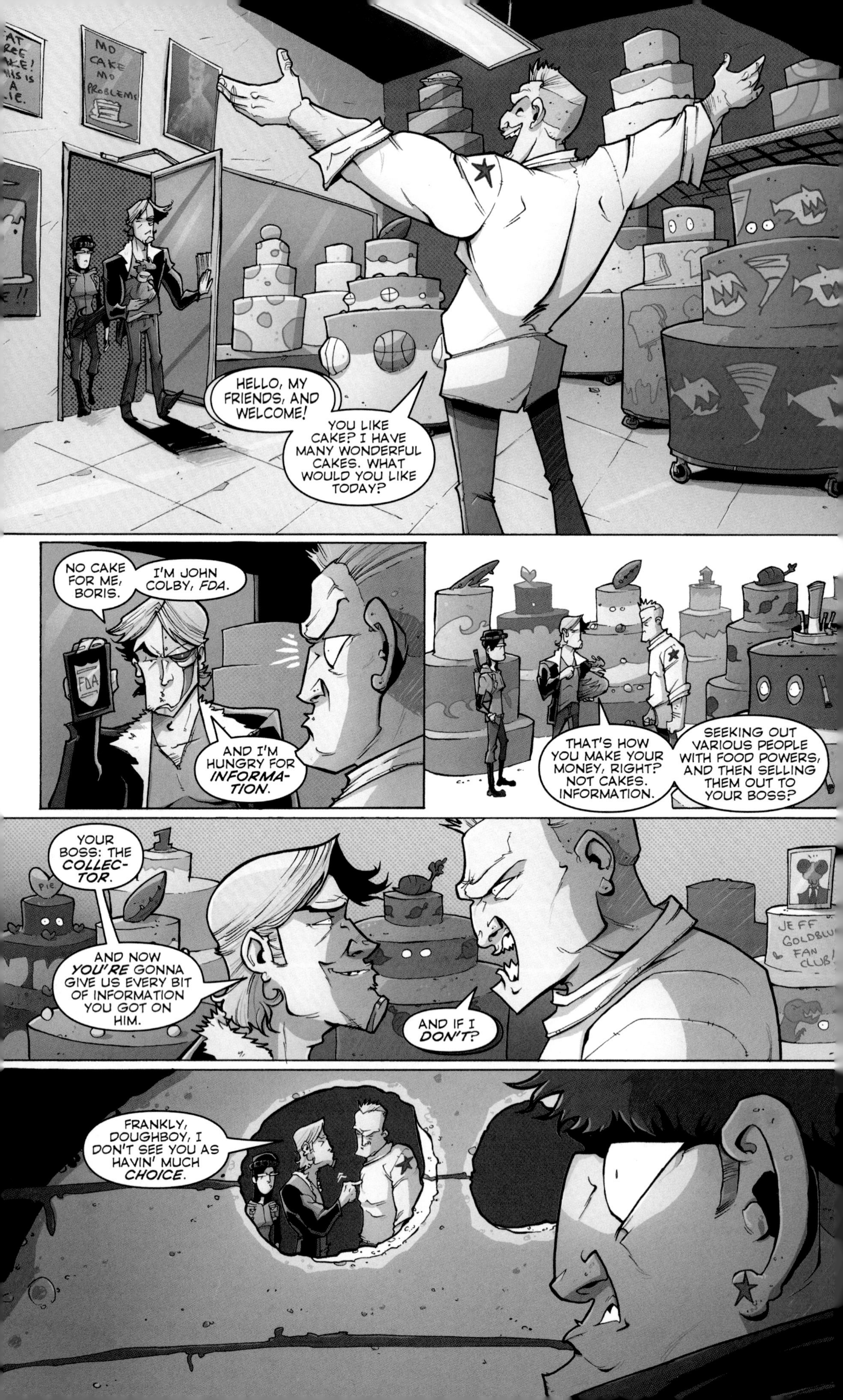
MO CAKE MO PROBLEMS
HELLO, MY FRIENDS, AND WELCOME!
YOU LIKE CAKE? I HAVE MANY WONDERFUL CAKES. WHAT WOULD YOU LIKE TODAY?
NO CAKE FOR ME, BORIS.
I'M JOHN COLBY, *FDA*.
FDA
AND I'M HUNGRY FOR *INFORMATION*.
THAT'S HOW YOU MAKE YOUR MONEY, RIGHT? NOT CAKES. INFORMATION.
SEEKING OUT VARIOUS PEOPLE WITH FOOD POWERS, AND THEN SELLING THEM OUT TO YOUR BOSS?
YOUR BOSS: THE *COLLECTOR*.
PIE
AND NOW *YOU'RE* GONNA GIVE US EVERY BIT OF INFORMATION YOU GOT ON HIM.
AND IF I *DON'T*?
JEFF GOLDBLUM FAN CLUB!
FRANKLY, DOUGHBOY, I DON'T SEE YOU AS HAVIN' MUCH *CHOICE*.

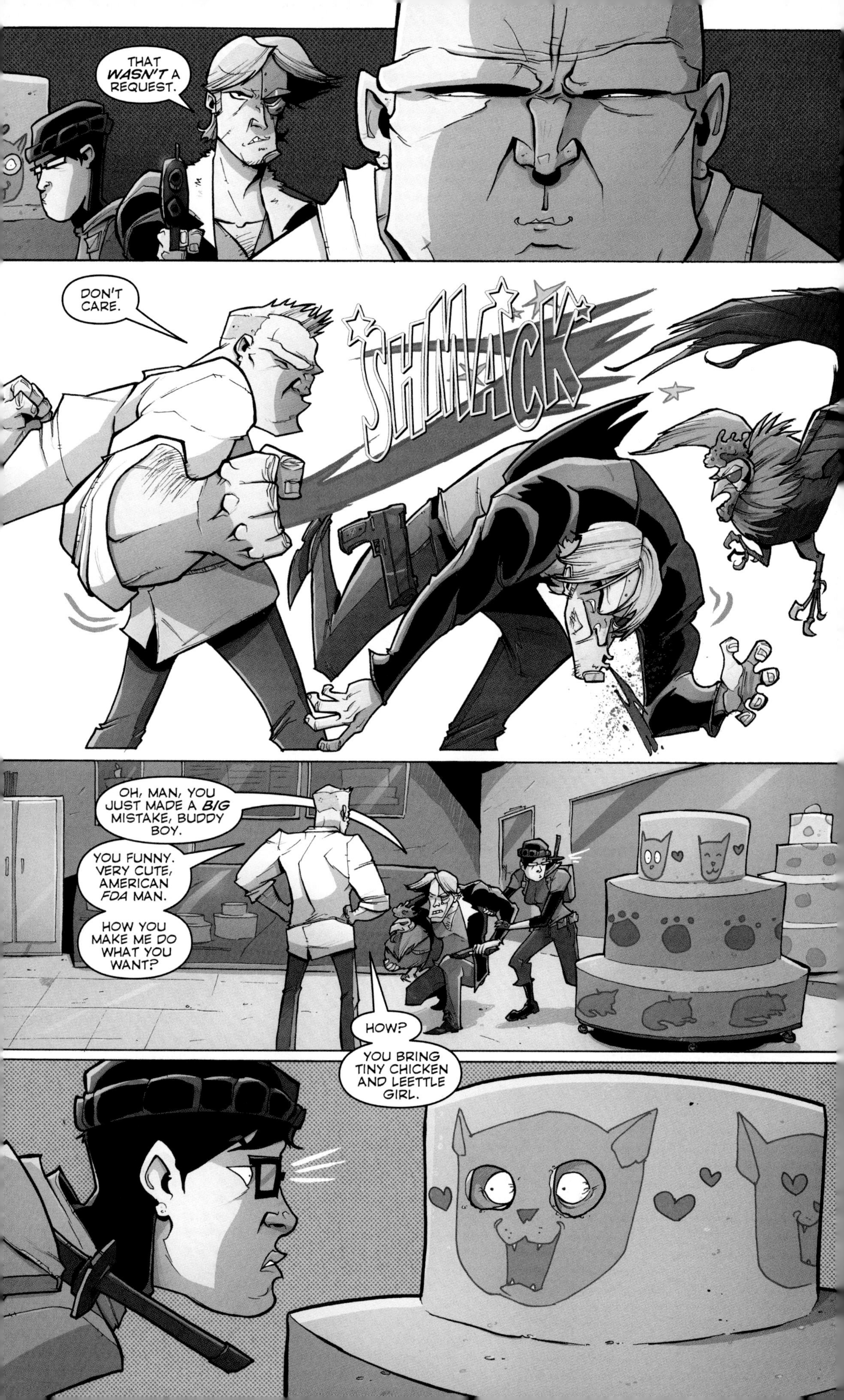
THAT WASN'T A REQUEST.
DON'T CARE.
SHMACK
OH, MAN, YOU JUST MADE A BIG MISTAKE, BUDDY BOY.
YOU FUNNY. VERY CUTE, AMERICAN FDA MAN.
HOW YOU MAKE ME DO WHAT YOU WANT?
HOW?
YOU BRING TINY CHICKEN AND LEETTLE GIRL.

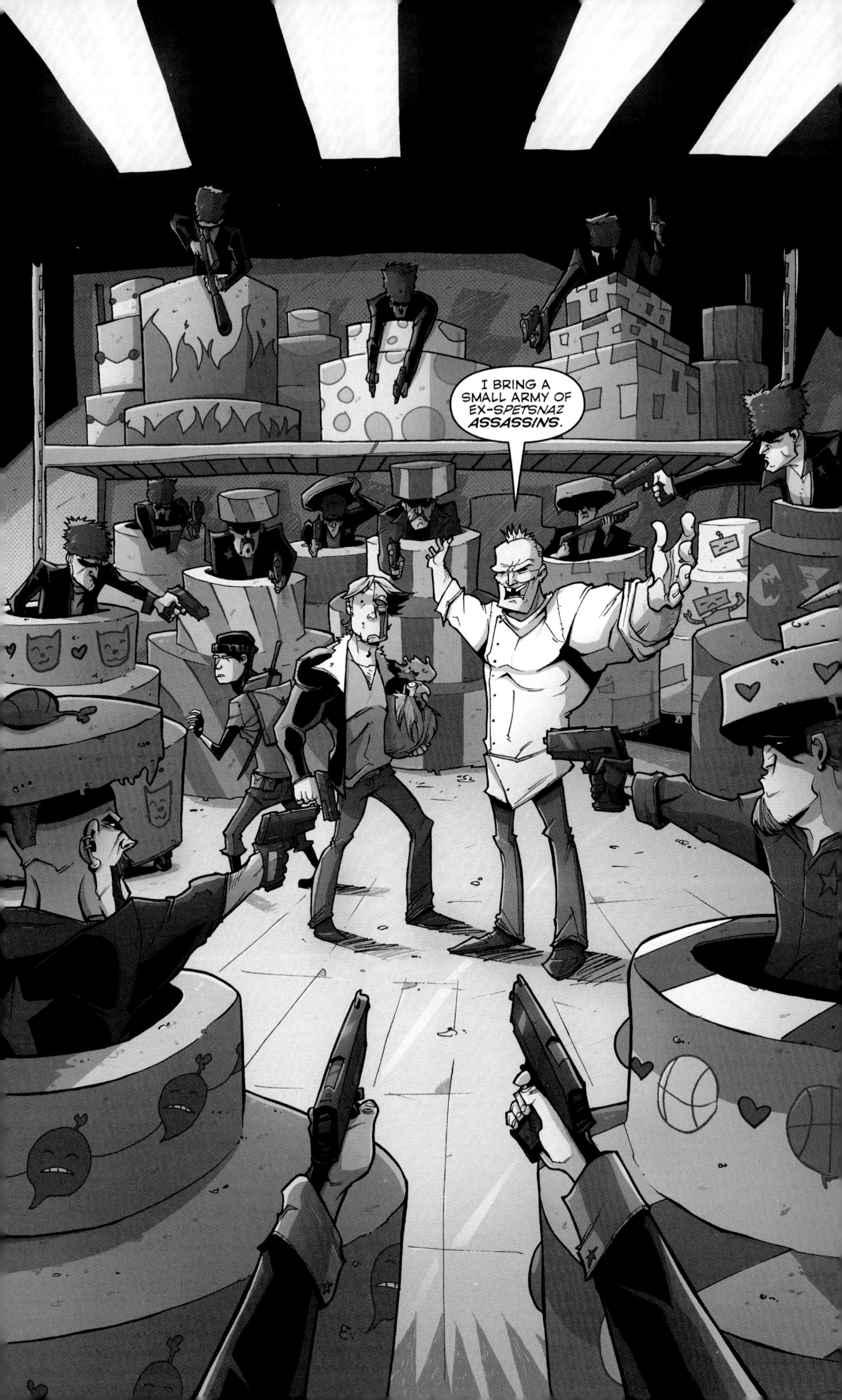
I BRING A SMALL ARMY OF EX-*SPETSNAZ* ***ASSASSINS***.

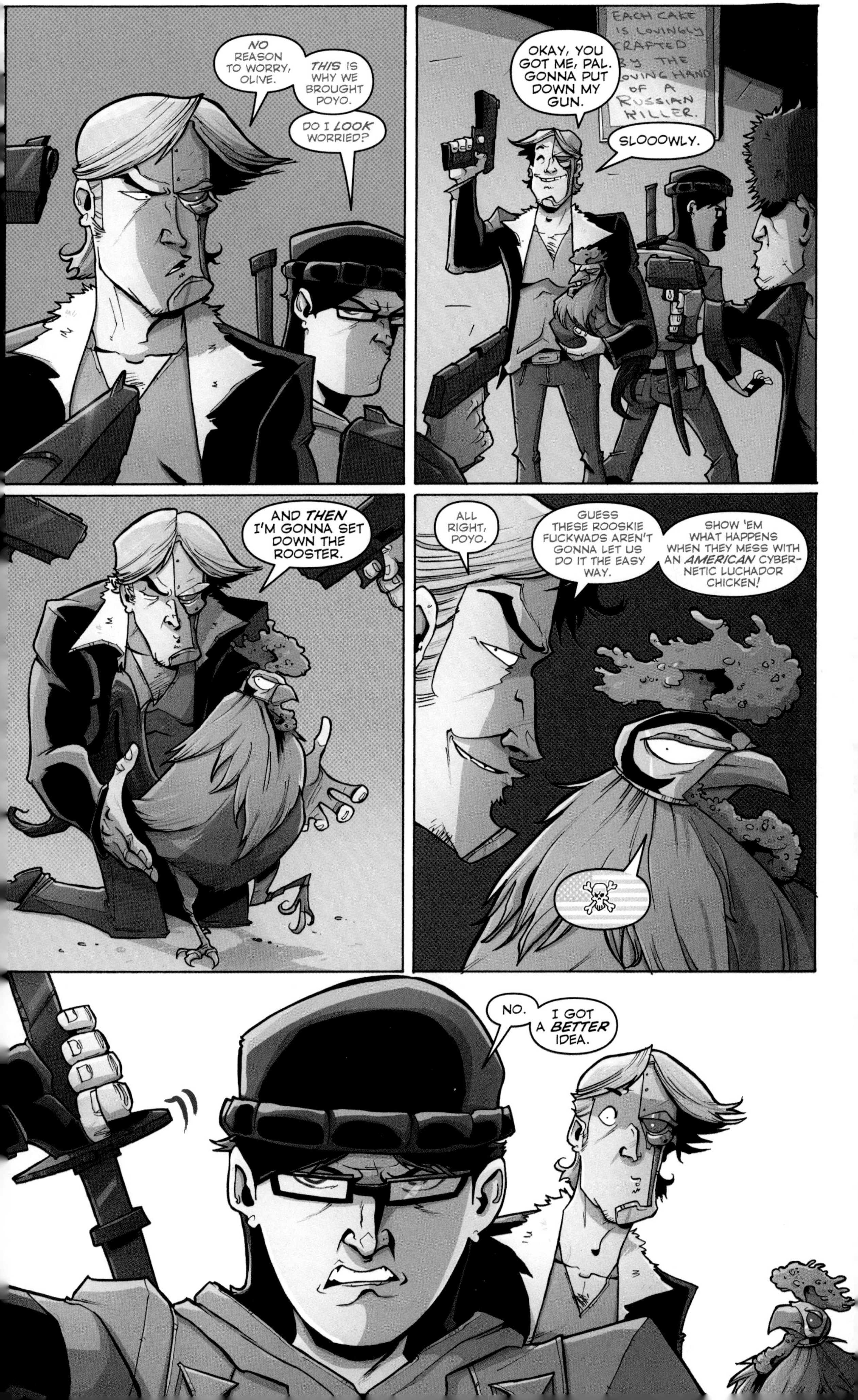
NO REASON TO WORRY, OLIVE.
THIS IS WHY WE BROUGHT POYO.
DO I LOOK WORRIED?
EACH CAKE IS LOVINGLY CRAFTED BY THE LOVING HAND OF A RUSSIAN KILLER.
OKAY, YOU GOT ME, PAL. GONNA PUT DOWN MY GUN.
SLOOOWLY.
AND THEN I'M GONNA SET DOWN THE ROOSTER.
ALL RIGHT, POYO.
GUESS THESE ROOSKIE FUCKWADS AREN'T GONNA LET US DO IT THE EASY WAY.
SHOW 'EM WHAT HAPPENS WHEN THEY MESS WITH AN AMERICAN CYBERNETIC LUCHADOR CHICKEN!
NO.
I GOT A BETTER IDEA.

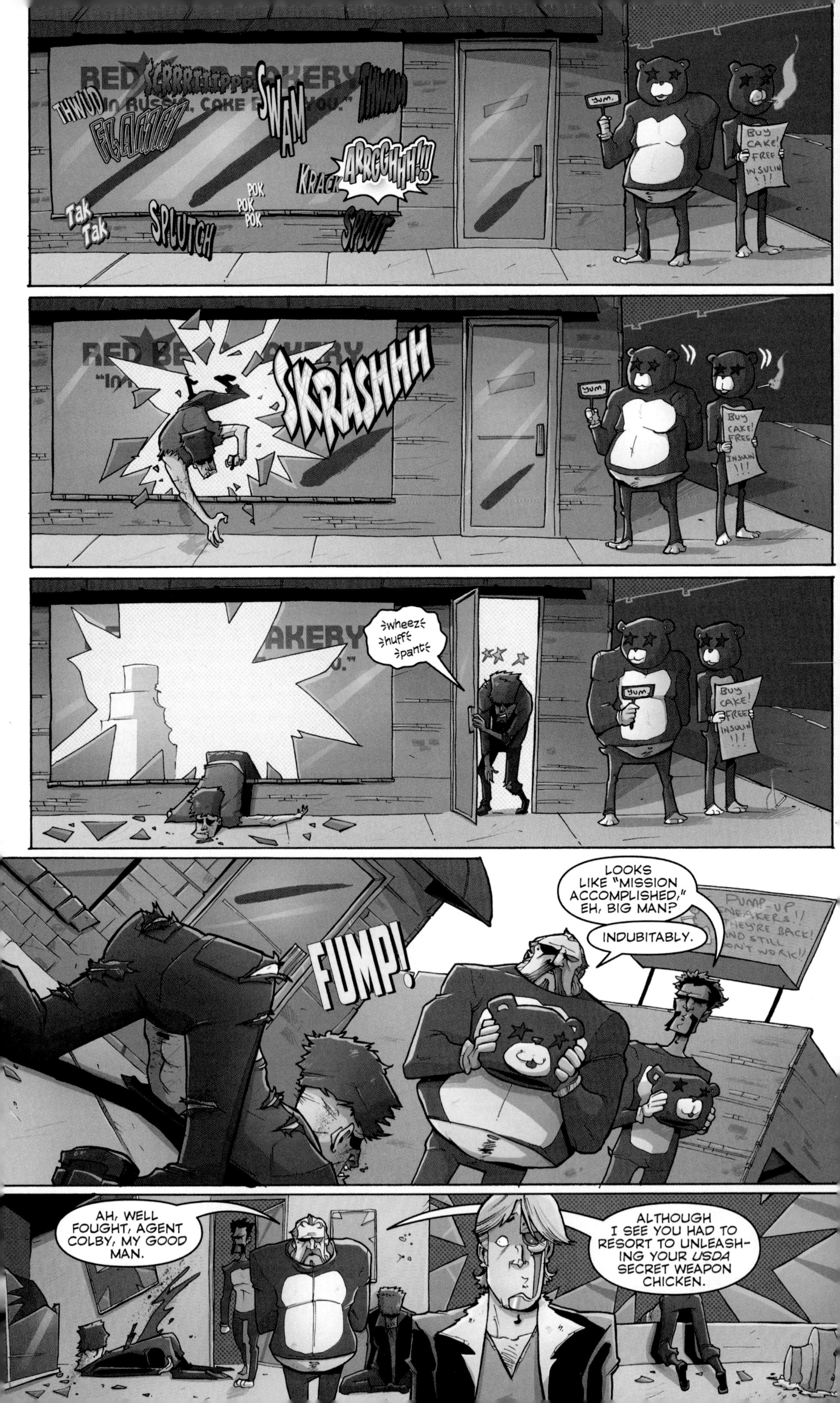
THWUD
SCRRRIIIPPP
SWAM
THWAM
KRACK
ARRGGHHH!!!
POK POK POK
Tak Tak
SPLUTCH
SPLUT
YUM.
BUY CAKE! FREE INSULIN !!!
SKRASHHH
YUM.
BUY CAKE! FREE INSULIN !!!
AKERY
wheez huff pant
YUM.
BUY CAKE! FREE INSULIN !!!
LOOKS LIKE "MISSION ACCOMPLISHED," EH, BIG MAN?
INDUBITABLY.
FUMP!
AH, WELL FOUGHT, AGENT COLBY, MY GOOD MAN.
ALTHOUGH I SEE YOU HAD TO RESORT TO UNLEASHING YOUR *USDA* SECRET WEAPON CHICKEN.

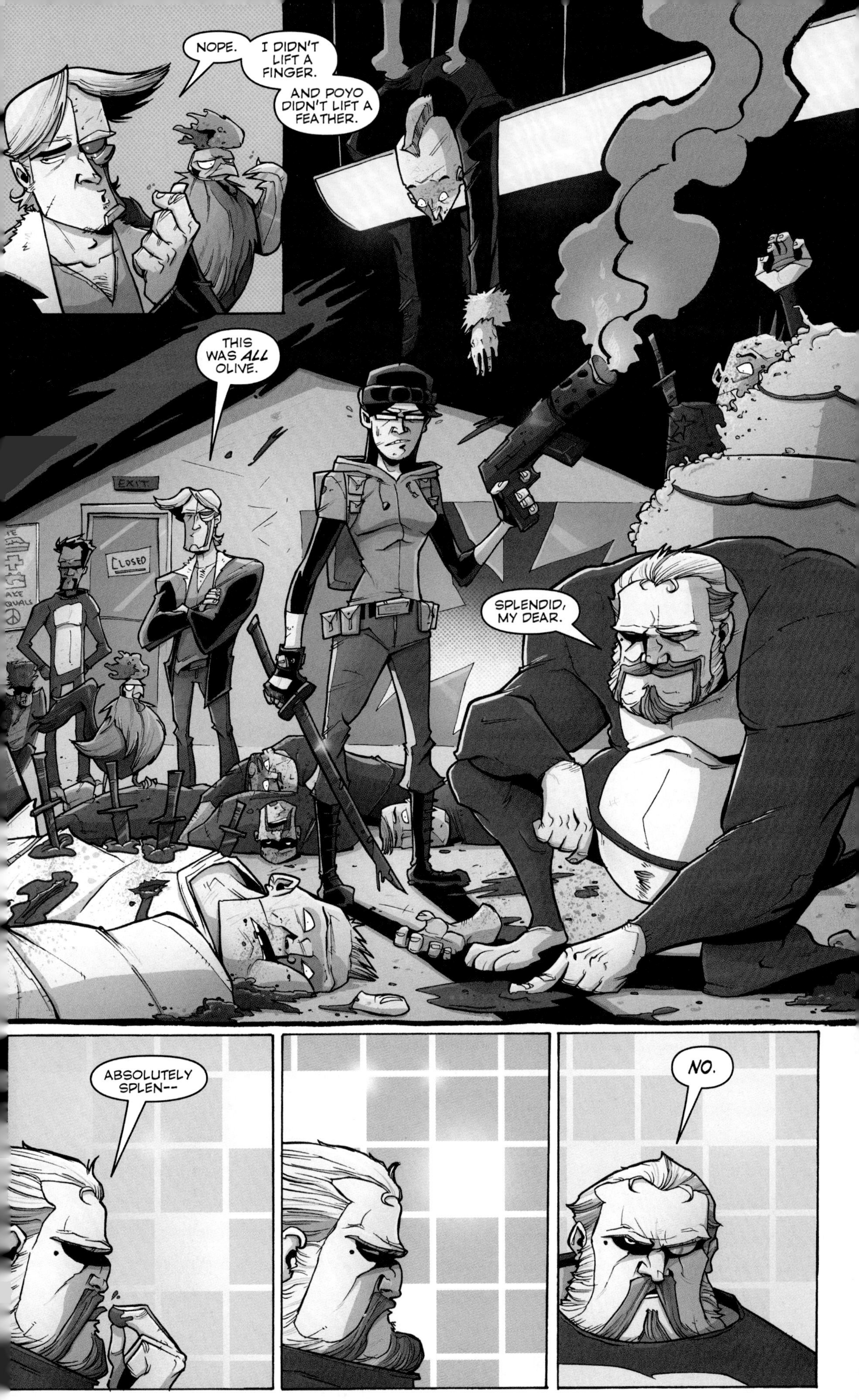
NOPE.
I DIDN'T LIFT A FINGER.
AND POYO DIDN'T LIFT A FEATHER.
THIS WAS ALL OLIVE.
EXIT
CLOSED
SPLENDID, MY DEAR.
ABSOLUTELY SPLEN--
NO.

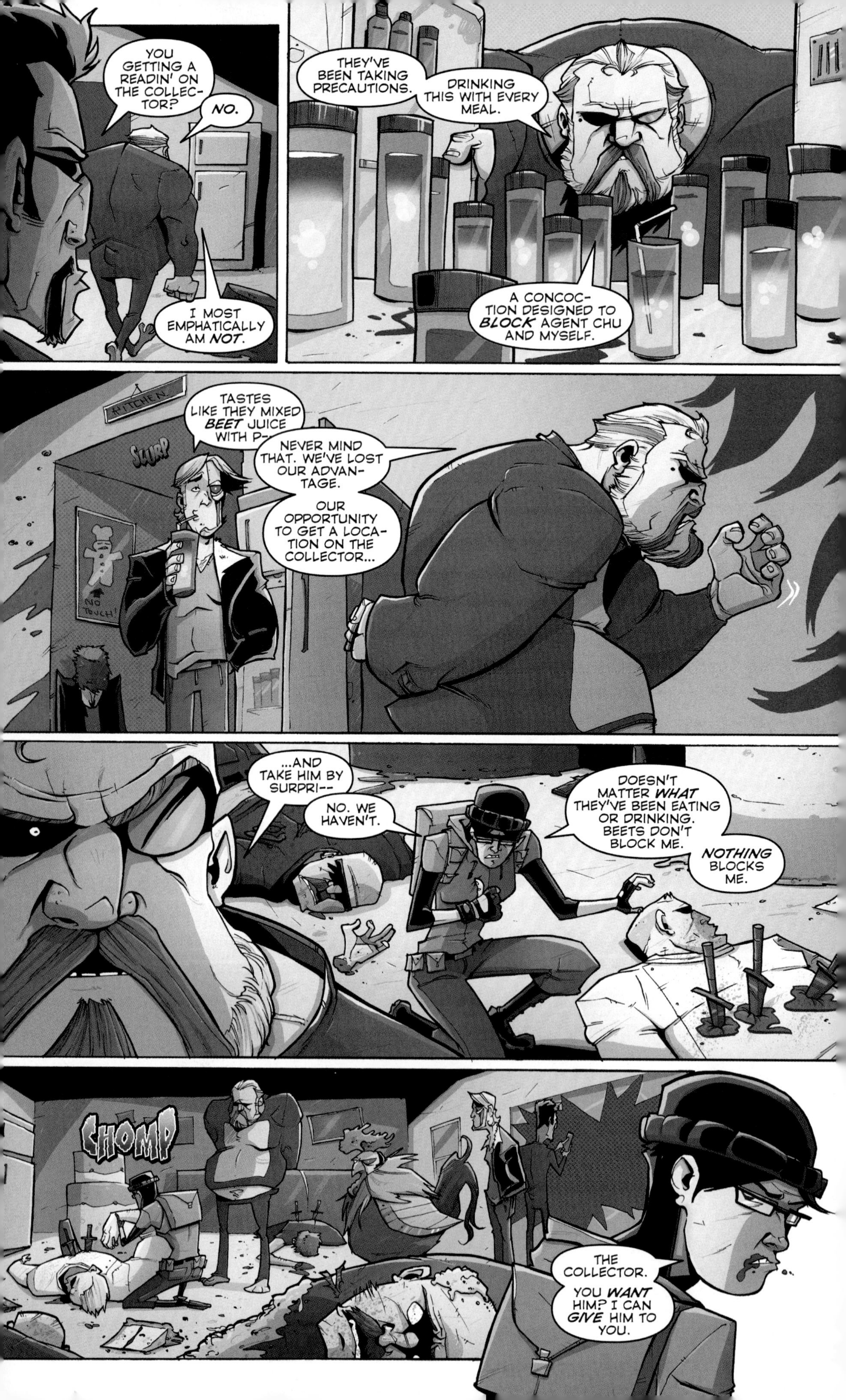
YOU GETTING A READIN' ON THE COLLECTOR?
NO.
I MOST EMPHATICALLY AM NOT.
THEY'VE BEEN TAKING PRECAUTIONS.
DRINKING THIS WITH EVERY MEAL.
A CONCOCTION DESIGNED TO BLOCK AGENT CHU AND MYSELF.
KITCHEN
SLURP
TASTES LIKE THEY MIXED BEET JUICE WITH P--
NEVER MIND THAT. WE'VE LOST OUR ADVANTAGE.
OUR OPPORTUNITY TO GET A LOCATION ON THE COLLECTOR...
NO TOUCH!
...AND TAKE HIM BY SURPRI--
NO. WE HAVEN'T.
DOESN'T MATTER WHAT THEY'VE BEEN EATING OR DRINKING. BEETS DON'T BLOCK ME.
NOTHING BLOCKS ME.
CHOMP
THE COLLECTOR.
YOU WANT HIM? I CAN GIVE HIM TO YOU.

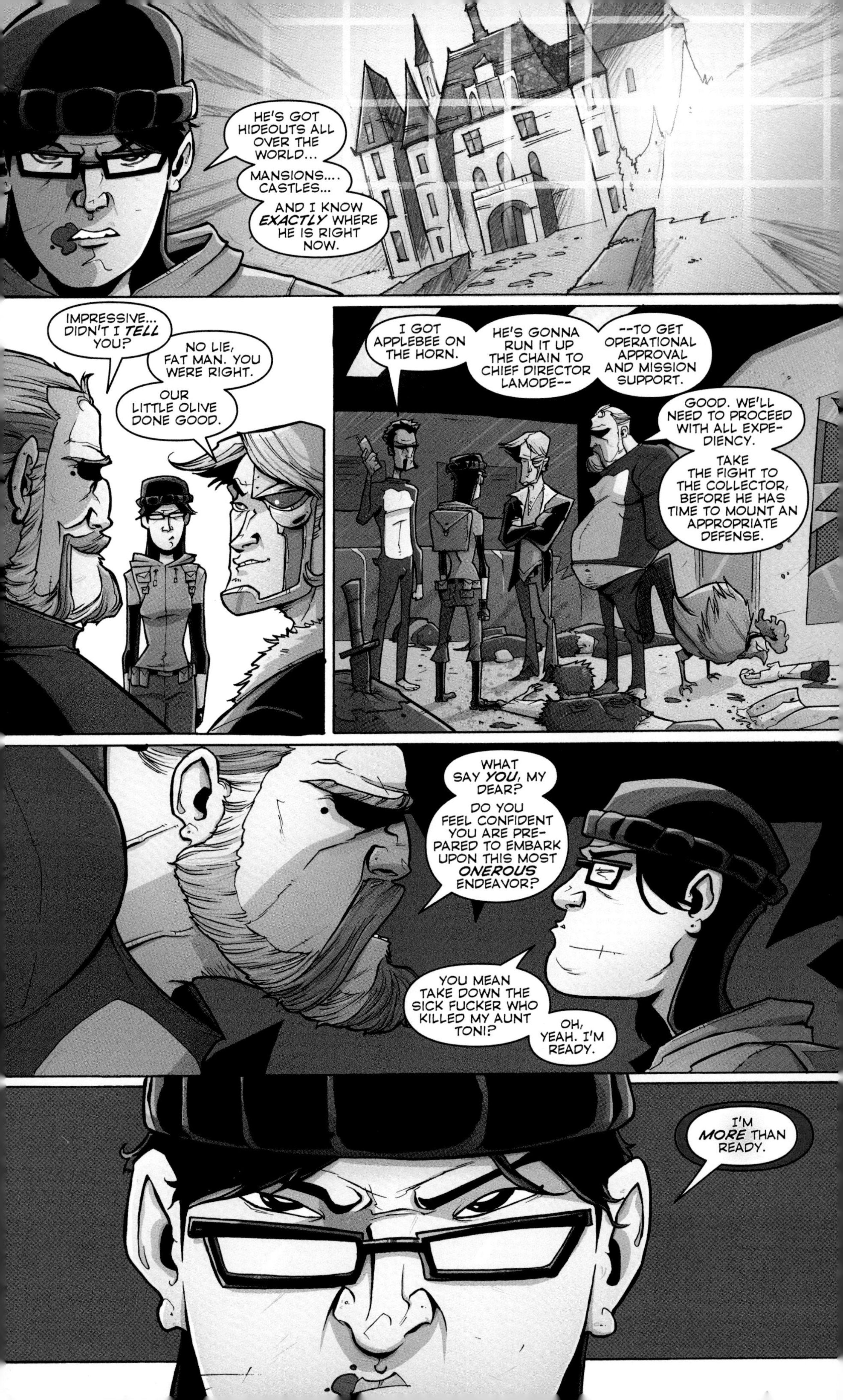

HE'S GOT HIDEOUTS ALL OVER THE WORLD...
MANSIONS.... CASTLES...
AND I KNOW EXACTLY WHERE HE IS RIGHT NOW.
IMPRESSIVE... DIDN'T I TELL YOU?
NO LIE, FAT MAN. YOU WERE RIGHT.
OUR LITTLE OLIVE DONE GOOD.
I GOT APPLEBEE ON THE HORN.
HE'S GONNA RUN IT UP THE CHAIN TO CHIEF DIRECTOR LAMODE--
--TO GET OPERATIONAL APPROVAL AND MISSION SUPPORT.
GOOD. WE'LL NEED TO PROCEED WITH ALL EXPE-DIENCY.
TAKE THE FIGHT TO THE COLLECTOR, BEFORE HE HAS TIME TO MOUNT AN APPROPRIATE DEFENSE.
WHAT SAY YOU, MY DEAR?
DO YOU FEEL CONFIDENT YOU ARE PRE-PARED TO EMBARK UPON THIS MOST ONEROUS ENDEAVOR?
YOU MEAN TAKE DOWN THE SICK FUCKER WHO KILLED MY AUNT TONI?
OH, YEAH. I'M READY.
I'M MORE THAN READY.

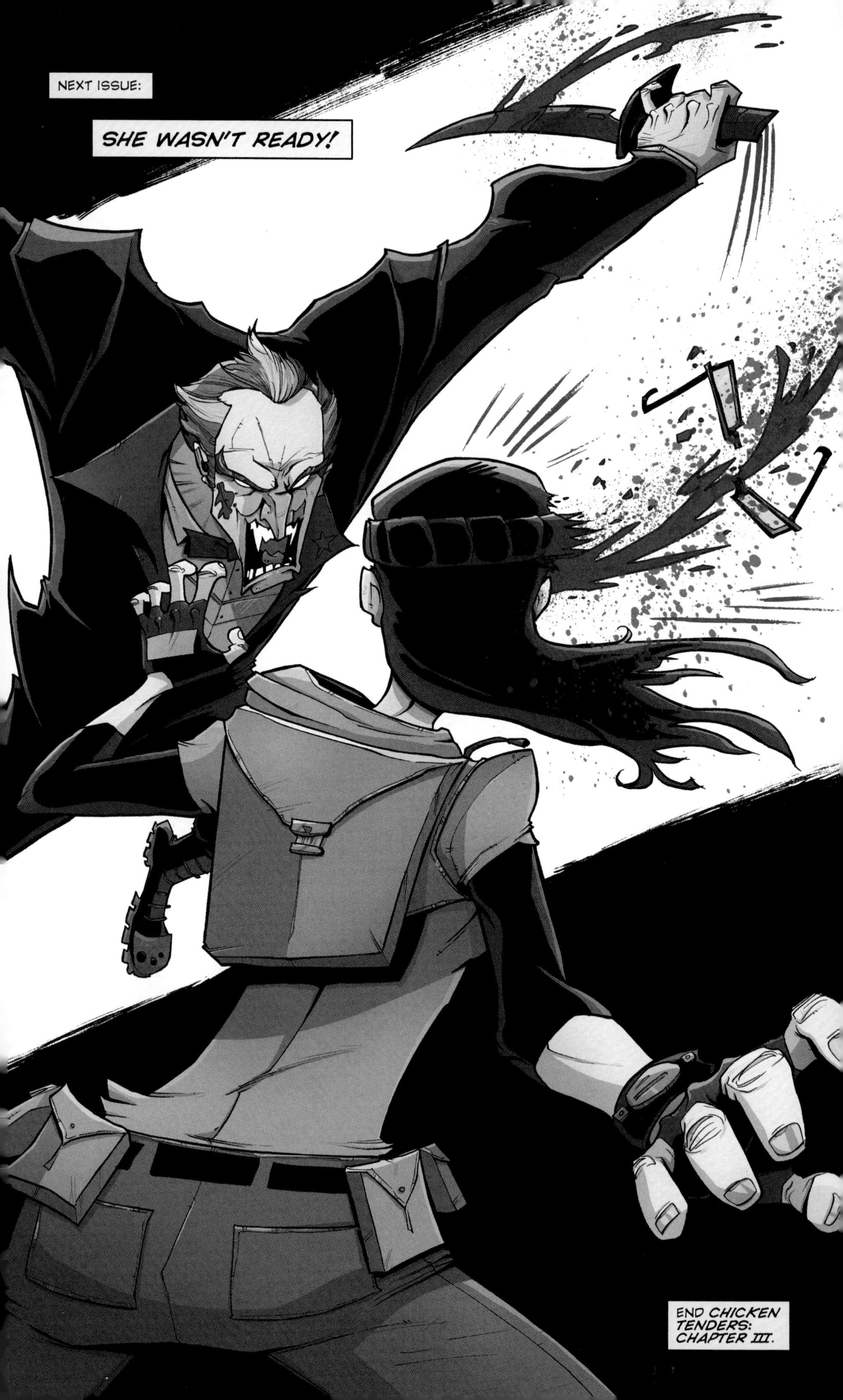
NEXT ISSUE:
SHE WASN'T READY!
END CHICKEN TENDERS: CHAPTER III.

Chapter Four

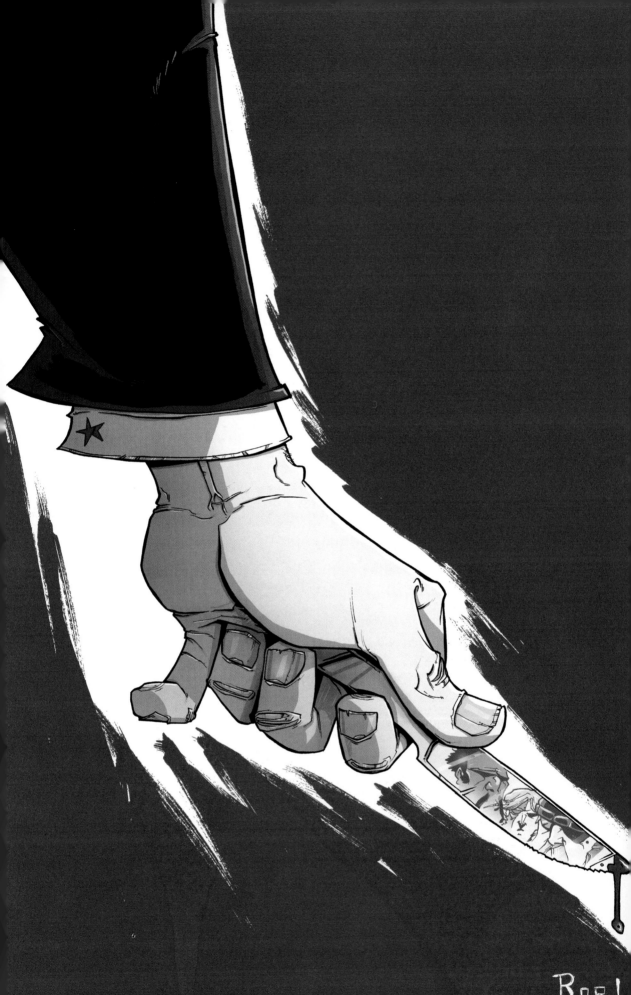

Issue #44 cover

RoB!

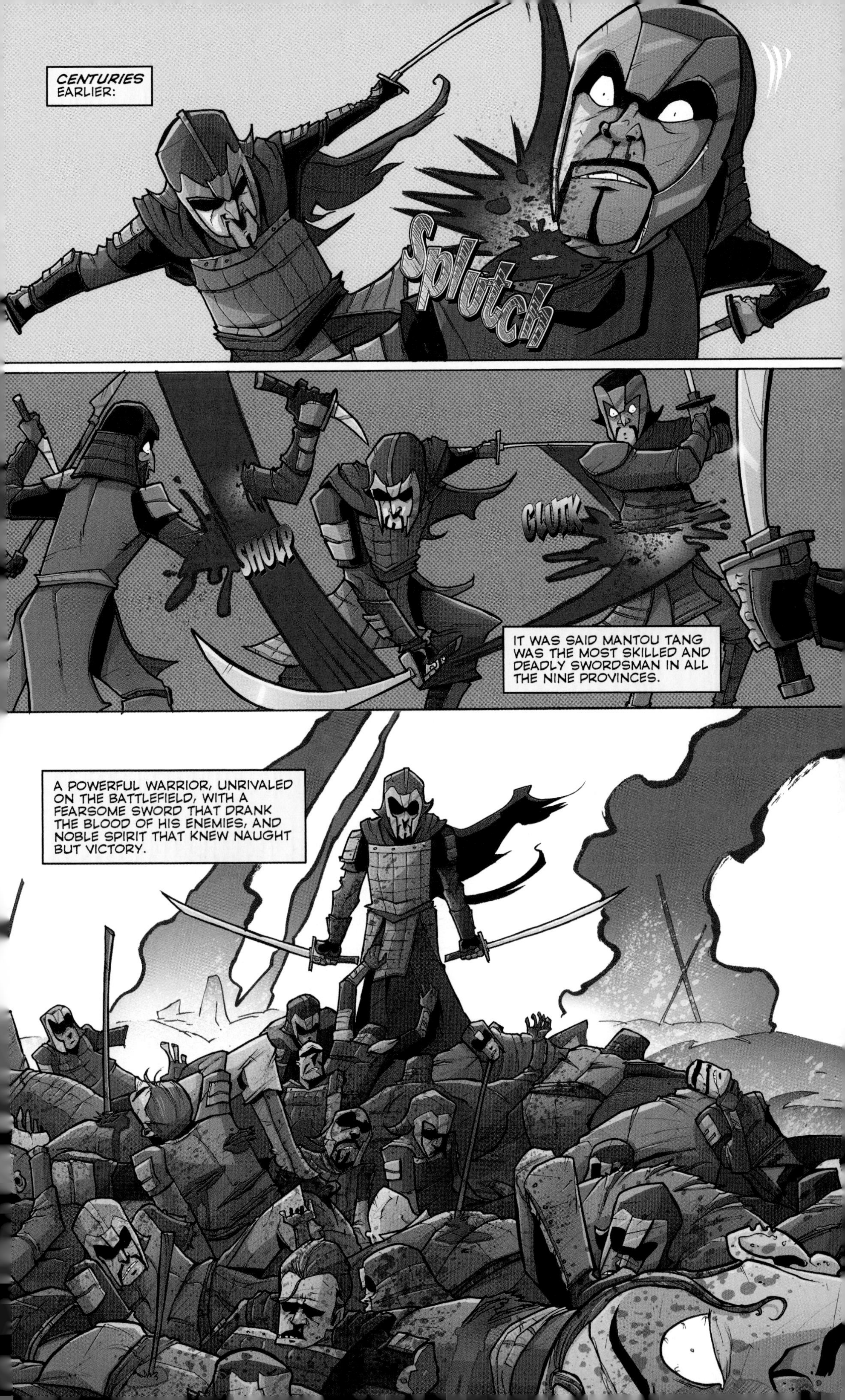
CENTURIES EARLIER:
Splutch
SHULP
GLUTK
IT WAS SAID MANTOU TANG WAS THE MOST SKILLED AND DEADLY SWORDSMAN IN ALL THE NINE PROVINCES.
A POWERFUL WARRIOR, UNRIVALED ON THE BATTLEFIELD, WITH A FEARSOME SWORD THAT DRANK THE BLOOD OF HIS ENEMIES, AND NOBLE SPIRIT THAT KNEW NAUGHT BUT VICTORY.

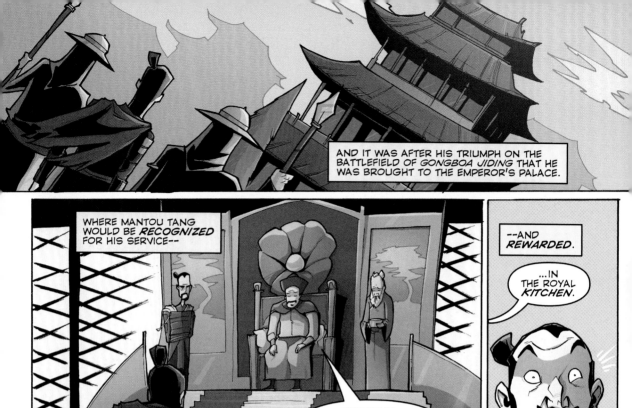

AND IT WAS AFTER HIS TRIUMPH ON THE BATTLEFIELD OF *GONGBOA JIDING* THAT HE WAS BROUGHT TO THE EMPEROR'S PALACE.

WHERE MANTOU TANG WOULD BE *RECOGNIZED* FOR HIS SERVICE--

FOR YOUR LOYALTY, FOR YOUR SERVICE, FOR YOUR BRAVERY AND DEDICATION, YOU ARE TO BE ASSIGNED A NEW POST, AND NEW DUTIES...

--AND *REWARDED*.

...IN THE ROYAL *KITCHEN*.

I-- *WHAT??*

MY LORD! THERE MUST BE SOME SORT OF *MIS-TAKE*.

THERE IS *NO* MISTAKE.

THE NOODLEREADER ORACLE HAS *SEEN* YOUR FUTURE.

AND YOUR FUTURE IS *BRIGHT*.

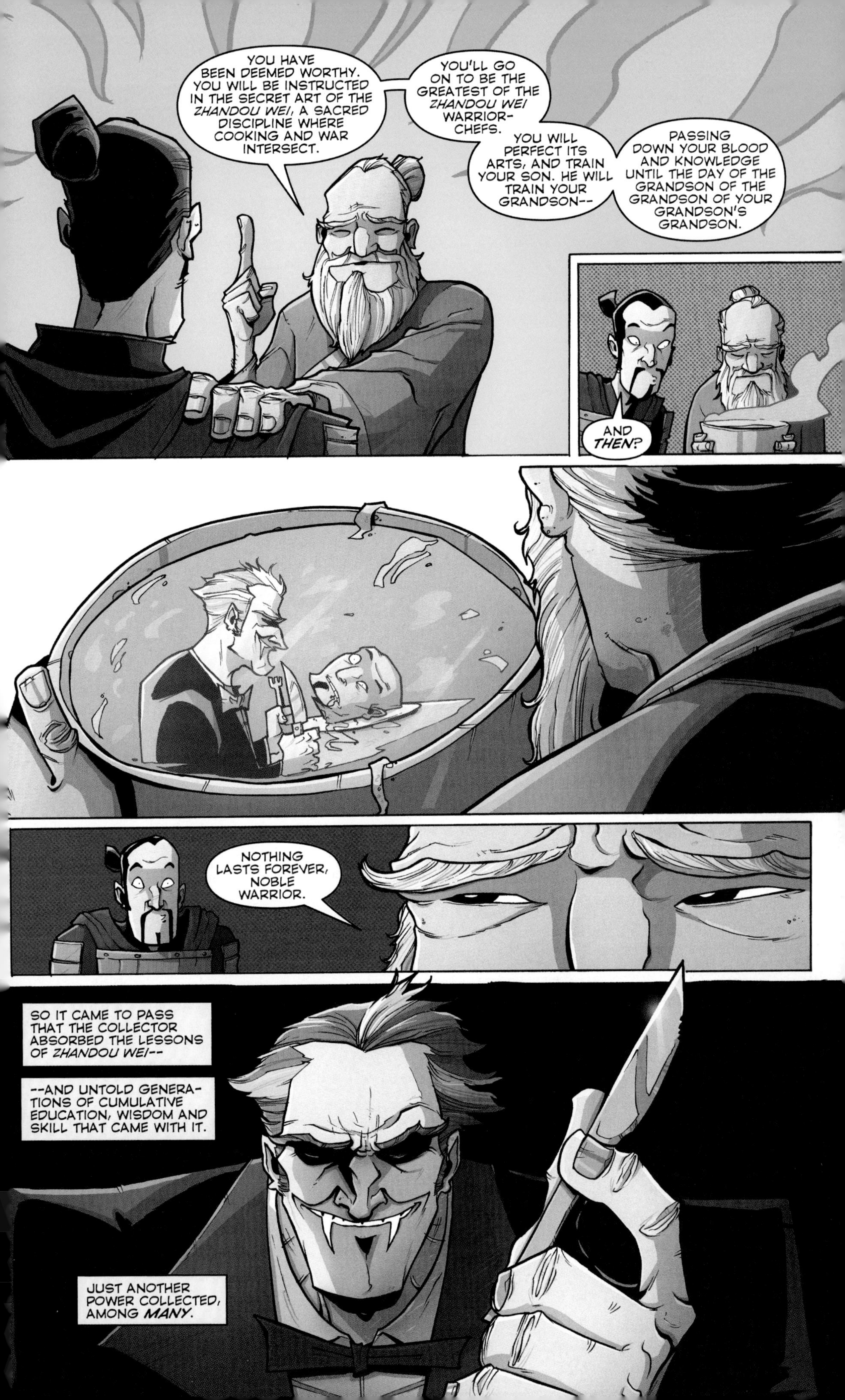
YOU HAVE BEEN DEEMED WORTHY. YOU WILL BE INSTRUCTED IN THE SECRET ART OF THE *ZHANDOU WEI*, A SACRED DISCIPLINE WHERE COOKING AND WAR INTERSECT.
YOU'LL GO ON TO BE THE GREATEST OF THE *ZHANDOU WEI* WARRIOR-CHEFS.
YOU WILL PERFECT ITS ARTS, AND TRAIN YOUR SON. HE WILL TRAIN YOUR GRANDSON--
PASSING DOWN YOUR BLOOD AND KNOWLEDGE UNTIL THE DAY OF THE GRANDSON OF THE GRANDSON OF YOUR GRANDSON'S GRANDSON.
AND *THEN*?
NOTHING LASTS FOREVER, NOBLE WARRIOR.
SO IT CAME TO PASS THAT THE COLLECTOR ABSORBED THE LESSONS OF *ZHANDOU WEI*--
--AND UNTOLD GENERATIONS OF CUMULATIVE EDUCATION, WISDOM AND SKILL THAT CAME WITH IT.
JUST ANOTHER POWER COLLECTED, AMONG *MANY*.

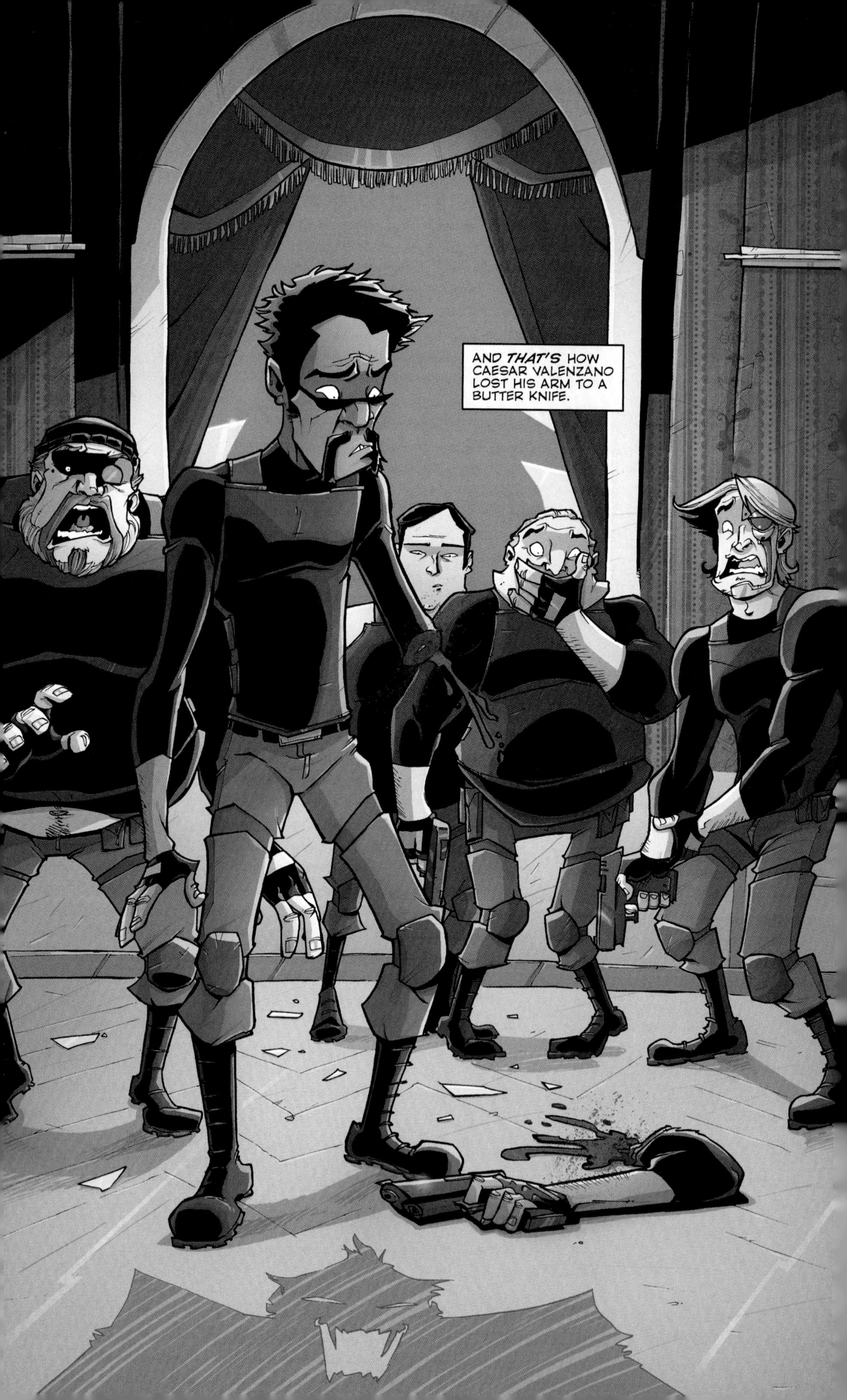
AND *THAT'S* HOW CAESAR VALENZANO LOST HIS ARM TO A BUTTER KNIFE.

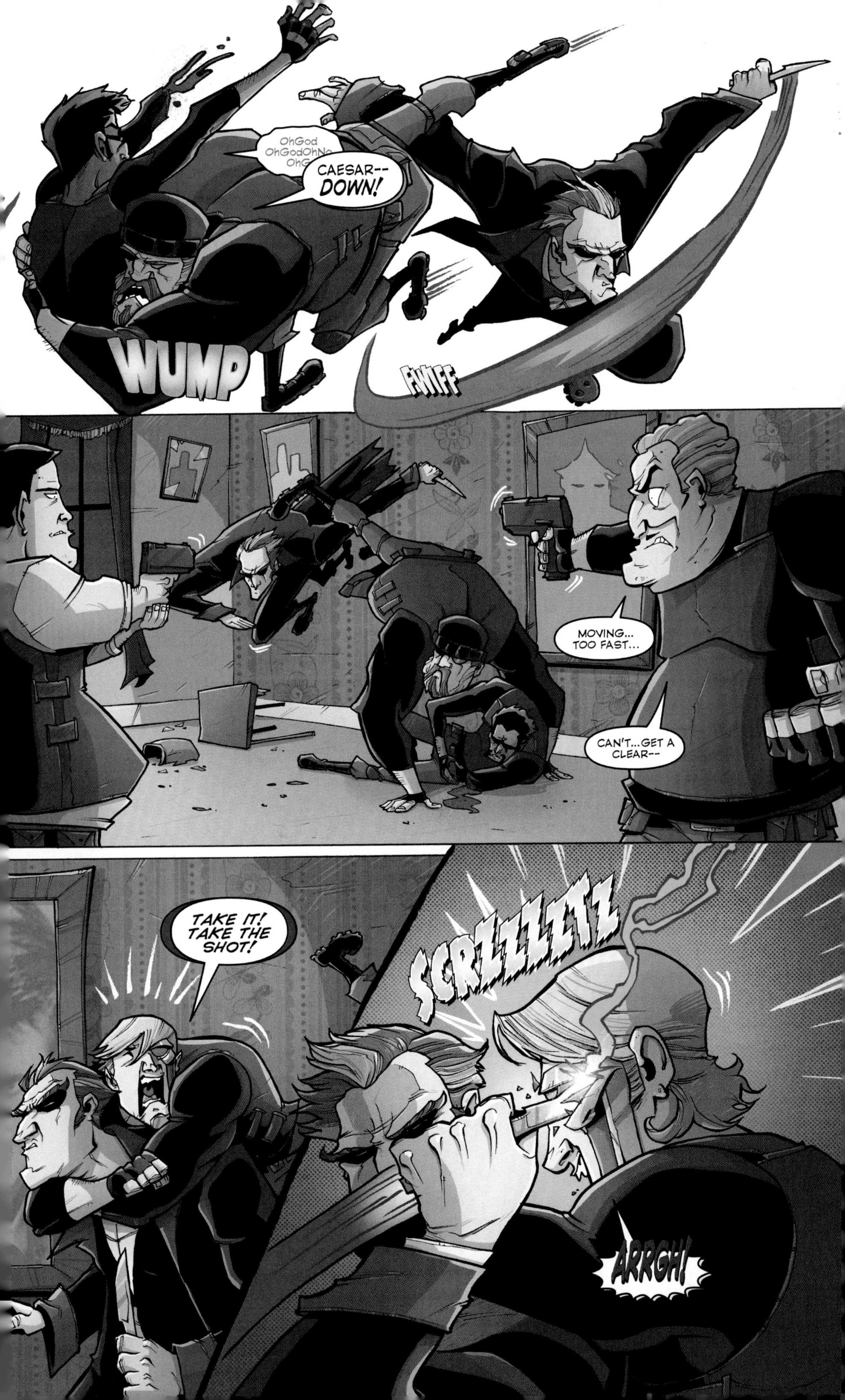
OhGod
OhGodOhNo
CAESAR-- DOWN!
WUMP
FWIFF
MOVING... TOO FAST...
CAN'T...GET A CLEAR--
TAKE IT! TAKE THE SHOT!
SCRZZZZZTZ
ARRGH!

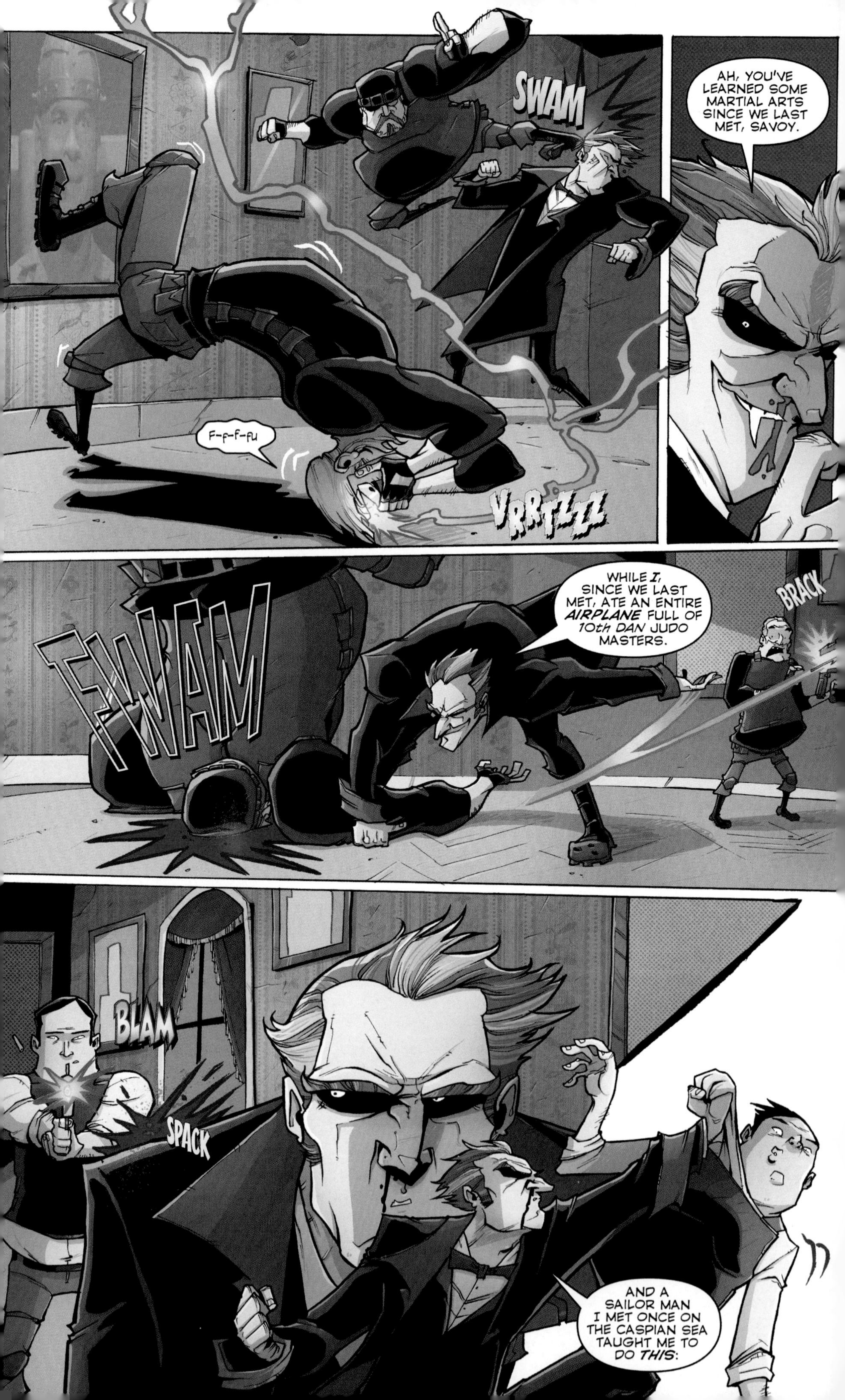
SWAM
F-f-f-fu
VRRTZZZZ
AH, YOU'VE LEARNED SOME MARTIAL ARTS SINCE WE LAST MET, SAVOY.
FWAM
WHILE *I*, SINCE WE LAST MET, ATE AN ENTIRE *AIRPLANE* FULL OF *10th DAN* JUDO MASTERS.
BRACK
BLAM
SPACK
AND A SAILOR MAN I MET ONCE ON THE CASPIAN SEA TAUGHT ME TO DO *THIS*:

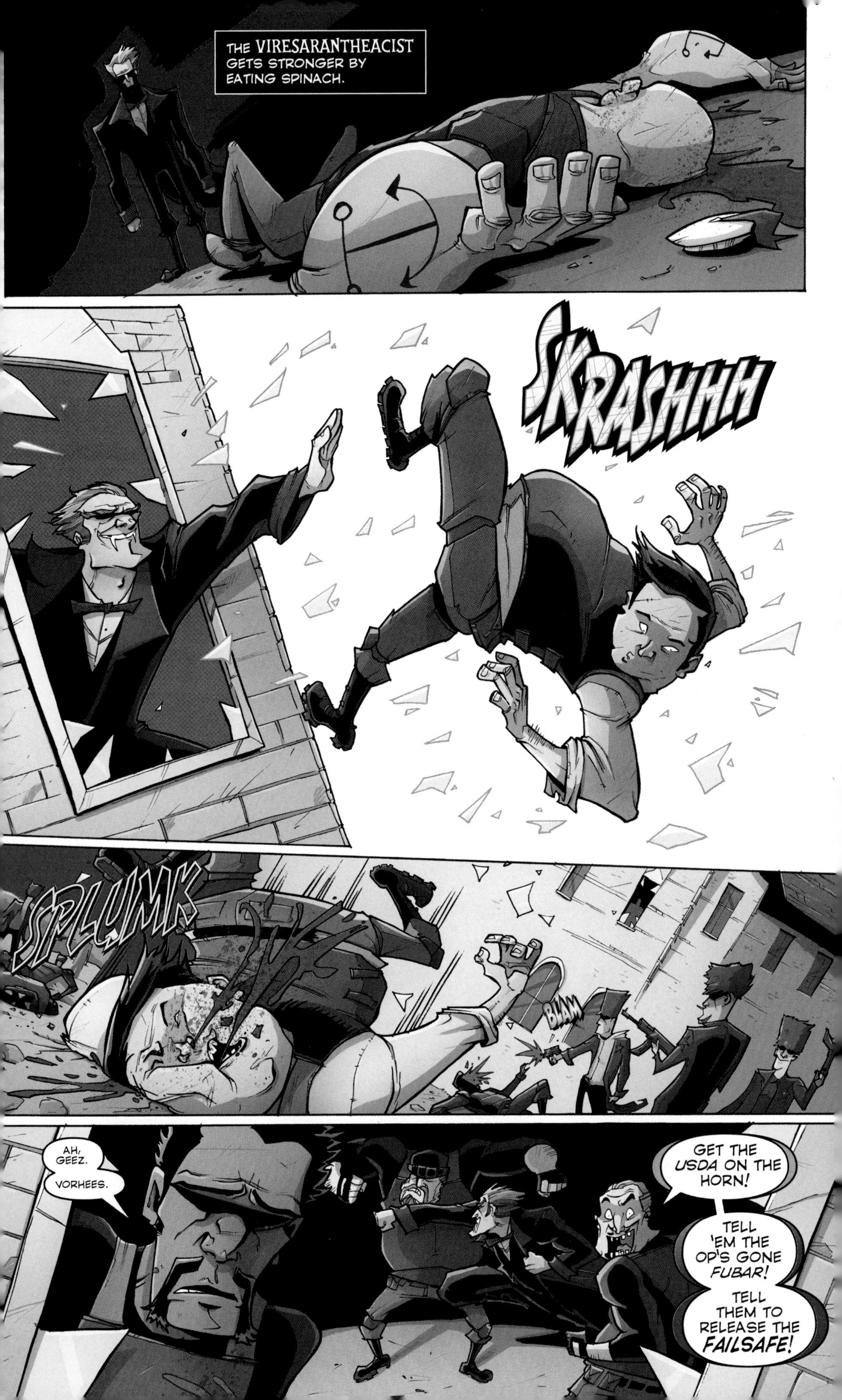
THE VIRESARANTHEACIST GETS STRONGER BY EATING SPINACH.
SKRASHHH
SPLUMK
BLAM
AH, GEEZ.
VORHEES.
GET THE *USDA* ON THE HORN!
TELL 'EM THE OP'S GONE *FUBAR*!
TELL THEM TO RELEASE THE ***FAILSAFE***!

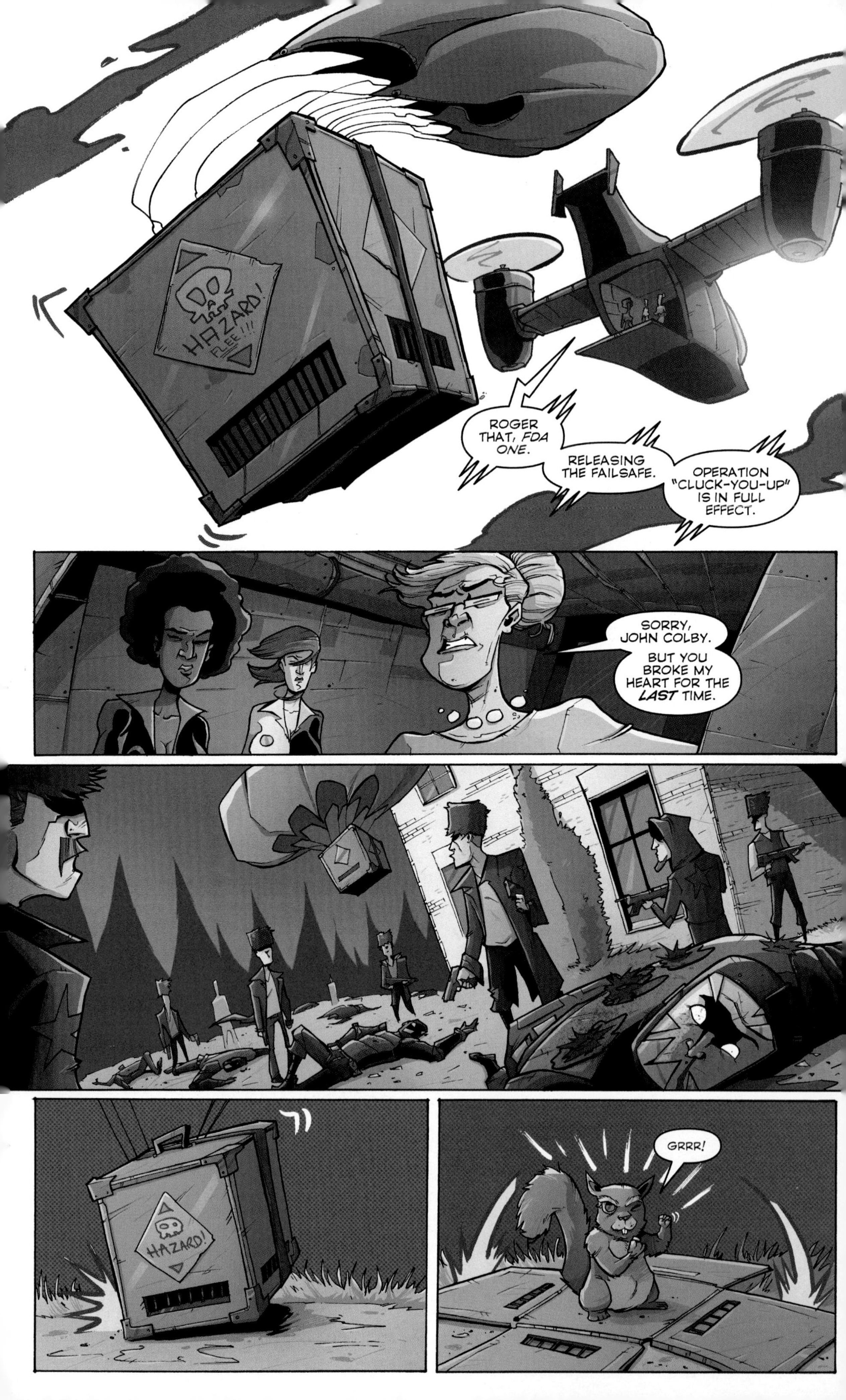
HAZARD!
FLEE!!!
ROGER THAT, *FDA ONE*.
RELEASING THE FAILSAFE.
OPERATION "CLUCK-YOU-UP" IS IN FULL EFFECT.
SORRY, JOHN COLBY.
BUT YOU BROKE MY HEART FOR THE ***LAST*** TIME.
HAZARD!
GRRR!

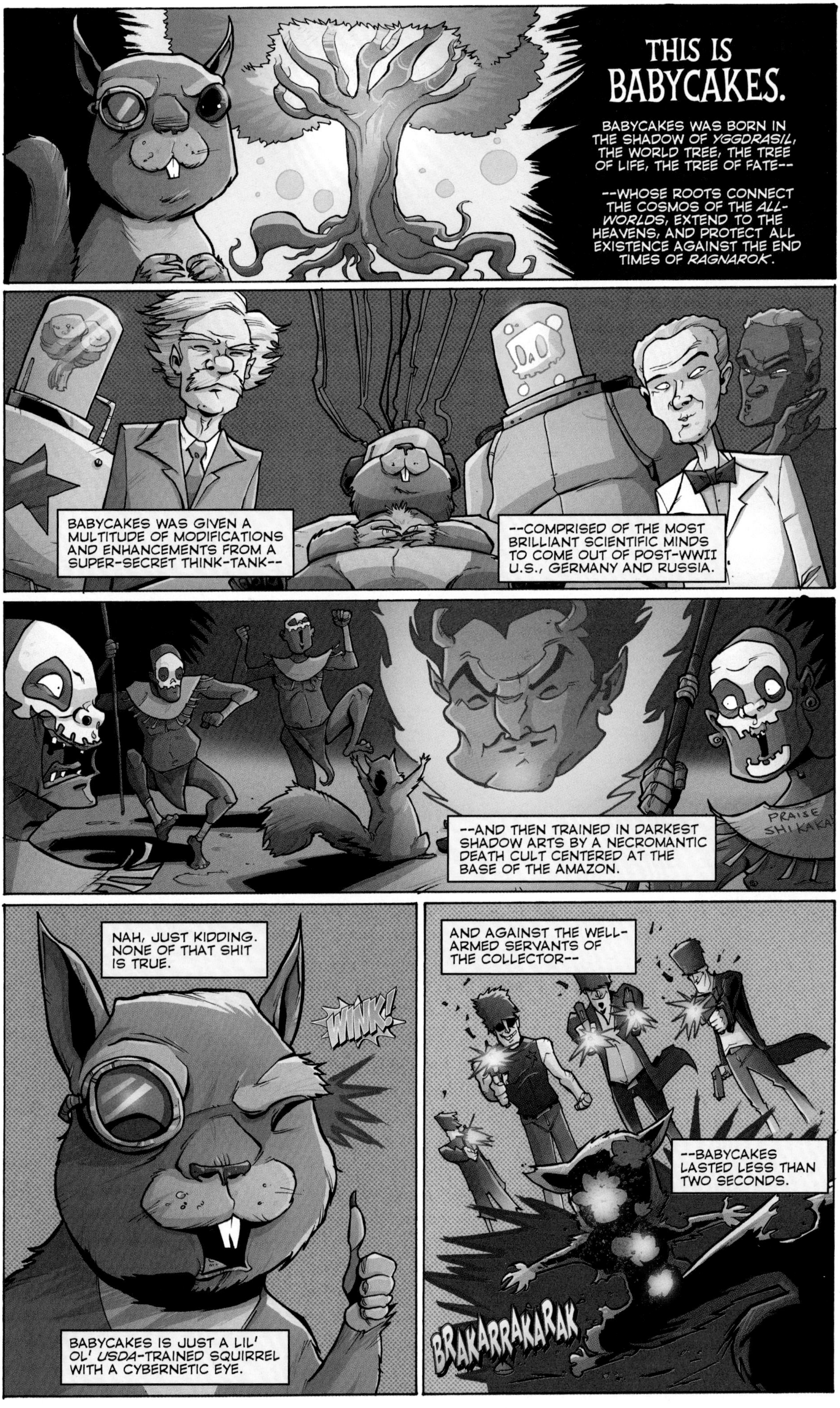
THIS IS BABYCAKES.
BABYCAKES WAS BORN IN THE SHADOW OF YGGDRASIL, THE WORLD TREE, THE TREE OF LIFE, THE TREE OF FATE--
--WHOSE ROOTS CONNECT THE COSMOS OF THE ALL-WORLDS, EXTEND TO THE HEAVENS, AND PROTECT ALL EXISTENCE AGAINST THE END TIMES OF RAGNAROK.
BABYCAKES WAS GIVEN A MULTITUDE OF MODIFICATIONS AND ENHANCEMENTS FROM A SUPER-SECRET THINK-TANK--
--COMPRISED OF THE MOST BRILLIANT SCIENTIFIC MINDS TO COME OUT OF POST-WWII U.S., GERMANY AND RUSSIA.
--AND THEN TRAINED IN DARKEST SHADOW ARTS BY A NECROMANTIC DEATH CULT CENTERED AT THE BASE OF THE AMAZON.
PRAISE SHIKAKA
NAH, JUST KIDDING. NONE OF THAT SHIT IS TRUE.
WINK!
BABYCAKES IS JUST A LIL' OL' USDA-TRAINED SQUIRREL WITH A CYBERNETIC EYE.
AND AGAINST THE WELL-ARMED SERVANTS OF THE COLLECTOR--
--BABYCAKES LASTED LESS THAN TWO SECONDS.
BRAKARRAKARAK

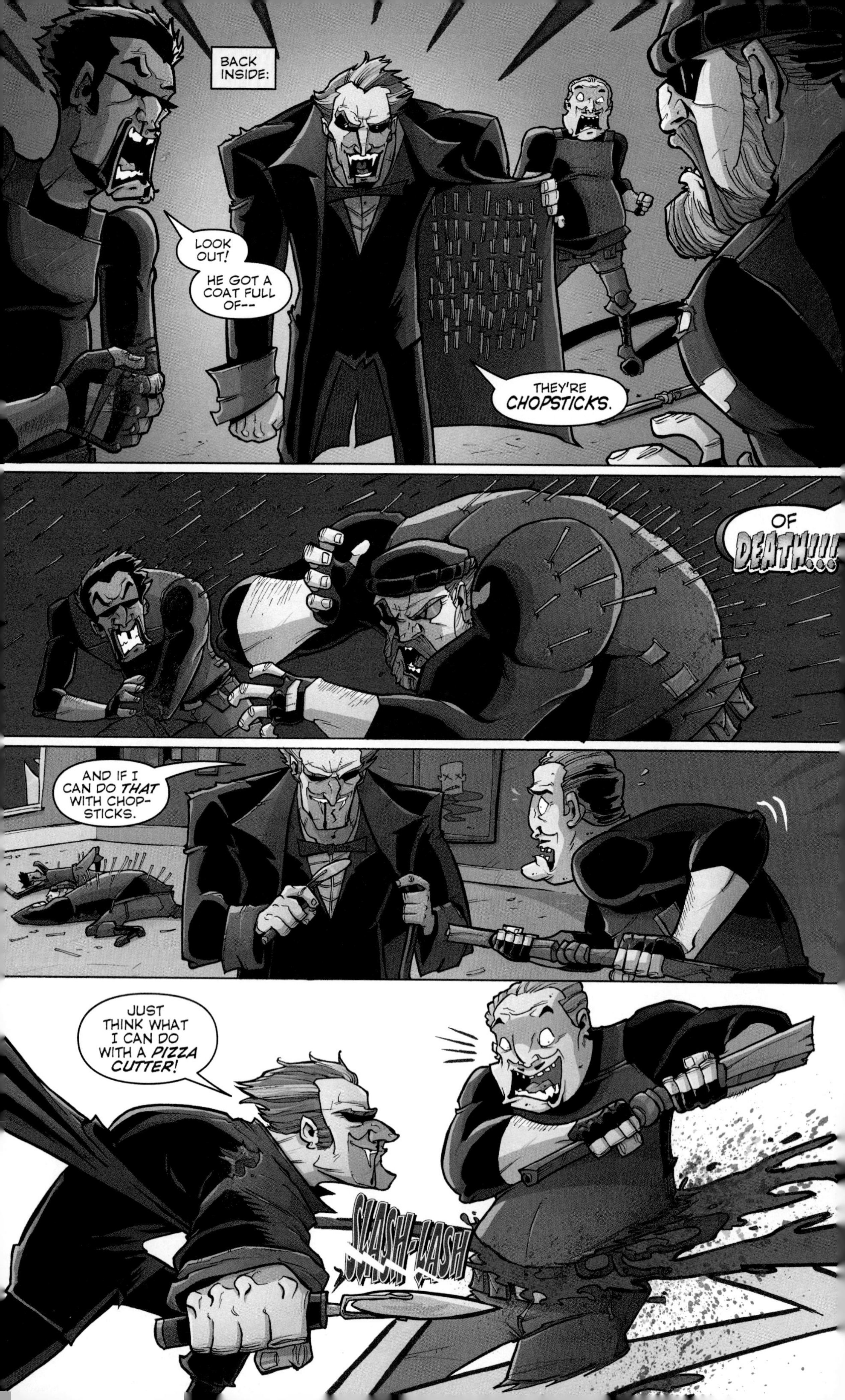
BACK INSIDE:
LOOK OUT!
HE GOT A COAT FULL OF--
THEY'RE CHOPSTICKS.
OF DEATH!!!
AND IF I CAN DO THAT WITH CHOP-STICKS.
JUST THINK WHAT I CAN DO WITH A PIZZA CUTTER!
SLASH-LASH

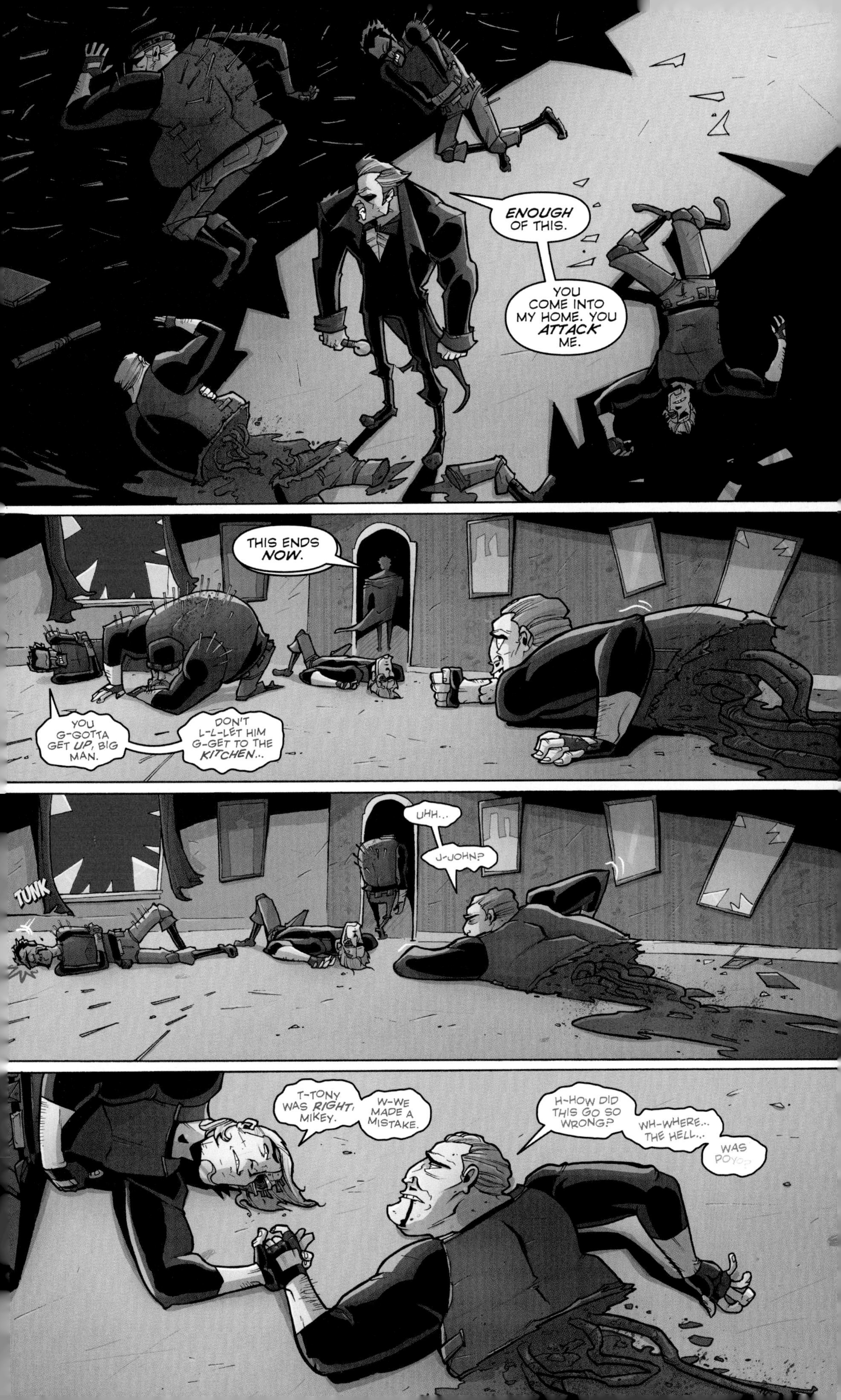
ENOUGH OF THIS.
YOU COME INTO MY HOME. YOU ATTACK ME.
THIS ENDS NOW.
YOU G-GOTTA GET UP, BIG MAN.
DON'T L-L-LET HIM G-GET TO THE KITCHEN...
TUNK
UHH...
J-JOHN?
T-TONY WAS RIGHT, MIKEY.
W-WE MADE A MISTAKE.
H-HOW DID THIS GO SO WRONG?
WH-WHERE... THE HELL...
WAS

MEANWHILE:
TWIN TERRORS!
OPPOSITE AFRICA
OPPOSITE EUROPE
PROPERTY OF OPPOSITE WORLD! IN DOG WE TRUST!!
OYOP!!!
VS.
DARK DIMENSION DOPPELGANGER!

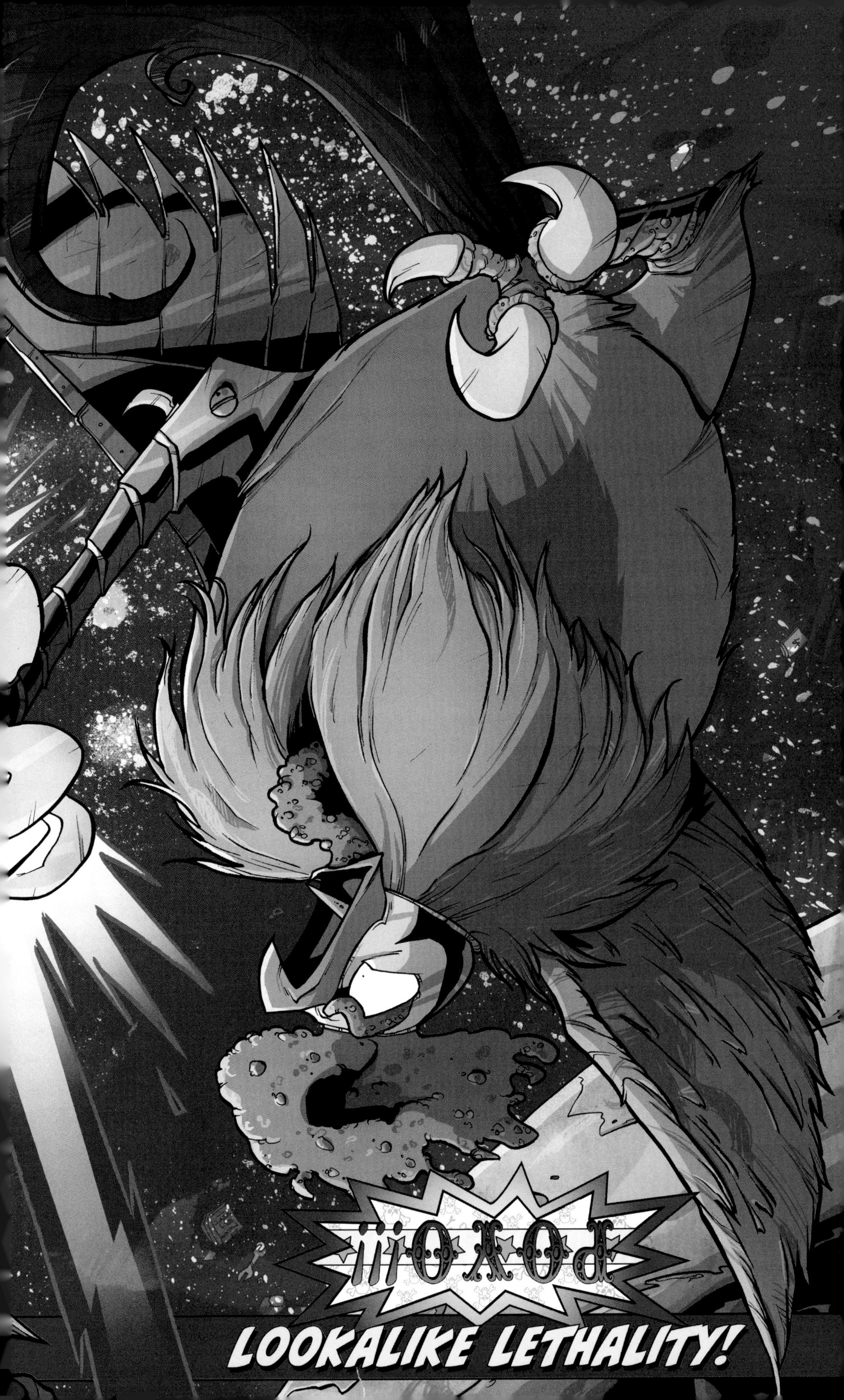
POXO!!!
LOOKALIKE LETHALITY!

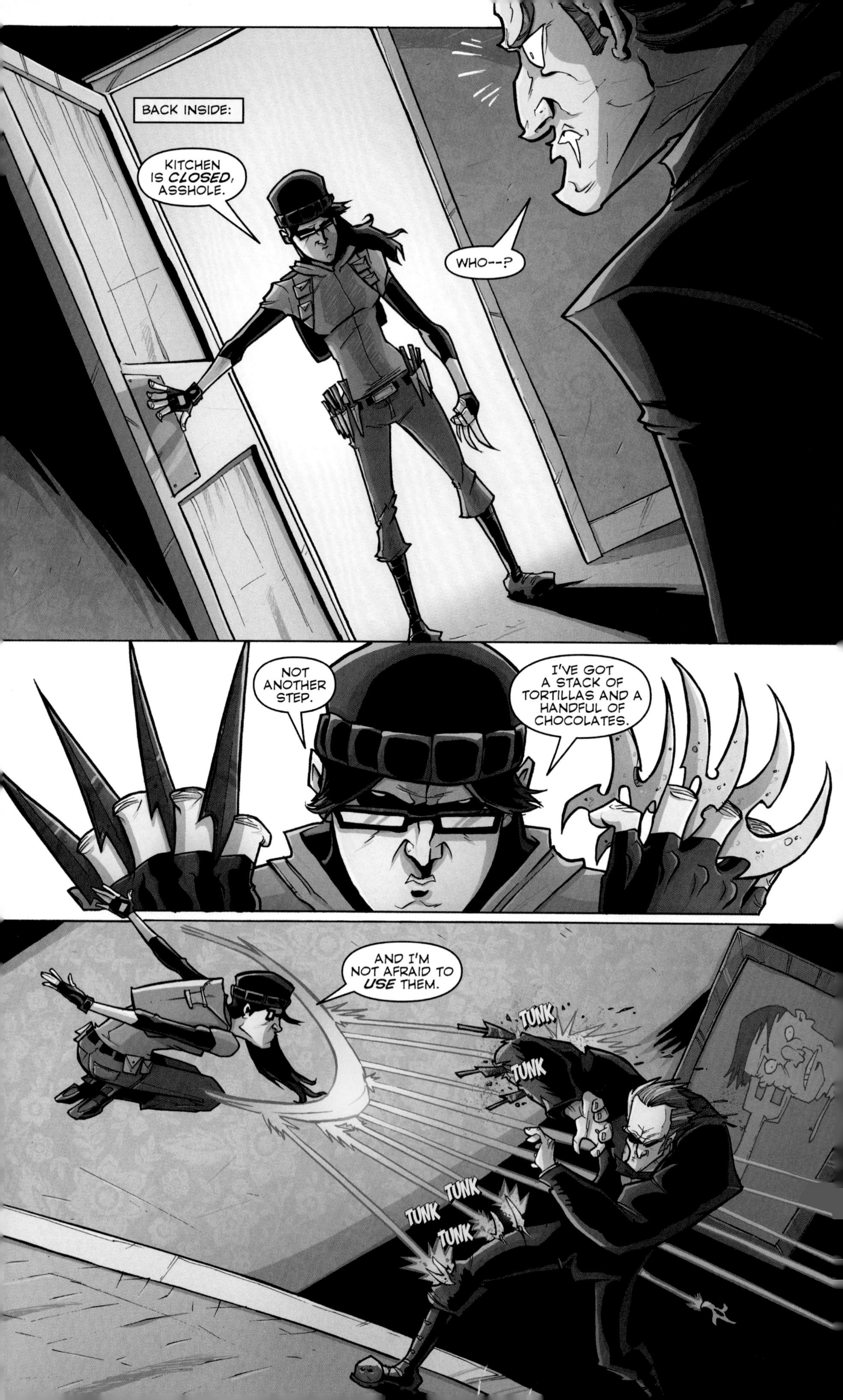
BACK INSIDE:
KITCHEN IS CLOSED, ASSHOLE.
WHO--?
NOT ANOTHER STEP.
I'VE GOT A STACK OF TORTILLAS AND A HANDFUL OF CHOCOLATES.
AND I'M NOT AFRAID TO USE THEM.
TUNK
TUNK
TUNK
TUNK
TUNK

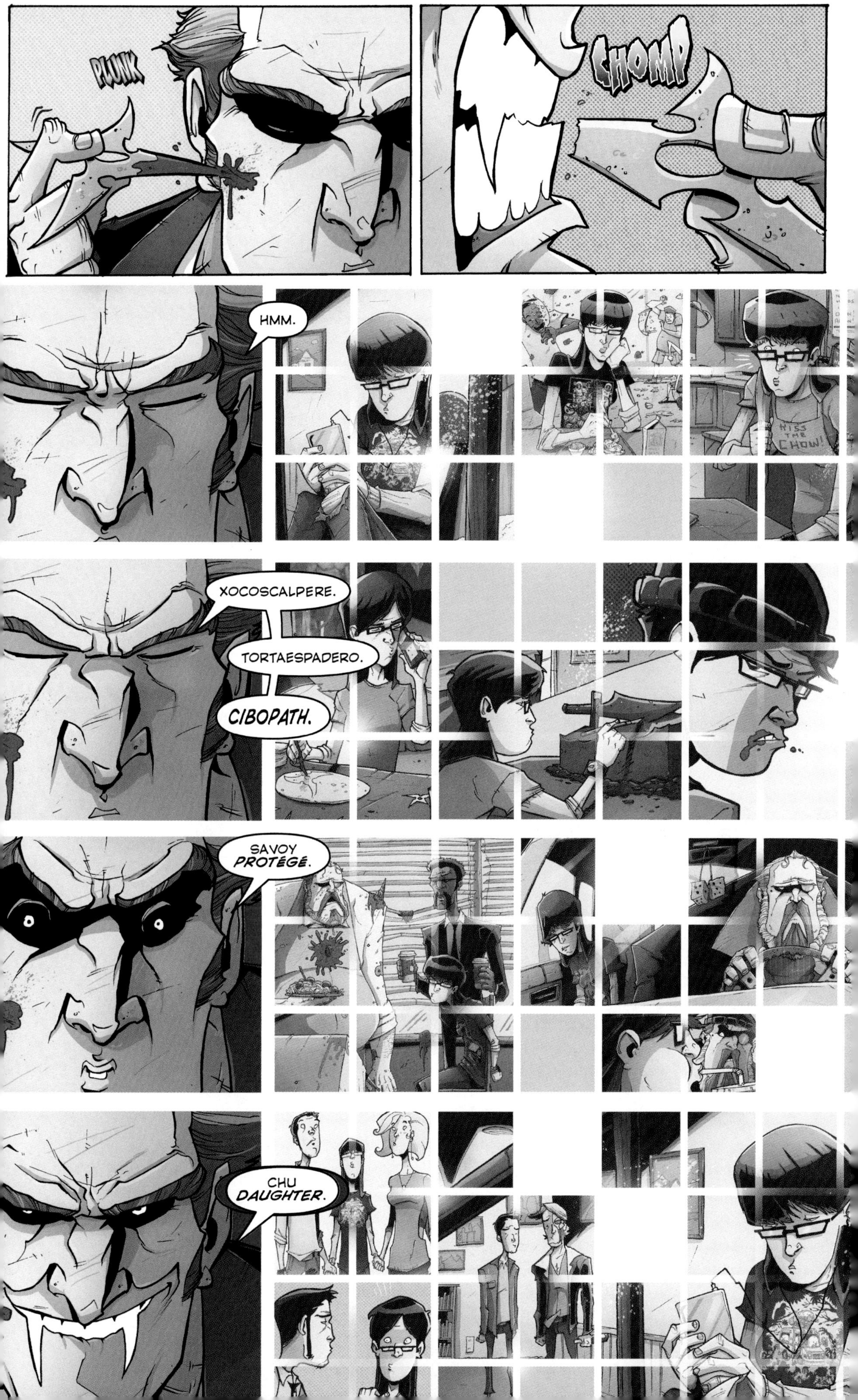
PLUNK
CHOMP
HMM.
KISS THE CHOW!
XOCOSCALPERE.
TORTAESPADERO.
CIBOPATH.
SAVOY PROTÉGÉ.
CHU DAUGHTER.

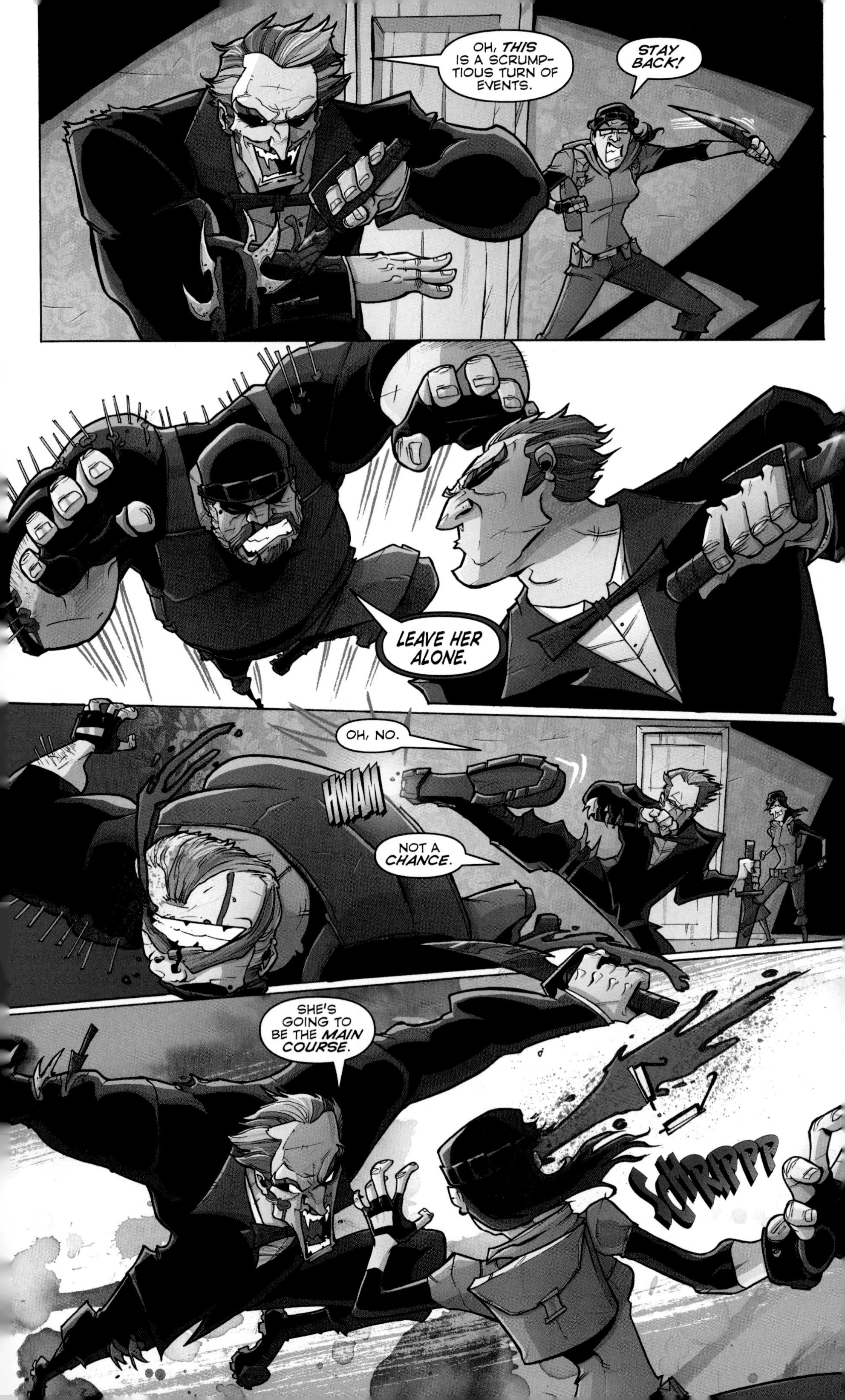
OH, THIS IS A SCRUMPTIOUS TURN OF EVENTS.
STAY BACK!
LEAVE HER ALONE.
OH, NO.
HWAM
NOT A CHANCE.
SHE'S GOING TO BE THE MAIN COURSE.
SCHRIPPP

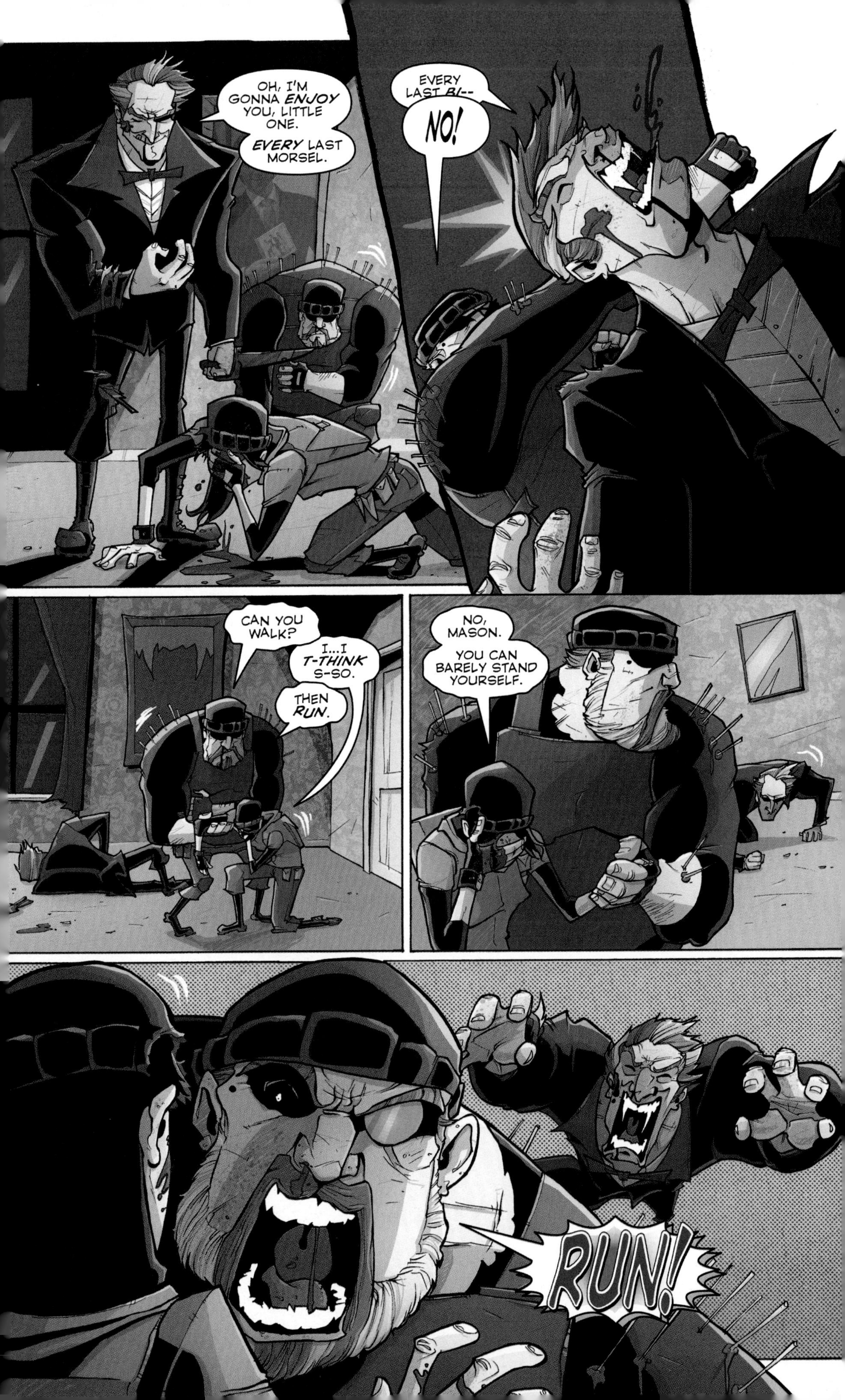
OH, I'M GONNA ENJOY YOU, LITTLE ONE.
EVERY LAST MORSEL.
EVERY LAST BI--
NO!
CAN YOU WALK?
I...I T-THINK S-SO.
THEN RUN.
NO, MASON.
YOU CAN BARELY STAND YOURSELF.
RUN!

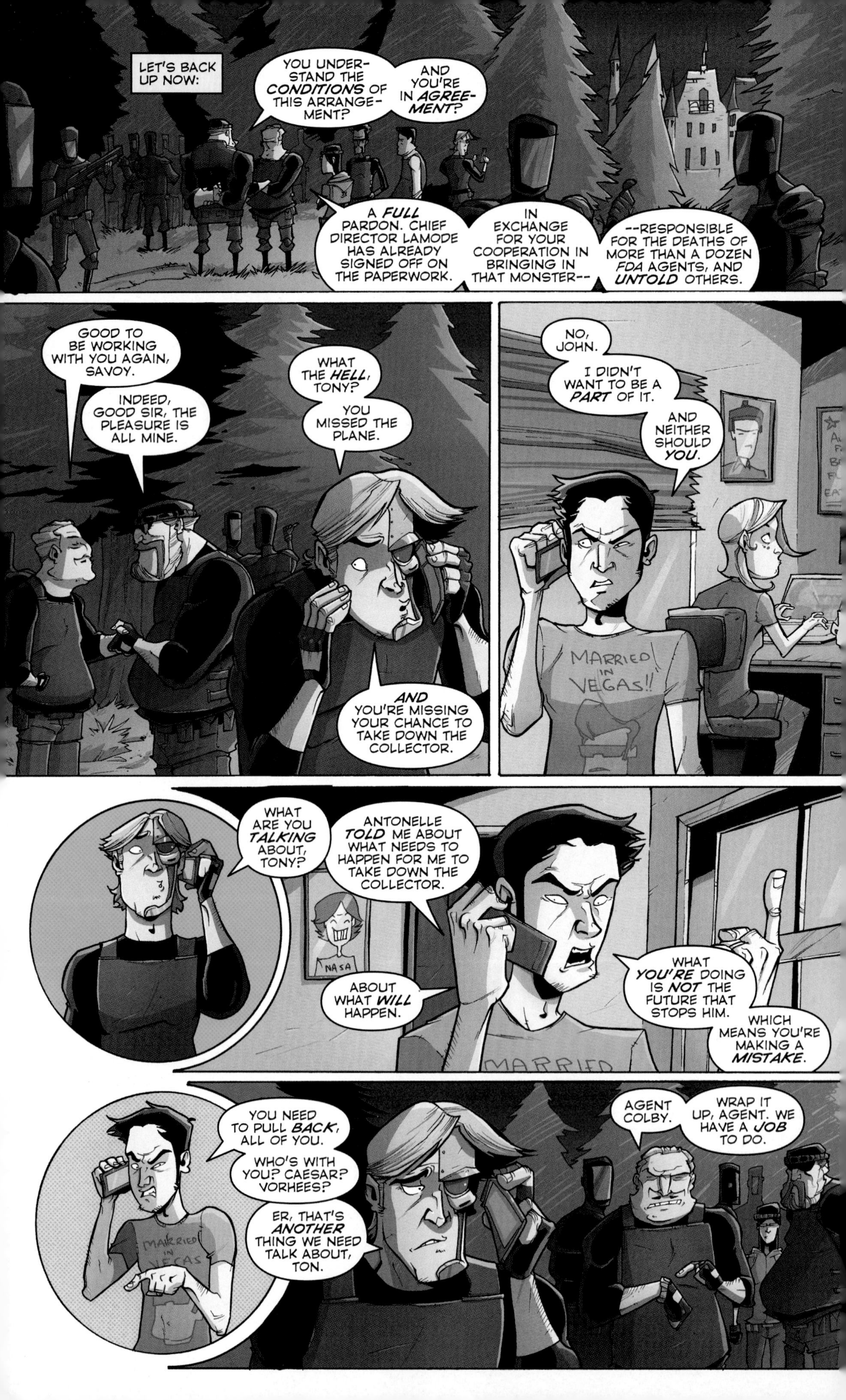
LET'S BACK UP NOW:
YOU UNDER-STAND THE CONDITIONS OF THIS ARRANGE-MENT?
AND YOU'RE IN AGREE-MENT?
A FULL PARDON. CHIEF DIRECTOR LAMODE HAS ALREADY SIGNED OFF ON THE PAPERWORK.
IN EXCHANGE FOR YOUR COOPERATION IN BRINGING IN THAT MONSTER--
--RESPONSIBLE FOR THE DEATHS OF MORE THAN A DOZEN FDA AGENTS, AND UNTOLD OTHERS.
GOOD TO BE WORKING WITH YOU AGAIN, SAVOY.
INDEED, GOOD SIR, THE PLEASURE IS ALL MINE.
WHAT THE HELL, TONY?
YOU MISSED THE PLANE.
AND YOU'RE MISSING YOUR CHANCE TO TAKE DOWN THE COLLECTOR.
NO, JOHN.
I DIDN'T WANT TO BE A PART OF IT.
AND NEITHER SHOULD YOU.
MARRIED IN VEGAS!!
WHAT ARE YOU TALKING ABOUT, TONY?
ANTONELLE TOLD ME ABOUT WHAT NEEDS TO HAPPEN FOR ME TO TAKE DOWN THE COLLECTOR.
ABOUT WHAT WILL HAPPEN.
NASA
WHAT YOU'RE DOING IS NOT THE FUTURE THAT STOPS HIM.
WHICH MEANS YOU'RE MAKING A MISTAKE.
YOU NEED TO PULL BACK, ALL OF YOU.
WHO'S WITH YOU? CAESAR? VORHEES?
ER, THAT'S ANOTHER THING WE NEED TALK ABOUT, TON.
AGENT COLBY.
WRAP IT UP, AGENT. WE HAVE A JOB TO DO.
MARRIED IN VEGAS

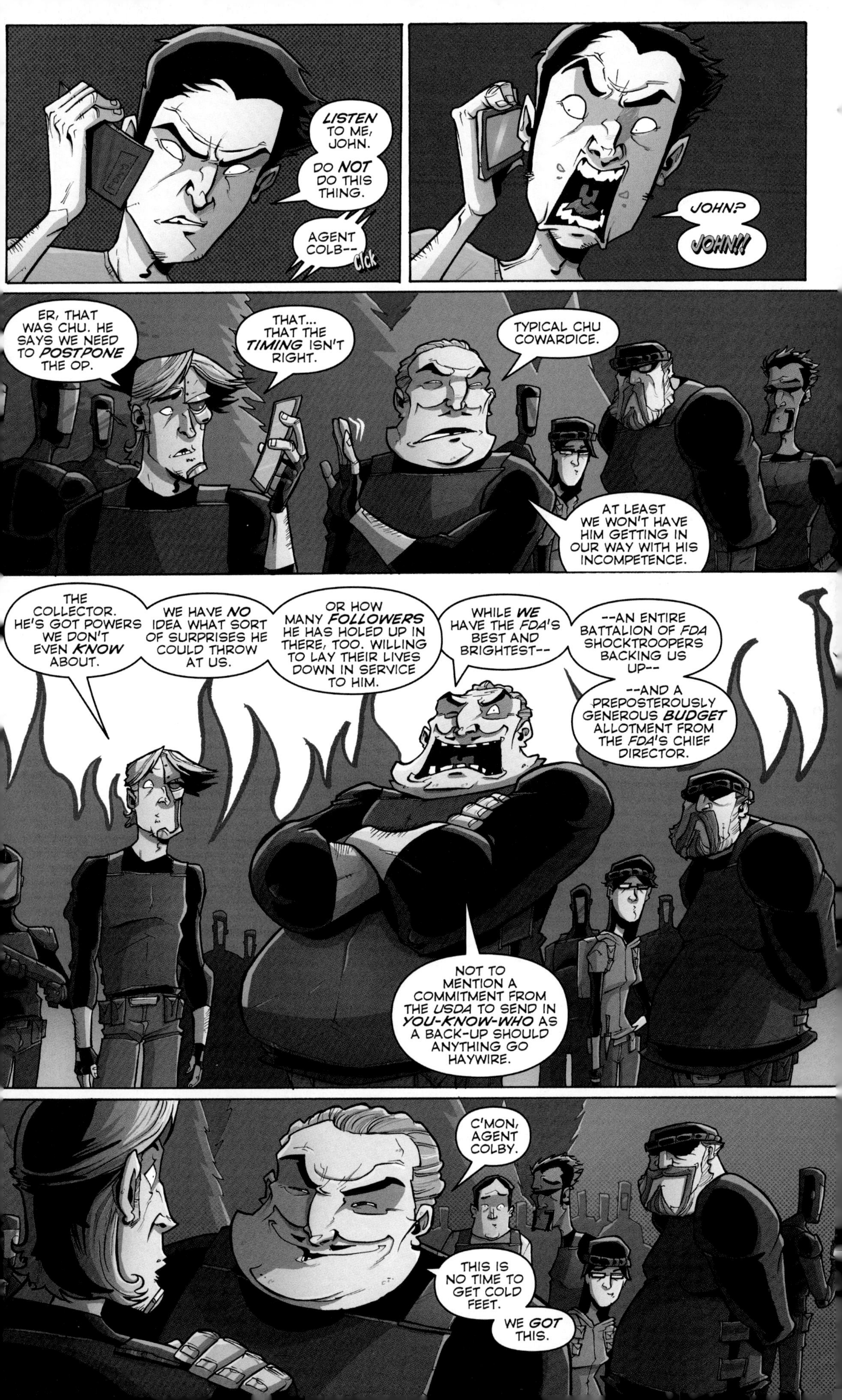

LISTEN TO ME, JOHN.
DO NOT DO THIS THING.
AGENT COLB--
CLCK
JOHN?
JOHN!!
ER, THAT WAS CHU. HE SAYS WE NEED TO POSTPONE THE OP.
THAT... THAT THE TIMING ISN'T RIGHT.
TYPICAL CHU COWARDICE.
AT LEAST WE WON'T HAVE HIM GETTING IN OUR WAY WITH HIS INCOMPETENCE.
THE COLLECTOR. HE'S GOT POWERS WE DON'T EVEN KNOW ABOUT.
WE HAVE NO IDEA WHAT SORT OF SURPRISES HE COULD THROW AT US.
OR HOW MANY FOLLOWERS HE HAS HOLED UP IN THERE, TOO. WILLING TO LAY THEIR LIVES DOWN IN SERVICE TO HIM.
WHILE WE HAVE THE FDA'S BEST AND BRIGHTEST--
--AN ENTIRE BATTALION OF FDA SHOCKTROOPERS BACKING US UP--
--AND A PREPOSTEROUSLY GENEROUS BUDGET ALLOTMENT FROM THE FDA'S CHIEF DIRECTOR.
NOT TO MENTION A COMMITMENT FROM THE USDA TO SEND IN YOU-KNOW-WHO AS A BACK-UP SHOULD ANYTHING GO HAYWIRE.
C'MON, AGENT COLBY.
THIS IS NO TIME TO GET COLD FEET.
WE GOT THIS.

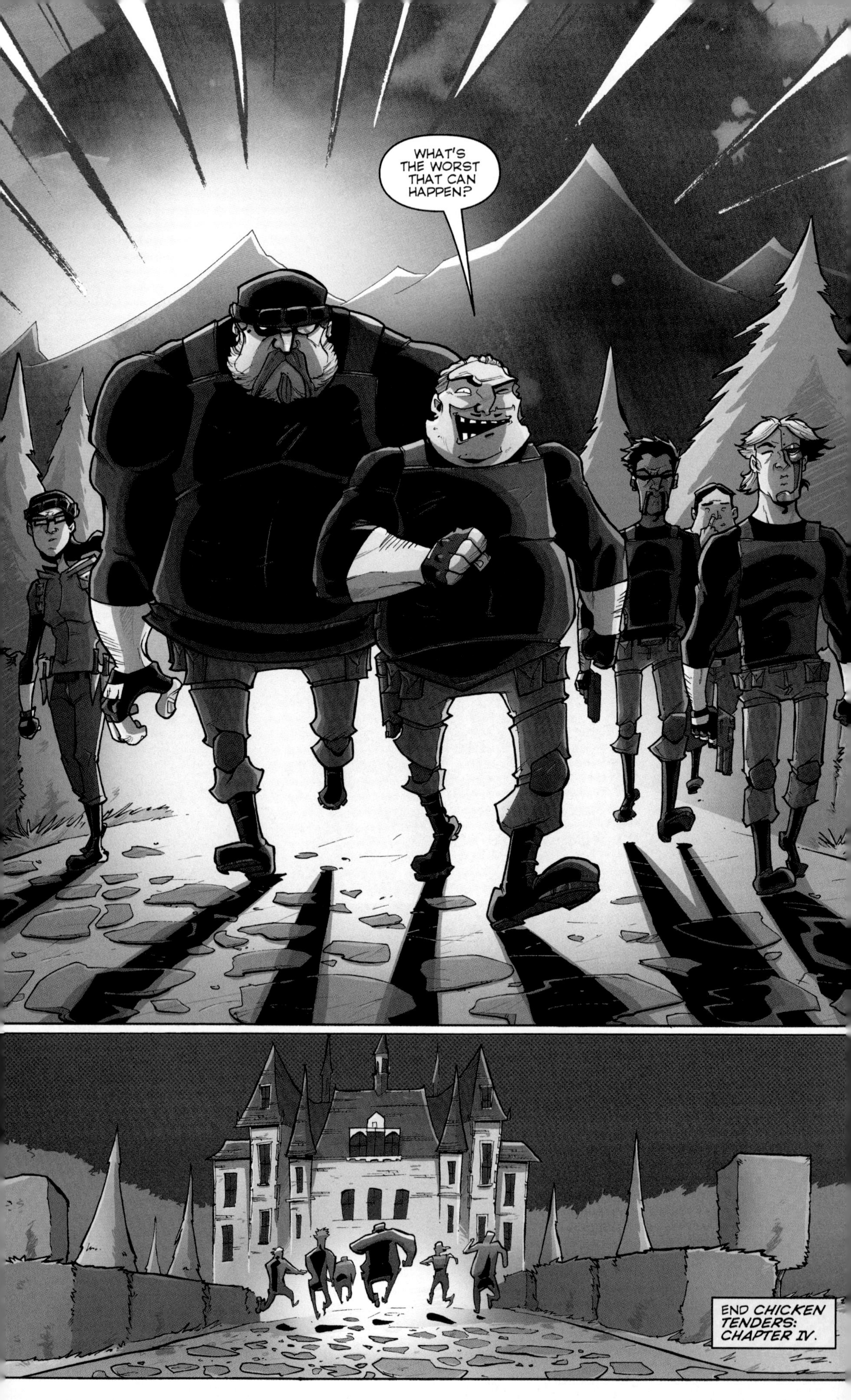
WHAT'S THE WORST THAT CAN HAPPEN?
END CHICKEN TENDERS: CHAPTER IV.

Chapter Five

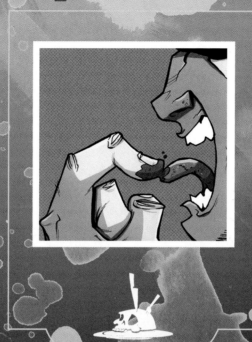

Issue #45 trifold cover

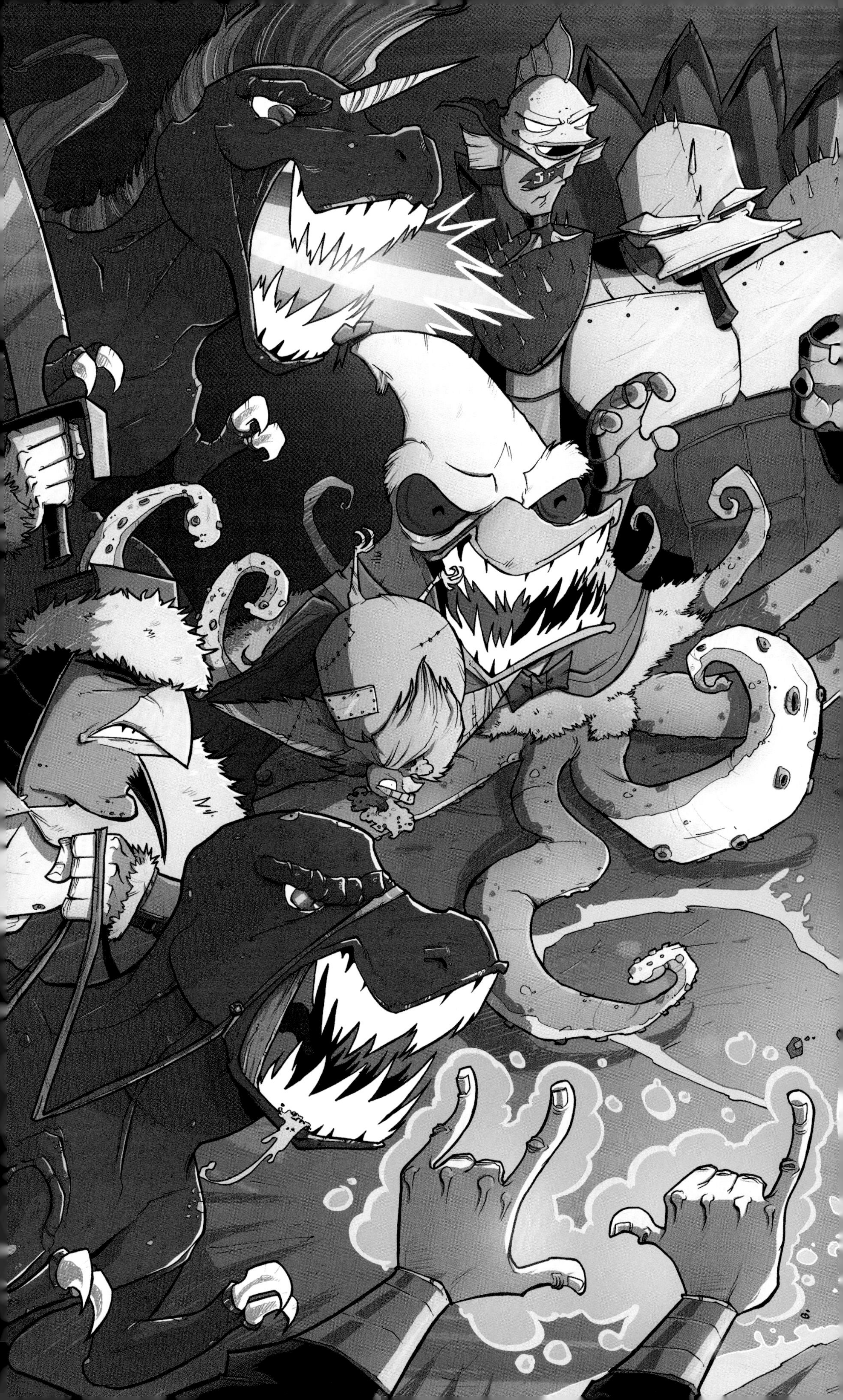

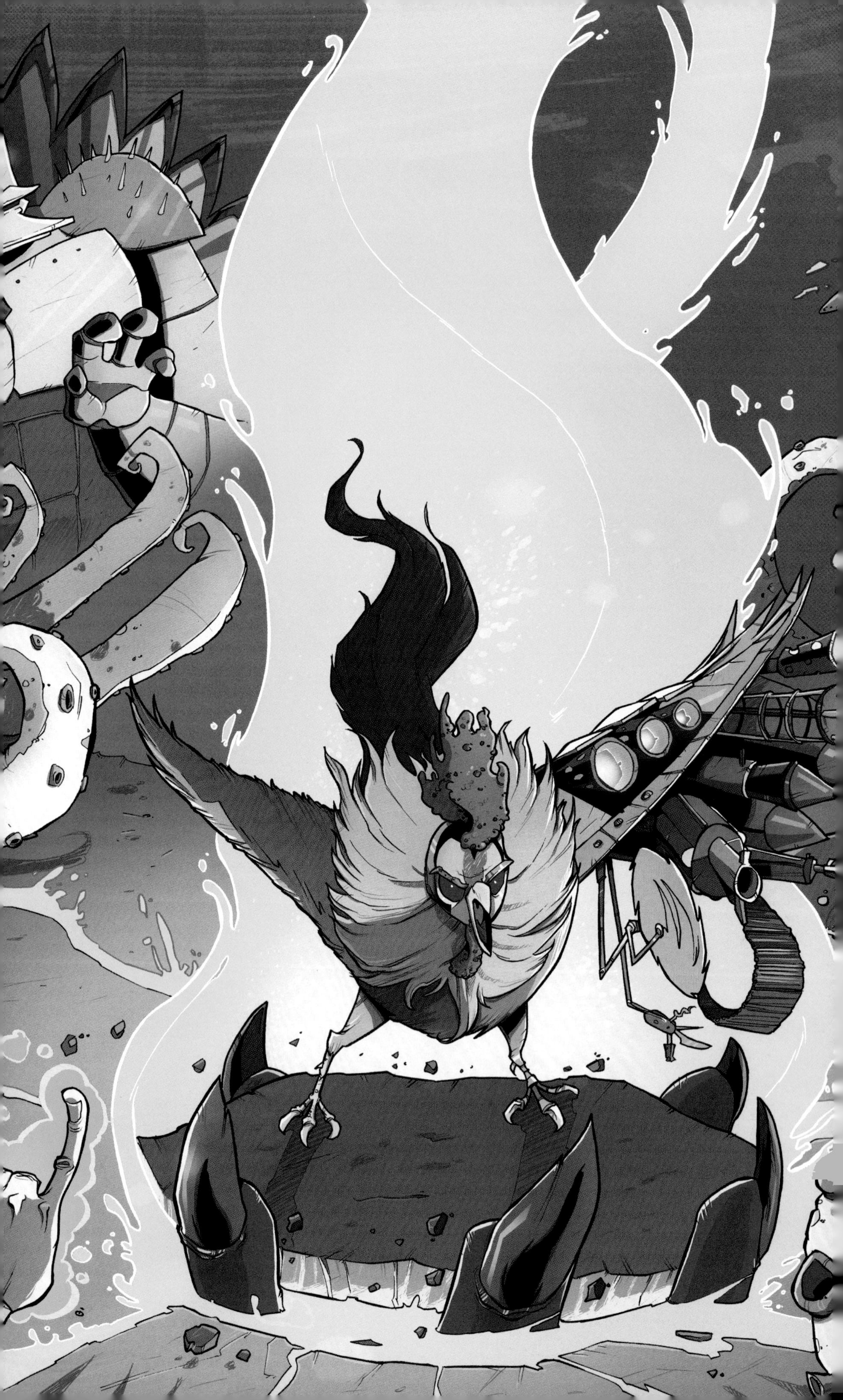

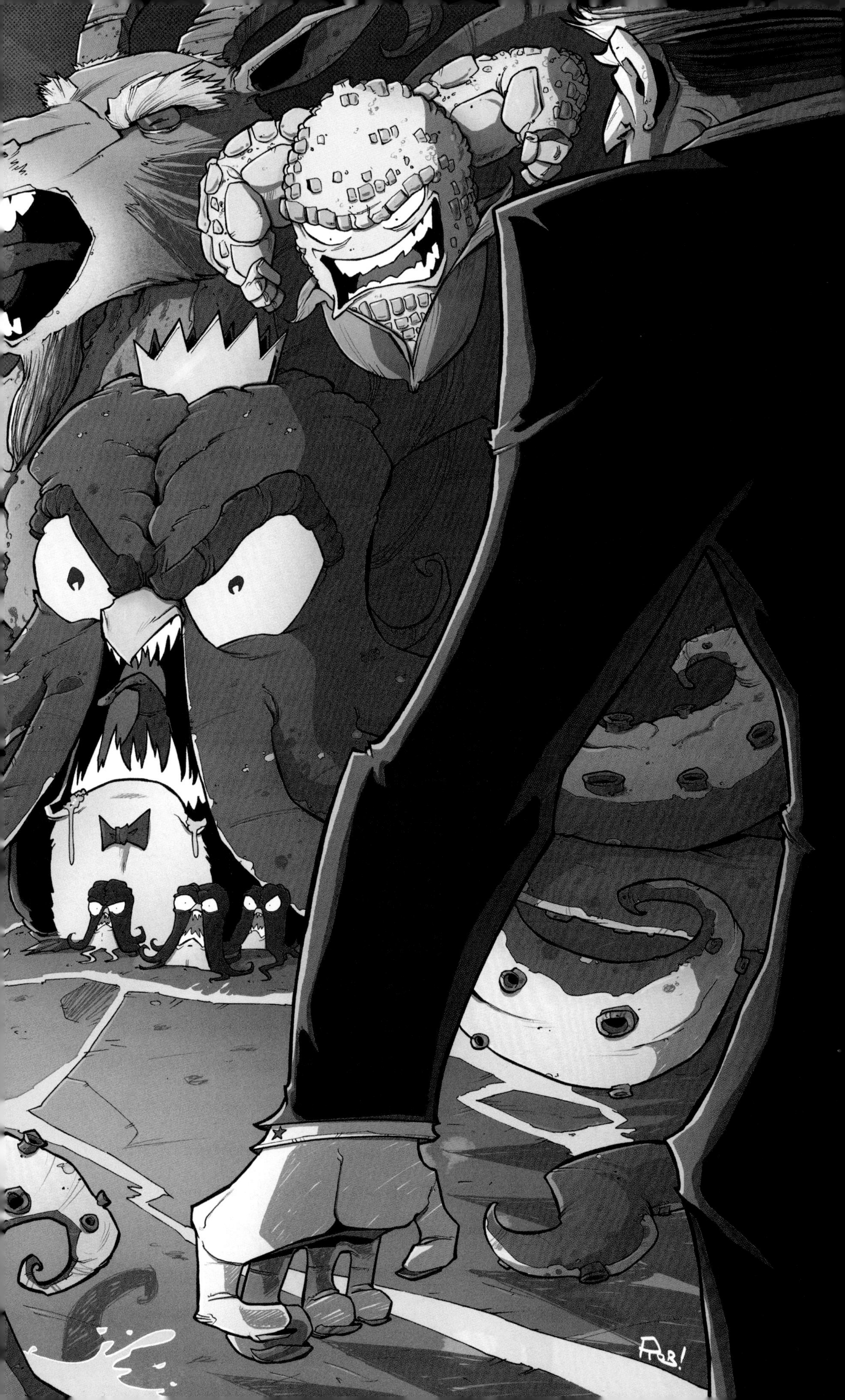

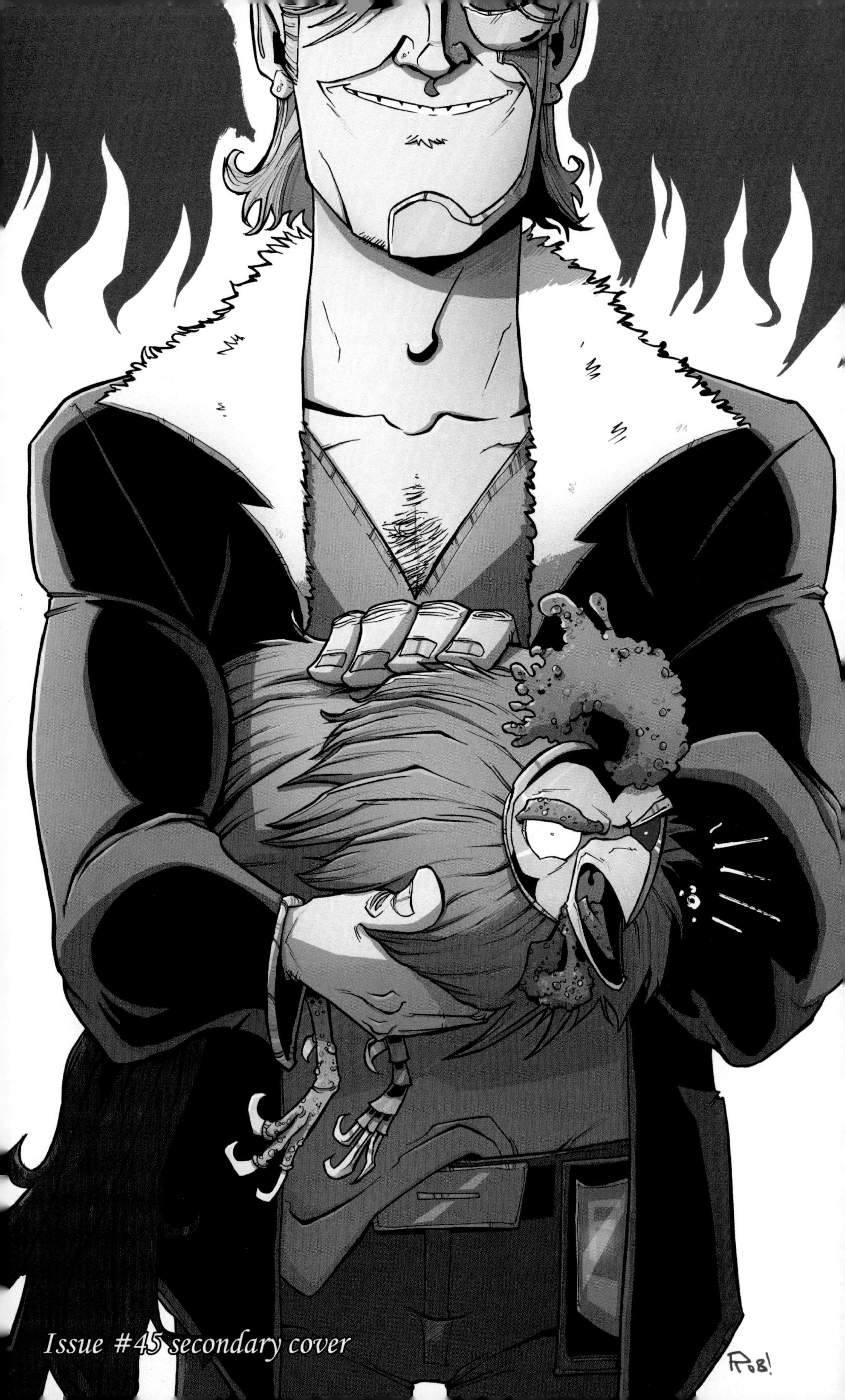

R 08!

Issue #45 secondary cover

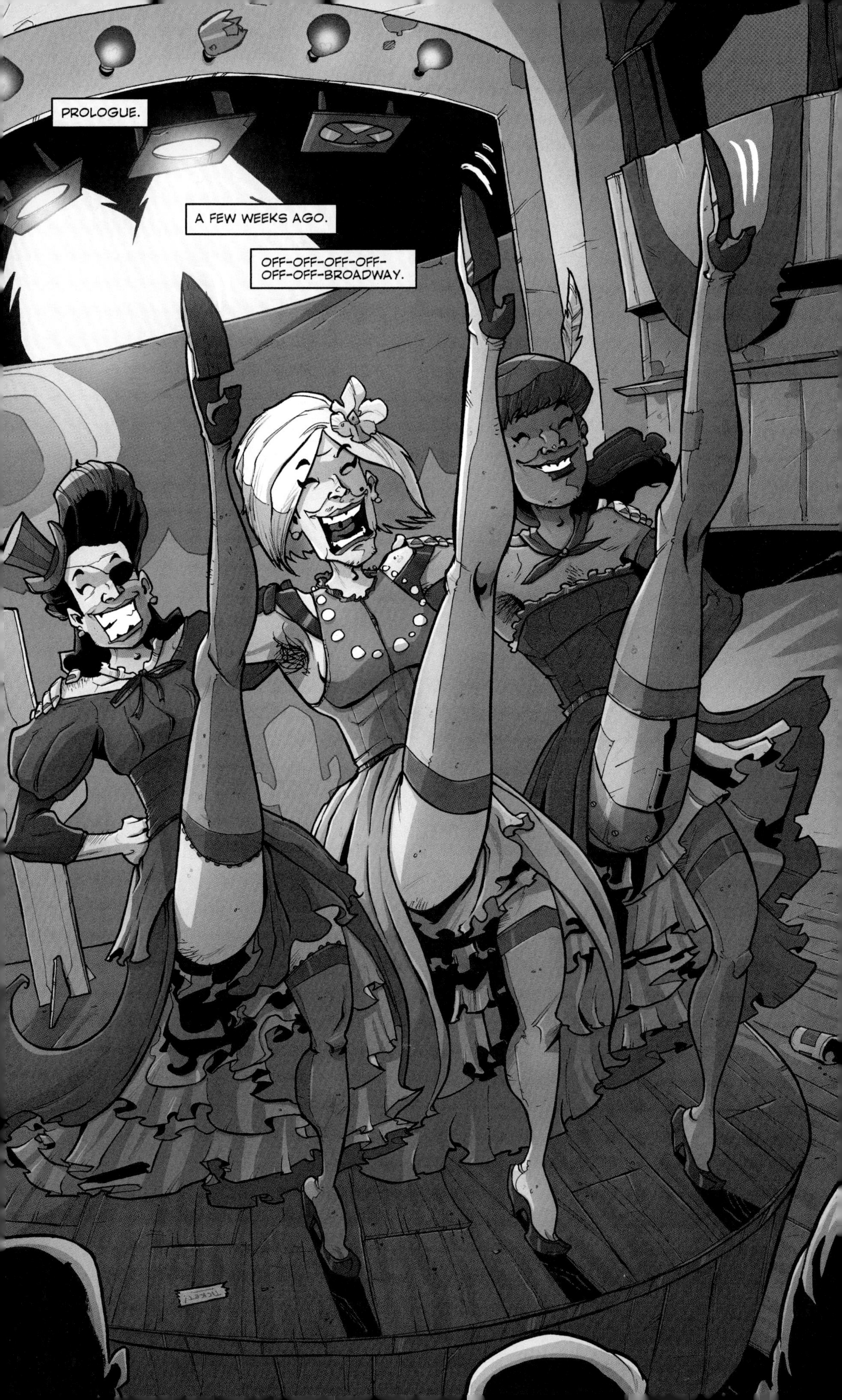
PROLOGUE.
A FEW WEEKS AGO.
OFF-OFF-OFF-OFF-
OFF-OFF-BROADWAY.

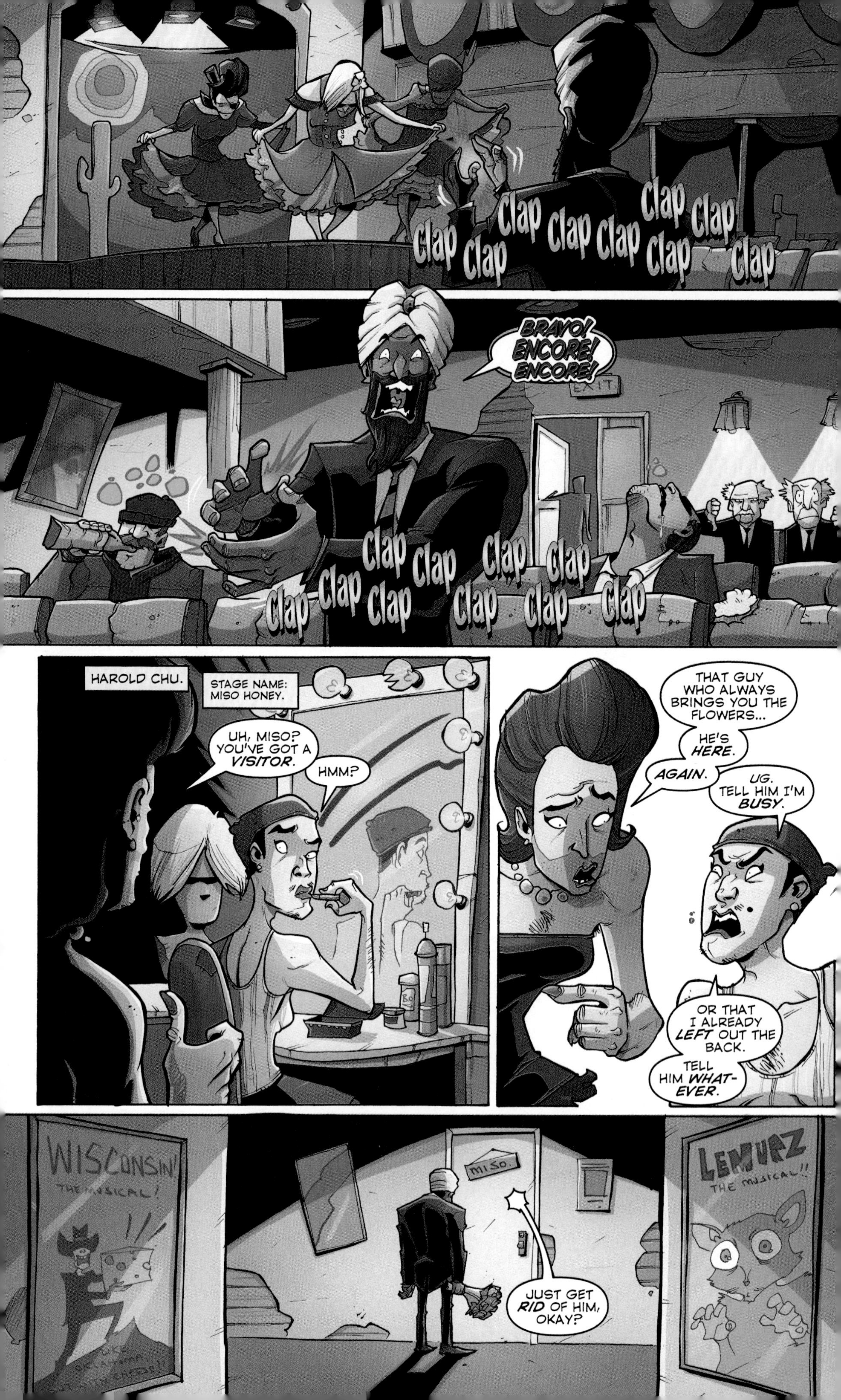

Clap Clap Clap Clap Clap Clap Clap Clap Clap
BRAVO! ENCORE! ENCORE!
EXIT
Clap Clap Clap Clap Clap Clap Clap Clap Clap Clap
HAROLD CHU.
STAGE NAME: MISO HONEY.
UH, MISO? YOU'VE GOT A *VISITOR*.
HMM?
THAT GUY WHO ALWAYS BRINGS YOU THE FLOWERS...
HE'S *HERE*.
AGAIN.
UG. TELL HIM I'M *BUSY*.
OR THAT I ALREADY *LEFT* OUT THE BACK.
TELL HIM *WHAT-EVER*.
WISCONSIN! THE MUSICAL!
LIKE OKLAHOMA, BUT WITH CHEESE!!
MISO.
LEMURZ THE MUSICAL!!
JUST GET *RID* OF HIM, OKAY?

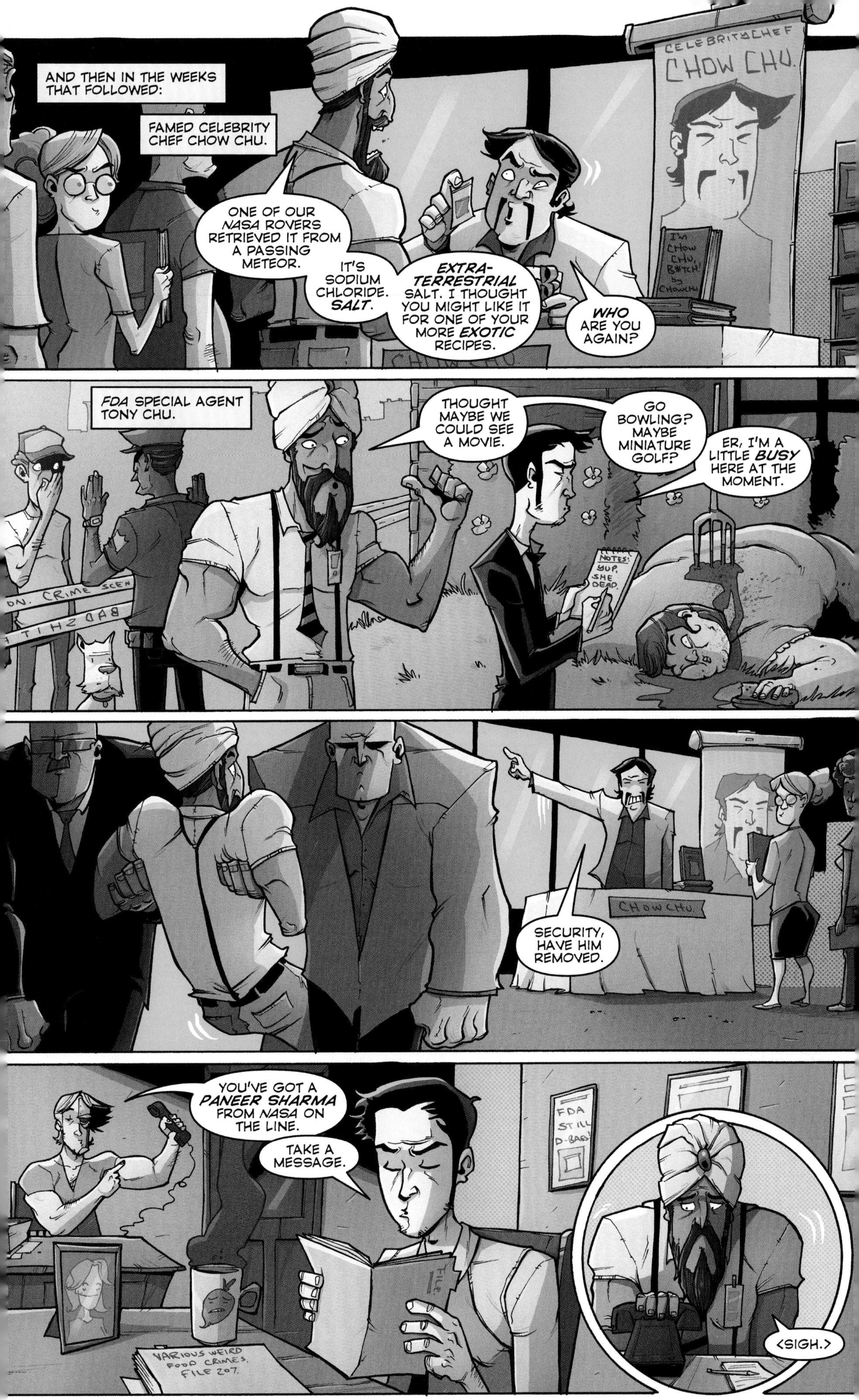
AND THEN IN THE WEEKS THAT FOLLOWED:
FAMED CELEBRITY CHEF CHOW CHU.
CELEBRITY CHEF CHOW CHU.
ONE OF OUR *NASA* ROVERS RETRIEVED IT FROM A PASSING METEOR.
IT'S SODIUM CHLORIDE. ***SALT***.
EXTRA-TERRESTRIAL SALT. I THOUGHT YOU MIGHT LIKE IT FOR ONE OF YOUR MORE ***EXOTIC*** RECIPES.
I'M CHOW CHU, B#TCH! by ChowChu
WHO ARE YOU AGAIN?
FDA SPECIAL AGENT TONY CHU.
THOUGHT MAYBE WE COULD SEE A MOVIE.
GO BOWLING? MAYBE MINIATURE GOLF?
ER, I'M A LITTLE ***BUSY*** HERE AT THE MOMENT.
NOTES: YUP, SHE DEAD.
CRIME SCENE
BAD SHIT
CHOW CHU
SECURITY, HAVE HIM REMOVED.
YOU'VE GOT A ***PANEER SHARMA*** FROM *NASA* ON THE LINE.
TAKE A MESSAGE.
FDA STILL D-BAGS!
VARIOUS WEIRD FOOD CRIMES. FILE 207.
<SIGH.>

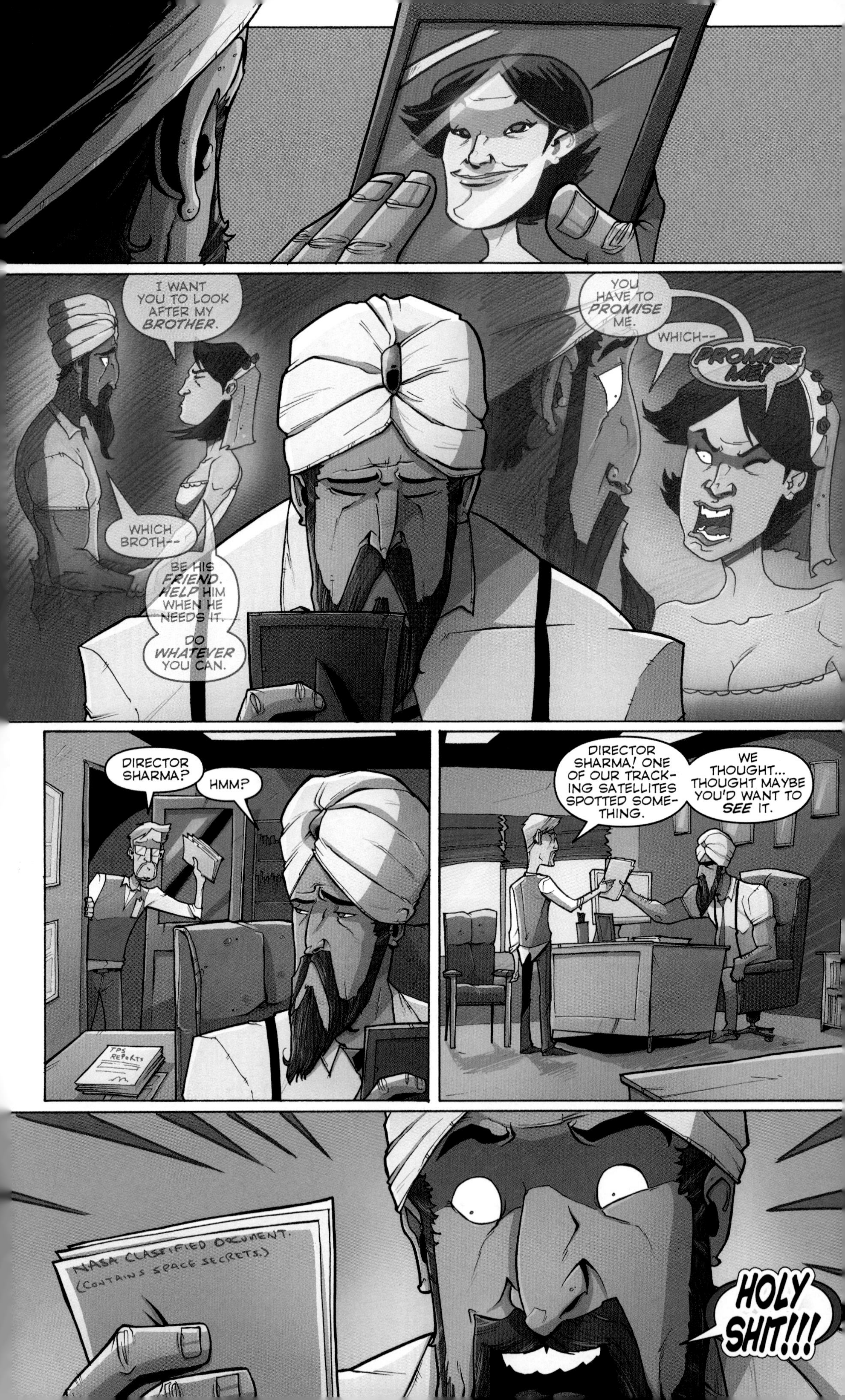
I WANT YOU TO LOOK AFTER MY BROTHER.
WHICH BROTH--
BE HIS FRIEND. HELP HIM WHEN HE NEEDS IT.
DO WHATEVER YOU CAN.
YOU HAVE TO PROMISE ME.
WHICH--
PROMISE ME!
DIRECTOR SHARMA?
HMM?
TPS REPORTS
DIRECTOR SHARMA! ONE OF OUR TRACKING SATELLITES SPOTTED SOMETHING.
WE THOUGHT... THOUGHT MAYBE YOU'D WANT TO SEE IT.
NASA CLASSIFIED DOCUMENT.
(CONTAINS SPACE SECRETS.)
HOLY SHIT!!!

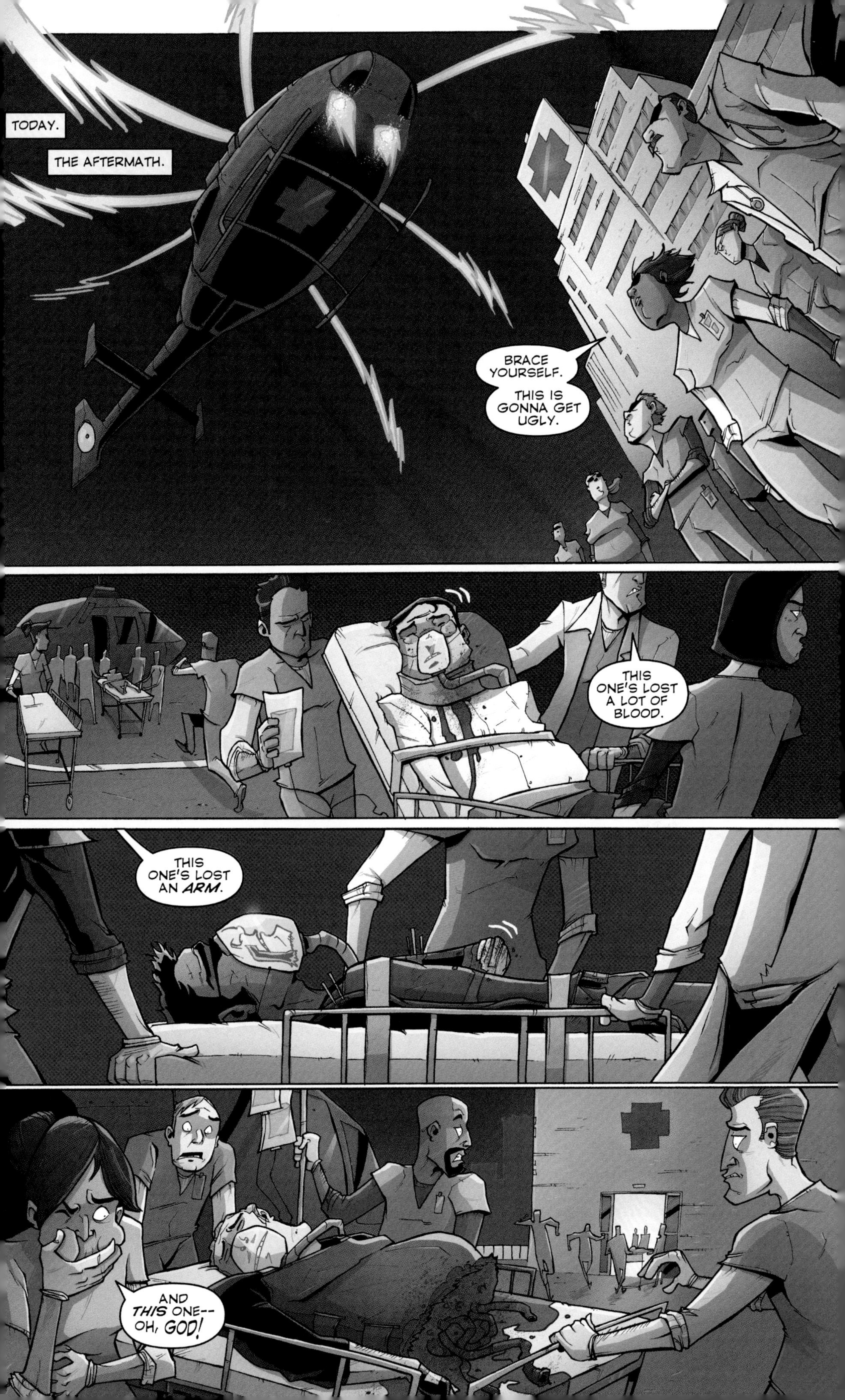
TODAY.
THE AFTERMATH.
BRACE YOURSELF.
THIS IS GONNA GET UGLY.
THIS ONE'S LOST A LOT OF BLOOD.
THIS ONE'S LOST AN *ARM*.
AND *THIS* ONE-- OH, *GOD!*

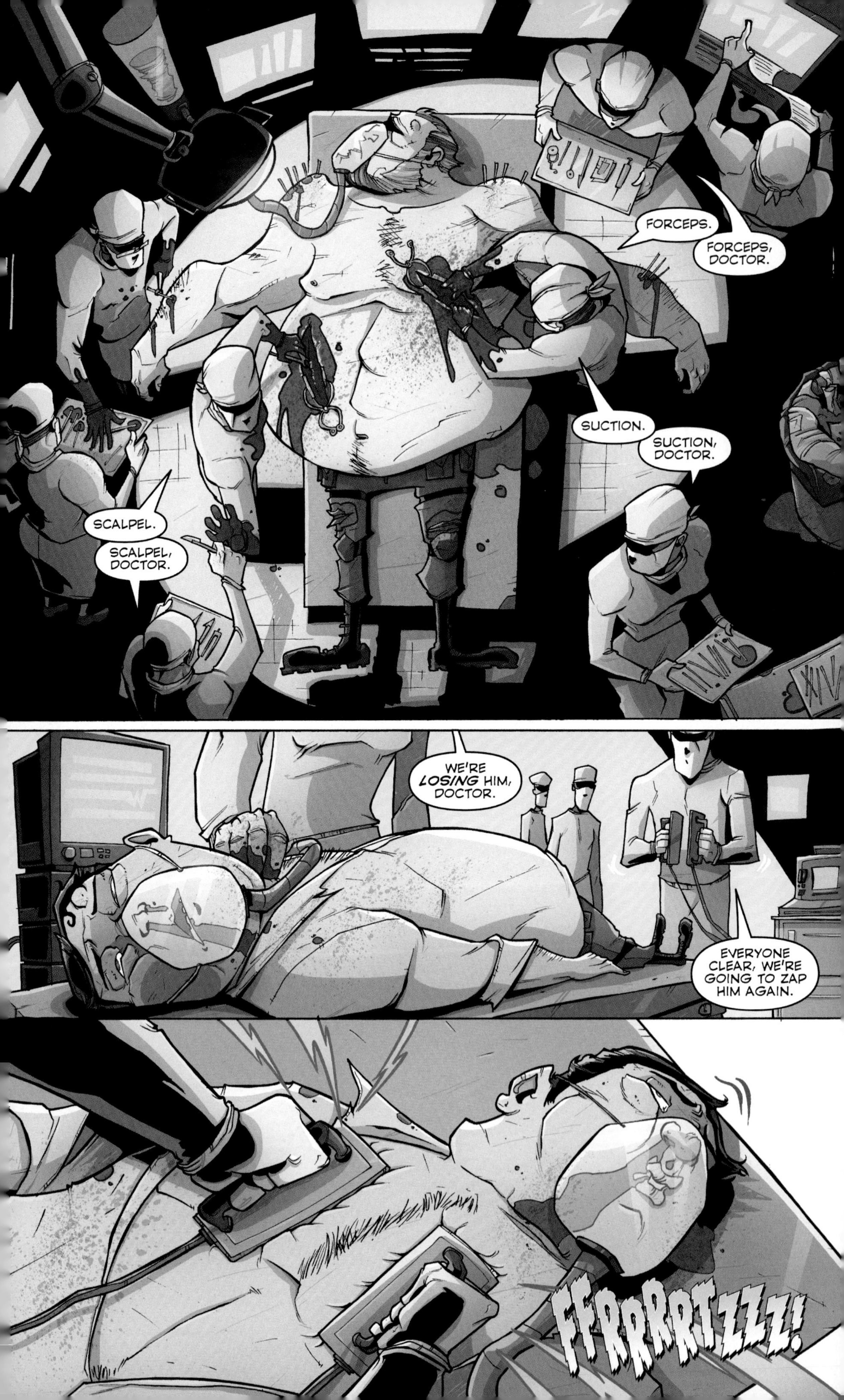
FORCEPS.
FORCEPS, DOCTOR.
SUCTION.
SUCTION, DOCTOR.
SCALPEL.
SCALPEL, DOCTOR.
WE'RE *LOSING* HIM, DOCTOR.
EVERYONE CLEAR, WE'RE GOING TO ZAP HIM AGAIN.
FFRRRRTZZZZ!

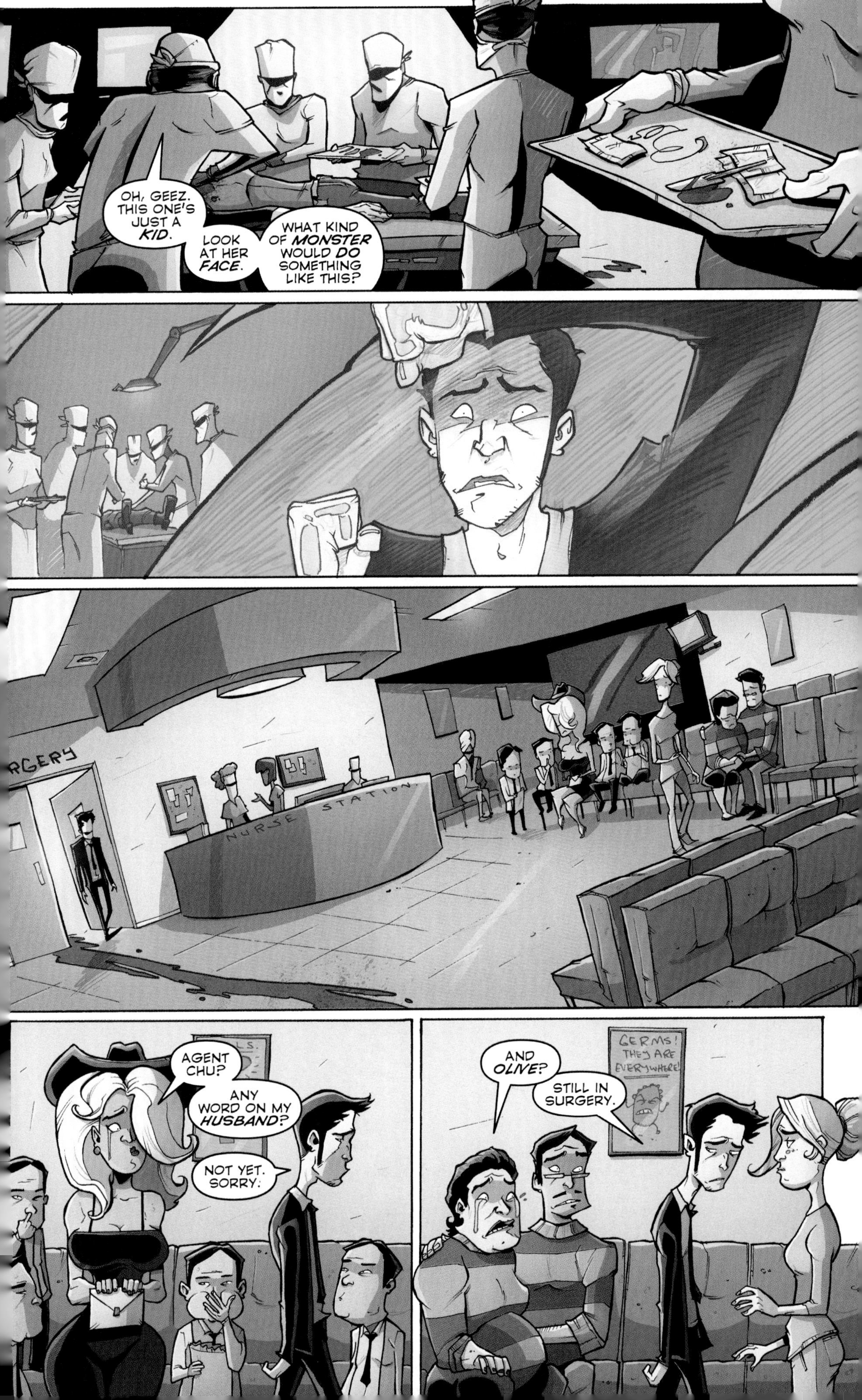

OH, GEEZ. THIS ONE'S JUST A *KID*.
LOOK AT HER *FACE*.
WHAT KIND OF *MONSTER* WOULD *DO* SOMETHING LIKE THIS?
RGERY
NURSE STATION
AGENT CHU?
ANY WORD ON MY *HUSBAND*?
NOT YET. SORRY.
GERMS! THEY ARE EVERYWHERE!
AND *OLIVE*?
STILL IN SURGERY.

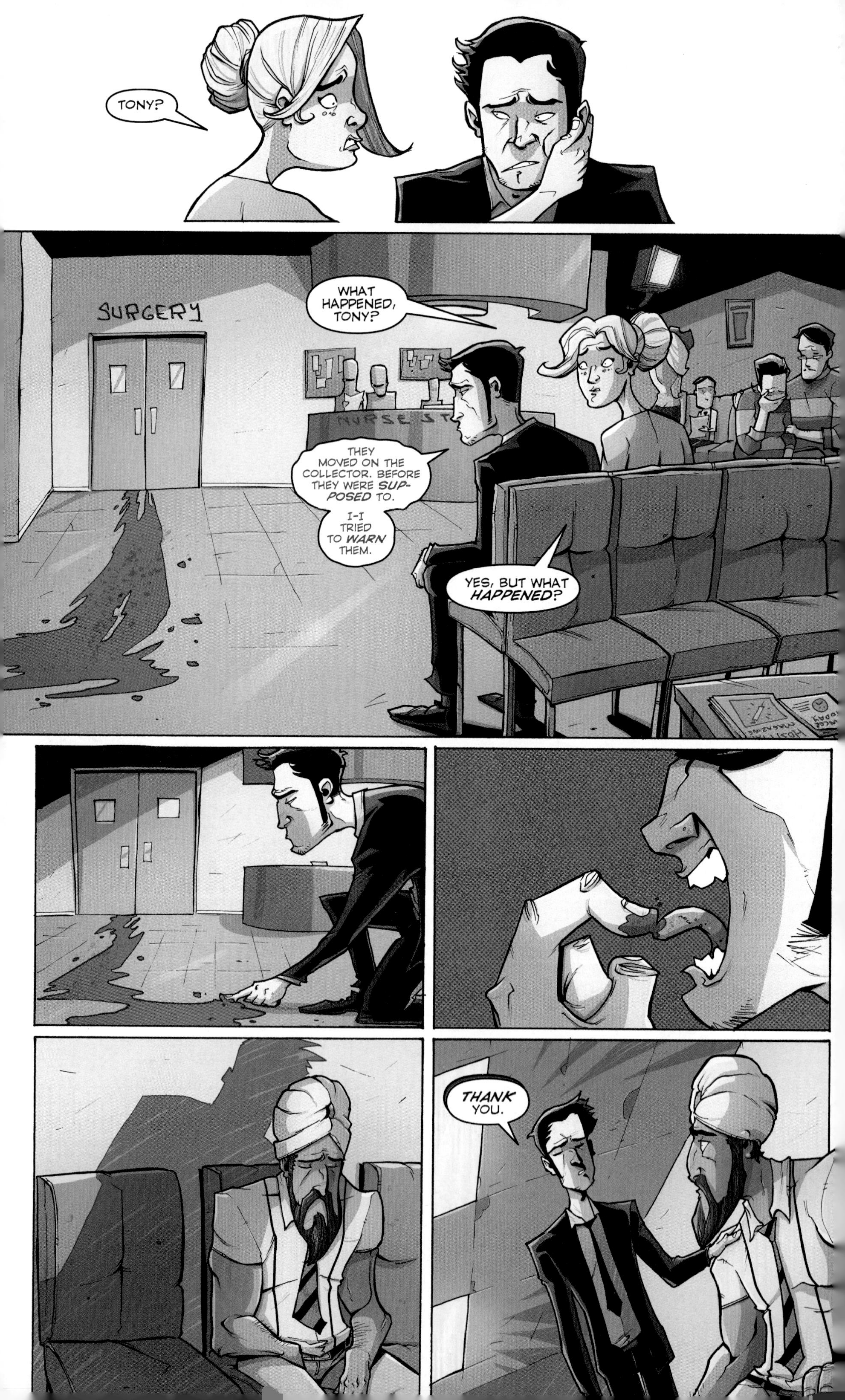
TONY?
SURGERY
WHAT HAPPENED, TONY?
NURSE ST
THEY MOVED ON THE COLLECTOR. BEFORE THEY WERE *SUPPOSED* TO.
I-I TRIED TO *WARN* THEM.
YES, BUT WHAT *HAPPENED*?
THANK YOU.

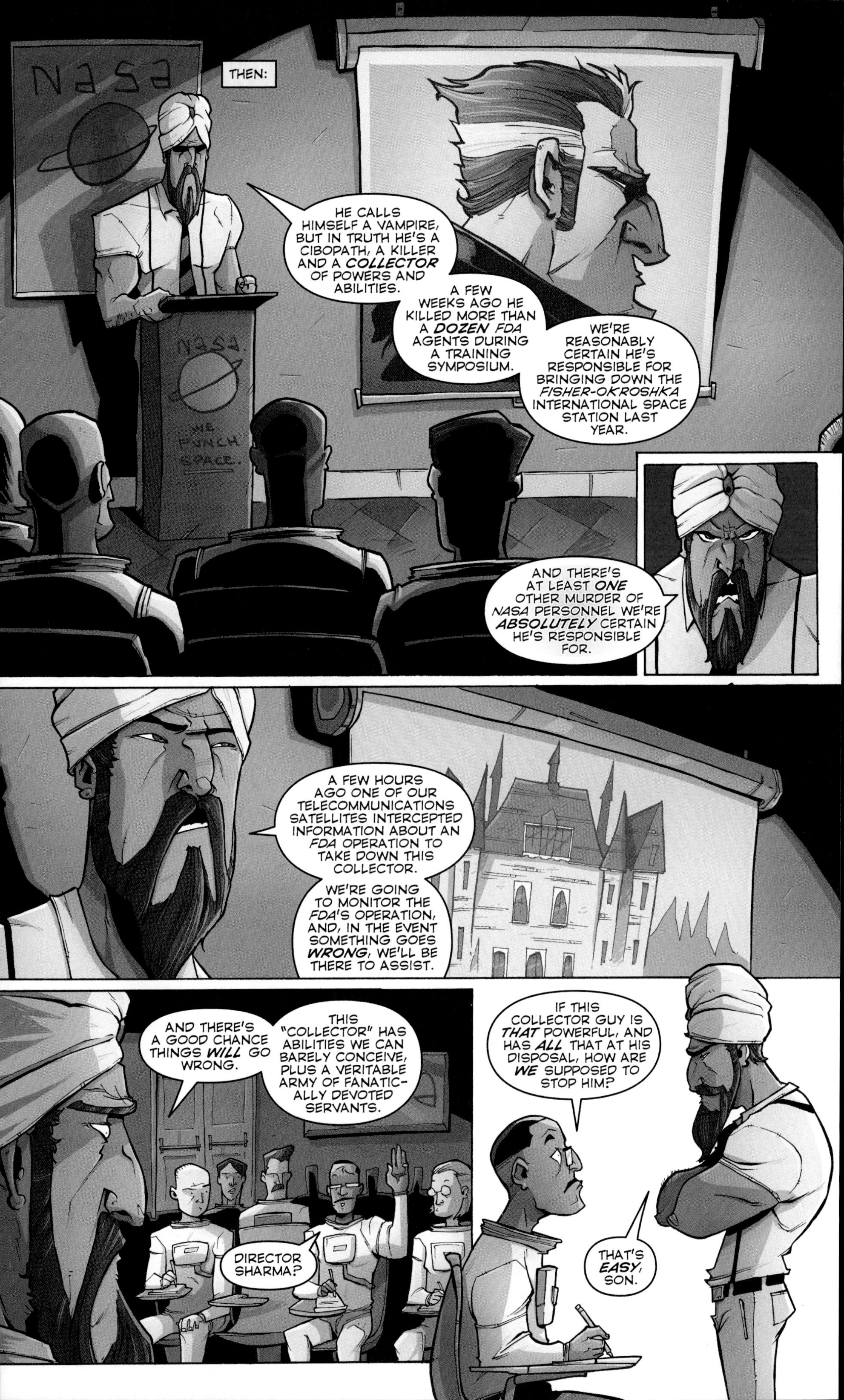
NASA
THEN:
HE CALLS HIMSELF A VAMPIRE, BUT IN TRUTH HE'S A CIBOPATH, A KILLER AND A *COLLECTOR* OF POWERS AND ABILITIES.
A FEW WEEKS AGO HE KILLED MORE THAN A *DOZEN FDA* AGENTS DURING A TRAINING SYMPOSIUM.
WE'RE REASONABLY CERTAIN HE'S RESPONSIBLE FOR BRINGING DOWN THE *FISHER-OKROSHKA* INTERNATIONAL SPACE STATION LAST YEAR.
NASA. WE PUNCH SPACE.
AND THERE'S AT LEAST *ONE* OTHER MURDER OF *NASA* PERSONNEL WE'RE *ABSOLUTELY* CERTAIN HE'S RESPONSIBLE FOR.
A FEW HOURS AGO ONE OF OUR TELECOMMUNICATIONS SATELLITES INTERCEPTED INFORMATION ABOUT AN *FDA* OPERATION TO TAKE DOWN THIS COLLECTOR.
WE'RE GOING TO MONITOR THE *FDA*'S OPERATION, AND, IN THE EVENT SOMETHING GOES *WRONG*, WE'LL BE THERE TO ASSIST.
AND THERE'S A GOOD CHANCE THINGS *WILL* GO WRONG.
THIS "COLLECTOR" HAS ABILITIES WE CAN BARELY CONCEIVE, PLUS A VERITABLE ARMY OF FANATICALLY DEVOTED SERVANTS.
DIRECTOR SHARMA?
IF THIS COLLECTOR GUY IS *THAT* POWERFUL, AND HAS *ALL* THAT AT HIS DISPOSAL, HOW ARE *WE* SUPPOSED TO STOP HIM?
THAT'S *EASY*, SON.

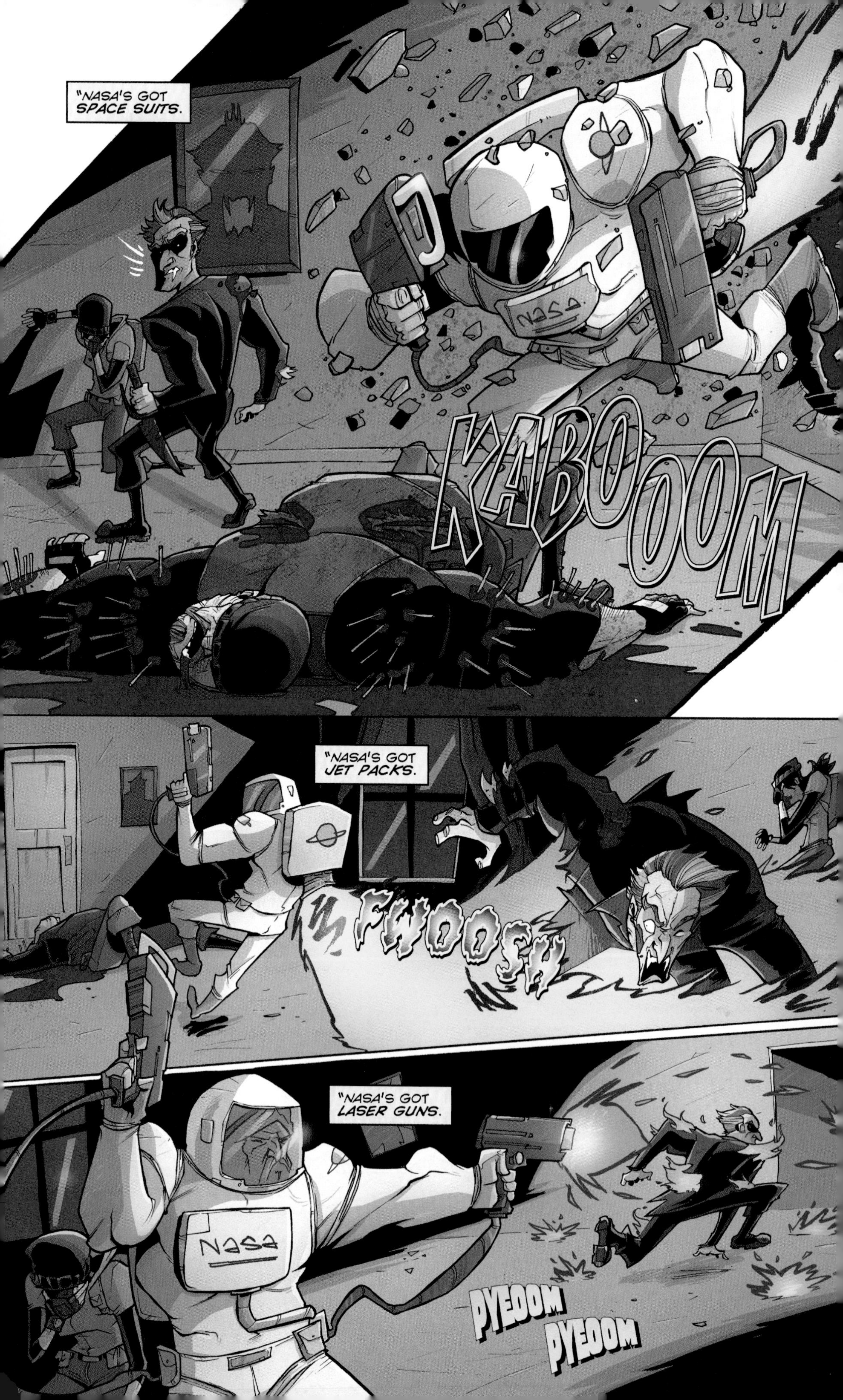
"NASA'S GOT SPACE SUITS.
KABOOOOM
"NASA'S GOT JET PACKS.
FWOOSH
"NASA'S GOT LASER GUNS.
PYEOOM
PYEOOM

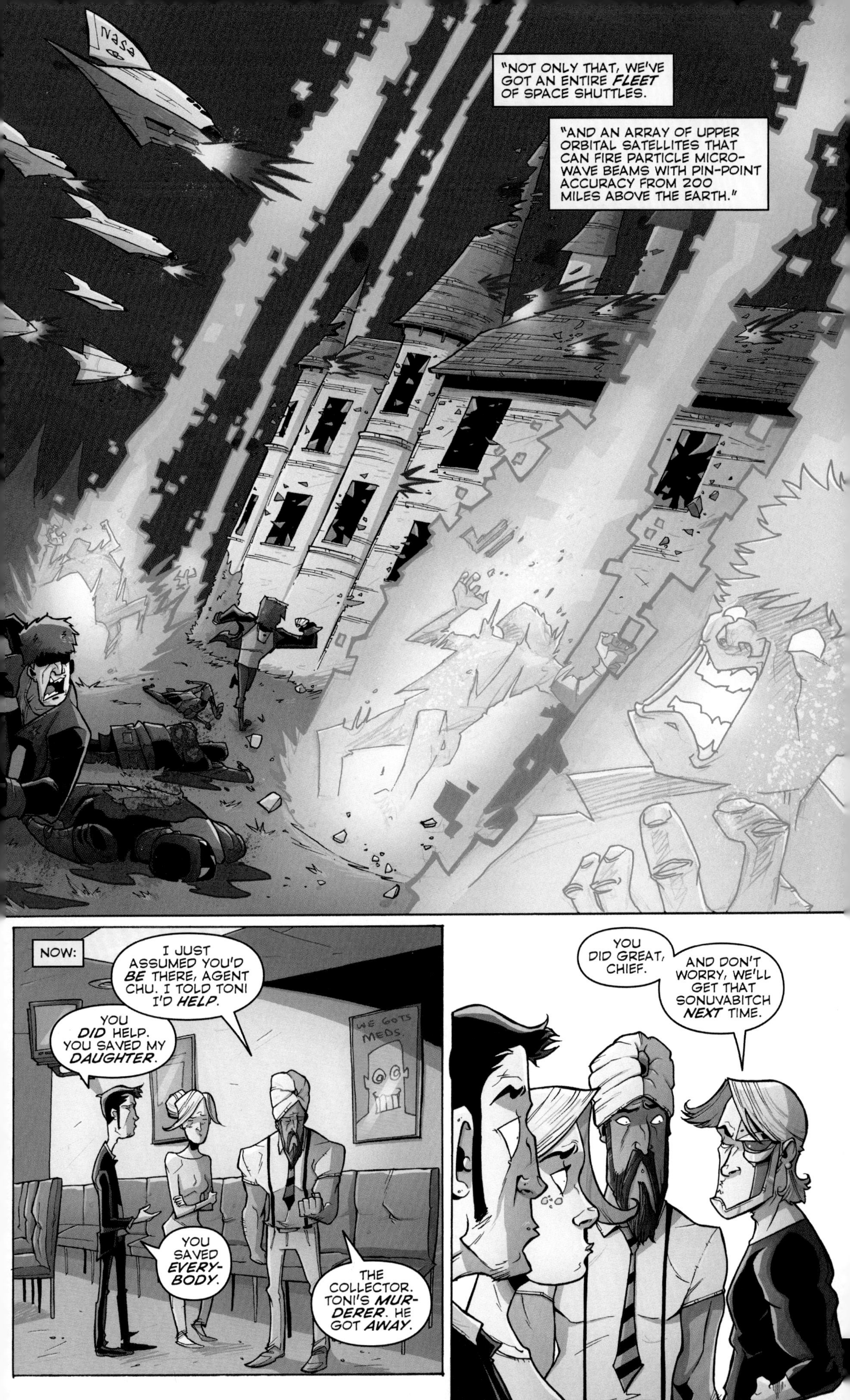
"NOT ONLY THAT, WE'VE GOT AN ENTIRE *FLEET* OF SPACE SHUTTLES.
"AND AN ARRAY OF UPPER ORBITAL SATELLITES THAT CAN FIRE PARTICLE MICRO-WAVE BEAMS WITH PIN-POINT ACCURACY FROM 200 MILES ABOVE THE EARTH."
NOW:
I JUST ASSUMED YOU'D *BE* THERE, AGENT CHU. I TOLD TONI I'D *HELP*.
YOU *DID* HELP. YOU SAVED MY *DAUGHTER*.
WE GOTS MEDS.
YOU SAVED *EVERY-BODY*.
THE COLLECTOR. TONI'S *MUR-DERER*. HE GOT *AWAY*.
YOU DID GREAT, CHIEF.
AND DON'T WORRY, WE'LL GET THAT SONUVABITCH *NEXT* TIME.

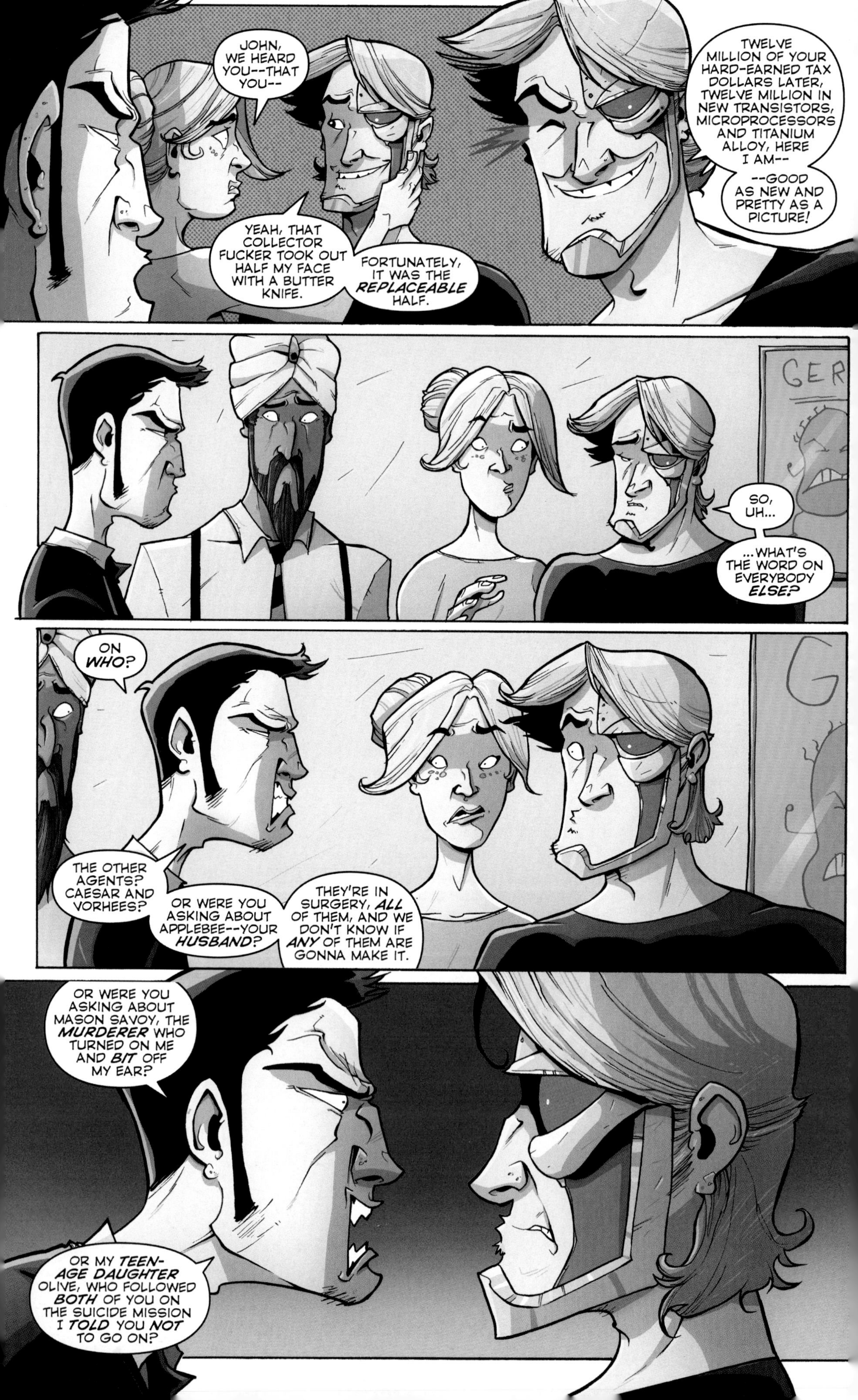
JOHN, WE HEARD YOU--THAT YOU--
YEAH, THAT COLLECTOR FUCKER TOOK OUT HALF MY FACE WITH A BUTTER KNIFE.
FORTUNATELY, IT WAS THE *REPLACEABLE* HALF.
TWELVE MILLION OF YOUR HARD-EARNED TAX DOLLARS LATER, TWELVE MILLION IN NEW TRANSISTORS, MICROPROCESSORS AND TITANIUM ALLOY, HERE I AM--
--GOOD AS NEW AND PRETTY AS A PICTURE!
GER
SO, UH...
...WHAT'S THE WORD ON EVERYBODY *ELSE?*
ON *WHO?*
THE OTHER AGENTS? CAESAR AND VORHEES?
OR WERE YOU ASKING ABOUT APPLEBEE--YOUR *HUSBAND?*
THEY'RE IN SURGERY, *ALL* OF THEM, AND WE DON'T KNOW IF *ANY* OF THEM ARE GONNA MAKE IT.
OR WERE YOU ASKING ABOUT MASON SAVOY, THE *MURDERER* WHO TURNED ON ME AND *BIT* OFF MY EAR?
OR MY *TEEN-AGE DAUGHTER* OLIVE, WHO FOLLOWED *BOTH* OF YOU ON THE SUICIDE MISSION I *TOLD* YOU *NOT* TO GO ON?

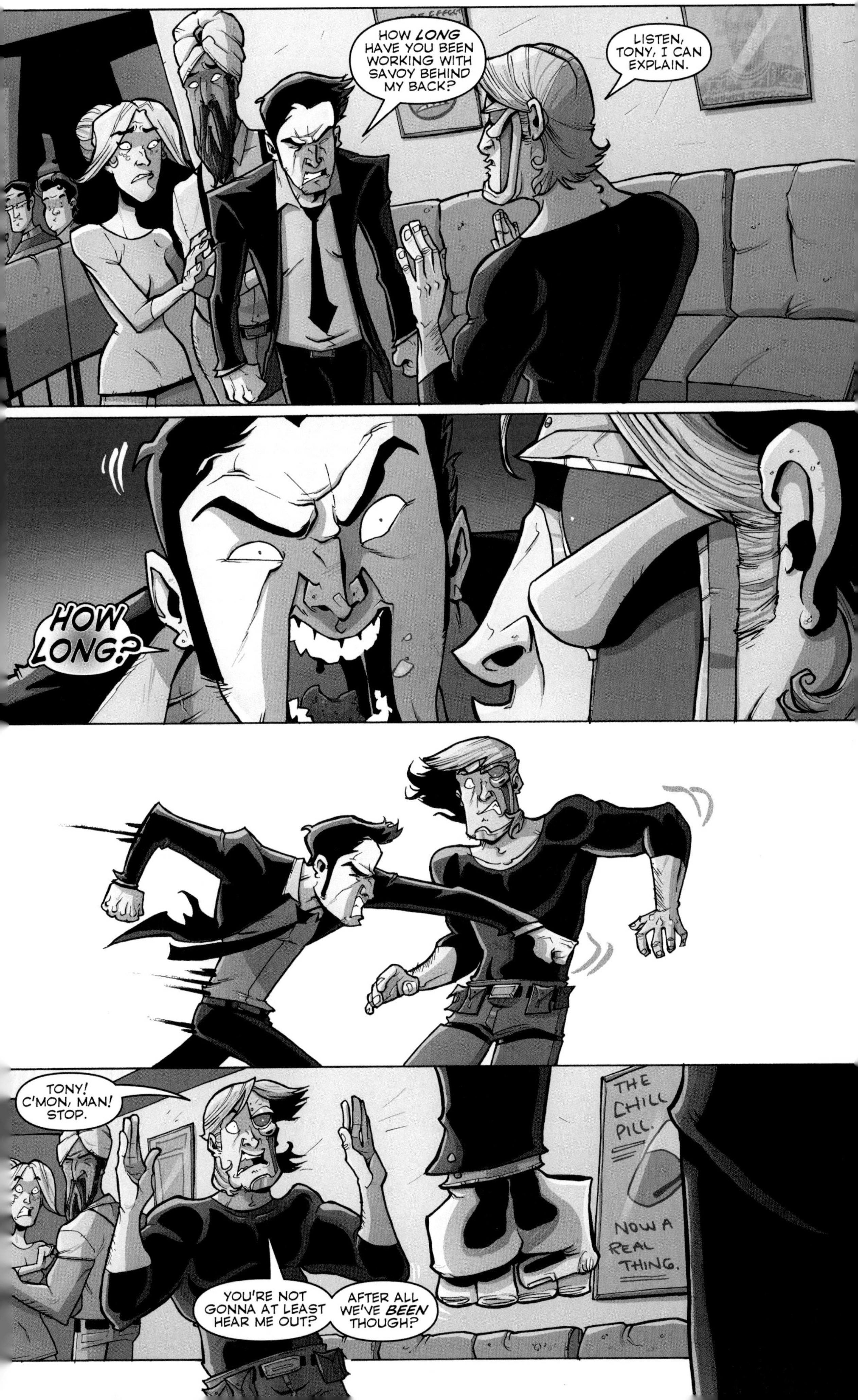
HOW *LONG* HAVE YOU BEEN WORKING WITH SAVOY BEHIND MY BACK?
LISTEN, TONY, I CAN EXPLAIN.
HOW LONG?
TONY! C'MON, MAN! STOP.
THE CHILL PILL. NOW A REAL THING.
YOU'RE NOT GONNA AT LEAST HEAR ME OUT?
AFTER ALL WE'VE *BEEN* THOUGH?

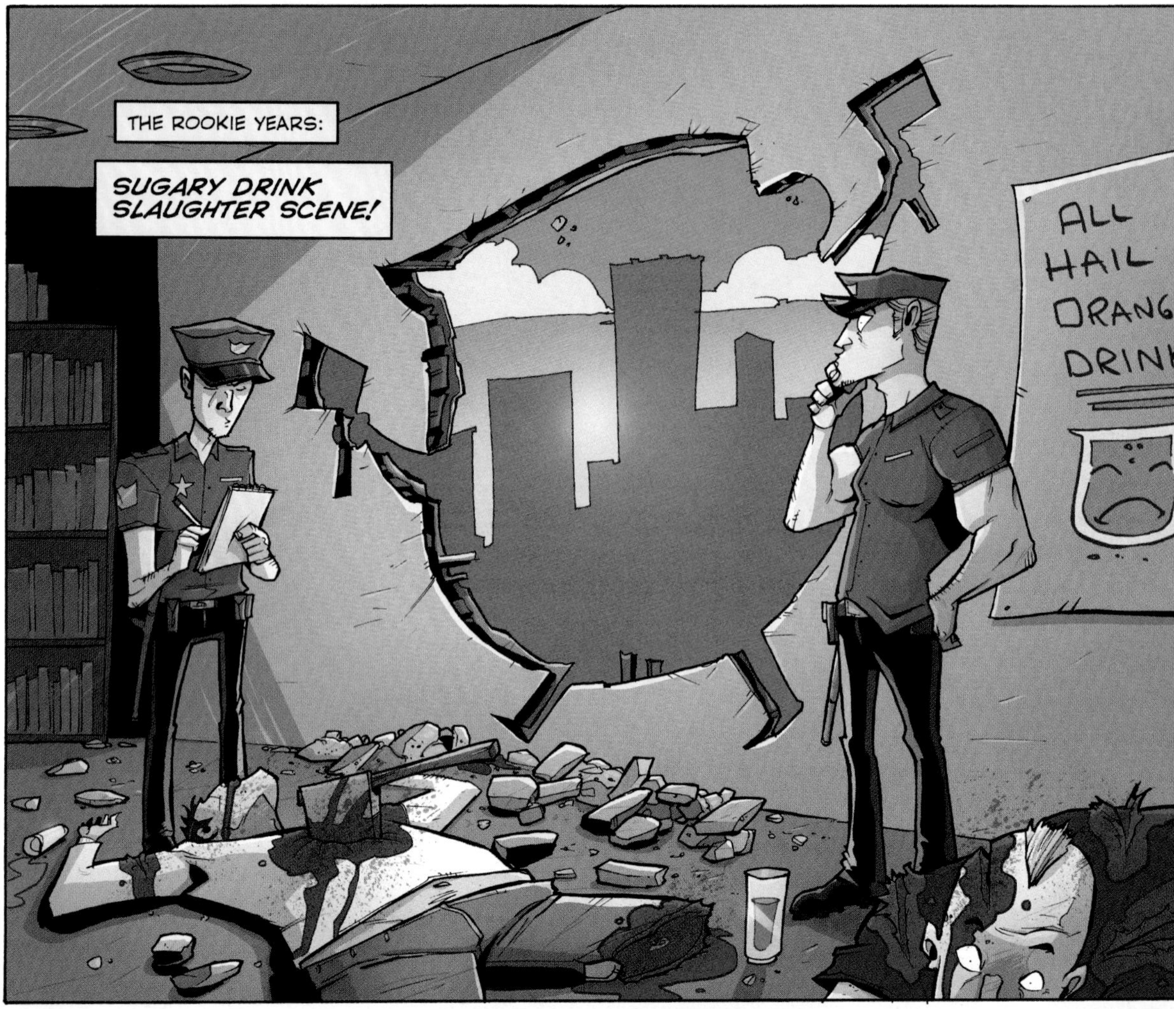
THE ROOKIE YEARS:
SUGARY DRINK SLAUGHTER SCENE!
ALL HAIL ORANGE DRINK.

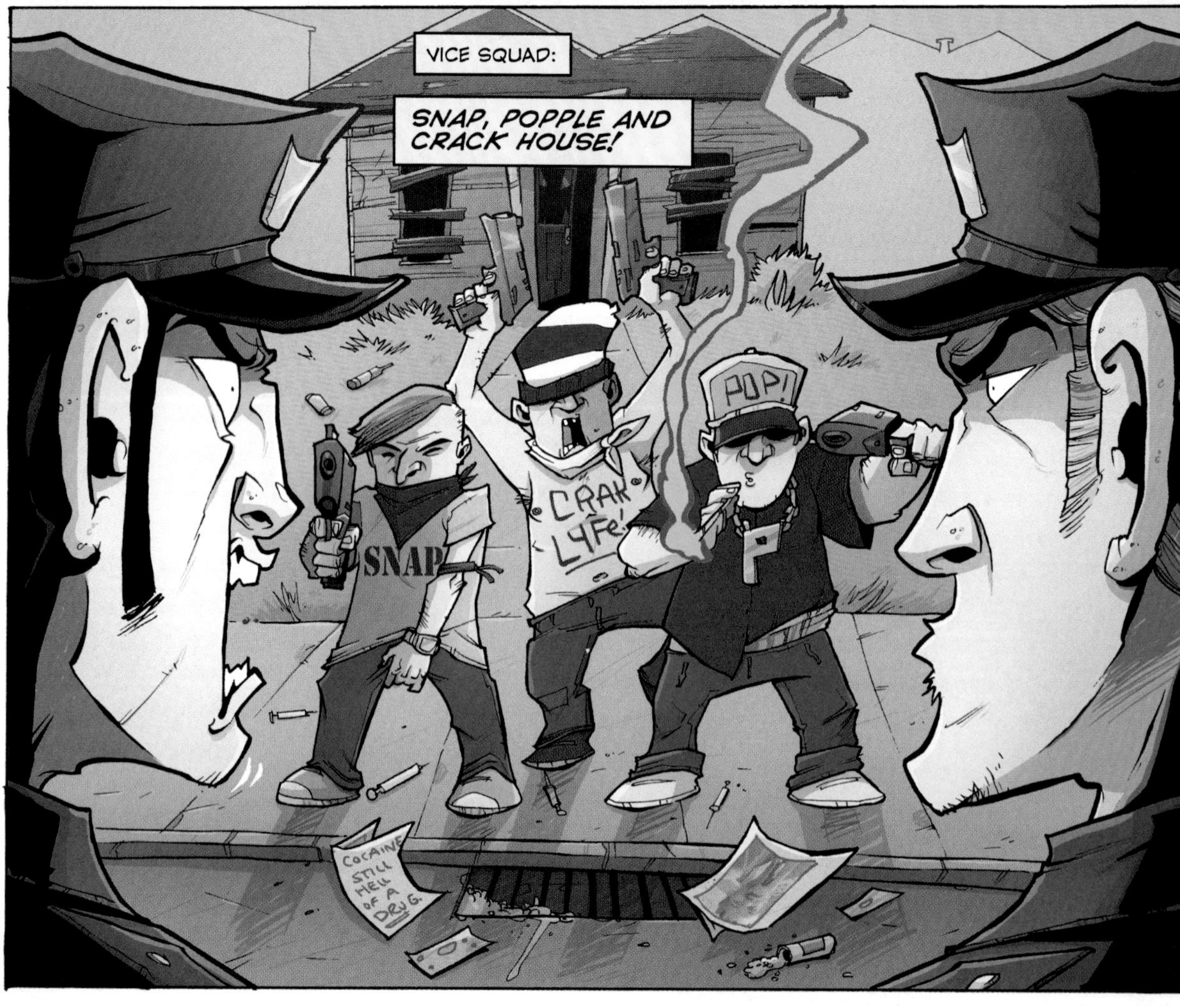
VICE SQUAD:
SNAP, POPPLE AND CRACK HOUSE!
SNAP
CRAK LYFE
POP!
P
COCAINE STILL HELL OF A DRUG.

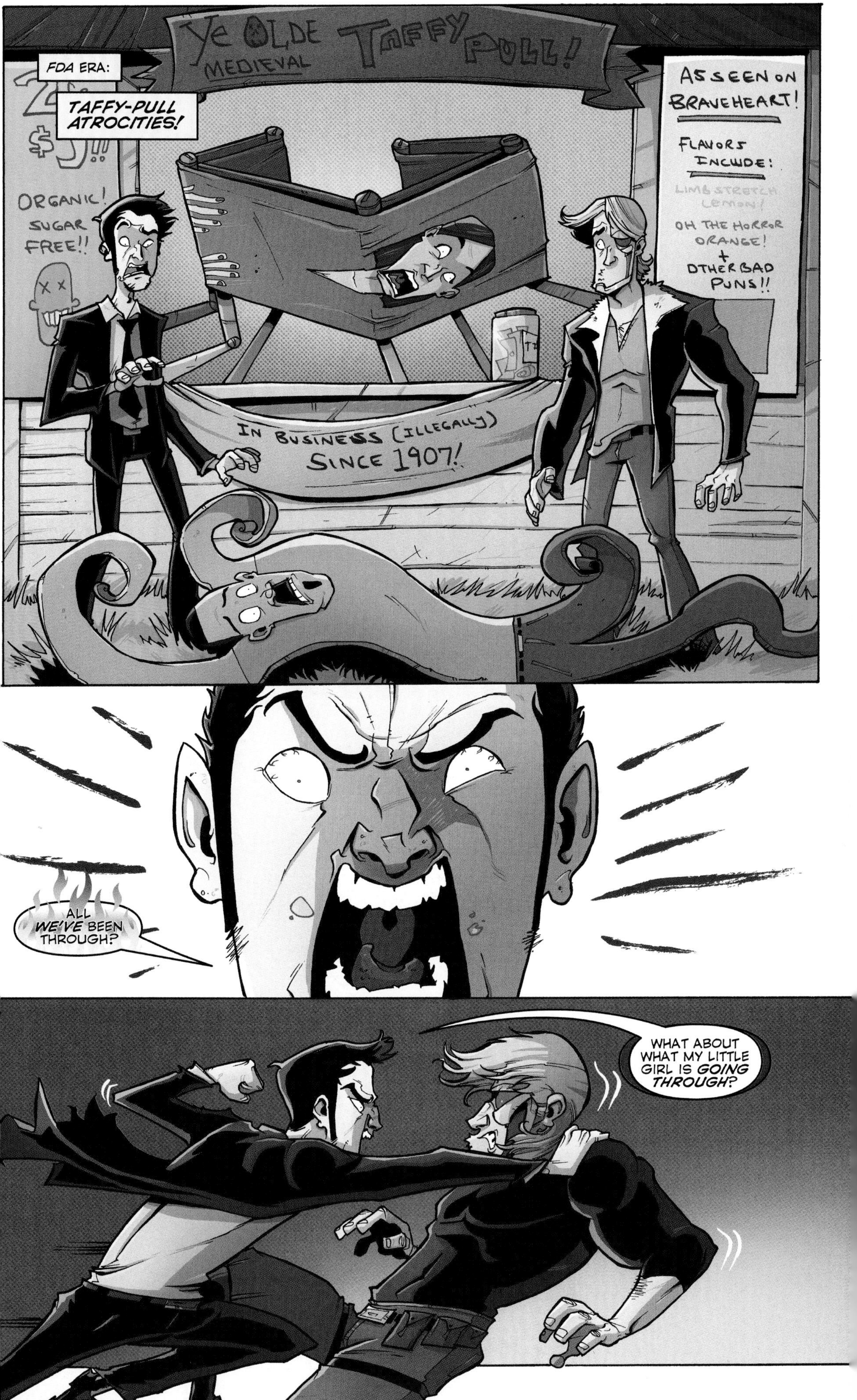
FDA ERA:
TAFFY-PULL ATROCITIES!
Ye OLDE MEDIEVAL TAFFY PULL!
ORGANIC! SUGAR FREE!!
AS SEEN ON BRAVEHEART!
FLAVORS INCLUDE:
LIMB STRETCH LEMON!
OH THE HORROR ORANGE!
+ OTHER BAD PUNS!!
IN BUSINESS (ILLEGALLY) SINCE 1907!
ALL *WE'VE* BEEN THROUGH?
WHAT ABOUT WHAT MY LITTLE GIRL IS *GOING THROUGH*?

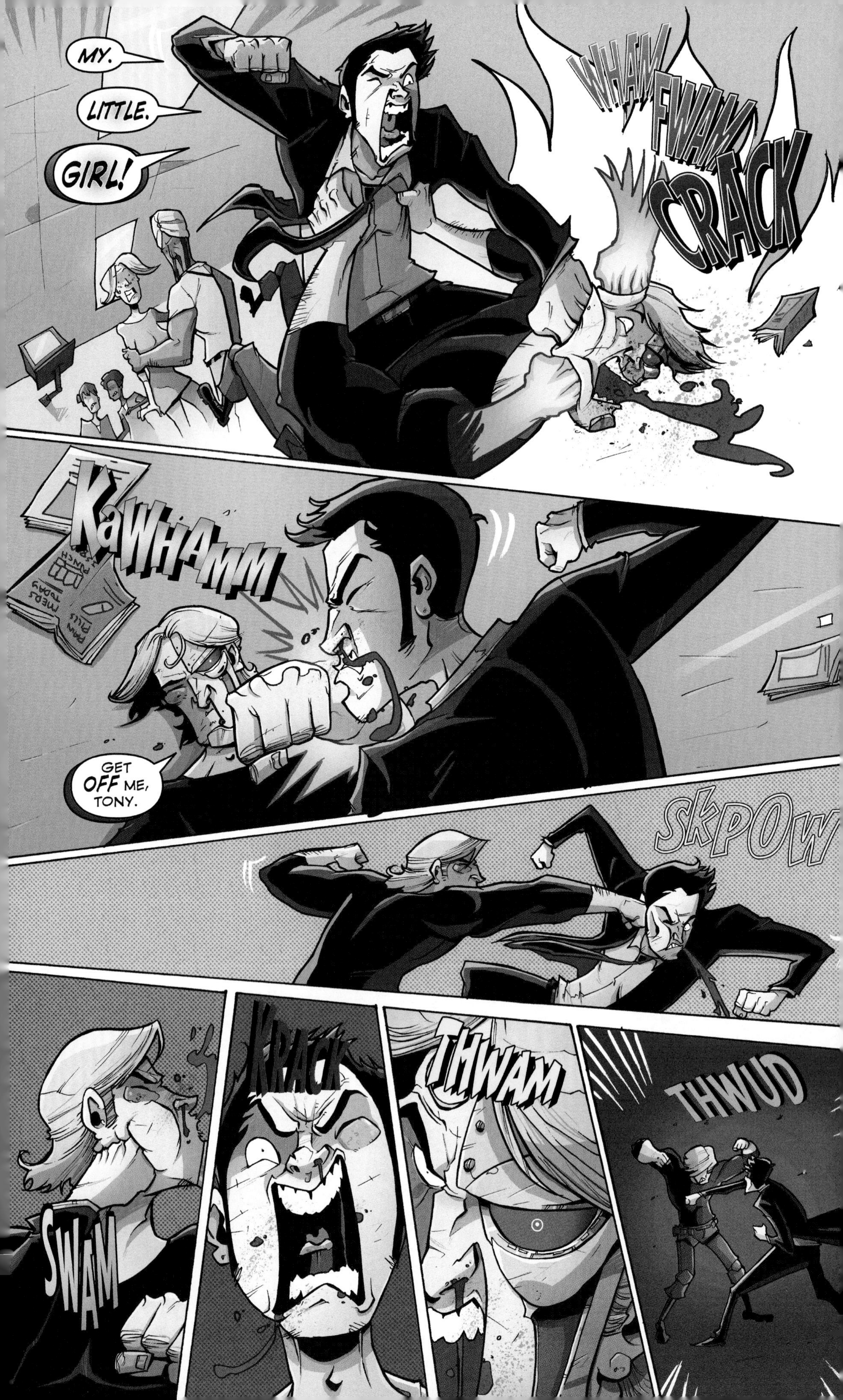
MY.
LITTLE.
GIRL!
WHAM
FWAM
CRACK
KaWHAMM
GET OFF ME, TONY.
SKPOW
SWAM
KRACK
THWAM
THWUD

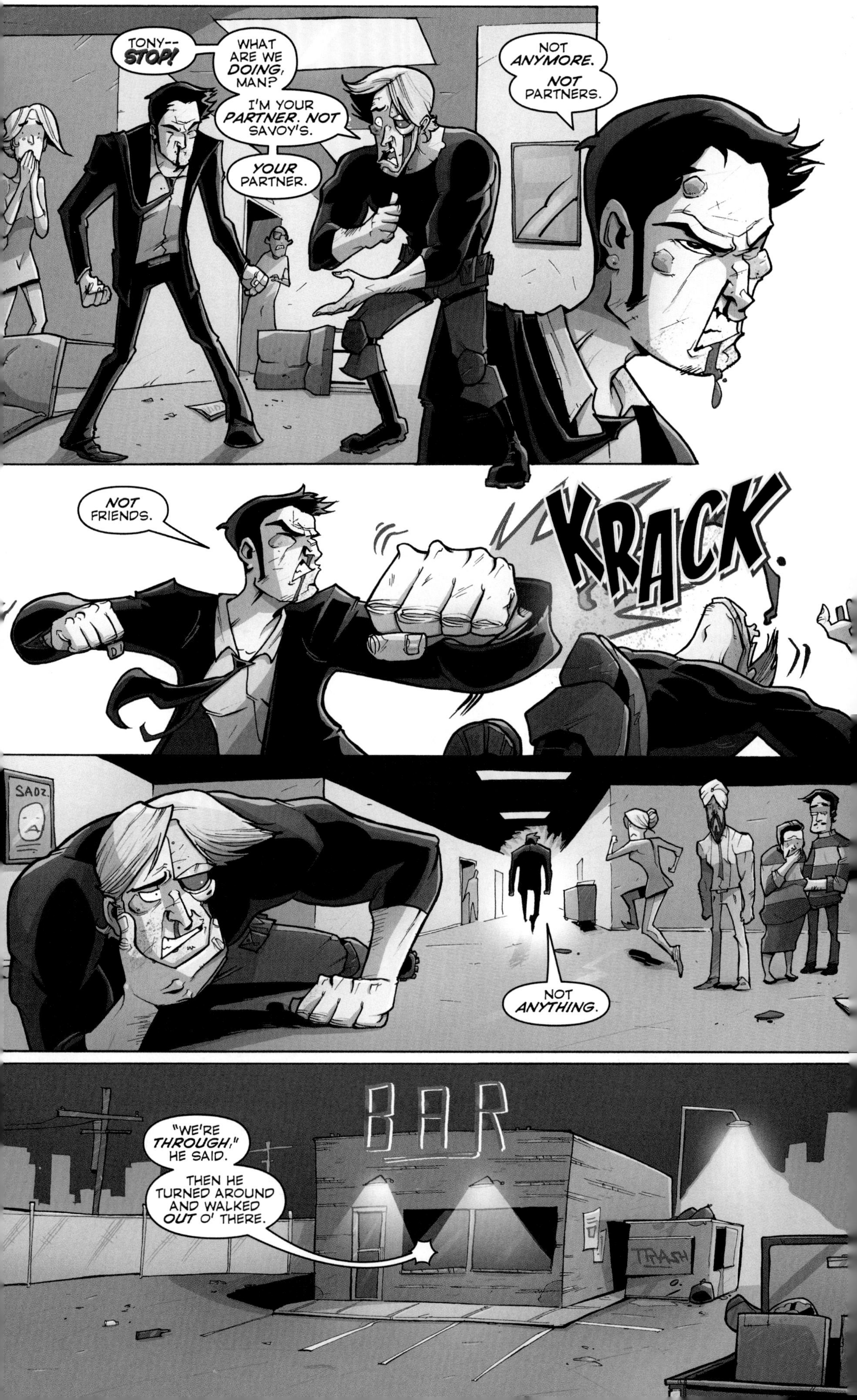
TONY-- STOP!
WHAT ARE WE DOING, MAN?
I'M YOUR PARTNER. NOT SAVOY'S.
YOUR PARTNER.
NOT ANYMORE.
NOT PARTNERS.
NOT FRIENDS.
KRACK.
SAOZ.
NOT ANYTHING.
BAR
"WE'RE THROUGH," HE SAID.
THEN HE TURNED AROUND AND WALKED OUT O' THERE.
TRASH

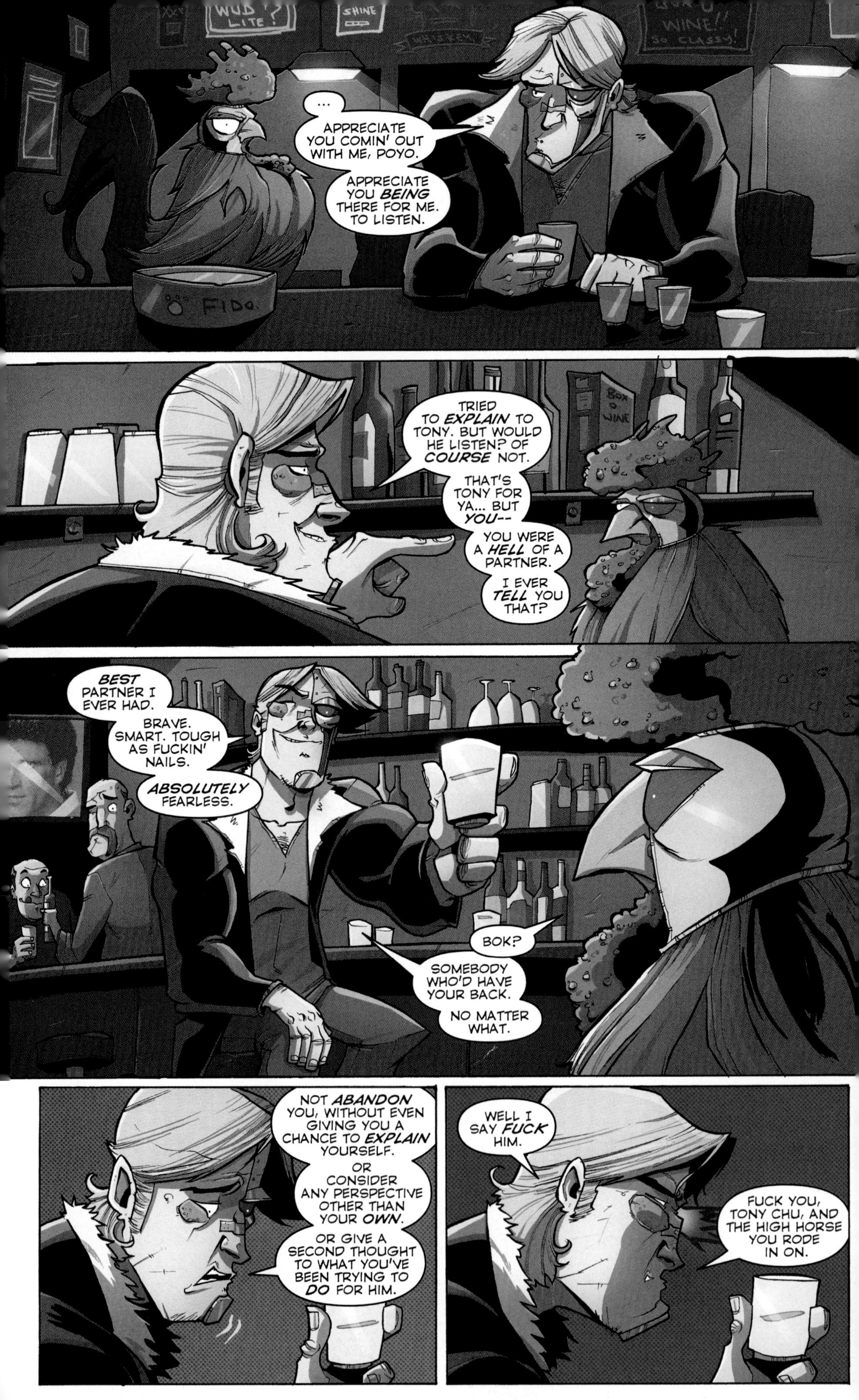

WUD? LITE
SHINE
WINE!! SO CLASSY!
FIDO
...
APPRECIATE YOU COMIN' OUT WITH ME, POYO.
APPRECIATE YOU *BEING* THERE FOR ME. TO LISTEN.
BOX O WINE
TRIED TO *EXPLAIN* TO TONY. BUT WOULD HE LISTEN? OF *COURSE* NOT.
THAT'S TONY FOR YA... BUT *YOU*--
YOU WERE A *HELL* OF A PARTNER.
I EVER *TELL* YOU THAT?
BEST PARTNER I EVER HAD.
BRAVE. SMART. TOUGH AS FUCKIN' NAILS.
ABSOLUTELY FEARLESS.
BOK?
SOMEBODY WHO'D HAVE YOUR BACK.
NO MATTER WHAT.
NOT *ABANDON* YOU, WITHOUT EVEN GIVING YOU A CHANCE TO *EXPLAIN* YOURSELF.
OR CONSIDER ANY PERSPECTIVE OTHER THAN YOUR *OWN*.
OR GIVE A SECOND THOUGHT TO WHAT YOU'VE BEEN TRYING TO *DO* FOR HIM.
WELL I SAY *FUCK* HIM.
FUCK YOU, TONY CHU, AND THE HIGH HORSE YOU RODE IN ON.

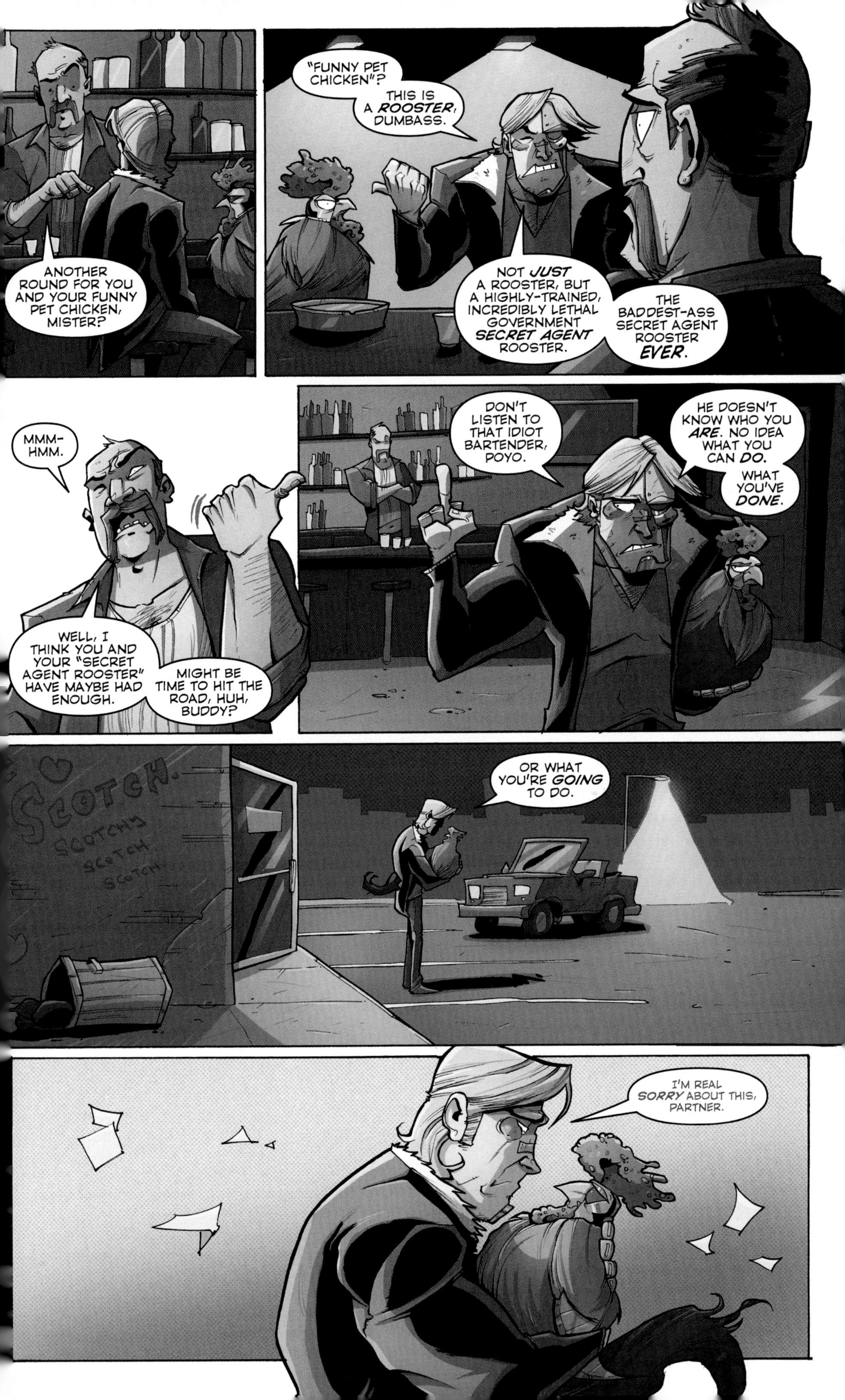
ANOTHER ROUND FOR YOU AND YOUR FUNNY PET CHICKEN, MISTER?
"FUNNY PET CHICKEN"?
THIS IS A ROOSTER, DUMBASS.
NOT JUST A ROOSTER, BUT A HIGHLY-TRAINED, INCREDIBLY LETHAL GOVERNMENT SECRET AGENT ROOSTER.
THE BADDEST-ASS SECRET AGENT ROOSTER EVER.
MMM-HMM.
WELL, I THINK YOU AND YOUR "SECRET AGENT ROOSTER" HAVE MAYBE HAD ENOUGH.
MIGHT BE TIME TO HIT THE ROAD, HUH, BUDDY?
DON'T LISTEN TO THAT IDIOT BARTENDER, POYO.
HE DOESN'T KNOW WHO YOU ARE. NO IDEA WHAT YOU CAN DO.
WHAT YOU'VE DONE.
SCOTCH
SCOTCH
SCOTCH
SCOTCH
OR WHAT YOU'RE GOING TO DO.
I'M REAL SORRY ABOUT THIS, PARTNER.

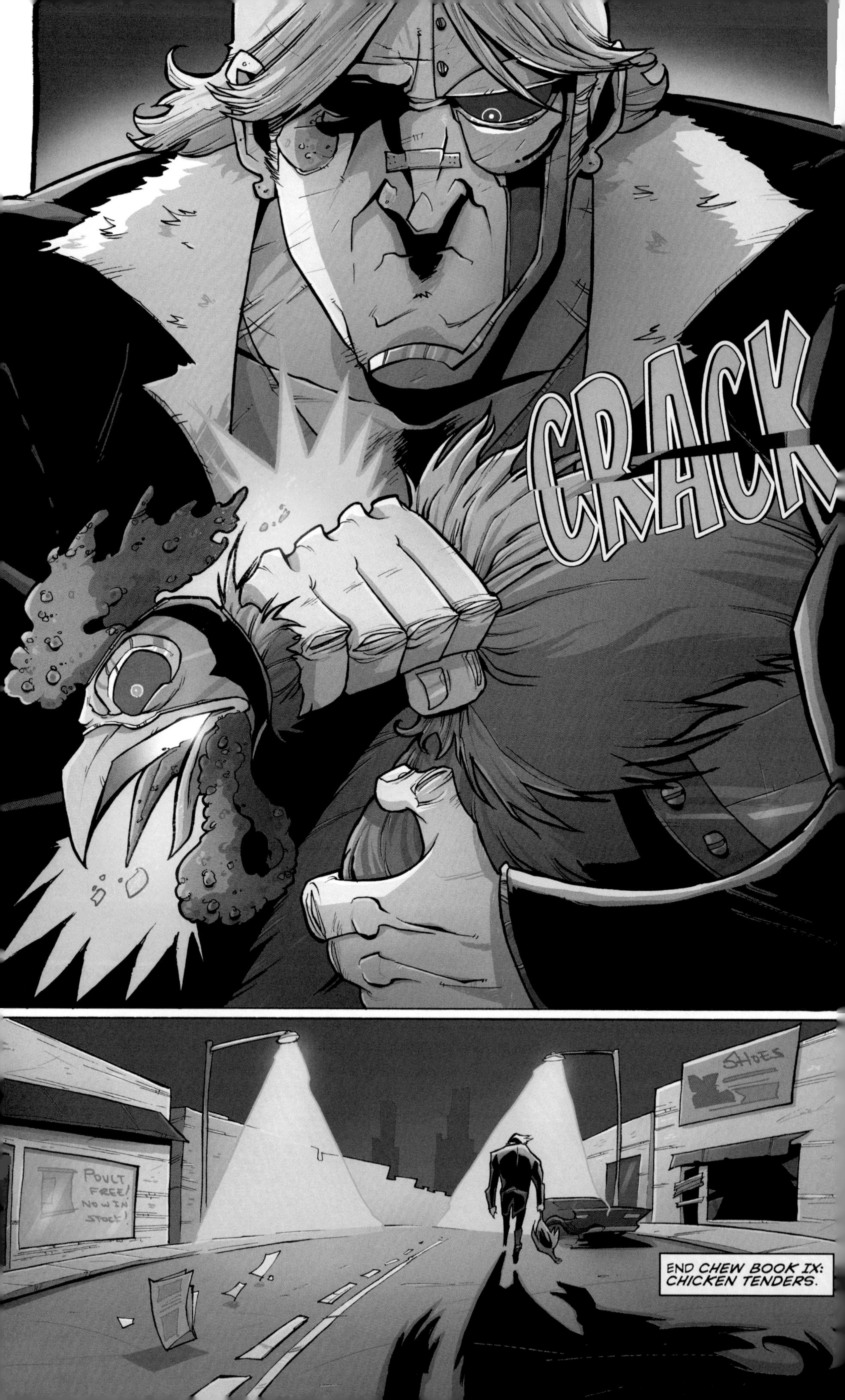
CRACK
SHOES
POULT FREE! NOW IN STOCK!
END CHEW BOOK IX: CHICKEN TENDERS.

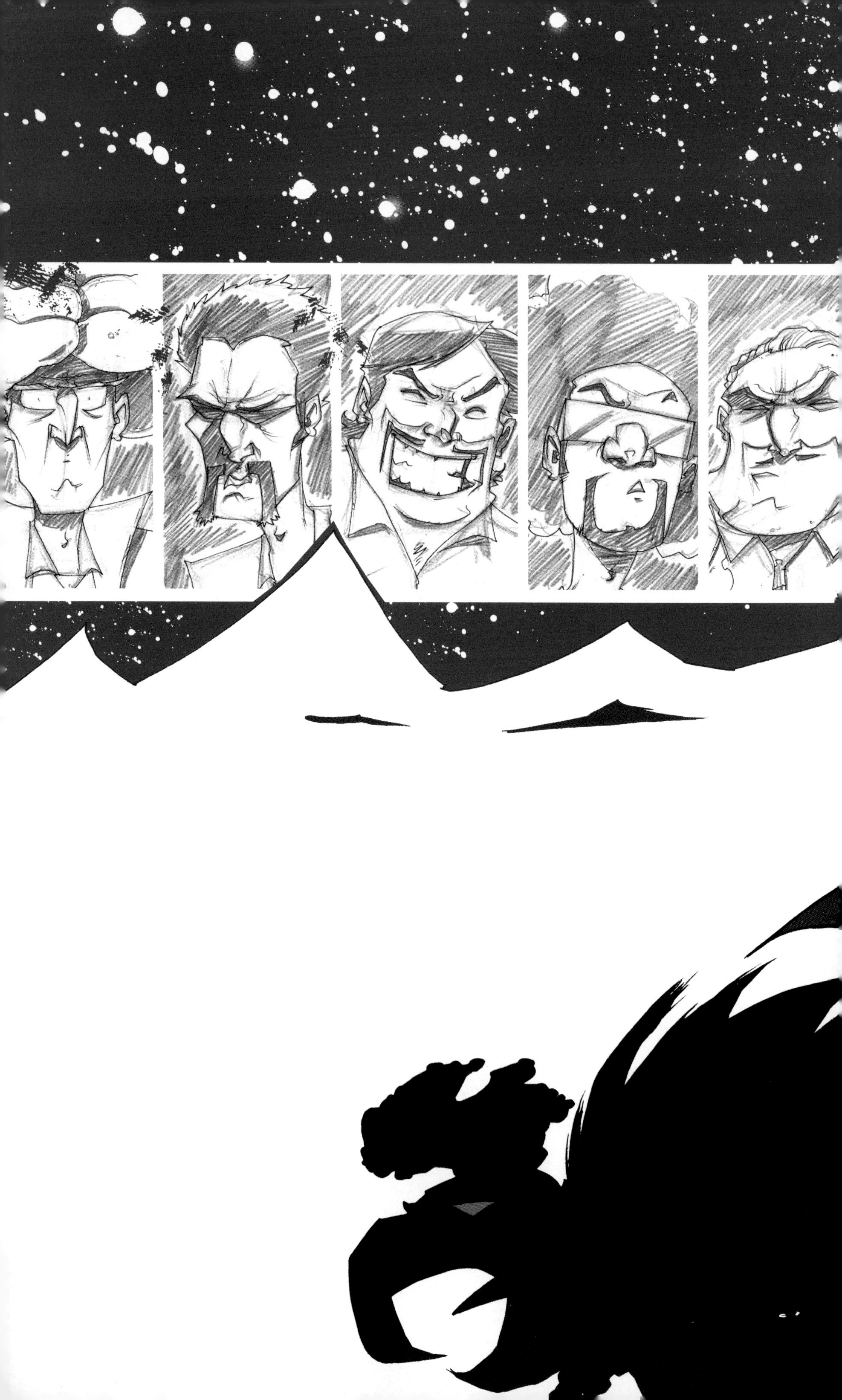

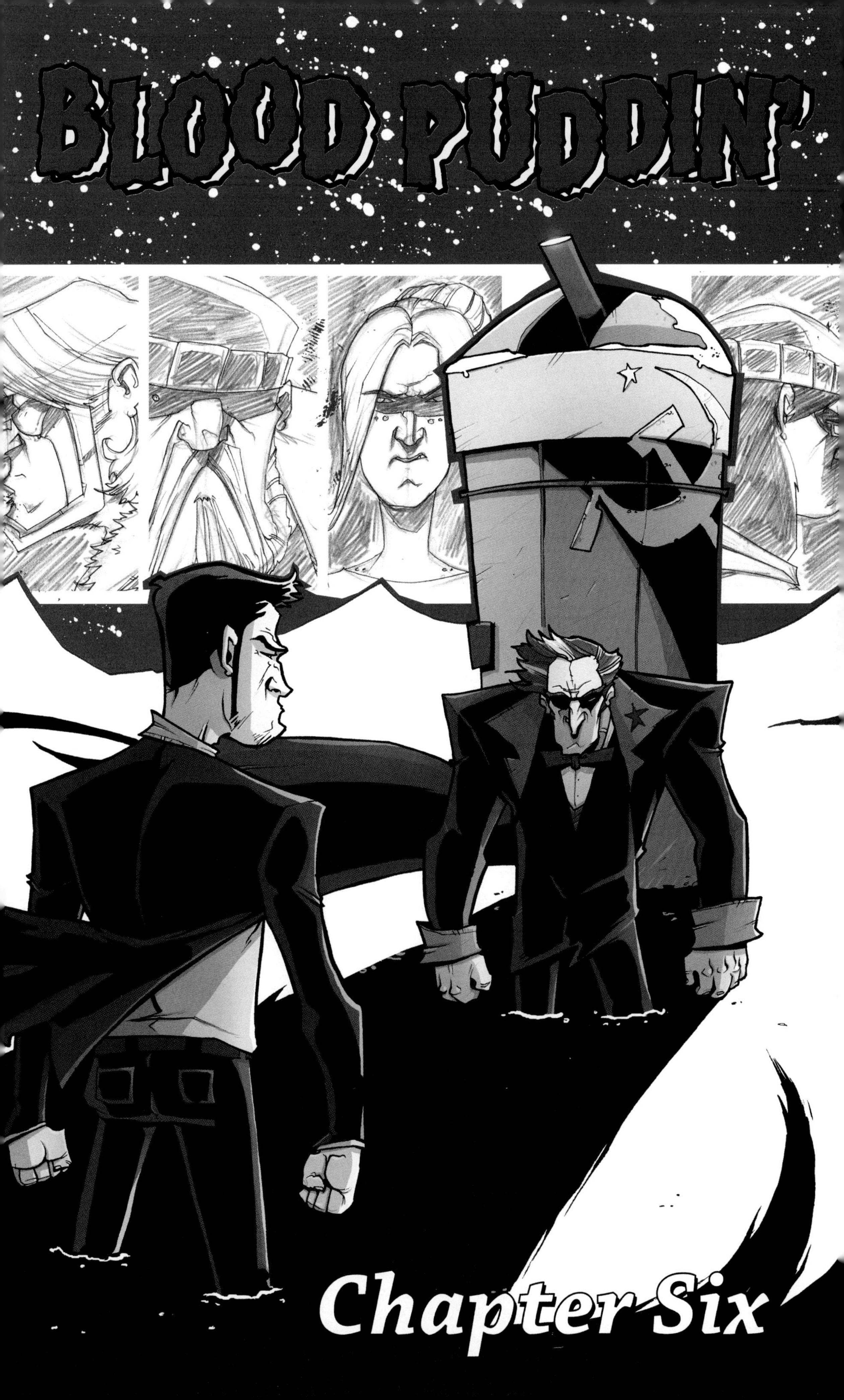
BLOOD PUDDIN'
Chapter Six

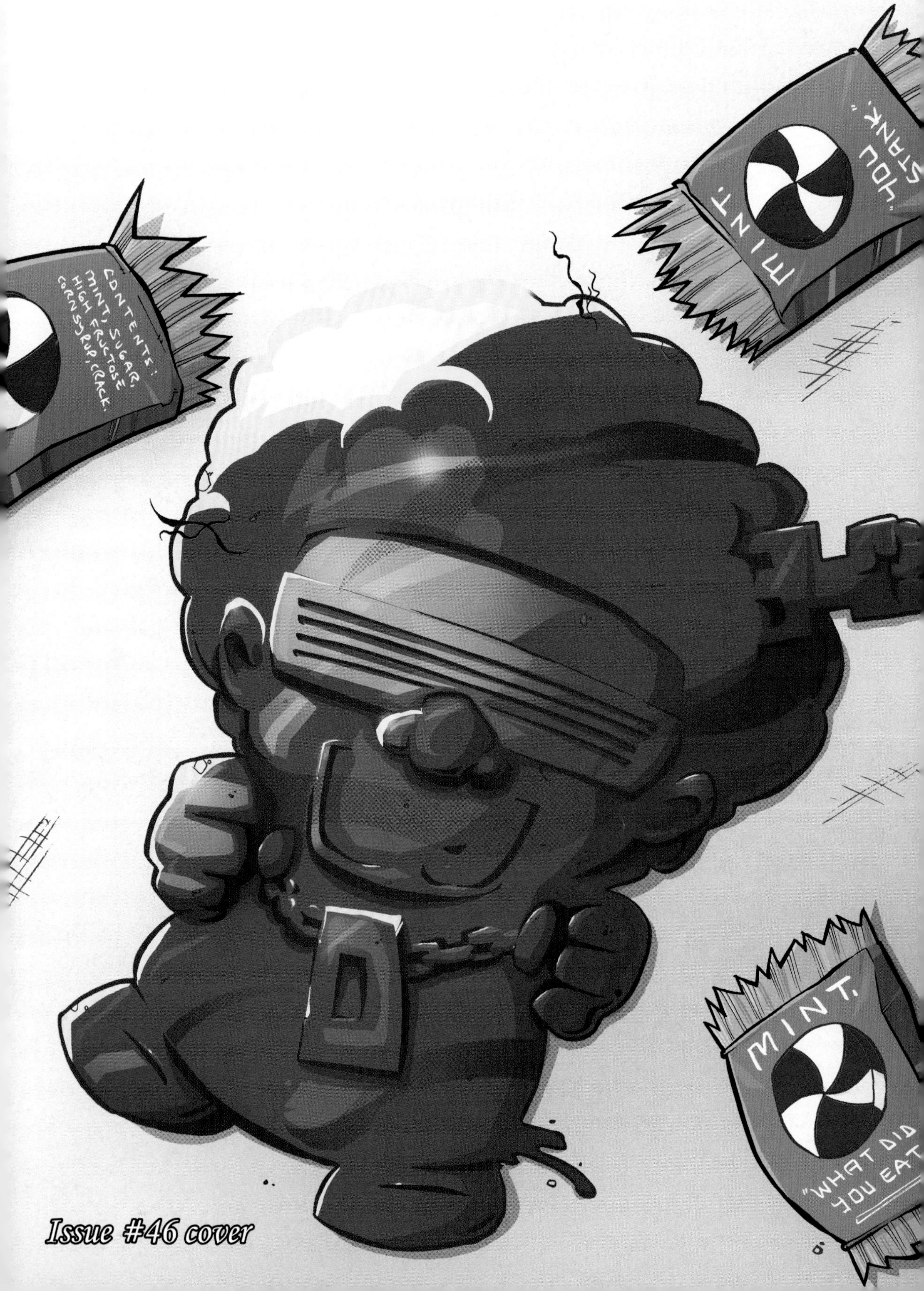
CONTENTS: MINT, SUGAR, HIGH FRUCTOSE CORNSYRUP, CRACK.
MINT.
"YOU STANK."
MINT.
"WHAT DID YOU EAT

Issue #46 cover

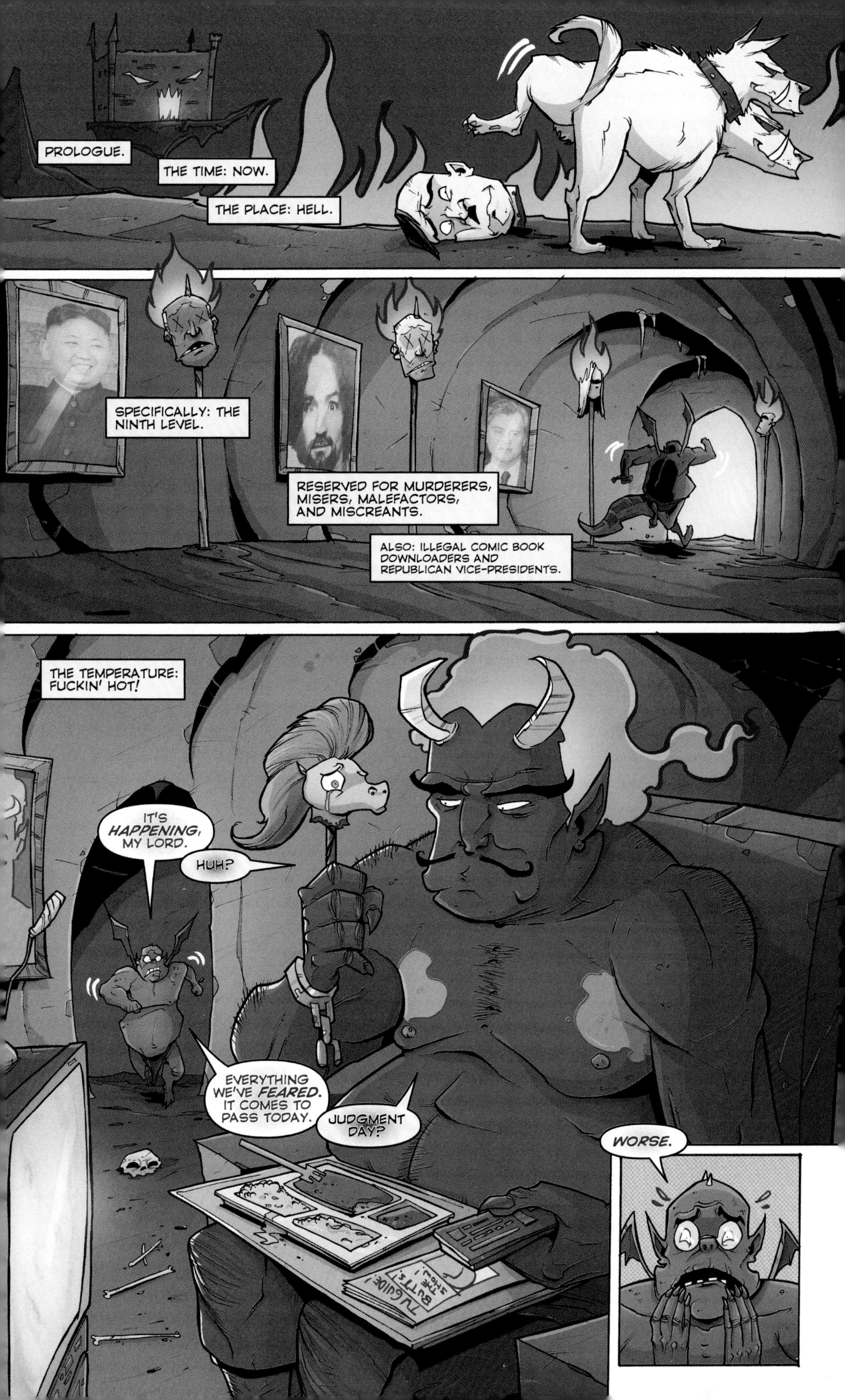
PROLOGUE.
THE TIME: NOW.
THE PLACE: HELL.
SPECIFICALLY: THE NINTH LEVEL.
RESERVED FOR MURDERERS, MISERS, MALEFACTORS, AND MISCREANTS.
ALSO: ILLEGAL COMIC BOOK DOWNLOADERS AND REPUBLICAN VICE-PRESIDENTS.
THE TEMPERATURE: FUCKIN' HOT!
IT'S *HAPPENING*, MY LORD.
HUH?
EVERYTHING WE'VE *FEARED*. IT COMES TO PASS TODAY.
JUDGMENT DAY?
WORSE.
TV GUIDE!
BUTTS!
THE SHOW!

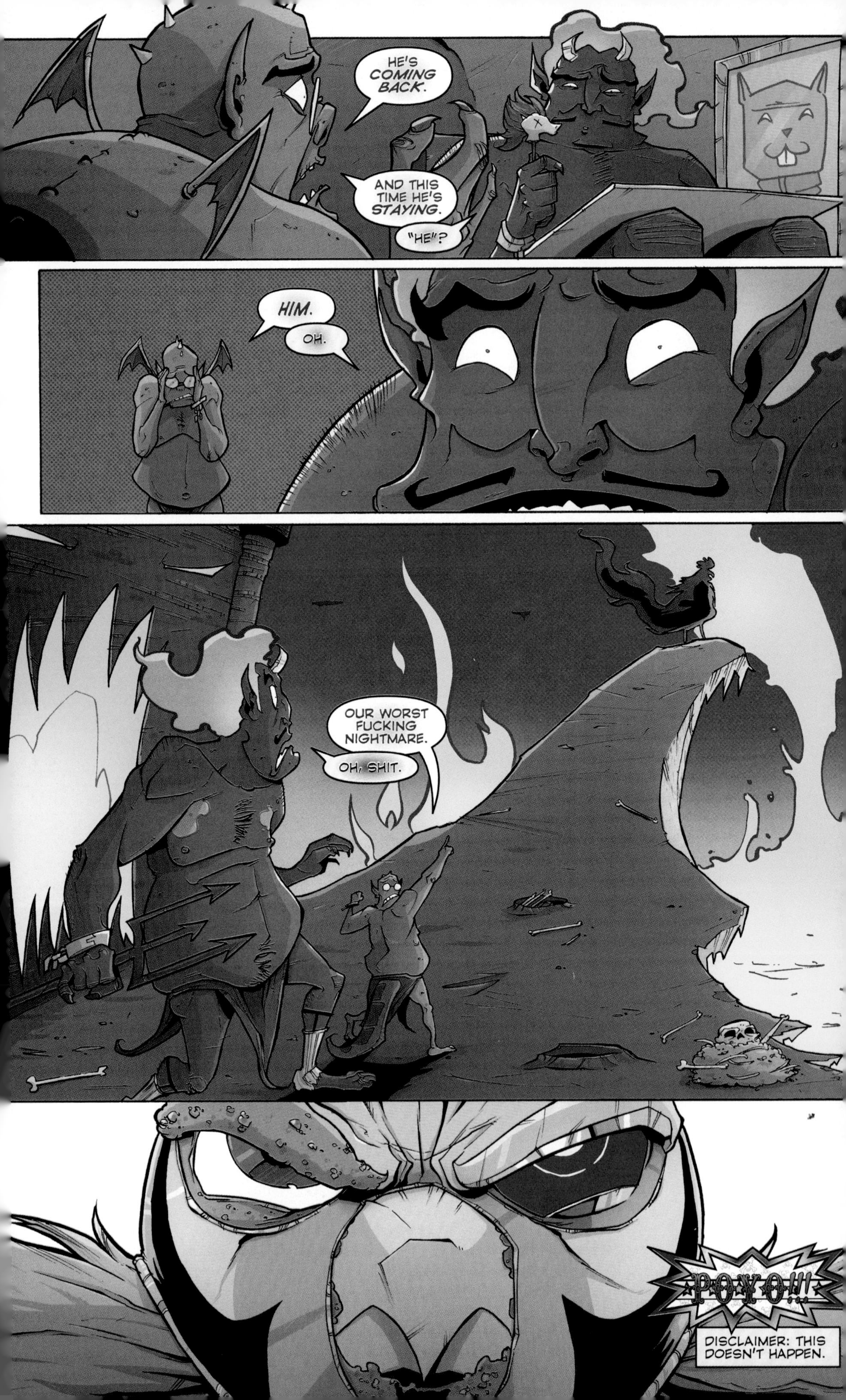
HE'S COMING BACK.
AND THIS TIME HE'S STAYING.
"HE"?
HIM.
OH.
OUR WORST FUCKING NIGHTMARE.
OH, SHIT.
POYO!!!
DISCLAIMER: THIS DOESN'T HAPPEN.

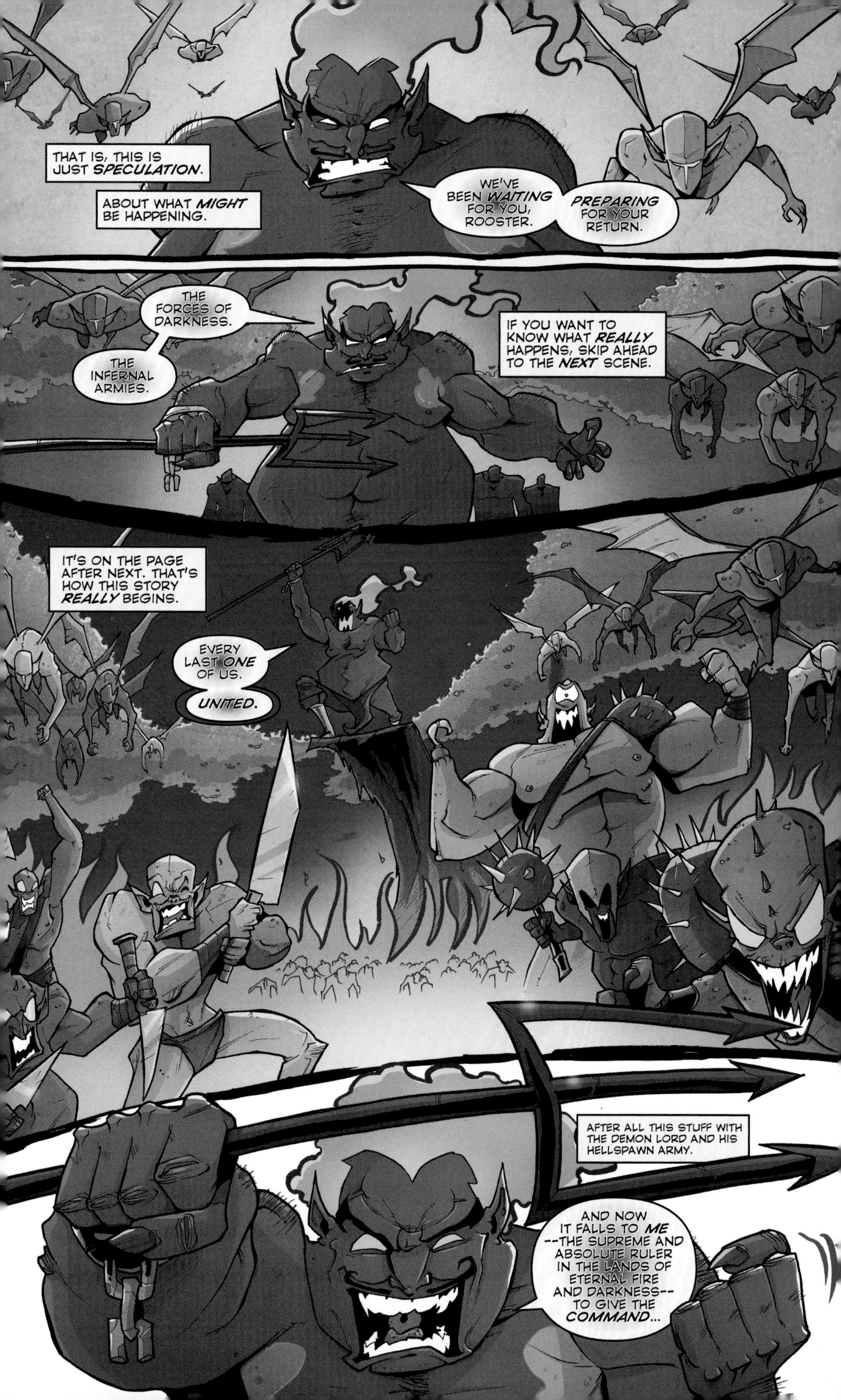
THAT IS, THIS IS JUST SPECULATION.
ABOUT WHAT MIGHT BE HAPPENING.
WE'VE BEEN WAITING FOR YOU, ROOSTER.
PREPARING FOR YOUR RETURN.
THE FORCES OF DARKNESS.
THE INFERNAL ARMIES.
IF YOU WANT TO KNOW WHAT REALLY HAPPENS, SKIP AHEAD TO THE NEXT SCENE.
IT'S ON THE PAGE AFTER NEXT. THAT'S HOW THIS STORY REALLY BEGINS.
EVERY LAST ONE OF US.
UNITED.
AFTER ALL THIS STUFF WITH THE DEMON LORD AND HIS HELLSPAWN ARMY.
AND NOW IT FALLS TO ME --THE SUPREME AND ABSOLUTE RULER IN THE LANDS OF ETERNAL FIRE AND DARKNESS-- TO GIVE THE COMMAND...

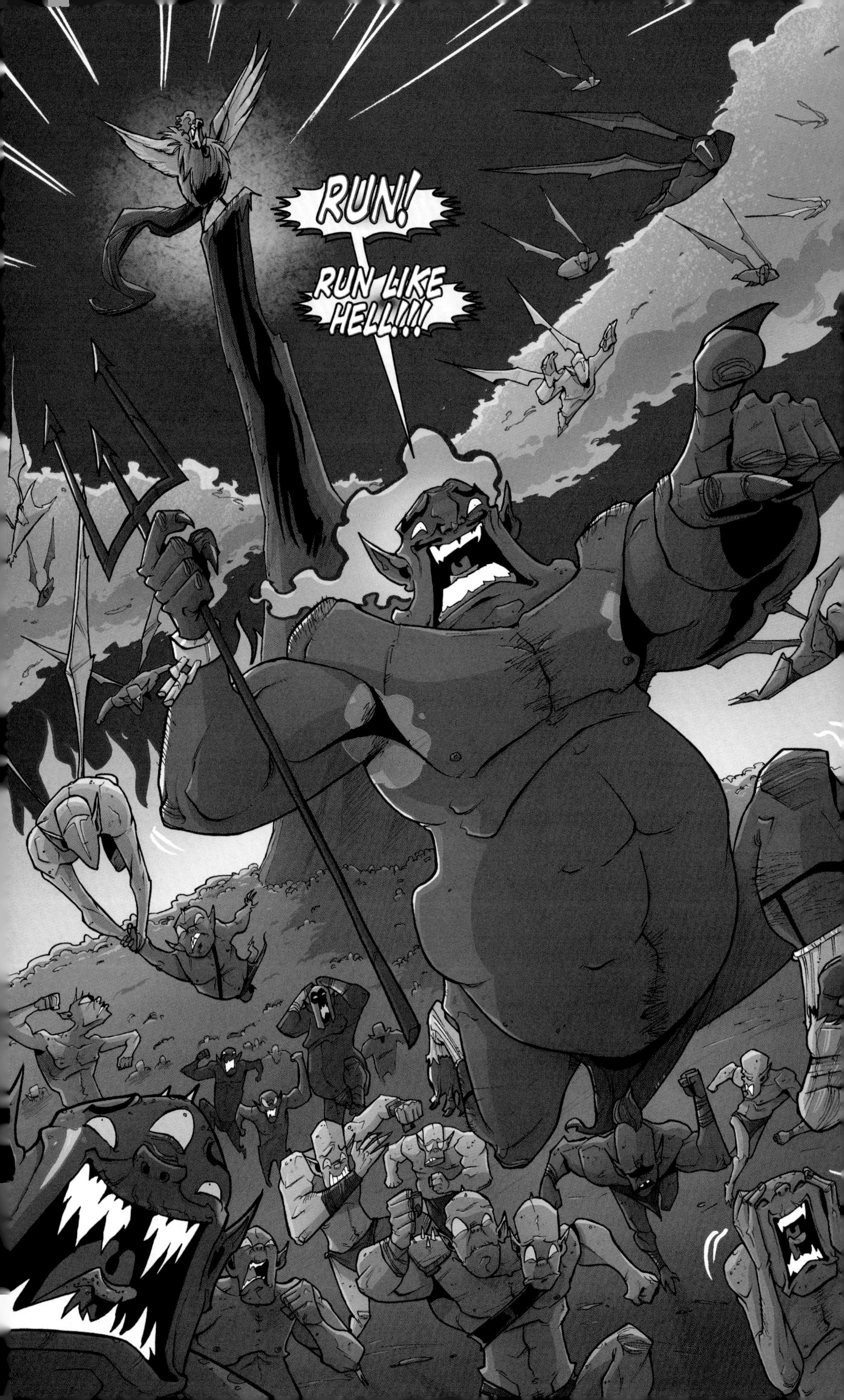
RUN!
RUN LIKE HELL!!!

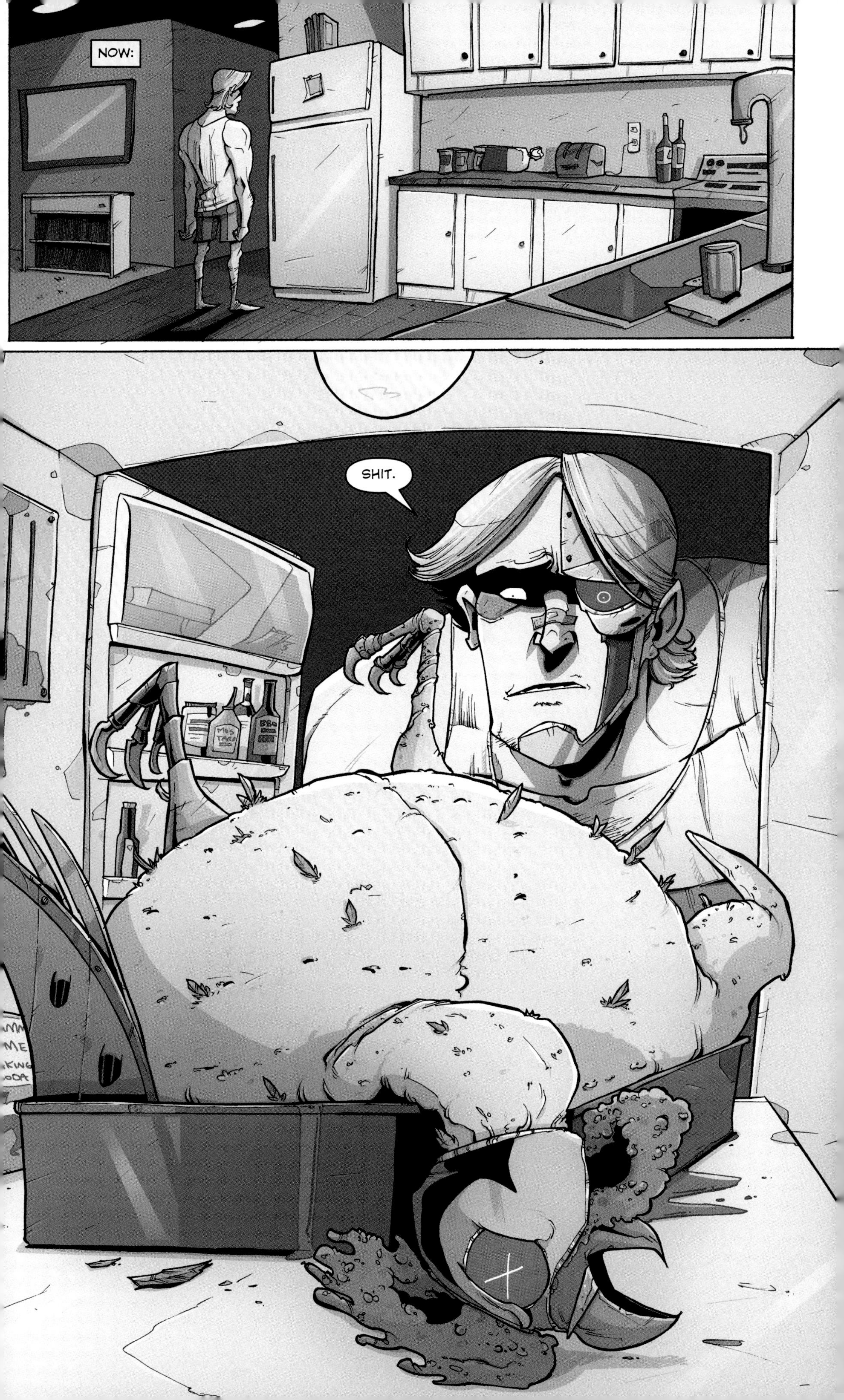
NOW:
SHIT.

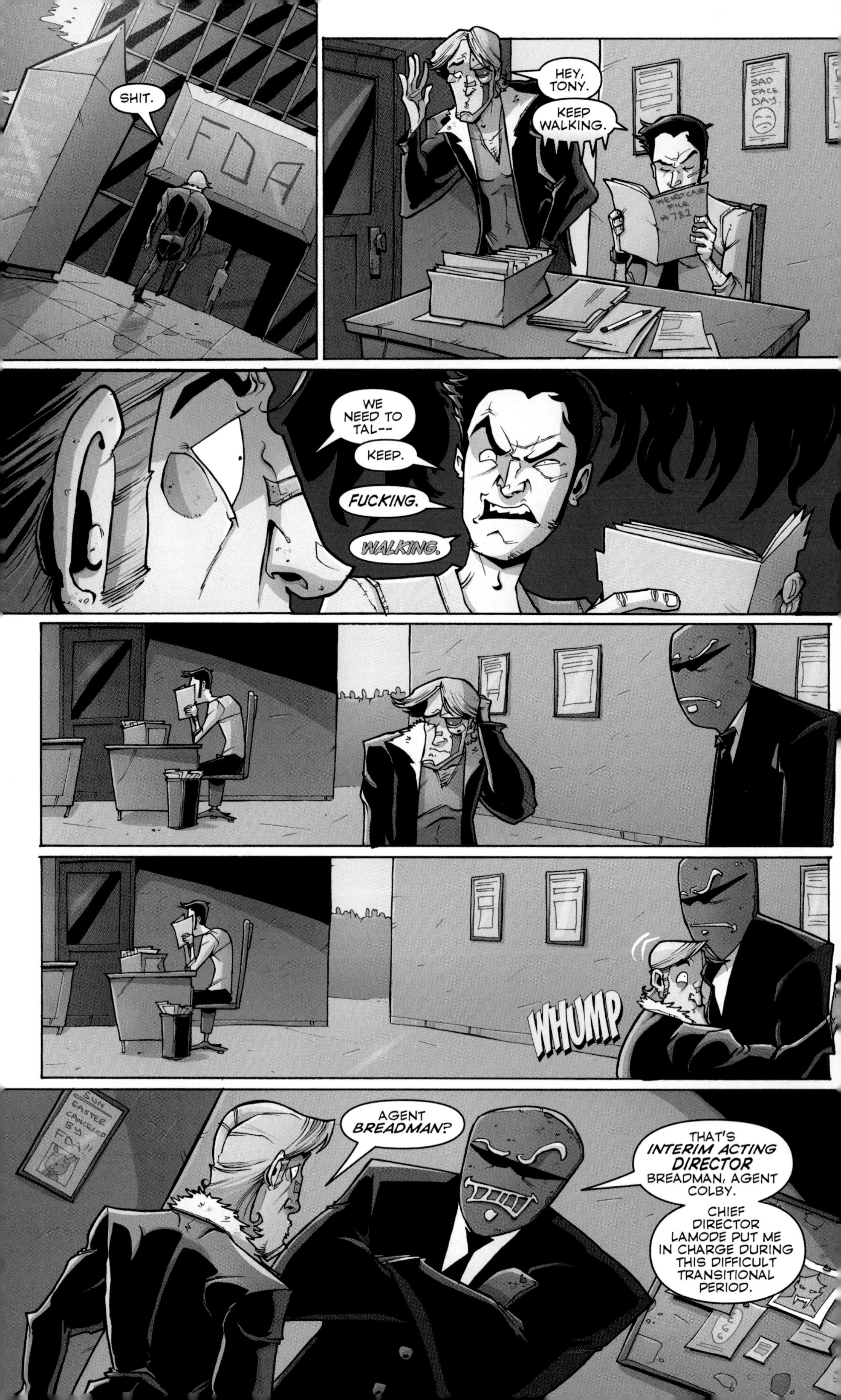
FDA
SHIT.
HEY, TONY.
KEEP WALKING.
SAD FACE DAY.
WEIRD CASE FILE #781
WE NEED TO TAL--
KEEP.
FUCKING.
WALKING.
WHUMP
SUN
EASTER CANCELLED BY FDA!!
AGENT BREADMAN?
THAT'S INTERIM ACTING DIRECTOR BREADMAN, AGENT COLBY.
CHIEF DIRECTOR LAMODE PUT ME IN CHARGE DURING THIS DIFFICULT TRANSITIONAL PERIOD.

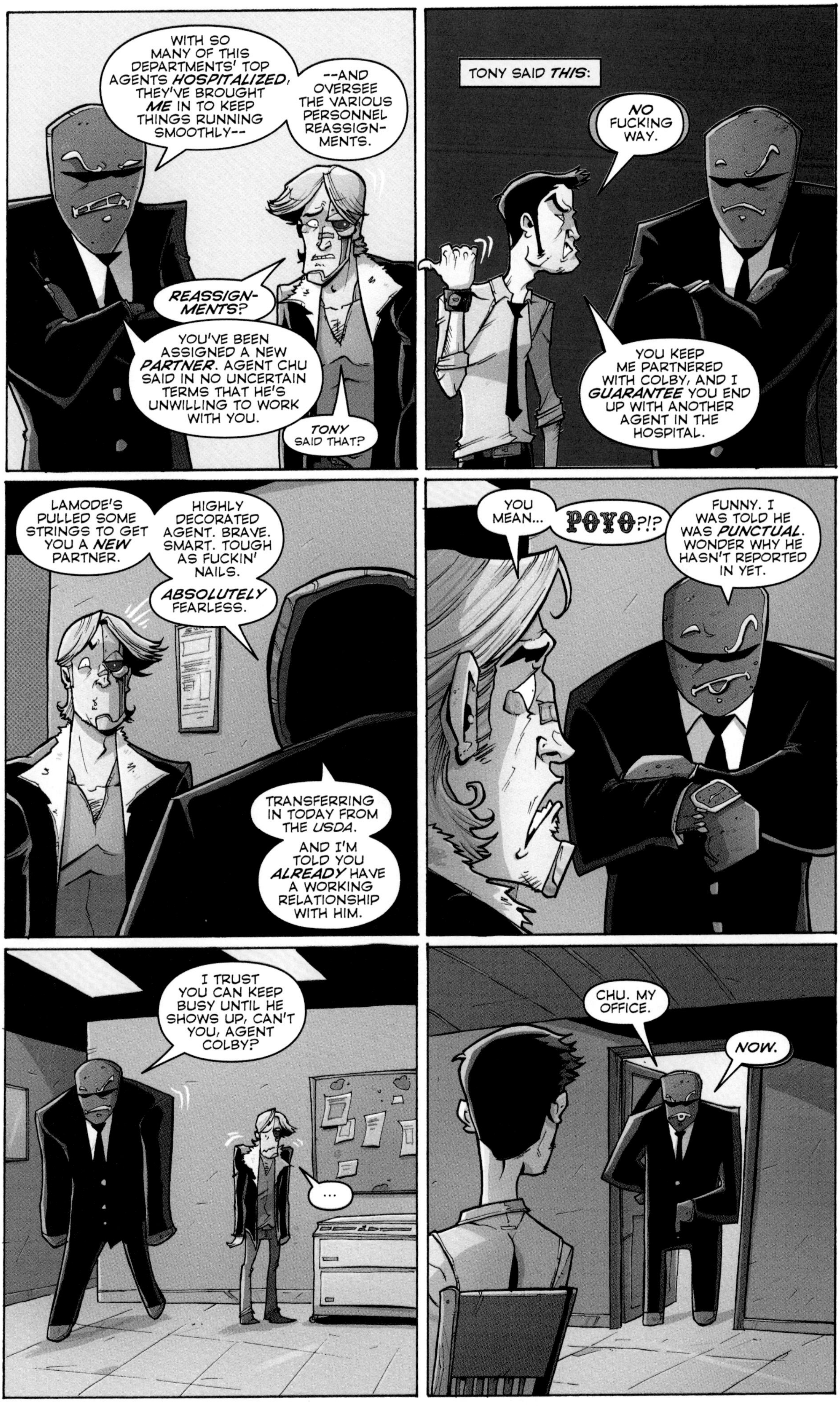
WITH SO MANY OF THIS DEPARTMENTS' TOP AGENTS *HOSPITALIZED*, THEY'VE BROUGHT *ME* IN TO KEEP THINGS RUNNING SMOOTHLY--
--AND OVERSEE THE VARIOUS PERSONNEL REASSIGNMENTS.
REASSIGNMENTS?
YOU'VE BEEN ASSIGNED A NEW *PARTNER*. AGENT CHU SAID IN NO UNCERTAIN TERMS THAT HE'S UNWILLING TO WORK WITH YOU.
TONY SAID THAT?
TONY SAID *THIS*:
NO FUCKING WAY.
YOU KEEP ME PARTNERED WITH COLBY, AND I *GUARANTEE* YOU END UP WITH ANOTHER AGENT IN THE HOSPITAL.
LAMODE'S PULLED SOME STRINGS TO GET YOU A *NEW* PARTNER.
HIGHLY DECORATED AGENT. BRAVE. SMART. TOUGH AS FUCKIN' NAILS.
ABSOLUTELY FEARLESS.
TRANSFERRING IN TODAY FROM THE *USDA*.
AND I'M TOLD YOU *ALREADY* HAVE A WORKING RELATIONSHIP WITH HIM.
YOU MEAN...
POYO?!?
FUNNY. I WAS TOLD HE WAS *PUNCTUAL*. WONDER WHY HE HASN'T REPORTED IN YET.
I TRUST YOU CAN KEEP BUSY UNTIL HE SHOWS UP, CAN'T YOU, AGENT COLBY?
...
CHU. MY OFFICE.
NOW.

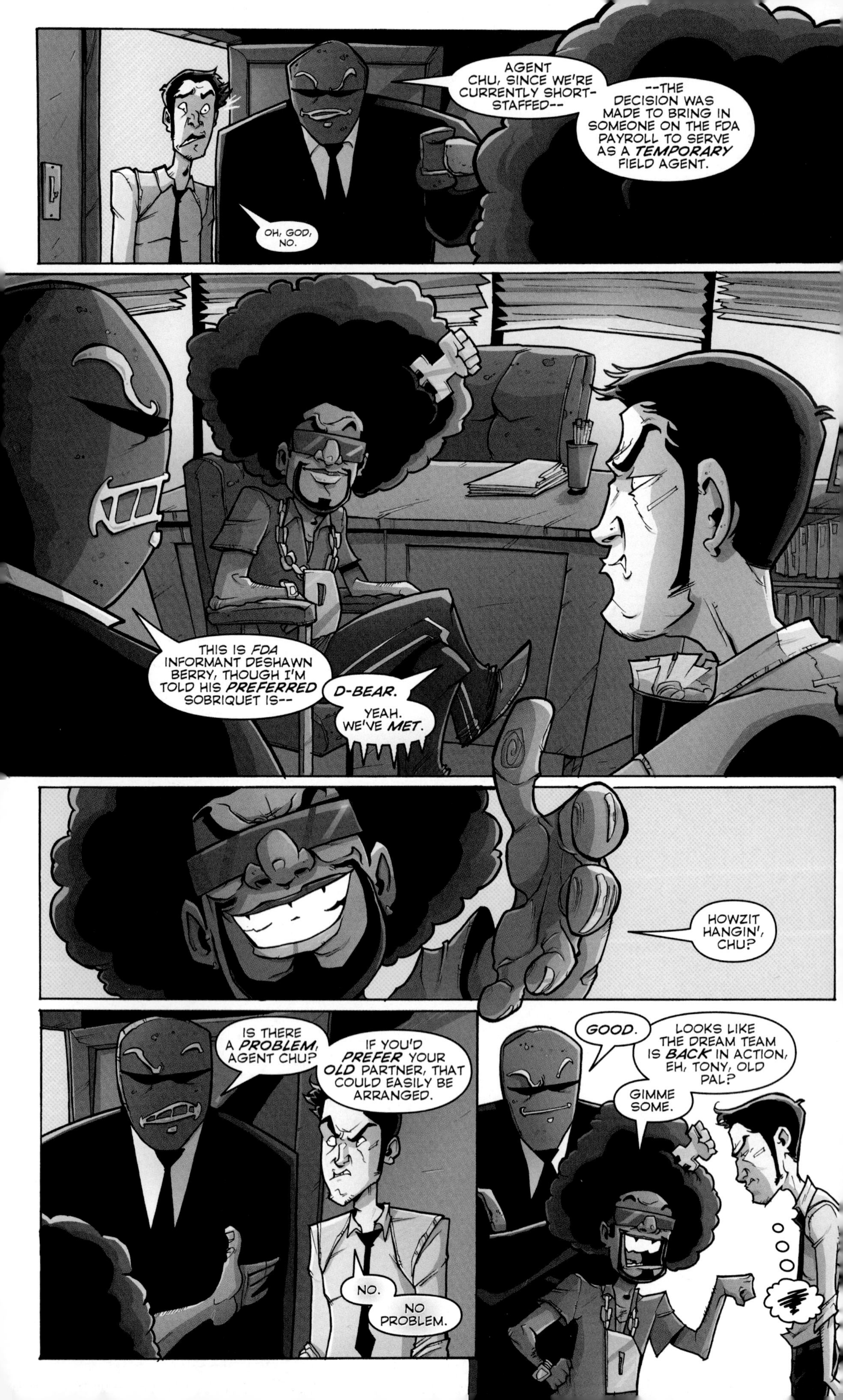
AGENT CHU, SINCE WE'RE CURRENTLY SHORT-STAFFED--
--THE DECISION WAS MADE TO BRING IN SOMEONE ON THE FDA PAYROLL TO SERVE AS A TEMPORARY FIELD AGENT.
OH, GOD, NO.
THIS IS FDA INFORMANT DESHAWN BERRY, THOUGH I'M TOLD HIS PREFERRED SOBRIQUET IS--
D-BEAR.
YEAH. WE'VE MET.
HOWZIT HANGIN', CHU?
IS THERE A PROBLEM, AGENT CHU?
IF YOU'D PREFER YOUR OLD PARTNER, THAT COULD EASILY BE ARRANGED.
NO.
NO PROBLEM.
GOOD.
LOOKS LIKE THE DREAM TEAM IS BACK IN ACTION, EH, TONY, OLD PAL?
GIMME SOME.

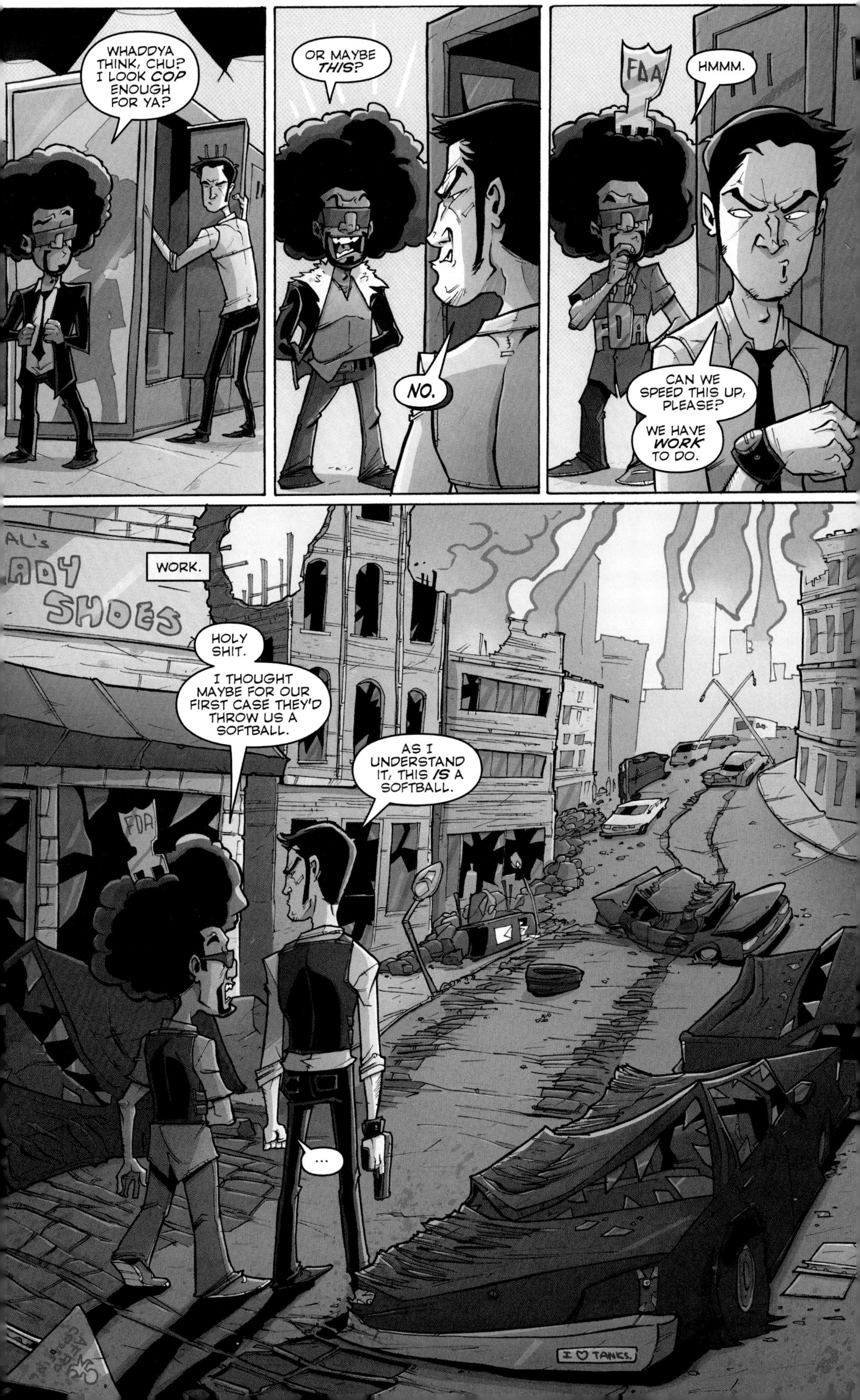

WHADDYA THINK, CHU? I LOOK COP ENOUGH FOR YA?
OR MAYBE THIS?
NO.
FDA
HMMM.
CAN WE SPEED THIS UP, PLEASE?
WE HAVE WORK TO DO.
AL's
ADY SHOES
WORK.
HOLY SHIT.
I THOUGHT MAYBE FOR OUR FIRST CASE THEY'D THROW US A SOFTBALL.
AS I UNDERSTAND IT, THIS IS A SOFTBALL.
...
I ♡ TANKS.

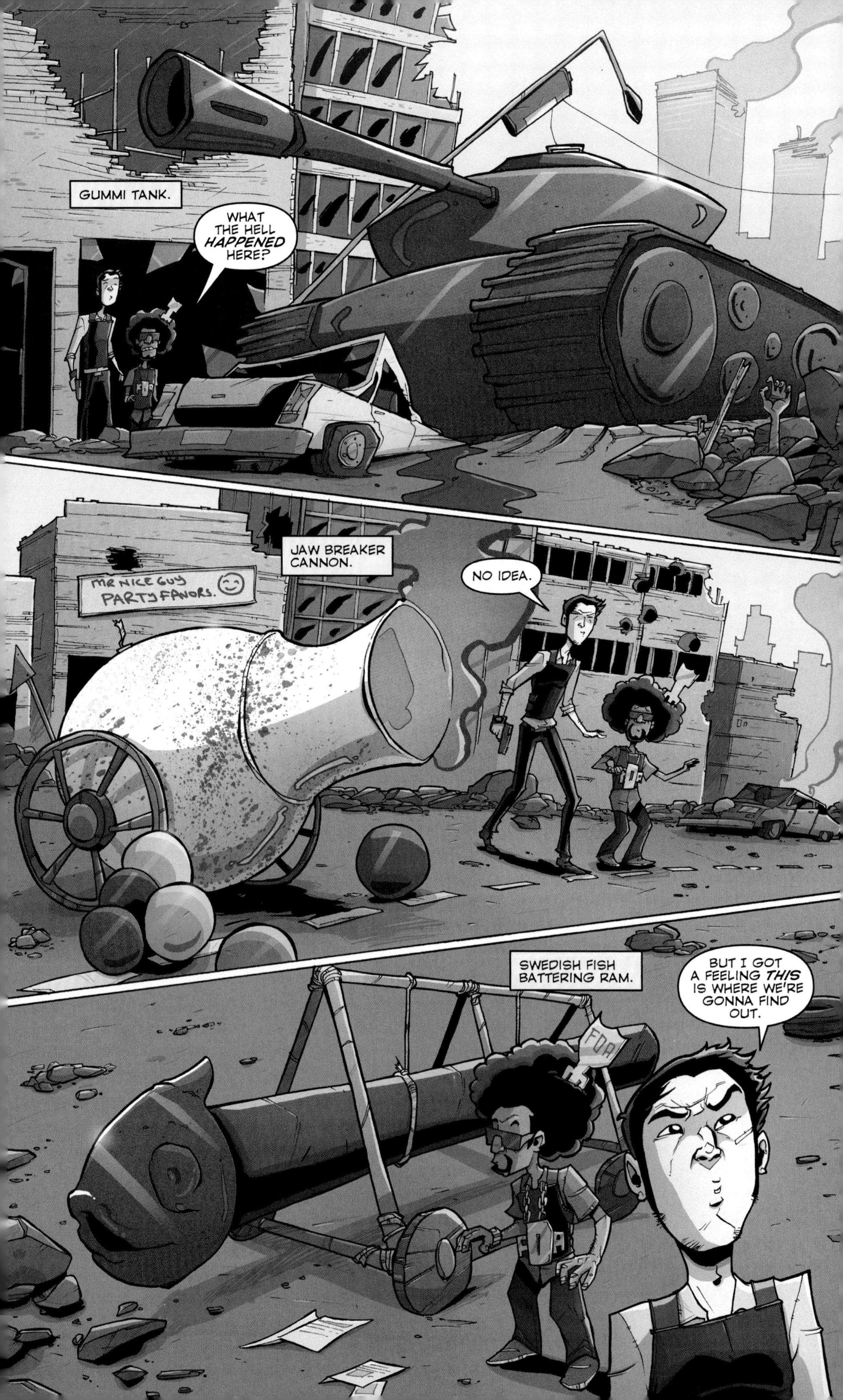
GUMMI TANK.
WHAT THE HELL HAPPENED HERE?
MR NICE GUY PARTY FAVORS.
JAW BREAKER CANNON.
NO IDEA.
SWEDISH FISH BATTERING RAM.
BUT I GOT A FEELING THIS IS WHERE WE'RE GONNA FIND OUT.

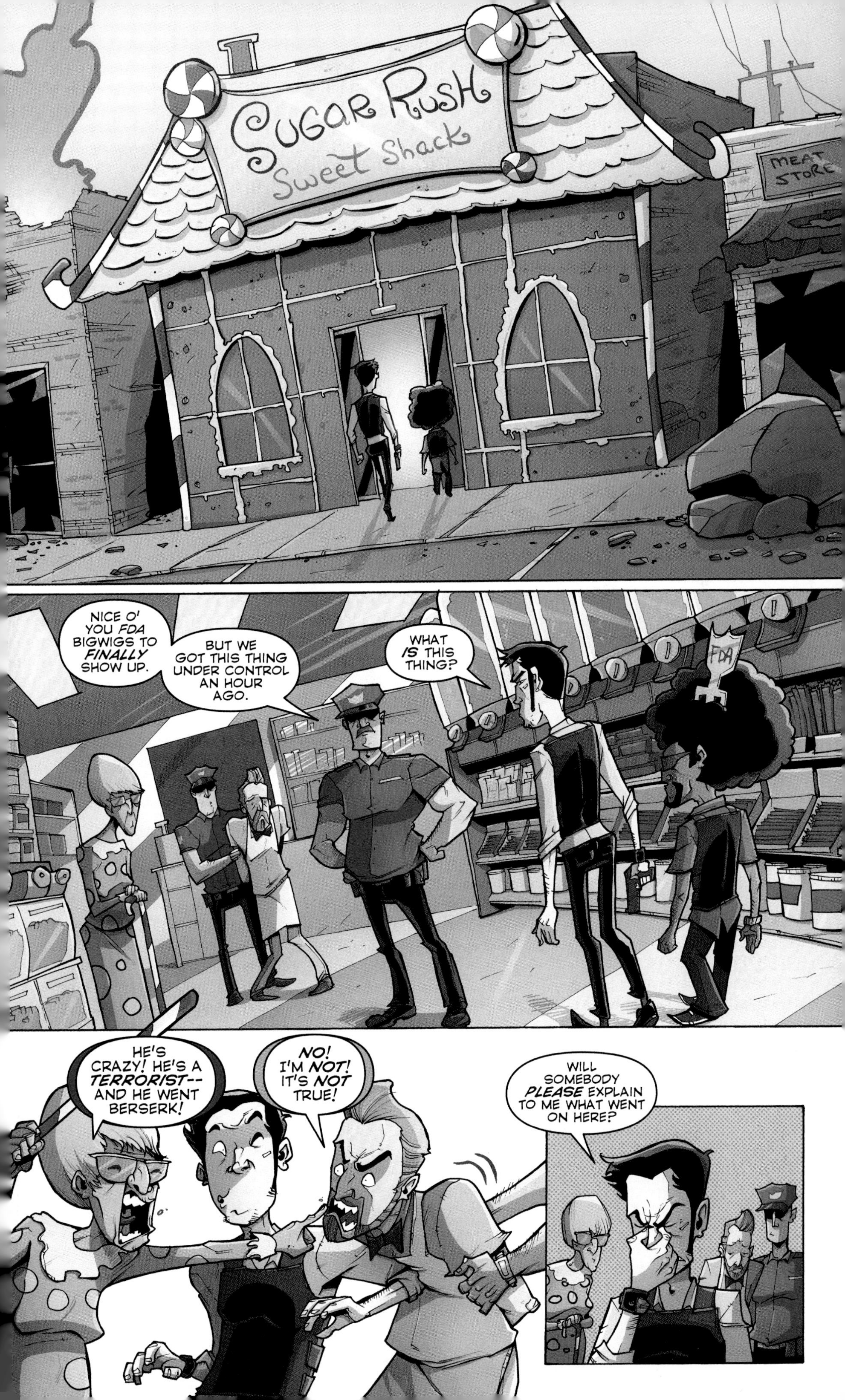
SUGAR RUSH
Sweet Shack
MEAT STORE
NICE O' YOU FDA BIGWIGS TO FINALLY SHOW UP.
BUT WE GOT THIS THING UNDER CONTROL AN HOUR AGO.
WHAT IS THIS THING?
FDA
HE'S CRAZY! HE'S A TERRORIST-- AND HE WENT BERSERK!
NO! I'M NOT! IT'S NOT TRUE!
WILL SOMEBODY PLEASE EXPLAIN TO ME WHAT WENT ON HERE?

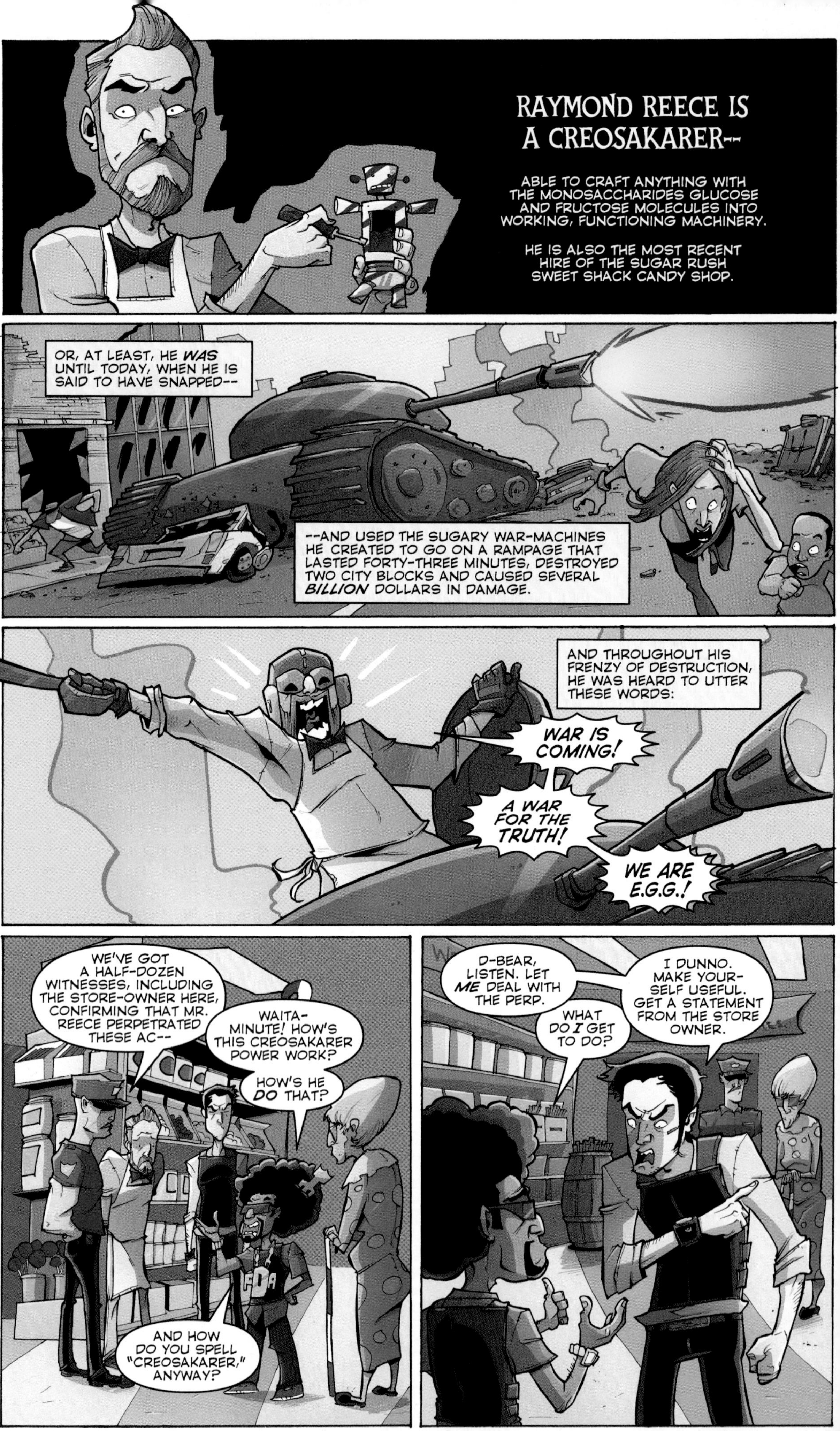
RAYMOND REECE IS A CREOSAKARER--
ABLE TO CRAFT ANYTHING WITH THE MONOSACCHARIDES GLUCOSE AND FRUCTOSE MOLECULES INTO WORKING, FUNCTIONING MACHINERY.
HE IS ALSO THE MOST RECENT HIRE OF THE SUGAR RUSH SWEET SHACK CANDY SHOP.
OR, AT LEAST, HE *WAS* UNTIL TODAY, WHEN HE IS SAID TO HAVE SNAPPED--
--AND USED THE SUGARY WAR-MACHINES HE CREATED TO GO ON A RAMPAGE THAT LASTED FORTY-THREE MINUTES, DESTROYED TWO CITY BLOCKS AND CAUSED SEVERAL *BILLION* DOLLARS IN DAMAGE.
AND THROUGHOUT HIS FRENZY OF DESTRUCTION, HE WAS HEARD TO UTTER THESE WORDS:
WAR IS COMING!
A WAR FOR THE TRUTH!
WE ARE E.G.G.!
WE'VE GOT A HALF-DOZEN WITNESSES, INCLUDING THE STORE-OWNER HERE, CONFIRMING THAT MR. REECE PERPETRATED THESE AC--
WAITA-MINUTE! HOW'S THIS CREOSAKARER POWER WORK?
HOW'S HE *DO* THAT?
AND HOW DO YOU SPELL "CREOSAKARER," ANYWAY?
D-BEAR, LISTEN. LET *ME* DEAL WITH THE PERP.
WHAT DO *I* GET TO DO?
I DUNNO. MAKE YOUR-SELF USEFUL. GET A STATEMENT FROM THE STORE OWNER.

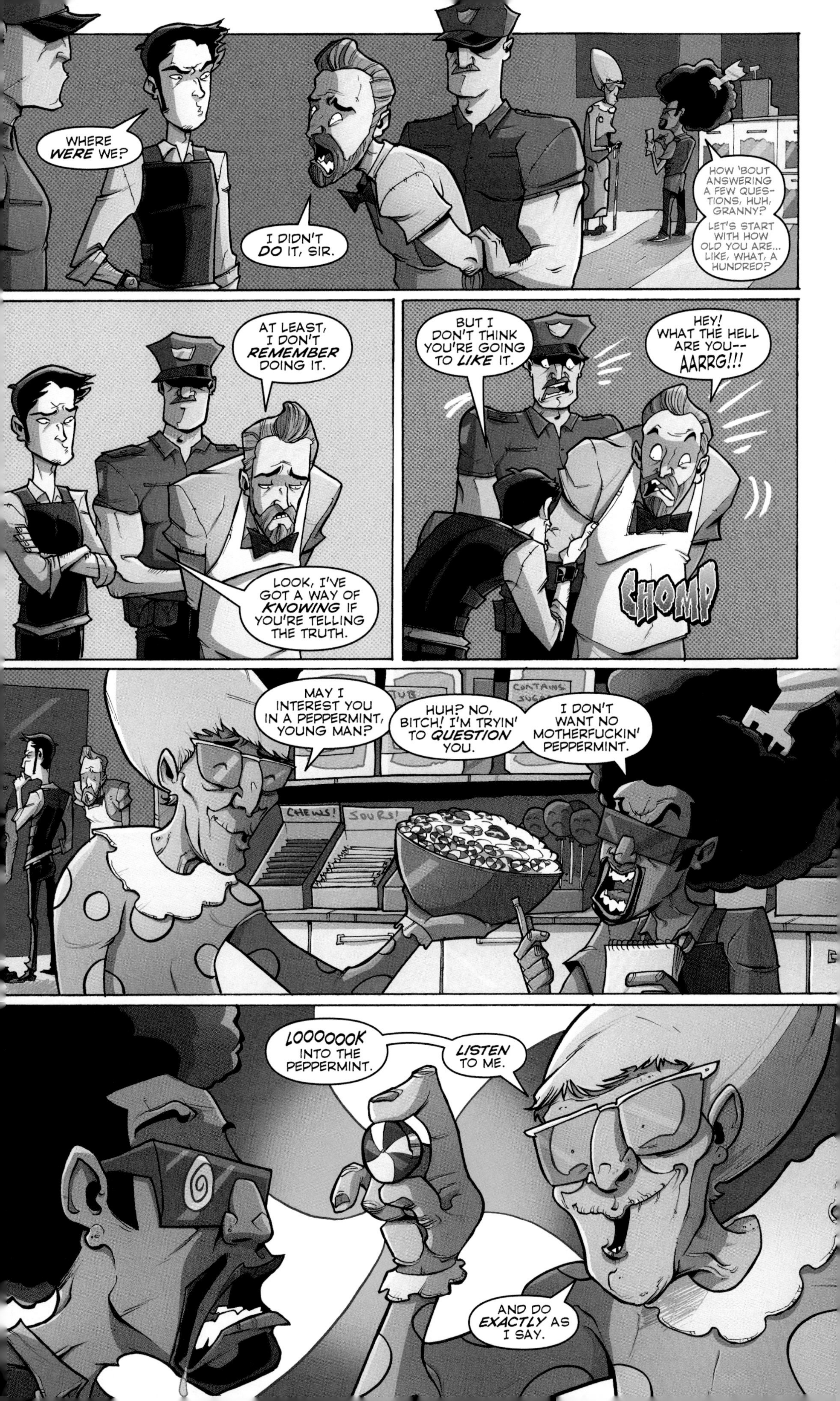

WHERE WERE WE?
I DIDN'T DO IT, SIR.
HOW 'BOUT ANSWERING A FEW QUESTIONS, HUH, GRANNY?
LET'S START WITH HOW OLD YOU ARE... LIKE, WHAT, A HUNDRED?
AT LEAST, I DON'T REMEMBER DOING IT.
LOOK, I'VE GOT A WAY OF KNOWING IF YOU'RE TELLING THE TRUTH.
BUT I DON'T THINK YOU'RE GOING TO LIKE IT.
HEY! WHAT THE HELL ARE YOU-- AARRG!!!
CHOMP
MAY I INTEREST YOU IN A PEPPERMINT, YOUNG MAN?
HUH? NO, BITCH! I'M TRYIN' TO QUESTION YOU.
I DON'T WANT NO MOTHERFUCKIN' PEPPERMINT.
CHEWS!
SOURS!
LOOOOOOK INTO THE PEPPERMINT.
LISTEN TO ME.
AND DO EXACTLY AS I SAY.

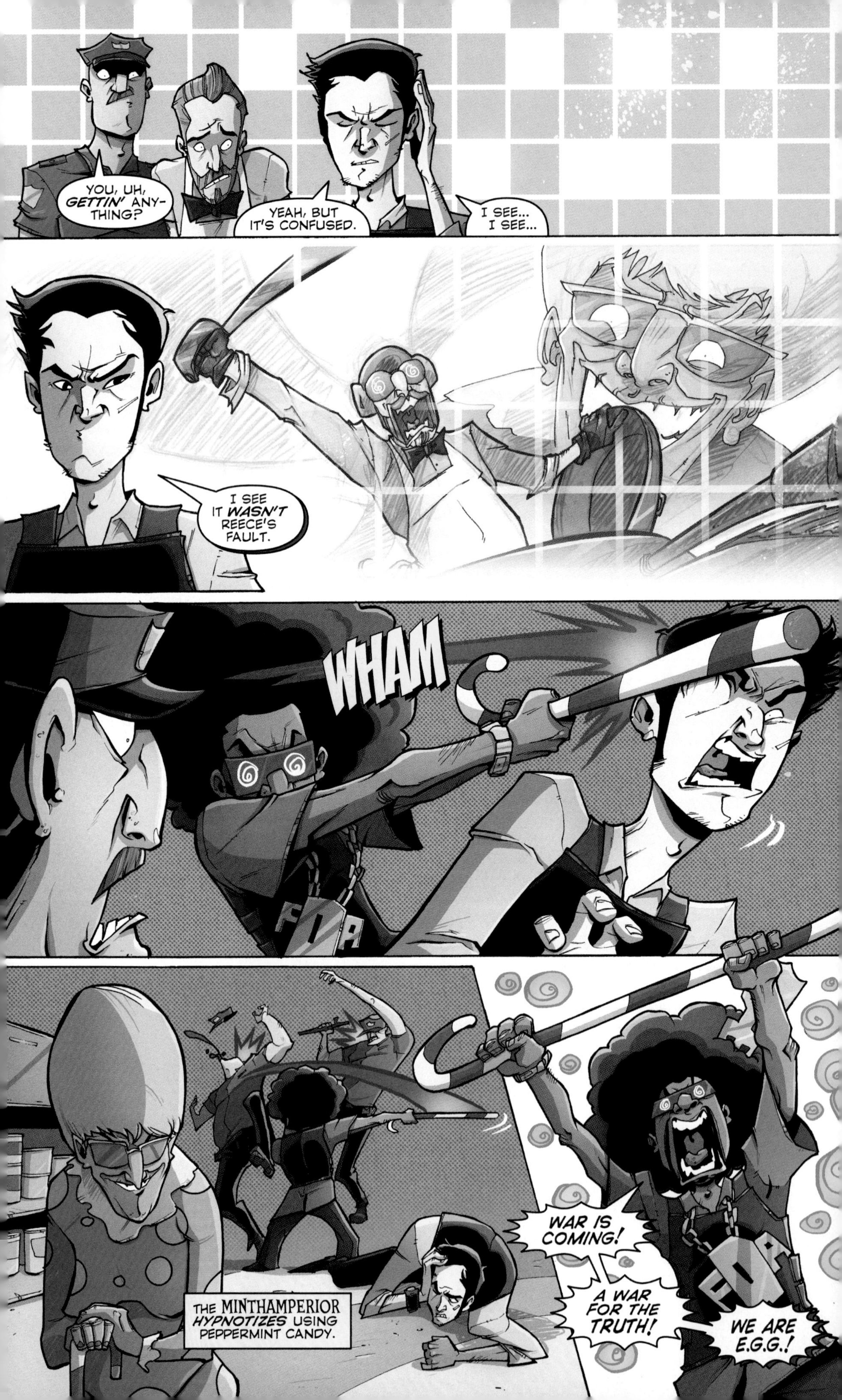
YOU, UH, GETTIN' ANY-THING?
YEAH, BUT IT'S CONFUSED.
I SEE... I SEE...
I SEE IT WASN'T REECE'S FAULT.
WHAM
THE MINTHAMPERIOR HYPNOTIZES USING PEPPERMINT CANDY.
WAR IS COMING!
A WAR FOR THE TRUTH!
WE ARE E.G.G.!

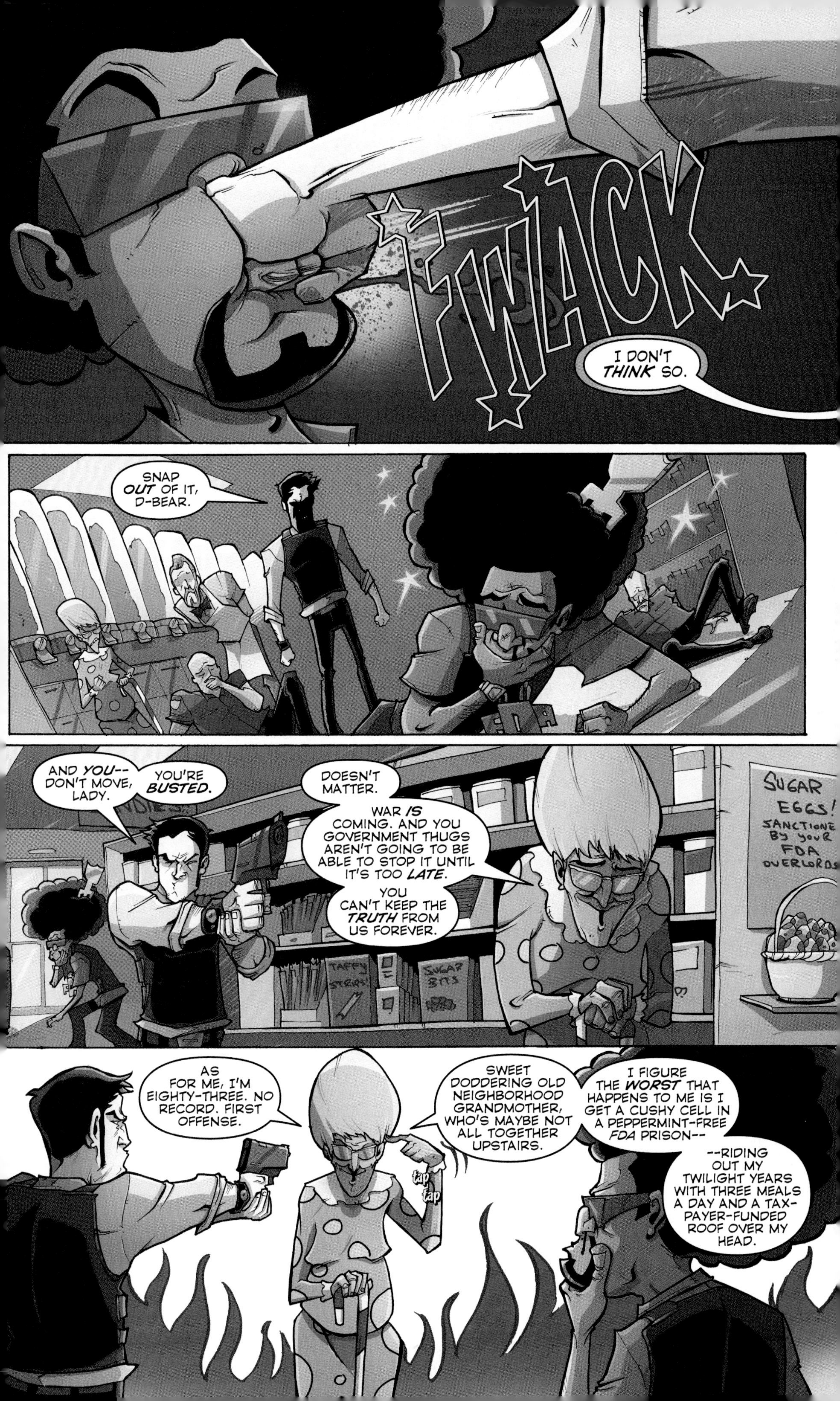
FWACK
I DON'T THINK SO.
SNAP OUT OF IT, D-BEAR.
AND YOU-- DON'T MOVE, LADY.
YOU'RE BUSTED.
DOESN'T MATTER.
WAR IS COMING. AND YOU GOVERNMENT THUGS AREN'T GOING TO BE ABLE TO STOP IT UNTIL IT'S TOO LATE.
YOU CAN'T KEEP THE TRUTH FROM US FOREVER.
SUGAR EGGS! SANCTIONE BY YOUR FDA OVERLORDS
TAFFY STRIPS!
SUGAR BITS
AS FOR ME, I'M EIGHTY-THREE. NO RECORD. FIRST OFFENSE.
SWEET DODDERING OLD NEIGHBORHOOD GRANDMOTHER, WHO'S MAYBE NOT ALL TOGETHER UPSTAIRS.
tap tap
I FIGURE THE WORST THAT HAPPENS TO ME IS I GET A CUSHY CELL IN A PEPPERMINT-FREE FDA PRISON--
--RIDING OUT MY TWILIGHT YEARS WITH THREE MEALS A DAY AND A TAX-PAYER-FUNDED ROOF OVER MY HEAD.

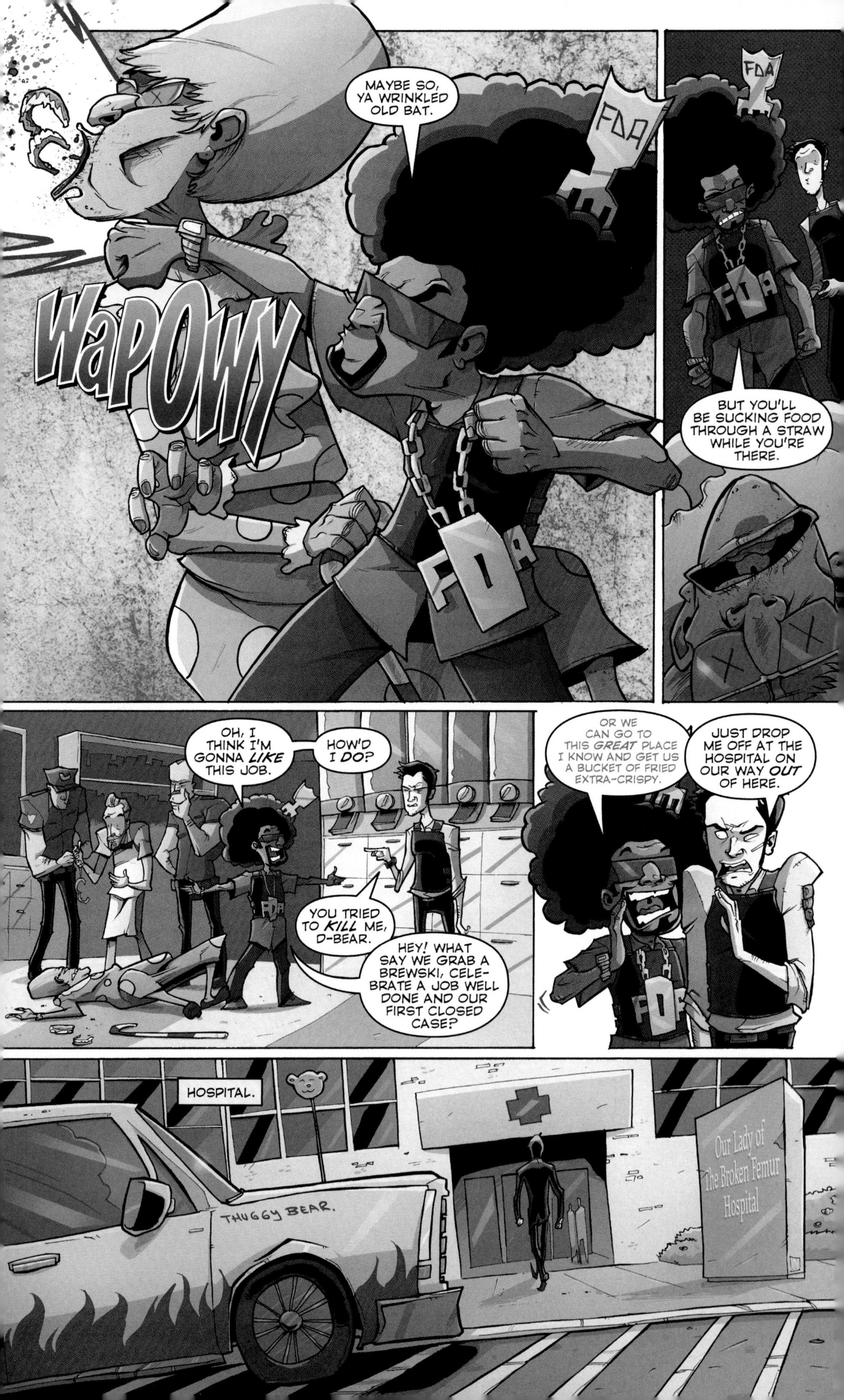
MAYBE SO, YA WRINKLED OLD BAT.
FDA
WAPOWY
BUT YOU'LL BE SUCKING FOOD THROUGH A STRAW WHILE YOU'RE THERE.
OH, I THINK I'M GONNA *LIKE* THIS JOB.
HOW'D I *DO*?
YOU TRIED TO *KILL* ME, D-BEAR.
HEY! WHAT SAY WE GRAB A BREWSKI, CELE-BRATE A JOB WELL DONE AND OUR FIRST CLOSED CASE?
OR WE CAN GO TO THIS *GREAT* PLACE I KNOW AND GET US A BUCKET OF FRIED EXTRA-CRISPY.
JUST DROP ME OFF AT THE HOSPITAL ON OUR WAY *OUT* OF HERE.
HOSPITAL.
THUGGY BEAR.
Our Lady of The Broken Femur Hospital

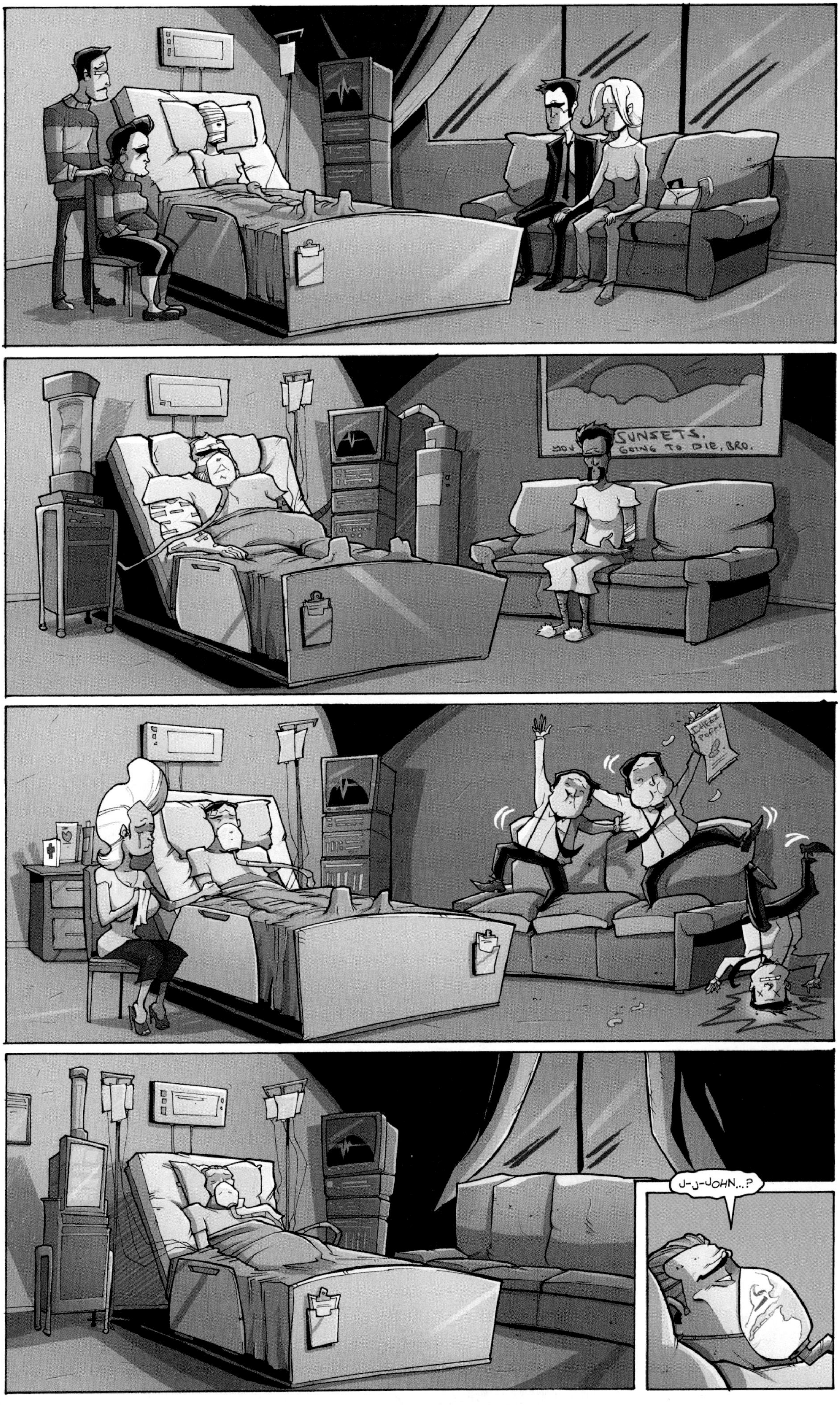
SUNSETS.
YOU
GOING TO DIE, BRO.
CHEEZ POFFS
J-J-JOHN...?

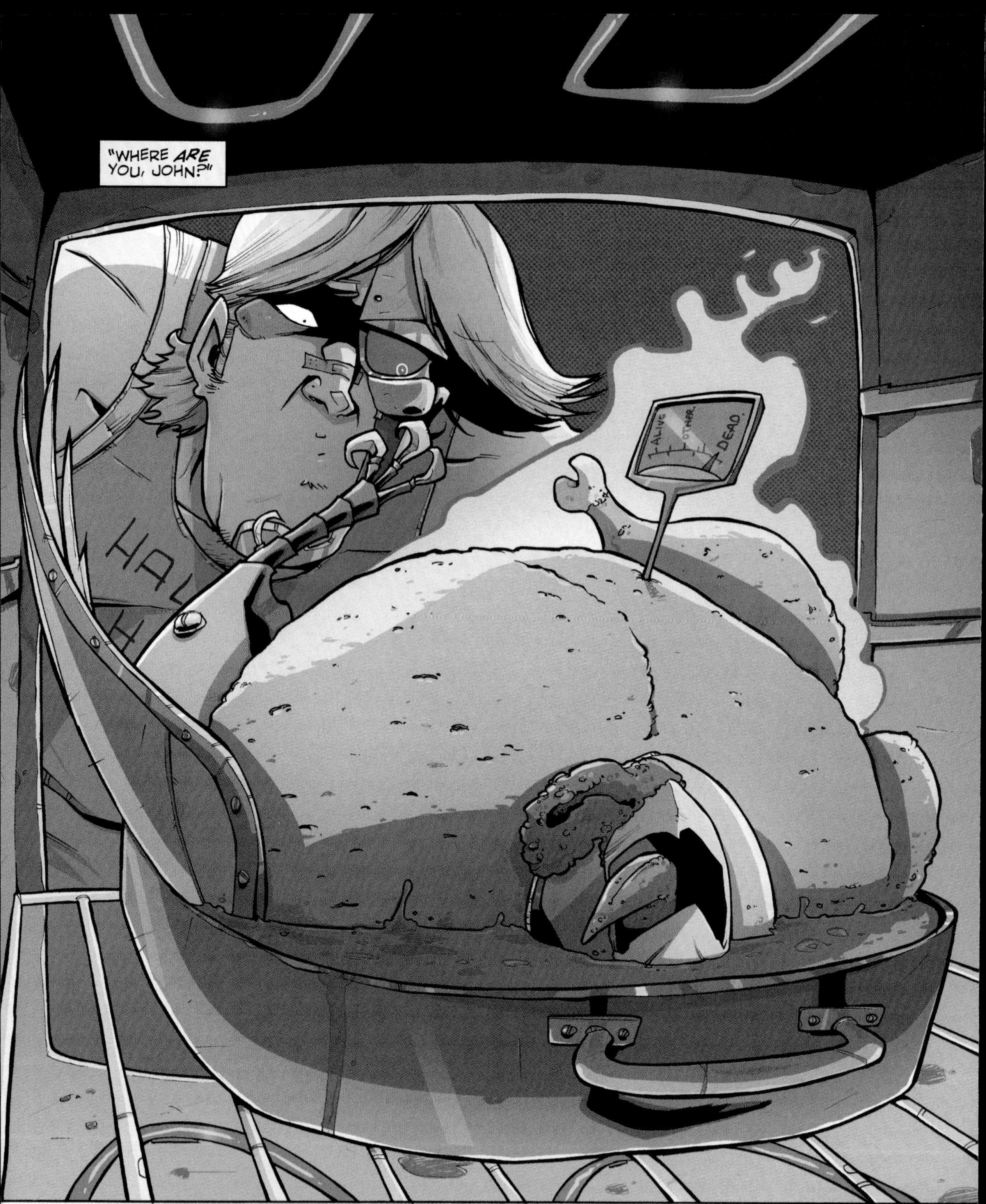
"WHERE ARE YOU, JOHN?"
ALIVE OTHER DEAD

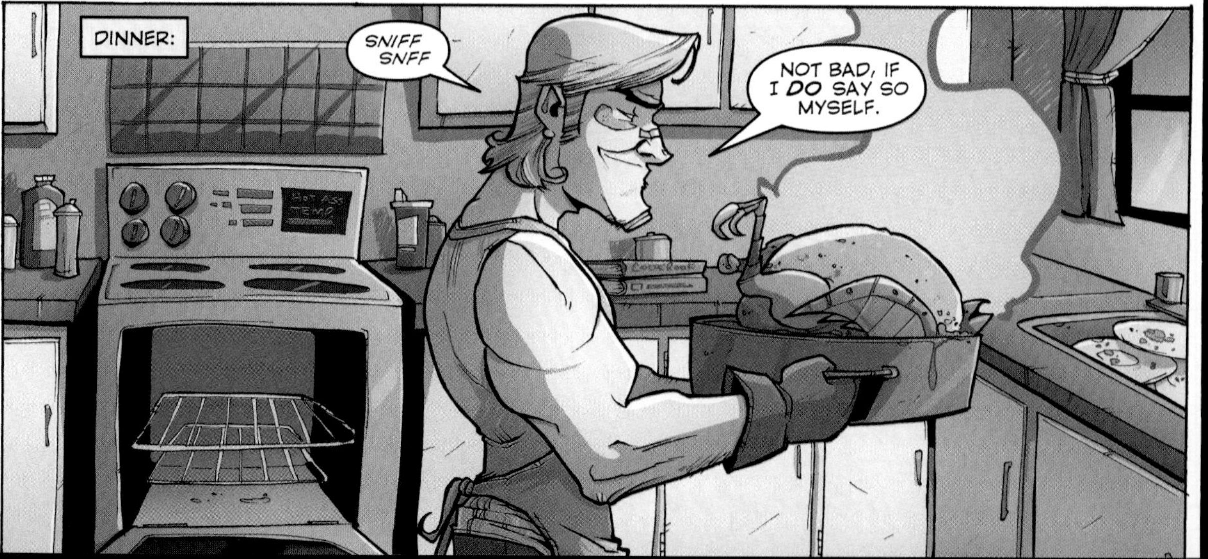
DINNER:
SNIFF SNFF
NOT BAD, IF I DO SAY SO MYSELF.

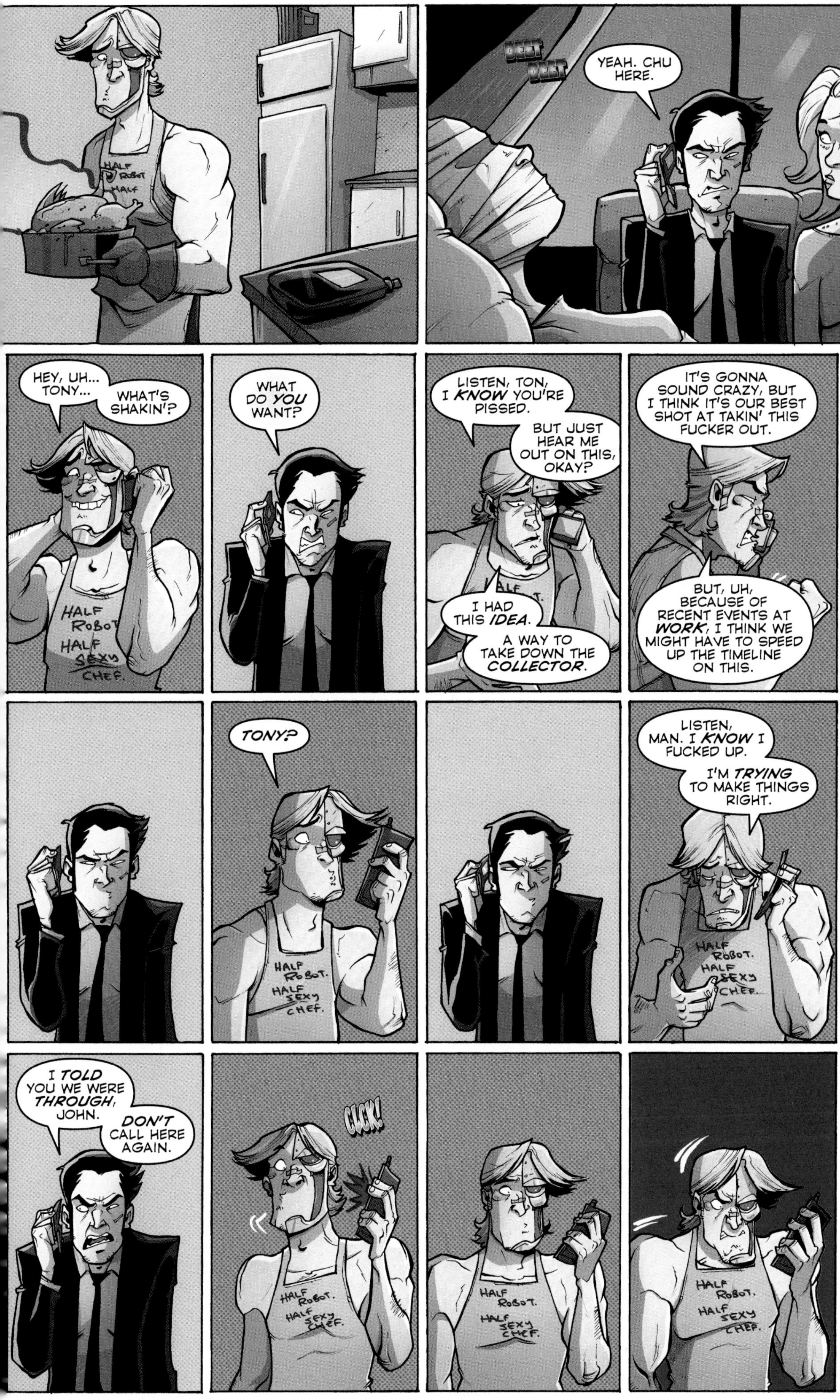
HALF ROBOT HALF
DEET DEET
YEAH. CHU HERE.
HEY, UH... TONY...
WHAT'S SHAKIN'?
WHAT DO YOU WANT?
LISTEN, TON, I KNOW YOU'RE PISSED.
BUT JUST HEAR ME OUT ON THIS, OKAY?
I HAD THIS IDEA.
A WAY TO TAKE DOWN THE COLLECTOR.
IT'S GONNA SOUND CRAZY, BUT I THINK IT'S OUR BEST SHOT AT TAKIN' THIS FUCKER OUT.
BUT, UH, BECAUSE OF RECENT EVENTS AT WORK, I THINK WE MIGHT HAVE TO SPEED UP THE TIMELINE ON THIS.
TONY?
LISTEN, MAN. I KNOW I FUCKED UP.
I'M TRYING TO MAKE THINGS RIGHT.
HALF ROBOT. HALF SEXY CHEF.
I TOLD YOU WE WERE THROUGH, JOHN.
DON'T CALL HERE AGAIN.
CLICK!

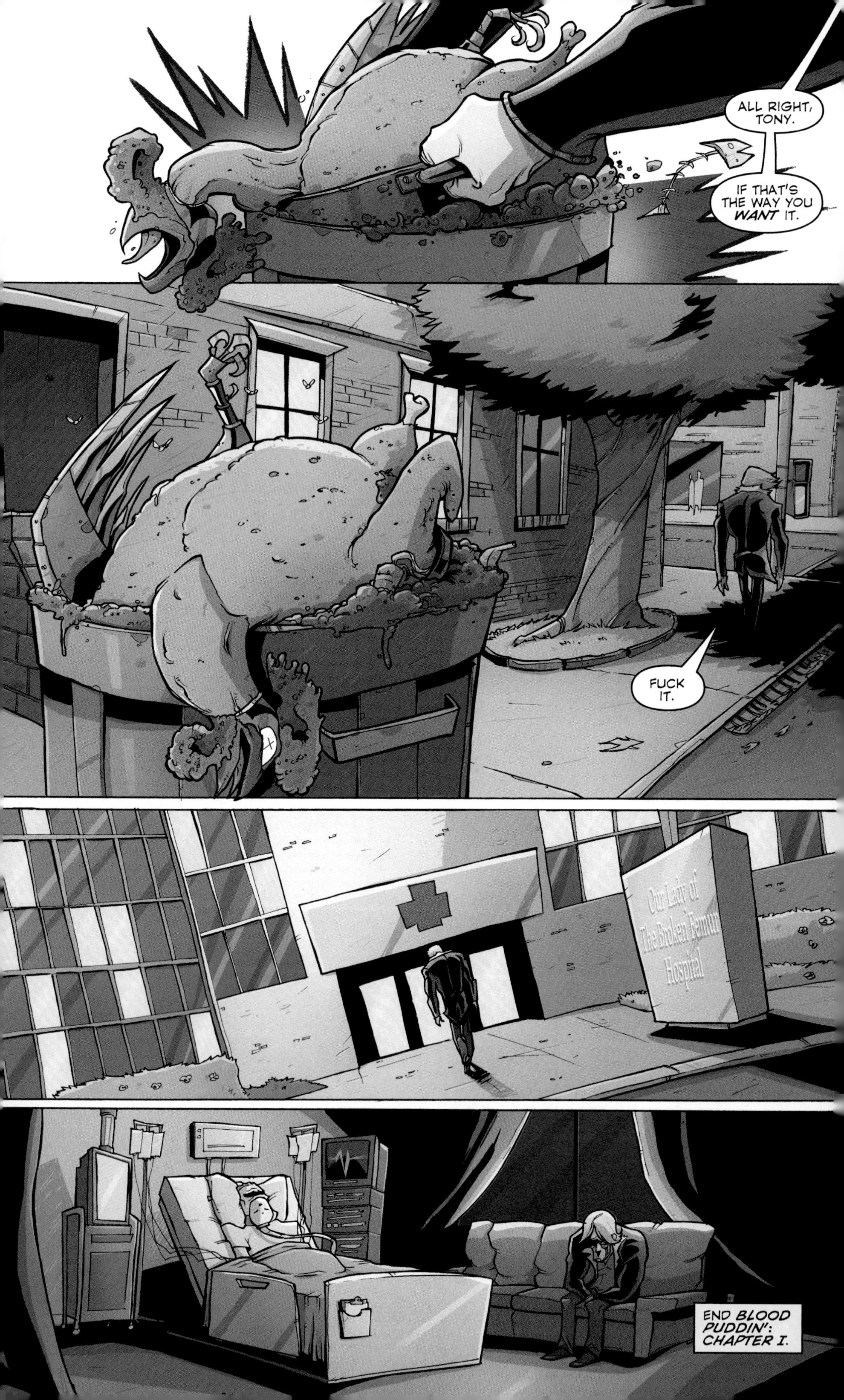
ALL RIGHT, TONY.
IF THAT'S THE WAY YOU *WANT* IT.
FUCK IT.
Our Lady of The Broken Femur Hospital
END *BLOOD PUDDIN': CHAPTER I.*

Chapter Seven

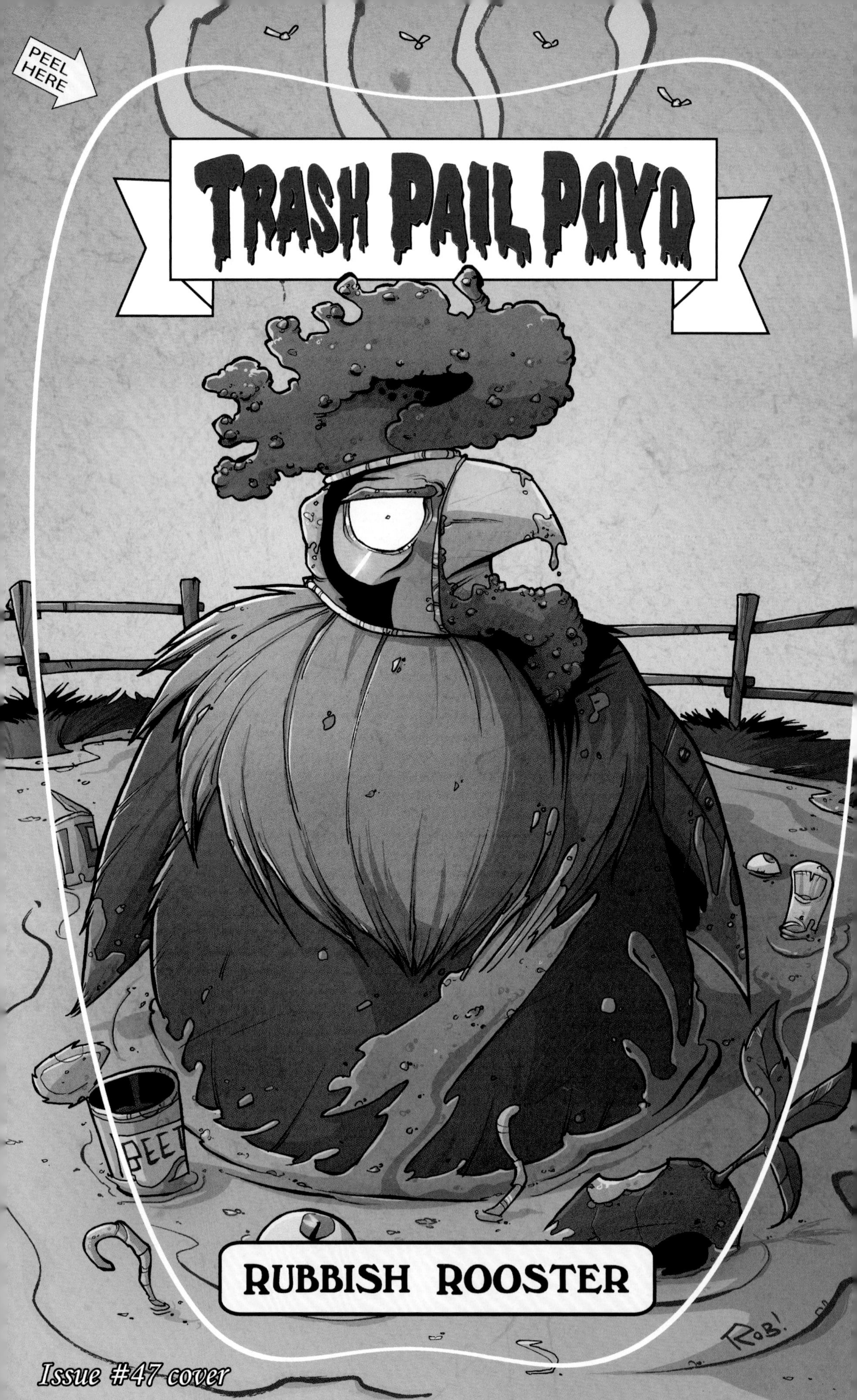
PEEL HERE
TRASH PAIL POYD
BEET
RUBBISH ROOSTER
ROB!
Issue #47 cover

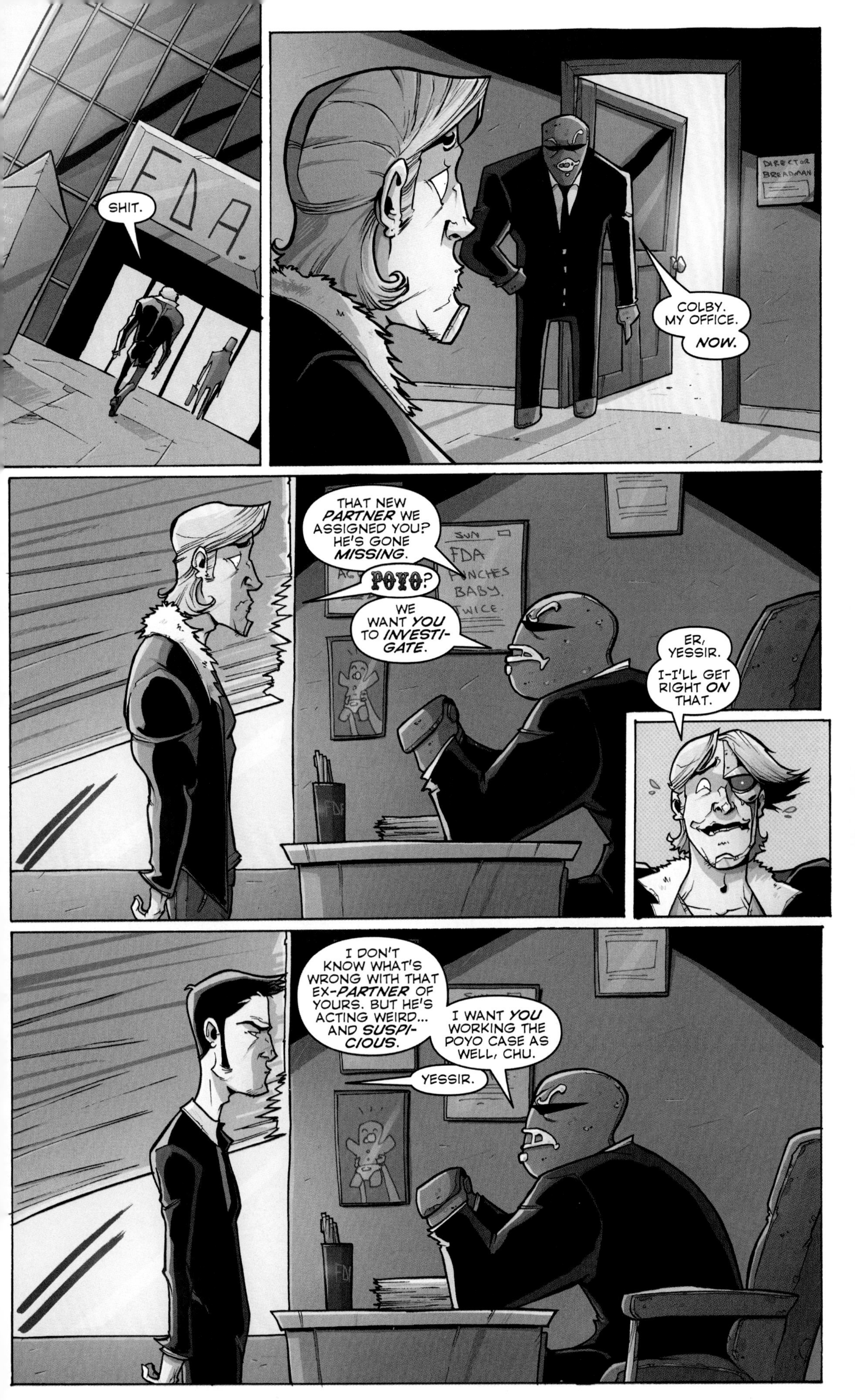

FDA
SHIT.
DIRECTOR BREADMAN
COLBY. MY OFFICE. NOW.
SUN
FDA PUNCHES BABY. TWICE.
THAT NEW PARTNER WE ASSIGNED YOU? HE'S GONE MISSING.
POYO?
WE WANT YOU TO INVESTIGATE.
ER, YESSIR.
I-I'LL GET RIGHT ON THAT.
I DON'T KNOW WHAT'S WRONG WITH THAT EX-PARTNER OF YOURS. BUT HE'S ACTING WEIRD... AND SUSPICIOUS.
I WANT YOU WORKING THE POYO CASE AS WELL, CHU.
YESSIR.

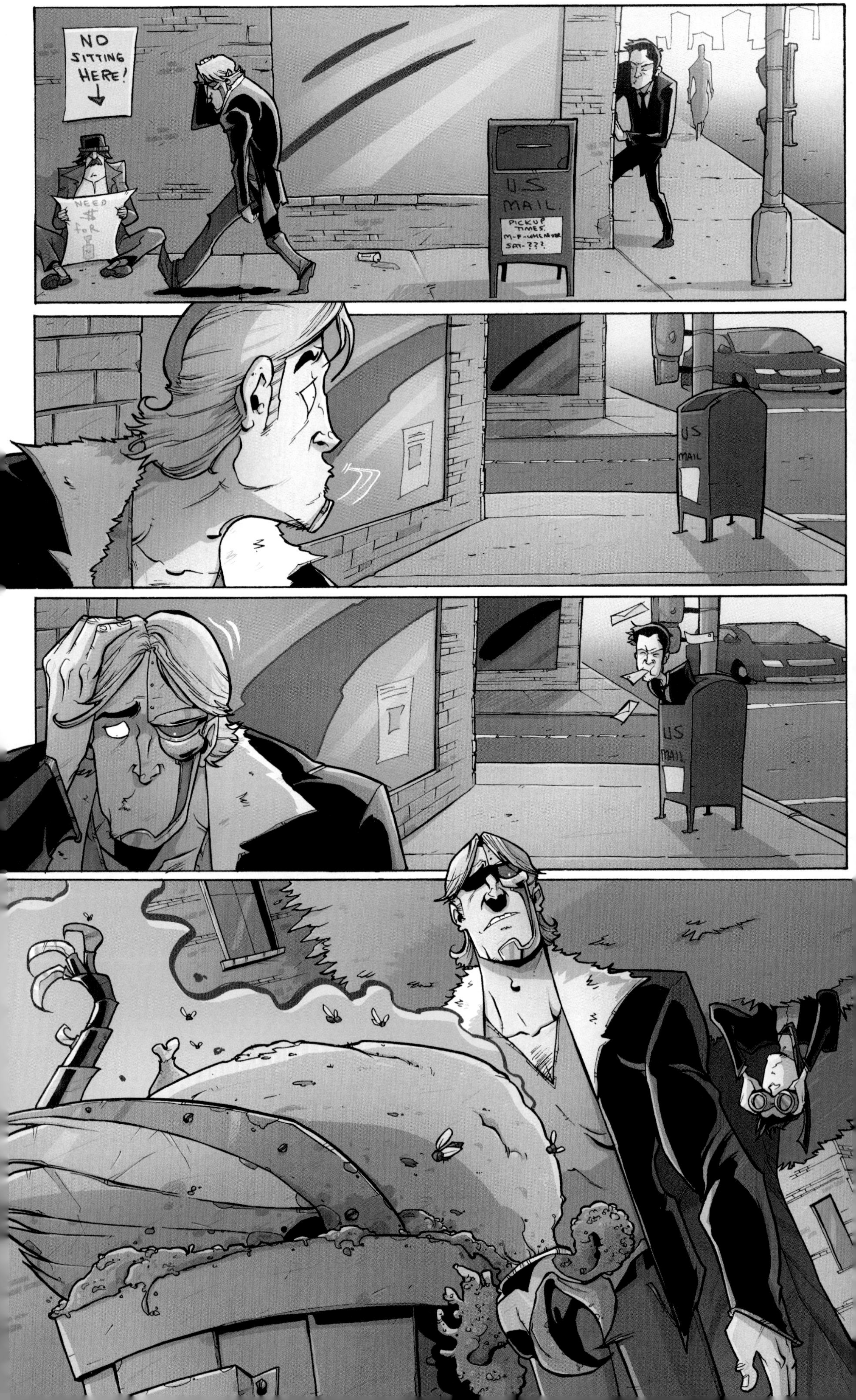
NO SITTING HERE!
NEED $ FOR
U.S. MAIL
PICKUP TIMES:
US MAIL
US MAIL

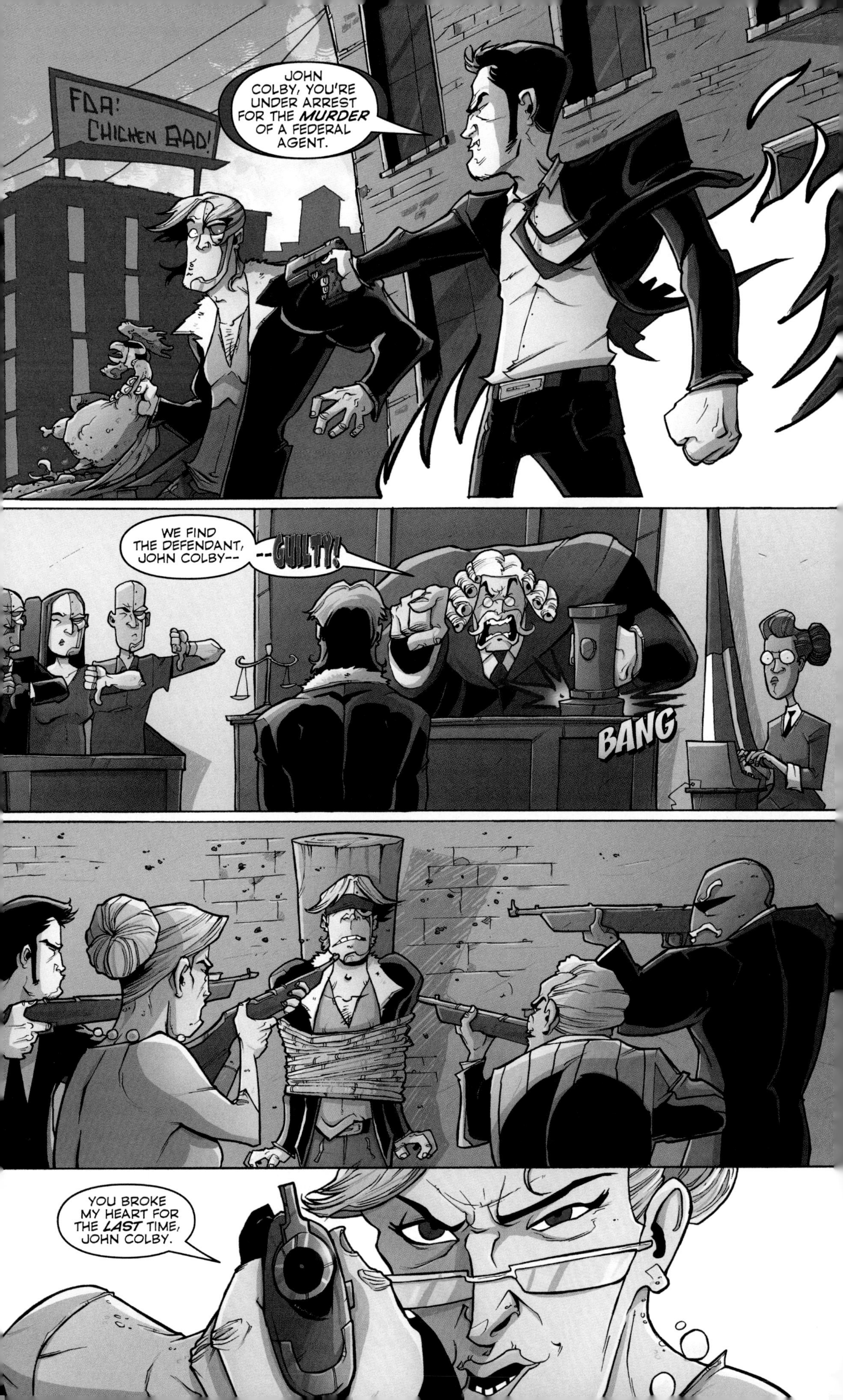
FOR CHICKEN BAD!
JOHN COLBY, YOU'RE UNDER ARREST FOR THE *MURDER* OF A FEDERAL AGENT.
WE FIND THE DEFENDANT, JOHN COLBY--
--GUILTY!
BANG
YOU BROKE MY HEART FOR THE *LAST* TIME, JOHN COLBY.

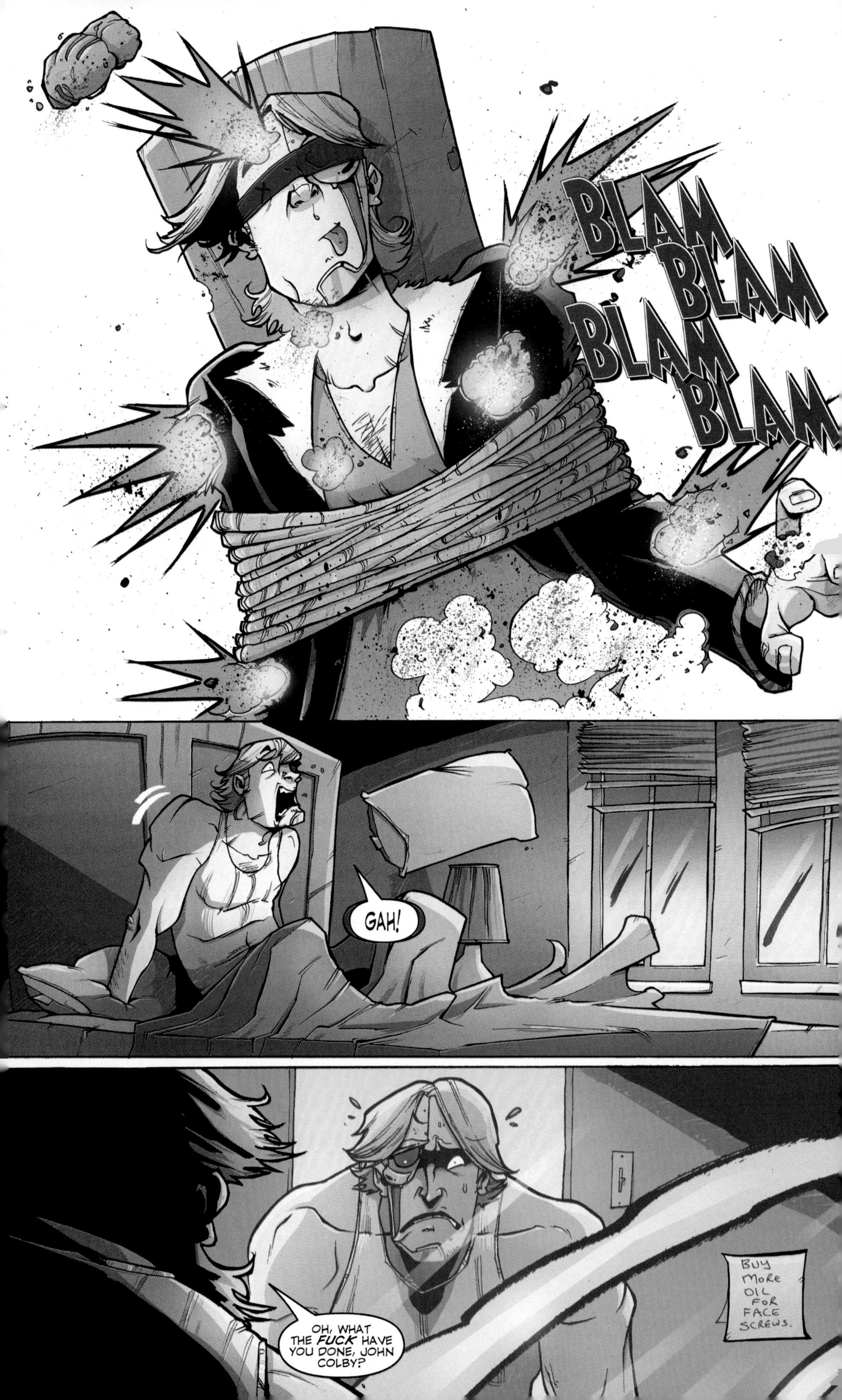
BLAM
BLAM
BLAM
BLAM
GAH!
OH, WHAT THE *FUCK* HAVE YOU DONE, JOHN COLBY?
BUY MORE OIL FOR FACE SCREWS.

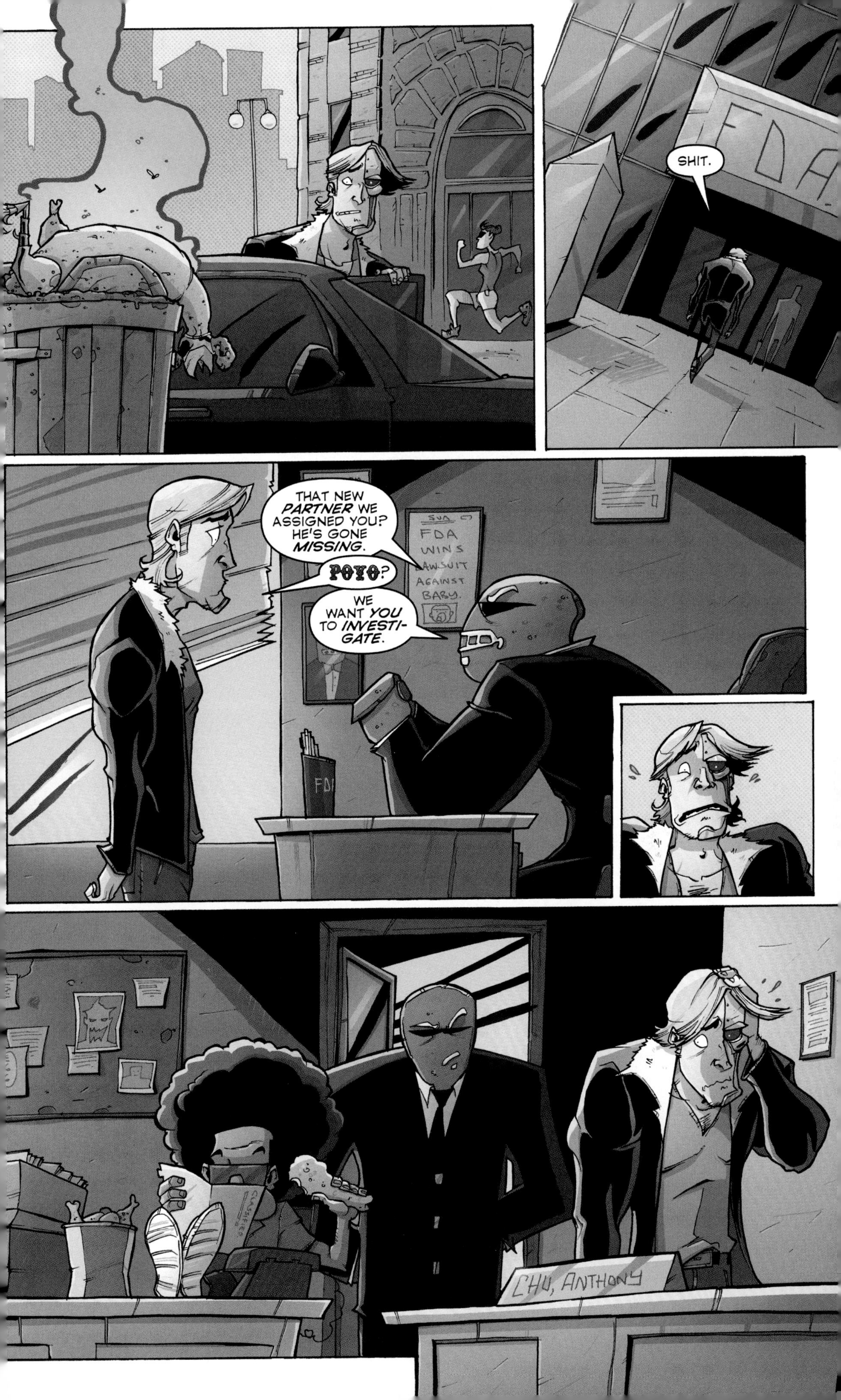

SHIT.
FDA
THAT NEW PARTNER WE ASSIGNED YOU? HE'S GONE MISSING.
POYO?
WE WANT YOU TO INVESTI-GATE.
FDA WINS LAWSUIT AGAINST BABY.
FDA
CHU, ANTHONY

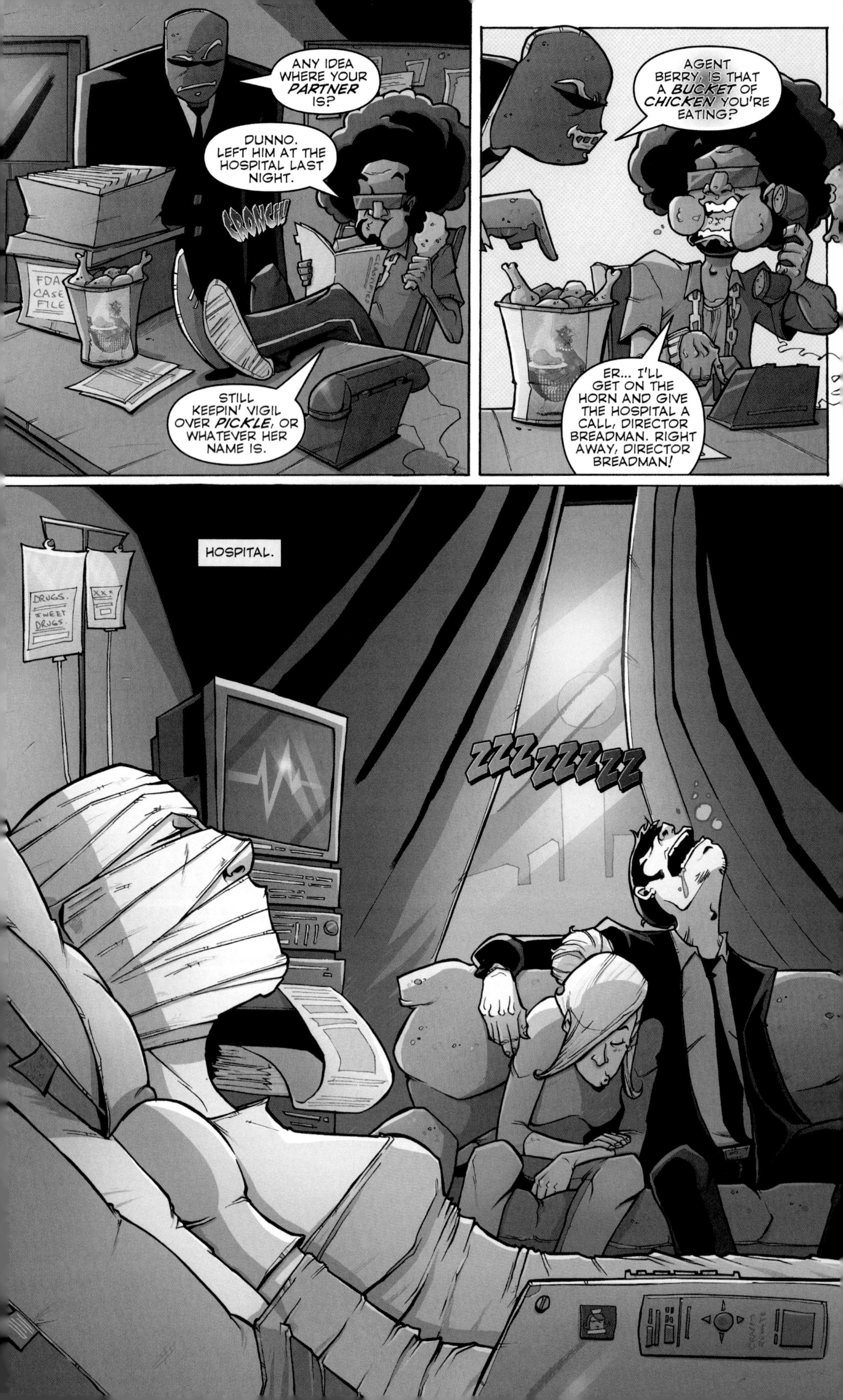

ANY IDEA WHERE YOUR *PARTNER* IS?
DUNNO. LEFT HIM AT THE HOSPITAL LAST NIGHT.
CRONCH!!
STILL KEEPIN' VIGIL OVER *PICKLE*, OR WHATEVER HER NAME IS.
FDA CASE FILE
AGENT BERRY, IS THAT A *BUCKET* OF *CHICKEN* YOU'RE EATING?
ER... I'LL GET ON THE HORN AND GIVE THE HOSPITAL A CALL, DIRECTOR BREADMAN. RIGHT AWAY, DIRECTOR BREADMAN!
HOSPITAL.
DRUGS. SWEET DRUGS.
ZZZZZZZZ

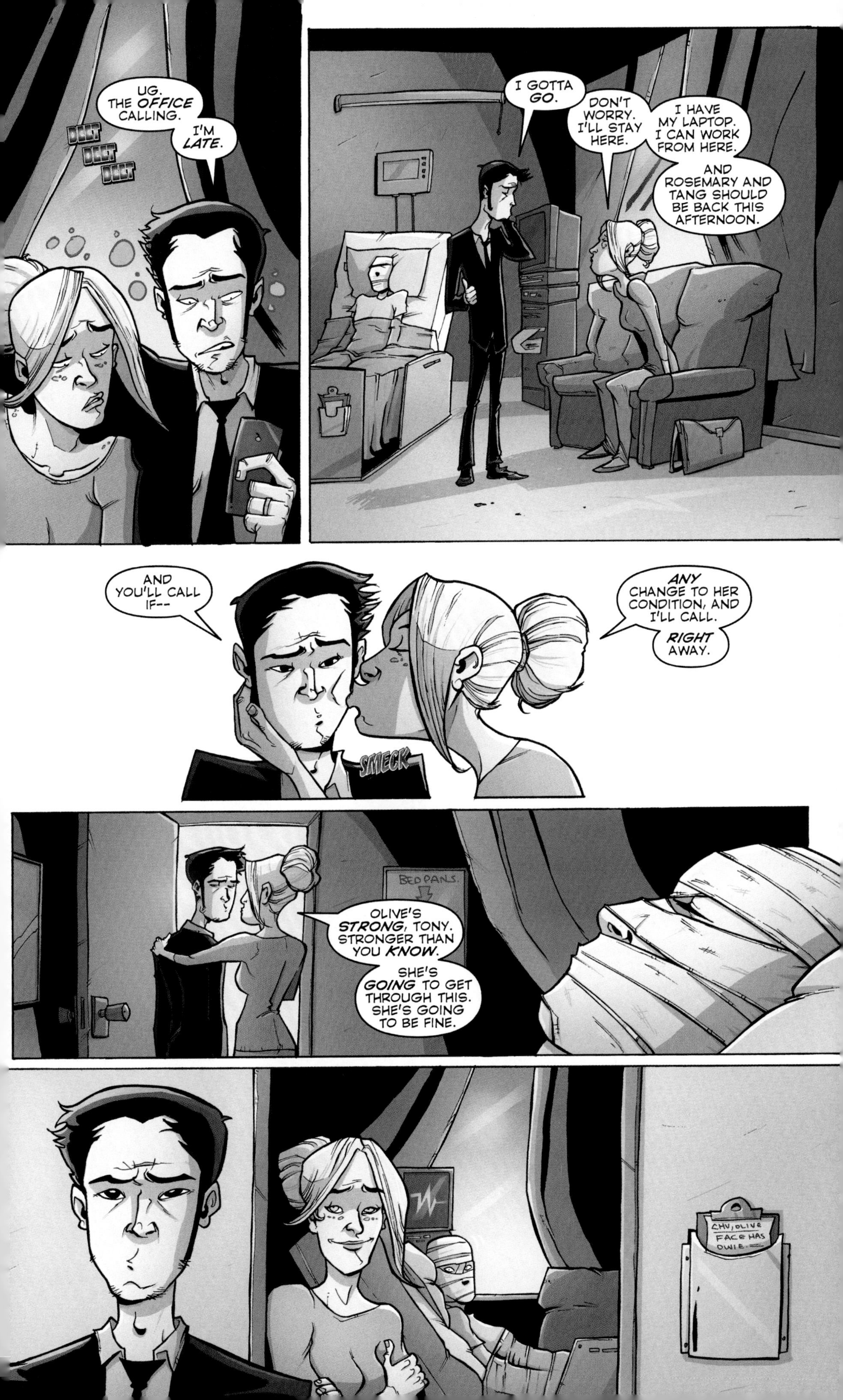
DEET DEET DEET
UG. THE OFFICE CALLING.
I'M LATE.
I GOTTA GO.
DON'T WORRY. I'LL STAY HERE.
I HAVE MY LAPTOP. I CAN WORK FROM HERE.
AND ROSEMARY AND TANG SHOULD BE BACK THIS AFTERNOON.
AND YOU'LL CALL IF--
ANY CHANGE TO HER CONDITION, AND I'LL CALL.
RIGHT AWAY.
SMECK
BEDPANS.
OLIVE'S STRONG, TONY. STRONGER THAN YOU KNOW.
SHE'S GOING TO GET THROUGH THIS. SHE'S GOING TO BE FINE.
CHU, OLIVE
FACE HAS OWIE.

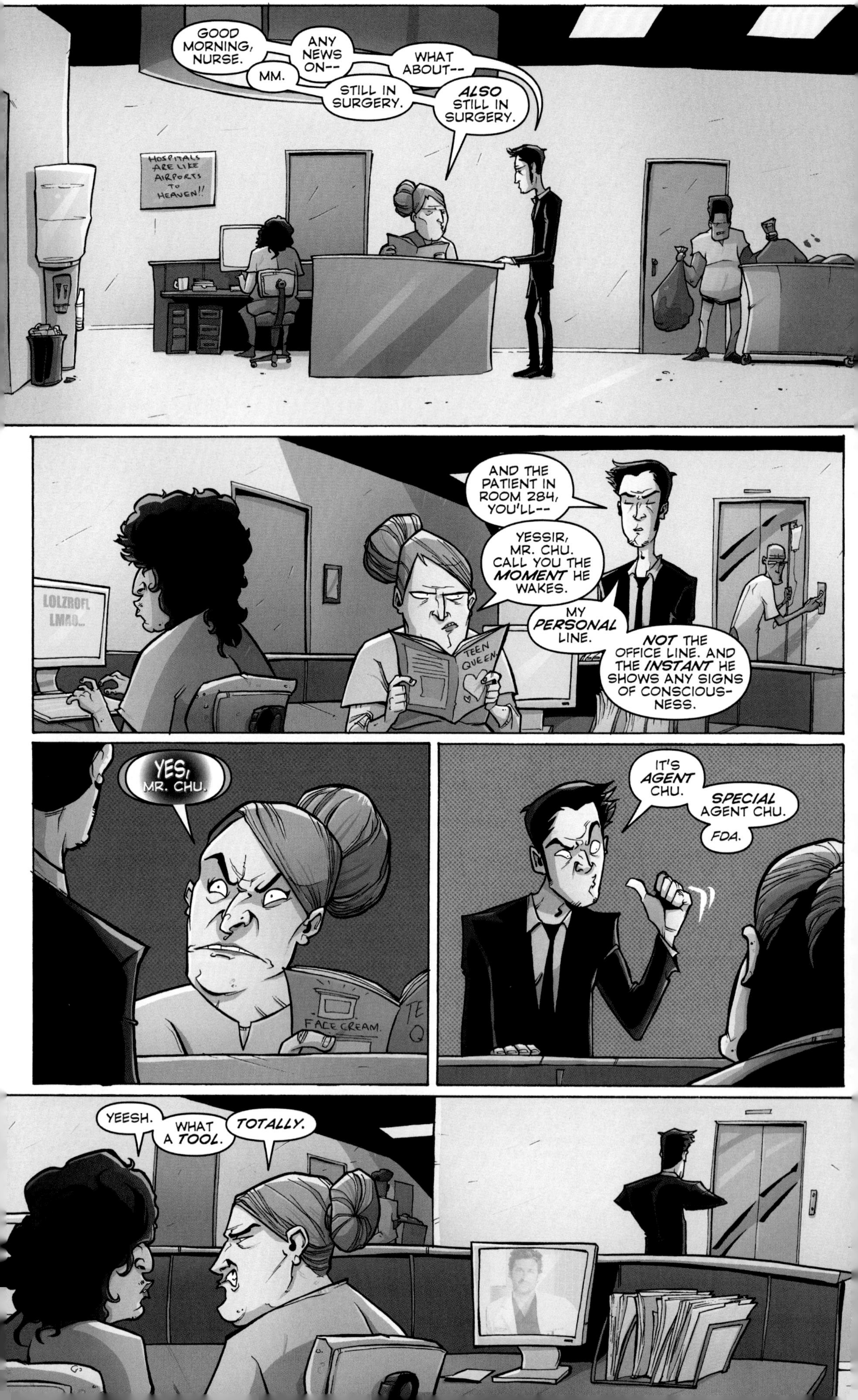
GOOD MORNING, NURSE.
MM.
ANY NEWS ON--
STILL IN SURGERY.
WHAT ABOUT--
ALSO STILL IN SURGERY.
HOSPITALS ARE LIKE AIRPORTS TO HEAVEN!!
AND THE PATIENT IN ROOM 284, YOU'LL--
YESSIR, MR. CHU. CALL YOU THE MOMENT HE WAKES.
MY PERSONAL LINE.
NOT THE OFFICE LINE. AND THE INSTANT HE SHOWS ANY SIGNS OF CONSCIOUS-NESS.
LOLZROFL LMAO...
TEEN QUEEN
YES, MR. CHU.
FACE CREAM
IT'S AGENT CHU.
SPECIAL AGENT CHU.
FDA.
YEESH.
WHAT A TOOL.
TOTALLY.

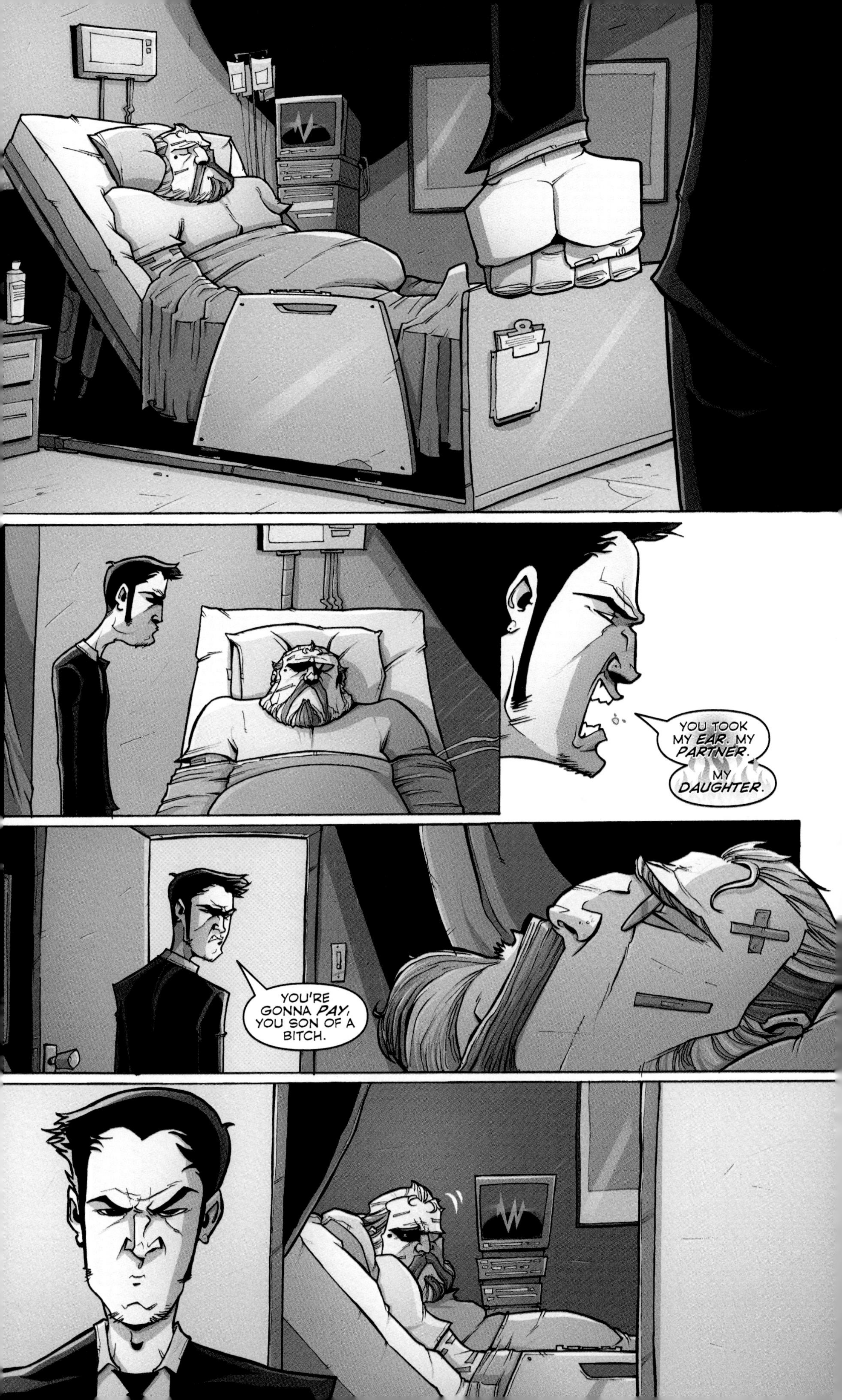
YOU TOOK MY EAR. MY PARTNER.
MY DAUGHTER.
YOU'RE GONNA PAY, YOU SON OF A BITCH.

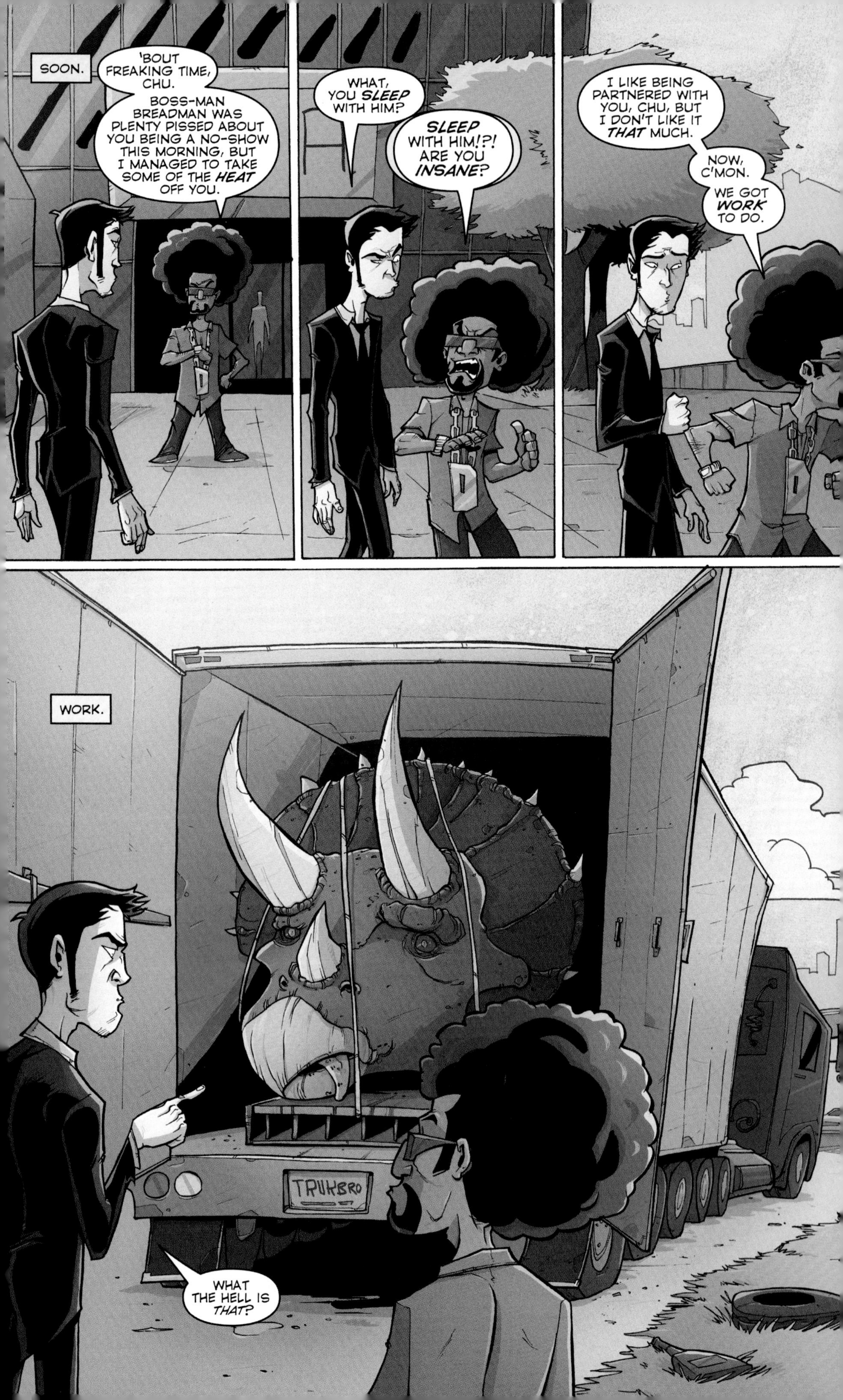

SOON.
'BOUT FREAKING TIME, CHU.
BOSS-MAN BREADMAN WAS PLENTY PISSED ABOUT YOU BEING A NO-SHOW THIS MORNING, BUT I MANAGED TO TAKE SOME OF THE *HEAT* OFF YOU.
WHAT, YOU *SLEEP* WITH HIM?
SLEEP WITH HIM!?! ARE YOU *INSANE*?
I LIKE BEING PARTNERED WITH YOU, CHU, BUT I DON'T LIKE IT *THAT* MUCH.
NOW, C'MON.
WE GOT *WORK* TO DO.
WORK.
TRUKBRO
WHAT THE HELL IS *THAT*?

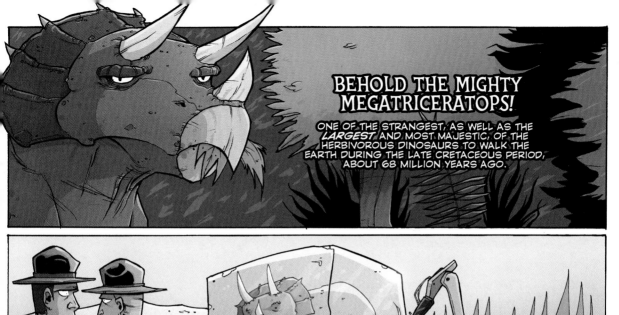

BEHOLD THE MIGHTY MEGATRICERATOPS!

ONE OF THE STRANGEST, AS WELL AS THE *LARGEST* AND MOST MAJESTIC, OF THE HERBIVOROUS DINOSAURS TO WALK THE EARTH DURING THE LATE CRETACEOUS PERIOD, ABOUT 68 MILLION YEARS AGO.

A SPECIMEN OF WHICH, ALMOST *COMPLETELY INTACT*, WAS RECENTLY UNEARTHED IN THE FROZEN NORTHERN TERRITORIES OF CANADA.

AND THEN DONATED FOR CUTTING-EDGE RESEARCH, CLONING, GENETIC-ENGINEERING AND DE-EXTINCTION EXPERIMENTATION.

HIGHWAY PATROL PULLED THIS RIG OVER ON A ROUTINE TRAFFIC STOP.

DIDN'T KNOW WHAT TO MAKE OF ITS *CARGO*, SO THEY GAVE *US* A CALL.

TRUCK WAS EN ROUTE TO A DINNER EVENT FOR THE *BON VIVANTS*, BUNCH OF HOITY-TOITY ONE-PERCENTERS WHO GET OFF ON CHOWING DOWN ON THINGS THAT ARE ENDANGERED OR EXTINCT.

THE *BON VIVANTS*?

I *BUSTED* THE *BON VIVANTS.*

I SHUT THEM *DOWN.*

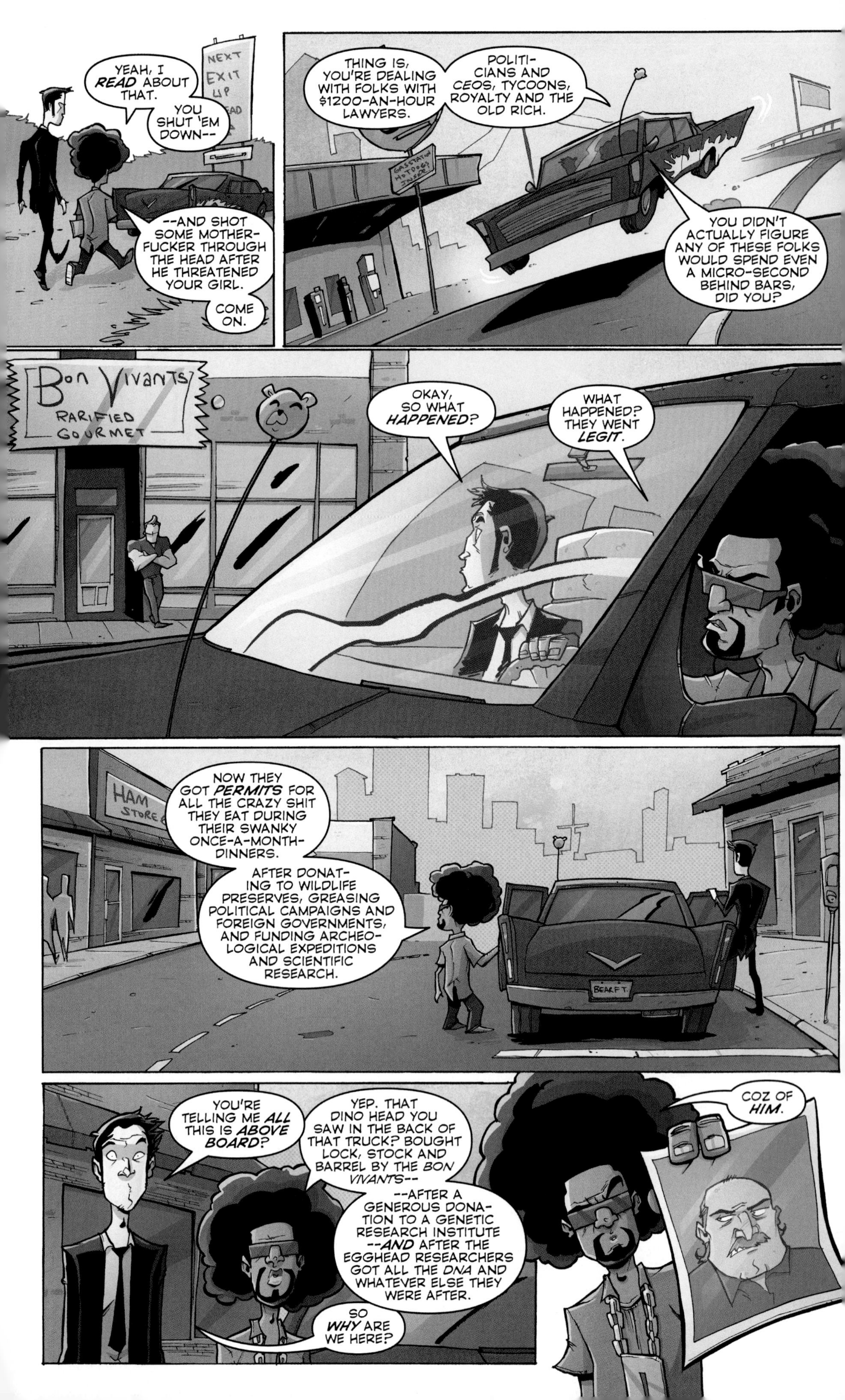
NEXT EXIT
YEAH, I *READ* ABOUT THAT.
YOU SHUT 'EM DOWN--
--AND SHOT SOME MOTHER-FUCKER THROUGH THE HEAD AFTER HE THREATENED YOUR GIRL.
COME ON.
THING IS, YOU'RE DEALING WITH FOLKS WITH $1200-AN-HOUR LAWYERS.
POLITI-CIANS AND CEOS, TYCOONS, ROYALTY AND THE OLD RICH.
YOU DIDN'T ACTUALLY FIGURE ANY OF THESE FOLKS WOULD SPEND EVEN A MICRO-SECOND BEHIND BARS, DID YOU?
Bon Vivants
RARIFIED GOURMET
OKAY, SO WHAT *HAPPENED*?
WHAT HAPPENED? THEY WENT *LEGIT*.
HAM STORE
NOW THEY GOT *PERMITS* FOR ALL THE CRAZY SHIT THEY EAT DURING THEIR SWANKY ONCE-A-MONTH-DINNERS.
AFTER DONATING TO WILDLIFE PRESERVES, GREASING POLITICAL CAMPAIGNS AND FOREIGN GOVERNMENTS, AND FUNDING ARCHEO-LOGICAL EXPEDITIONS AND SCIENTIFIC RESEARCH.
BEARFT.
YOU'RE TELLING ME *ALL* THIS IS *ABOVE BOARD*?
YEP. THAT DINO HEAD YOU SAW IN THE BACK OF THAT TRUCK? BOUGHT LOCK, STOCK AND BARREL BY THE *BON VIVANTS*--
--AFTER A GENEROUS DONA-TION TO A GENETIC RESEARCH INSTITUTE *--AND* AFTER THE EGGHEAD RESEARCHERS GOT ALL THE *DNA* AND WHATEVER ELSE THEY WERE AFTER.
SO *WHY* ARE WE HERE?
COZ OF *HIM*.

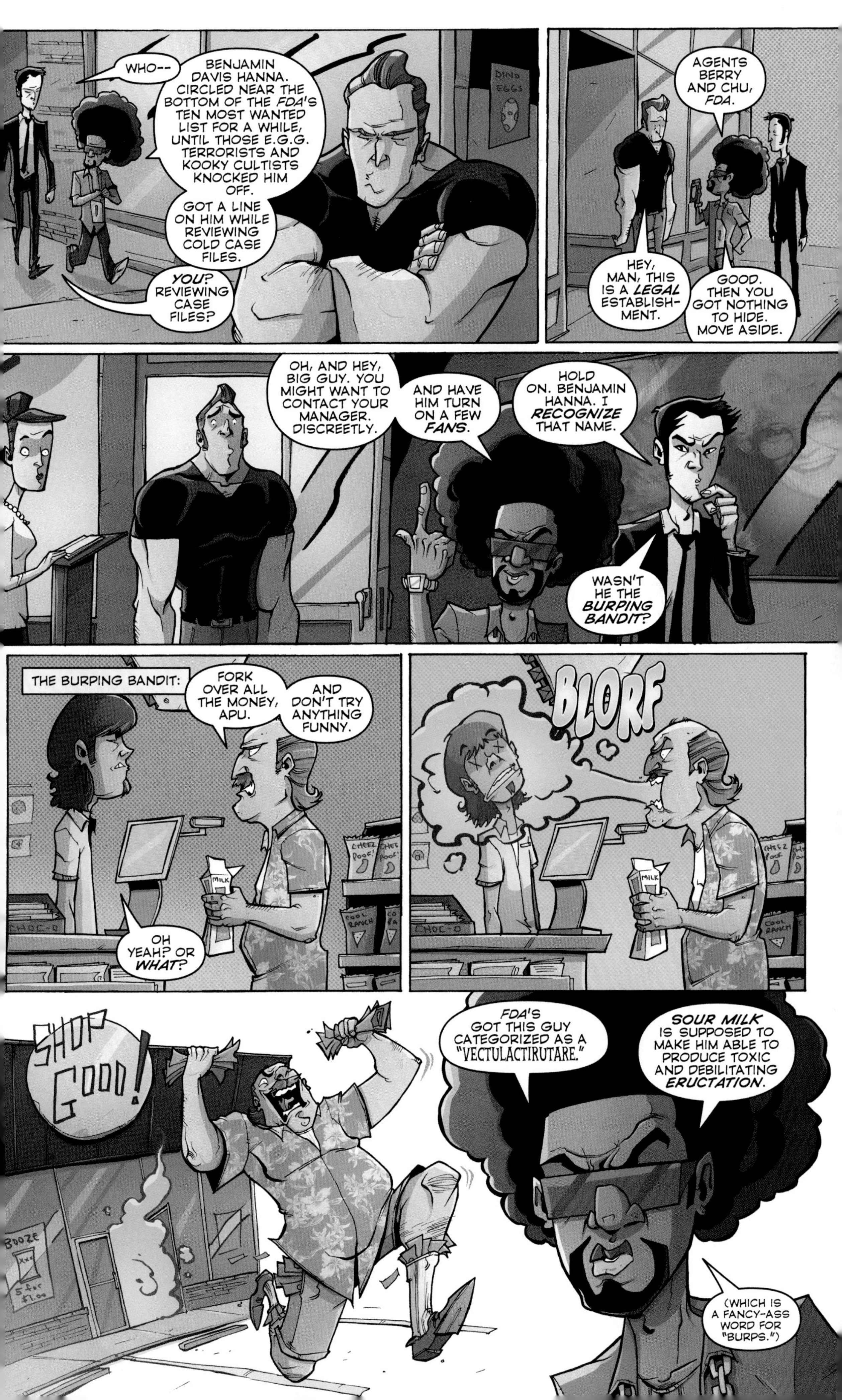
WHO--
BENJAMIN DAVIS HANNA. CIRCLED NEAR THE BOTTOM OF THE FDA'S TEN MOST WANTED LIST FOR A WHILE, UNTIL THOSE E.G.G. TERRORISTS AND KOOKY CULTISTS KNOCKED HIM OFF.
GOT A LINE ON HIM WHILE REVIEWING COLD CASE FILES.
YOU? REVIEWING CASE FILES?
DINO EGGS
AGENTS BERRY AND CHU, FDA.
HEY, MAN, THIS IS A LEGAL ESTABLISH-MENT.
GOOD. THEN YOU GOT NOTHING TO HIDE. MOVE ASIDE.
OH, AND HEY, BIG GUY. YOU MIGHT WANT TO CONTACT YOUR MANAGER. DISCREETLY.
AND HAVE HIM TURN ON A FEW FANS.
HOLD ON. BENJAMIN HANNA. I RECOGNIZE THAT NAME.
WASN'T HE THE BURPING BANDIT?
THE BURPING BANDIT:
FORK OVER ALL THE MONEY, APU.
AND DON'T TRY ANYTHING FUNNY.
OH YEAH? OR WHAT?
MILK
BLORF
SHOP GOOD!
BOOZE
5 for $1.00
FDA'S GOT THIS GUY CATEGORIZED AS A "VECTULACTIRUTARE."
SOUR MILK IS SUPPOSED TO MAKE HIM ABLE TO PRODUCE TOXIC AND DEBILITATING ERUCTATION.
(WHICH IS A FANCY-ASS WORD FOR "BURPS.")

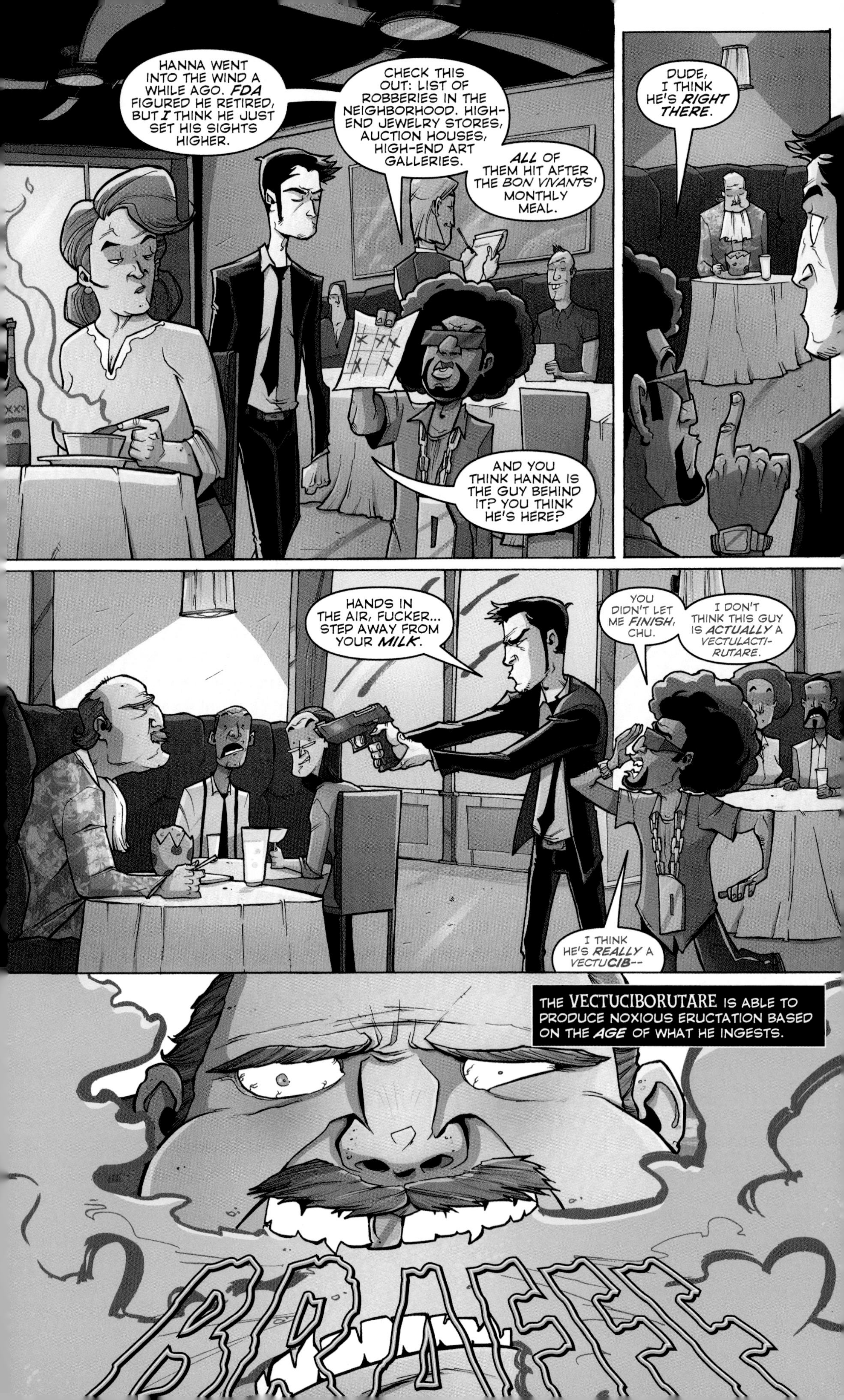

HANNA WENT INTO THE WIND A WHILE AGO. FDA FIGURED HE RETIRED, BUT I THINK HE JUST SET HIS SIGHTS HIGHER.
CHECK THIS OUT: LIST OF ROBBERIES IN THE NEIGHBORHOOD. HIGH-END JEWELRY STORES, AUCTION HOUSES, HIGH-END ART GALLERIES.
ALL OF THEM HIT AFTER THE BON VIVANTS' MONTHLY MEAL.
AND YOU THINK HANNA IS THE GUY BEHIND IT? YOU THINK HE'S HERE?
DUDE, I THINK HE'S RIGHT THERE.
HANDS IN THE AIR, FUCKER... STEP AWAY FROM YOUR MILK.
YOU DIDN'T LET ME FINISH, CHU.
I DON'T THINK THIS GUY IS ACTUALLY A VECTULACTI-RUTARE.
I THINK HE'S REALLY A VECTUCIB--
THE VECTUCIBORUTARE IS ABLE TO PRODUCE NOXIOUS ERUCTATION BASED ON THE AGE OF WHAT HE INGESTS.

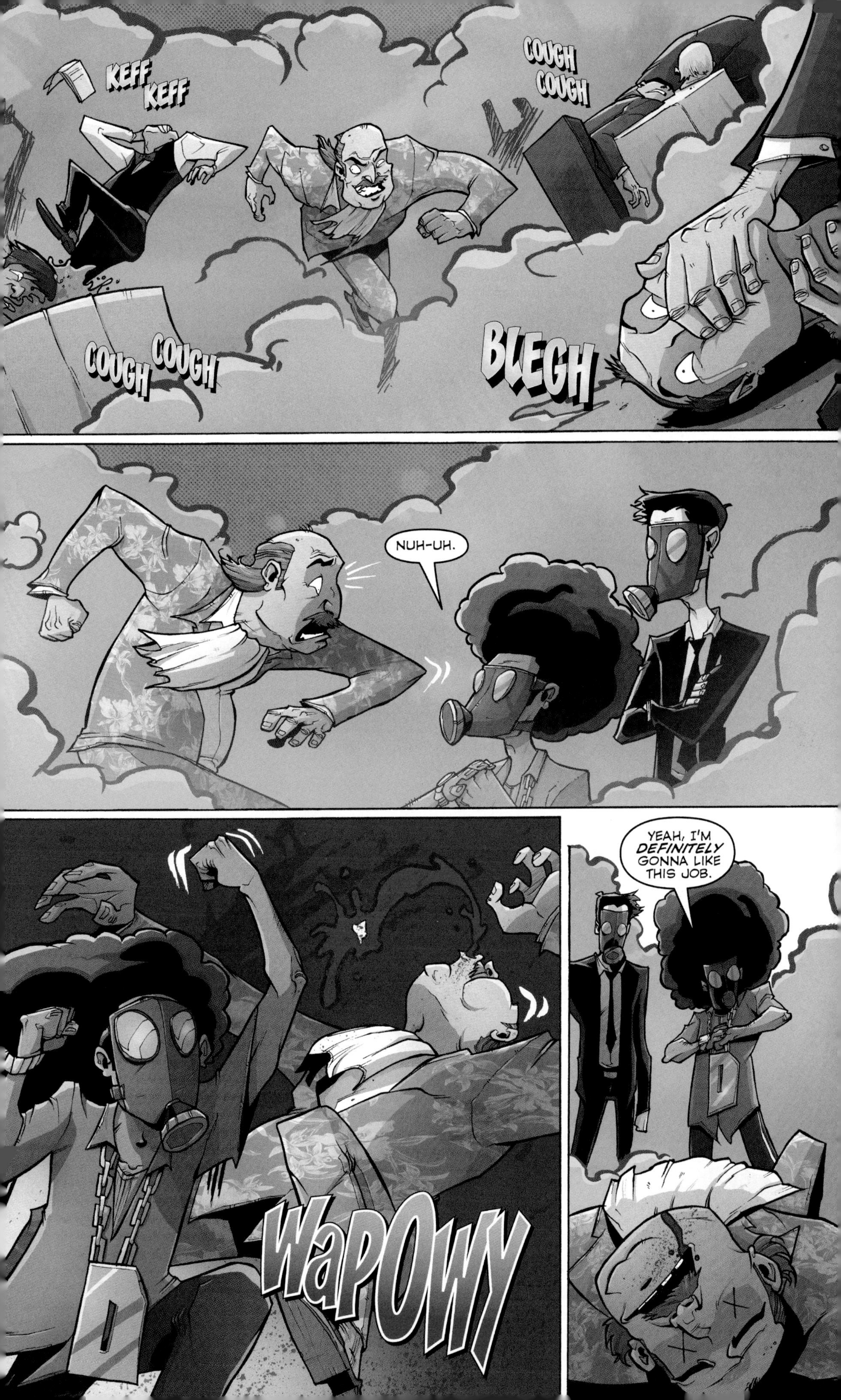
KEFF KEFF
COUGH COUGH
COUGH COUGH
BLEGH
NUH-UH.
WAPOWY
YEAH, I'M *DEFINITELY* GONNA LIKE THIS JOB.

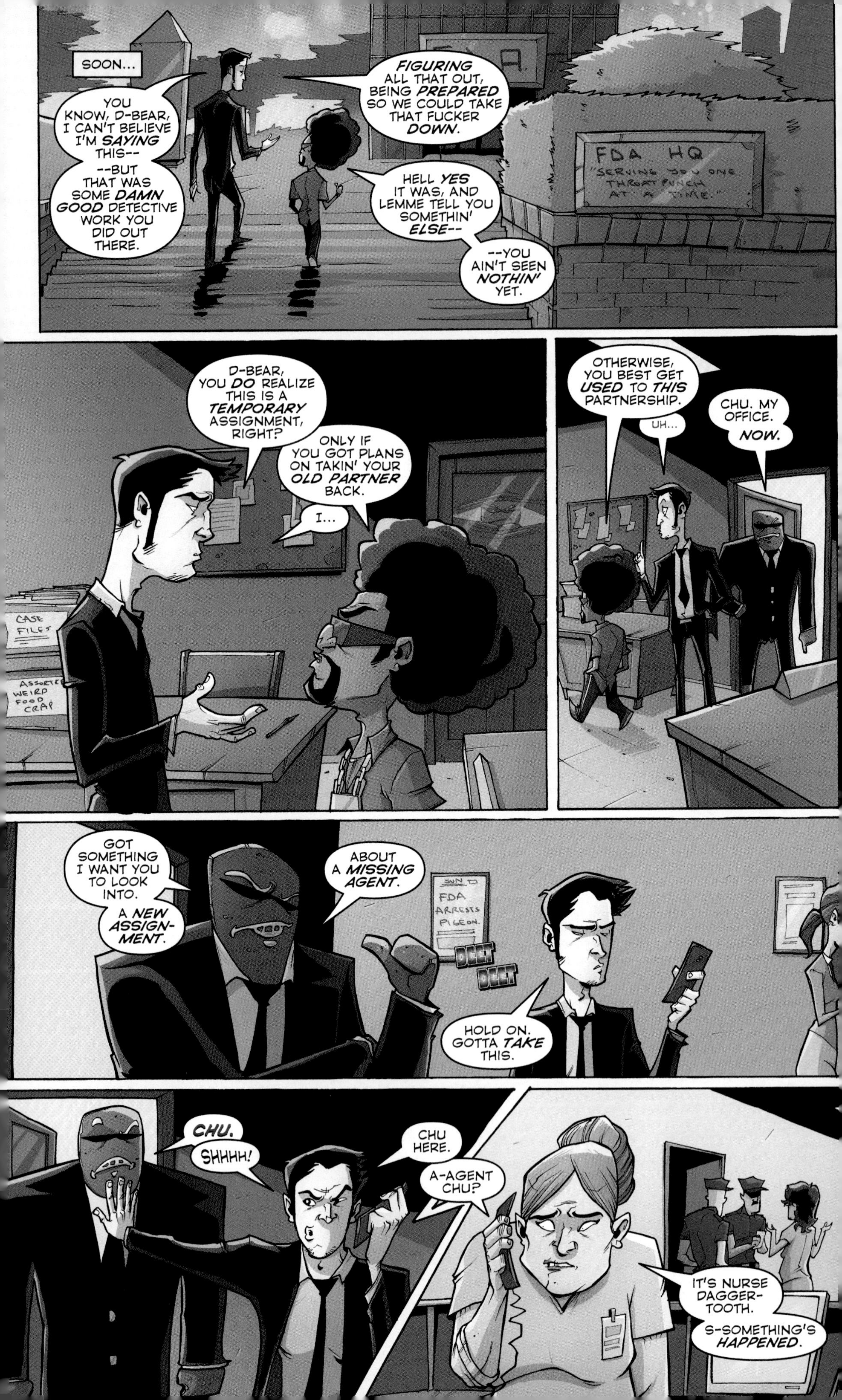
SOON...
YOU KNOW, D-BEAR, I CAN'T BELIEVE I'M SAYING THIS--
--BUT THAT WAS SOME DAMN GOOD DETECTIVE WORK YOU DID OUT THERE.
FIGURING ALL THAT OUT, BEING PREPARED SO WE COULD TAKE THAT FUCKER DOWN.
HELL YES IT WAS, AND LEMME TELL YOU SOMETHIN' ELSE--
--YOU AIN'T SEEN NOTHIN' YET.
FDA HQ
"SERVING YOU ONE THROAT PUNCH AT A TIME."
D-BEAR, YOU DO REALIZE THIS IS A TEMPORARY ASSIGNMENT, RIGHT?
ONLY IF YOU GOT PLANS ON TAKIN' YOUR OLD PARTNER BACK.
I...
CASE FILES
ASSORTED WEIRD FOOD CRAP
OTHERWISE, YOU BEST GET USED TO THIS PARTNERSHIP.
UH...
CHU. MY OFFICE. NOW.
GOT SOMETHING I WANT YOU TO LOOK INTO.
A NEW ASSIGNMENT.
ABOUT A MISSING AGENT.
FDA ARRESTS PIGEON.
DEET DEET
HOLD ON. GOTTA TAKE THIS.
CHU.
SHHHH!
CHU HERE.
A-AGENT CHU?
IT'S NURSE DAGGERTOOTH.
S-SOMETHING'S HAPPENED.

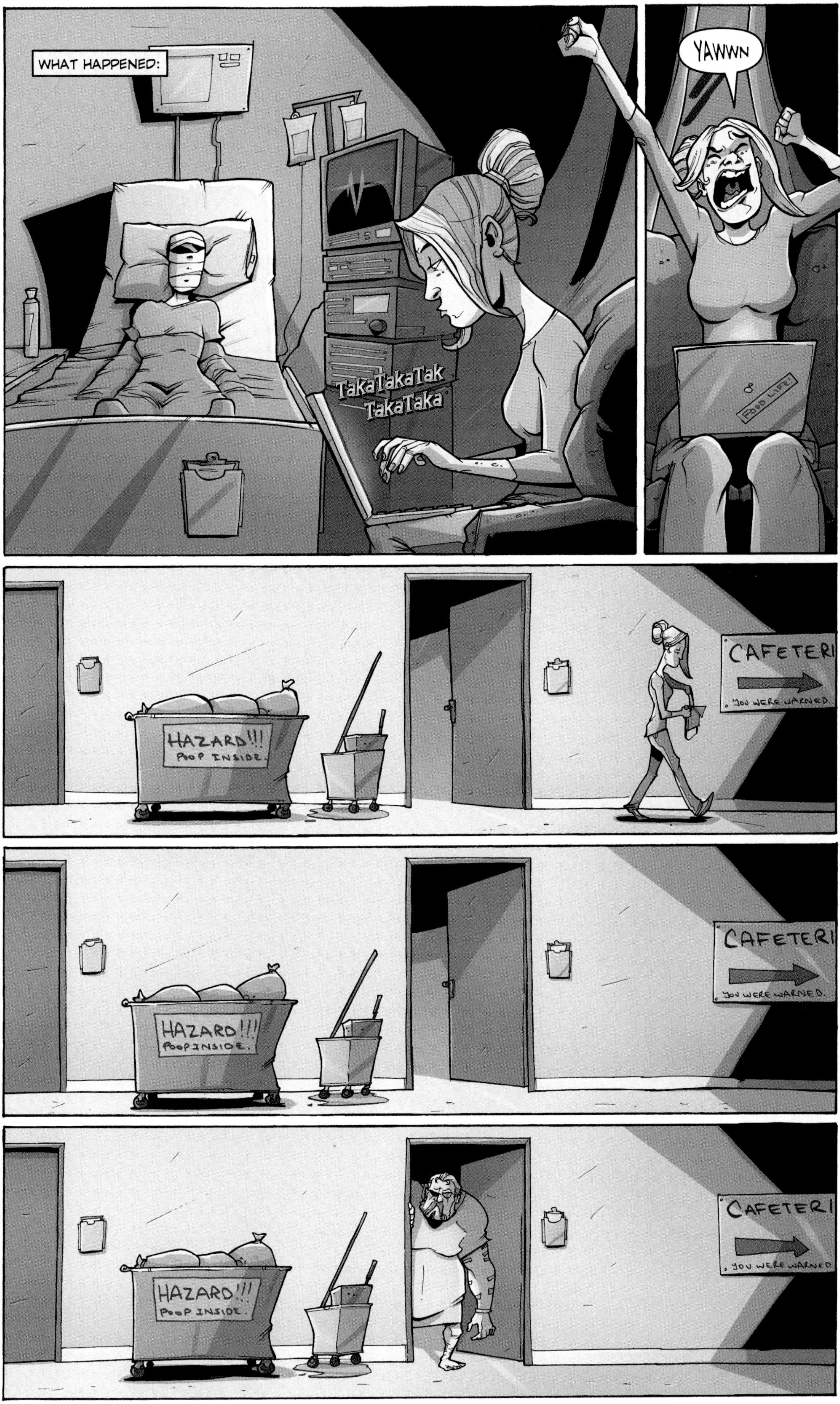
WHAT HAPPENED:
TakaTakaTak
TakaTaka
YAWWN
FOOD LIFE!
HAZARD!!!
POOP INSIDE.
CAFETERI
YOU WERE WARNED.
HAZARD!!!
POOP INSIDE.
CAFETERI
YOU WERE WARNED.
HAZARD!!!
POOP INSIDE.
CAFETERI
YOU WERE WARNED.

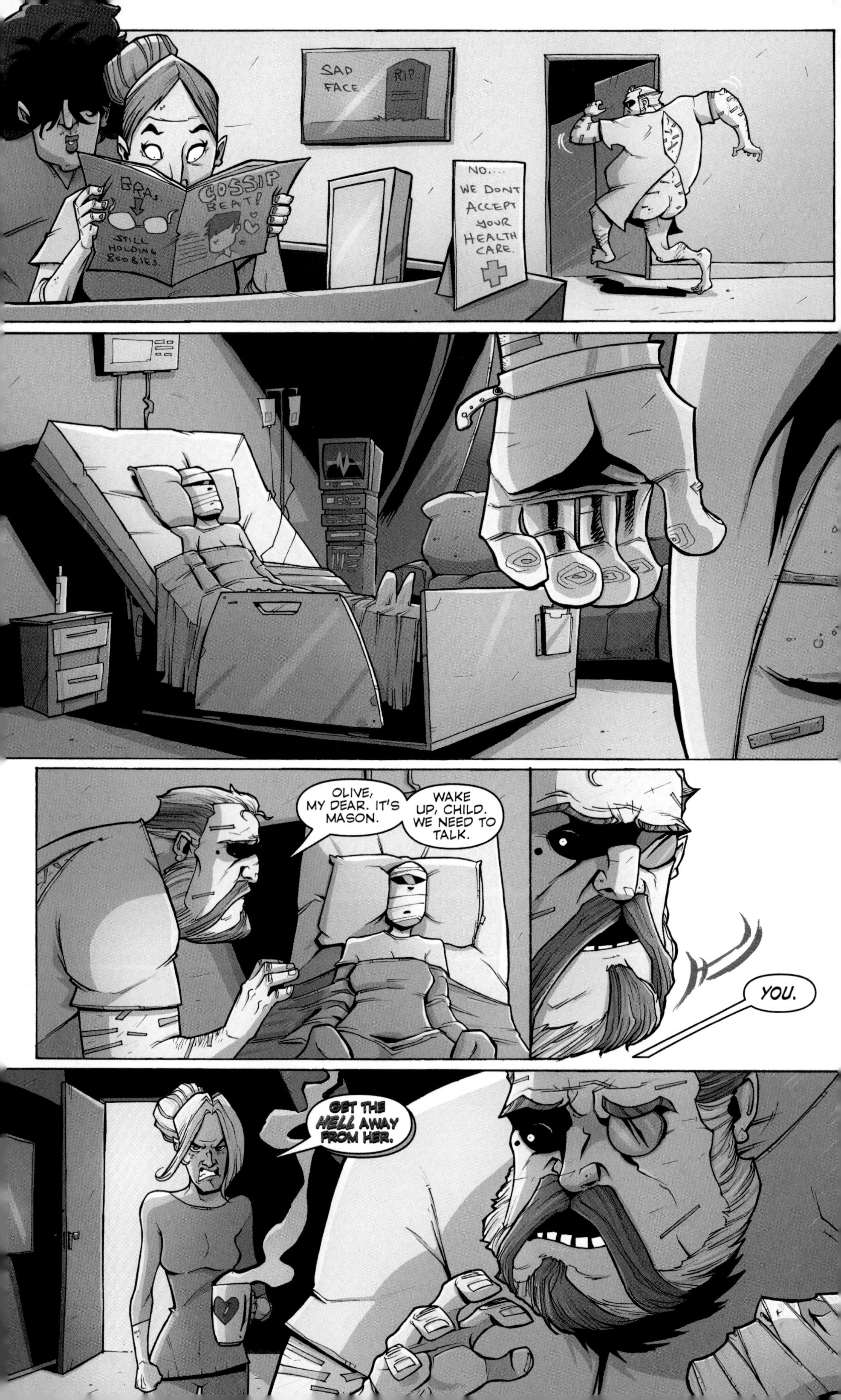

SAD FACE.
RIP
BRAS.
STILL HOLDING BOOBIES.
GOSSIP BEAT!
NO.... WE DONT ACCEPT YOUR HEALTH CARE.
OLIVE, MY DEAR. IT'S MASON.
WAKE UP, CHILD. WE NEED TO TALK.
YOU.
GET THE HELL AWAY FROM HER.

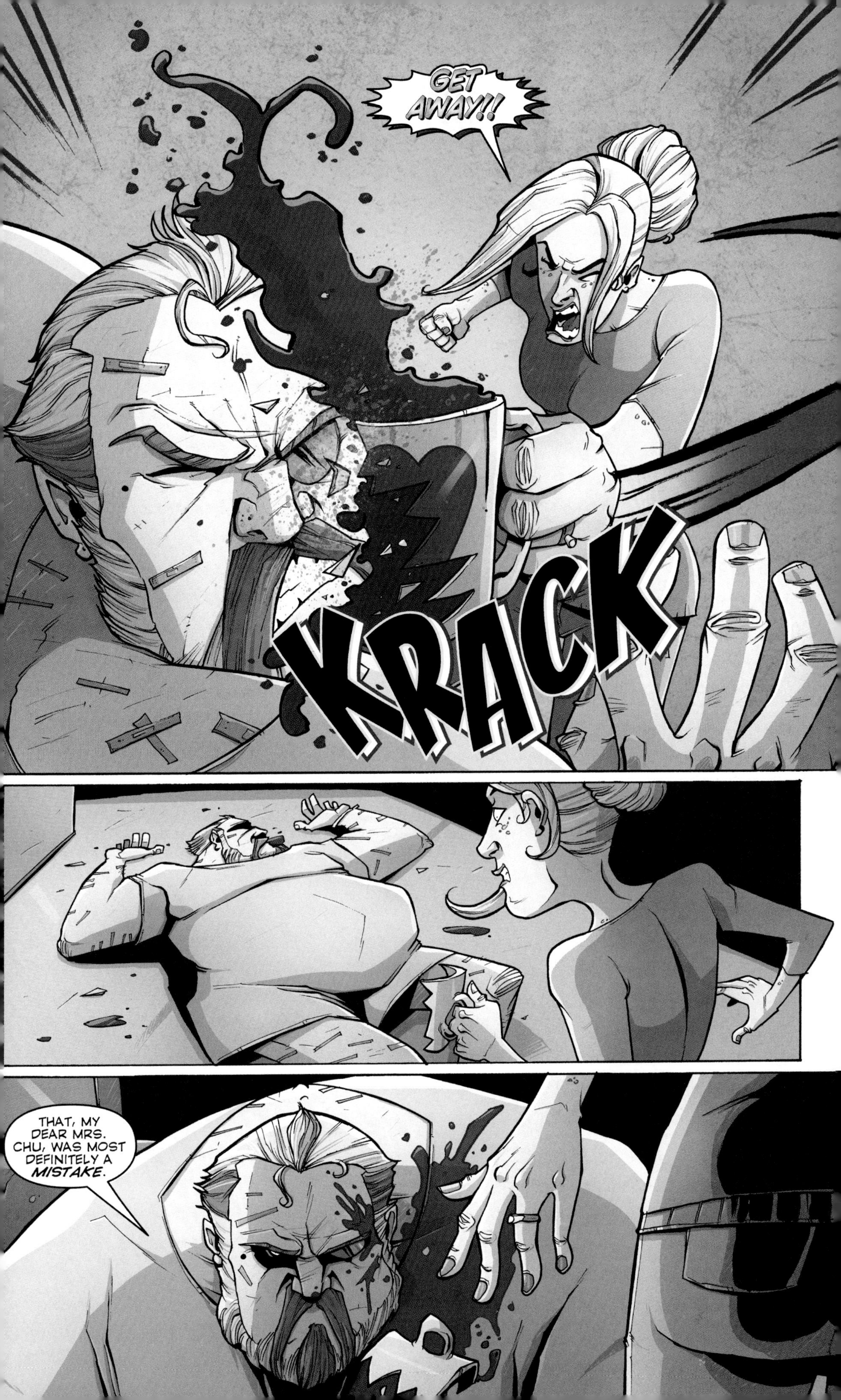
GET AWAY!!
KRACK
THAT, MY DEAR MRS. CHU, WAS MOST DEFINITELY A *MISTAKE*.

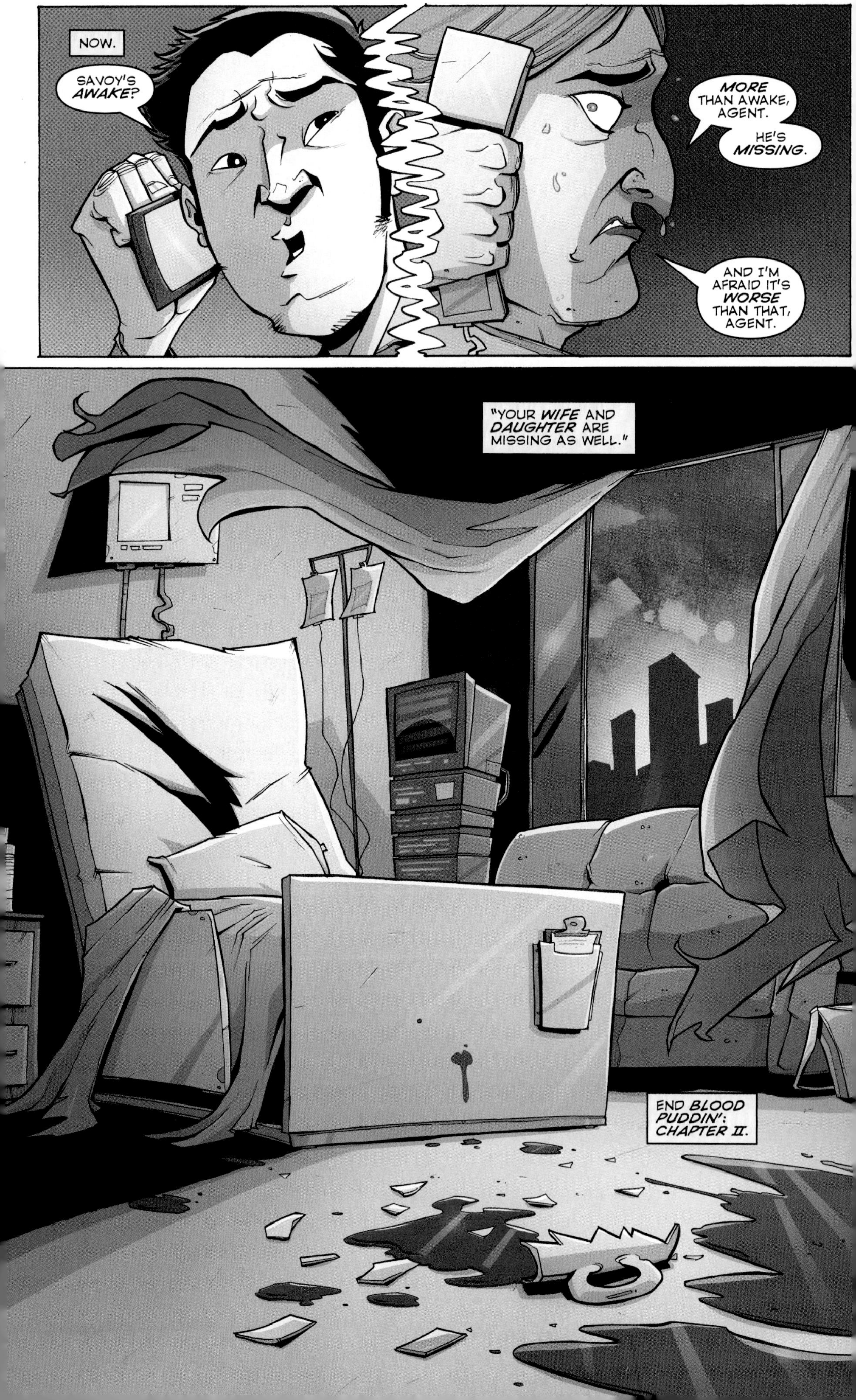
NOW.
SAVOY'S AWAKE?
MORE THAN AWAKE, AGENT.
HE'S MISSING.
AND I'M AFRAID IT'S WORSE THAN THAT, AGENT.
"YOUR WIFE AND DAUGHTER ARE MISSING AS WELL."
END BLOOD PUDDIN': CHAPTER II.

Chapter Eight

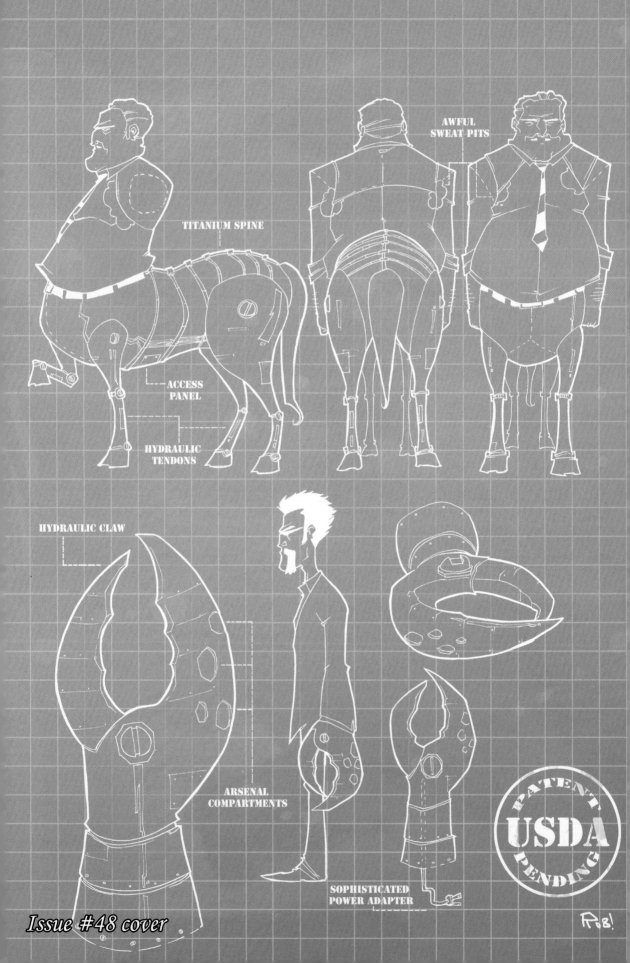

TITANIUM SPINE

AWFUL
SWEAT PITS

ACCESS
PANEL

HYDRAULIC
TENDONS

HYDRAULIC CLAW

ARSENAL
COMPARTMENTS

SOPHISTICATED
POWER ADAPTER

PATENT PENDING
USDA

Issue #48 cover

Rob!

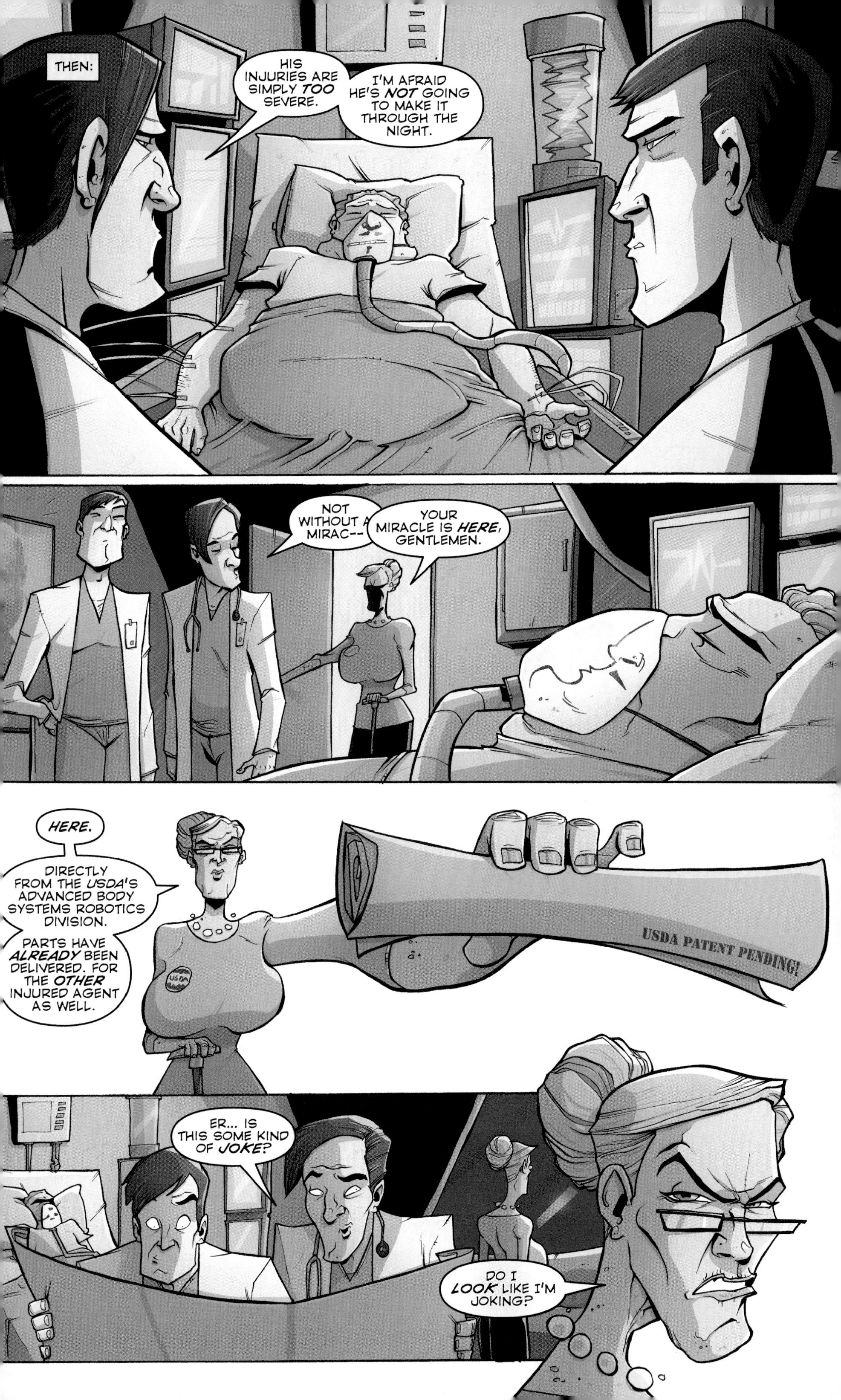
THEN:
HIS INJURIES ARE SIMPLY TOO SEVERE.
I'M AFRAID HE'S NOT GOING TO MAKE IT THROUGH THE NIGHT.
NOT WITHOUT A MIRAC--
YOUR MIRACLE IS HERE, GENTLEMEN.
HERE.
DIRECTLY FROM THE USDA'S ADVANCED BODY SYSTEMS ROBOTICS DIVISION.
PARTS HAVE ALREADY BEEN DELIVERED. FOR THE OTHER INJURED AGENT AS WELL.
USDA PATENT PENDING!
ER... IS THIS SOME KIND OF JOKE?
DO I LOOK LIKE I'M JOKING?

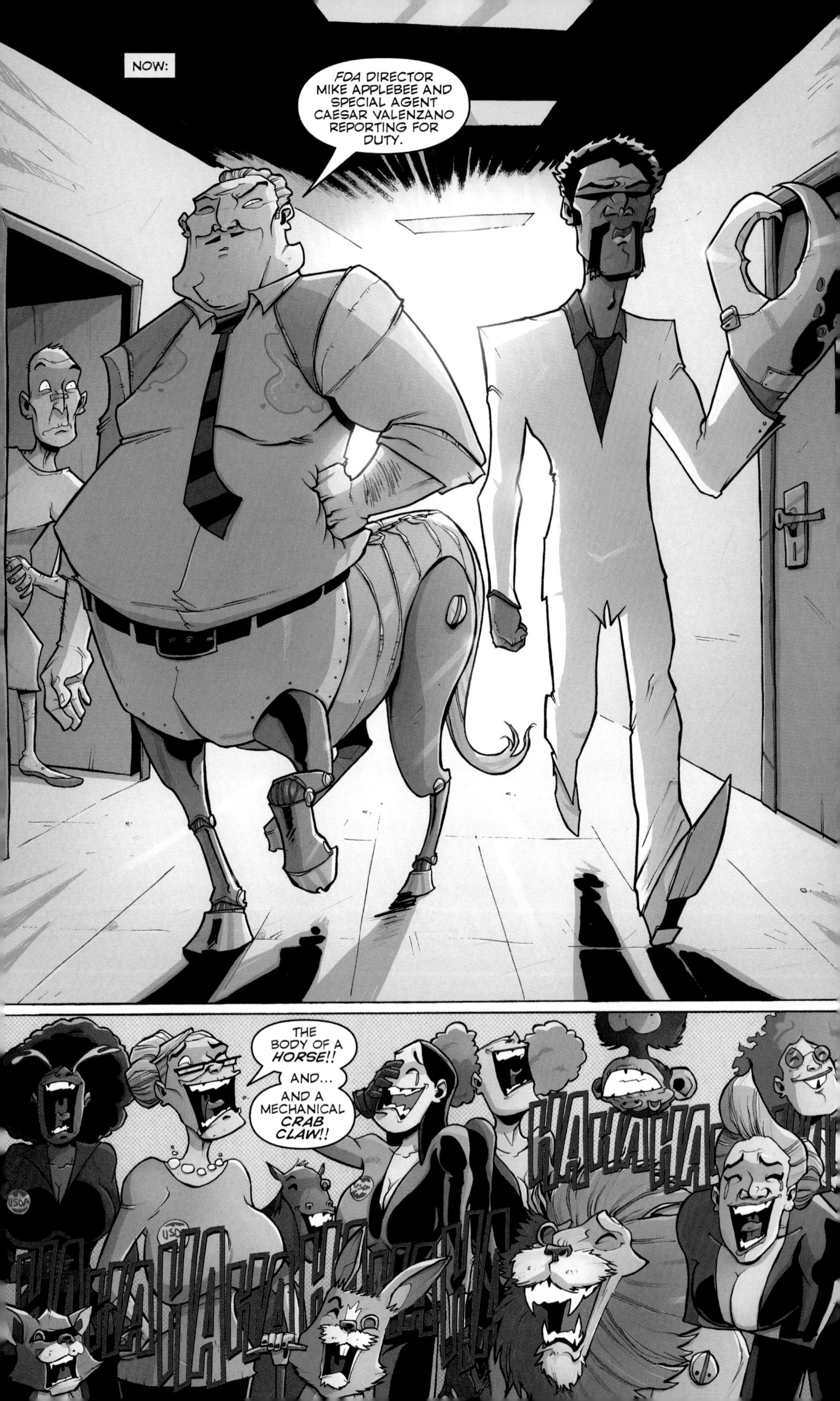
NOW:
FDA DIRECTOR MIKE APPLEBEE AND SPECIAL AGENT CAESAR VALENZANO REPORTING FOR DUTY.
THE BODY OF A HORSE!!
AND...
AND A MECHANICAL CRAB CLAW!!

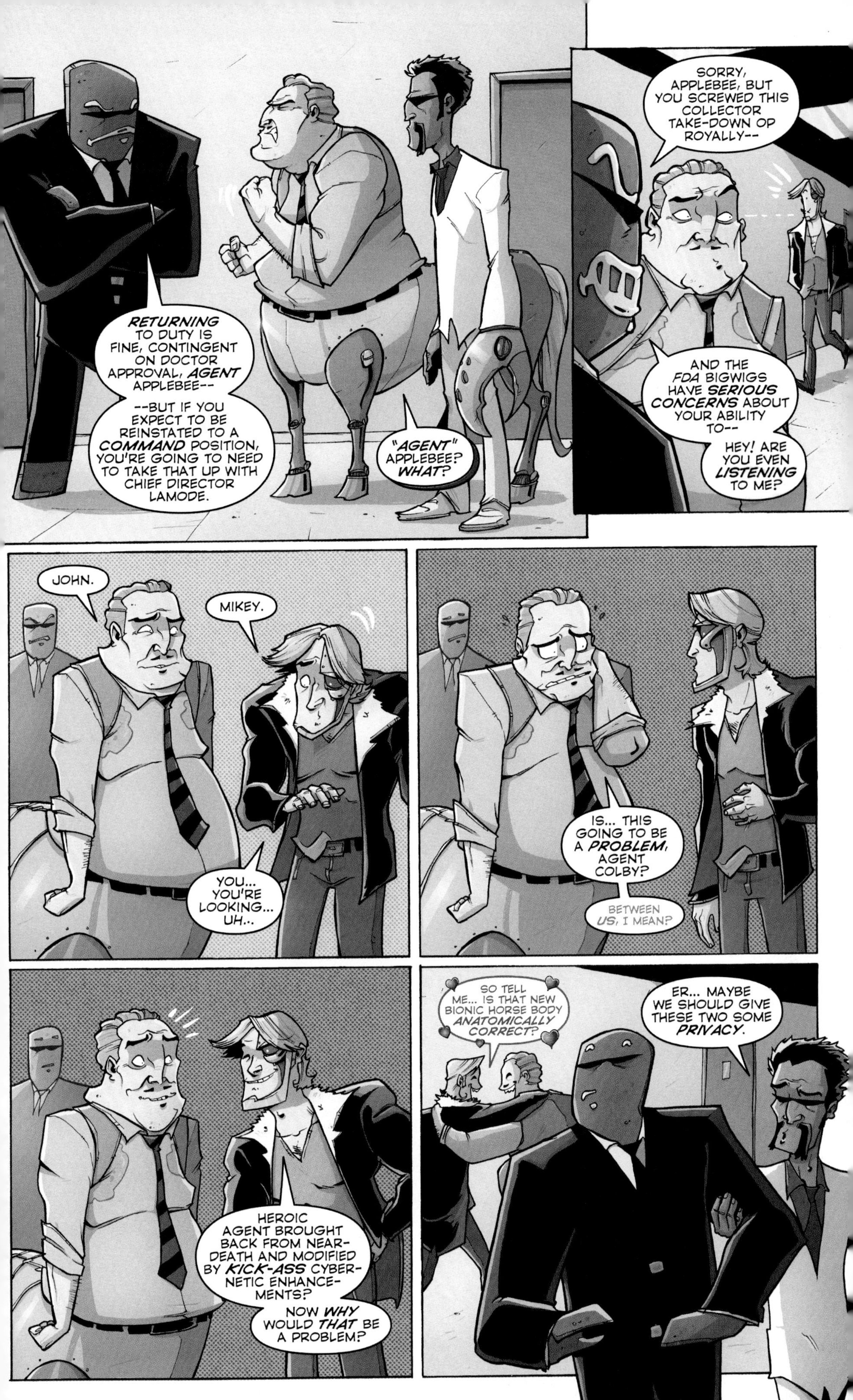
RETURNING TO DUTY IS FINE, CONTINGENT ON DOCTOR APPROVAL, AGENT APPLEBEE--
--BUT IF YOU EXPECT TO BE REINSTATED TO A COMMAND POSITION, YOU'RE GOING TO NEED TO TAKE THAT UP WITH CHIEF DIRECTOR LAMODE.
"AGENT" APPLEBEE? WHAT?
SORRY, APPLEBEE, BUT YOU SCREWED THIS COLLECTOR TAKE-DOWN OP ROYALLY--
AND THE FDA BIGWIGS HAVE SERIOUS CONCERNS ABOUT YOUR ABILITY TO--
HEY! ARE YOU EVEN LISTENING TO ME?
JOHN.
MIKEY.
YOU... YOU'RE LOOKING... UH...
IS... THIS GOING TO BE A PROBLEM, AGENT COLBY?
BETWEEN US, I MEAN?
HEROIC AGENT BROUGHT BACK FROM NEAR-DEATH AND MODIFIED BY KICK-ASS CYBER-NETIC ENHANCE-MENTS?
NOW WHY WOULD THAT BE A PROBLEM?
SO TELL ME... IS THAT NEW BIONIC HORSE BODY ANATOMICALLY CORRECT?
ER... MAYBE WE SHOULD GIVE THESE TWO SOME PRIVACY.

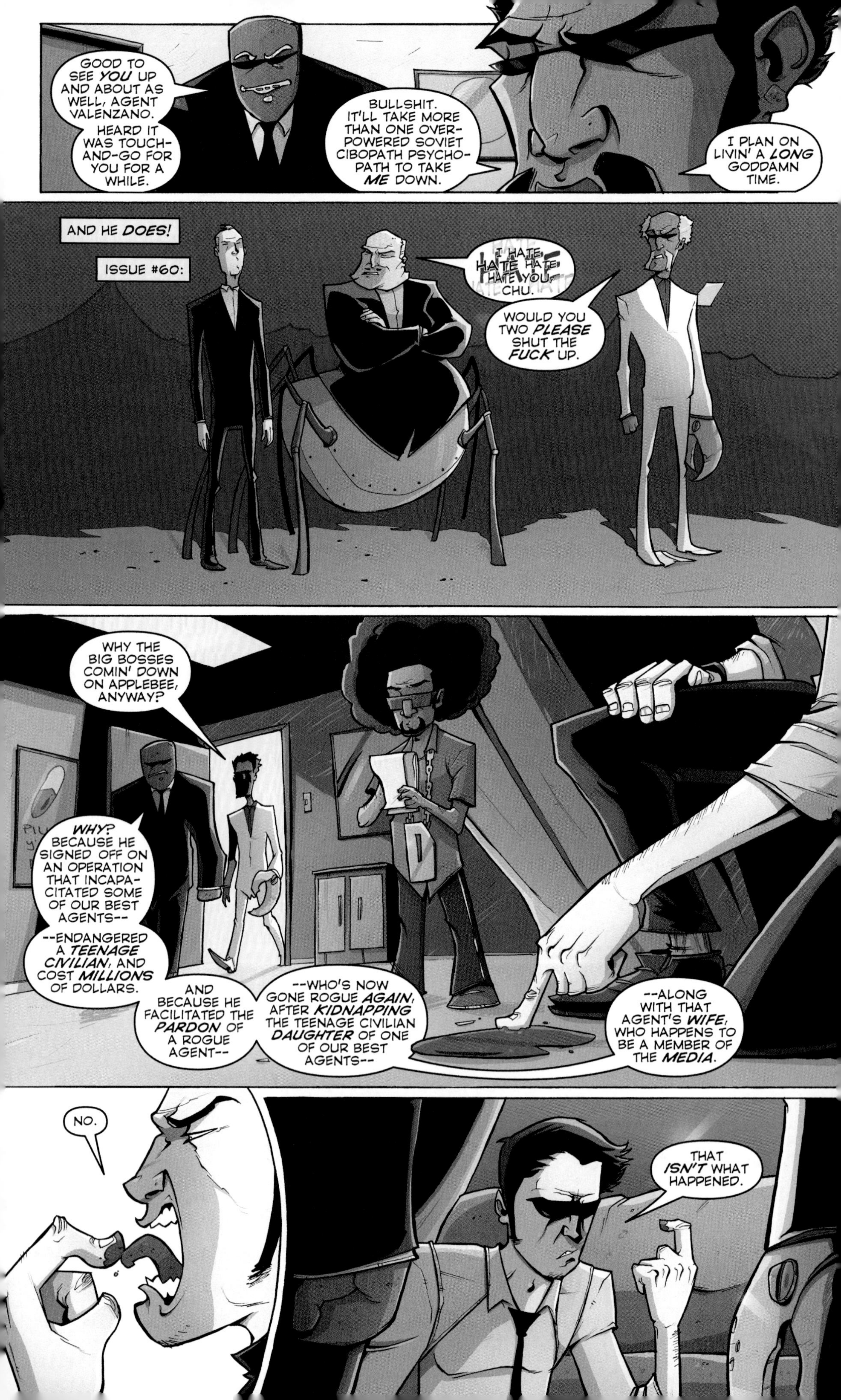

GOOD TO SEE *YOU* UP AND ABOUT AS WELL, AGENT VALENZANO.
HEARD IT WAS TOUCH-AND-GO FOR YOU FOR A WHILE.
BULLSHIT. IT'LL TAKE MORE THAN ONE OVER-POWERED SOVIET CIBOPATH PSYCHO-PATH TO TAKE *ME* DOWN.
I PLAN ON LIVIN' A *LONG* GODDAMN TIME.
AND HE *DOES!*
ISSUE #60:
I HATE HATE HATE HATE YOU, CHU.
WOULD YOU TWO *PLEASE* SHUT THE *FUCK* UP.
WHY THE BIG BOSSES COMIN' DOWN ON APPLEBEE, ANYWAY?
WHY? BECAUSE HE SIGNED OFF ON AN OPERATION THAT INCAPACITATED SOME OF OUR BEST AGENTS--
--ENDANGERED A *TEENAGE CIVILIAN*, AND COST *MILLIONS* OF DOLLARS.
AND BECAUSE HE FACILITATED THE *PARDON* OF A ROGUE AGENT--
--WHO'S NOW GONE ROGUE *AGAIN*, AFTER *KIDNAPPING* THE TEENAGE CIVILIAN *DAUGHTER* OF ONE OF OUR BEST AGENTS--
--ALONG WITH THAT AGENT'S *WIFE*, WHO HAPPENS TO BE A MEMBER OF THE *MEDIA*.
NO.
THAT *ISN'T* WHAT HAPPENED.

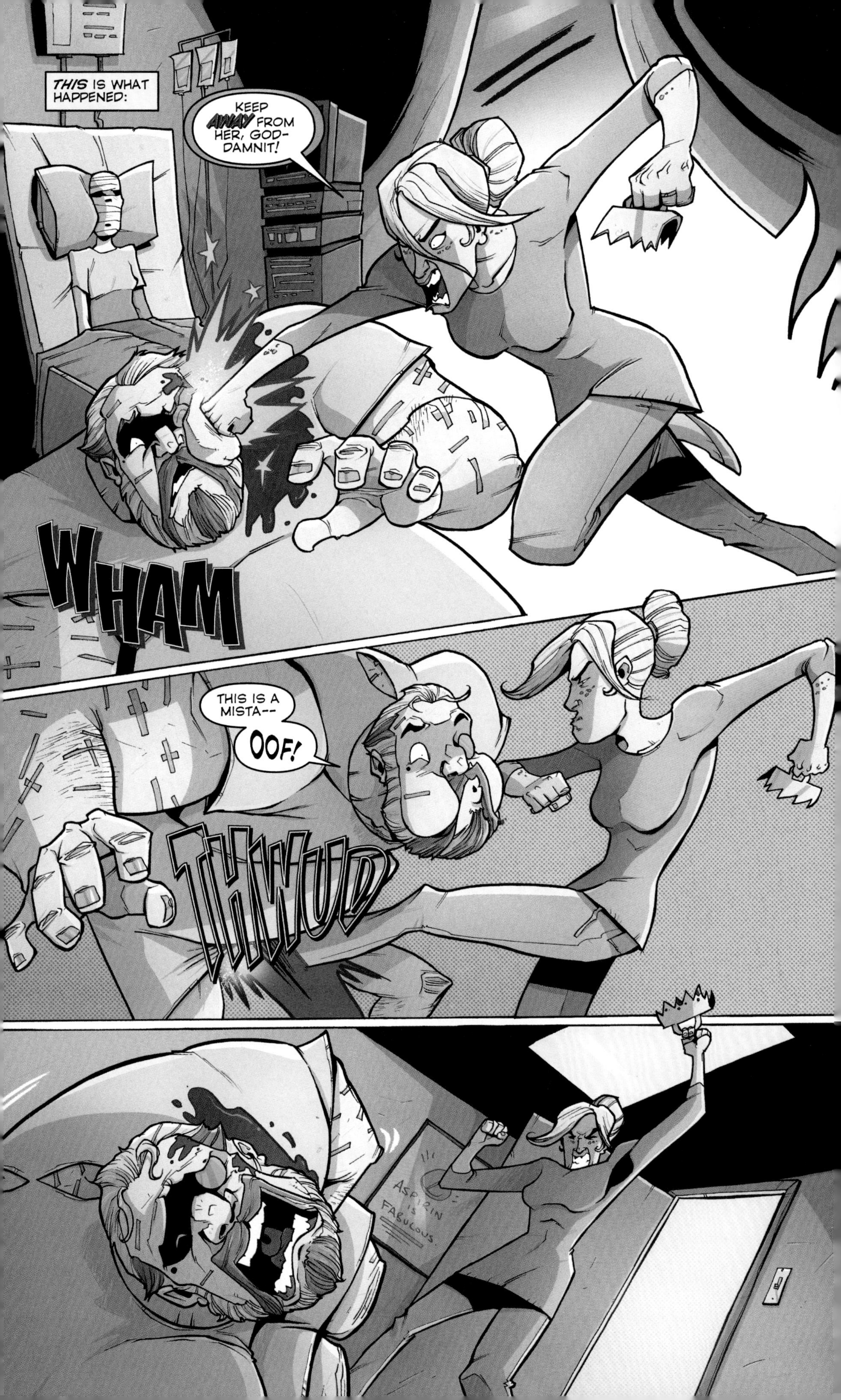
THIS IS WHAT HAPPENED:
KEEP AWAY FROM HER, GOD-DAMNIT!
WHAM
THIS IS A MISTA--
OOF!
THWUD
ASPIRIN IS FABULOUS

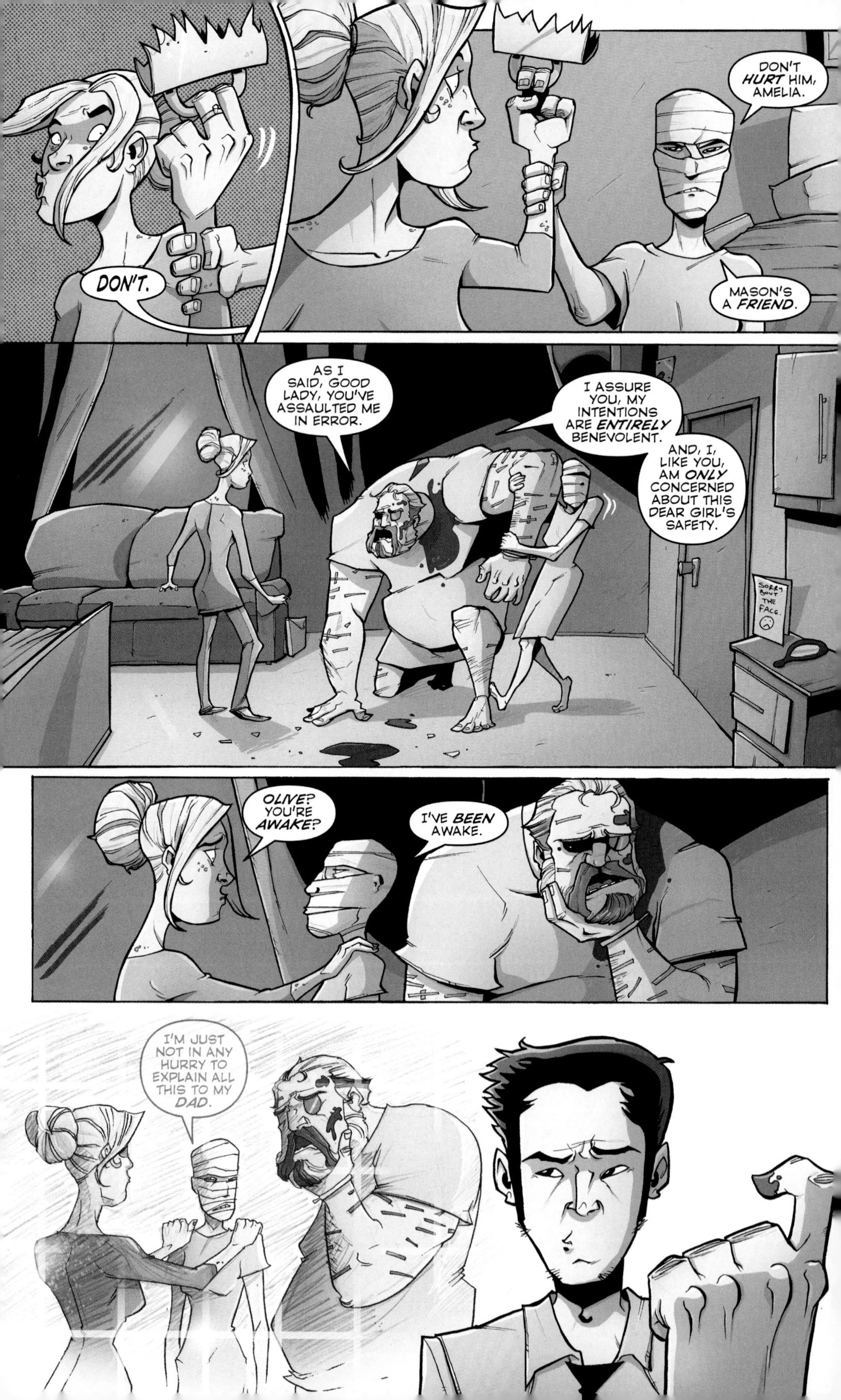
DON'T.
DON'T HURT HIM, AMELIA.
MASON'S A FRIEND.
AS I SAID, GOOD LADY, YOU'VE ASSAULTED ME IN ERROR.
I ASSURE YOU, MY INTENTIONS ARE ENTIRELY BENEVOLENT.
AND, I, LIKE YOU, AM ONLY CONCERNED ABOUT THIS DEAR GIRL'S SAFETY.
SORRY BOUT THE FACE.
OLIVE? YOU'RE AWAKE?
I'VE BEEN AWAKE.
I'M JUST NOT IN ANY HURRY TO EXPLAIN ALL THIS TO MY DAD.

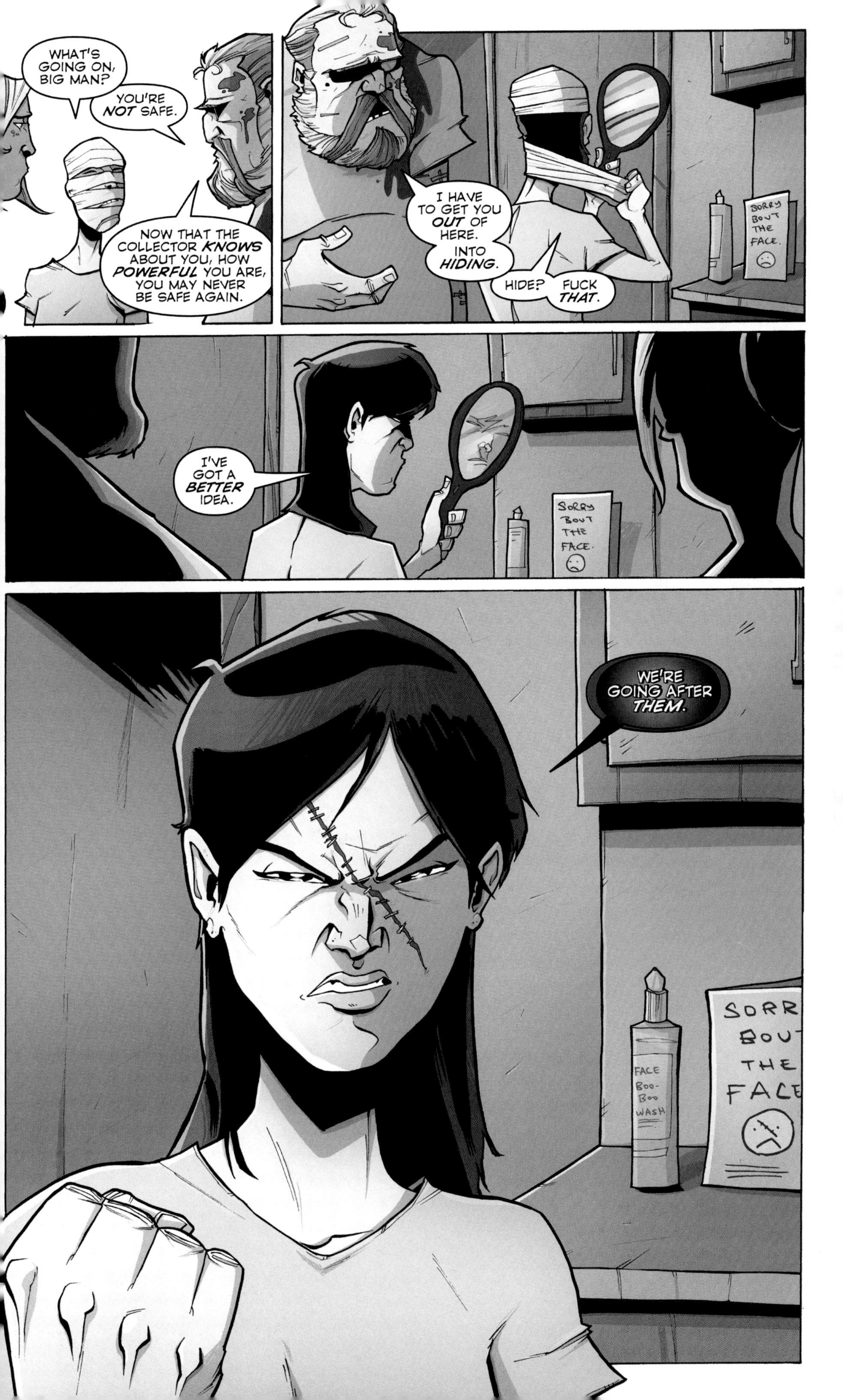
WHAT'S GOING ON, BIG MAN?
YOU'RE NOT SAFE.
NOW THAT THE COLLECTOR KNOWS ABOUT YOU, HOW POWERFUL YOU ARE, YOU MAY NEVER BE SAFE AGAIN.
I HAVE TO GET YOU OUT OF HERE.
INTO HIDING.
SORRY BOUT THE FACE.
HIDE?
FUCK THAT.
I'VE GOT A BETTER IDEA.
SORRY BOUT THE FACE.
WE'RE GOING AFTER THEM.
FACE BOO-BOO WASH
SORR BOUT THE FACE

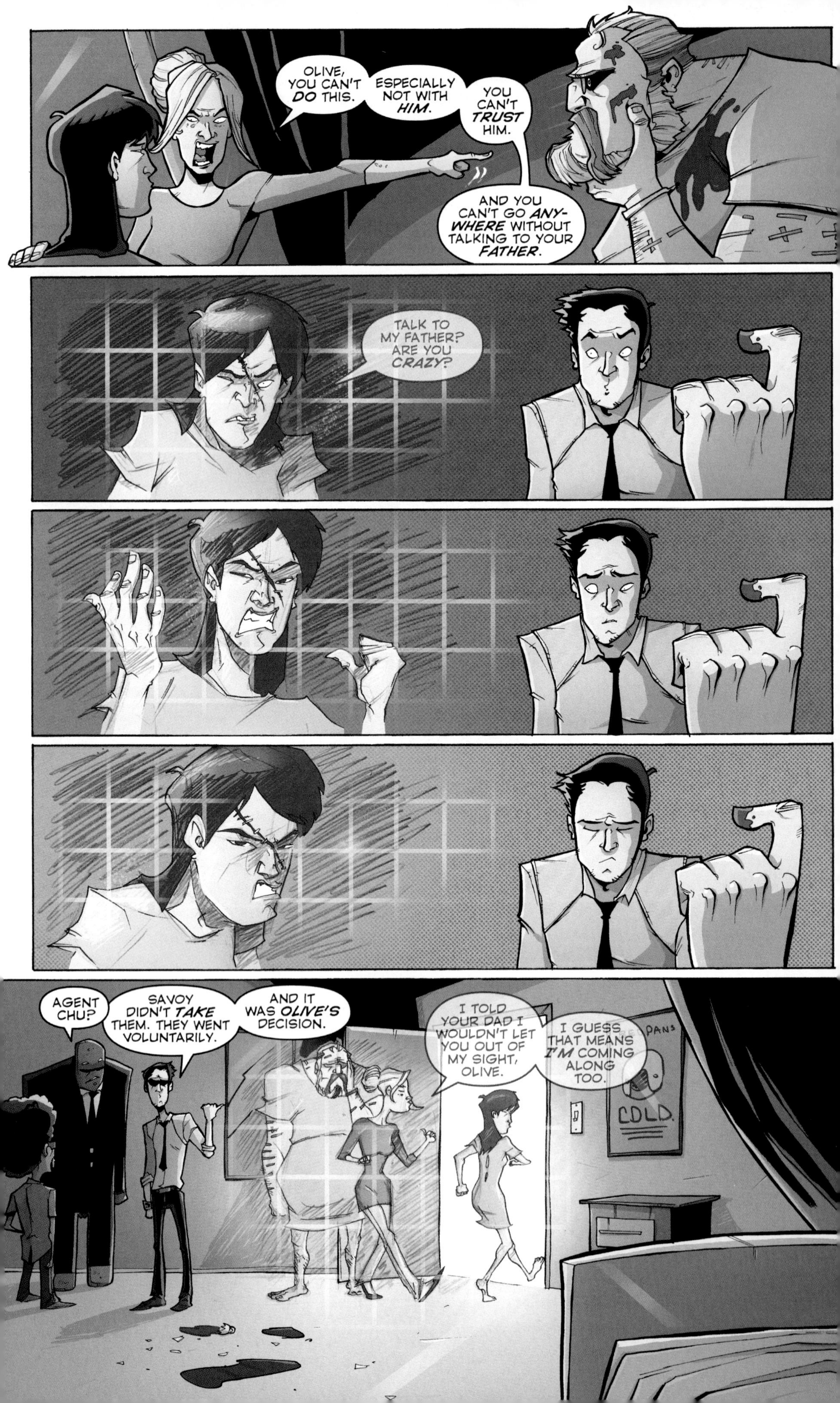
OLIVE, YOU CAN'T DO THIS.
ESPECIALLY NOT WITH HIM.
YOU CAN'T TRUST HIM.
AND YOU CAN'T GO ANY-WHERE WITHOUT TALKING TO YOUR FATHER.
TALK TO MY FATHER? ARE YOU CRAZY?
AGENT CHU?
SAVOY DIDN'T TAKE THEM. THEY WENT VOLUNTARILY.
AND IT WAS OLIVE'S DECISION.
I TOLD YOUR DAD I WOULDN'T LET YOU OUT OF MY SIGHT, OLIVE.
I GUESS THAT MEANS I'M COMING ALONG TOO.
C.D.L.D.

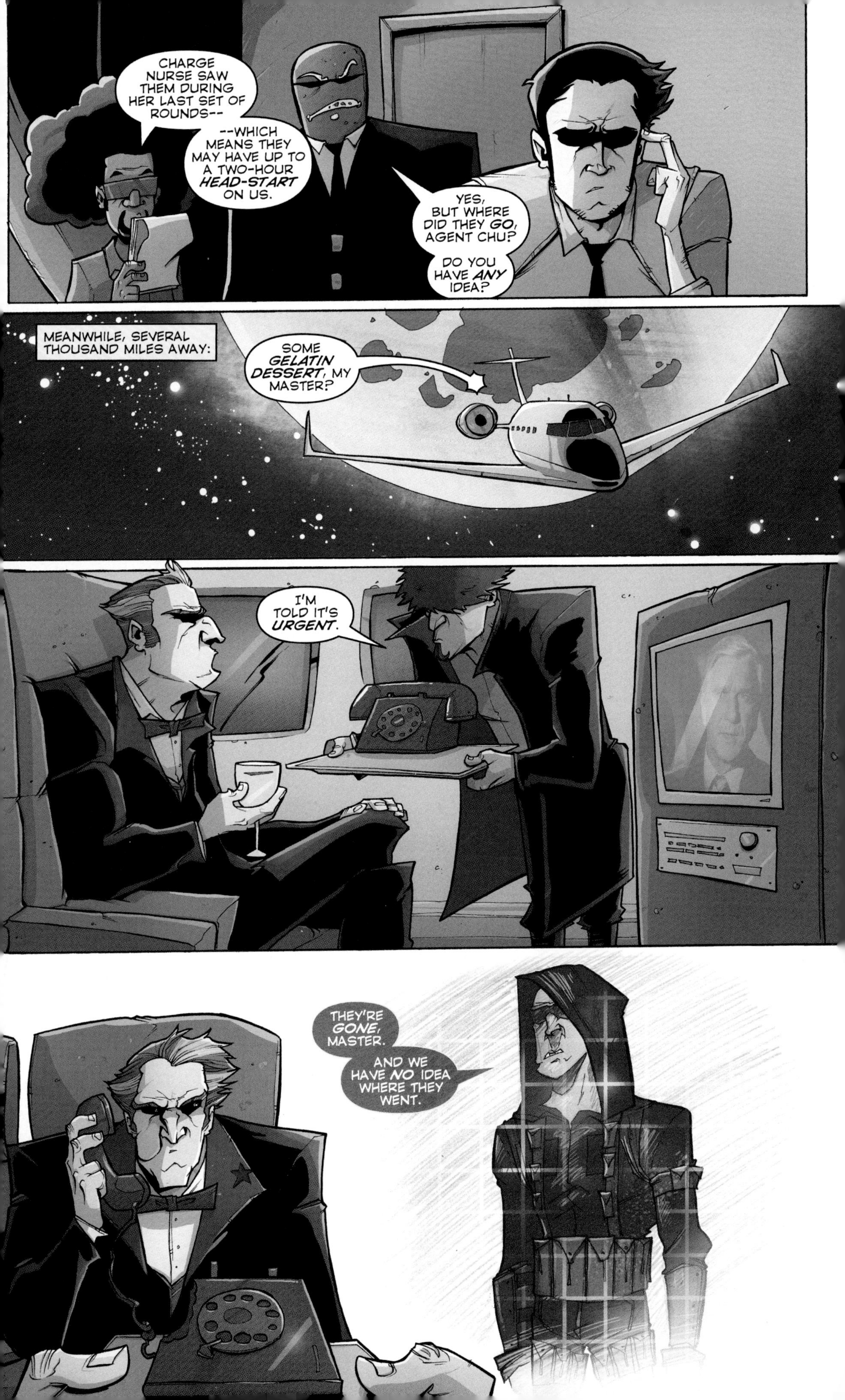
CHARGE NURSE SAW THEM DURING HER LAST SET OF ROUNDS--
--WHICH MEANS THEY MAY HAVE UP TO A TWO-HOUR HEAD-START ON US.
YES, BUT WHERE DID THEY GO, AGENT CHU?
DO YOU HAVE ANY IDEA?
MEANWHILE, SEVERAL THOUSAND MILES AWAY:
SOME GELATIN DESSERT, MY MASTER?
I'M TOLD IT'S URGENT.
THEY'RE GONE, MASTER.
AND WE HAVE NO IDEA WHERE THEY WENT.

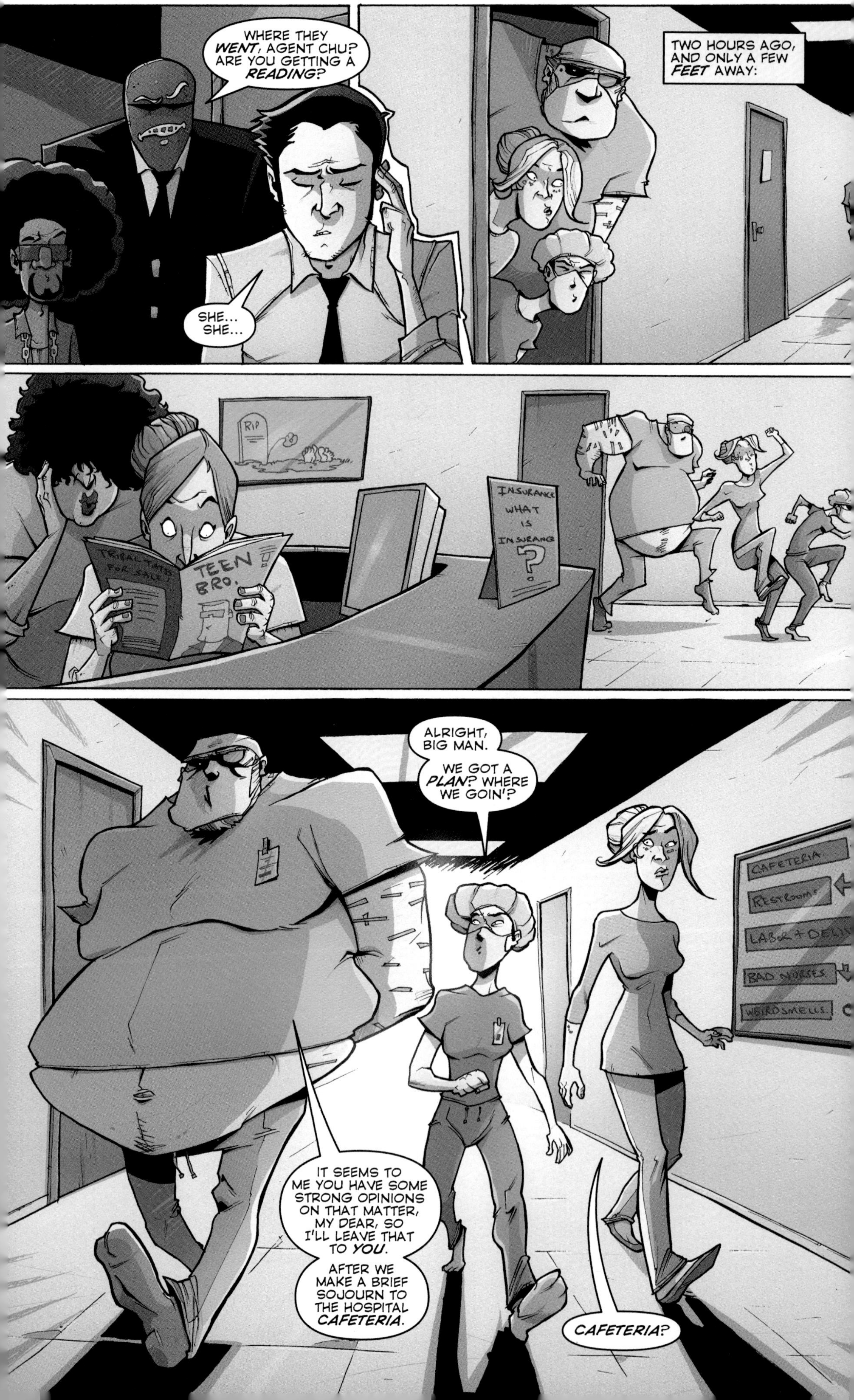

WHERE THEY *WENT*, AGENT CHU? ARE YOU GETTING A *READING*?
SHE... SHE...
TWO HOURS AGO, AND ONLY A FEW *FEET* AWAY:
RIP
TRIBAL TATTS FOR SALE!
TEEN BRO.
INSURANCE WHAT IS INSURANCE ?
ALRIGHT, BIG MAN.
WE GOT A *PLAN*? WHERE WE GOIN'?
CAFETERIA
RESTROOMS
LABOR + DELI
BAD NURSES
WEIRD SMELLS
IT SEEMS TO ME YOU HAVE SOME STRONG OPINIONS ON THAT MATTER, MY DEAR, SO I'LL LEAVE THAT TO *YOU*.
AFTER WE MAKE A BRIEF SOJOURN TO THE HOSPITAL *CAFETERIA*.
CAFETERIA?

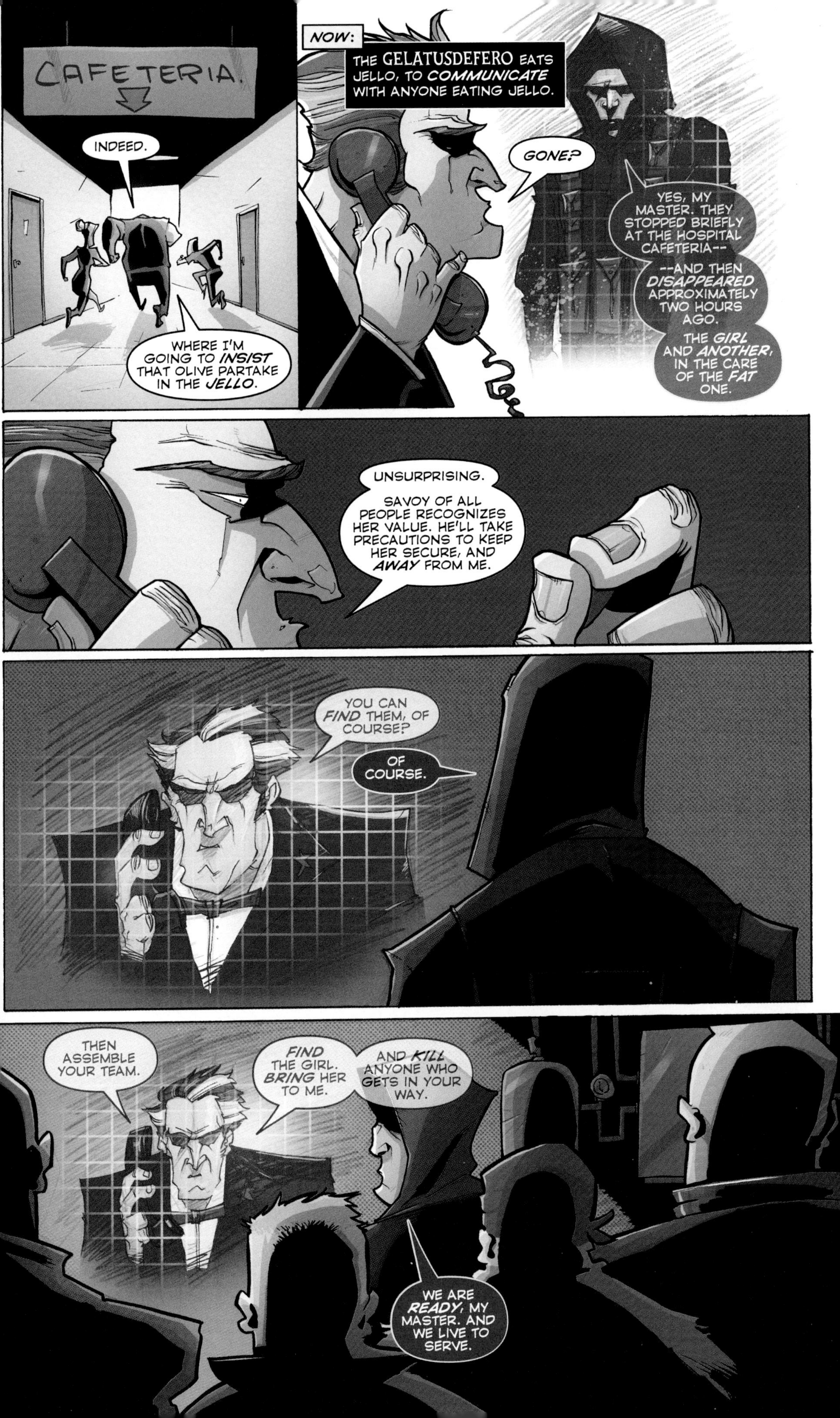
CAFETERIA
INDEED.
WHERE I'M GOING TO INSIST THAT OLIVE PARTAKE IN THE JELLO.
NOW:
THE GELATUSDEFERO EATS JELLO, TO COMMUNICATE WITH ANYONE EATING JELLO.
GONE?
YES, MY MASTER. THEY STOPPED BRIEFLY AT THE HOSPITAL CAFETERIA--
--AND THEN DISAPPEARED APPROXIMATELY TWO HOURS AGO.
THE GIRL AND ANOTHER, IN THE CARE OF THE FAT ONE.
UNSURPRISING.
SAVOY OF ALL PEOPLE RECOGNIZES HER VALUE. HE'LL TAKE PRECAUTIONS TO KEEP HER SECURE, AND AWAY FROM ME.
YOU CAN FIND THEM, OF COURSE?
OF COURSE.
THEN ASSEMBLE YOUR TEAM.
FIND THE GIRL. BRING HER TO ME.
AND KILL ANYONE WHO GETS IN YOUR WAY.
WE ARE READY, MY MASTER. AND WE LIVE TO SERVE.

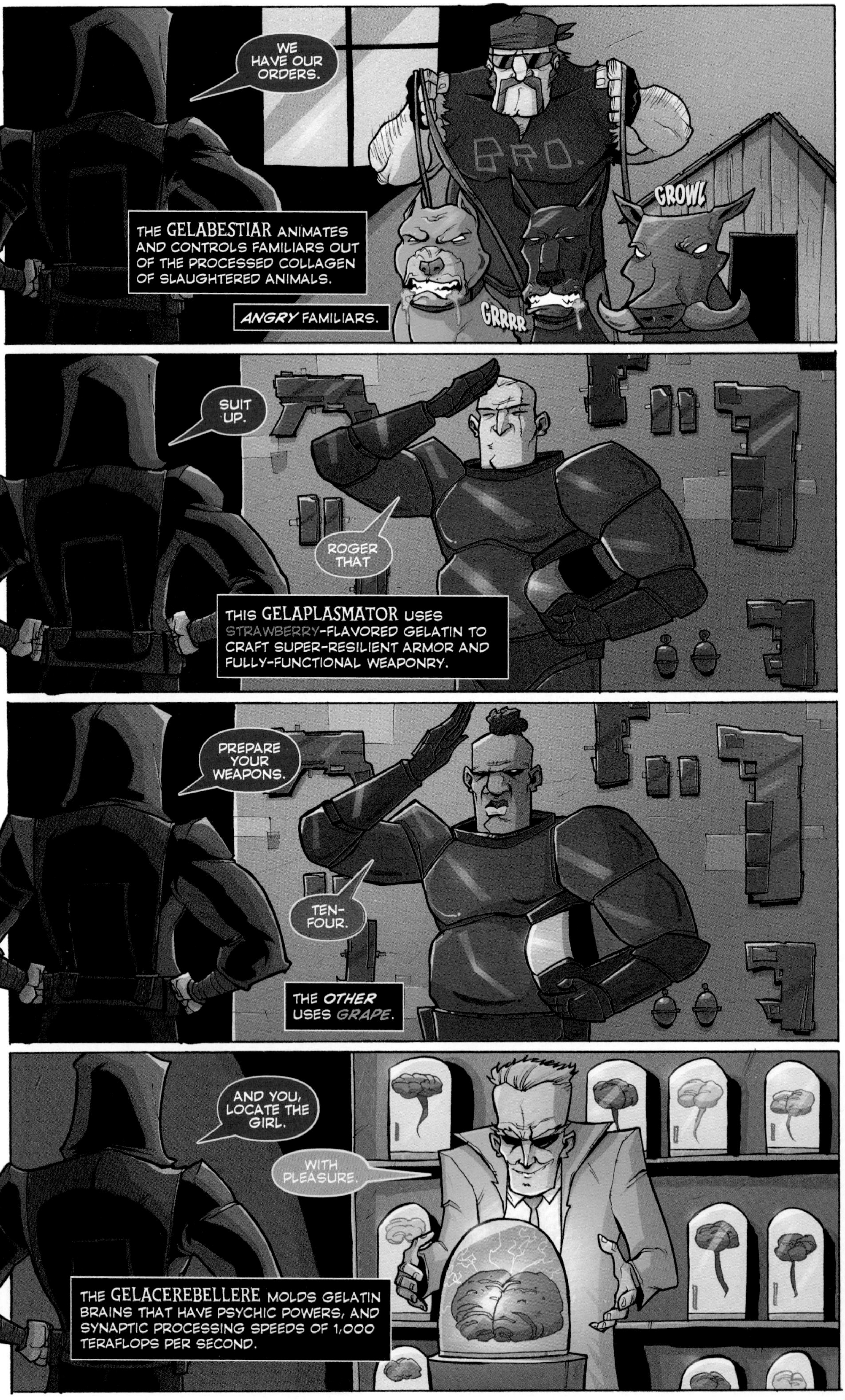
WE HAVE OUR ORDERS.
THE GELABESTIAR ANIMATES AND CONTROLS FAMILIARS OUT OF THE PROCESSED COLLAGEN OF SLAUGHTERED ANIMALS.
ANGRY FAMILIARS.
BRO.
GROWL
GRRRR
SUIT UP.
ROGER THAT
THIS GELAPLASMATOR USES STRAWBERRY-FLAVORED GELATIN TO CRAFT SUPER-RESILIENT ARMOR AND FULLY-FUNCTIONAL WEAPONRY.
PREPARE YOUR WEAPONS.
TEN-FOUR.
THE OTHER USES GRAPE.
AND YOU, LOCATE THE GIRL.
WITH PLEASURE.
THE GELACEREBELLERE MOLDS GELATIN BRAINS THAT HAVE PSYCHIC POWERS, AND SYNAPTIC PROCESSING SPEEDS OF 1,000 TERAFLOPS PER SECOND.

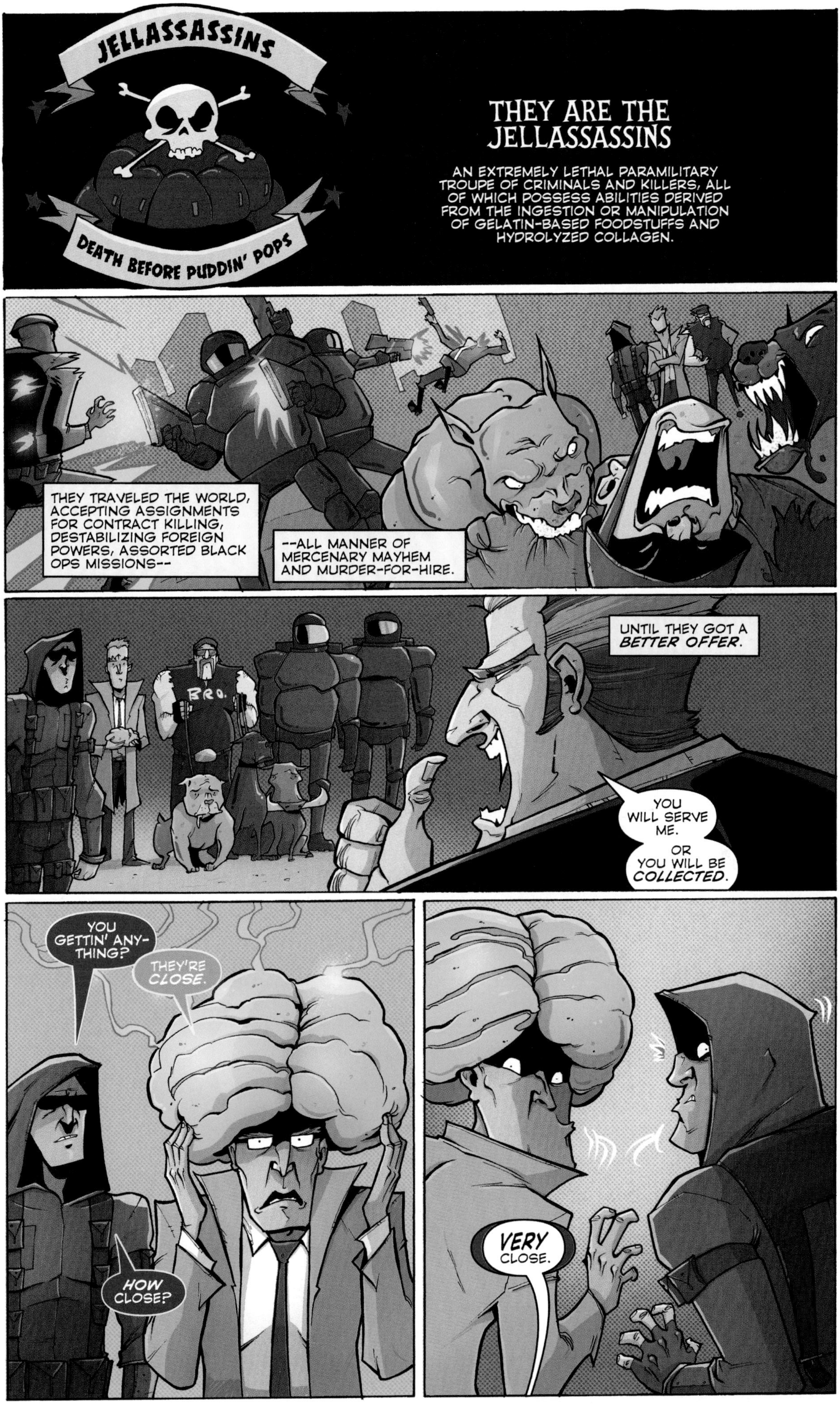
JELLASSASSINS
DEATH BEFORE PUDDIN' POPS
THEY ARE THE JELLASSASSINS
AN EXTREMELY LETHAL PARAMILITARY TROUPE OF CRIMINALS AND KILLERS, ALL OF WHICH POSSESS ABILITIES DERIVED FROM THE INGESTION OR MANIPULATION OF GELATIN-BASED FOODSTUFFS AND HYDROLYZED COLLAGEN.
THEY TRAVELED THE WORLD, ACCEPTING ASSIGNMENTS FOR CONTRACT KILLING, DESTABILIZING FOREIGN POWERS, ASSORTED BLACK OPS MISSIONS--
--ALL MANNER OF MERCENARY MAYHEM AND MURDER-FOR-HIRE.
UNTIL THEY GOT A BETTER OFFER.
BRO.
YOU WILL SERVE ME.
OR YOU WILL BE COLLECTED.
YOU GETTIN' ANY-THING?
THEY'RE CLOSE.
HOW CLOSE?
VERY CLOSE.

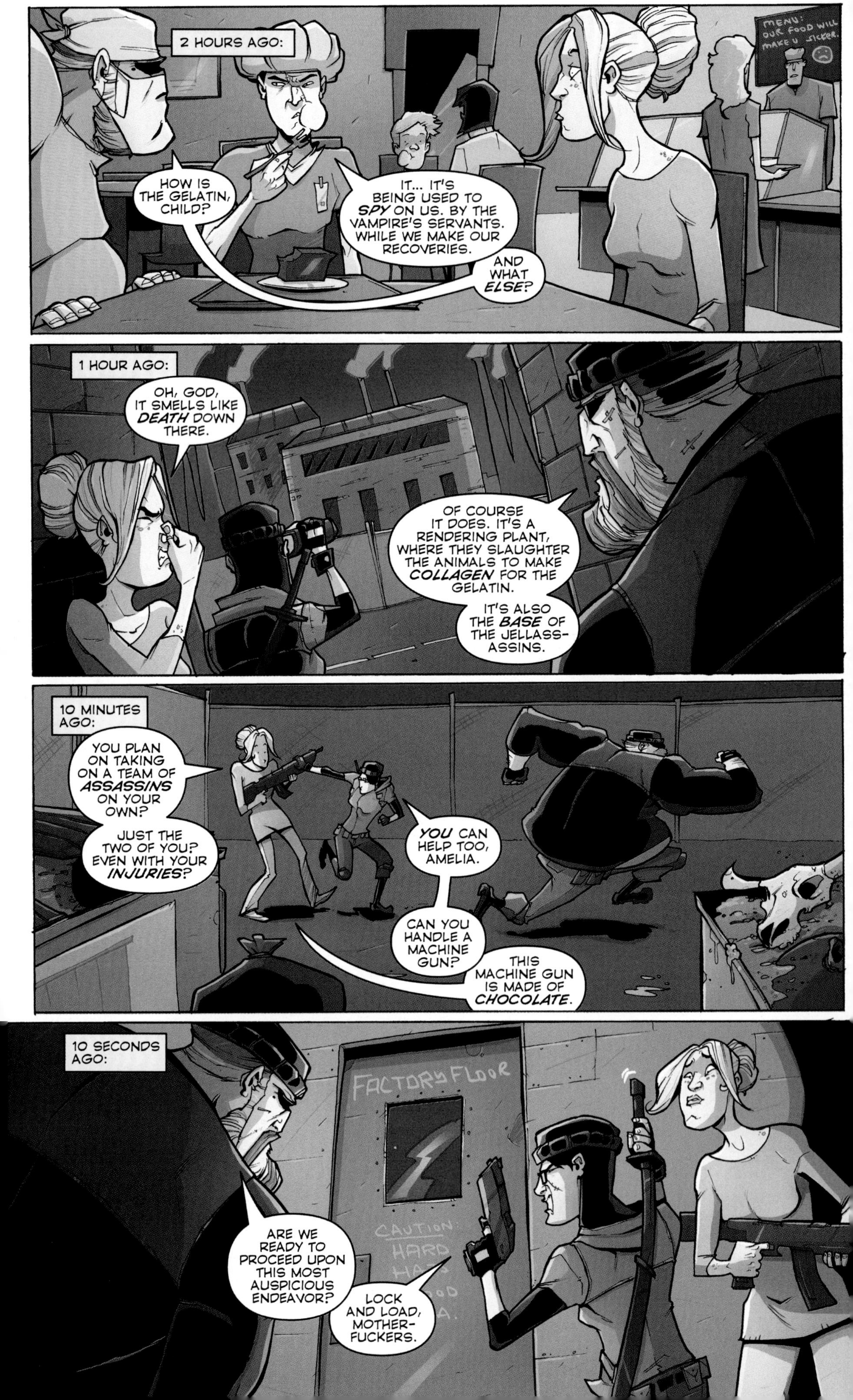
2 HOURS AGO:
MENU: OUR FOOD WILL MAKE U SICKER.
HOW IS THE GELATIN, CHILD?
IT... IT'S BEING USED TO SPY ON US. BY THE VAMPIRE'S SERVANTS. WHILE WE MAKE OUR RECOVERIES.
AND WHAT ELSE?
1 HOUR AGO:
OH, GOD, IT SMELLS LIKE DEATH DOWN THERE.
OF COURSE IT DOES. IT'S A RENDERING PLANT, WHERE THEY SLAUGHTER THE ANIMALS TO MAKE COLLAGEN FOR THE GELATIN.
IT'S ALSO THE BASE OF THE JELLASS-ASSINS.
10 MINUTES AGO:
YOU PLAN ON TAKING ON A TEAM OF ASSASSINS ON YOUR OWN?
JUST THE TWO OF YOU? EVEN WITH YOUR INJURIES?
YOU CAN HELP TOO, AMELIA.
CAN YOU HANDLE A MACHINE GUN?
THIS MACHINE GUN IS MADE OF CHOCOLATE.
10 SECONDS AGO:
FACTORY FLOOR
ARE WE READY TO PROCEED UPON THIS MOST AUSPICIOUS ENDEAVOR?
LOCK AND LOAD, MOTHER-FUCKERS.

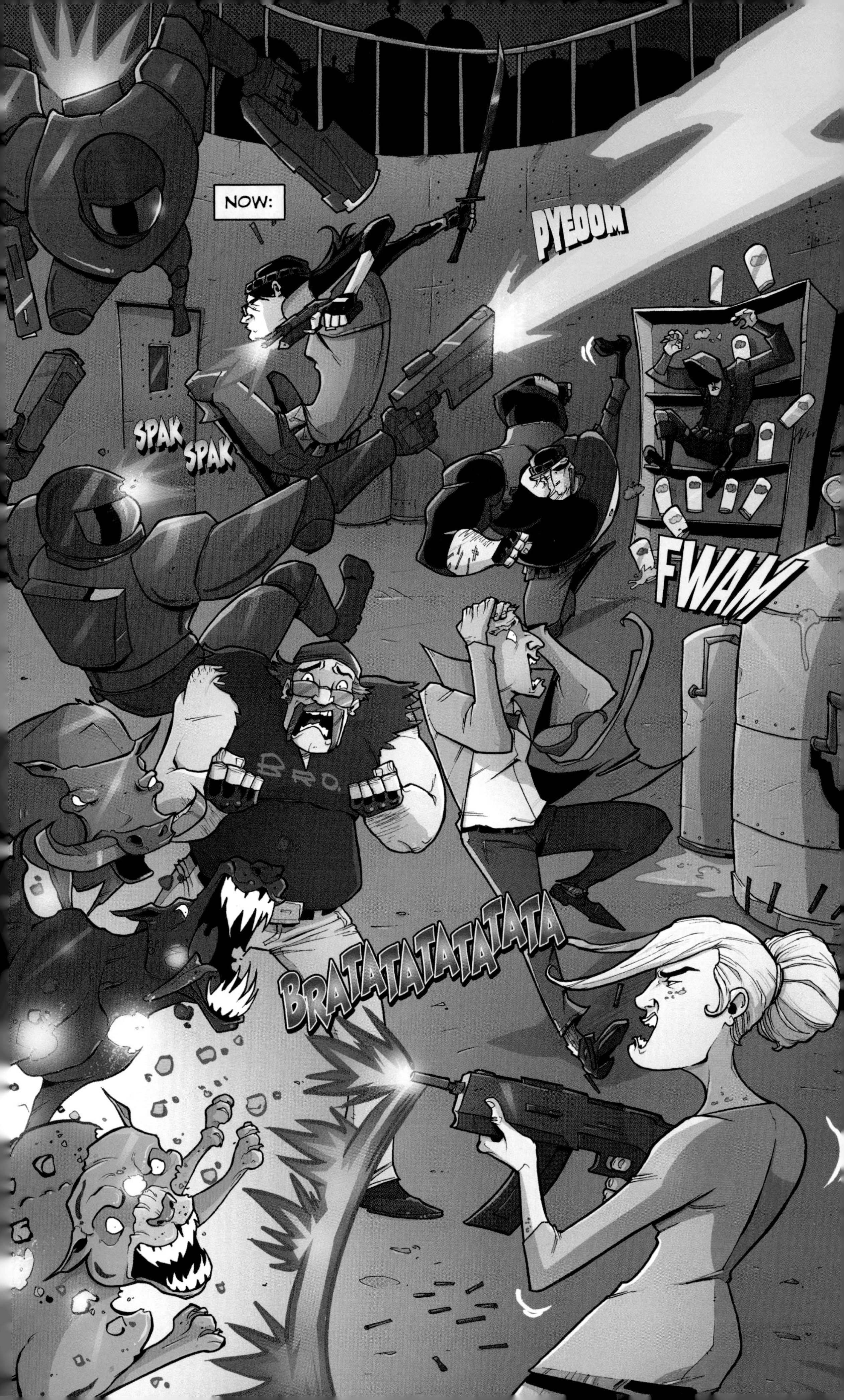
NOW:
PYEOOM
SPAK
SPAK
FWAM
BRATATATATATATA

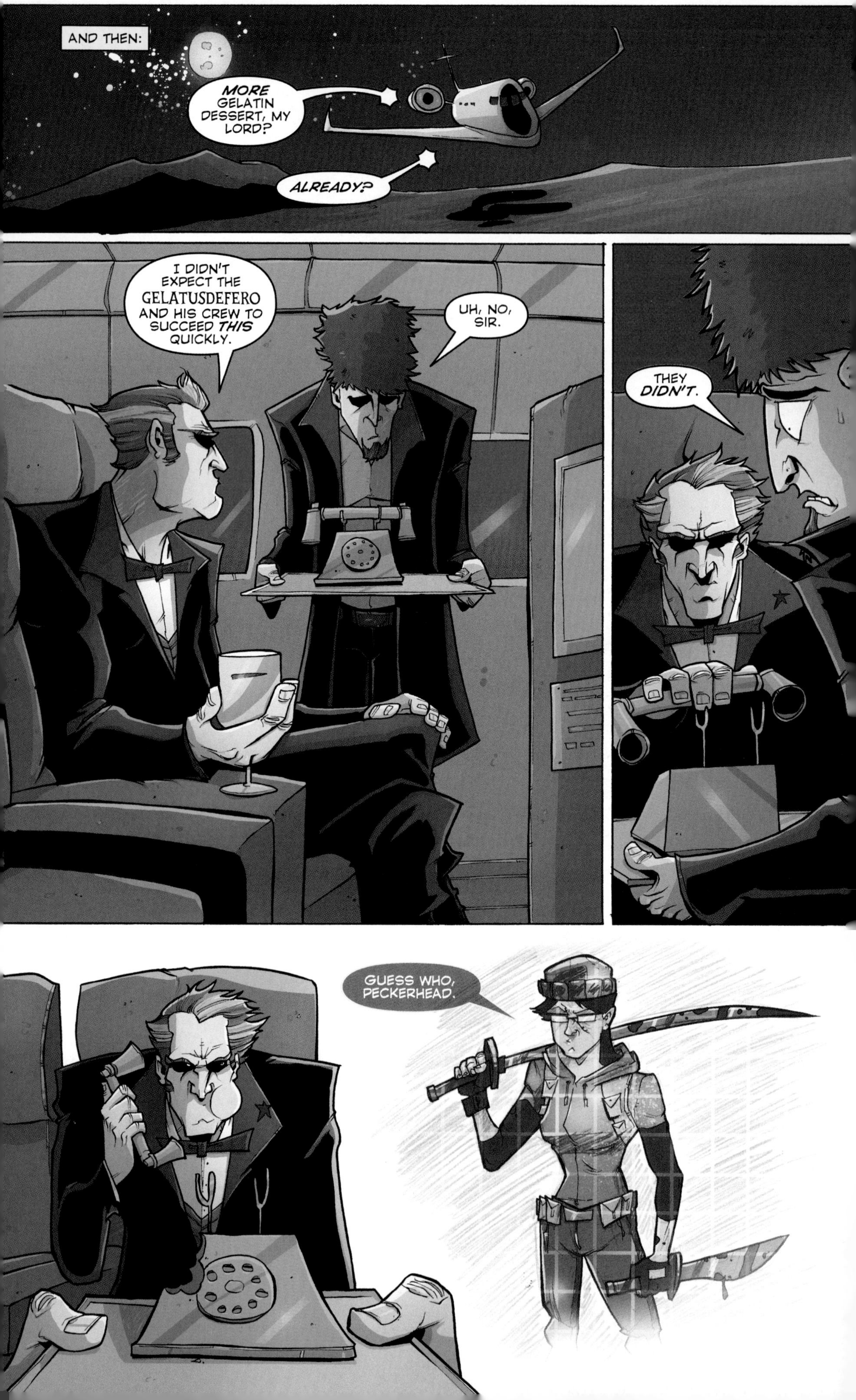
AND THEN:
MORE GELATIN DESSERT, MY LORD?
ALREADY?
I DIDN'T EXPECT THE GELATUSDEFERO AND HIS CREW TO SUCCEED THIS QUICKLY.
UH, NO, SIR.
THEY DIDN'T.
GUESS WHO, PECKERHEAD.

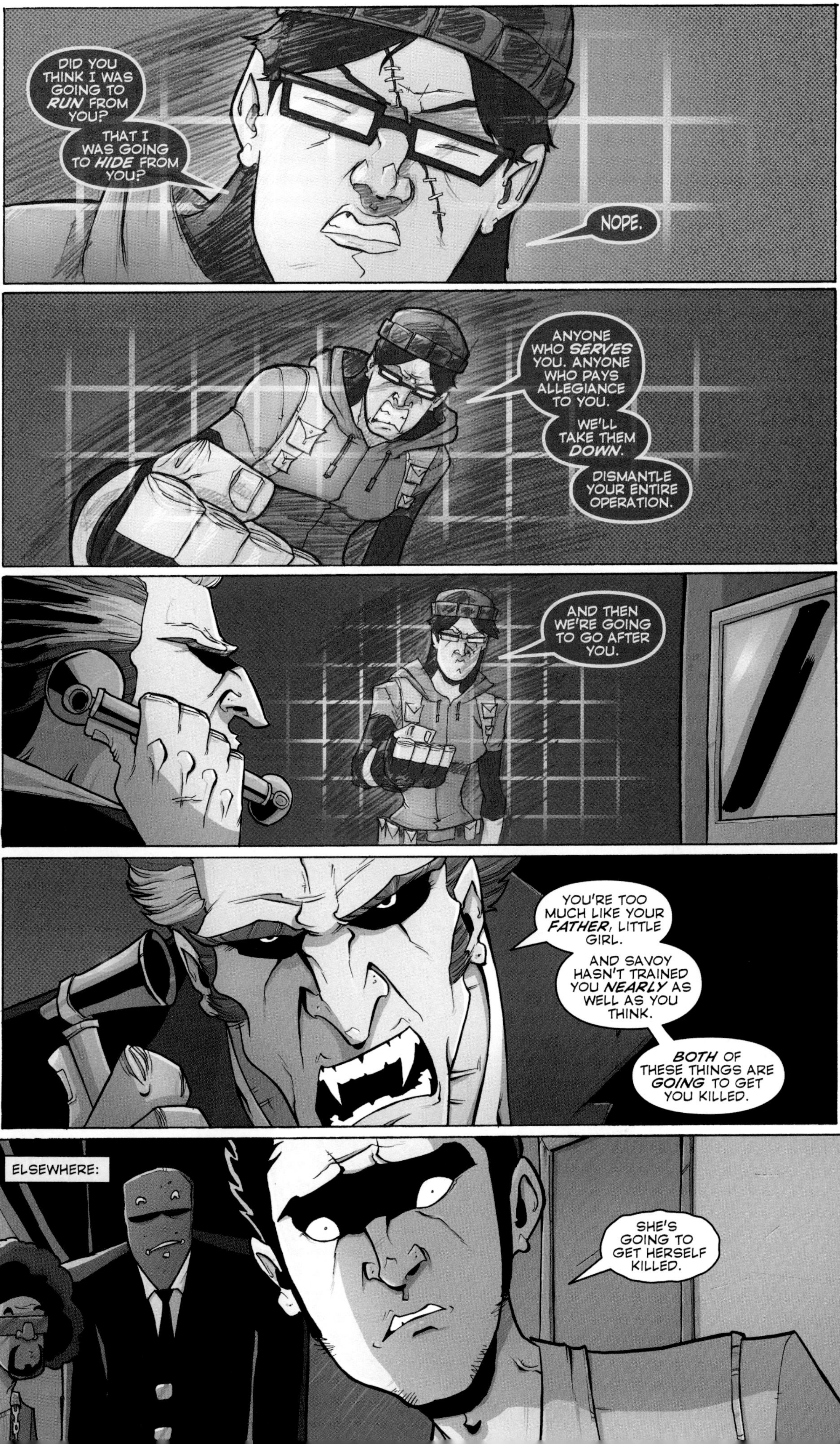

DID YOU THINK I WAS GOING TO RUN FROM YOU?
THAT I WAS GOING TO HIDE FROM YOU?
NOPE.
ANYONE WHO SERVES YOU. ANYONE WHO PAYS ALLEGIANCE TO YOU.
WE'LL TAKE THEM DOWN.
DISMANTLE YOUR ENTIRE OPERATION.
AND THEN WE'RE GOING TO GO AFTER YOU.
YOU'RE TOO MUCH LIKE YOUR FATHER, LITTLE GIRL.
AND SAVOY HASN'T TRAINED YOU NEARLY AS WELL AS YOU THINK.
BOTH OF THESE THINGS ARE GOING TO GET YOU KILLED.
ELSEWHERE:
SHE'S GOING TO GET HERSELF KILLED.

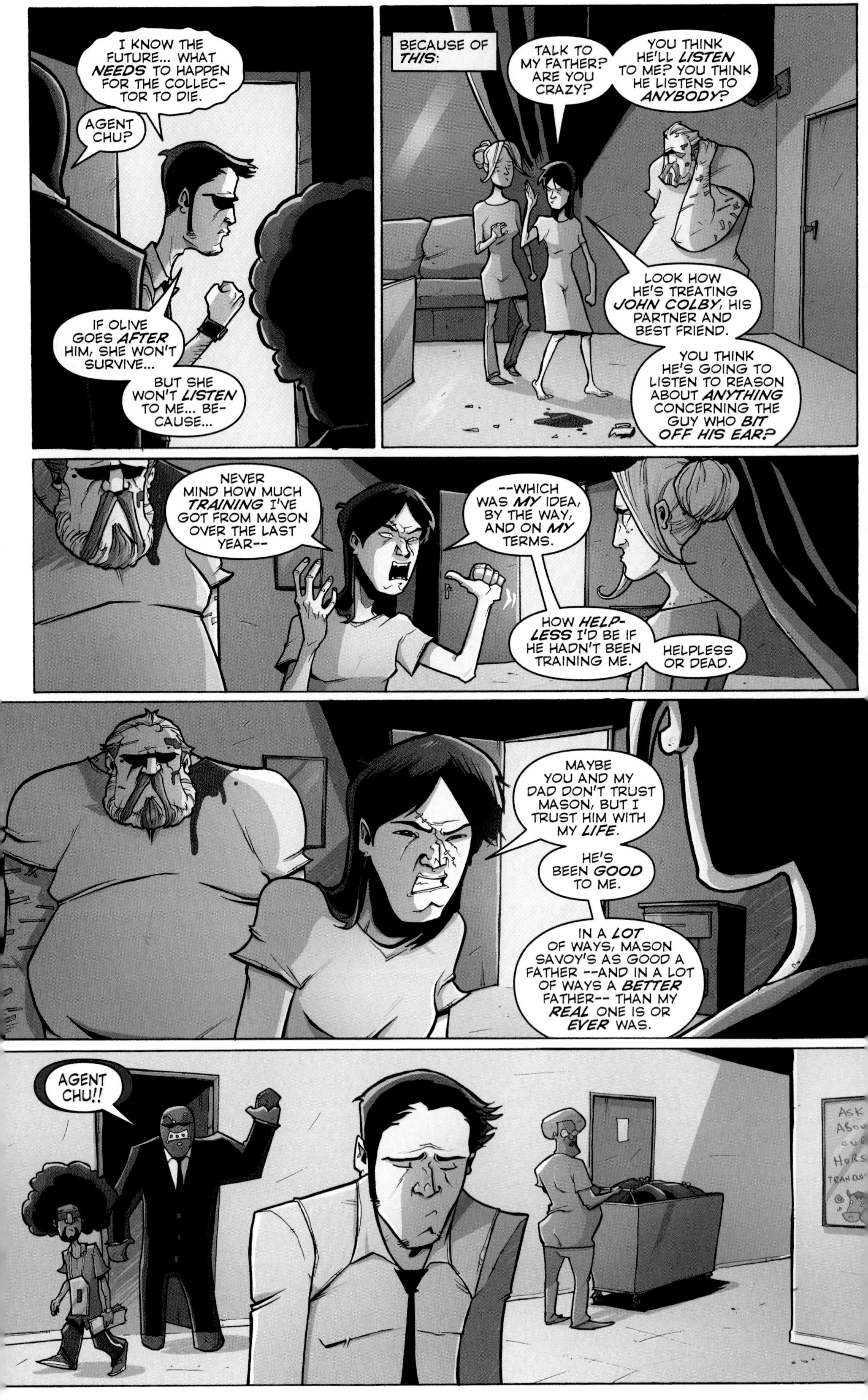

I KNOW THE FUTURE... WHAT NEEDS TO HAPPEN FOR THE COLLECTOR TO DIE.
AGENT CHU?
IF OLIVE GOES AFTER HIM, SHE WON'T SURVIVE...
BUT SHE WON'T LISTEN TO ME... BECAUSE...
BECAUSE OF THIS:
TALK TO MY FATHER? ARE YOU CRAZY?
YOU THINK HE'LL LISTEN TO ME? YOU THINK HE LISTENS TO ANYBODY?
LOOK HOW HE'S TREATING JOHN COLBY, HIS PARTNER AND BEST FRIEND.
YOU THINK HE'S GOING TO LISTEN TO REASON ABOUT ANYTHING CONCERNING THE GUY WHO BIT OFF HIS EAR?
NEVER MIND HOW MUCH TRAINING I'VE GOT FROM MASON OVER THE LAST YEAR--
--WHICH WAS MY IDEA, BY THE WAY, AND ON MY TERMS.
HOW HELPLESS I'D BE IF HE HADN'T BEEN TRAINING ME.
HELPLESS OR DEAD.
MAYBE YOU AND MY DAD DON'T TRUST MASON, BUT I TRUST HIM WITH MY LIFE.
HE'S BEEN GOOD TO ME.
IN A LOT OF WAYS, MASON SAVOY'S AS GOOD A FATHER --AND IN A LOT OF WAYS A BETTER FATHER-- THAN MY REAL ONE IS OR EVER WAS.
AGENT CHU!!

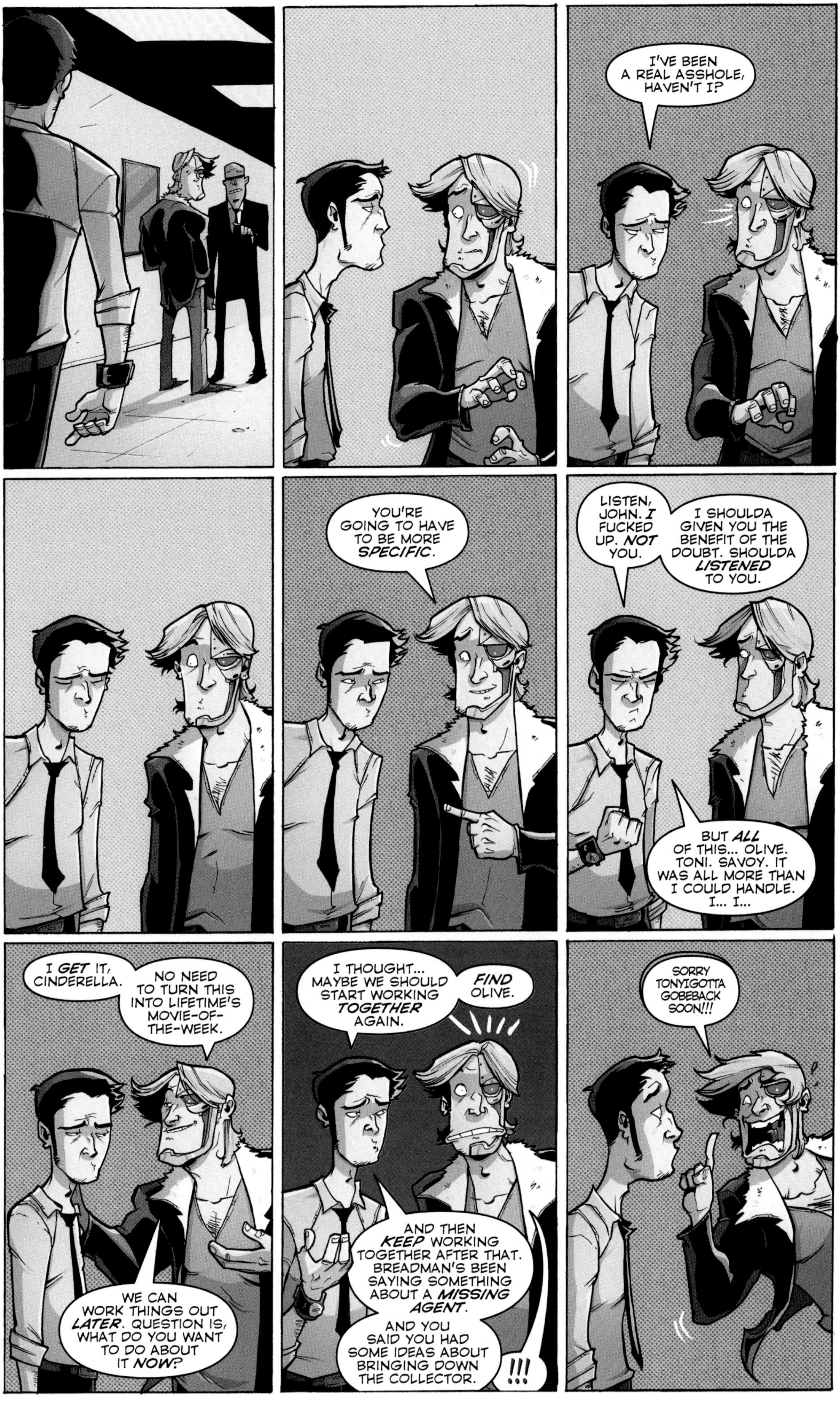
I'VE BEEN A REAL ASSHOLE, HAVEN'T I?
YOU'RE GOING TO HAVE TO BE MORE SPECIFIC.
LISTEN, JOHN. I FUCKED UP. NOT YOU.
I SHOULDA GIVEN YOU THE BENEFIT OF THE DOUBT. SHOULDA LISTENED TO YOU.
BUT ALL OF THIS... OLIVE. TONI. SAVOY. IT WAS ALL MORE THAN I COULD HANDLE. I... I...
I GET IT, CINDERELLA.
NO NEED TO TURN THIS INTO LIFETIME'S MOVIE-OF-THE-WEEK.
WE CAN WORK THINGS OUT LATER. QUESTION IS, WHAT DO YOU WANT TO DO ABOUT IT NOW?
I THOUGHT... MAYBE WE SHOULD START WORKING TOGETHER AGAIN.
FIND OLIVE.
AND THEN KEEP WORKING TOGETHER AFTER THAT. BREADMAN'S BEEN SAYING SOMETHING ABOUT A MISSING AGENT.
AND YOU SAID YOU HAD SOME IDEAS ABOUT BRINGING DOWN THE COLLECTOR.
!!!
SORRY TONYIGOTTA GOBEBACK SOON!!!

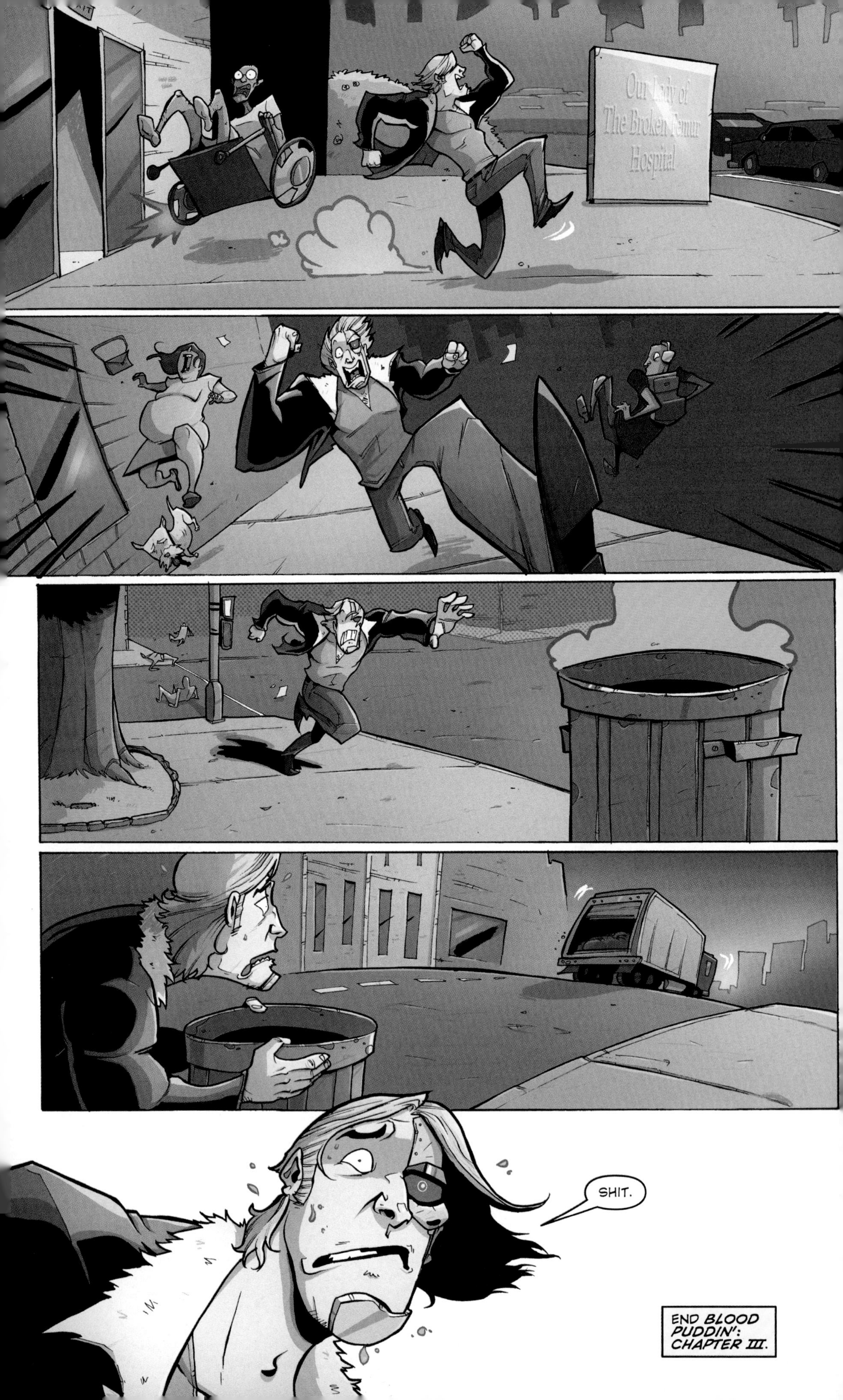
Our Lady of
The Broken Femur
Hospital
SHIT.
END BLOOD PUDDIN': CHAPTER III.

Chapter Nine

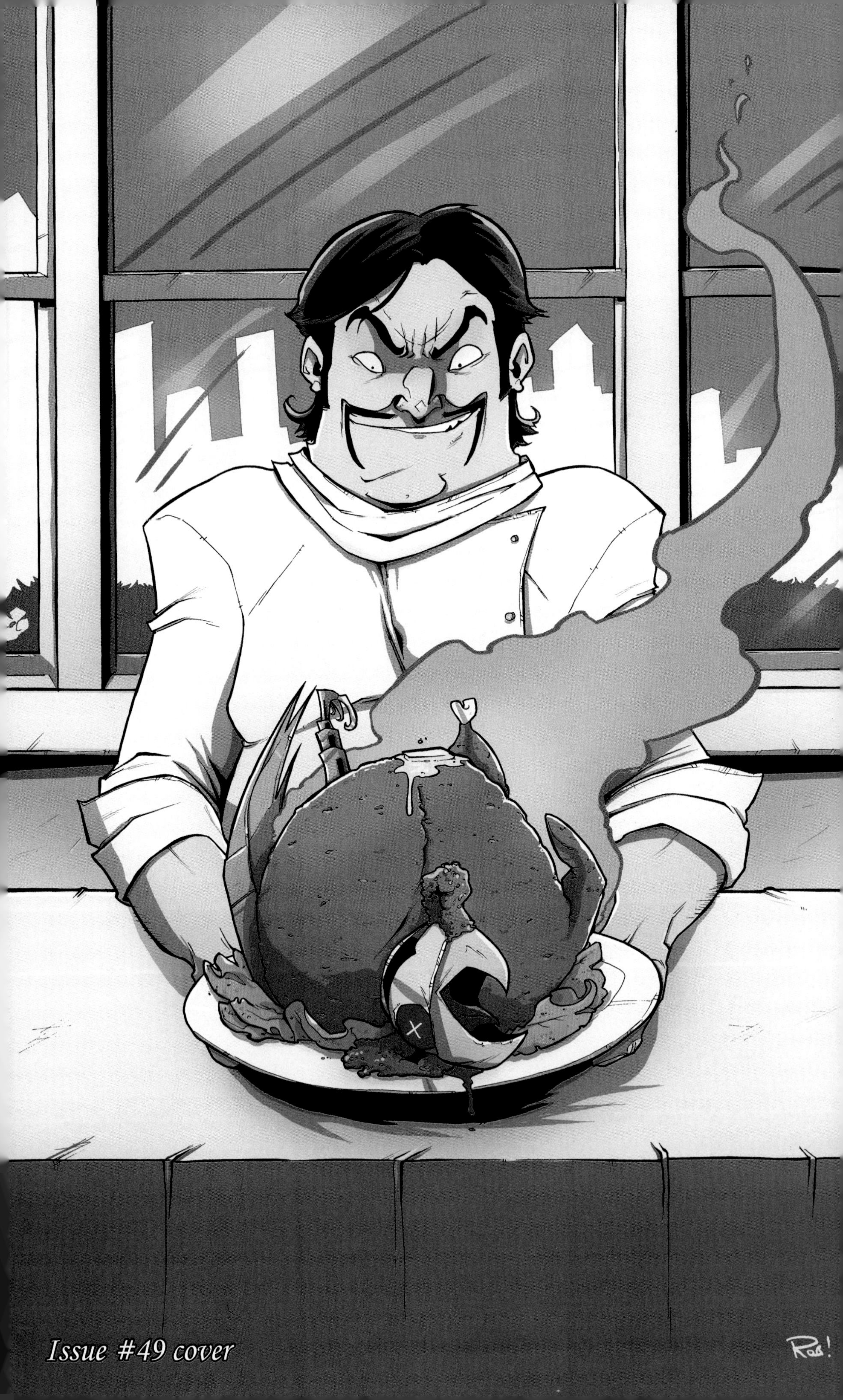
Rob!

Issue #49 cover

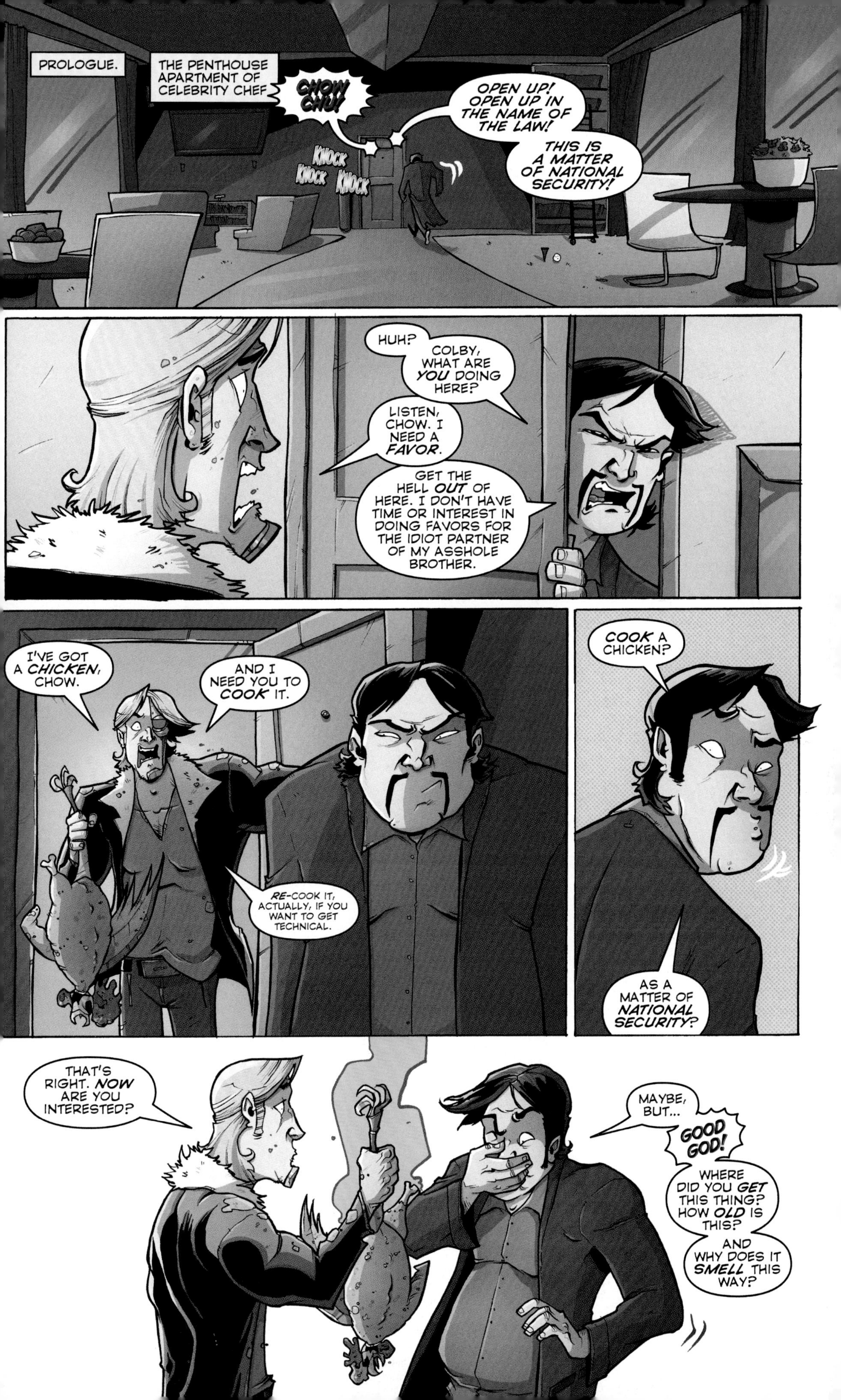
PROLOGUE.
THE PENTHOUSE APARTMENT OF CELEBRITY CHEF
CHOW CHU!
KNOCK KNOCK KNOCK
OPEN UP! OPEN UP IN THE NAME OF THE LAW!
THIS IS A MATTER OF NATIONAL SECURITY!
HUH?
COLBY, WHAT ARE YOU DOING HERE?
LISTEN, CHOW. I NEED A FAVOR.
GET THE HELL OUT OF HERE. I DON'T HAVE TIME OR INTEREST IN DOING FAVORS FOR THE IDIOT PARTNER OF MY ASSHOLE BROTHER.
I'VE GOT A CHICKEN, CHOW.
AND I NEED YOU TO COOK IT.
RE-COOK IT, ACTUALLY, IF YOU WANT TO GET TECHNICAL.
COOK A CHICKEN?
AS A MATTER OF NATIONAL SECURITY?
THAT'S RIGHT. NOW ARE YOU INTERESTED?
MAYBE, BUT...
GOOD GOD!
WHERE DID YOU GET THIS THING? HOW OLD IS THIS?
AND WHY DOES IT SMELL THIS WAY?

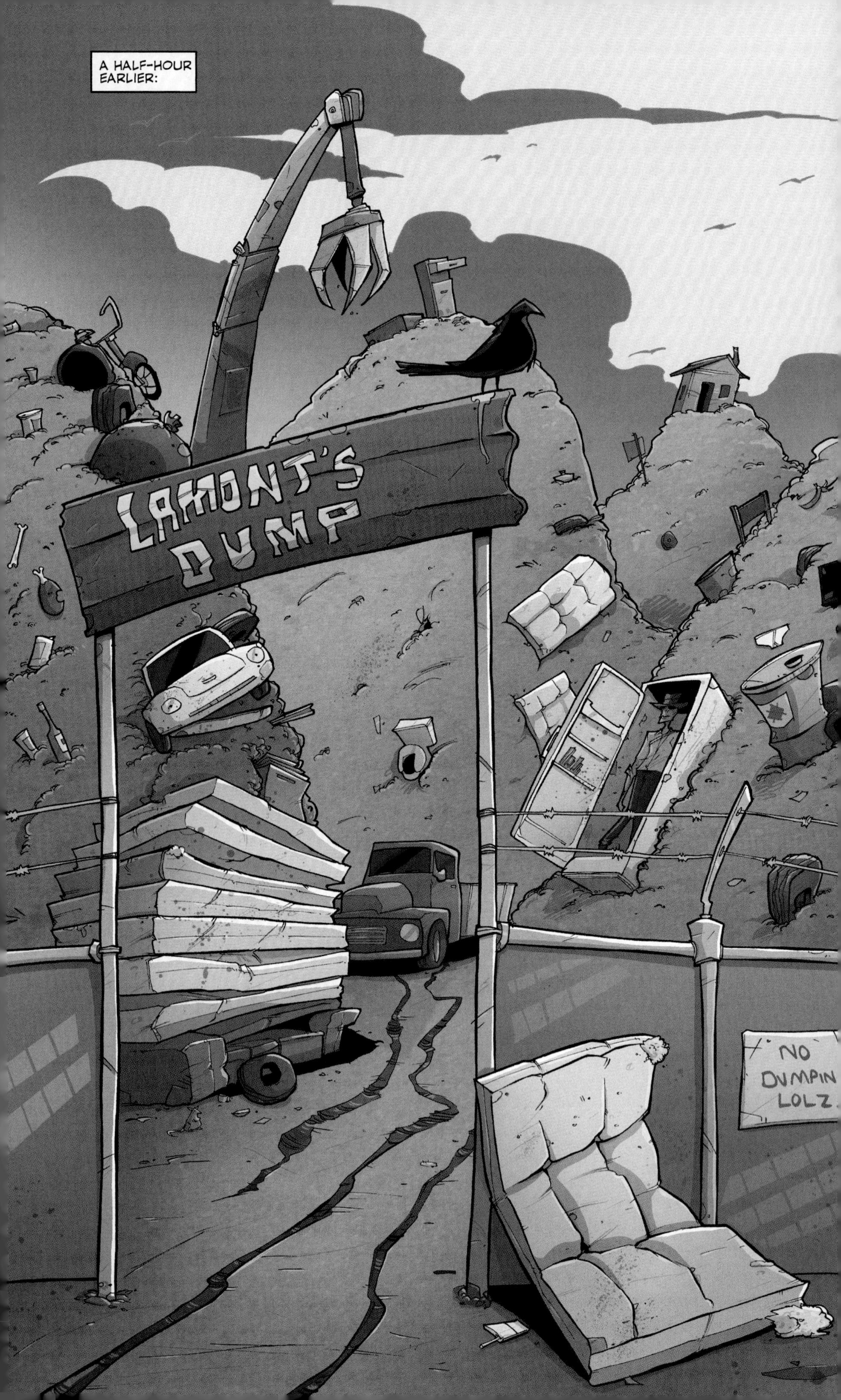
A HALF-HOUR EARLIER:
LAMONT'S DUMP
NO DUMPIN LOLZ

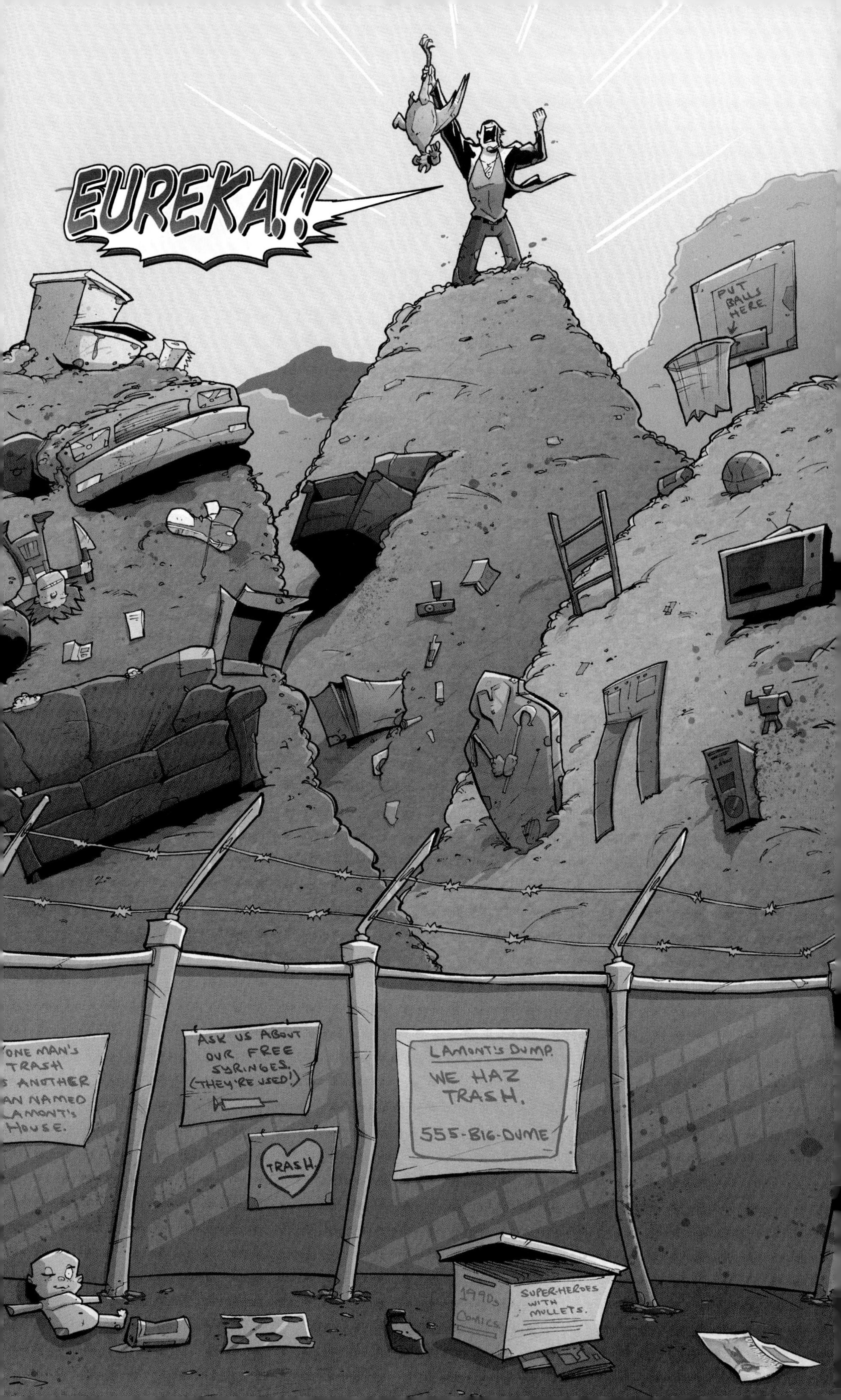
EUREKA!!
PUT BALLS HERE
ONE MAN'S
TRASH
S ANOTHER
AN NAMED
LAMONT'S
HOUSE.
ASK US ABOUT OUR FREE SYRINGES. (THEY'RE USED!)
TRASH.
LAMONT'S DUMP.
WE HAZ TRASH.
555-816-DUMP
1990s COMICS
SUPER-HEROES WITH MULLETS.

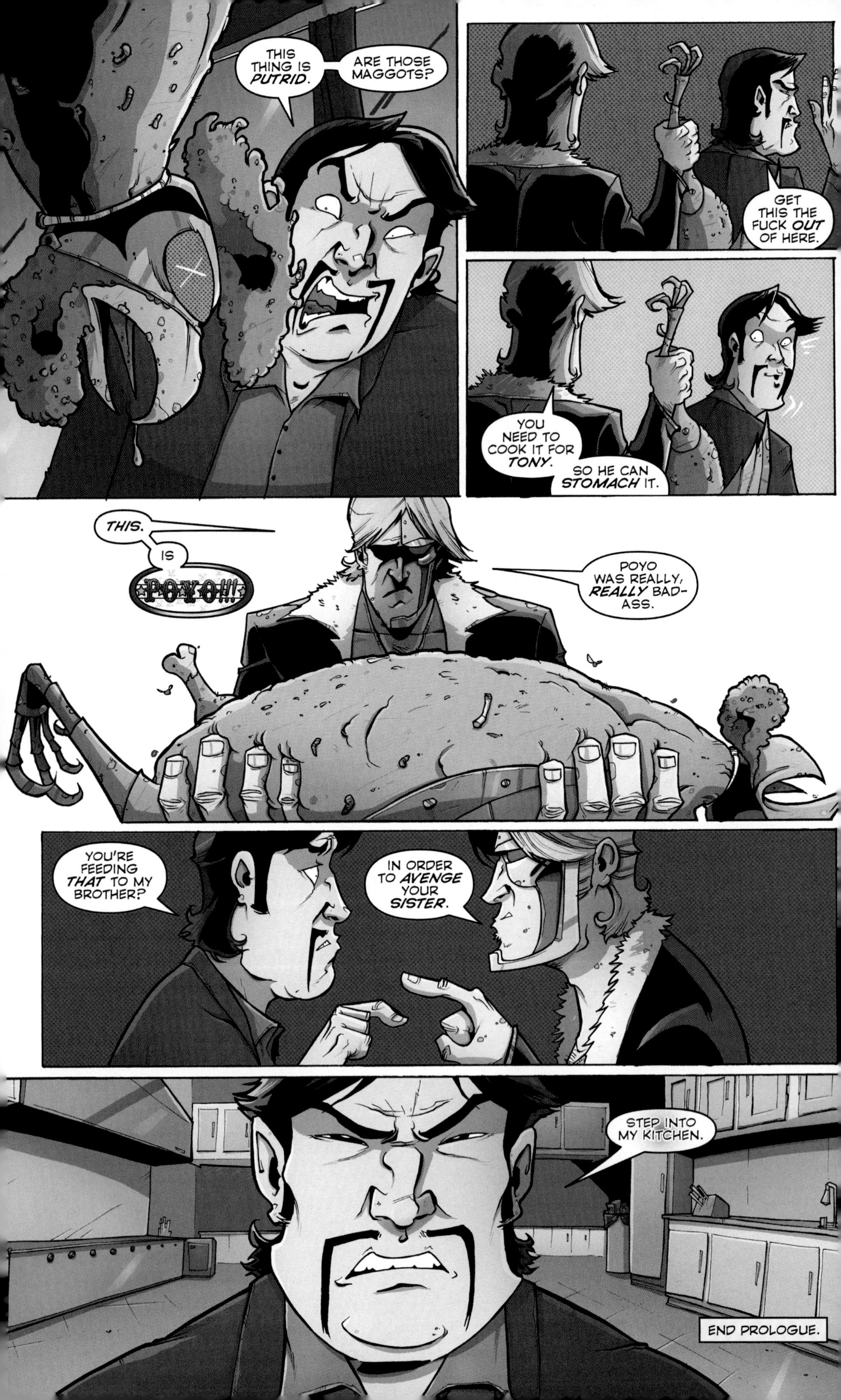

THIS THING IS PUTRID.
ARE THOSE MAGGOTS?
GET THIS THE FUCK OUT OF HERE.
YOU NEED TO COOK IT FOR TONY.
SO HE CAN STOMACH IT.
THIS.
IS
POYO!!!
POYO WAS REALLY, REALLY BAD-ASS.
YOU'RE FEEDING THAT TO MY BROTHER?
IN ORDER TO AVENGE YOUR SISTER.
STEP INTO MY KITCHEN.
END PROLOGUE.

ELSEWHERE:

THE SHIT HITS THE FAN.

KNOCK KNOCK KNOCK

KNOCK KNOCK

UHHH...

YOU GUYS *HEAR* THAT?

SCIENCE. BRO. E=MC HAMMER.

KNOCK KNOCK

SOME- BODY AT THE DOOR?

OUT *HERE*?

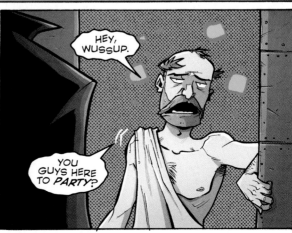

HEY, WUSSUP.

YOU GUYS HERE TO *PARTY*?

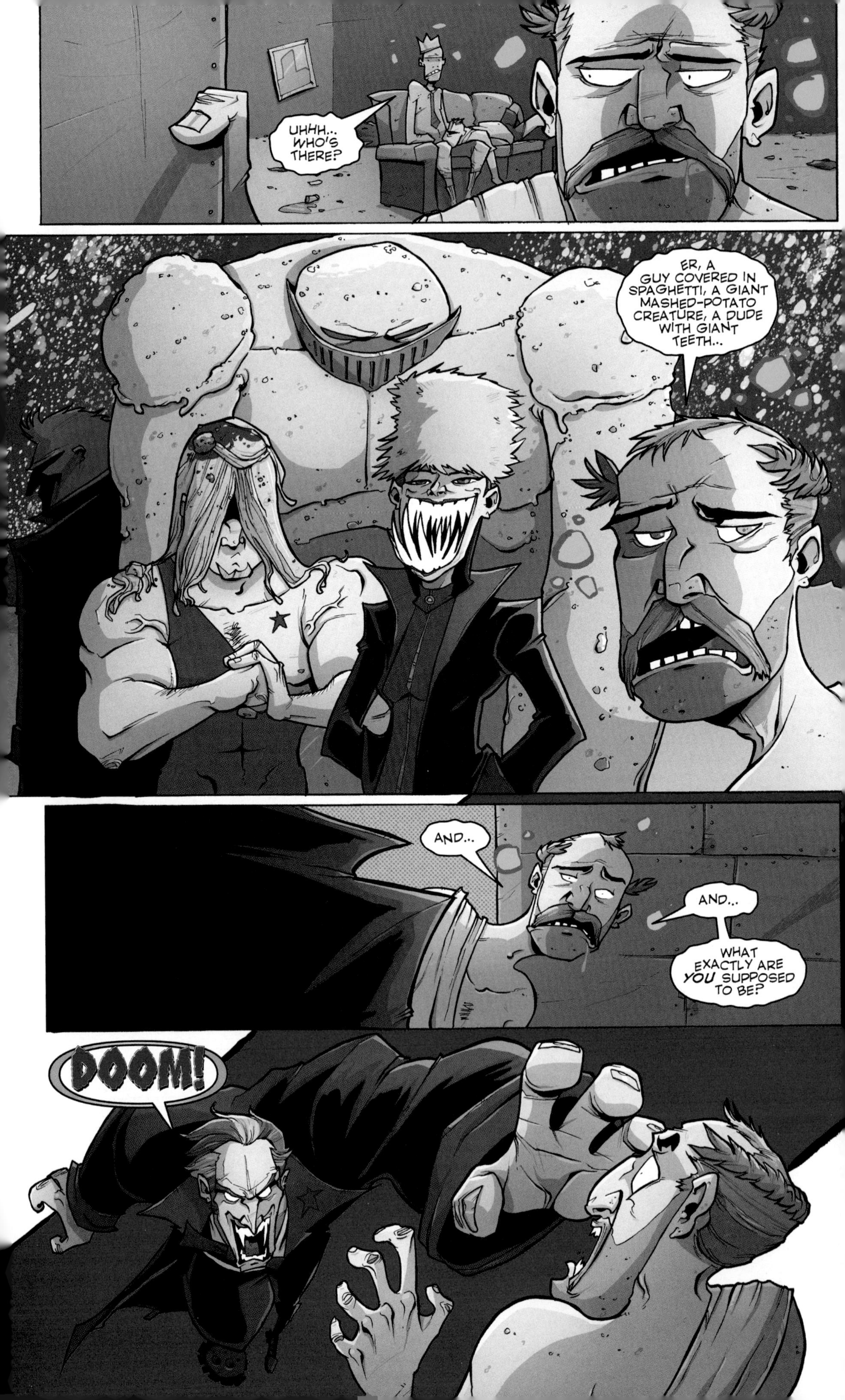
UHHH... WHO'S THERE?
ER, A GUY COVERED IN SPAGHETTI, A GIANT MASHED-POTATO CREATURE, A DUDE WITH GIANT TEETH...
AND...
AND...
WHAT EXACTLY ARE YOU SUPPOSED TO BE?
DOOM!

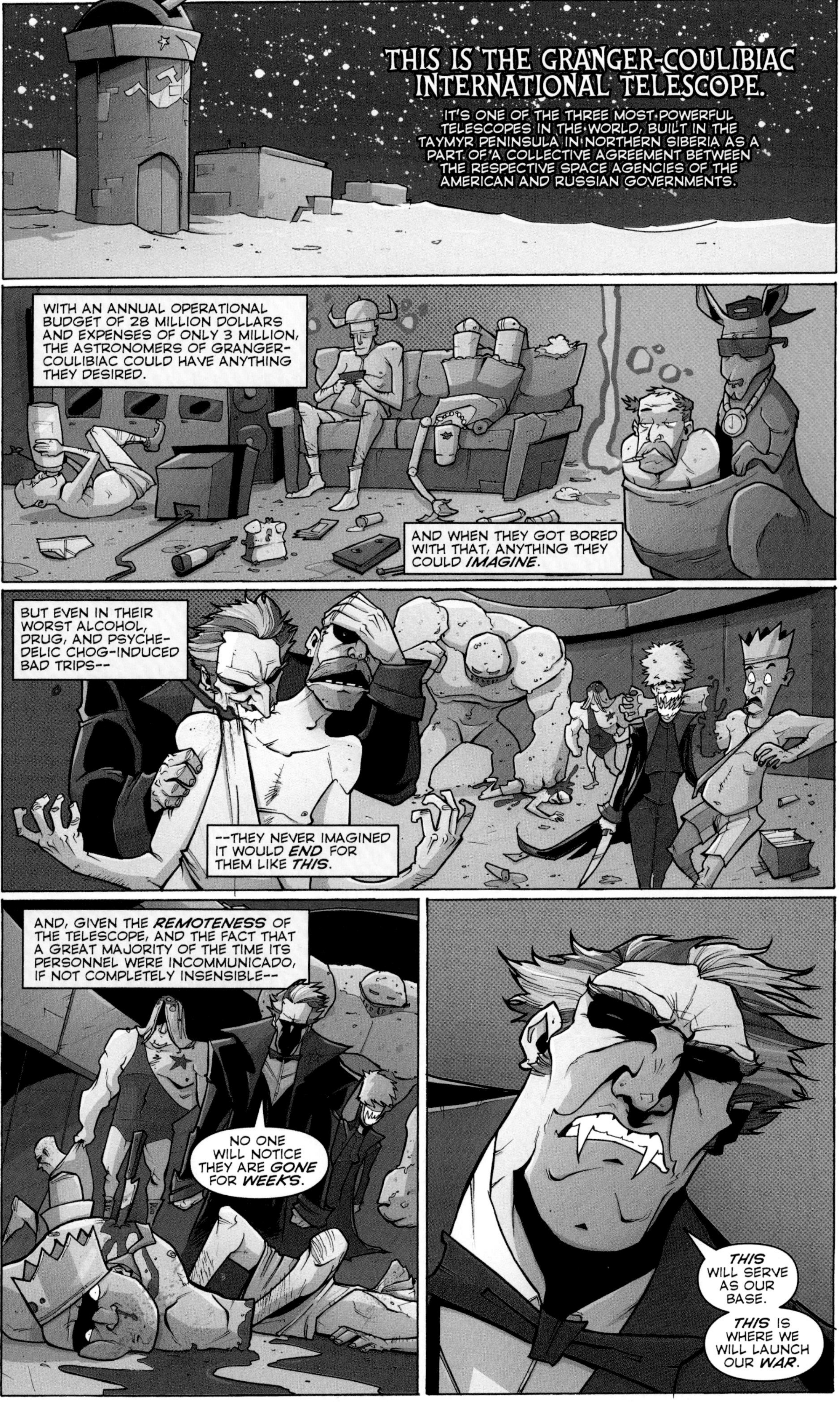
THIS IS THE GRANGER-COULIBIAC INTERNATIONAL TELESCOPE.
IT'S ONE OF THE THREE MOST POWERFUL TELESCOPES IN THE WORLD, BUILT IN THE TAYMYR PENINSULA IN NORTHERN SIBERIA AS A PART OF A COLLECTIVE AGREEMENT BETWEEN THE RESPECTIVE SPACE AGENCIES OF THE AMERICAN AND RUSSIAN GOVERNMENTS.
WITH AN ANNUAL OPERATIONAL BUDGET OF 28 MILLION DOLLARS AND EXPENSES OF ONLY 3 MILLION, THE ASTRONOMERS OF GRANGER-COULIBIAC COULD HAVE ANYTHING THEY DESIRED.
AND WHEN THEY GOT BORED WITH THAT, ANYTHING THEY COULD IMAGINE.
BUT EVEN IN THEIR WORST ALCOHOL, DRUG, AND PSYCHEDELIC CHOG-INDUCED BAD TRIPS--
--THEY NEVER IMAGINED IT WOULD END FOR THEM LIKE THIS.
AND, GIVEN THE REMOTENESS OF THE TELESCOPE, AND THE FACT THAT A GREAT MAJORITY OF THE TIME ITS PERSONNEL WERE INCOMMUNICADO, IF NOT COMPLETELY INSENSIBLE--
NO ONE WILL NOTICE THEY ARE GONE FOR WEEKS.
THIS WILL SERVE AS OUR BASE.
THIS IS WHERE WE WILL LAUNCH OUR WAR.

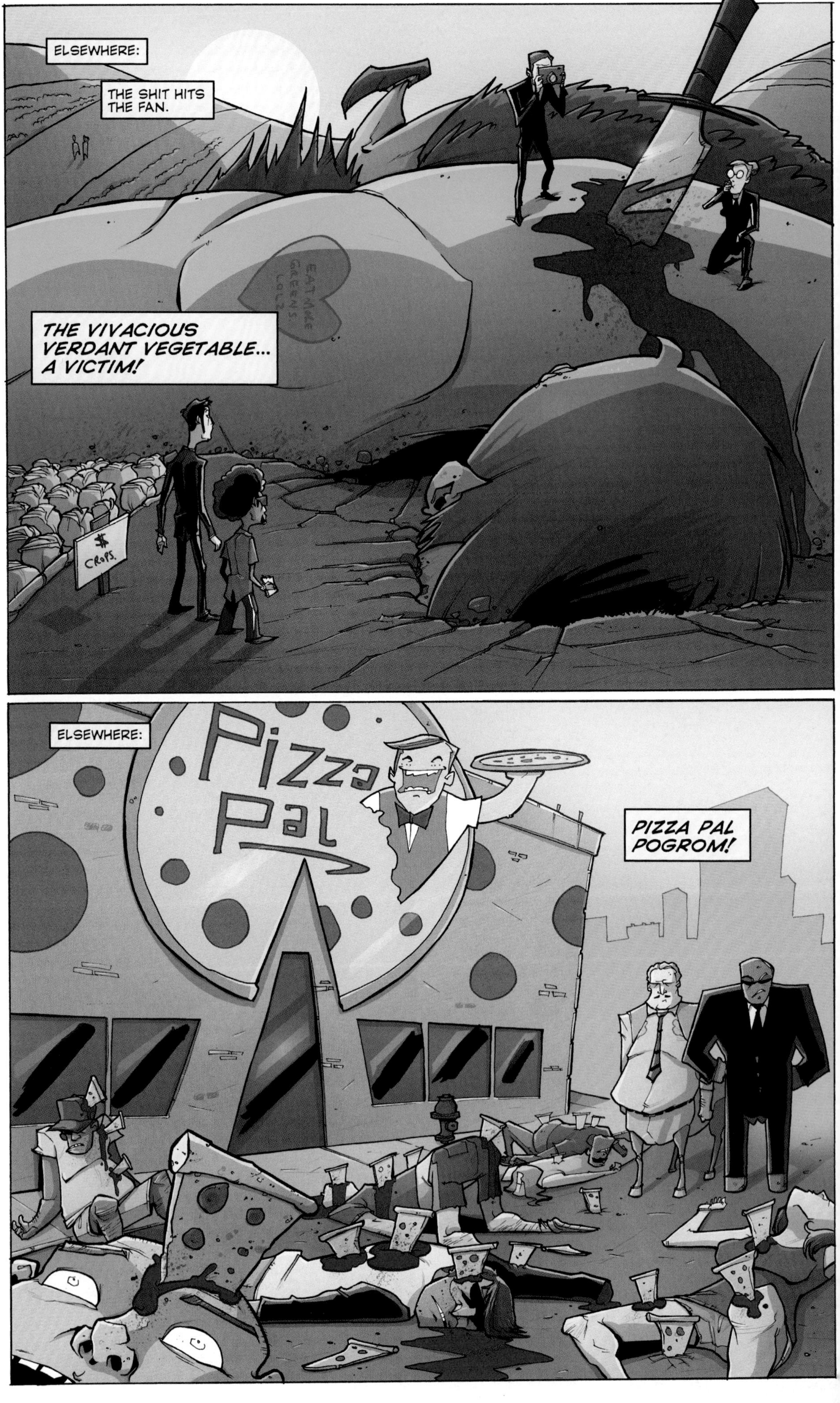
ELSEWHERE:
THE SHIT HITS THE FAN.
EAT MORE GREENS LOL
THE VIVACIOUS VERDANT VEGETABLE... A VICTIM!
$ CROPS.
ELSEWHERE:
Pizza Pal
PIZZA PAL POGROM!

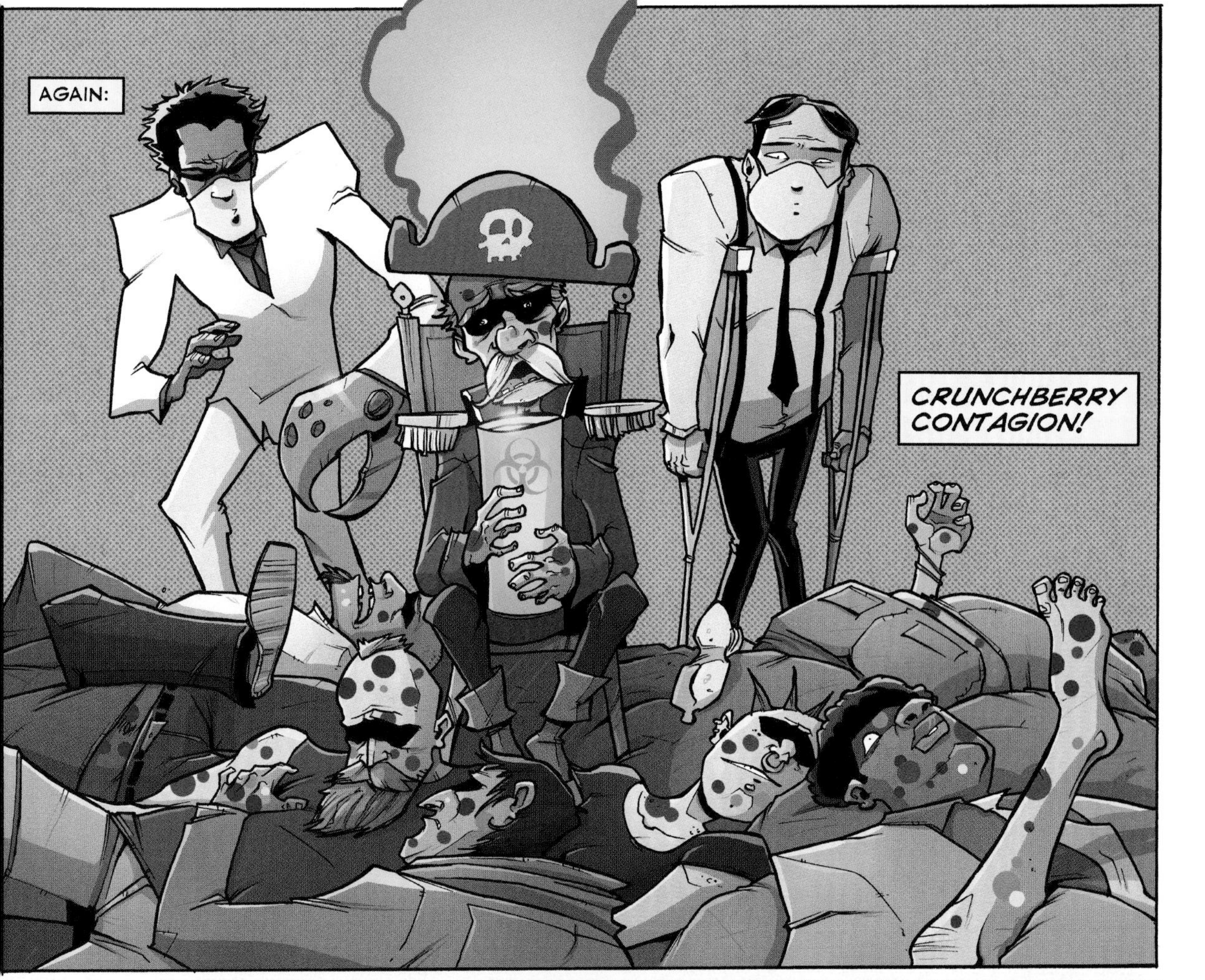
AGAIN:
CRUNCHBERRY CONTAGION!

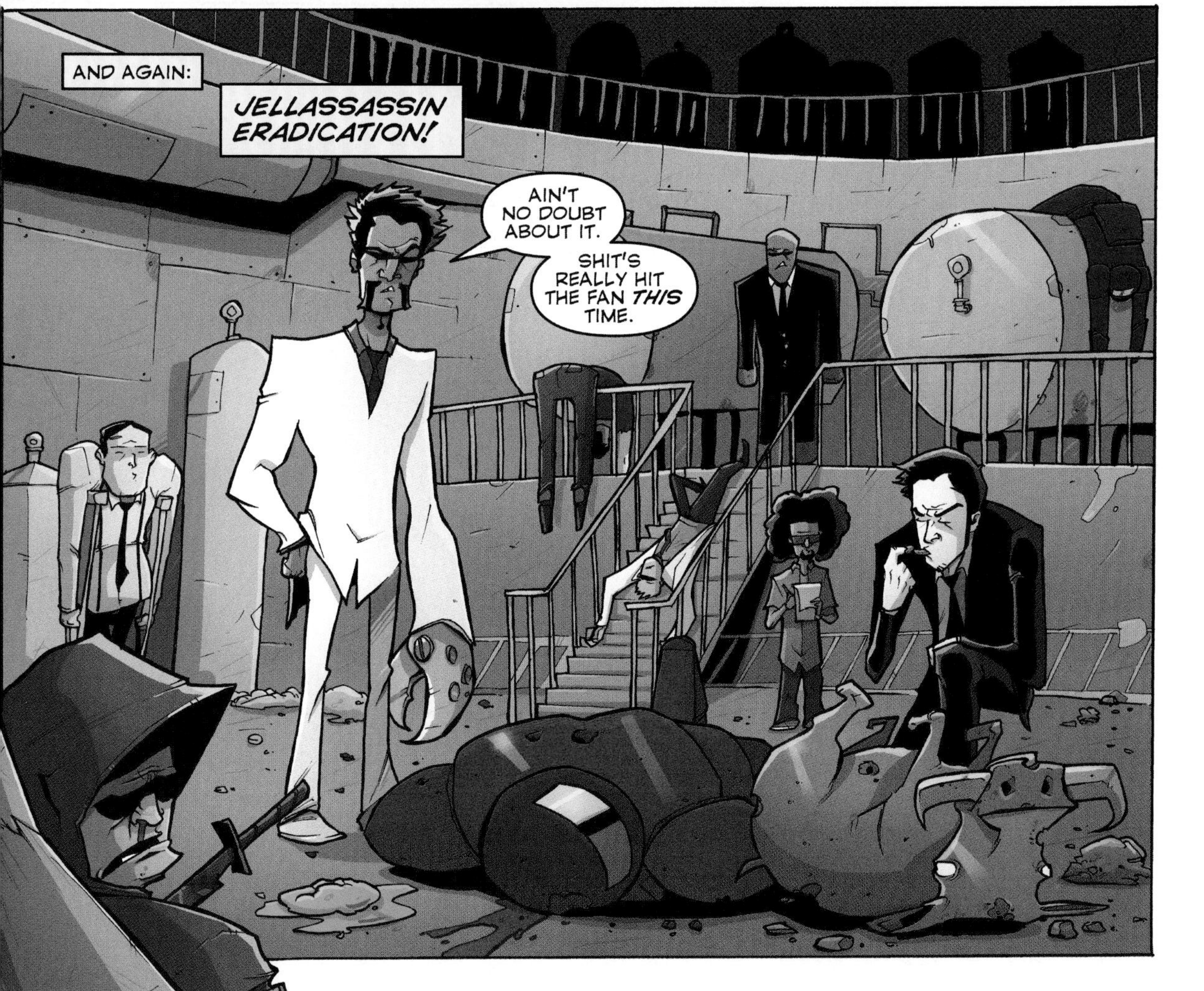
AND AGAIN:
JELLASSASSIN ERADICATION!
AIN'T NO DOUBT ABOUT IT.
SHIT'S REALLY HIT THE FAN THIS TIME.

INDEED IT HAS. THIS COLLECTOR MONSTER IS OUT OF CONTROL.

IT SEEMS HE'S DECLARED *WAR*.

ACCELERATING HIS COLLECTING, SENDING HIS SERVANTS TO FORCE EVERYBODY WITH FOOD POWERS INTO HIS SERVICE--

AND KILLING *ANY-BODY* WHO RESISTS.

HE'S GOING TO BE TOO POWERFUL TO STOP SOON, IF HE ISN'T ALREADY.

OF COURSE, TO *STOP* HIM, FIRST WE'RE GOING TO HAVE TO *FIND* HIM.

HE'S BEEN IN *HIDING* SINCE THE FDA'S DISASTROUS OFFENSIVE ON THE COLLECTOR'S CASTLE.

DAYS SINCE LAST TERROR "ACCIDENT" -5

DIRECTOR *BREADMAN*, I GOT A *READING* ON THAT WHICH CAN HELP.

A LEAD ON THE COLLECTOR'S *LOCALE*.

GONNA NEED AGENT VALENZANO WITH ME ON THIS ASSIGN-MENT.

FINE. JUST GET ME *RESULTS*, AGENTS! AND DO IT *QUICKLY!*

YO. WHAT ABOUT *ME*, BOSS?

DOCTORS HAVE CLEARED AGENT *VORHEES* FOR RETURN TO DUTY.

YOU CAN BE TEAMED WITH *HIM*, AGENT BERRY.

THE CRIPPLED RETARDED GUY?

SHIT.

FUCK.

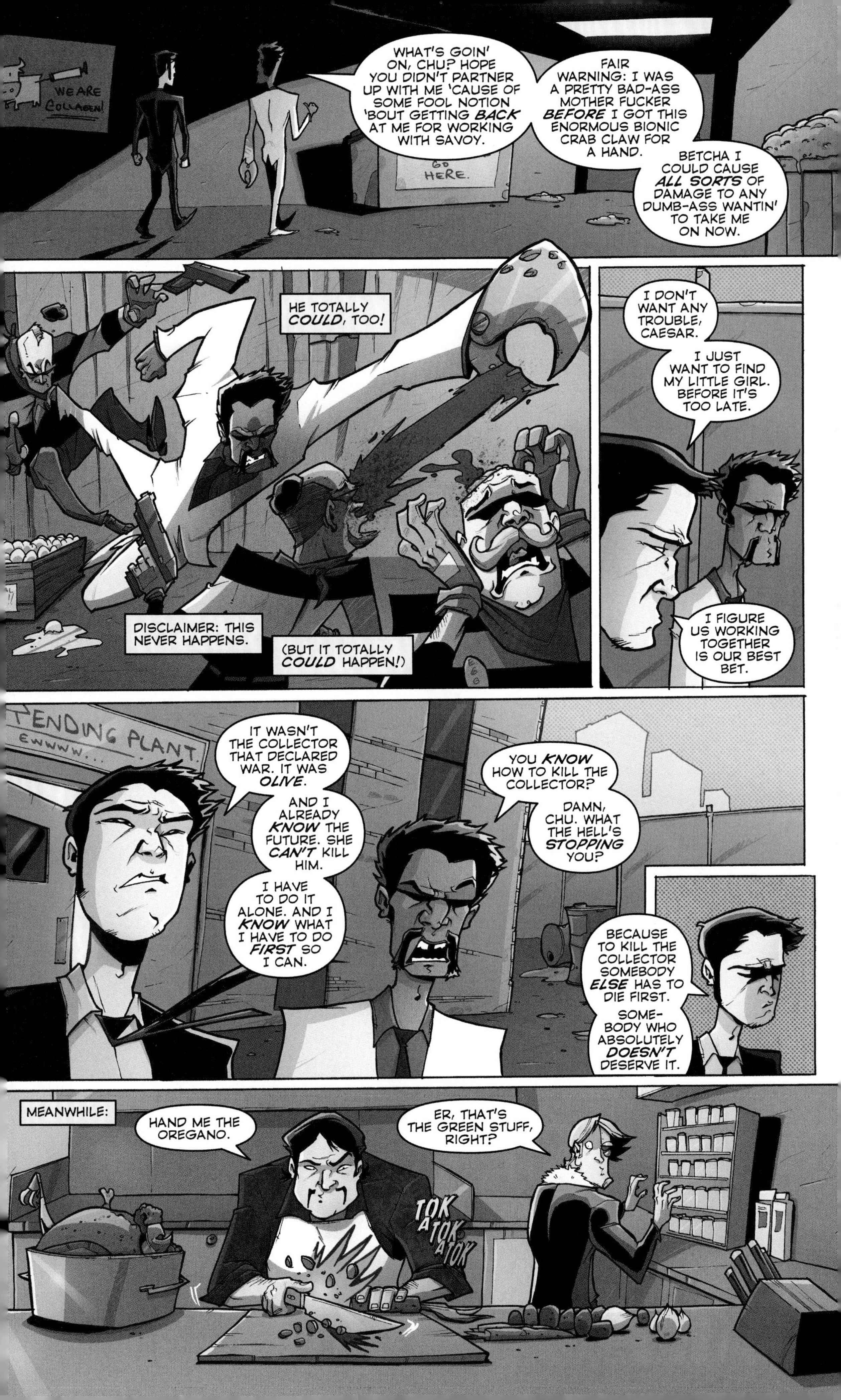
WE ARE COLLAGEN!
GO HERE.
WHAT'S GOIN' ON, CHU? HOPE YOU DIDN'T PARTNER UP WITH ME 'CAUSE OF SOME FOOL NOTION 'BOUT GETTING BACK AT ME FOR WORKING WITH SAVOY.
FAIR WARNING: I WAS A PRETTY BAD-ASS MOTHER FUCKER BEFORE I GOT THIS ENORMOUS BIONIC CRAB CLAW FOR A HAND.
BETCHA I COULD CAUSE ALL SORTS OF DAMAGE TO ANY DUMB-ASS WANTIN' TO TAKE ME ON NOW.
HE TOTALLY COULD, TOO!
DISCLAIMER: THIS NEVER HAPPENS.
(BUT IT TOTALLY COULD HAPPEN!)
I DON'T WANT ANY TROUBLE, CAESAR.
I JUST WANT TO FIND MY LITTLE GIRL. BEFORE IT'S TOO LATE.
I FIGURE US WORKING TOGETHER IS OUR BEST BET.
RENDING PLANT. EWWWW...
IT WASN'T THE COLLECTOR THAT DECLARED WAR. IT WAS OLIVE.
AND I ALREADY KNOW THE FUTURE. SHE CAN'T KILL HIM.
I HAVE TO DO IT ALONE. AND I KNOW WHAT I HAVE TO DO FIRST SO I CAN.
YOU KNOW HOW TO KILL THE COLLECTOR?
DAMN, CHU. WHAT THE HELL'S STOPPING YOU?
BECAUSE TO KILL THE COLLECTOR SOMEBODY ELSE HAS TO DIE FIRST.
SOME-BODY WHO ABSOLUTELY DOESN'T DESERVE IT.
MEANWHILE:
HAND ME THE OREGANO.
ER, THAT'S THE GREEN STUFF, RIGHT?
TOK A TOK A TOK

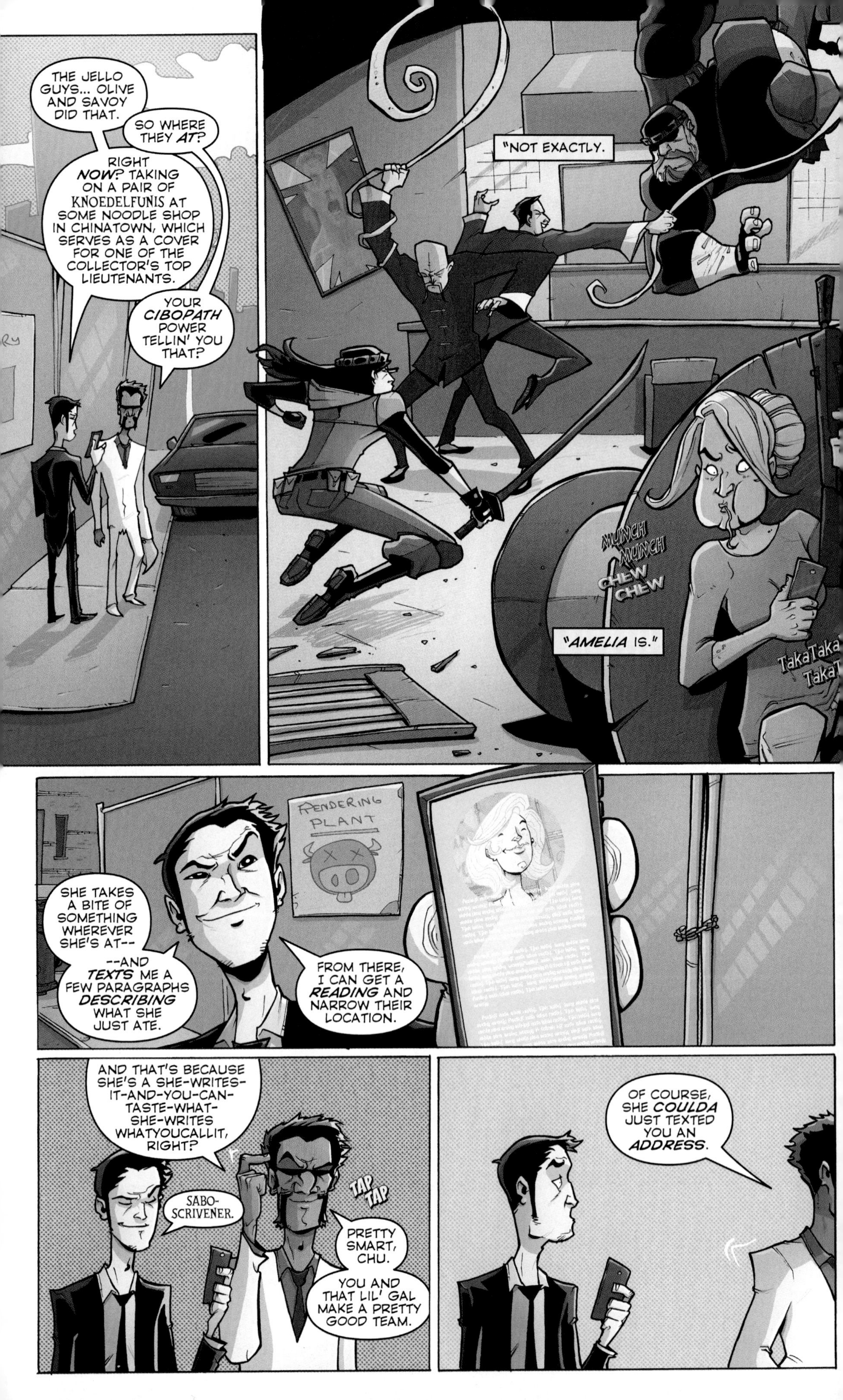
THE JELLO GUYS... OLIVE AND SAVOY DID THAT.
SO WHERE THEY *AT*?
RIGHT *NOW*? TAKING ON A PAIR OF KNOEDELFUNIS AT SOME NOODLE SHOP IN CHINATOWN, WHICH SERVES AS A COVER FOR ONE OF THE COLLECTOR'S TOP LIEUTENANTS.
YOUR *CIBOPATH* POWER TELLIN' YOU THAT?
"NOT EXACTLY.
MUNCH MUNCH
CHEW CHEW
"*AMELIA* IS."
TakaTaka TakaT
RENDERING PLANT
SHE TAKES A BITE OF SOMETHING WHEREVER SHE'S AT--
--AND *TEXTS* ME A FEW PARAGRAPHS *DESCRIBING* WHAT SHE JUST ATE.
FROM THERE, I CAN GET A *READING* AND NARROW THEIR LOCATION.
AND THAT'S BECAUSE SHE'S A SHE-WRITES-IT-AND-YOU-CAN-TASTE-WHAT-SHE-WRITES WHATYOUCALLIT, RIGHT?
SABO-SCRIVENER.
TAP TAP
PRETTY SMART, CHU.
YOU AND THAT LIL' GAL MAKE A PRETTY GOOD TEAM.
OF COURSE, SHE *COULDA* JUST TEXTED YOU AN *ADDRESS*.

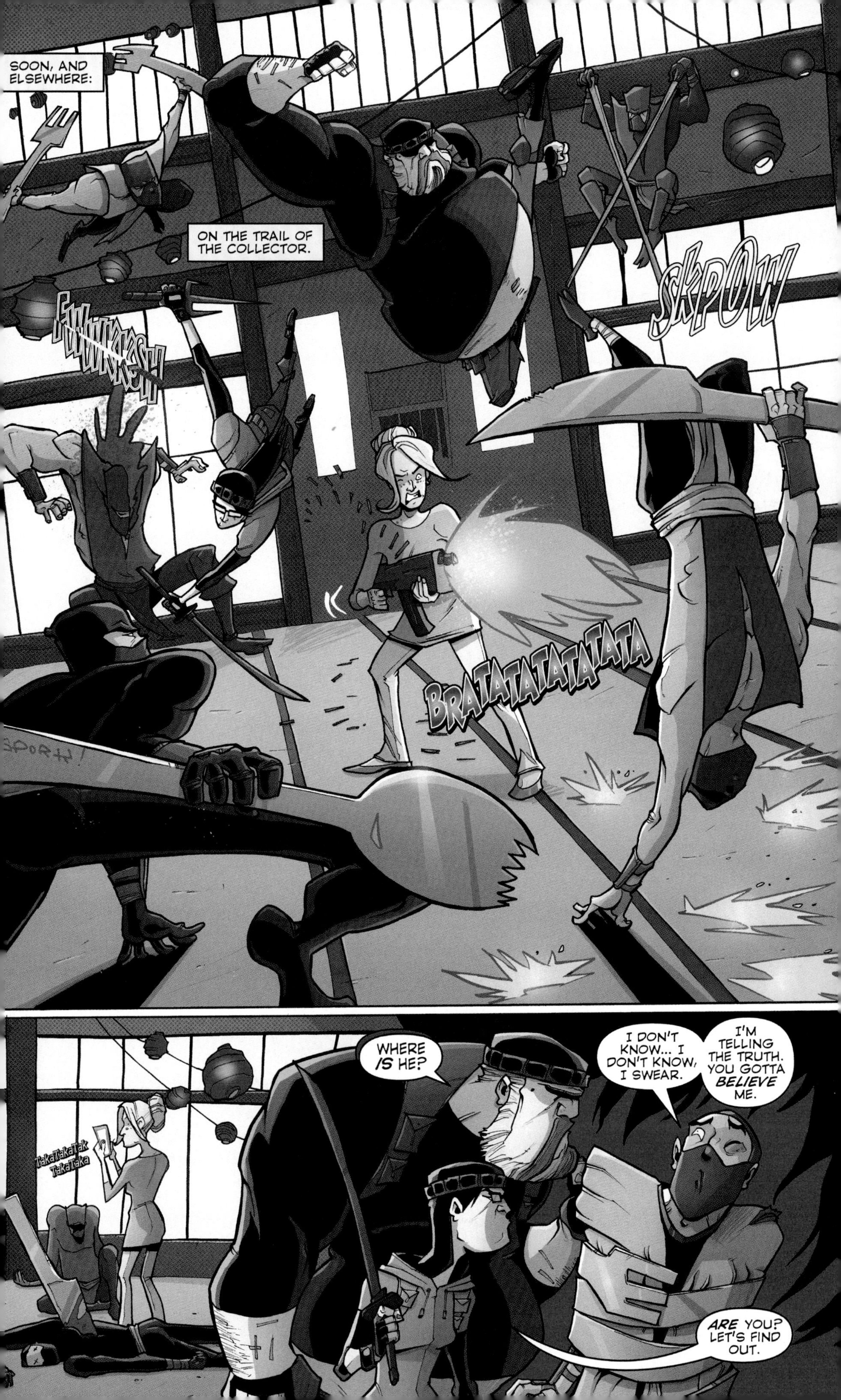

SOON, AND ELSEWHERE:
ON THE TRAIL OF THE COLLECTOR.
SKPOW
BRATATATATATATA
WHERE IS HE?
I DON'T KNOW... I DON'T KNOW, I SWEAR.
I'M TELLING THE TRUTH. YOU GOTTA BELIEVE ME.
TakaTakaTak TakaTaka
ARE YOU? LET'S FIND OUT.

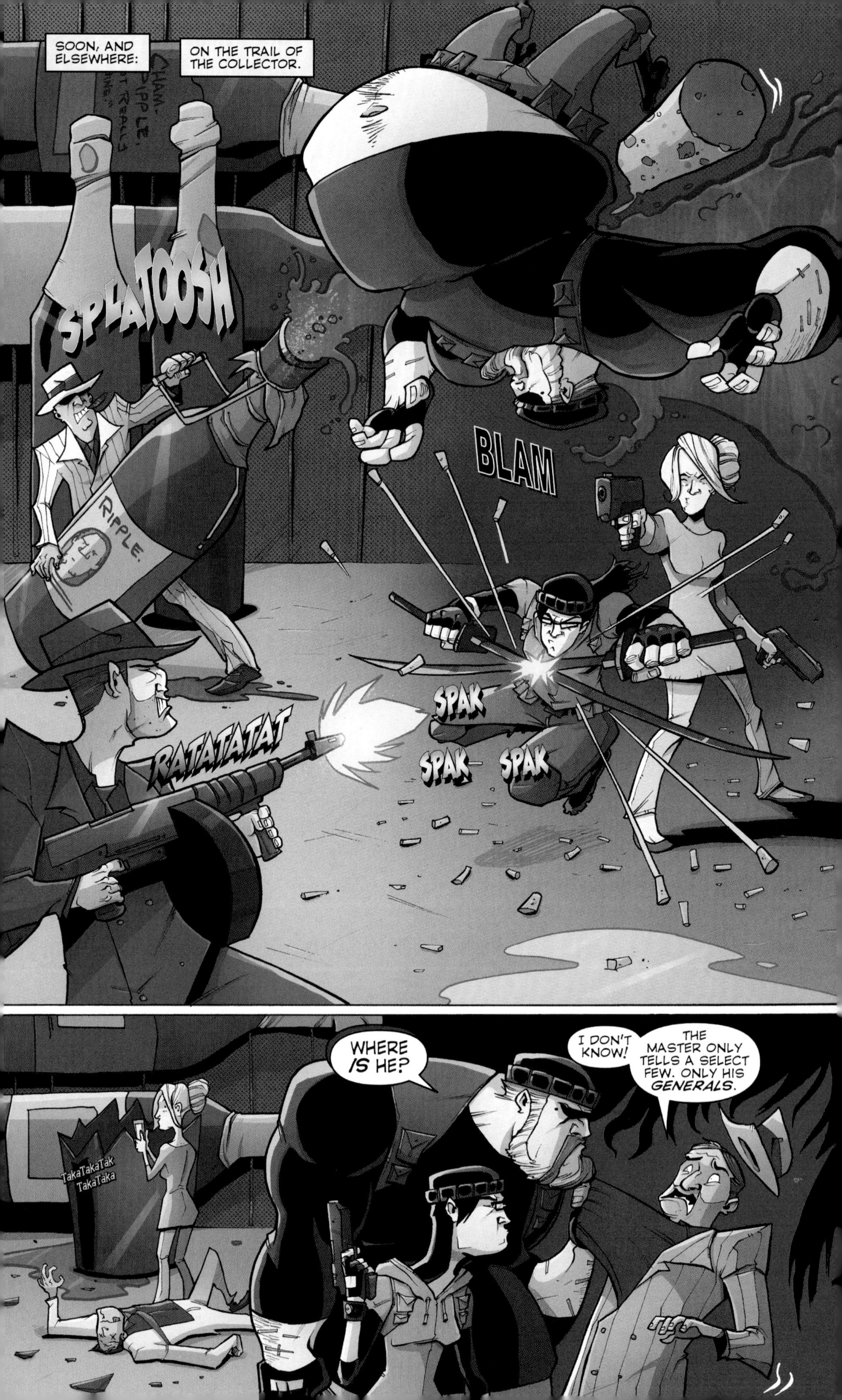
SOON, AND ELSEWHERE:
ON THE TRAIL OF THE COLLECTOR.
SPLATOOSH
RIPPLE.
BLAM
SPAK
RATATATAT
SPAK
SPAK
TakaTakaTak
TakaTaka
WHERE *IS* HE?
I DON'T KNOW!
THE MASTER ONLY TELLS A SELECT FEW. ONLY HIS *GENERALS*.

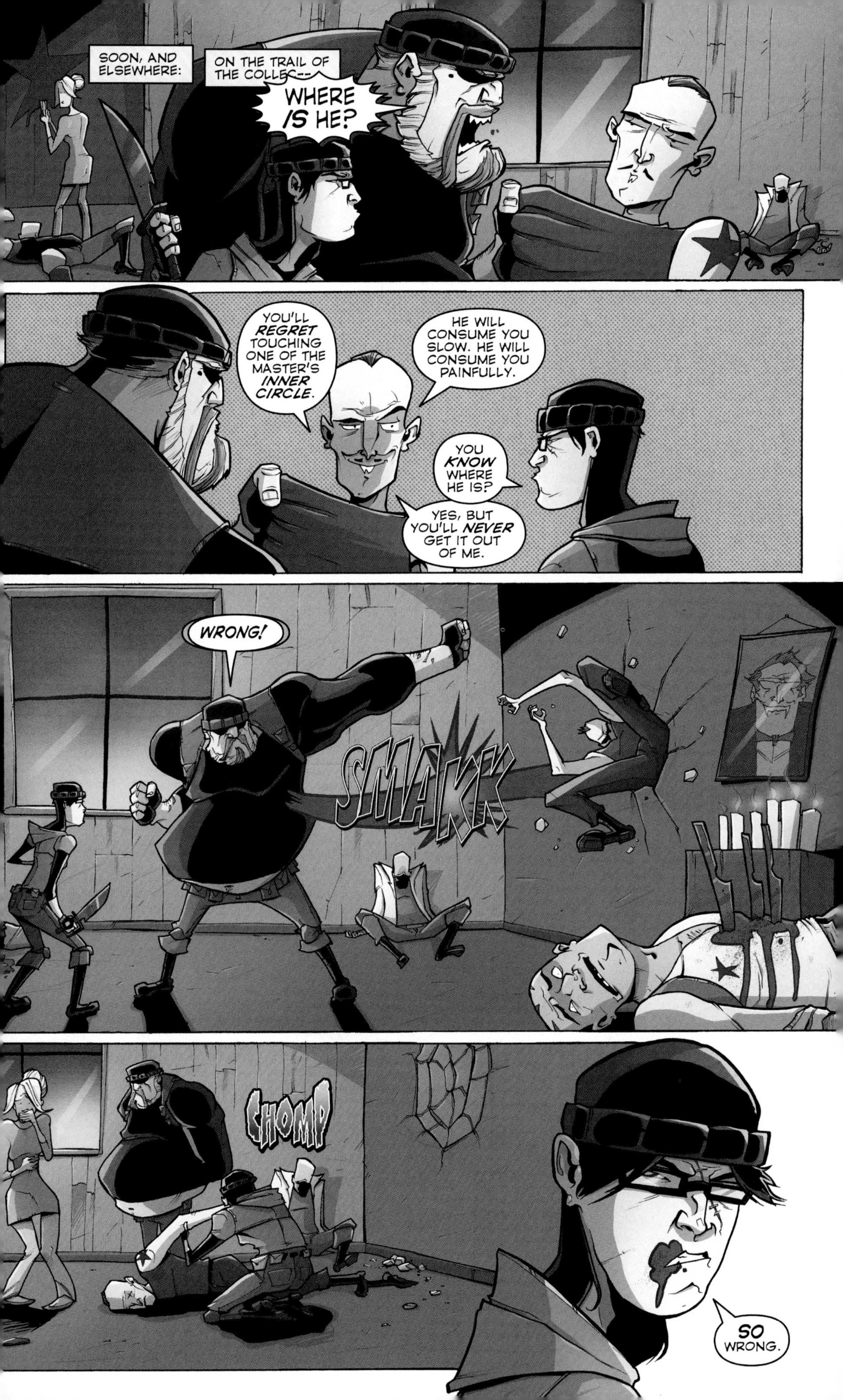
SOON, AND ELSEWHERE:
ON THE TRAIL OF THE COLLEC--
WHERE IS HE?
YOU'LL REGRET TOUCHING ONE OF THE MASTER'S INNER CIRCLE.
HE WILL CONSUME YOU SLOW. HE WILL CONSUME YOU PAINFULLY.
YOU KNOW WHERE HE IS?
YES, BUT YOU'LL NEVER GET IT OUT OF ME.
WRONG!
SMAKK
CHOMP
SO WRONG.

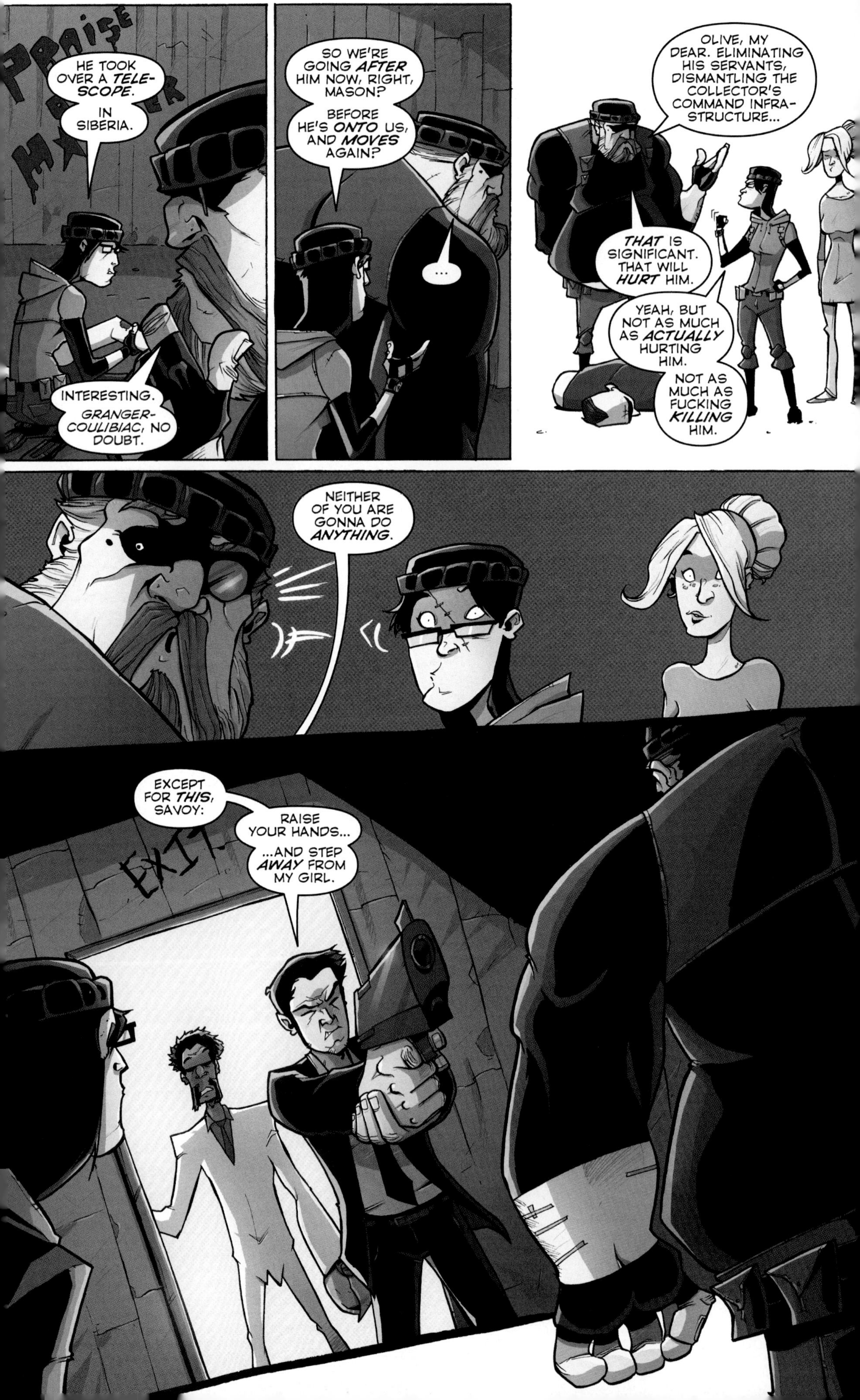
PRAISE
HE TOOK OVER A TELESCOPE.
IN SIBERIA.
INTERESTING. GRANGER-COULIBIAC, NO DOUBT.
SO WE'RE GOING AFTER HIM NOW, RIGHT, MASON?
BEFORE HE'S ONTO US, AND MOVES AGAIN?
...
OLIVE, MY DEAR. ELIMINATING HIS SERVANTS, DISMANTLING THE COLLECTOR'S COMMAND INFRASTRUCTURE...
THAT IS SIGNIFICANT. THAT WILL HURT HIM.
YEAH, BUT NOT AS MUCH AS ACTUALLY HURTING HIM.
NOT AS MUCH AS FUCKING KILLING HIM.
NEITHER OF YOU ARE GONNA DO ANYTHING.
EXCEPT FOR THIS, SAVOY:
RAISE YOUR HANDS...
...AND STEP AWAY FROM MY GIRL.
EXIT

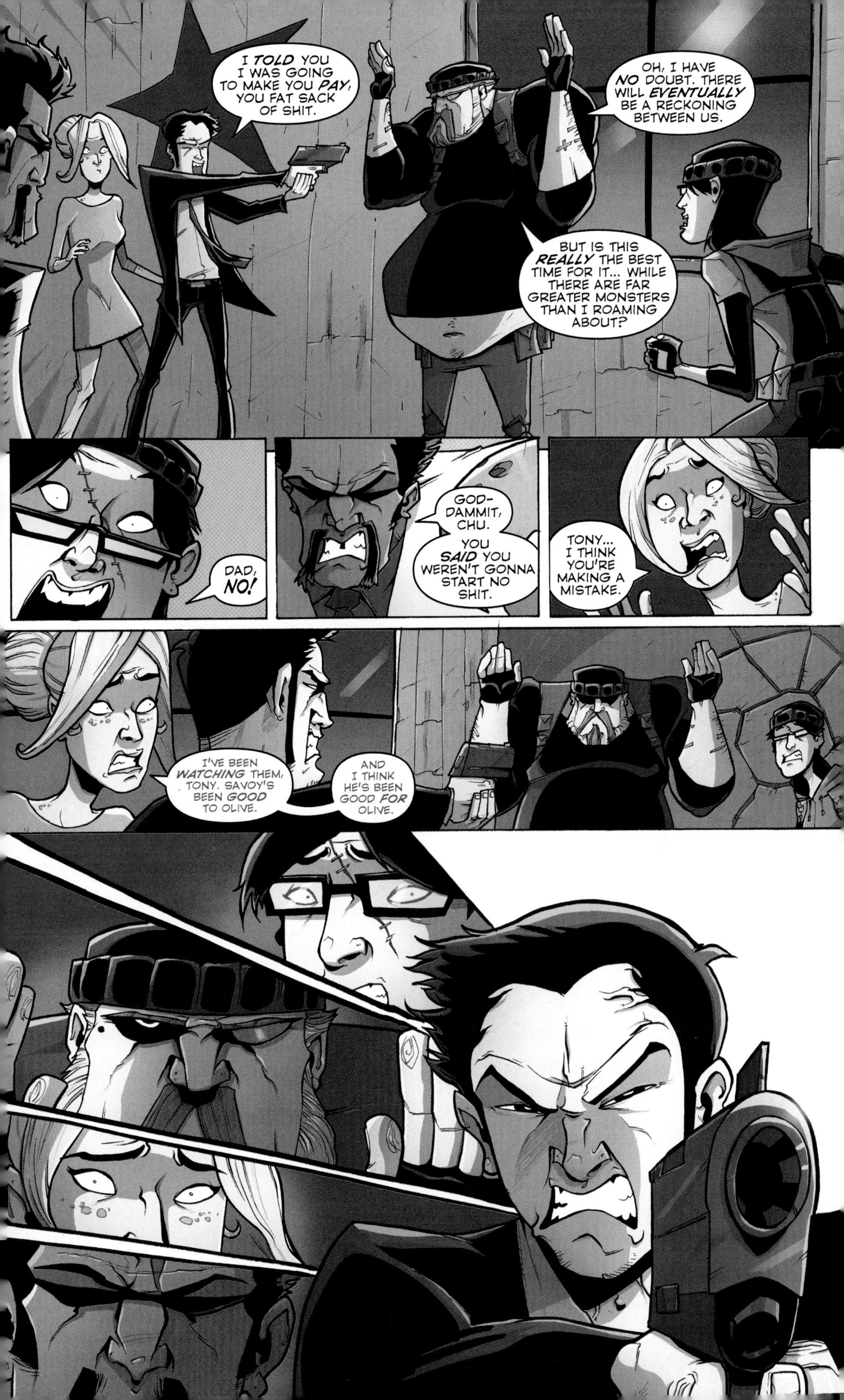
I TOLD YOU I WAS GOING TO MAKE YOU PAY, YOU FAT SACK OF SHIT.
OH, I HAVE NO DOUBT. THERE WILL EVENTUALLY BE A RECKONING BETWEEN US.
BUT IS THIS REALLY THE BEST TIME FOR IT... WHILE THERE ARE FAR GREATER MONSTERS THAN I ROAMING ABOUT?
DAD, NO!
GOD-DAMMIT, CHU.
YOU SAID YOU WEREN'T GONNA START NO SHIT.
TONY... I THINK YOU'RE MAKING A MISTAKE.
I'VE BEEN WATCHING THEM, TONY. SAVOY'S BEEN GOOD TO OLIVE.
AND I THINK HE'S BEEN GOOD FOR OLIVE.

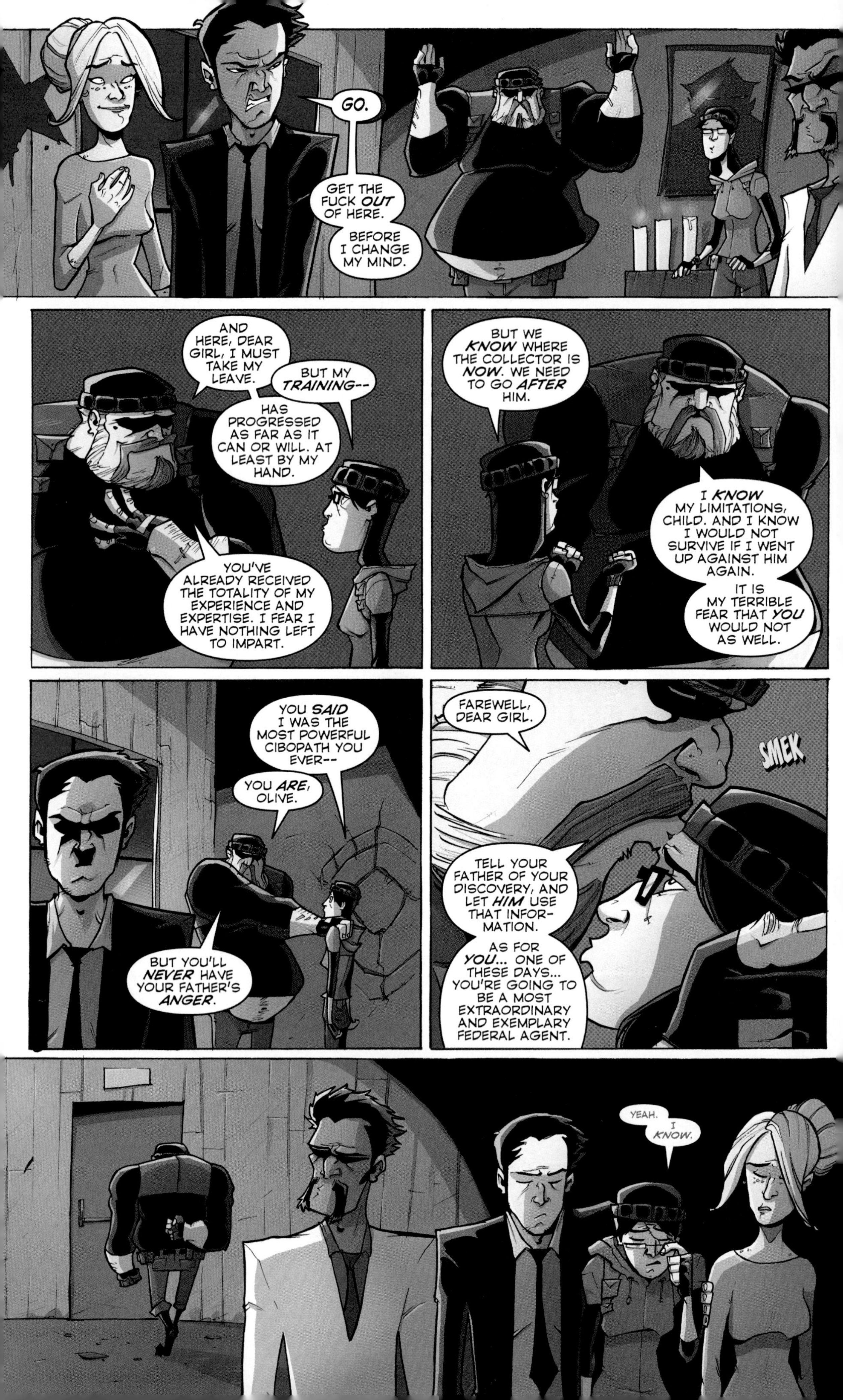
GO.
GET THE FUCK OUT OF HERE.
BEFORE I CHANGE MY MIND.
AND HERE, DEAR GIRL, I MUST TAKE MY LEAVE.
BUT MY TRAINING--
HAS PROGRESSED AS FAR AS IT CAN OR WILL. AT LEAST BY MY HAND.
YOU'VE ALREADY RECEIVED THE TOTALITY OF MY EXPERIENCE AND EXPERTISE. I FEAR I HAVE NOTHING LEFT TO IMPART.
BUT WE KNOW WHERE THE COLLECTOR IS NOW. WE NEED TO GO AFTER HIM.
I KNOW MY LIMITATIONS, CHILD. AND I KNOW I WOULD NOT SURVIVE IF I WENT UP AGAINST HIM AGAIN.
IT IS MY TERRIBLE FEAR THAT YOU WOULD NOT AS WELL.
YOU SAID I WAS THE MOST POWERFUL CIBOPATH YOU EVER--
YOU ARE, OLIVE.
BUT YOU'LL NEVER HAVE YOUR FATHER'S ANGER.
FAREWELL, DEAR GIRL.
SMEK
TELL YOUR FATHER OF YOUR DISCOVERY, AND LET HIM USE THAT INFORMATION.
AS FOR YOU... ONE OF THESE DAYS... YOU'RE GOING TO BE A MOST EXTRAORDINARY AND EXEMPLARY FEDERAL AGENT.
YEAH. I KNOW.

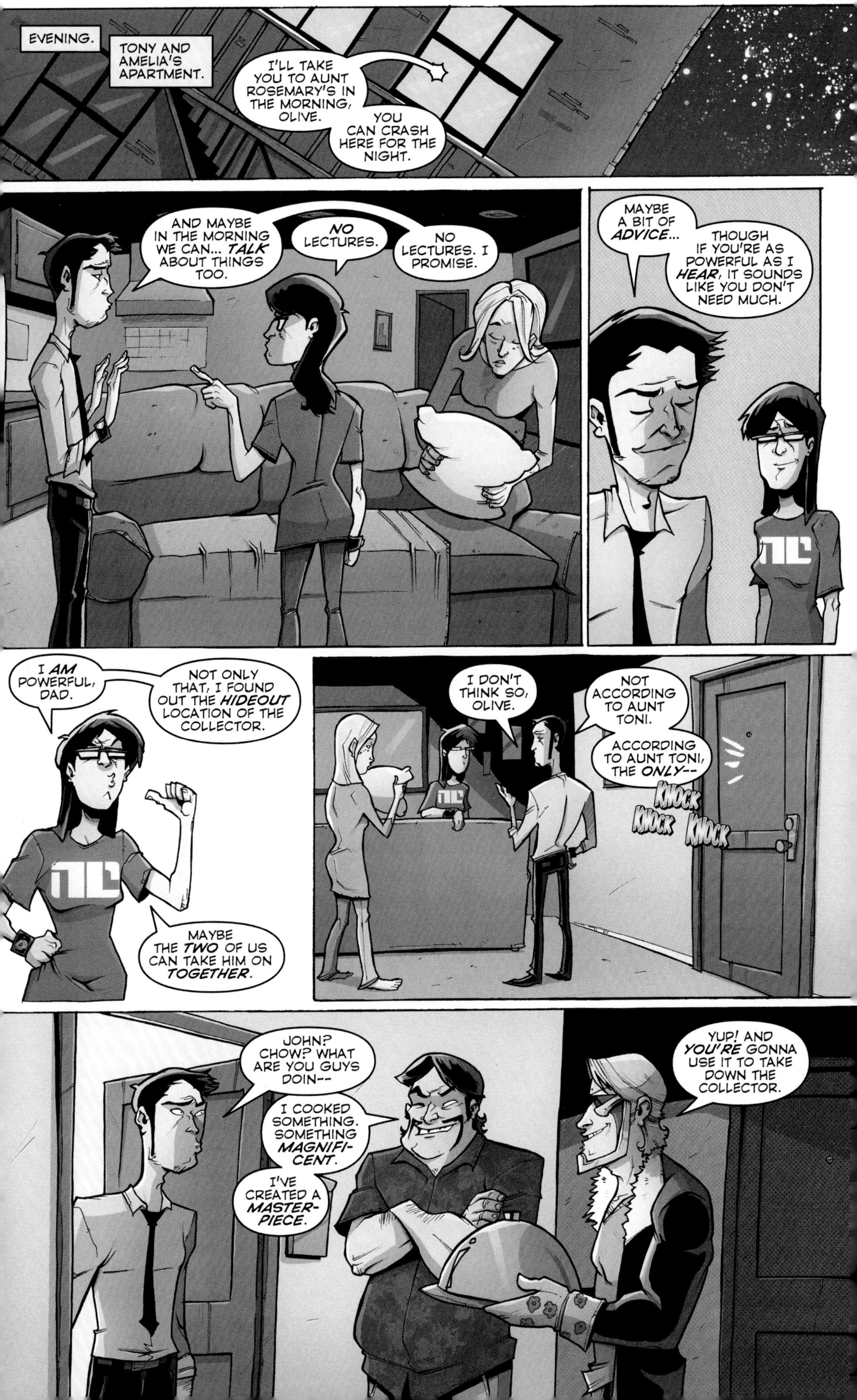
EVENING.
TONY AND AMELIA'S APARTMENT.
I'LL TAKE YOU TO AUNT ROSEMARY'S IN THE MORNING, OLIVE.
YOU CAN CRASH HERE FOR THE NIGHT.
AND MAYBE IN THE MORNING WE CAN... TALK ABOUT THINGS TOO.
NO LECTURES.
NO LECTURES. I PROMISE.
MAYBE A BIT OF ADVICE...
THOUGH IF YOU'RE AS POWERFUL AS I HEAR, IT SOUNDS LIKE YOU DON'T NEED MUCH.
I AM POWERFUL, DAD.
NOT ONLY THAT, I FOUND OUT THE HIDEOUT LOCATION OF THE COLLECTOR.
MAYBE THE TWO OF US CAN TAKE HIM ON TOGETHER.
I DON'T THINK SO, OLIVE.
NOT ACCORDING TO AUNT TONI.
ACCORDING TO AUNT TONI, THE ONLY--
KNOCK KNOCK KNOCK
JOHN? CHOW? WHAT ARE YOU GUYS DOIN--
I COOKED SOMETHING. SOMETHING MAGNIFI-CENT.
I'VE CREATED A MASTER-PIECE.
YUP! AND YOU'RE GONNA USE IT TO TAKE DOWN THE COLLECTOR.

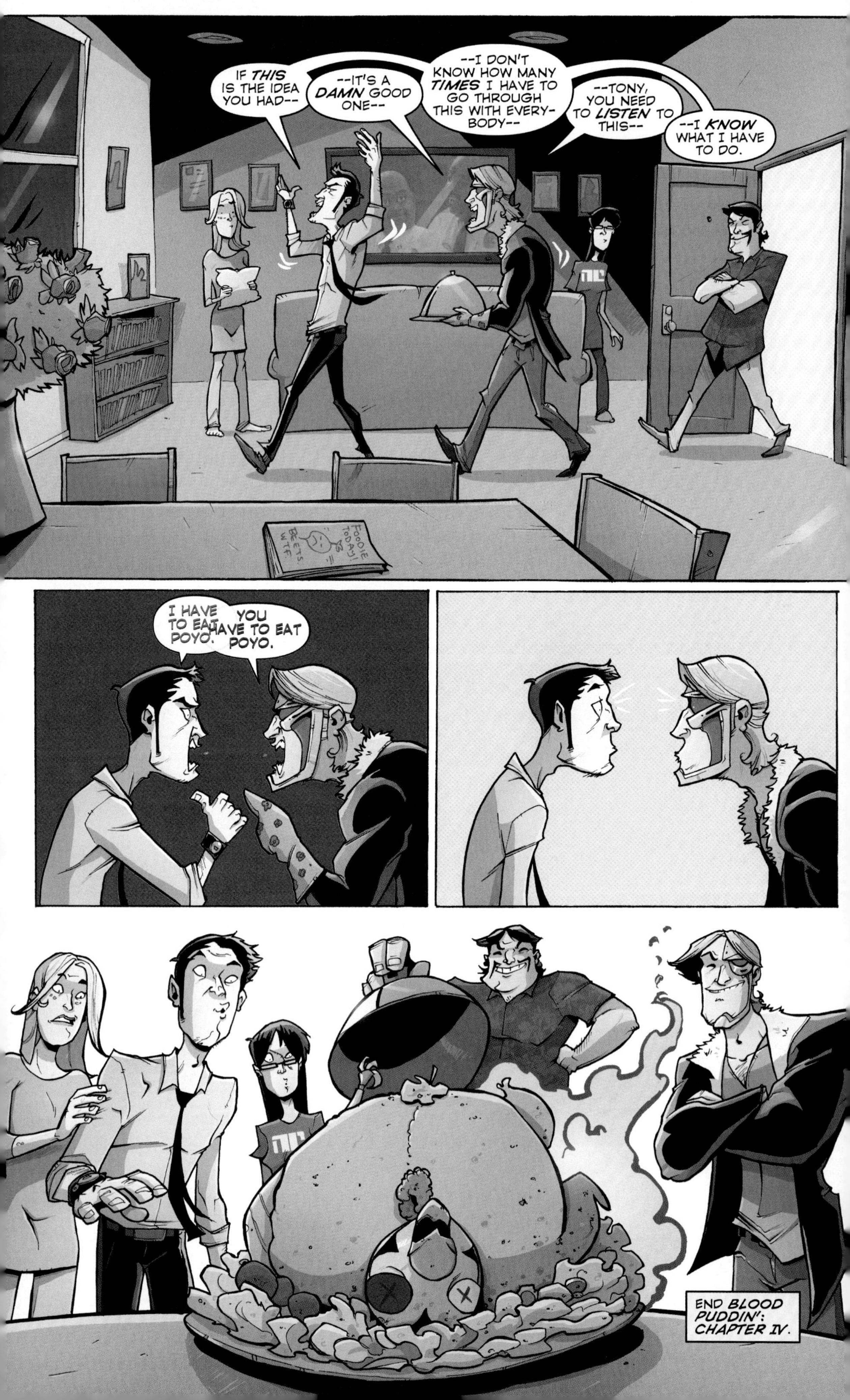
IF THIS IS THE IDEA YOU HAD--
--IT'S A DAMN GOOD ONE--
--I DON'T KNOW HOW MANY TIMES I HAVE TO GO THROUGH THIS WITH EVERY-BODY--
--TONY, YOU NEED TO LISTEN TO THIS--
--I KNOW WHAT I HAVE TO DO.
I HAVE TO EAT POYO.
YOU HAVE TO EAT POYO.
END BLOOD PUDDIN': CHAPTER IV.

Chapter Ten

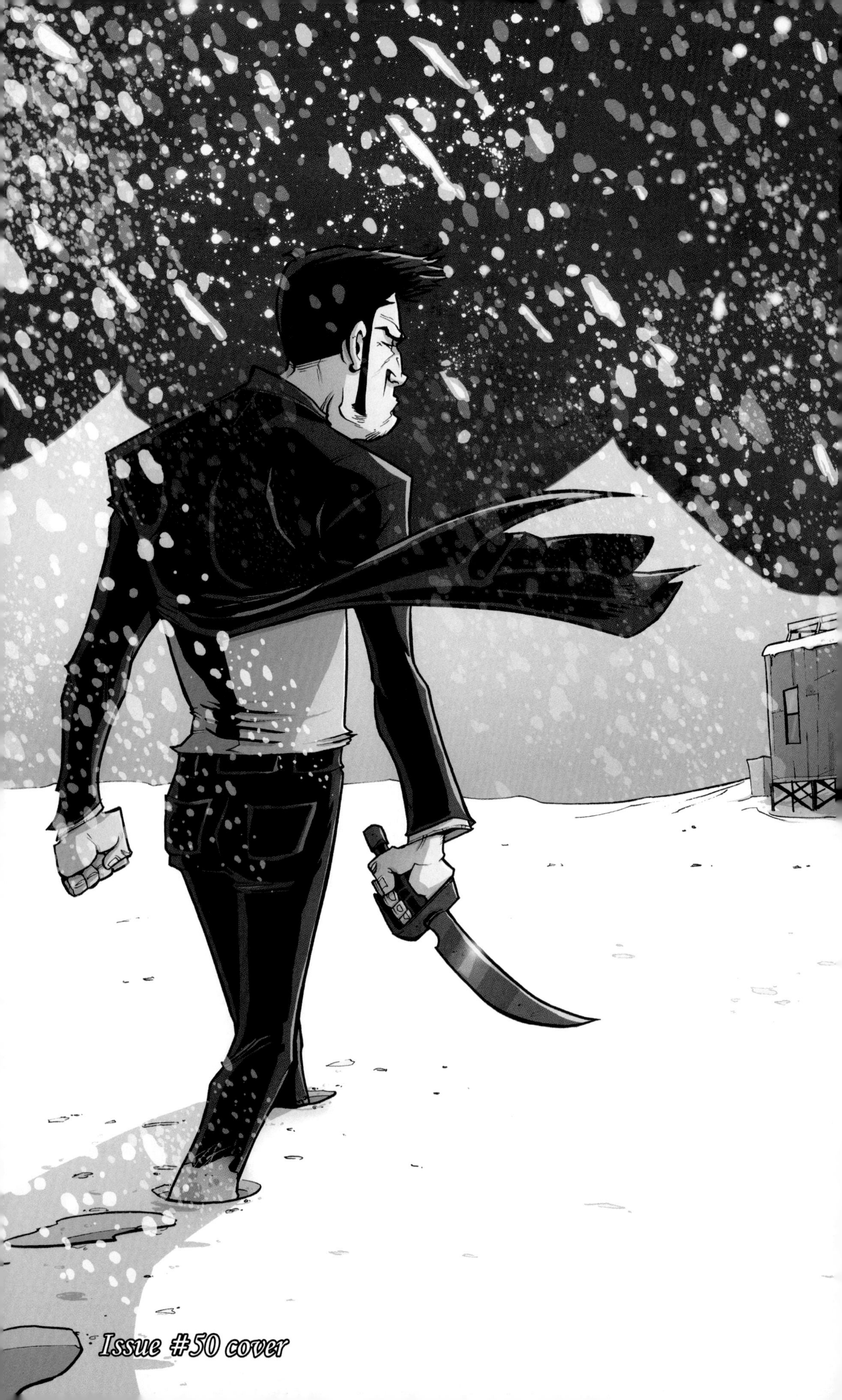

Issue #50 cover

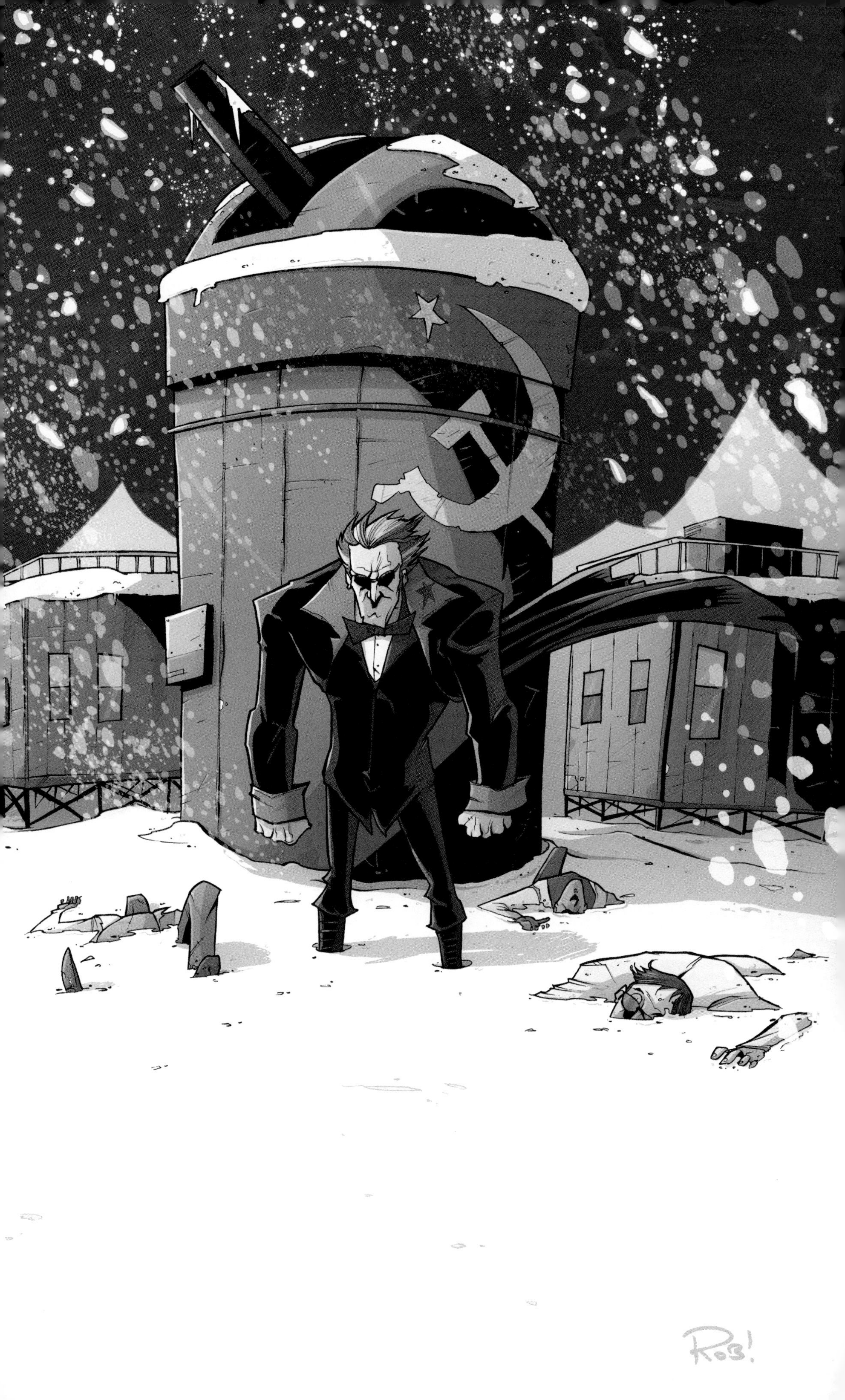

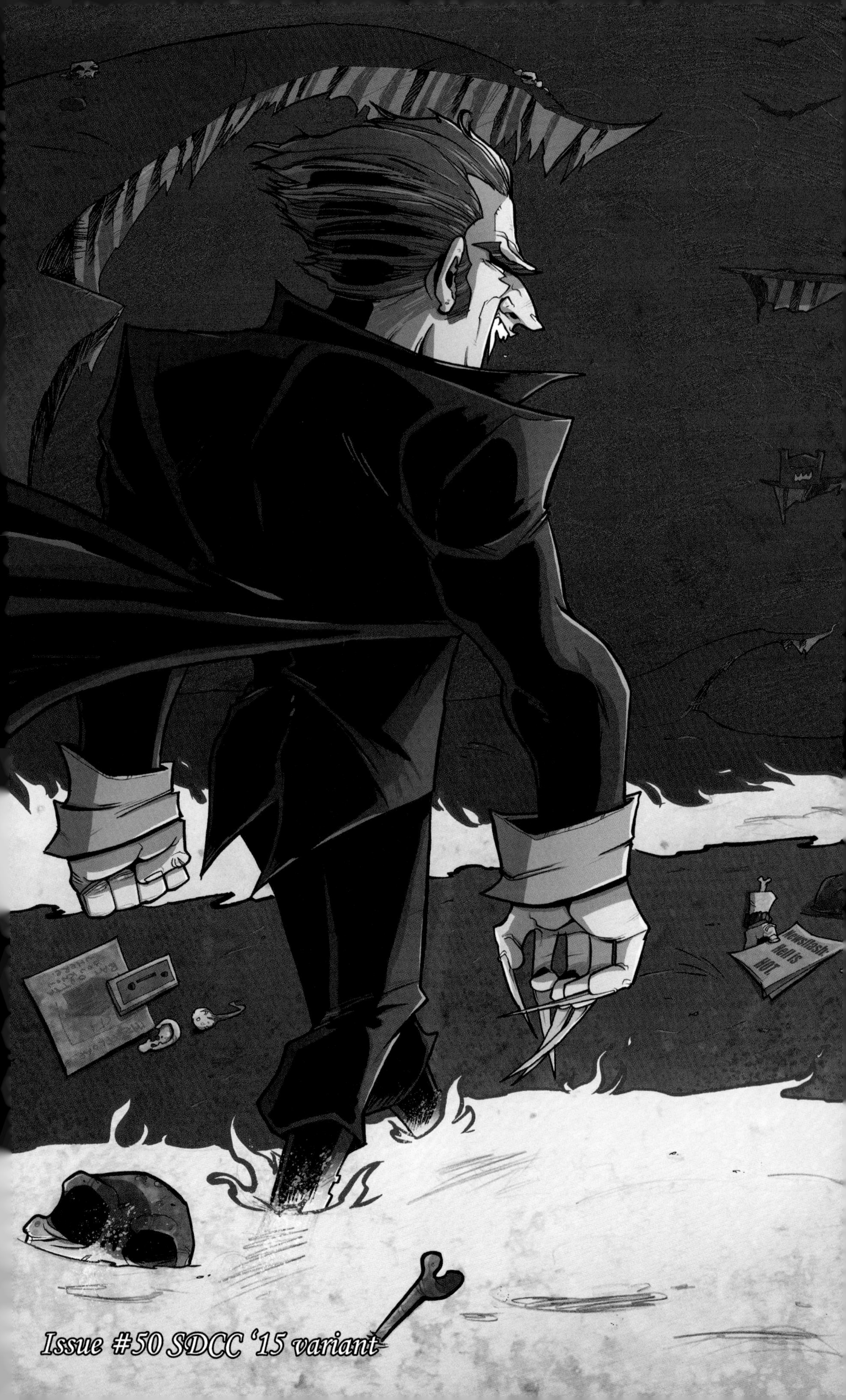
Newsflash:
Hell is
HOT.

Issue #50 SDCC '15 variant

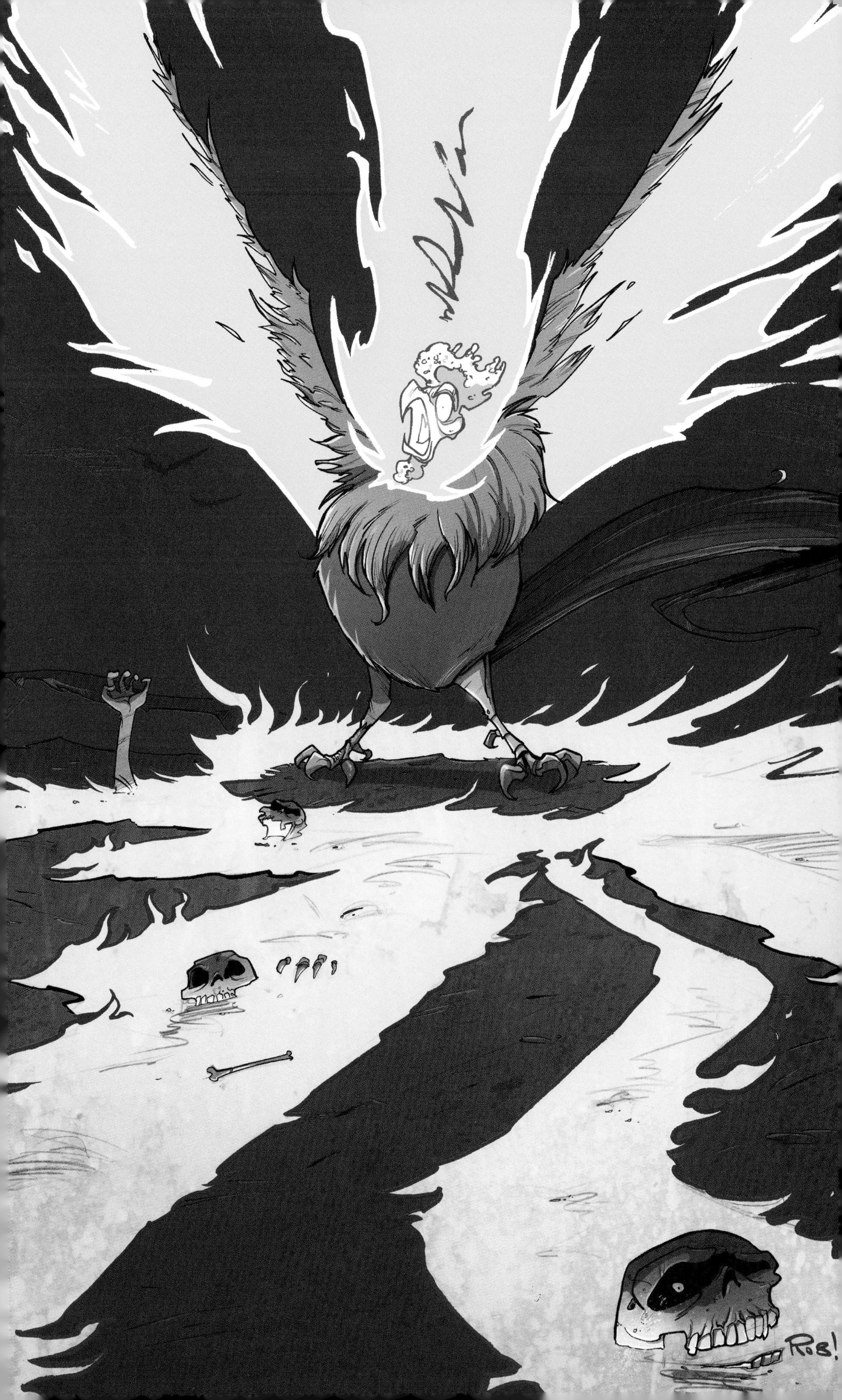
ROB!

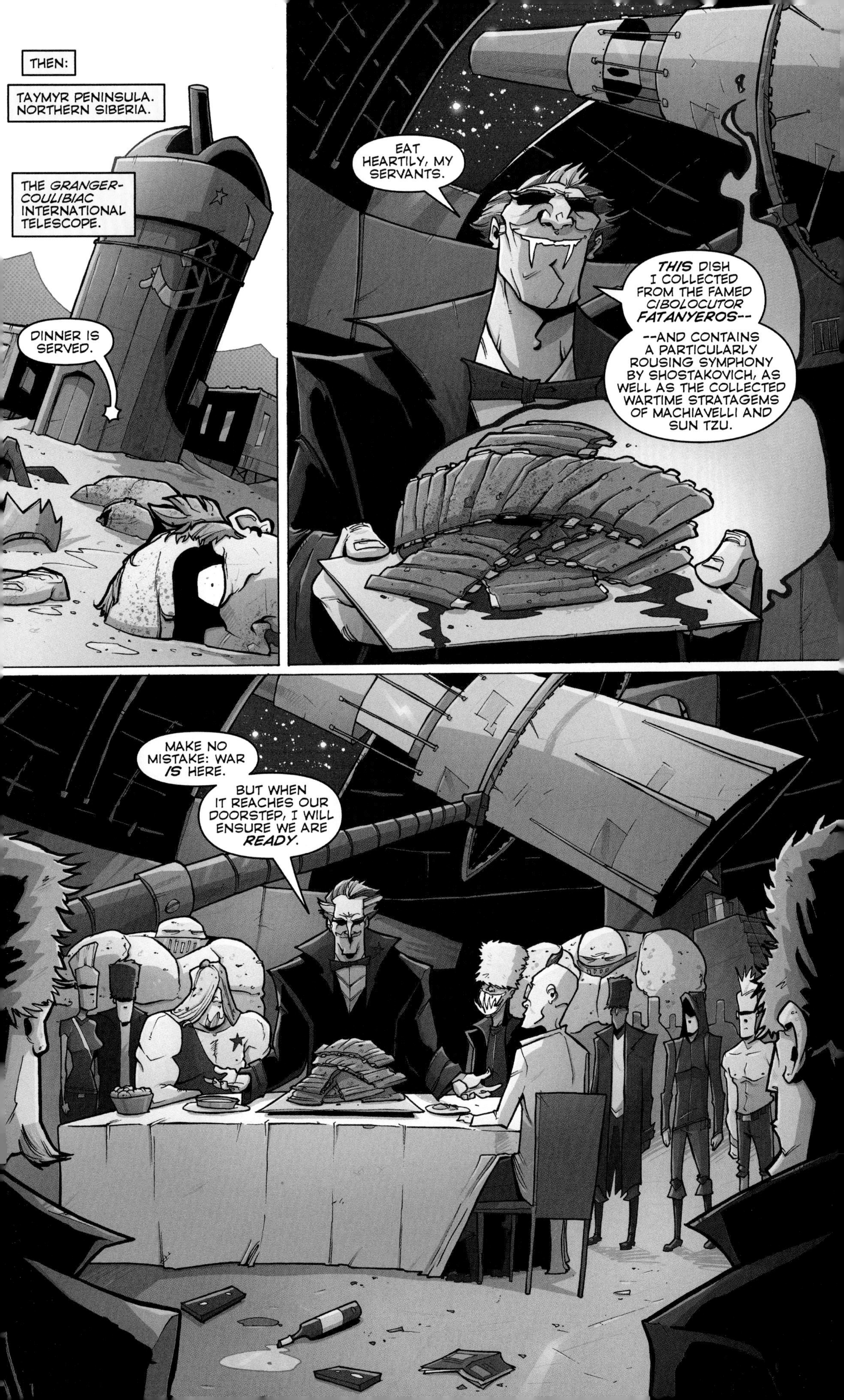
THEN:
TAYMYR PENINSULA. NORTHERN SIBERIA.
THE GRANGER-COULIBIAC INTERNATIONAL TELESCOPE.
DINNER IS SERVED.
EAT HEARTILY, MY SERVANTS.
THIS DISH I COLLECTED FROM THE FAMED CIBOLOCUTOR FATANYEROS--
--AND CONTAINS A PARTICULARLY ROUSING SYMPHONY BY SHOSTAKOVICH, AS WELL AS THE COLLECTED WARTIME STRATAGEMS OF MACHIAVELLI AND SUN TZU.
MAKE NO MISTAKE: WAR IS HERE.
BUT WHEN IT REACHES OUR DOORSTEP, I WILL ENSURE WE ARE READY.

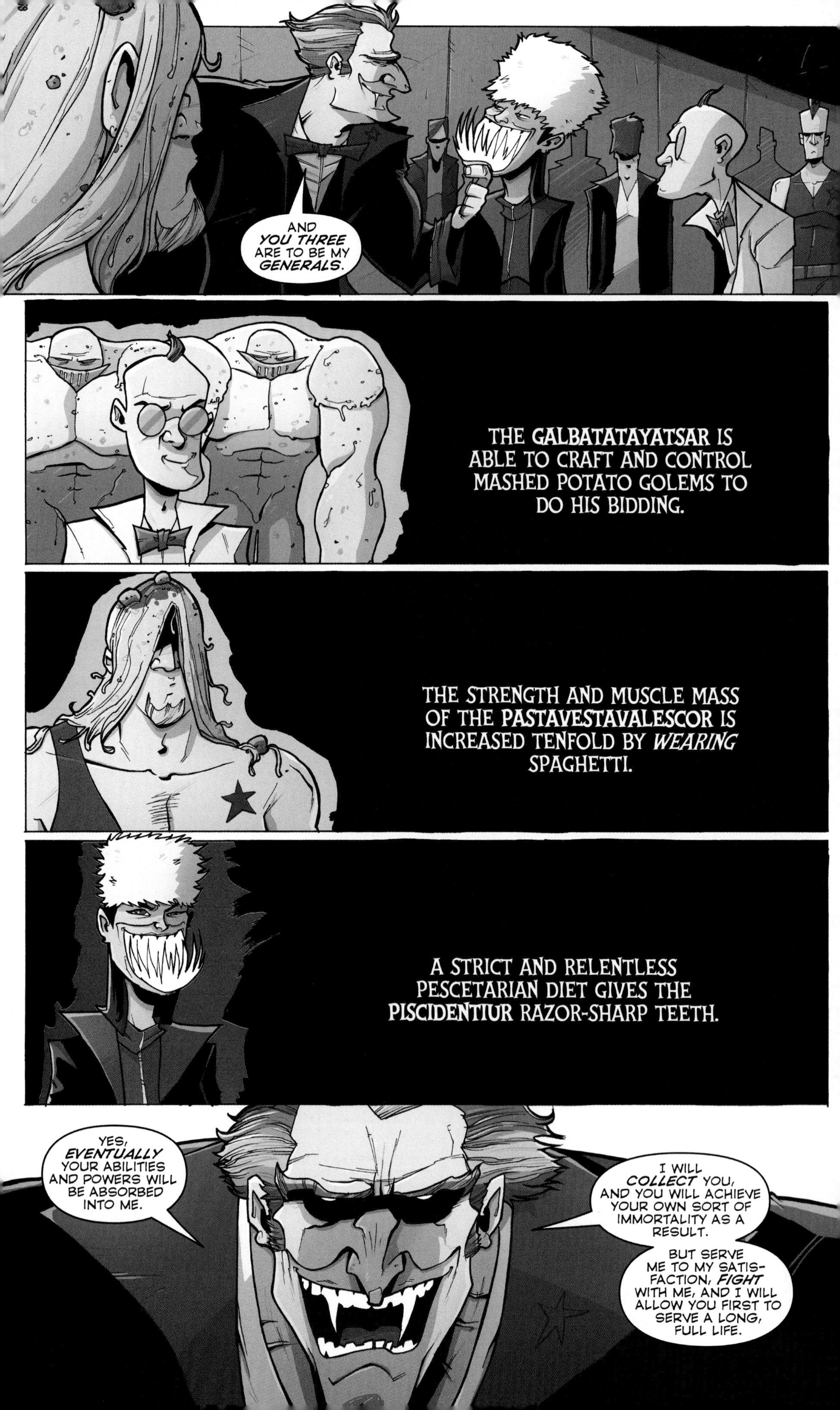

AND *YOU THREE* ARE TO BE MY *GENERALS*.
THE **GALBATATAYATSAR** IS ABLE TO CRAFT AND CONTROL MASHED POTATO GOLEMS TO DO HIS BIDDING.
THE STRENGTH AND MUSCLE MASS OF THE **PASTAVESTAVALESCOR** IS INCREASED TENFOLD BY *WEARING* SPAGHETTI.
A STRICT AND RELENTLESS PESCETARIAN DIET GIVES THE **PISCIDENTIUR** RAZOR-SHARP TEETH.
YES, ***EVENTUALLY*** YOUR ABILITIES AND POWERS WILL BE ABSORBED INTO ME.
I WILL ***COLLECT*** YOU, AND YOU WILL ACHIEVE YOUR OWN SORT OF IMMORTALITY AS A RESULT.
BUT SERVE ME TO MY SATIS-FACTION, ***FIGHT*** WITH ME, AND I WILL ALLOW YOU FIRST TO SERVE A LONG, FULL LIFE.

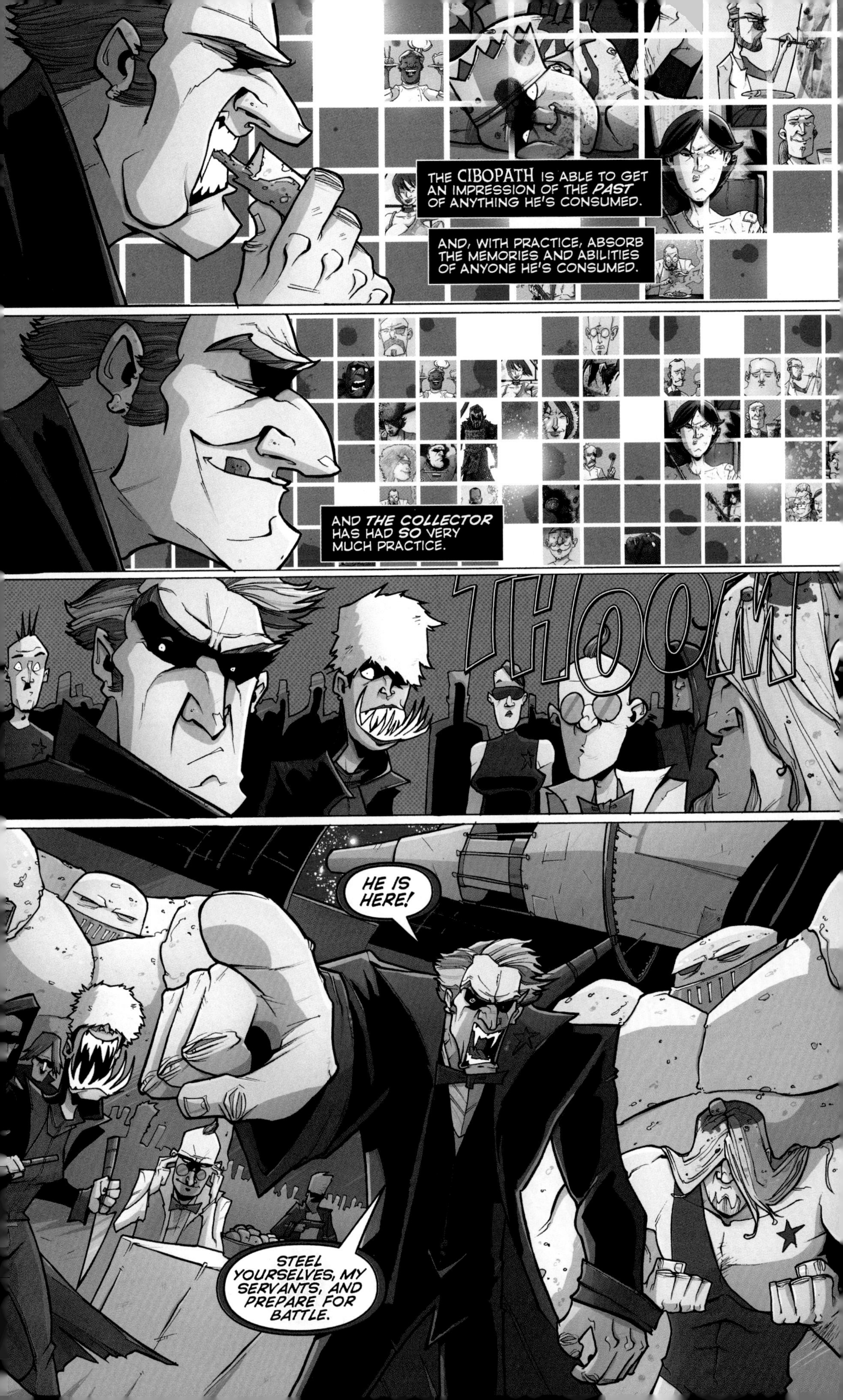
THE CIBOPATH IS ABLE TO GET AN IMPRESSION OF THE *PAST* OF ANYTHING HE'S CONSUMED.
AND, WITH PRACTICE, ABSORB THE MEMORIES AND ABILITIES OF ANYONE HE'S CONSUMED.
AND *THE COLLECTOR* HAS HAD *SO* VERY MUCH PRACTICE.
THOOM
HE IS HERE!
STEEL YOURSELVES, MY SERVANTS, AND PREPARE FOR BATTLE.

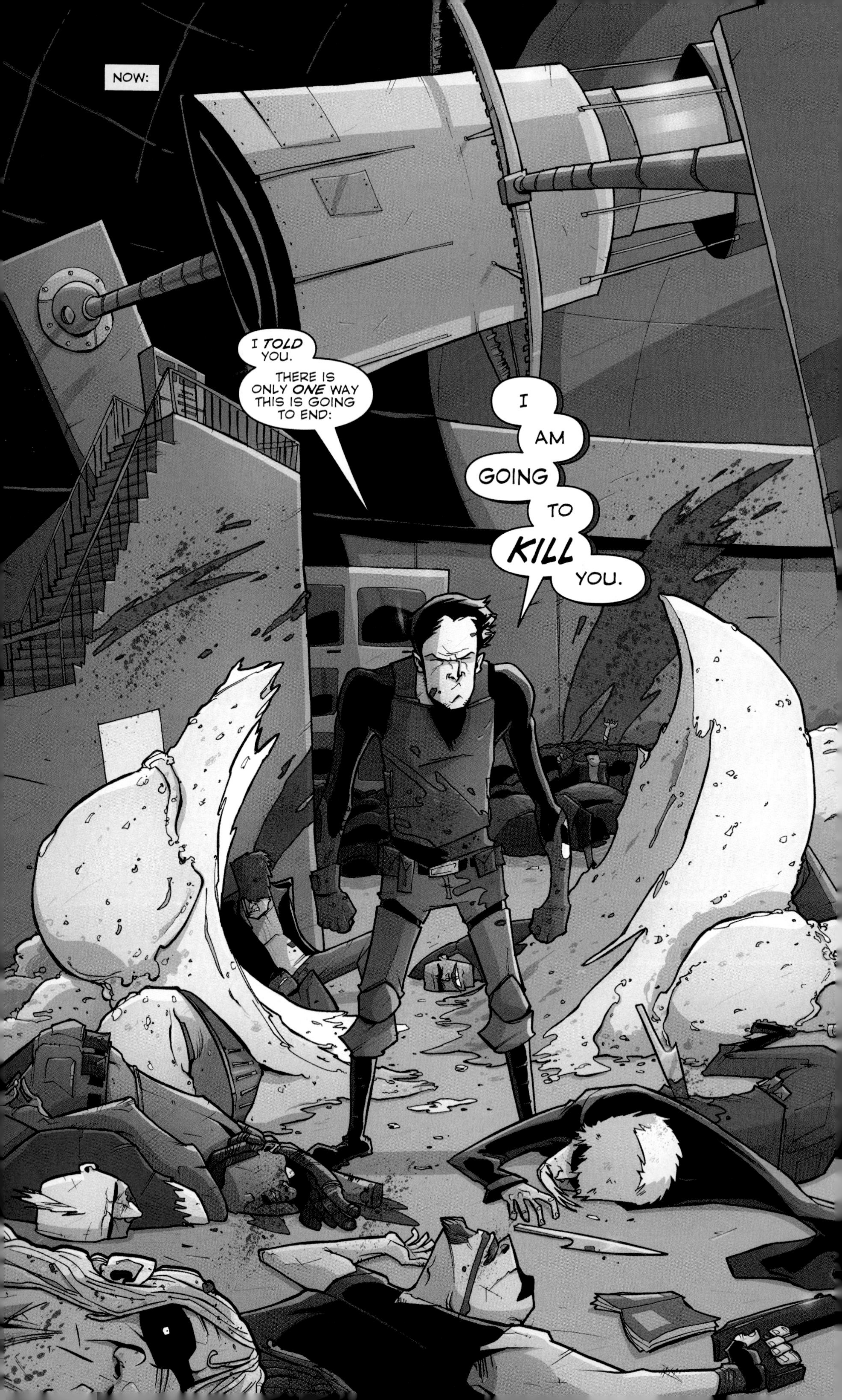
NOW:
I TOLD YOU. THERE IS ONLY ONE WAY THIS IS GOING TO END:
I AM GOING TO KILL YOU.

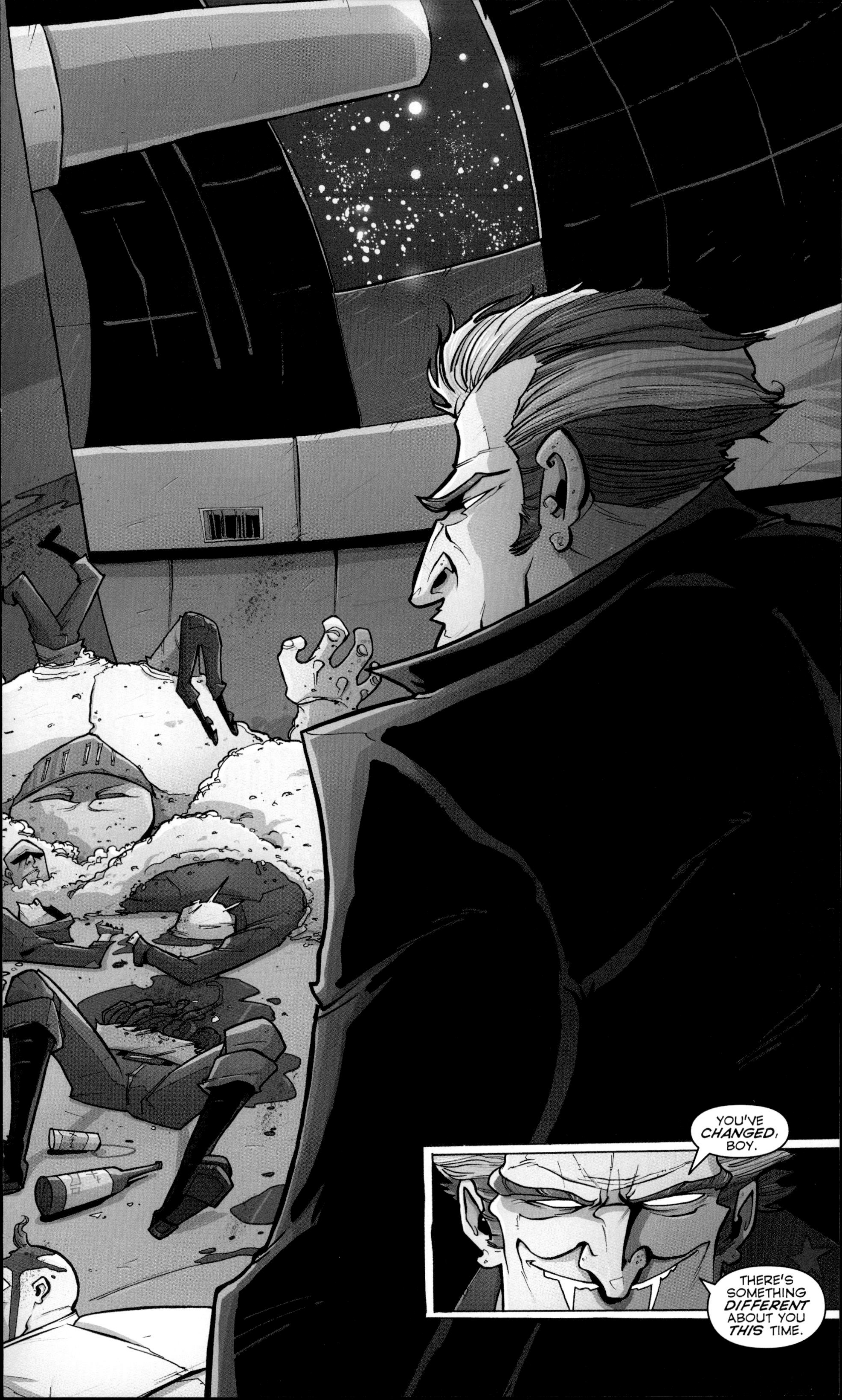

YOU'VE *CHANGED*, BOY.
THERE'S SOMETHING *DIFFERENT* ABOUT YOU *THIS* TIME.

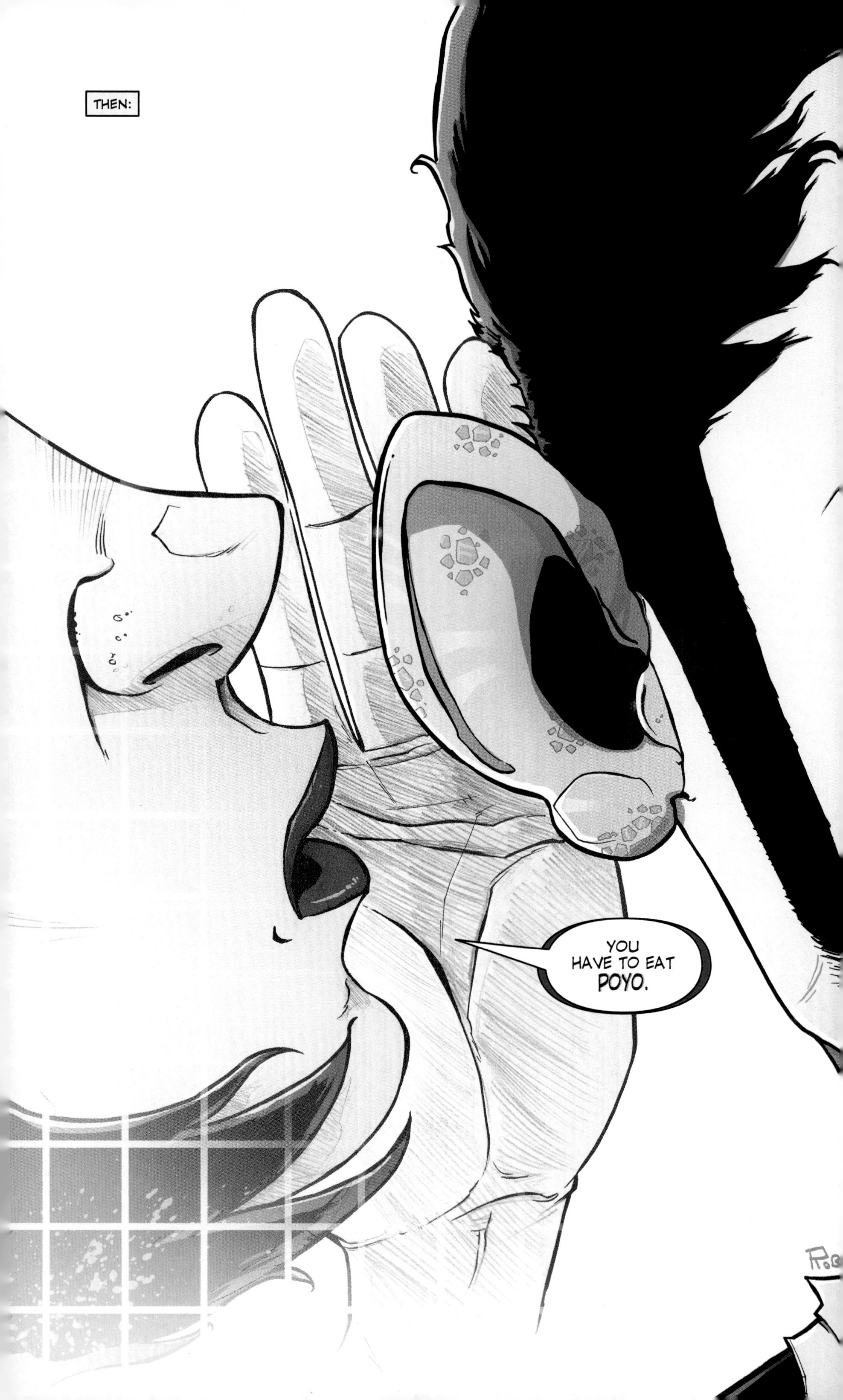
THEN:
YOU HAVE TO EAT POYO.

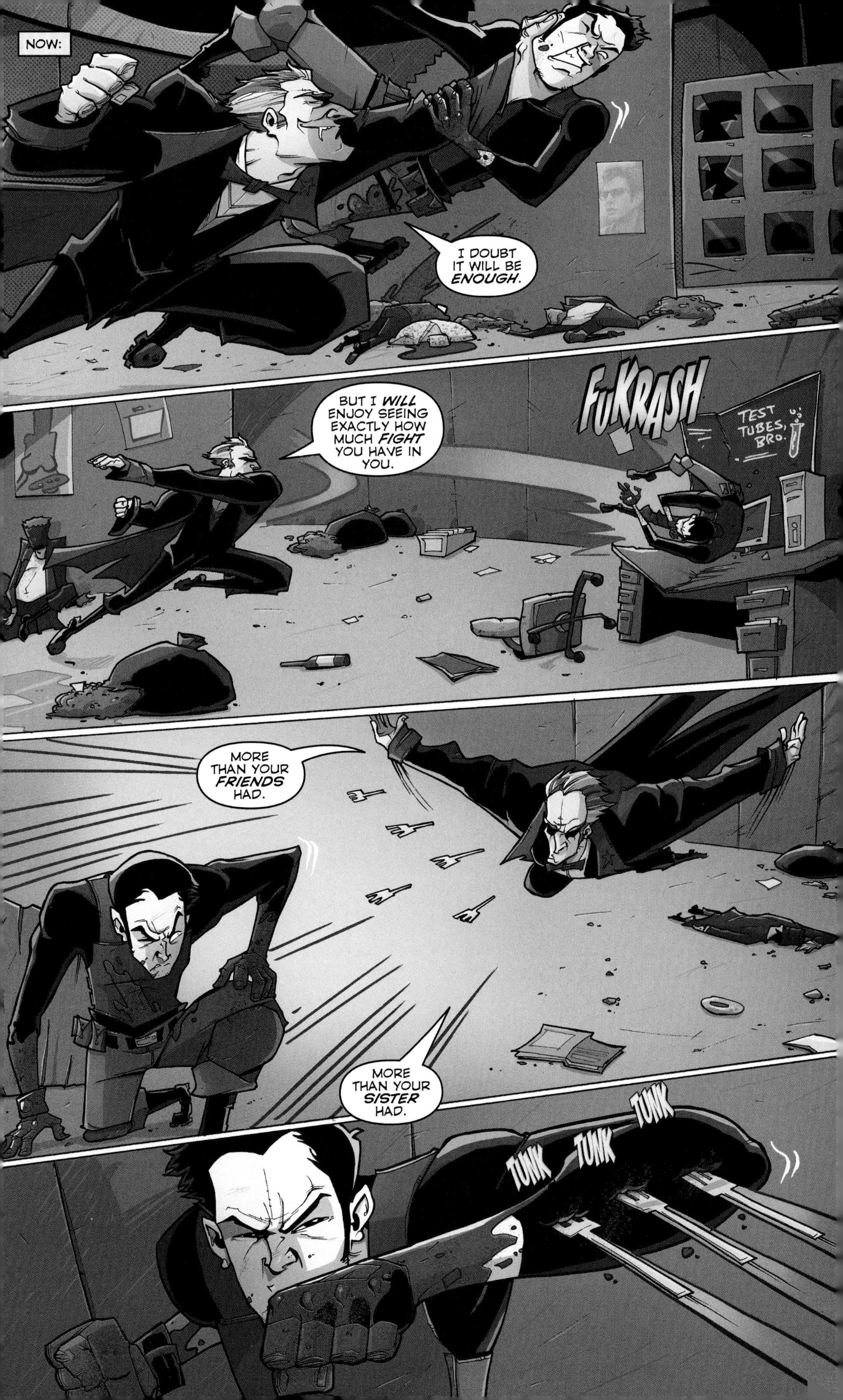
NOW:
I DOUBT IT WILL BE ENOUGH.
FUKRASH
TEST TUBES, BRO.
BUT I WILL ENJOY SEEING EXACTLY HOW MUCH FIGHT YOU HAVE IN YOU.
MORE THAN YOUR FRIENDS HAD.
MORE THAN YOUR SISTER HAD.
TUNK
TUNK
TUNK

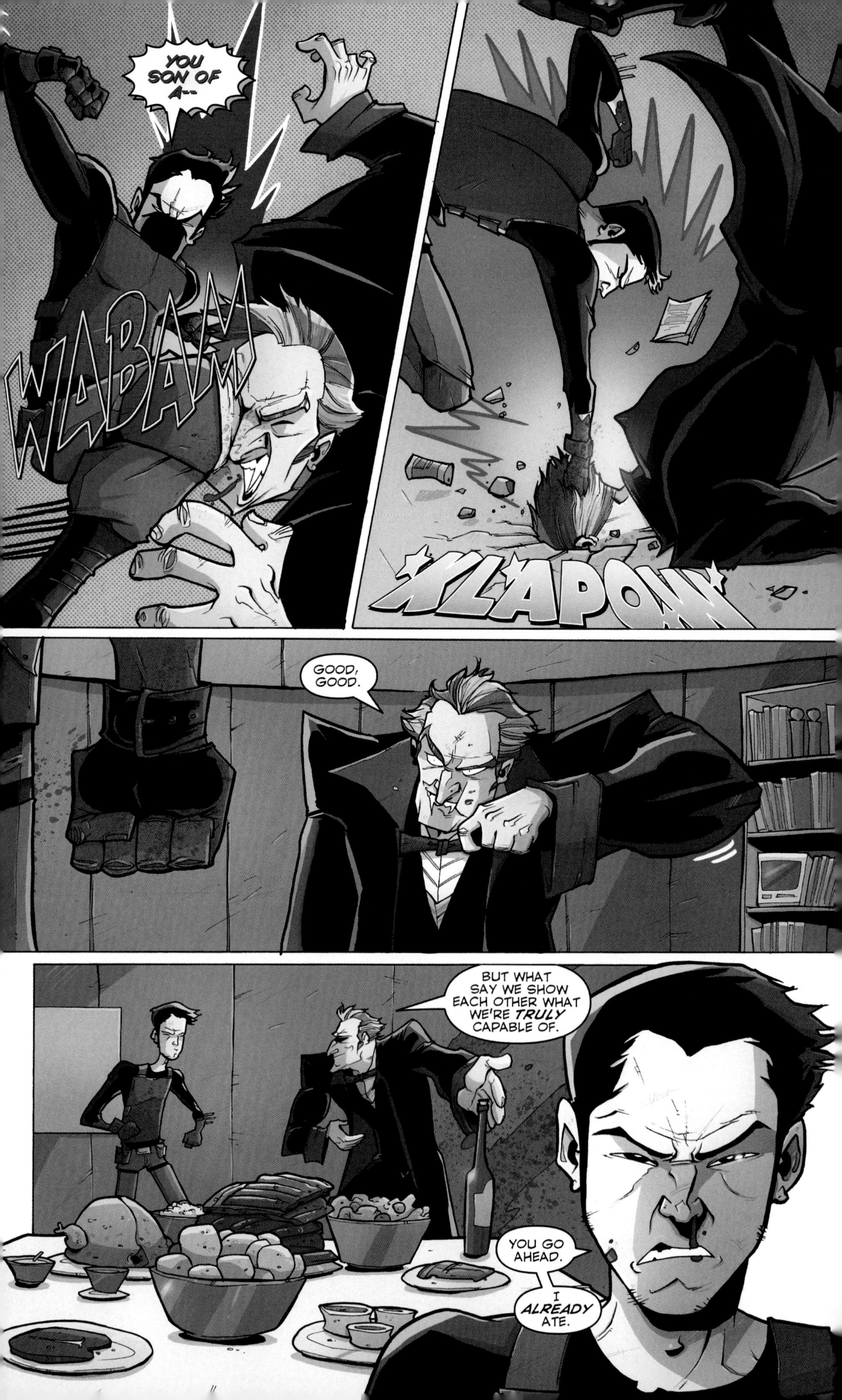
YOU SON OF A--
WABAM
KLAPOW
GOOD, GOOD.
BUT WHAT SAY WE SHOW EACH OTHER WHAT WE'RE *TRULY* CAPABLE OF.
YOU GO AHEAD.
I *ALREADY* ATE.

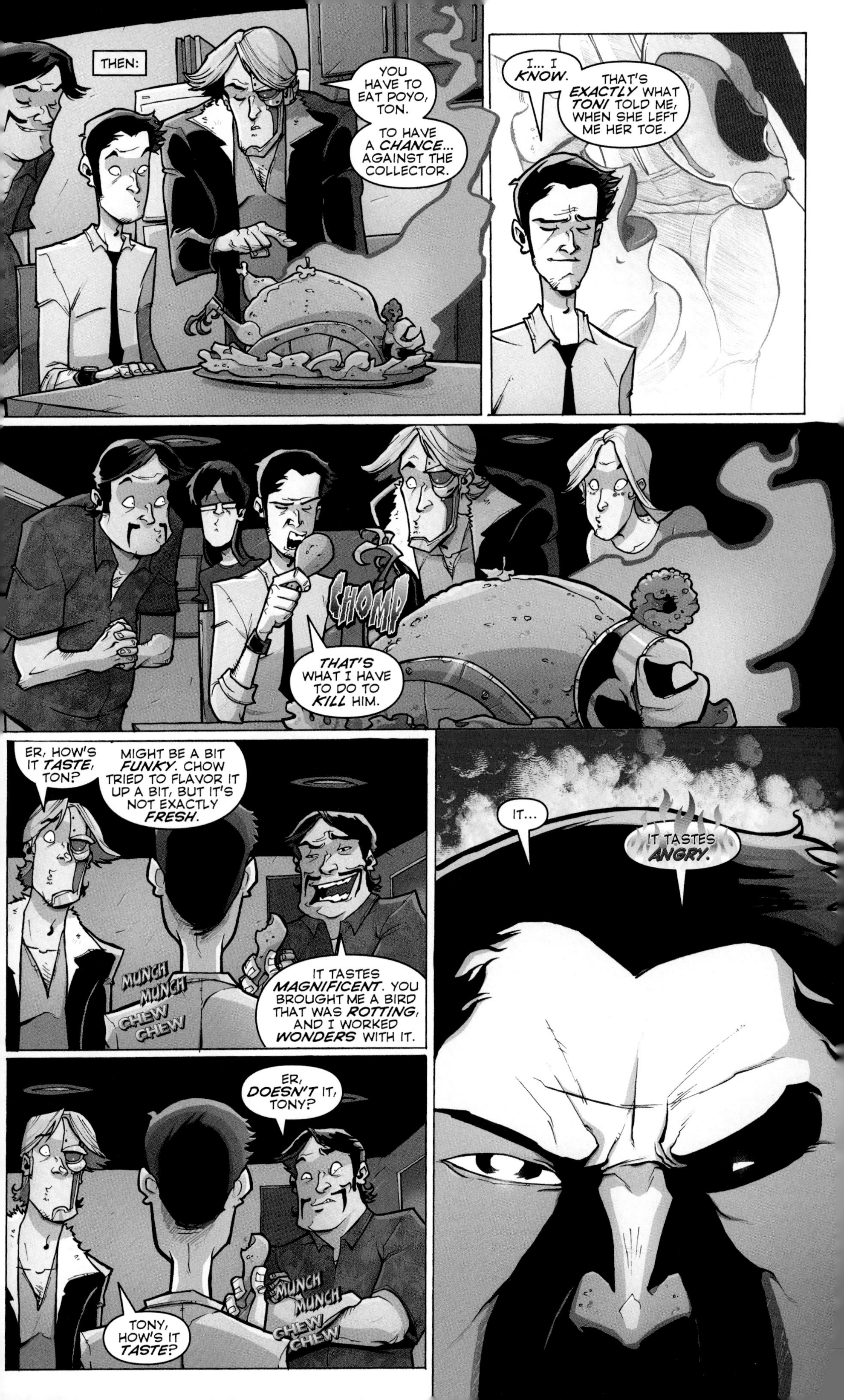
THEN:
YOU HAVE TO EAT POYO, TON.
TO HAVE A CHANCE... AGAINST THE COLLECTOR.
I... I KNOW.
THAT'S EXACTLY WHAT TONI TOLD ME, WHEN SHE LEFT ME HER TOE.
CHOMP
THAT'S WHAT I HAVE TO DO TO KILL HIM.
ER, HOW'S IT TASTE, TON?
MIGHT BE A BIT FUNKY. CHOW TRIED TO FLAVOR IT UP A BIT, BUT IT'S NOT EXACTLY FRESH.
MUNCH MUNCH CHEW CHEW
IT TASTES MAGNIFICENT. YOU BROUGHT ME A BIRD THAT WAS ROTTING, AND I WORKED WONDERS WITH IT.
ER, DOESN'T IT, TONY?
TONY, HOW'S IT TASTE?
MUNCH MUNCH CHEW CHEW
IT...
IT TASTES ANGRY.

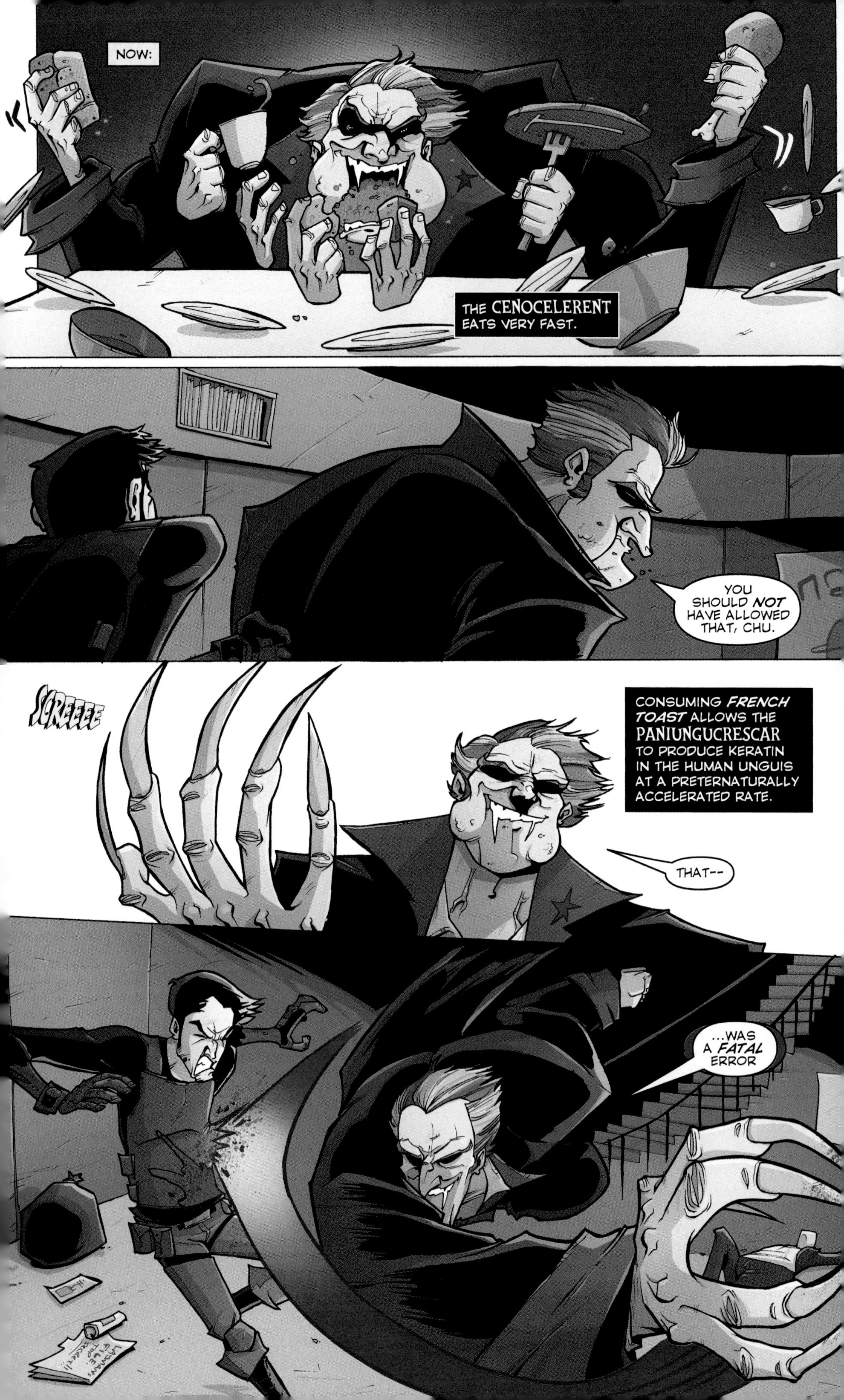
NOW:
THE CENOCELERENT EATS VERY FAST.
YOU SHOULD NOT HAVE ALLOWED THAT, CHU.
SCREEEEE
CONSUMING FRENCH TOAST ALLOWS THE PANIUNGUCRESCAR TO PRODUCE KERATIN IN THE HUMAN UNGUIS AT A PRETERNATURALLY ACCELERATED RATE.
THAT--
...WAS A FATAL ERROR

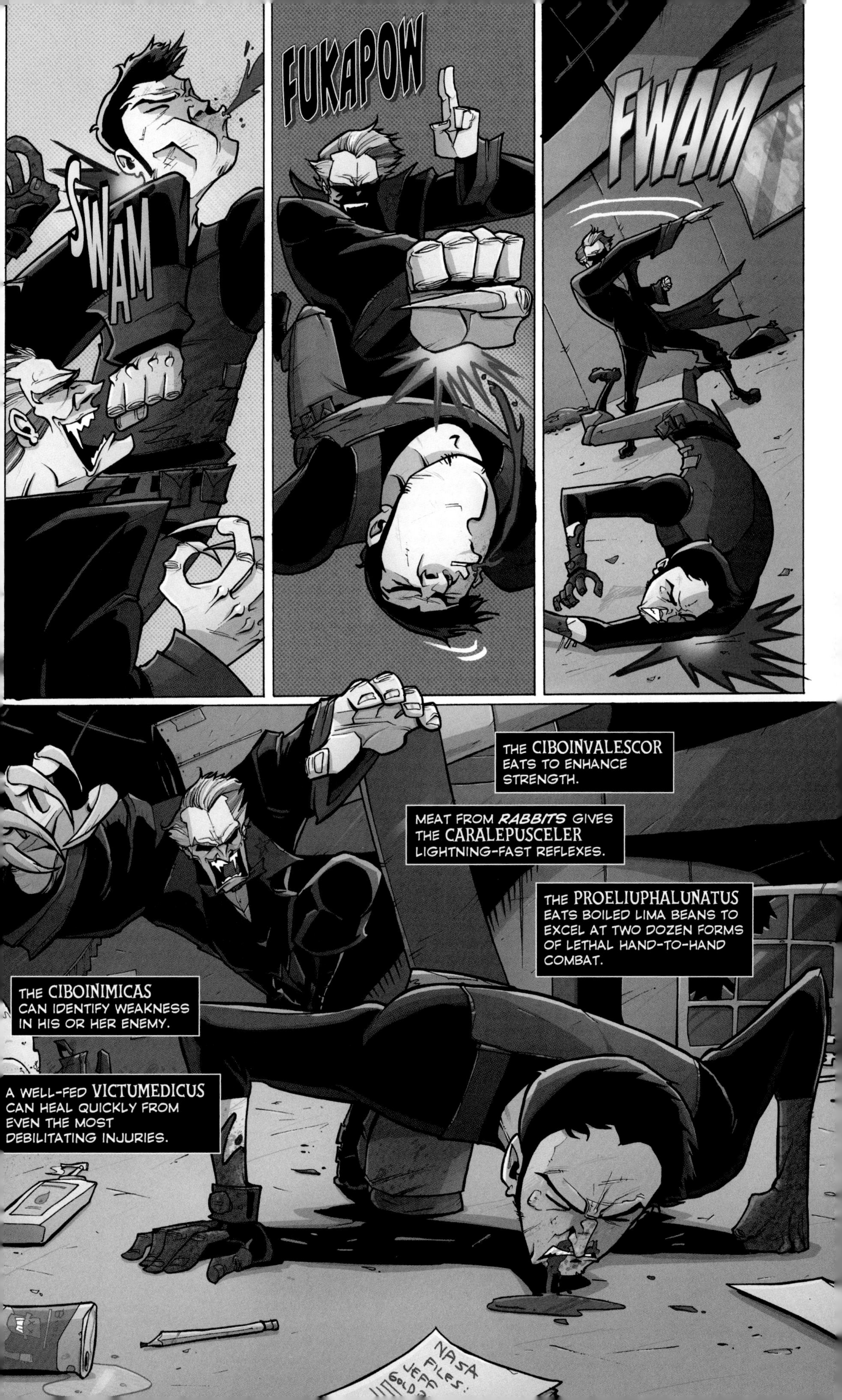
SWAM
FUKAPOW
FWAM
THE CIBOINVALESCOR EATS TO ENHANCE STRENGTH.
MEAT FROM *RABBITS* GIVES THE CARALEPUSCELER LIGHTNING-FAST REFLEXES.
THE PROELIUPHALUNATUS EATS BOILED LIMA BEANS TO EXCEL AT TWO DOZEN FORMS OF LETHAL HAND-TO-HAND COMBAT.
THE CIBOINIMICAS CAN IDENTIFY WEAKNESS IN HIS OR HER ENEMY.
A WELL-FED VICTUMEDICUS CAN HEAL QUICKLY FROM EVEN THE MOST DEBILITATING INJURIES.
NASA FILES: JEFF

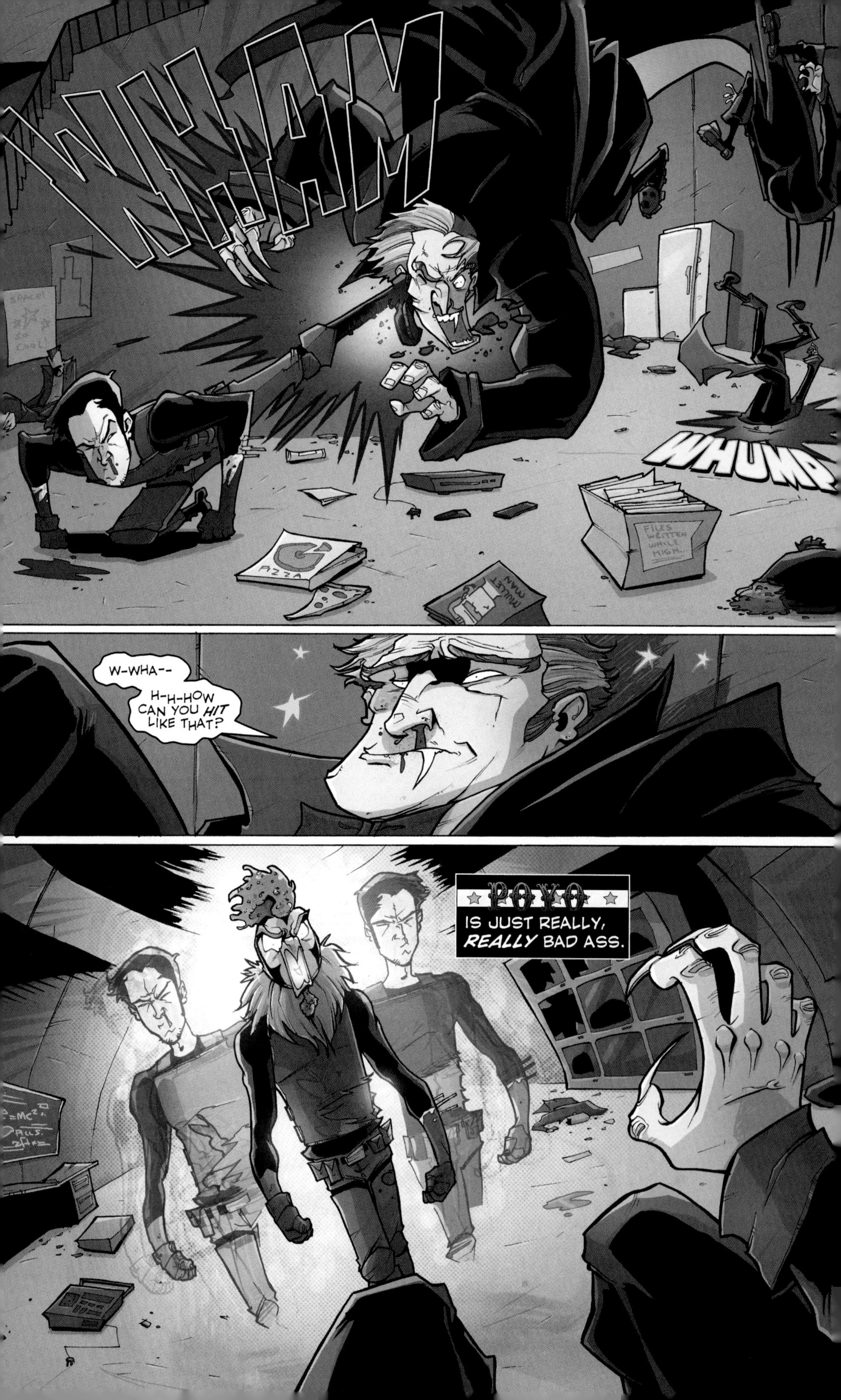
WHAM
SPACE! SO COOL!
WHUMP
FILES WRITTEN WHILE HIGH
PIZZA
MULLET MAN
W-WHA--
H-H-HOW CAN YOU *HIT* LIKE THAT?
POYO
IS JUST REALLY, *REALLY* BAD ASS.

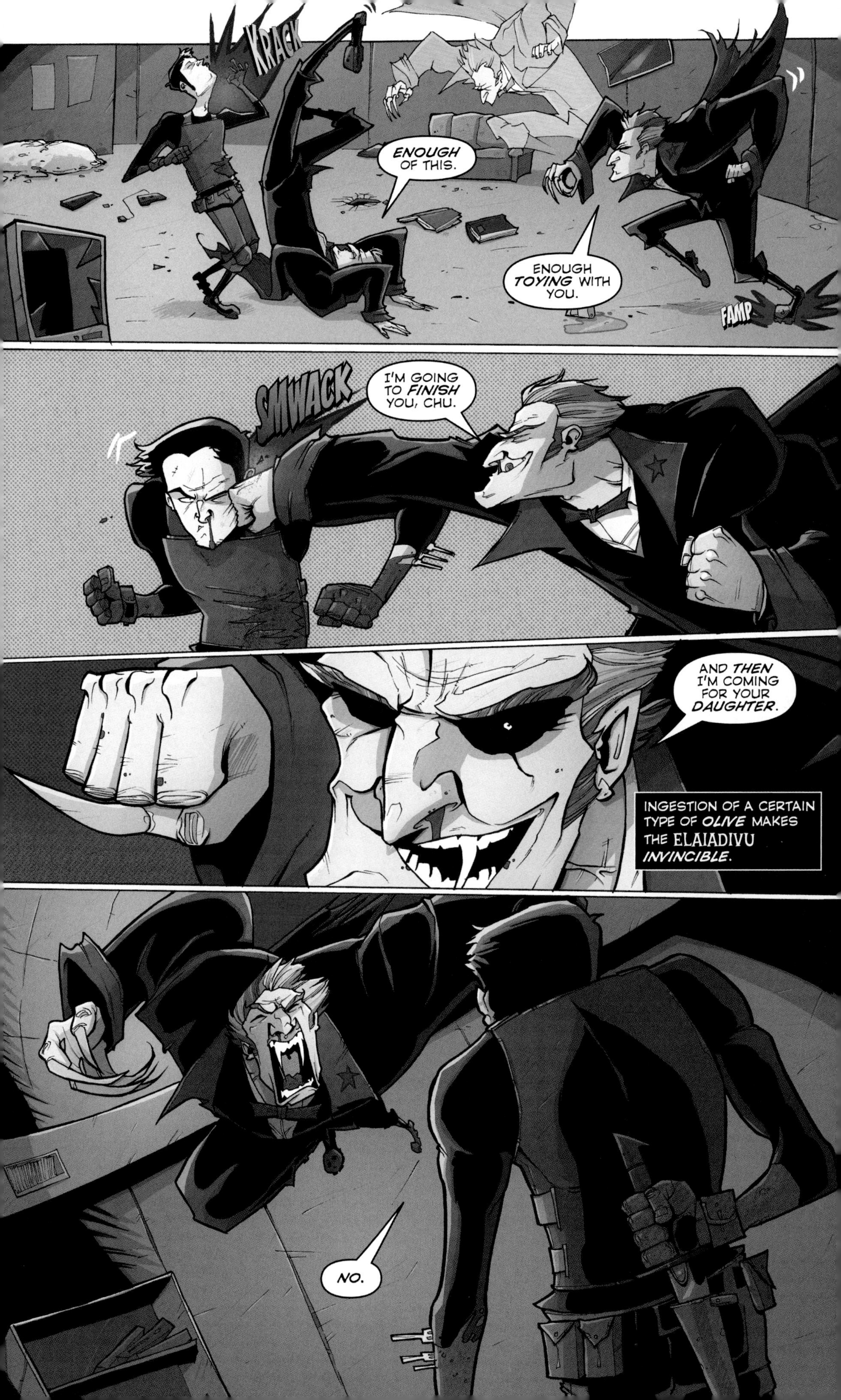
KRACK
ENOUGH OF THIS.
ENOUGH TOYING WITH YOU.
FAMP
SMWACK
I'M GOING TO FINISH YOU, CHU.
AND THEN I'M COMING FOR YOUR DAUGHTER.
INGESTION OF A CERTAIN TYPE OF OLIVE MAKES THE ELAIADIVU INVINCIBLE.
NO.

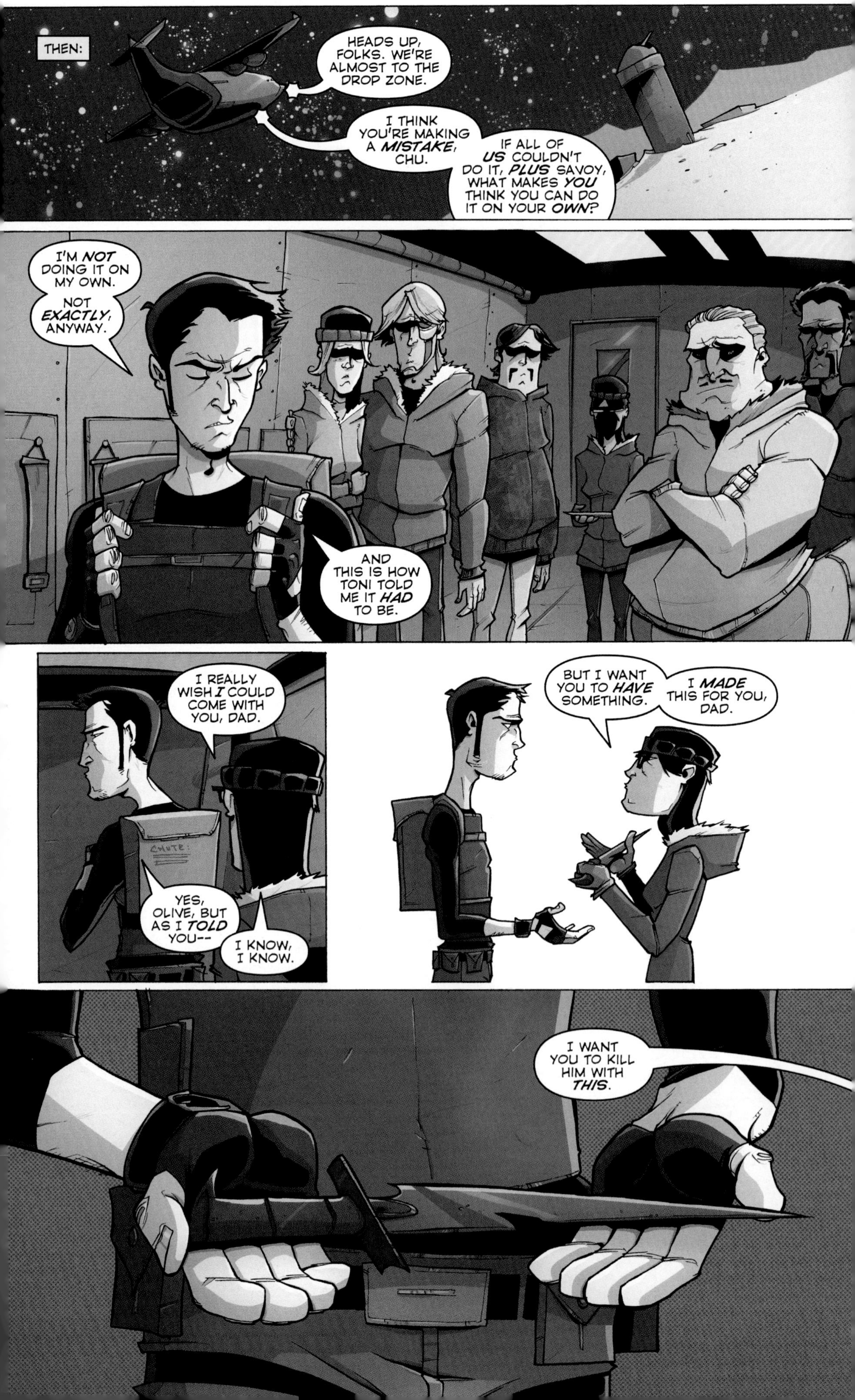
THEN:
HEADS UP, FOLKS. WE'RE ALMOST TO THE DROP ZONE.
I THINK YOU'RE MAKING A *MISTAKE*, CHU.
IF ALL OF *US* COULDN'T DO IT, *PLUS* SAVOY, WHAT MAKES *YOU* THINK YOU CAN DO IT ON YOUR *OWN*?
I'M *NOT* DOING IT ON MY OWN.
NOT *EXACTLY*, ANYWAY.
AND THIS IS HOW TONI TOLD ME IT *HAD* TO BE.
I REALLY WISH *I* COULD COME WITH YOU, DAD.
CHUTE:
YES, OLIVE, BUT AS I *TOLD* YOU--
I KNOW, I KNOW.
BUT I WANT YOU TO *HAVE* SOMETHING.
I *MADE* THIS FOR YOU, DAD.
I WANT YOU TO KILL HIM WITH *THIS*.

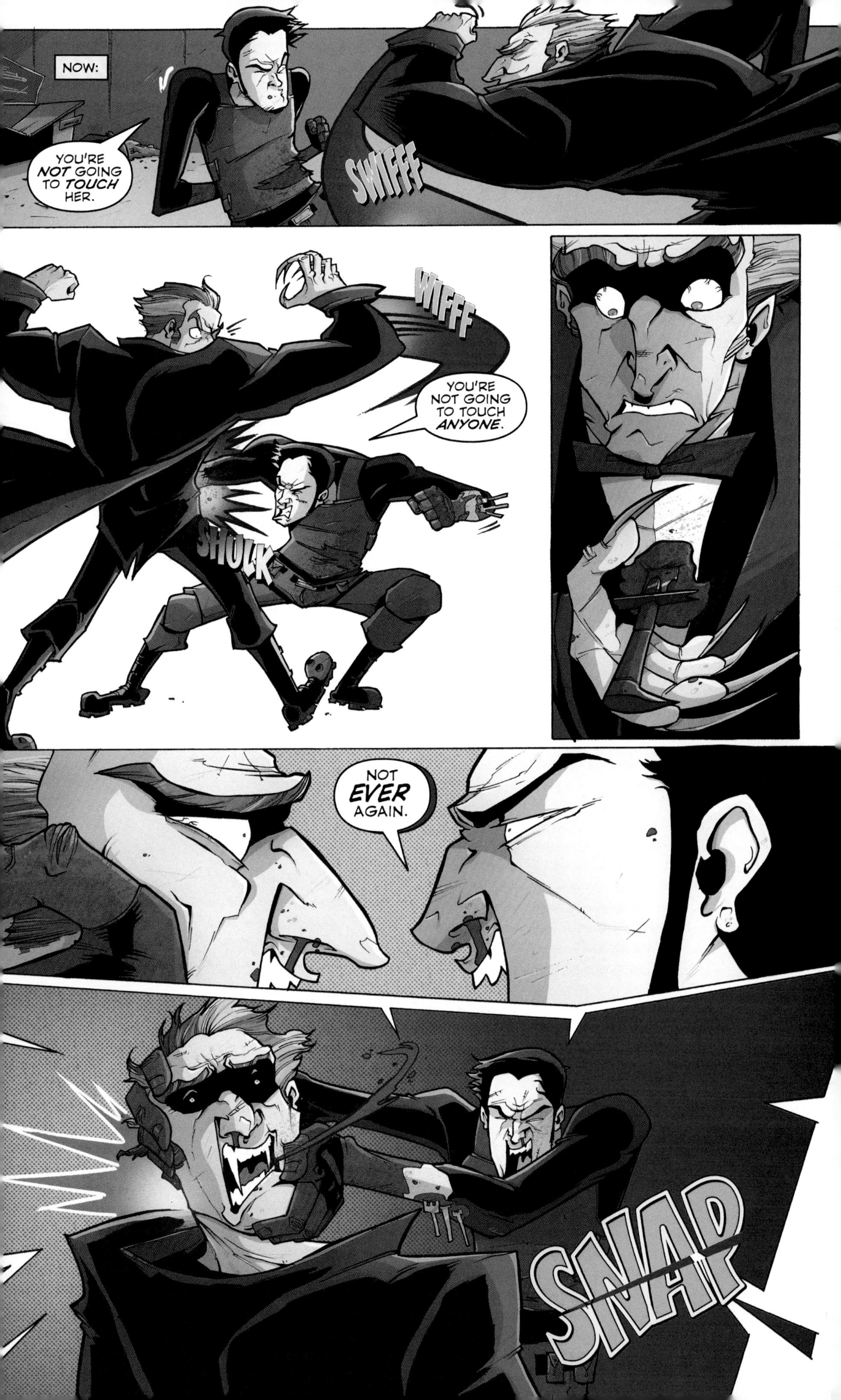
NOW:
YOU'RE NOT GOING TO TOUCH HER.
SWIFFF
WIFFF
YOU'RE NOT GOING TO TOUCH ANYONE.
SHULK
NOT EVER AGAIN.
SNAP

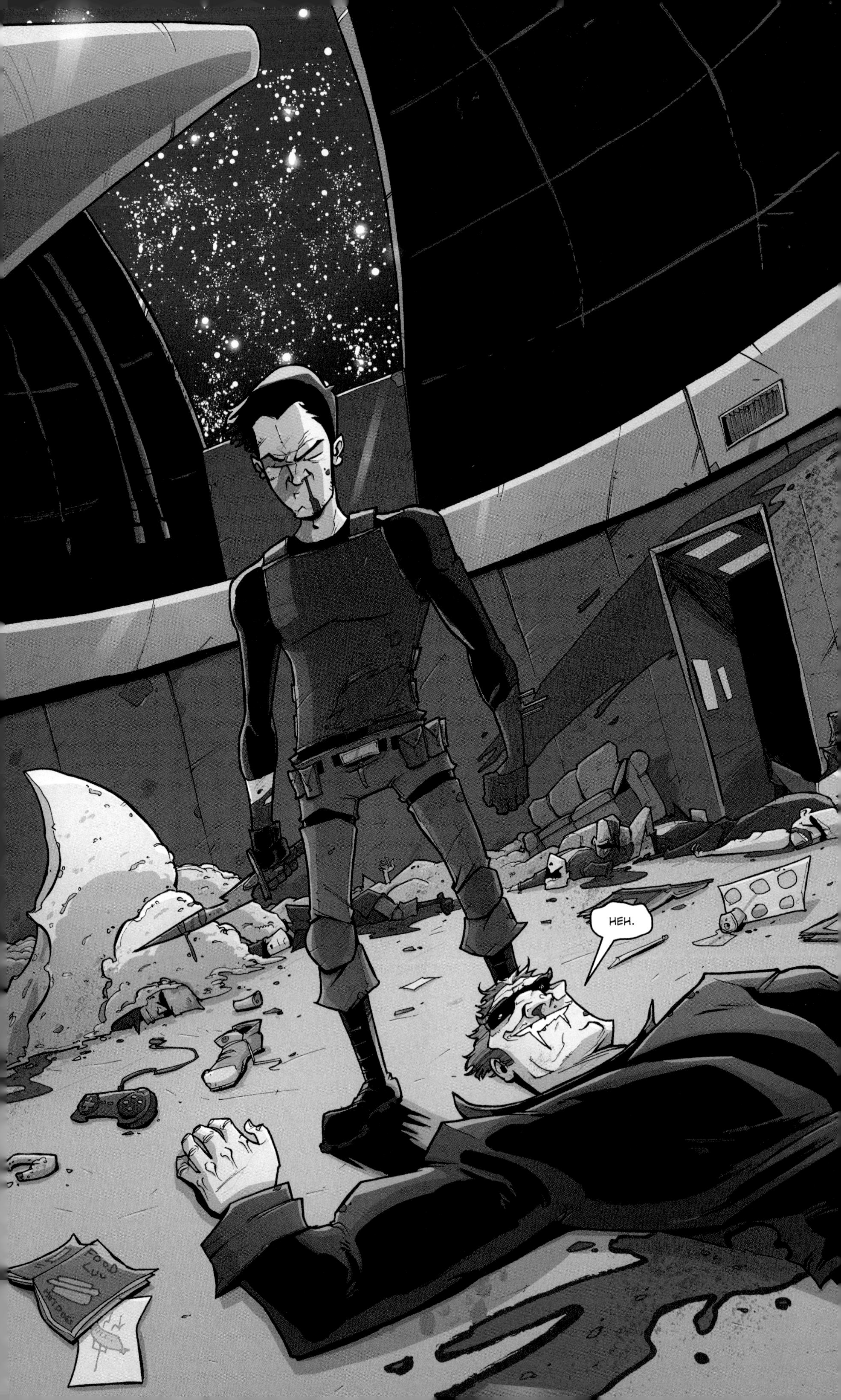
HEH.

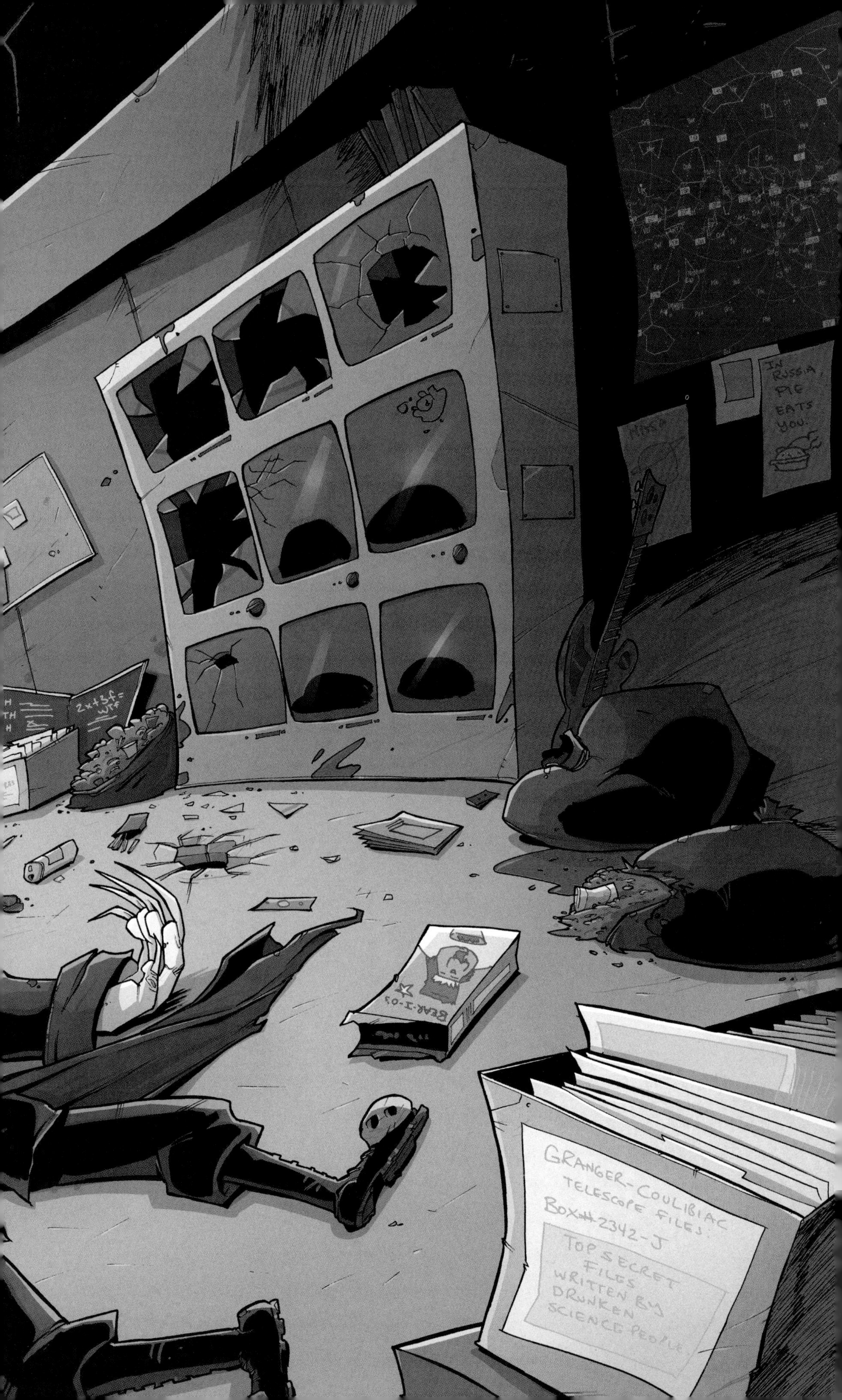
IN RUSSIA, PIG EATS YOU.
BEAR-I-03
GRANGER-COULIBIAC TELESCOPE FILES
BOX#2342-J
TOP SECRET FILES WRITTEN BY DRUNKEN SCIENCE PEOPLE

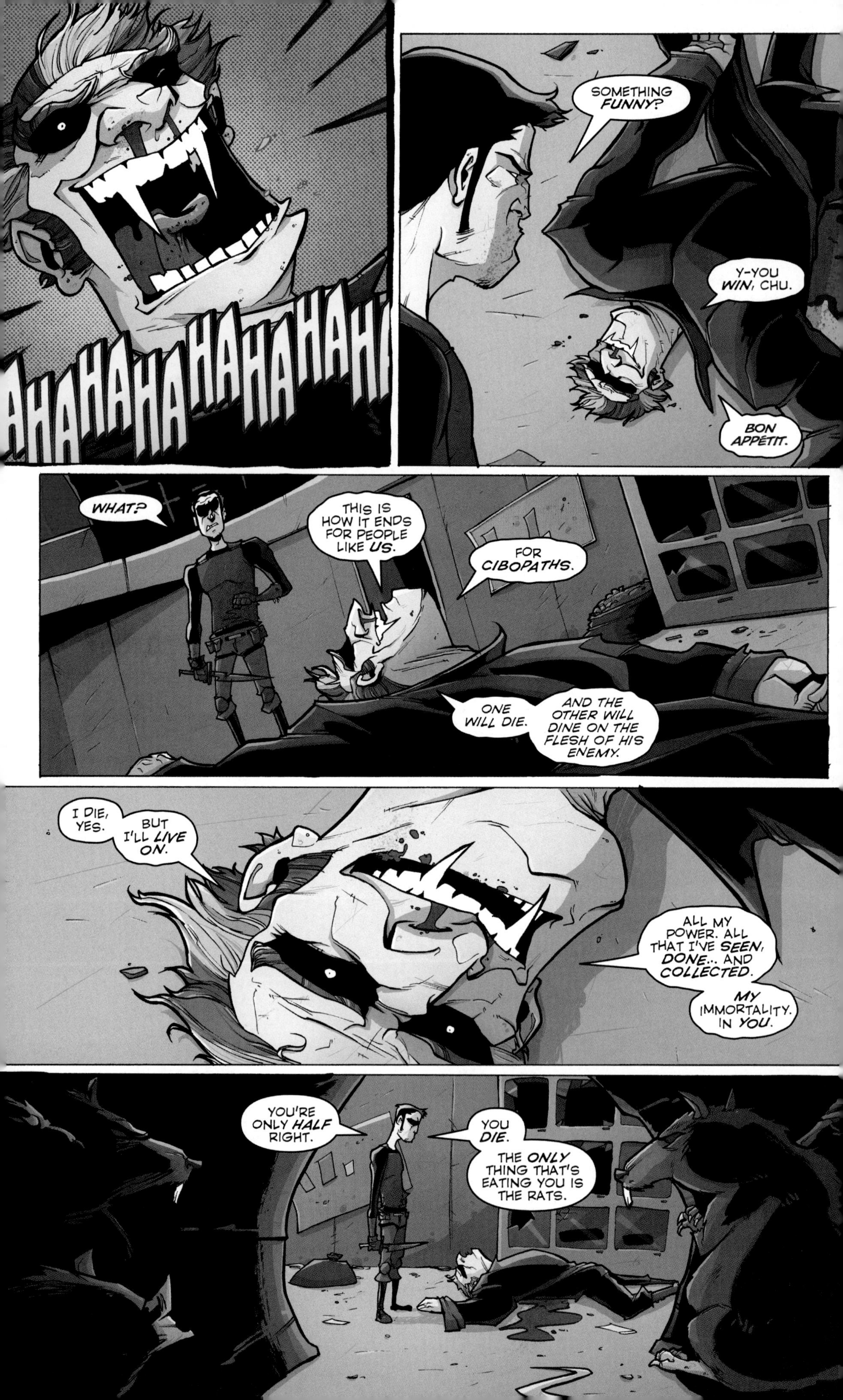

HAHAHAHAHAHAHAHAH
SOMETHING FUNNY?
Y-YOU WIN, CHU.
BON APPÉTIT.
WHAT?
THIS IS HOW IT ENDS FOR PEOPLE LIKE US.
FOR CIBOPATHS.
ONE WILL DIE.
AND THE OTHER WILL DINE ON THE FLESH OF HIS ENEMY.
I DIE, YES.
BUT I'LL LIVE ON.
ALL MY POWER. ALL THAT I'VE SEEN, DONE... AND COLLECTED.
MY IMMORTALITY. IN YOU.
YOU'RE ONLY HALF RIGHT.
YOU DIE.
THE ONLY THING THAT'S EATING YOU IS THE RATS.

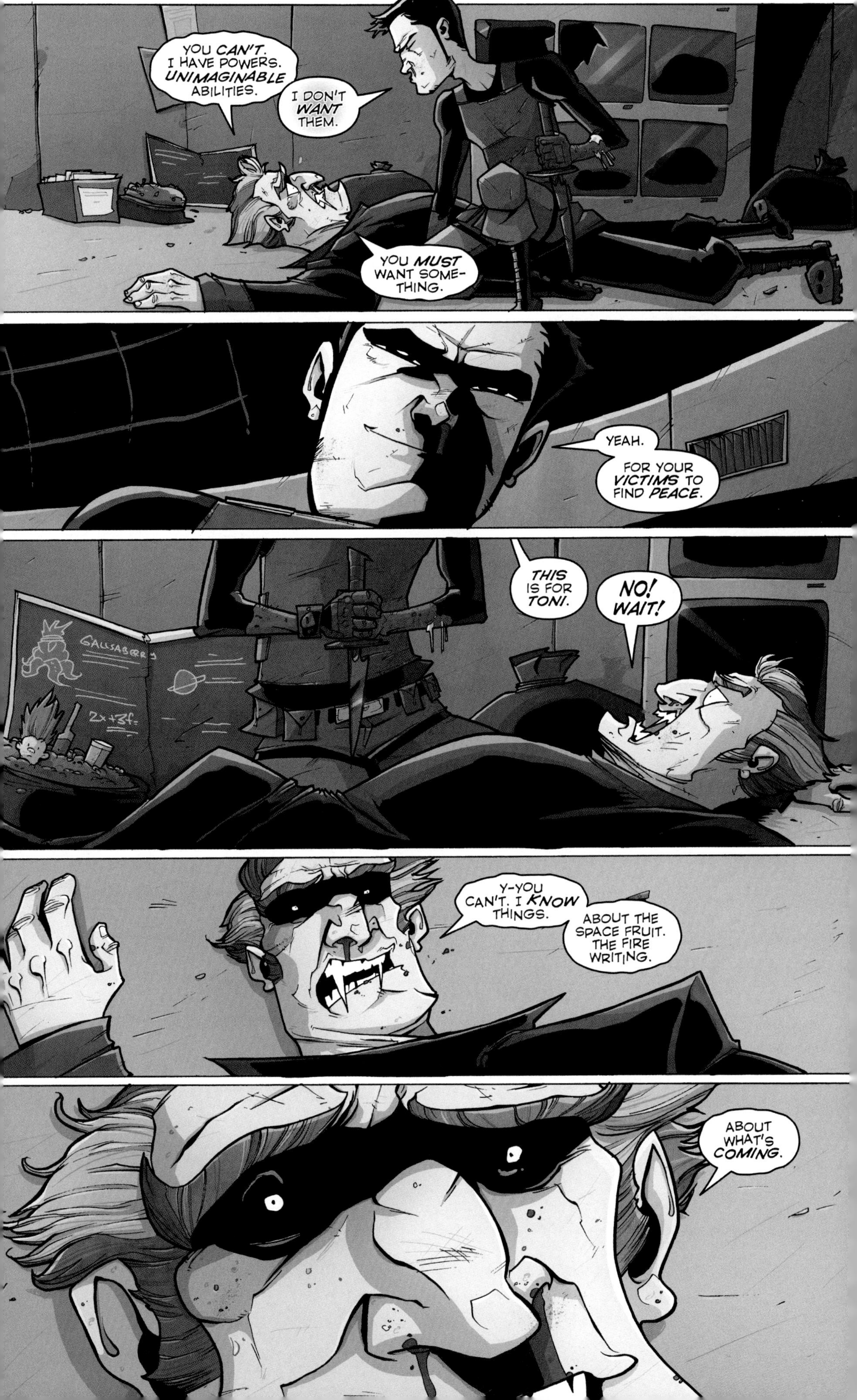

YOU CAN'T. I HAVE POWERS. UNIMAGINABLE ABILITIES.
I DON'T WANT THEM.
YOU MUST WANT SOME-THING.
YEAH.
FOR YOUR VICTIMS TO FIND PEACE.
THIS IS FOR TONI.
NO! WAIT!
Y-YOU CAN'T. I KNOW THINGS.
ABOUT THE SPACE FRUIT. THE FIRE WRITING.
ABOUT WHAT'S COMING.

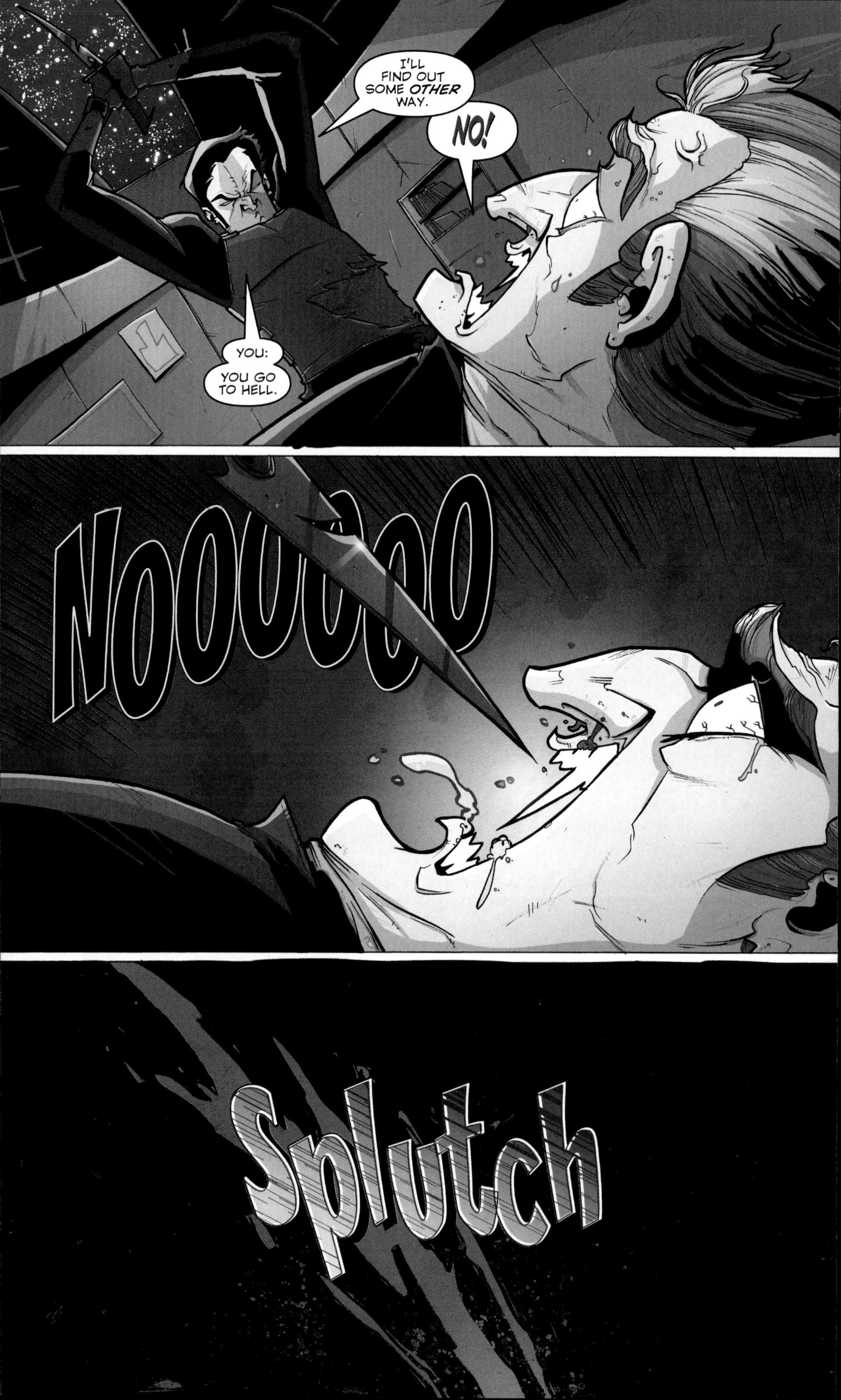

I'LL FIND OUT SOME *OTHER* WAY.
NO!
YOU: YOU GO TO HELL.
NOOOOOO
Splutch

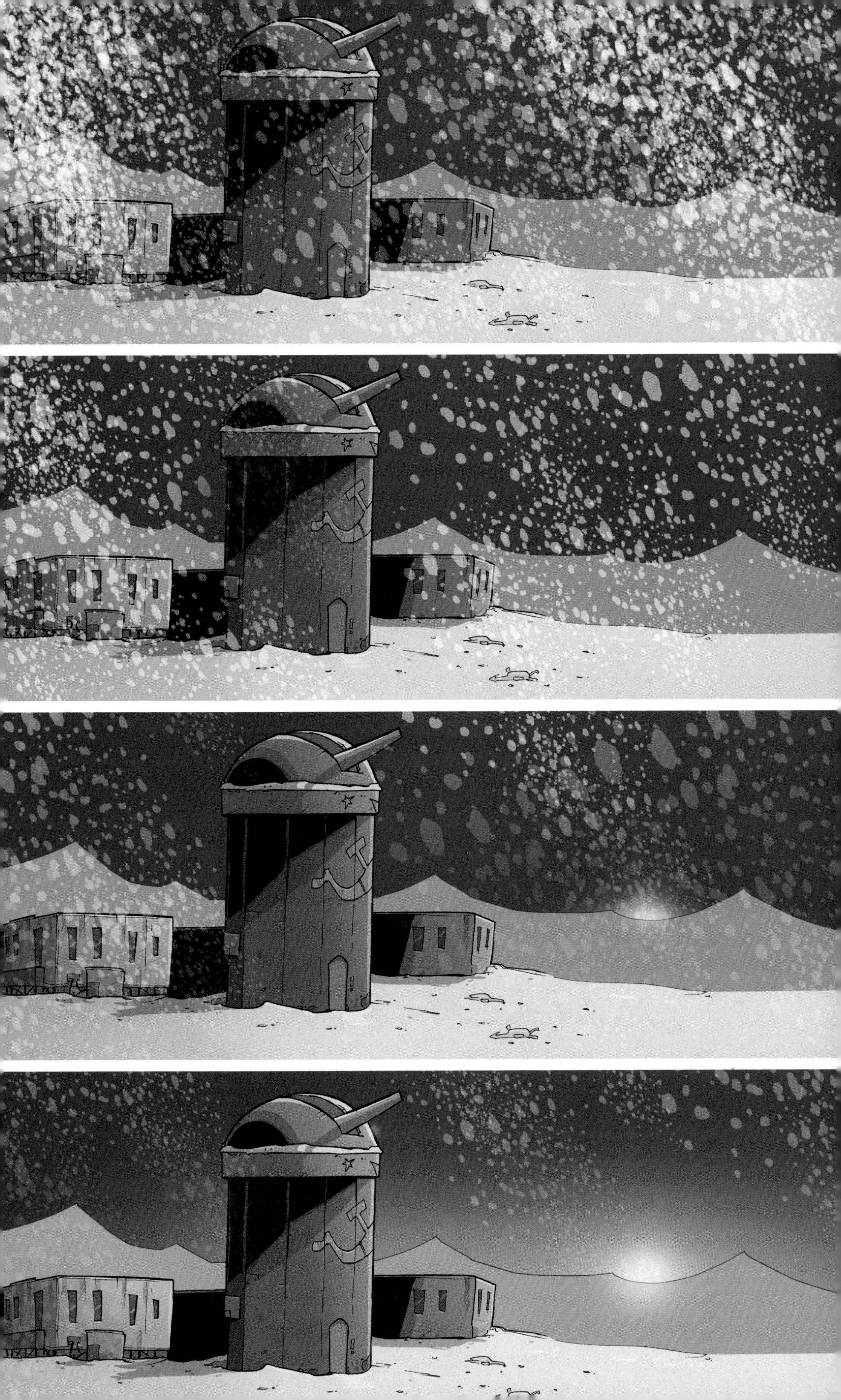

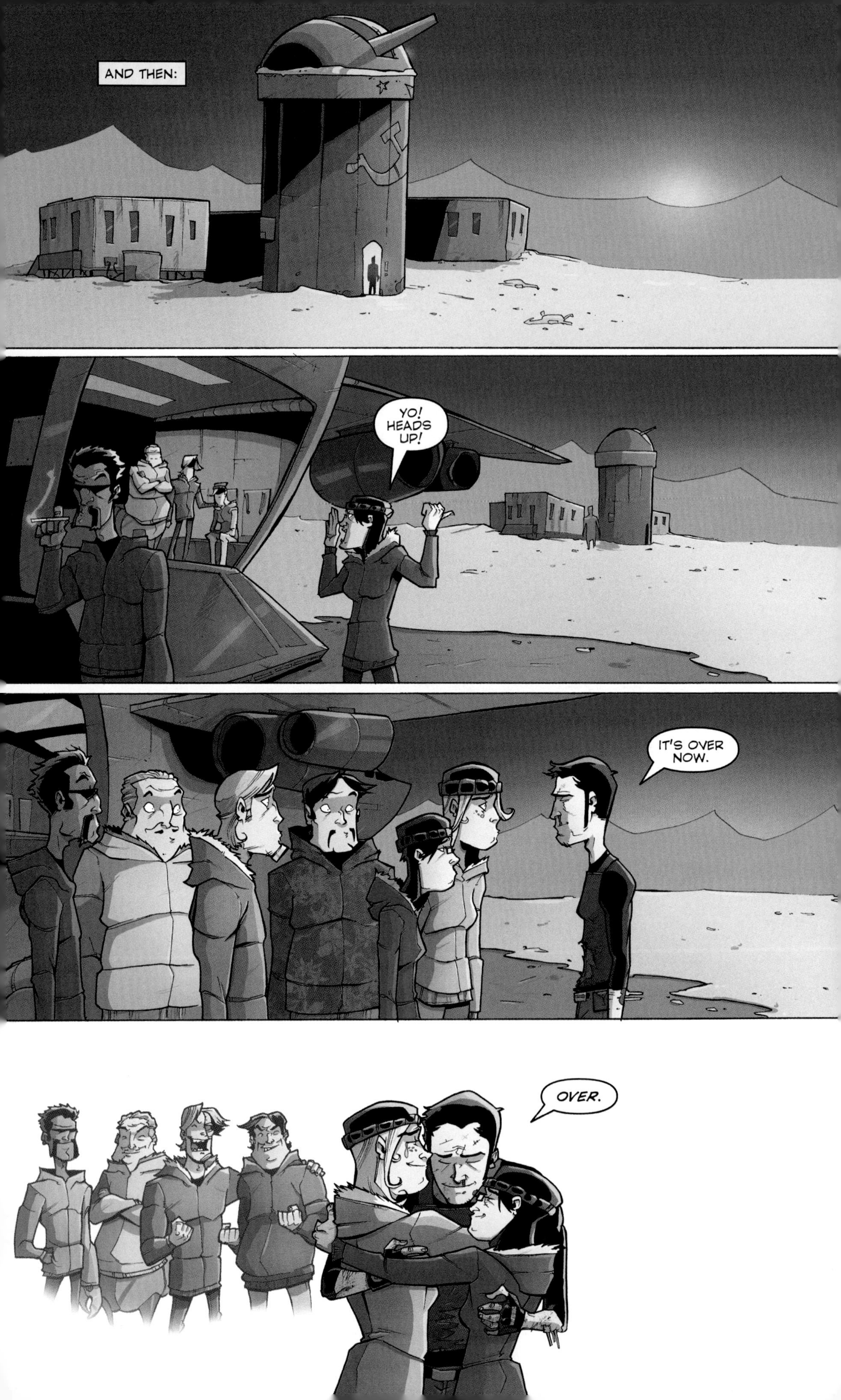
AND THEN:
YO! HEADS UP!
IT'S OVER NOW.
OVER.

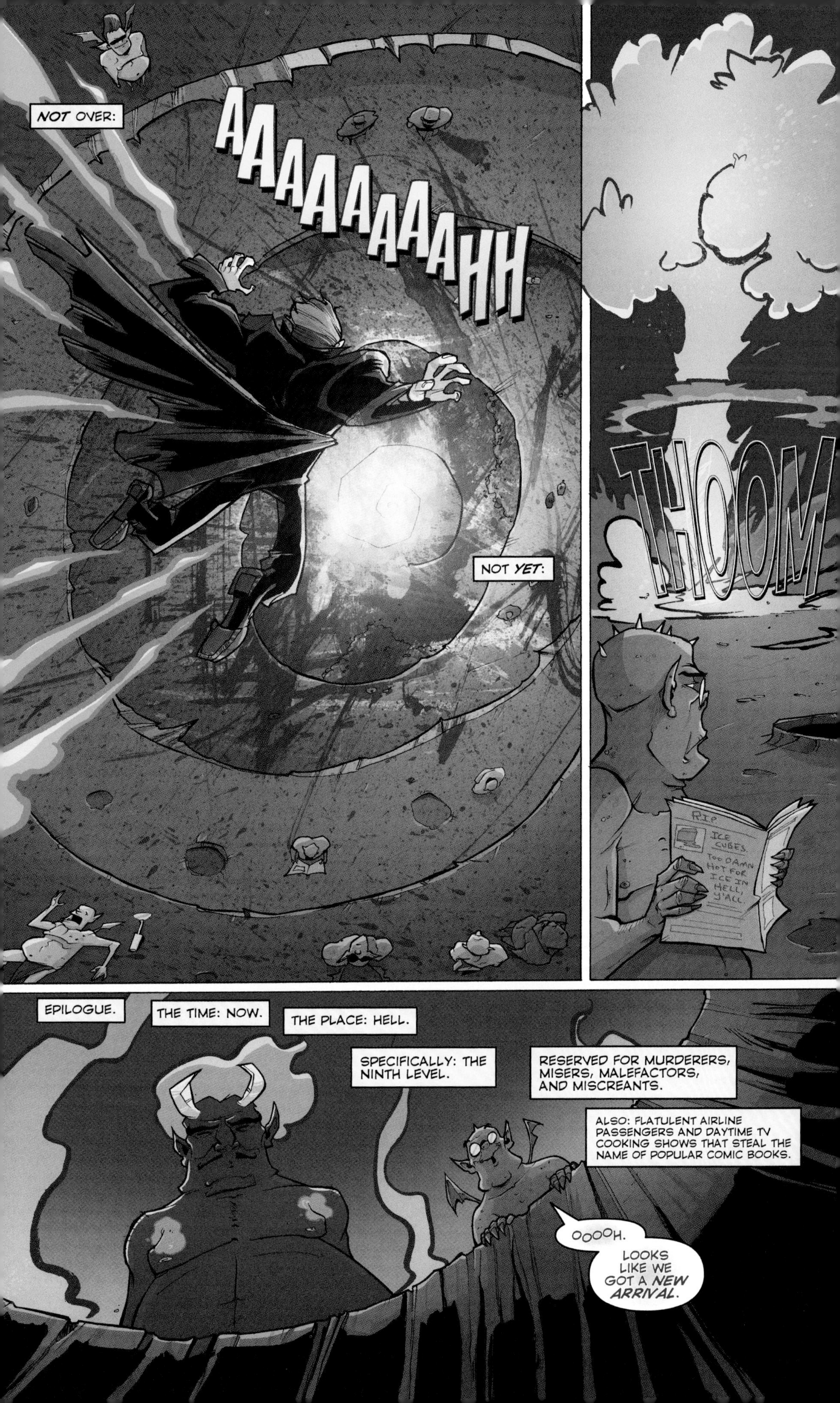

NOT OVER:
AAAAAAAAAAAHH
NOT YET:
THOOM
RIP
ICE CUBES.
TOO DAMN HOT FOR ICE IN HELL, Y'ALL.
EPILOGUE.
THE TIME: NOW.
THE PLACE: HELL.
SPECIFICALLY: THE NINTH LEVEL.
RESERVED FOR MURDERERS, MISERS, MALEFACTORS, AND MISCREANTS.
ALSO: FLATULENT AIRLINE PASSENGERS AND DAYTIME TV COOKING SHOWS THAT STEAL THE NAME OF POPULAR COMIC BOOKS.
OOOOH.
LOOKS LIKE WE GOT A NEW ARRIVAL.

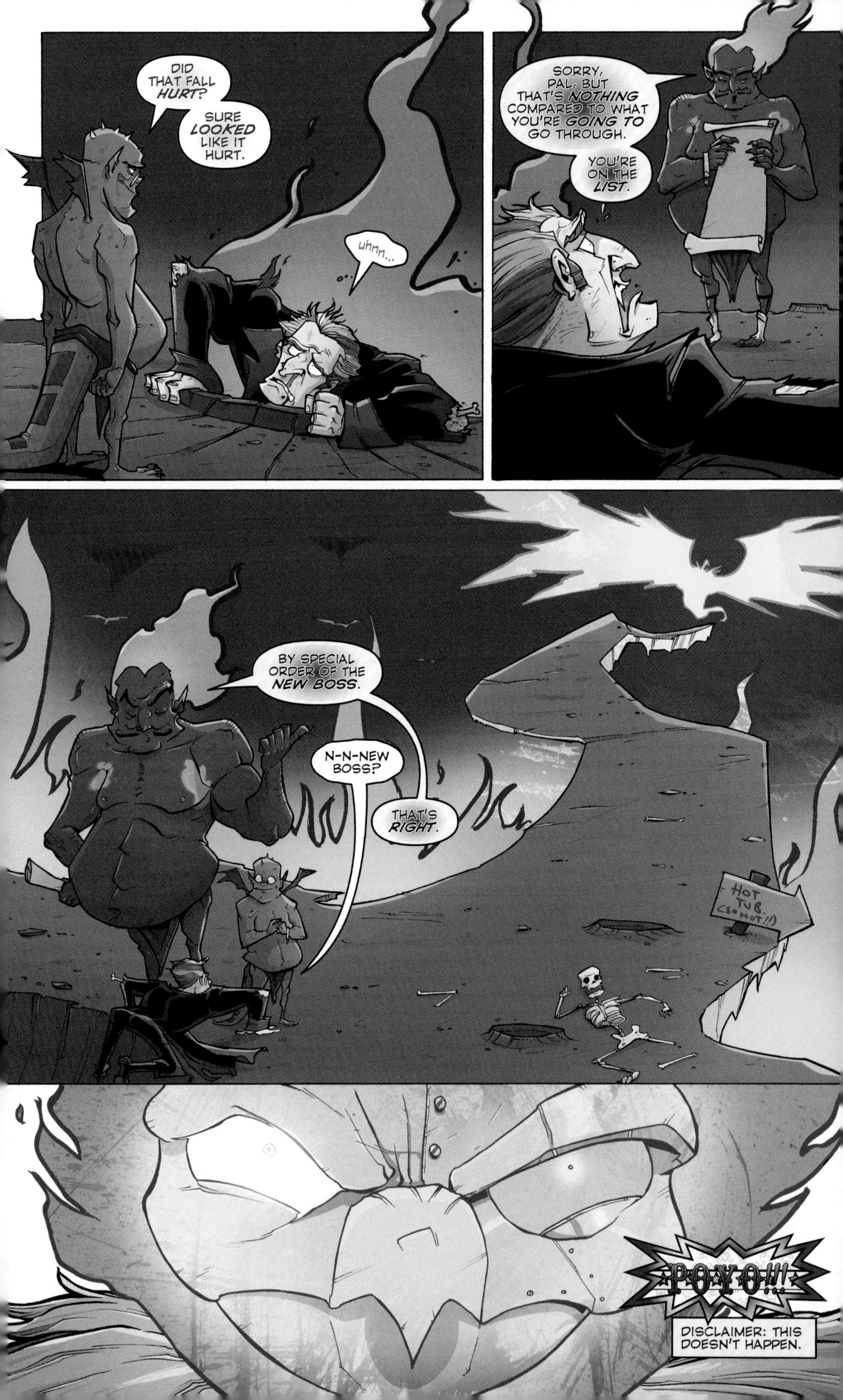

DID THAT FALL *HURT*?
SURE *LOOKED* LIKE IT HURT.
uhnn...
SORRY, PAL, BUT THAT'S *NOTHING* COMPARED TO WHAT YOU'RE *GOING TO* GO THROUGH.
YOU'RE ON THE *LIST*.
BY SPECIAL ORDER OF THE *NEW BOSS*.
N-N-NEW BOSS?
THAT'S *RIGHT*.
HOT TUB (SO HOT!!)
POYO!!!
DISCLAIMER: THIS DOESN'T HAPPEN.

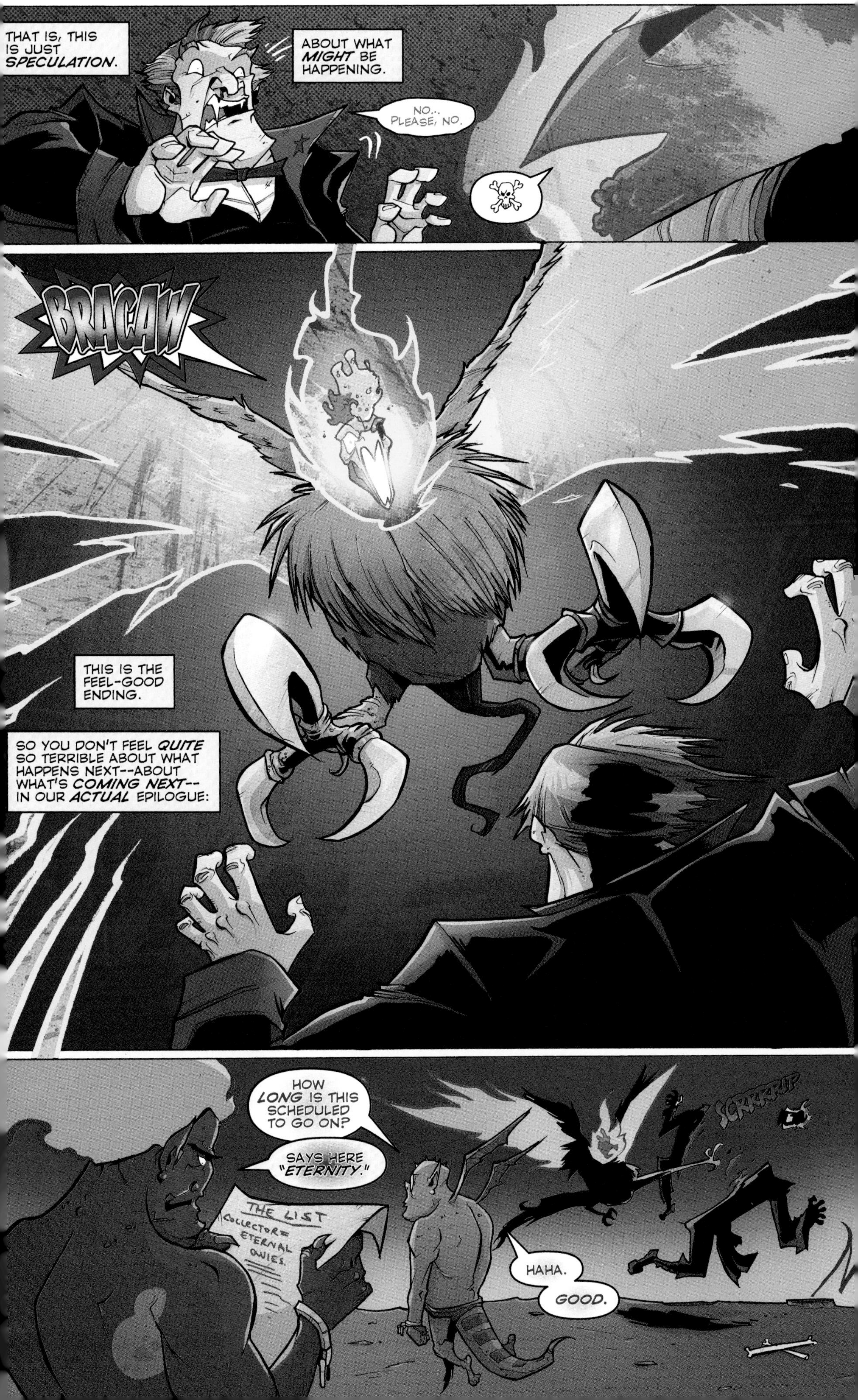
THAT IS, THIS IS JUST *SPECULATION*.
ABOUT WHAT *MIGHT* BE HAPPENING.
NO... PLEASE, NO.
BRACAW
THIS IS THE FEEL-GOOD ENDING.
SO YOU DON'T FEEL *QUITE* SO TERRIBLE ABOUT WHAT HAPPENS NEXT--ABOUT WHAT'S *COMING NEXT*-- IN OUR *ACTUAL* EPILOGUE:
HOW *LONG* IS THIS SCHEDULED TO GO ON?
SAYS HERE "*ETERNITY*."
THE LIST
COLLECTOR= ETERNAL OWIES.
SCRKKRIP
HAHA.
GOOD.

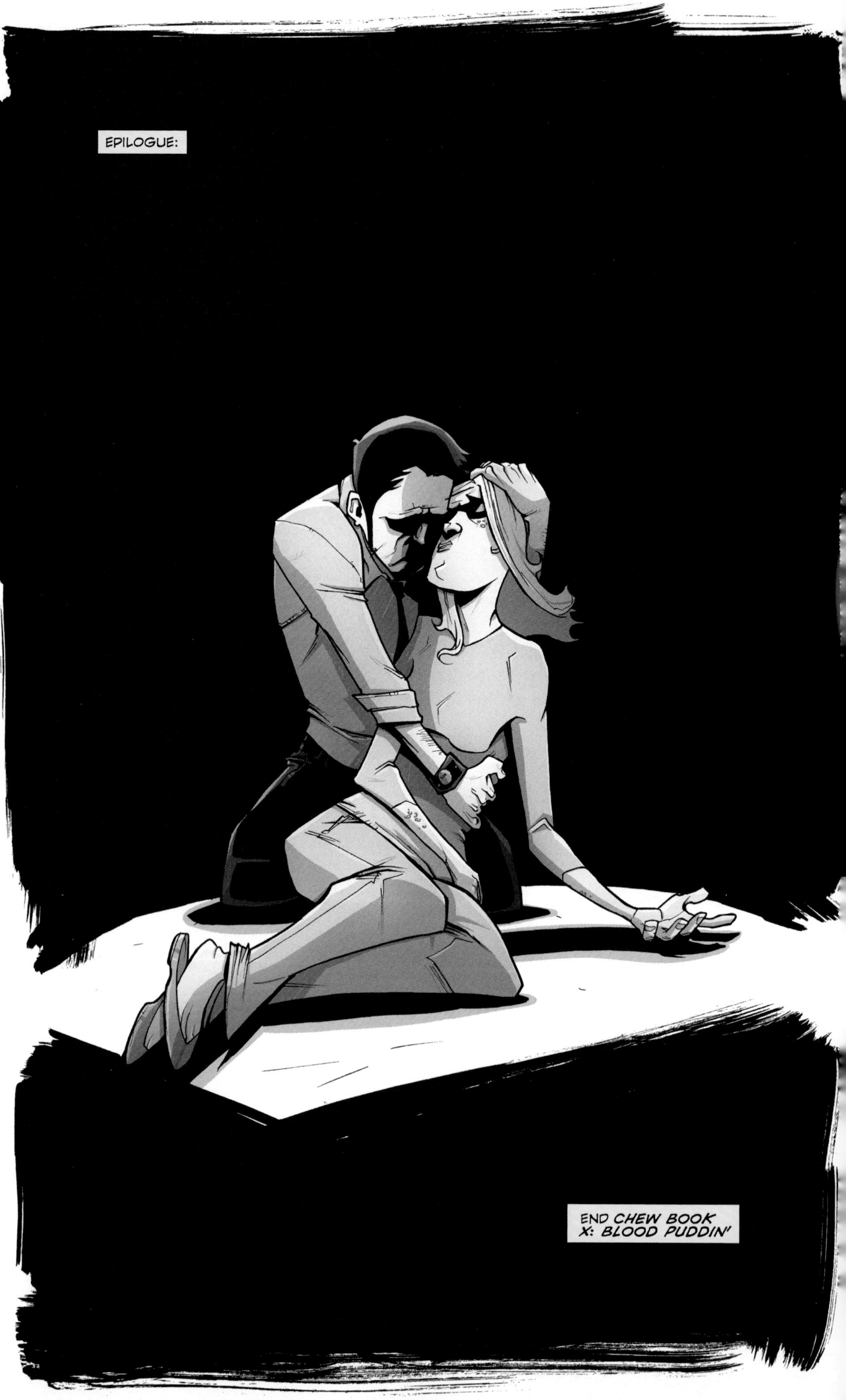
EPILOGUE:
END CHEW BOOK X: BLOOD PUDDIN'

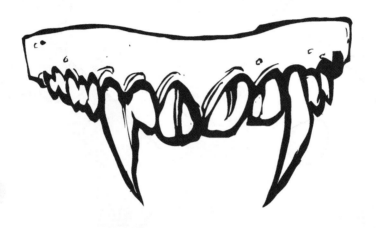

Extras

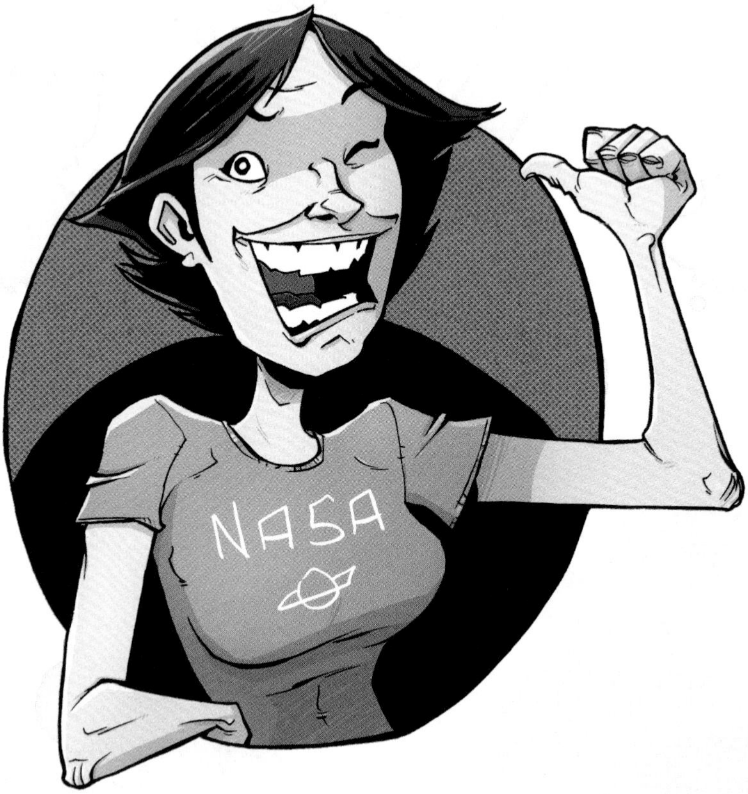
NASA

GALLERY

KODY CHAMBERLAIN
@KodyChamberlain

CHRIS BURNHAM
@TheBurnham
&
DAVID BARON
@myzombies

DANIEL WARREN JOHNSON
@danielwarrenart.

PAUL HANLEY
paulhanley.deviantart.com

DAN GOLDMAN
@dan_goldman
redlightproperties.com

IRENE STRYCHALSKI
@RenieDraws
reniedraws.tumblr.com

RAY FAWKES
@rayfawkes

RYAN BROWNE
@RyanBrowneArt.

SINA GRACE
@sinagrace
&
SHAUN STEVEN STRUBLE
@struble

JEREMY BASTIAN
@JeremyBastian

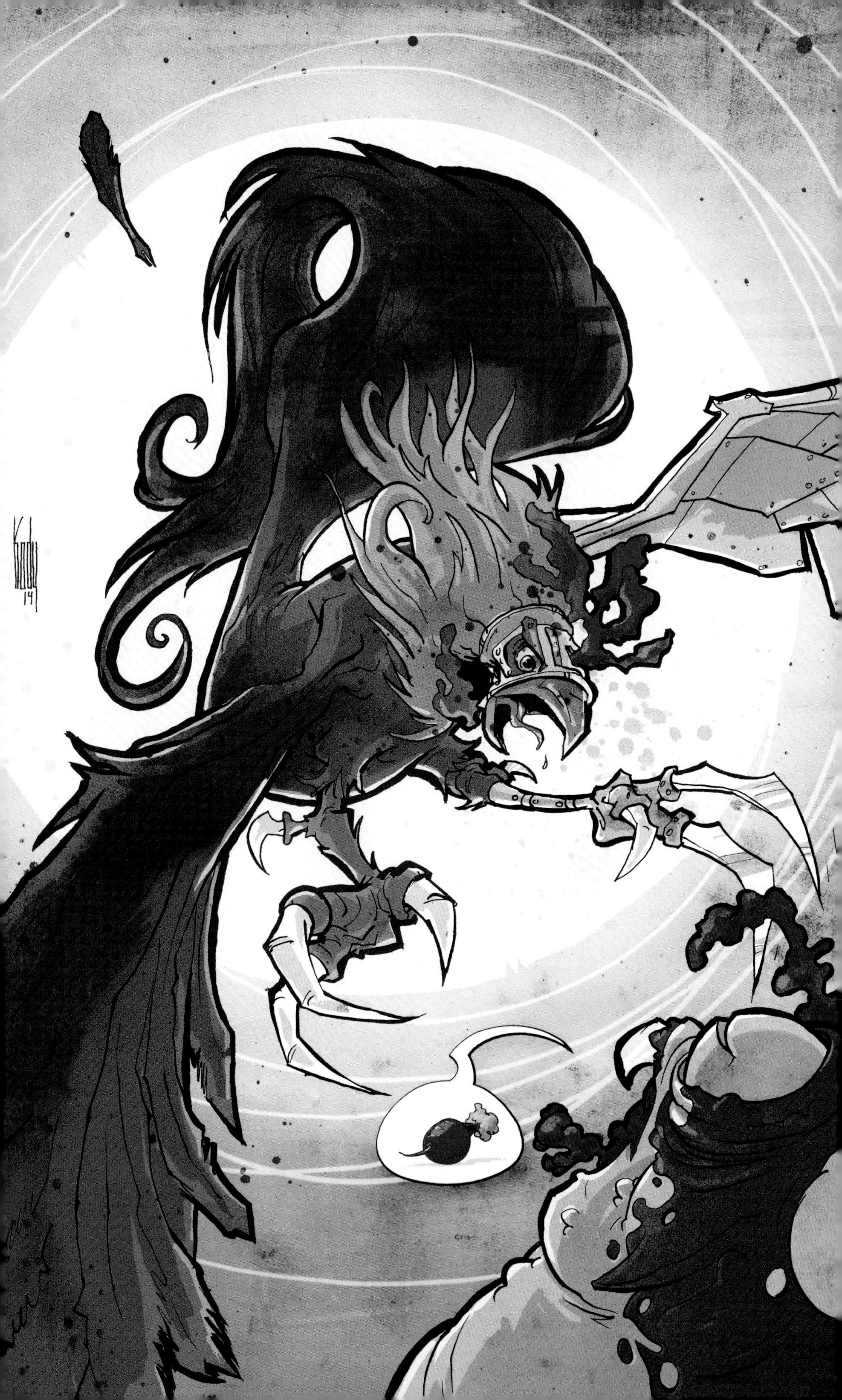

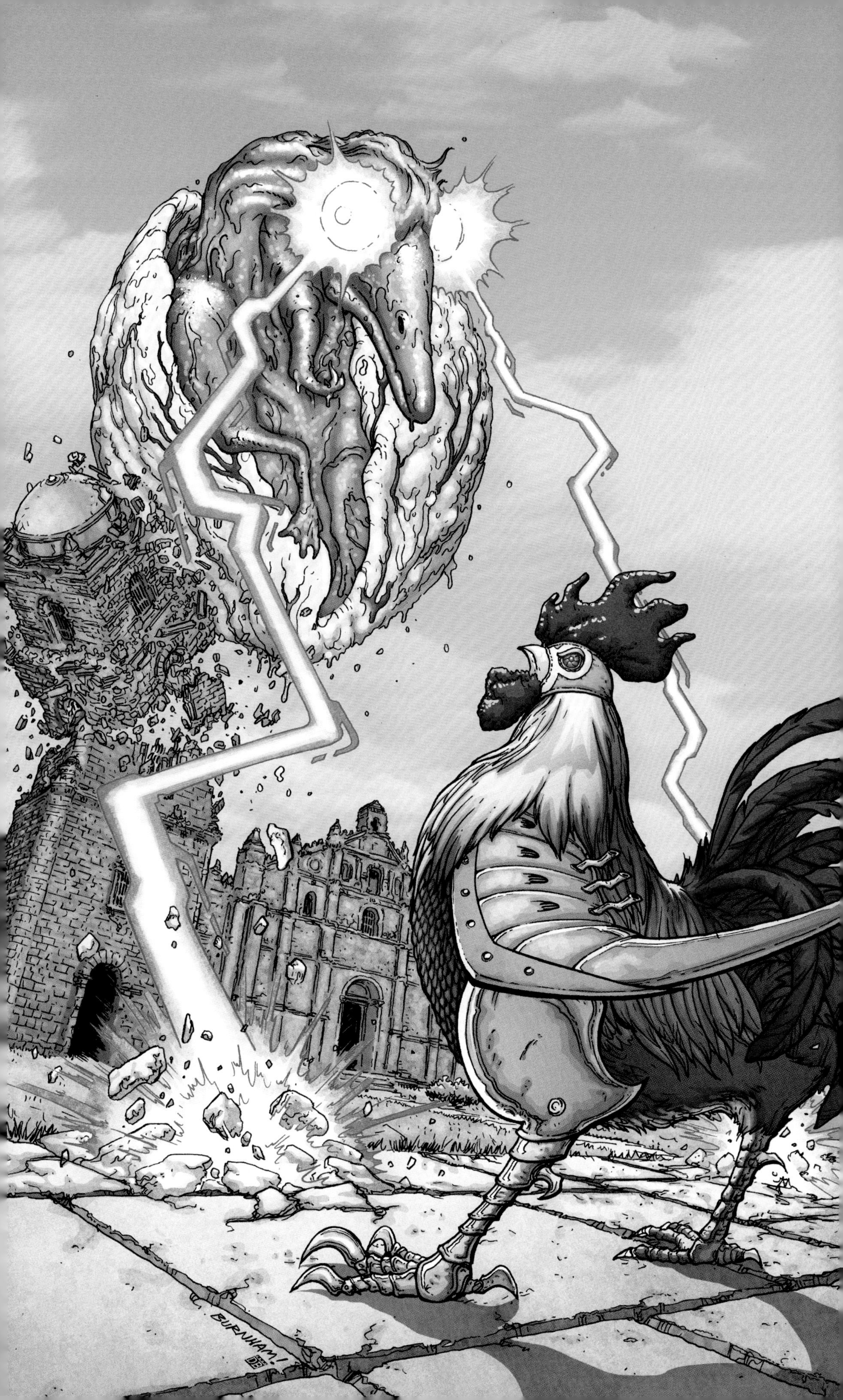

BURNHAM!

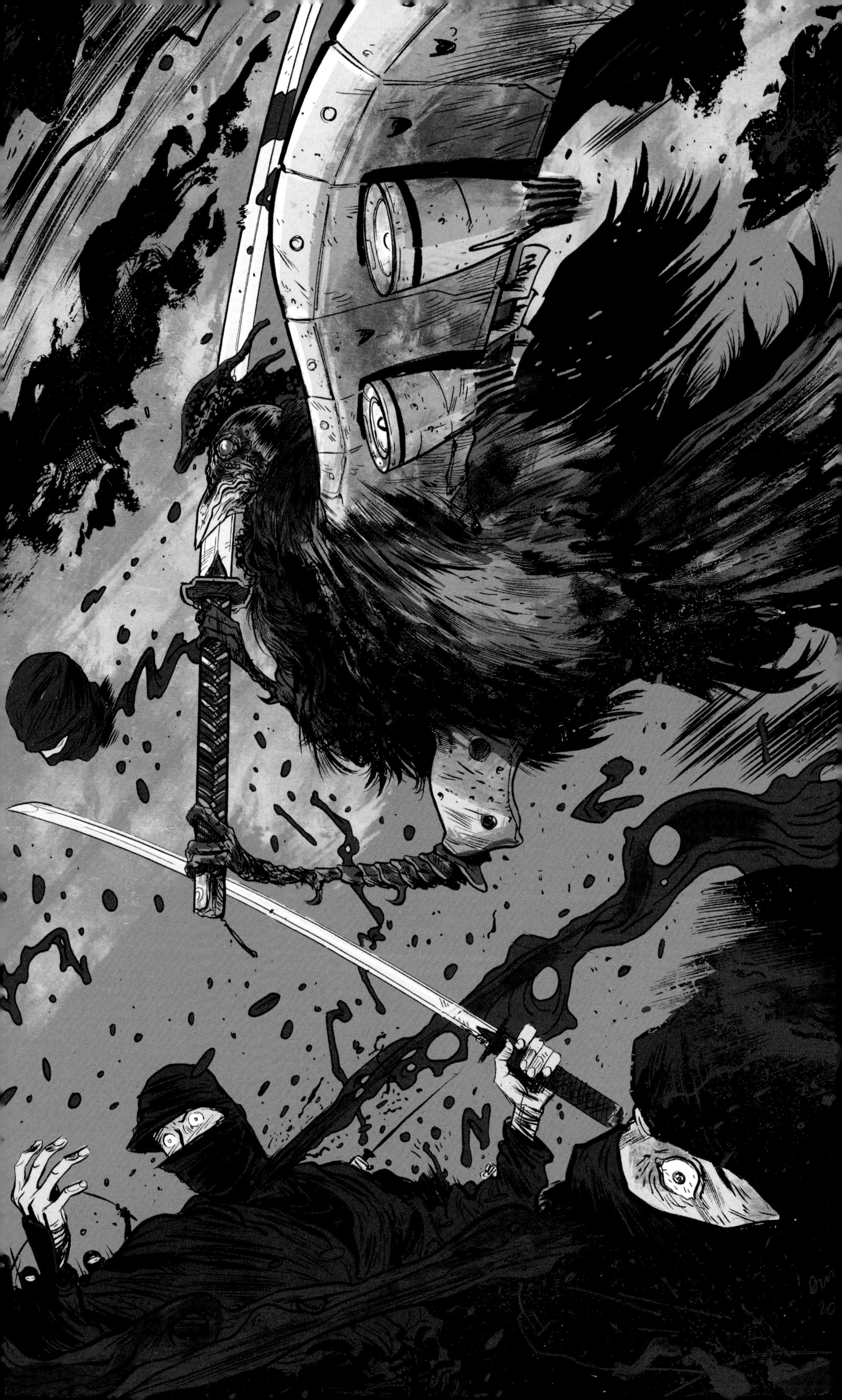

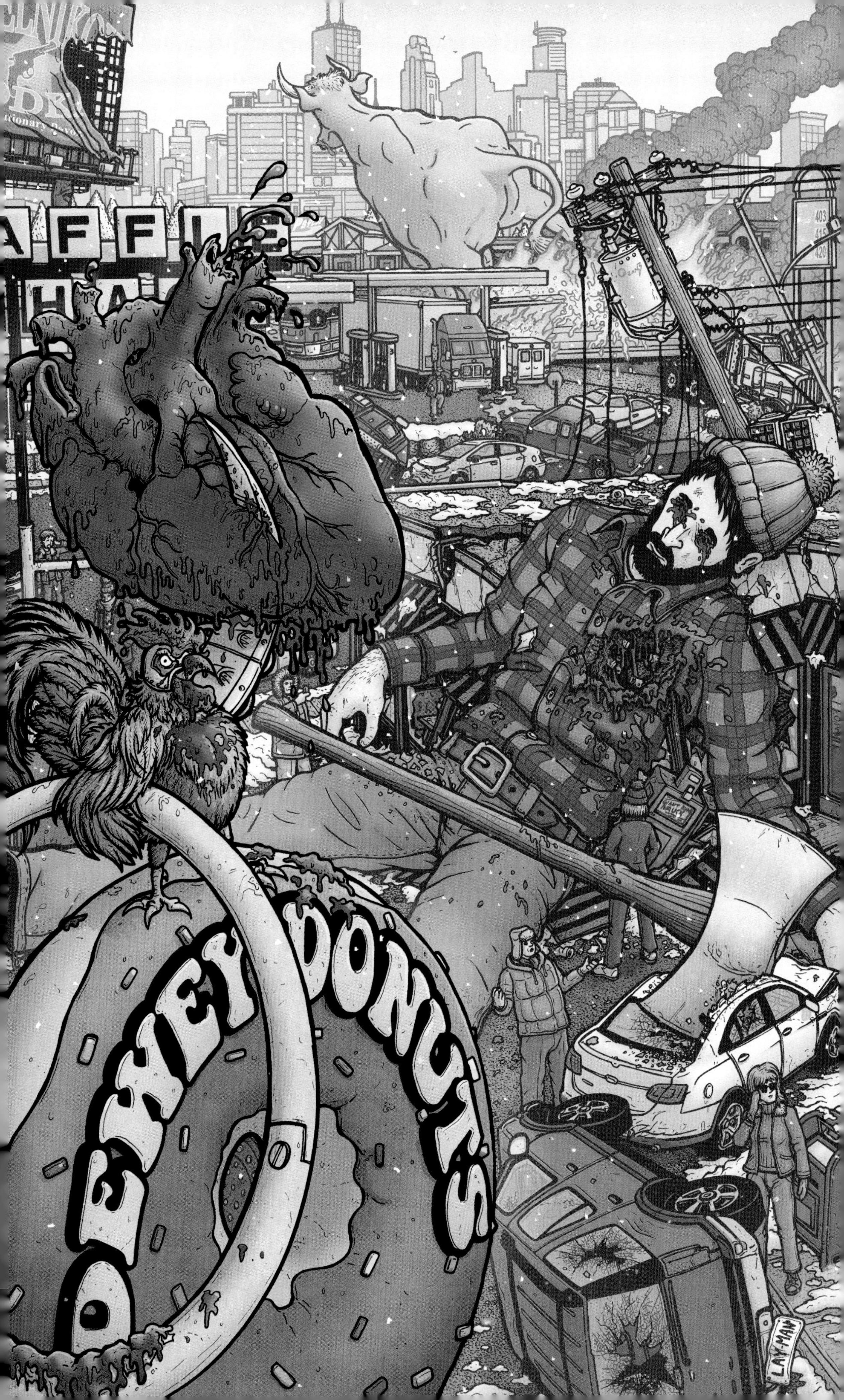
AFFLE
403
415
420
DONUTS
LAY-MAN

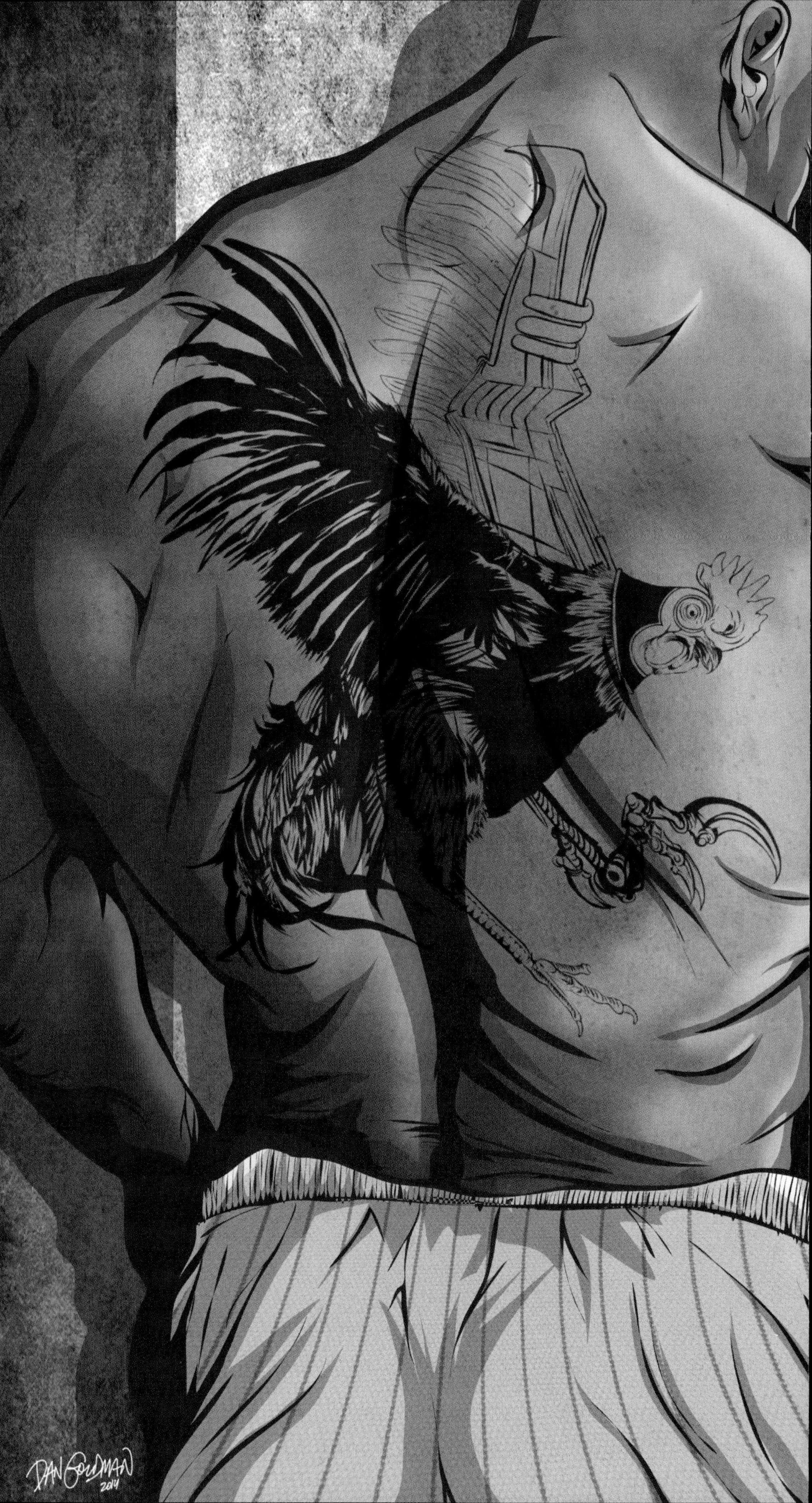
DAN GOLDMAN
2014

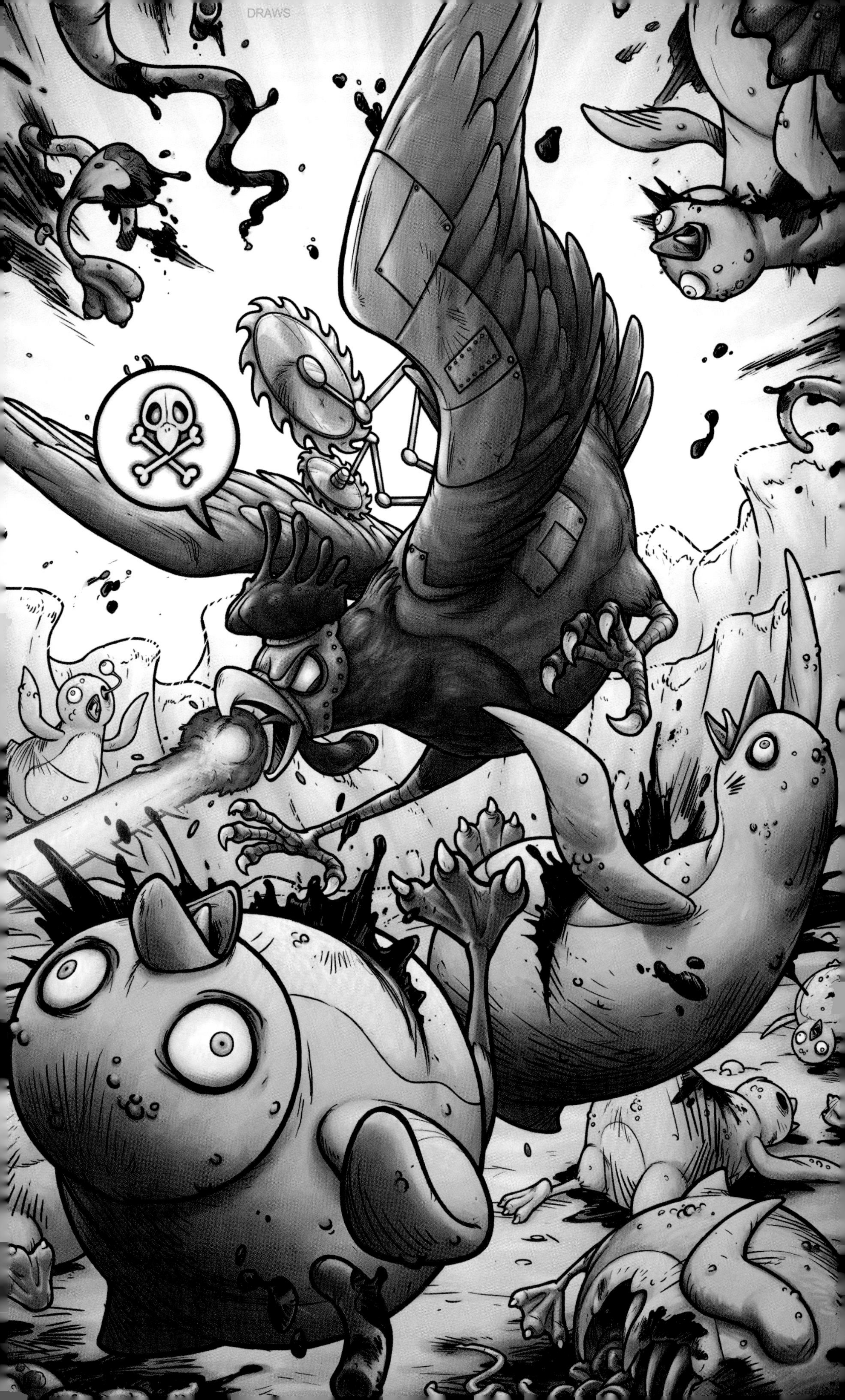

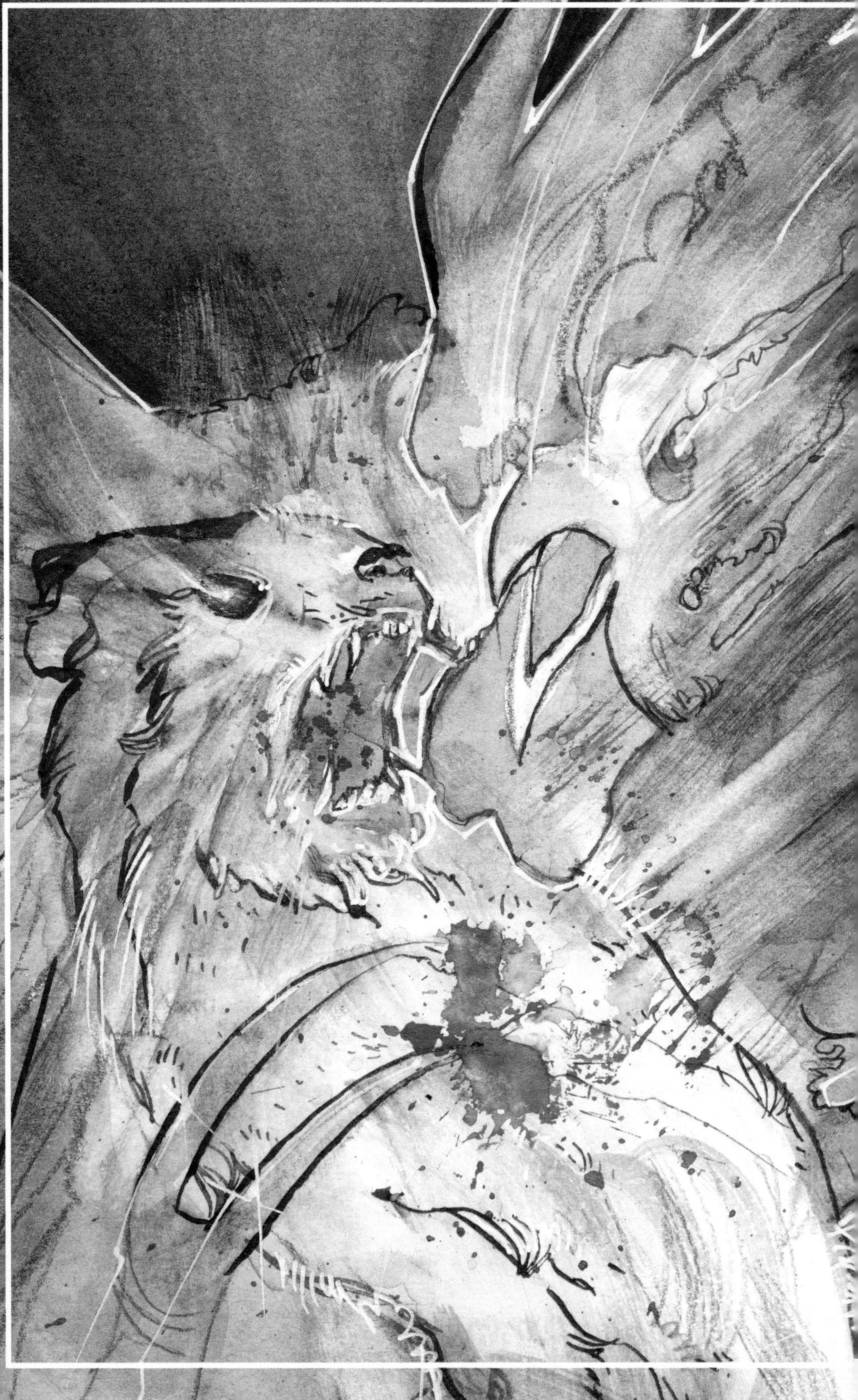

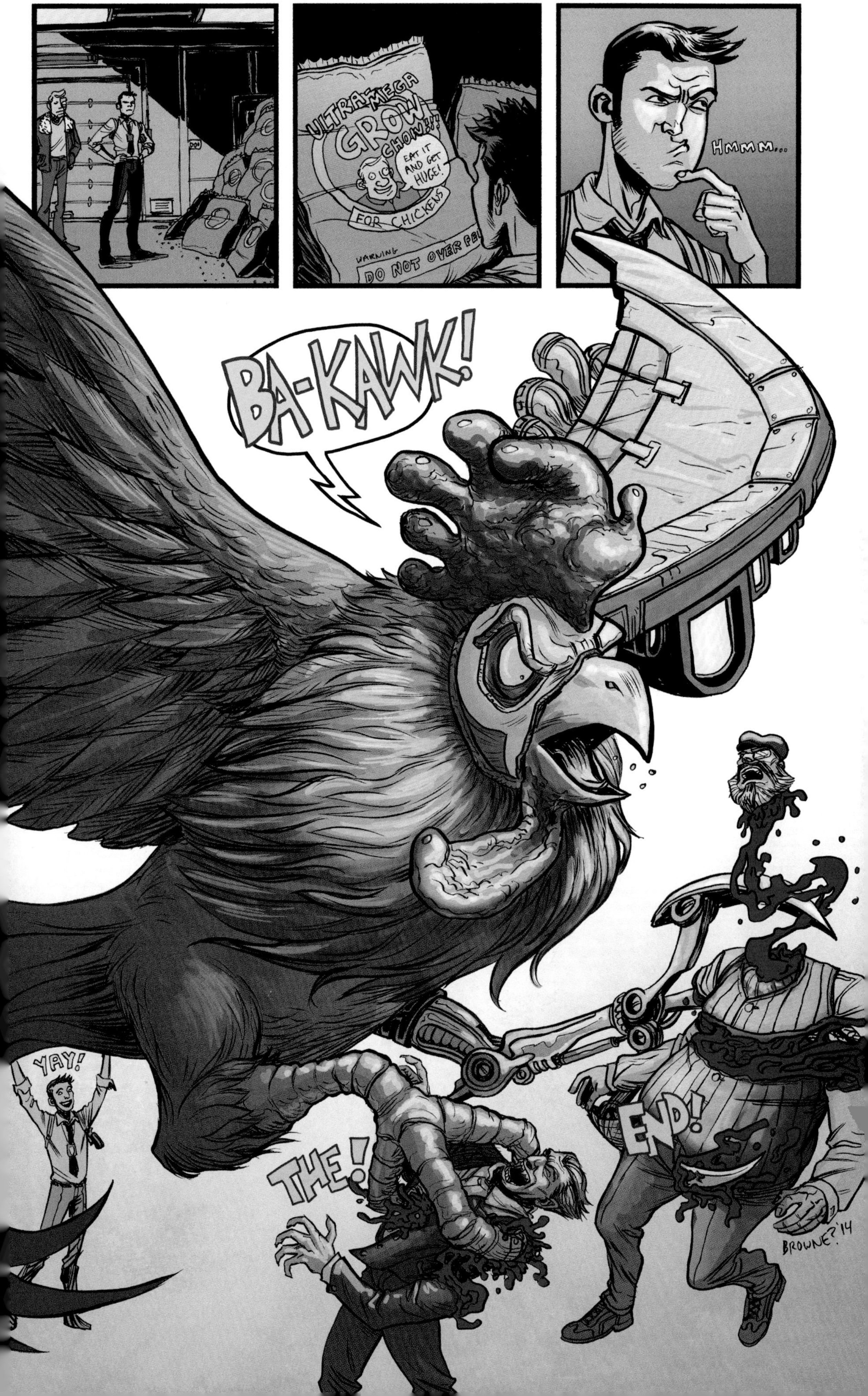

ULTRA MEGA GROW CHOW!!!
EAT IT AND GET HUGE!
FOR CHICKENS
WARNING
DO NOT OVER FE
HMMM...
BA-KAWK!
YAY!
THE!
END!
BROWNE? '14

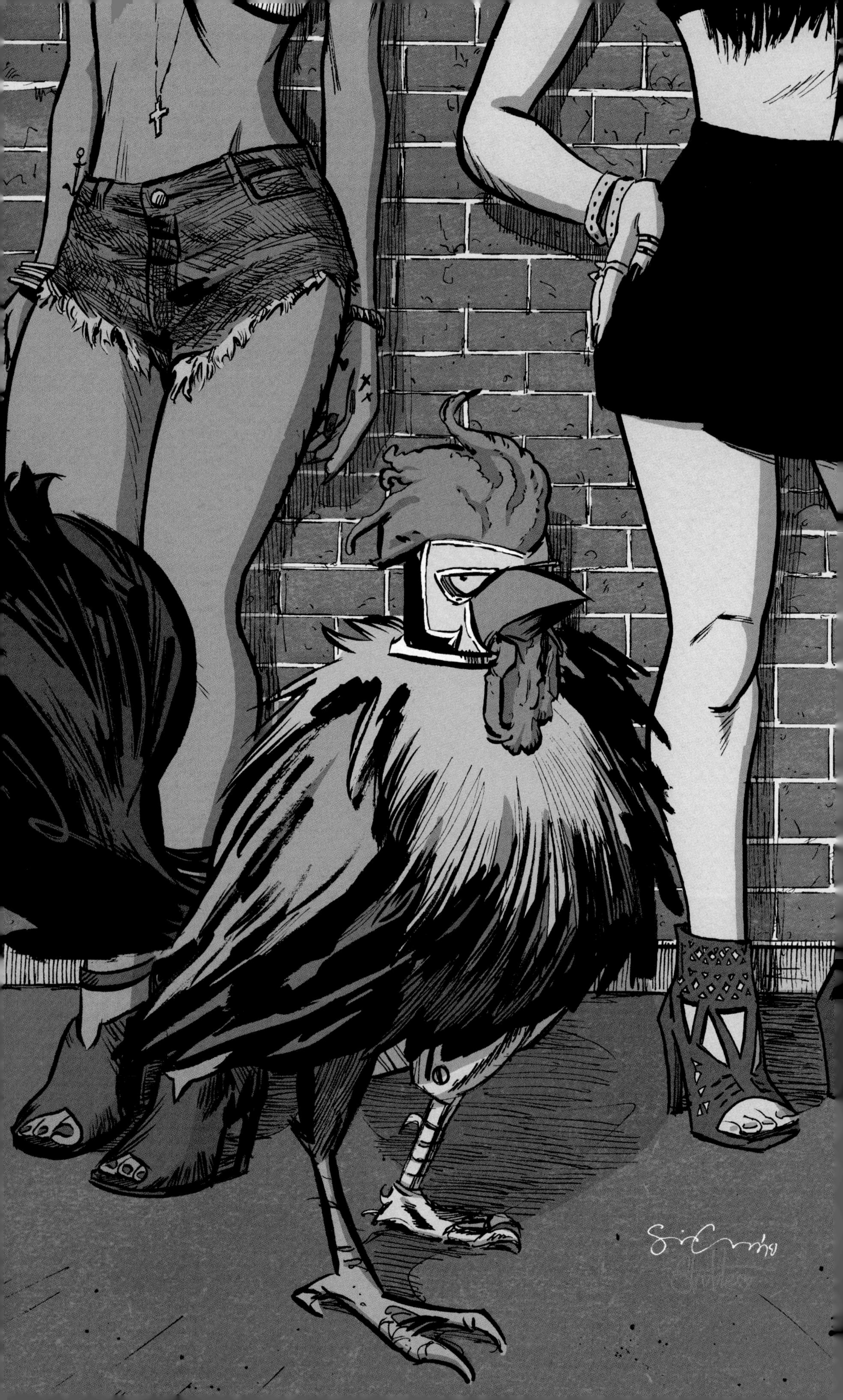

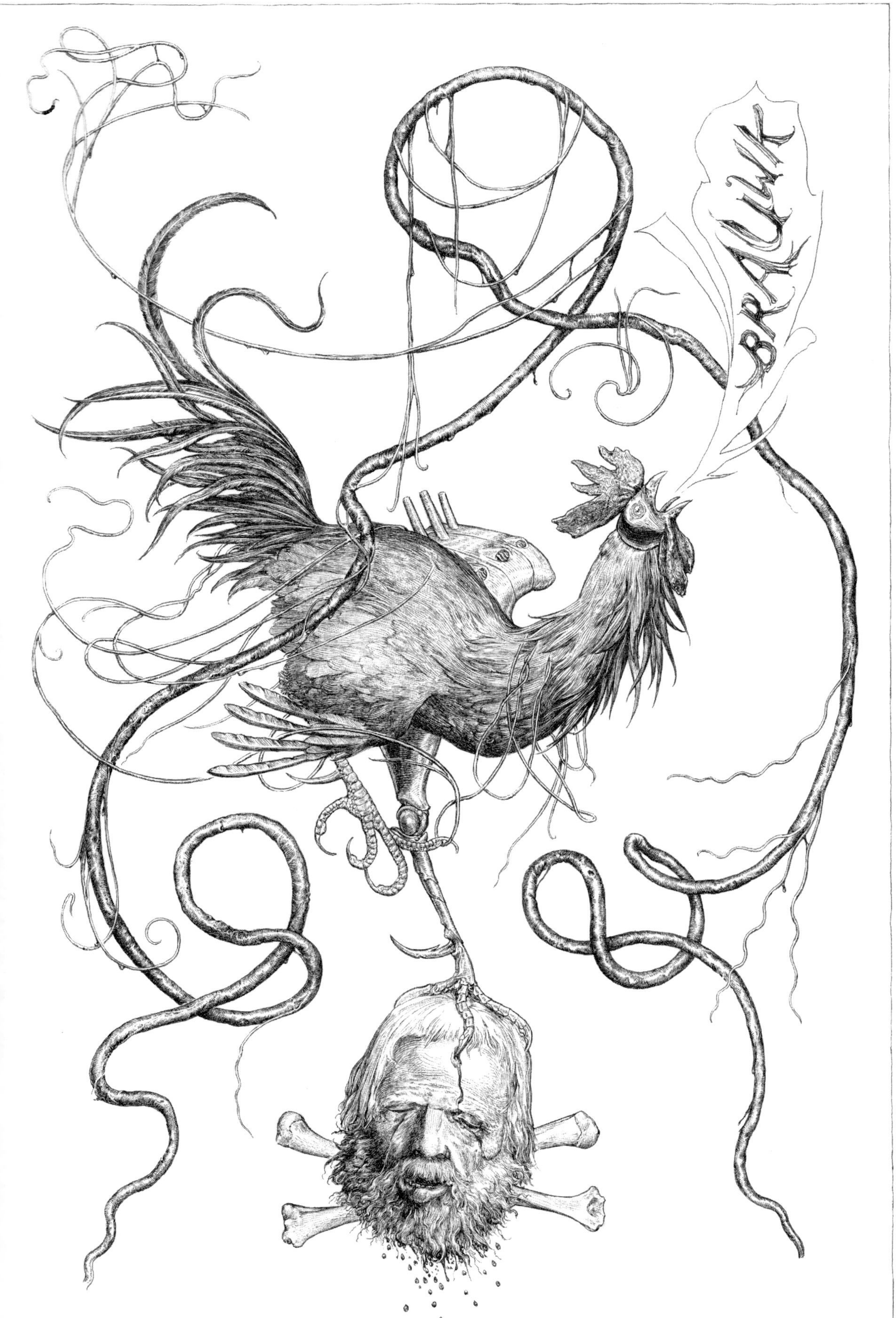
BRAUWK
JEREMY A. BASTIAN

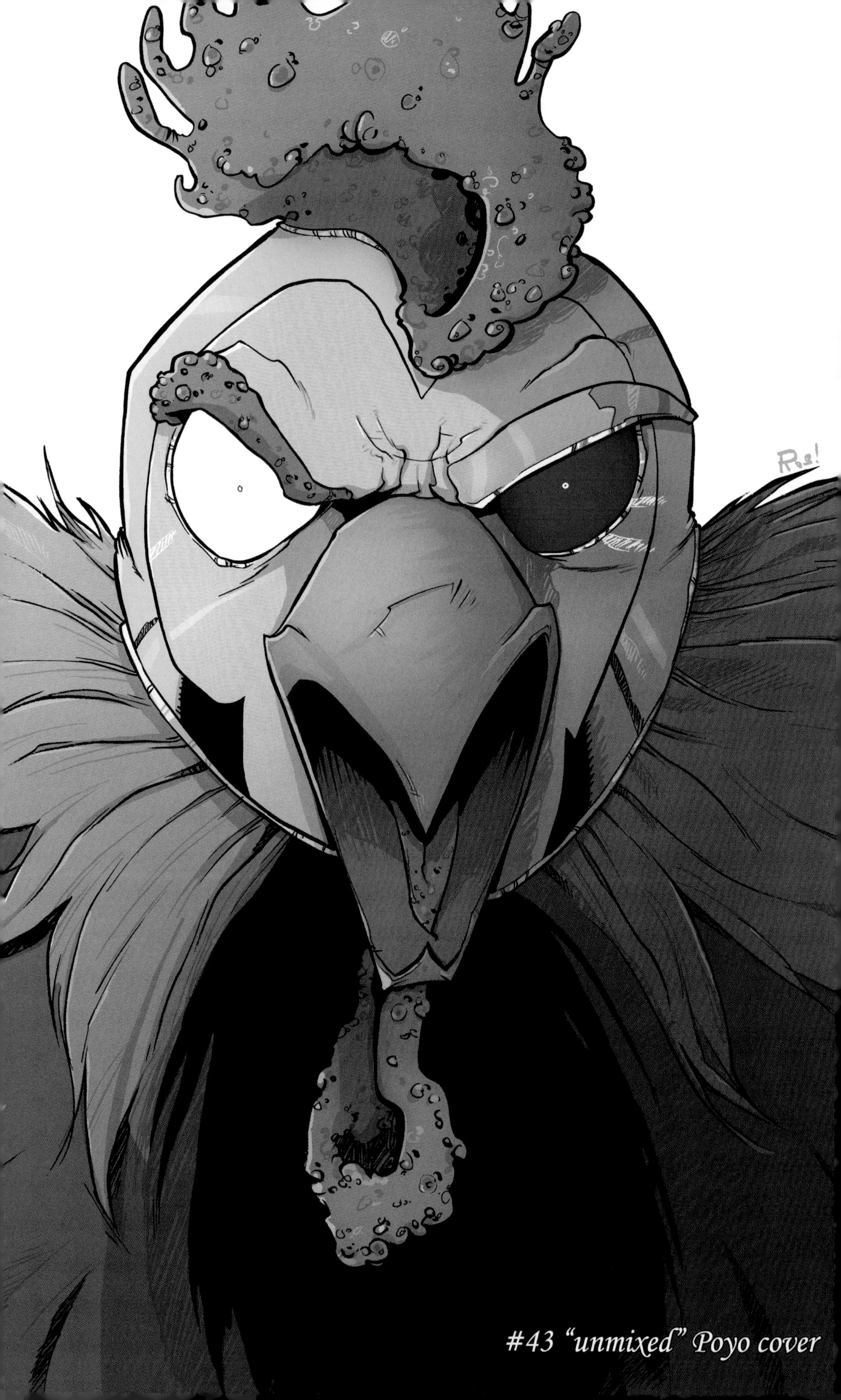

#43 "unmixed" Poyo cover

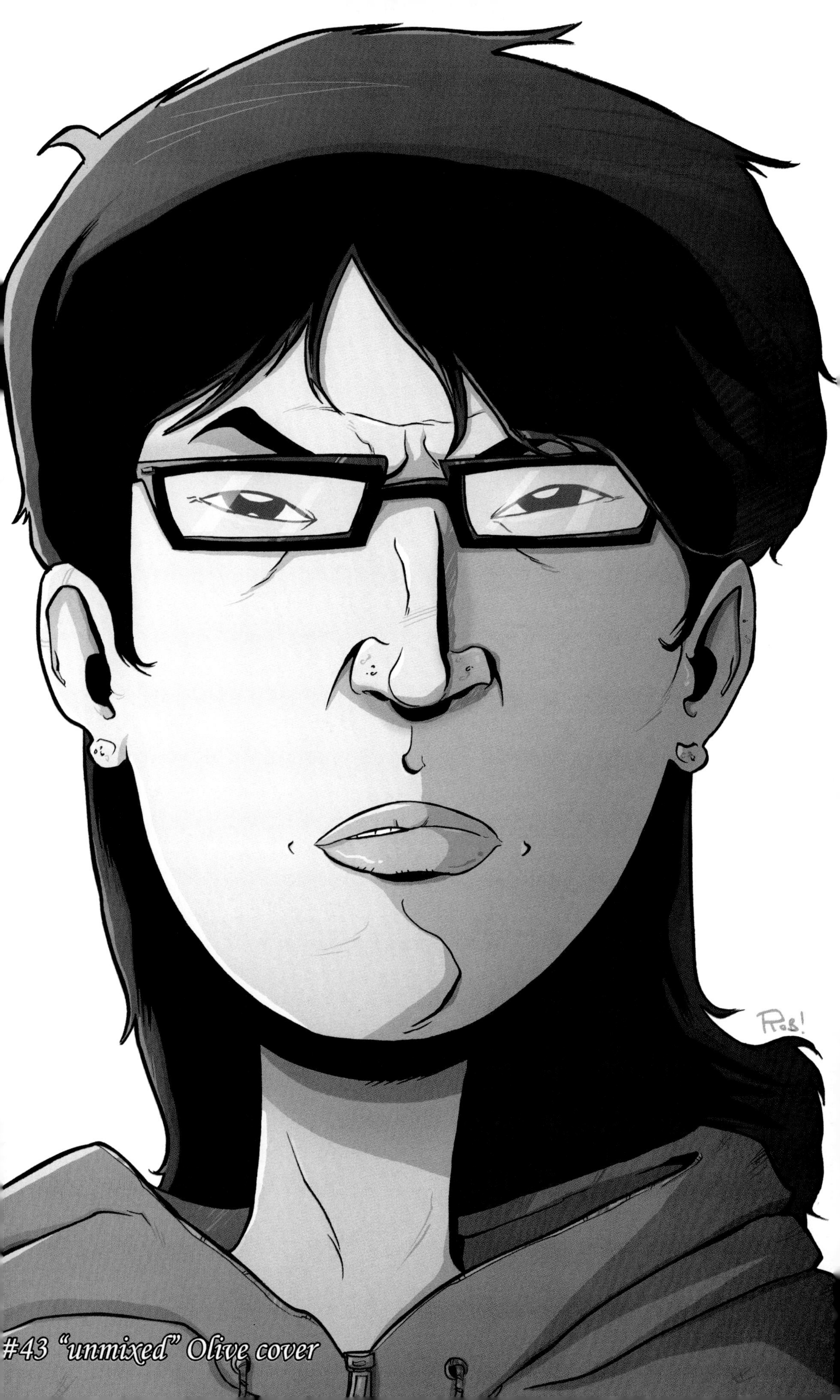
Ros!
#43 "unmixed" Olive cover

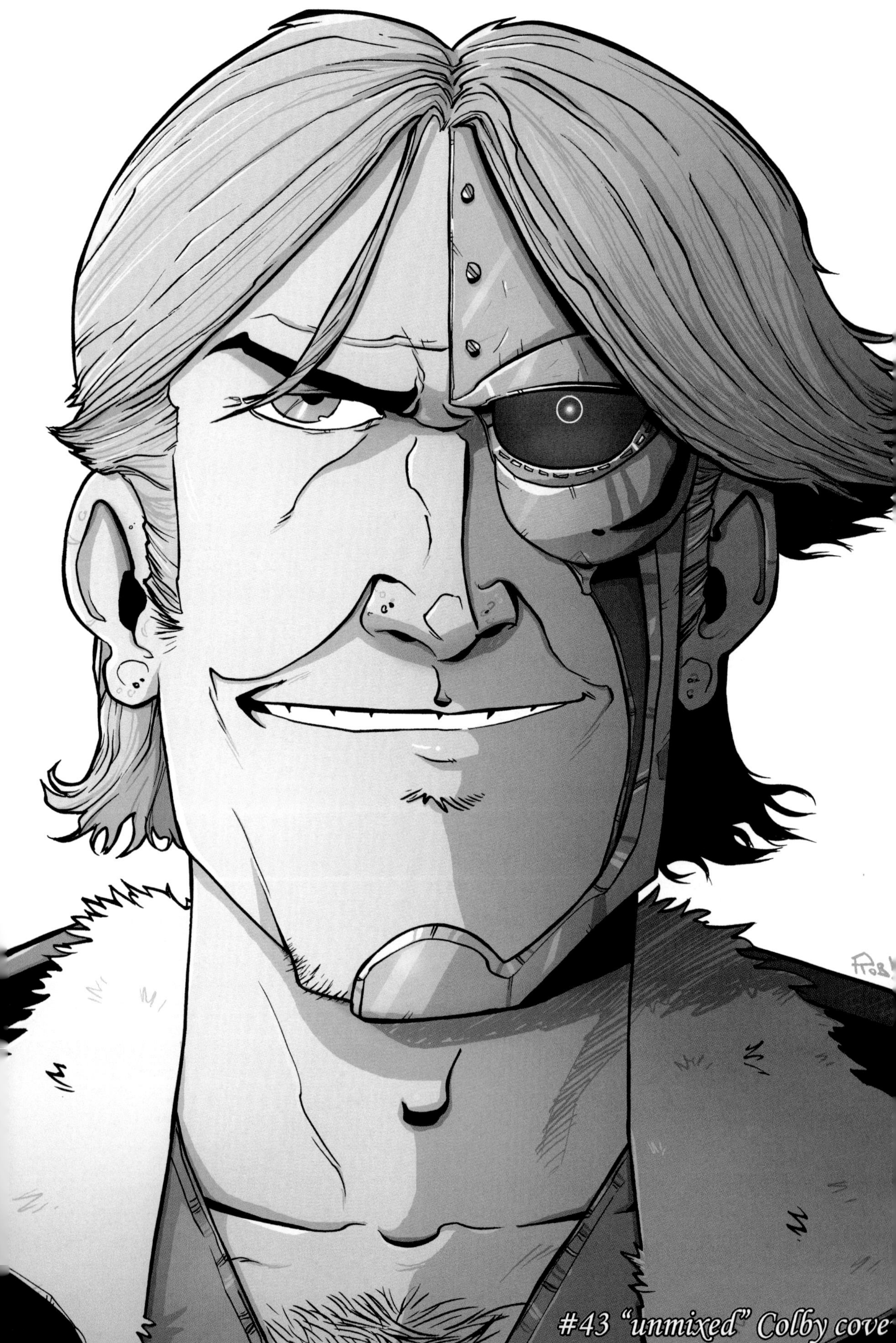

#43 "unmixed" Colby cove

1.

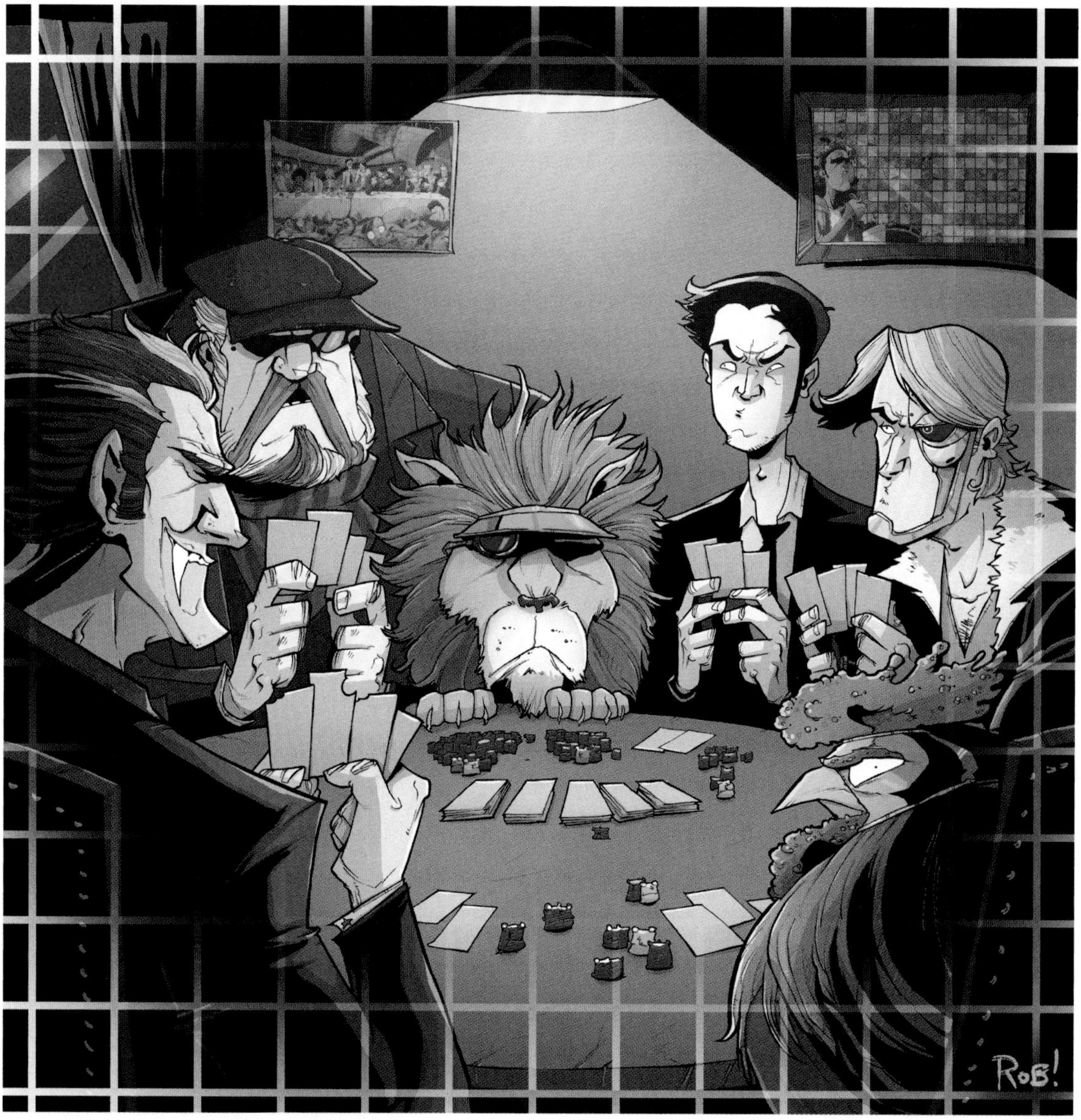

RoB!

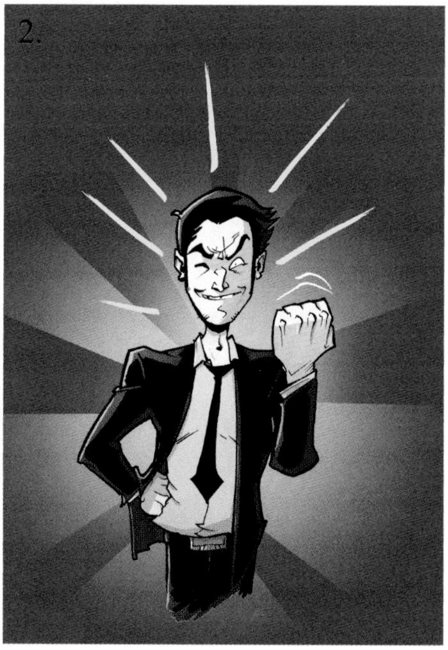

2.

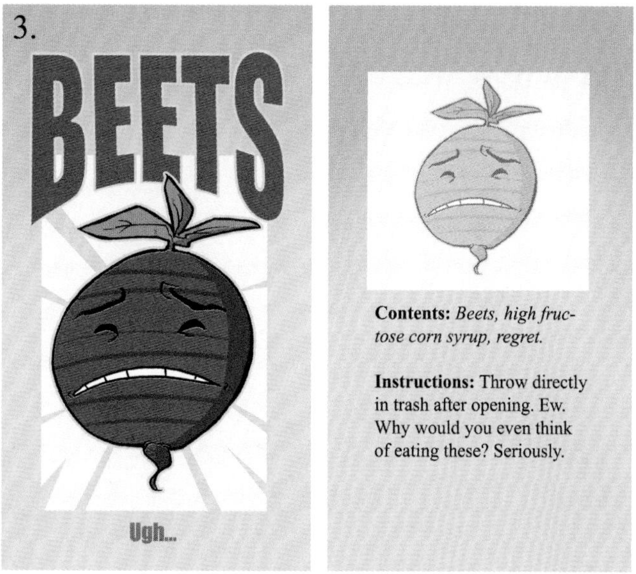

3.
BEETS
Ugh...
Contents: Beets, high fructose corn syrup, regret.
Instructions: Throw directly in trash after opening. Ew. Why would you even think of eating these? Seriously.

1. Cover for the CHEW Card Game.
2. Concept art for CHEW game.
3. Beets Label for Skelton Crew CHEW Merch.

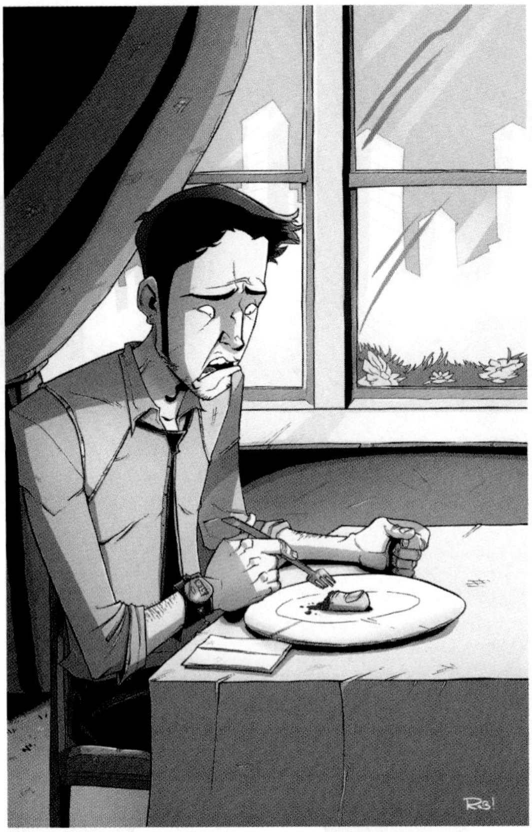

CHEW #37 A COVER

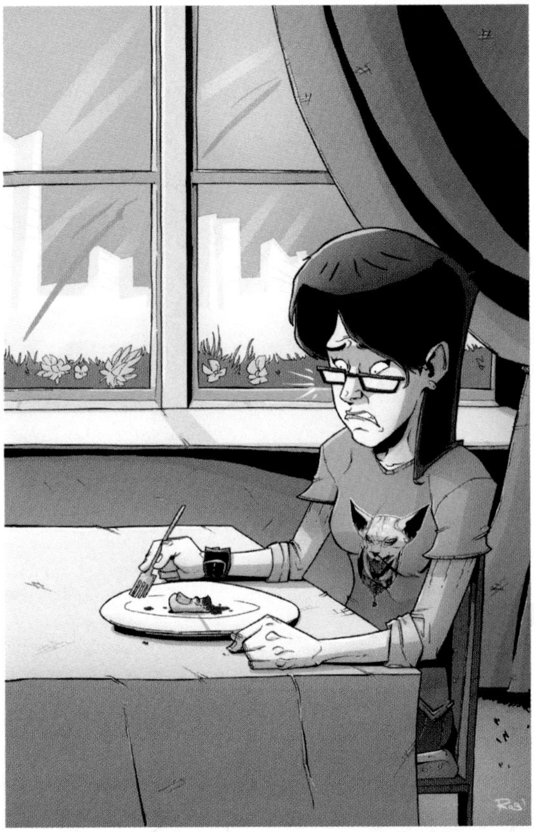

CHEW #37 B COVER

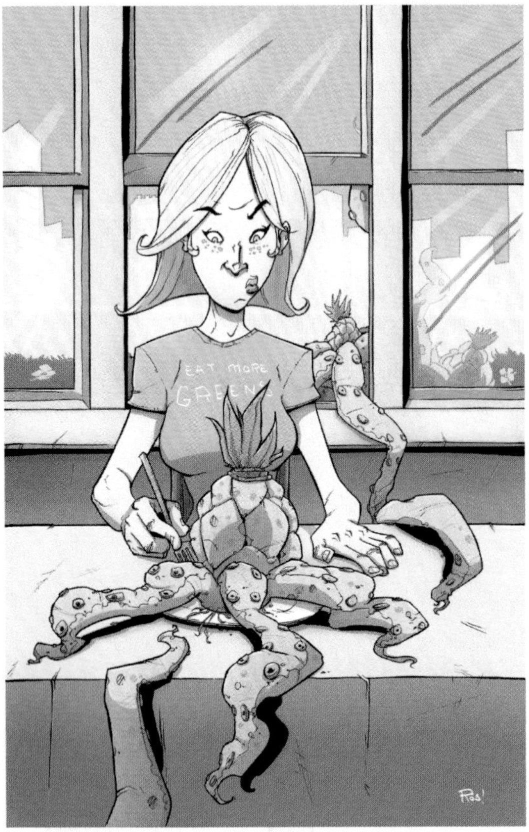
EAT MORE

CHEW #39 COVER

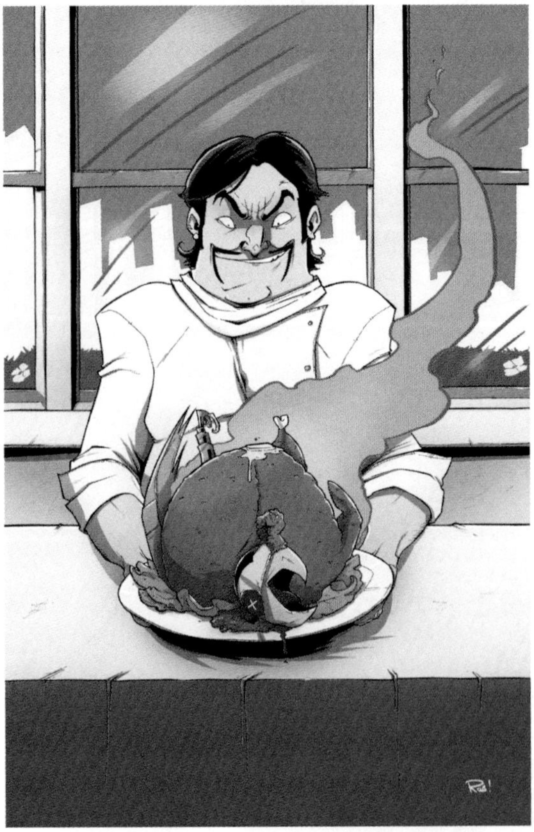

CHEW #49 COVER

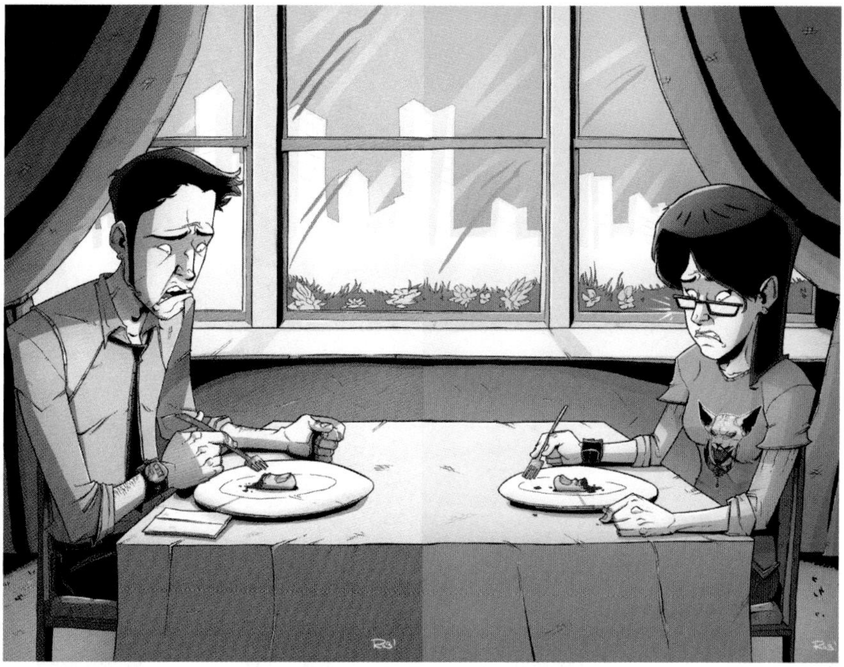

CHEW #37A + #37B

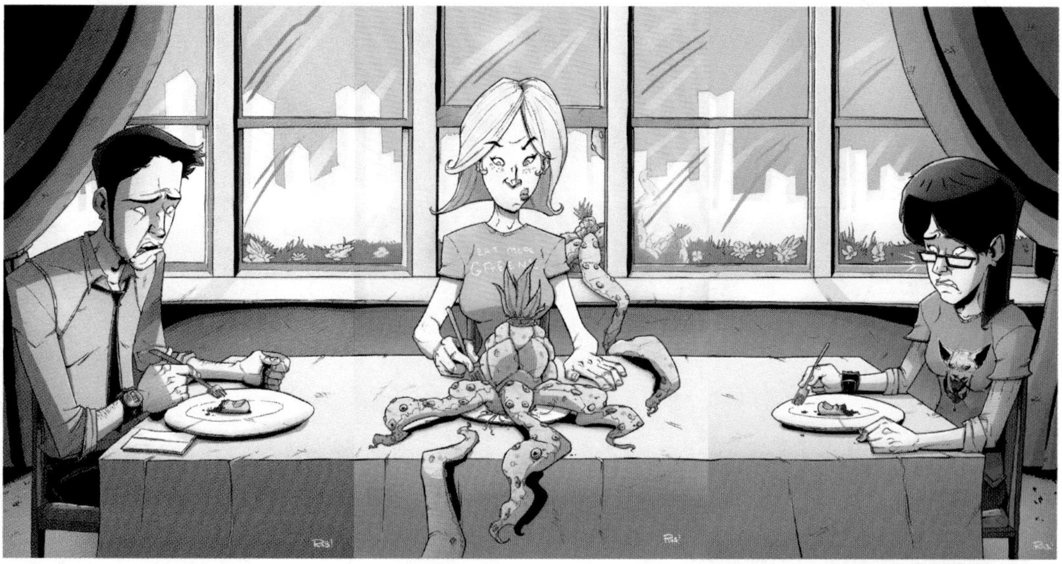

CHEW #37A + #39 + #37B

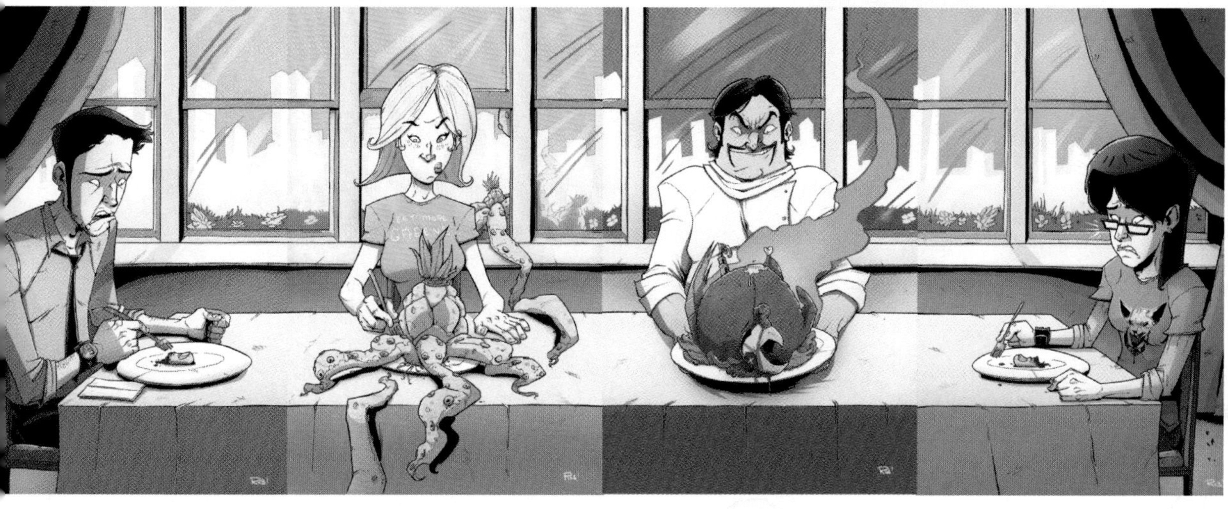

CHEW #37A + #39 + #49 + #37B

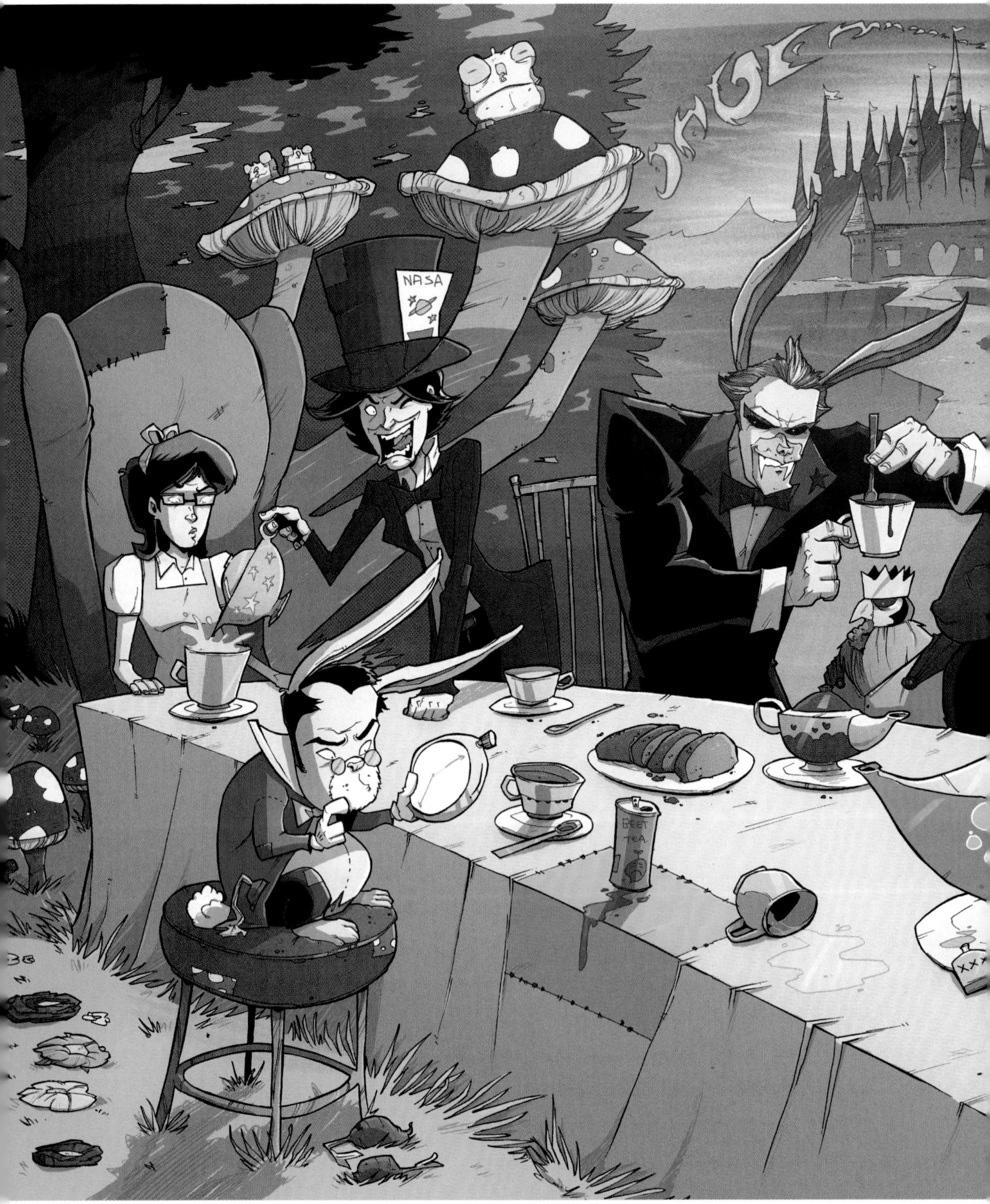
NASA
BEET TEA

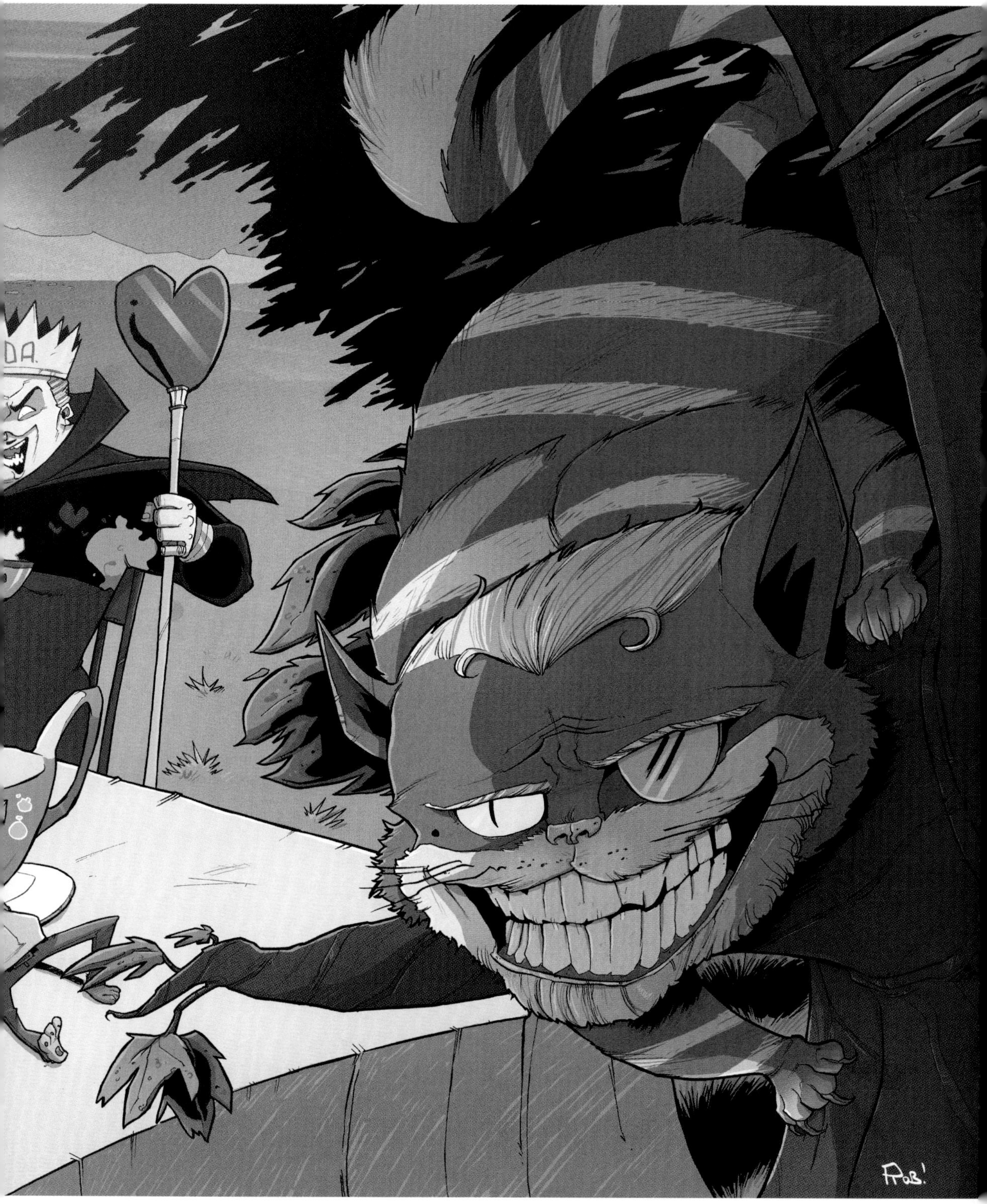

CHEW Wonderland Commission.

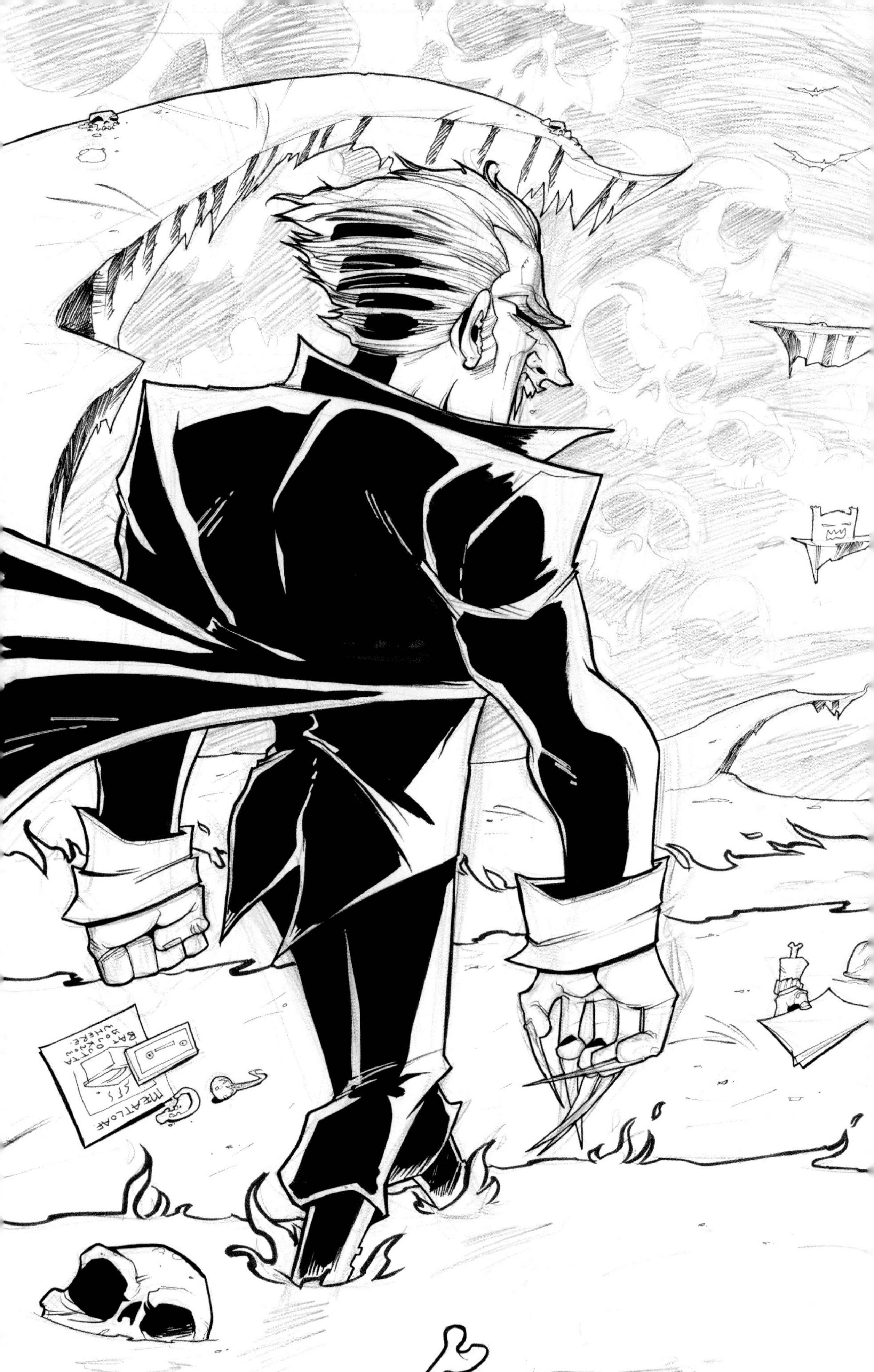
MEATLOAF
BAT OUTTA YOU KNOW WHERE.

CHEW #50 SDCC Cover pencils.

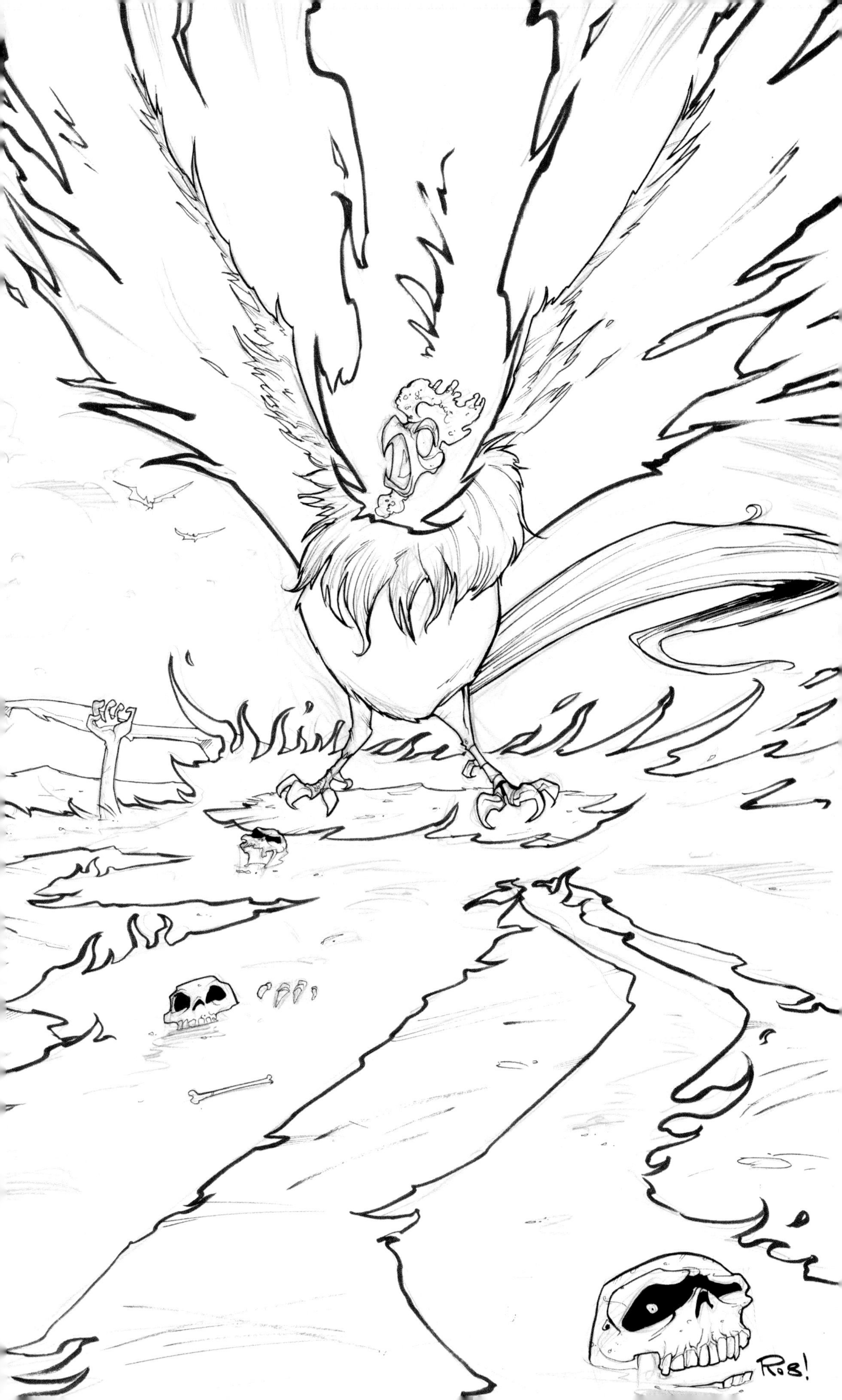
ROB!

Offensively violent Layman/Guillory cameo death scene
from *The Manhattan Projects* #17
by Jonathan Hickman, Nick Pitarra & Jordie Bellaire.

The Manhattan Projects © Jonathan Hickman & Nick Pitarra.

JOHN LAYMAN
Little is known about the reclusive writer of CHEW, but by all accounts
he is preternaturally handsome, and beloved by all.

ROB GUILLORY
Rob Guillory is still an artist living in Lafayette, Louisiana. In his free
time, he has no free time. In between his heroic work schedule, he enjoys
his wife's sweet company, as well as that of his two children, who have
made a blood pact never to allow Rob to sleep again. He is currently in
the midst of moving his family to a Sideways Universe where his cat
Freckles isn't such an idiot.

ChewComic.com
For original art: robguillory.com

Badass Chew stuff: http://www.skeltoncrewstudio.bigcartel.com

Layman on Twitter: @themightylayman   *Rob on Twitter: @Rob_guillory*